"YOU KNOW WHAT Will would say?" says Christina.

"What?" I say, my voice breaking.

"He would tell you to get over it," she says. "To stop being so irrational and take the stupid gun."

Will had little patience for the irrational. Christina must be right; she knew him better than I did.

And she—who lost someone dear to her that day, just as I did—was able to forgive me, an act that must have been nearly impossible. It would have been impossible for me, if the situation were reversed. So why is it so difficult for me to forgive myself?

"Roth knows how to write. The novel's love story, intricate plot, and unforgettable setting work in concert to deliver a novel that will rivet fans of the first book."

—PUBLISHERS WEEKLY

"In this addictive sequel to the acclaimed **DIVERGENT**, a bleak postapocalyptic Chicago collapses into all-out civil war. Another spectacular cliff-hanger."

—KIRKUS REVIEWS

"**INSURGENT** explores several critical themes, including the importance of family and the crippling power of grief at its loss."

—SLJ

"Packed with stunning twists and devastating betrayals, this sequel opens up the world-building to include some exploration of this society's origins and relationship to the world outside their societal limits, raising the stakes even higher. Fans of the first book will not be disappointed."

—BCCB

Also by Veronica Roth

DIVERGENT

ALLEGIANT

FOUR: A DIVERGENT COLLECTION

INSURGENT

VERONICA ROTH

KATHERINE TEGEN BOOKS
An Imprint of HarperCollins Publishers

Katherine Tegen Books is an imprint of HarperCollins Publishers.

Insurgent

www.epicreads.com

Library of Congress Cataloging-in-Publication Data

Roth, Veronica.

Insurgent / Veronica Roth. — 1st ed.

p.   cm.

Summary: "As war surges in the dystopian society around her, sixteen-year-old Divergent Tris Prior must continue trying to save those she loves—and herself—while grappling with haunting questions of grief and forgiveness, identity and loyalty, politics and love."— Provided by publisher.

ISBN 978-0-06-202405-3 (pbk.)

ISBN 978-0-06-238774-5 (Can.)

ISBN 978-0-06-237285-7 (movie tie-in pbk.)

ISBN 978-0-06-238775-2 (Can. movie tie-in pbk.)

ISBN 978-0-06-238845-2 (special edition)

ISBN 978-0-06-238849-0 (special edition)

ISBN 978-0-06-238848-3 (special edition)

ISBN 978-0-06-238846-9 (special edition)

[1. Identity—Fiction. 2. Families—Fiction. 3. Courage—Fiction. 4. Social classes—Fiction. 5. Science fiction.] I. Title.

PZ7.R7375Ins 2012   2011053287

[Fic]—dc22   CIP

                                                                              AC

Typography by Joel Tippie

14 15 16 17 18 PC/RRDH 10 9 8 7 6 5 4 3 2 1

❖

First paperback edition, 2015

To Nelson,
who was worth every risk

Like a wild animal, the truth is too powerful to remain caged.
—From the Candor faction manifesto

CHAPTER
ONE

I WAKE WITH his name in my mouth.

Will.

Before I open my eyes, I watch him crumple to the pavement again. Dead.

My doing.

Tobias crouches in front of me, his hand on my left shoulder. The train car bumps over the rails, and Marcus, Peter, and Caleb stand by the doorway. I take a deep breath and hold it in an attempt to relieve some of the pressure that is building in my chest.

An hour ago, nothing that happened felt real to me. Now it does.

I breathe out, and the pressure is still there.

"Tris, come on," Tobias says, his eyes searching mine.

"We have to jump."

It is too dark to see where we are, but if we are getting off, we are probably close to the fence. Tobias helps me to my feet and guides me toward the doorway.

The others jump off one by one: Peter first, then Marcus, then Caleb. I take Tobias's hand. The wind picks up as we stand at the edge of the car opening, like a hand pushing me back, toward safety.

But we launch ourselves into darkness and land hard on the ground. The impact hurts the bullet wound in my shoulder. I bite my lip to keep from crying out, and search for my brother.

"Okay?" I say when I see him sitting in the grass a few feet away, rubbing his knee.

He nods. I hear him sniff like he's fending off tears, and I have to turn away.

We landed in the grass near the fence, several yards away from the worn path that the Amity trucks travel to deliver food to the city, and the gate that lets them out—the gate that is currently shut, locking us in. The fence towers over us, too high and flexible to climb over, too sturdy to knock down.

"There are supposed to be Dauntless guards here," says Marcus. "Where are they?"

"They were probably under the simulation," Tobias

says, "and are now . . ." He pauses. "Who knows where, doing who knows what."

We stopped the simulation—the weight of the hard drive in my back pocket reminds me—but we didn't pause to see the aftermath. What happened to our friends, our peers, our leaders, our factions? There is no way to know.

Tobias approaches a small metal box on the right side of the gate and opens it, revealing a keypad.

"Let's hope the Erudite didn't think to change this combination," he says as he types in a series of numbers. He stops at the eighth one, and the gate clicks open.

"How did you know that?" says Caleb. His voice sounds thick with emotion, so thick I am surprised it does not choke him on the way out.

"I worked in the Dauntless control room, monitoring the security system. We only change the codes twice a year," Tobias says.

"How lucky," says Caleb. He gives Tobias a wary look.

"Luck has nothing to do with it," Tobias says. "I only worked there because I wanted to make sure I could get out."

I shiver. The way he talks about getting out—it's like he thinks we're trapped. I never thought about it that way before, and now that seems foolish.

We walk in a small pack, Peter cradling his bloody

arm to his chest—the arm that I shot—and Marcus with his hand on Peter's shoulder, keeping him stable. Caleb wipes his cheeks every few seconds, and I know he's crying but I don't know how to comfort him, or why I am not crying myself.

Instead I take the lead, Tobias silent at my side, and though he does not touch me, he steadies me.

+ + +

Pinpricks of light are the first sign that we are nearing Amity headquarters. Then squares of light that turn into glowing windows. A cluster of wooden and glass buildings.

Before we can reach them, we have to walk through an orchard. My feet sink into the ground, and above me, the branches grow into one another, forming a kind of tunnel. Dark fruit hangs among the leaves, ready to drop. The sharp, sweet smell of rotting apples mixes with the scent of wet earth in my nose.

When we get close, Marcus leaves Peter's side and walks in front. "I know where to go," he says.

He leads us past the first building to the second one on the left. All the buildings except the greenhouses are made of the same dark wood, unpainted, rough. I hear laughter through an open window. The contrast between the laughter and the stone stillness within me is jarring.

Marcus opens one of the doors. I would be shocked by the lack of security if we were not at Amity headquarters. They often straddle the line between trust and stupidity.

In this building the only sound is of our squeaking shoes. I don't hear Caleb crying anymore, but then, he was quiet about it before.

Marcus stops before an open room, where Johanna Reyes, representative of Amity, sits, staring out the window. I recognize her because it is hard to forget Johanna's face, whether you've seen her once or a thousand times. A scar stretches in a thick line from just above her right eyebrow to her lip, rendering her blind in one eye and giving her a lisp when she talks. I have only heard her speak once, but I remember. She would have been a beautiful woman if not for that scar.

"Oh, thank God," she says when she sees Marcus. She walks toward him with her arms open. Instead of embracing him, she just touches his shoulders, like she remembers the Abnegation's distaste for casual physical contact.

"The other members of your party got here a few hours ago, but they weren't sure if you had made it," she says. She is referring to the group of Abnegation who were with my father and Marcus in the safe house. I didn't even think to worry about them.

She looks over Marcus's shoulder, first at Tobias and Caleb, then at me, then at Peter.

"Oh my," she says, her eyes lingering on the blood soaking Peter's shirt. "I'll send for a doctor. I can grant you all permission to stay the night, but tomorrow, our community must decide together. And"—she eyes Tobias and me—"they will likely not be enthusiastic about a Dauntless presence in our compound. I of course ask you to turn over any weapons you might have."

I wonder, suddenly, how she knows that I am Dauntless. I am still wearing a gray shirt. My father's shirt.

At that moment, his smell, which is an even mixture of soap and sweat, wafts upward, and it fills my nose, fills my entire head with him. I clench my hands so hard into fists that my fingernails cut into my skin. *Not here. Not here.*

Tobias hands over his gun, but when I reach behind me to take out my own concealed weapon, he grabs my hand, guiding it away from my back. Then he laces his fingers with mine to cover up what he just did.

I know it's smart to keep one of our guns. But it would have been a relief to hand it over.

"My name is Johanna Reyes," she says, extending her

hand to me, and then Tobias. A Dauntless greeting. I am impressed by her awareness of the customs of other factions. I always forget how considerate the Amity are until I see it for myself.

"This is T—" Marcus starts, but Tobias interrupts him.

"My name is Four," he says. "This is Tris, Caleb, and Peter."

A few days ago, "Tobias" was a name only I knew, among the Dauntless; it was the piece of himself that he gave me. Outside Dauntless headquarters, I remember why he hid that name from the world. It binds him to Marcus.

"Welcome to the Amity compound." Johanna's eyes fix on my face, and she smiles crookedly. "Let us take care of you."

+ + +

We do let them. An Amity nurse gives me a salve—developed by Erudite to speed healing—to put on my shoulder, and then escorts Peter to the hospital ward to mend his arm. Johanna takes us to the cafeteria, where we find some of the Abnegation who were in the safe house with Caleb and my father. Susan is there, and some of our old neighbors, and rows of wooden tables as long as the room itself. They greet us—especially Marcus—with held-in tears and suppressed smiles.

I cling to Tobias's arm. I sag under the weight of the members of my parents' faction, their lives, their tears.

One of the Abnegation puts a cup of steaming liquid under my nose and says, "Drink this. It will help you sleep as it helped some of the others sleep. No dreams."

The liquid is pink-red, like strawberries. I grab the cup and drink it fast. For a few seconds the heat from the liquid makes me feel like I am full of something again. And as I drain the last drops from the cup, I feel myself relaxing. Someone leads me down the hallway, to a room with a bed in it. That is all.

CHAPTER
TWO

I OPEN MY eyes, terrified, my hands clutching at the sheets. But I am not running through the streets of the city or the corridors of Dauntless headquarters. I am in a bed in Amity headquarters, and the smell of sawdust is in the air.

I shift, and wince as something digs into my back. I reach behind me, and my fingers wrap around the gun.

For a moment I see Will standing before me, both our guns between us—*his hand, I could have shot his hand, why didn't I, why?*—and I almost scream his name.

Then he's gone.

I get out of bed and lift the mattress with one hand, propping it up on my knee. Then I shove the gun beneath it and let the mattress bury it. Once it is out of sight and no longer pressed to my skin, my head feels clearer.

Now that the adrenaline rush of yesterday is gone, and whatever made me sleep has worn off, the deep ache and shooting pains of my shoulder are intense. I am wearing the same clothes I wore last night. The corner of the hard drive peeks out from under my pillow, where I shoved it right before I fell asleep. On it is the simulation data that controlled the Dauntless, and the record of what the Erudite did. It feels too important for me to even touch, but I can't leave it here, so I grab it and wedge it between the dresser and the wall. Part of me thinks it would be a good idea to destroy it, but I know it contains the only record of my parents' deaths, so I'll settle for keeping it hidden.

Someone knocks on my door. I sit on the edge of the bed and try to smooth my hair down.

"Come in," I say.

The door opens, and Tobias steps halfway in, the door dividing his body in half. He wears the same jeans as yesterday, but a dark red T-shirt instead of his black one, probably borrowed from one of the Amity. It's a strange color on him, too bright, but when he leans his head back against the doorframe, I see that it makes the blue in his eyes lighter.

"The Amity are meeting in a half hour." He quirks his eyebrows and adds, with a touch of melodrama, *"To decide our fate."*

I shake my head. "Never thought my fate would be in the hands of a bunch of Amity."

"Me either. Oh, I brought you something." He unscrews the cap of a small bottle and holds out a dropper filled with clear liquid. "Pain medicine. Take a dropperful every six hours."

"Thanks." I squeeze the dropper into the back of my throat. The medicine tastes like old lemon.

He hooks a thumb in one of his belt loops and says, "How are you, Beatrice?"

"Did you just call me *Beatrice*?"

"Thought I would give it a try." He smiles. "Not good?"

"Maybe on special occasions only. Initiation days, Choosing Days . . ." I pause. I was about to rattle off a few more holidays, but only the Abnegation celebrate them. The Dauntless have holidays of their own, I assume, but I don't know what they are. And anyway, the idea that we would celebrate anything right now is so ludicrous I don't continue.

"It's a deal." His smile fades. "How are you, Tris?"

It's not a strange question, after what we've been through, but I tense up when he asks it, worried that he'll somehow see into my mind. I haven't told him about Will yet. I want to, but I don't know how. Just the thought of saying the words out loud makes me feel so heavy I could break through the floorboards.

"I'm . . ." I shake my head a few times. "I don't know, Four. I'm awake. I . . ." I am still shaking my head. He slides his hand over my cheek, one finger anchored behind my ear. Then he tilts his head down and kisses me, sending a warm ache through my body. I wrap my hands around his arm, holding him there as long as I can. When he touches me, the hollowed-out feeling in my chest and stomach is not as noticeable.

I don't have to tell him. I can just try to forget—he can help me forget.

"I know," he says. "Sorry. I shouldn't have asked."

For a moment all I can think is, *How could you* possibly *know?* But something about his expression reminds me that he does know something about loss. He lost his mother when he was young. I don't remember how she died, just that we attended her funeral.

Suddenly I remember him clutching the curtains in his living room, about nine years old, wearing gray, his dark eyes shut. The image is fleeting, and it could be my imagination, not a memory.

He releases me. "I'll let you get ready."

+ + +

The women's bathroom is two doors down. The floor is dark brown tile, and each shower stall has wooden walls and a plastic curtain separating it from the central aisle. A sign on the back wall says REMEMBER: TO CONSERVE RESOURCES, SHOWERS RUN FOR ONLY FIVE MINUTES.

The stream of water is cold, so I wouldn't want the extra minutes even if I could have them. I wash quickly with my left hand, leaving my right hand hanging at my side. The pain medicine Tobias gave me worked fast—the pain in my shoulder has already faded to a dull throb.

When I get out of the shower, a stack of clothes waits on my bed. It contains some yellow and red, from the Amity, and some gray, from the Abnegation, colors I rarely see side by side. If I had to guess, I would say that one of the Abnegation put the stack there for me. It's something they would think to do.

I pull on a pair of dark red pants made of denim—so long I have to roll them up three times—and a gray Abnegation shirt that is too big for me. The sleeves come down to my fingertips, and I roll them up too. It hurts to move my right hand, so I keep the movements small and slow.

Someone knocks on the door. "Beatrice?" The soft voice is Susan's.

I open the door for her. She carries a tray of food, which she sets down on the bed. I search her face for a sign of what she has lost—her father, an Abnegation leader, didn't survive the attack—but I see only the placid determination characteristic of my old faction.

"I'm sorry the clothes don't fit," she says. "I'm sure we can find some better ones for you if the Amity allow us to stay."

"They're fine," I say. "Thank you."

"I heard you were shot. Do you need my help with your hair? Or your shoes?"

I am about to refuse, but I really do need help.

"Yes, thank you."

I sit down on a stool in front of the mirror, and she stands behind me, her eyes dutifully trained on the task at hand rather than her reflection. They do not lift, not even for an instant, as she runs a comb through my hair. And she doesn't ask about my shoulder, how I was shot, what happened when I left the Abnegation safe house to stop the simulation. I get the sense that if I were to whittle her down to her core, she would be Abnegation all the way through.

"Have you seen Robert yet?" I say. Her brother, Robert, chose Amity when I chose Dauntless, so he is somewhere in this compound. I wonder if their reunion will be any-thing like Caleb's and mine.

"Briefly, last night," she says. "I left him to grieve with his faction as I grieve with mine. It is nice to see him again, though."

I hear a finality in her tone that tells me the subject is closed.

"It's a shame this happened when it did," Susan says. "Our leaders were about to do something wonderful."

"Really? What?"

"I don't know." Susan blushes. "I just knew that something was happening. I didn't mean to be curious; I just noticed things."

"I wouldn't blame you for being curious even if you had been."

She nods and keeps combing. I wonder what the Abnegation leaders—including my father—were doing. And I can't help but marvel at Susan's assumption that whatever they were doing was wonderful. I wish I could believe that of people again.

If I ever did.

"The Dauntless wear their hair down, right?" she says.

"Sometimes," I say. "Do you know how to braid?"

So her deft fingers tuck pieces of my hair into one braid that tickles the middle of my spine. I stare hard at my reflection until she finishes. I thank her when she's done, and she leaves with a small smile, closing the door behind her.

I keep staring, but I don't see myself. I can still feel her fingers brushing the back of my neck, so much like my mother's fingers, the last morning I spent with her. My eyes wet with tears, I rock back and forth on the stool, trying to push the memory from my mind. I am afraid that if I start to sob, I will never stop until I shrivel up like a raisin.

I see a sewing kit on the dresser. In it are two colors of thread, red and yellow, and a pair of scissors.

I feel calm as I undo the braid in my hair and comb it again. I part my hair down the middle and make sure that it is straight and flat. I close the scissors over the hair by my chin.

How can I look the same, when she's gone and everything is different? I can't.

I cut in as straight a line as I can, using my jaw as a guide. The tricky part is the back, which I can't see very well, so I do the best I can by touch instead of sight. Locks of blond hair surround me on the floor in a semicircle.

I leave the room without looking at my reflection again.

+ + +

When Tobias and Caleb come to get me later, they stare at me like I am not the person they knew yesterday.

"You cut your hair," says Caleb, his eyebrows high. Grabbing hold of facts in the midst of shock is very Erudite of him. His hair sticks up on one side from where he slept on it, and his eyes are bloodshot.

"Yeah," I say. "It's . . . too hot for long hair."

"Fair enough."

We walk down the hallway together. The floorboards creak beneath our feet. I miss the way my footsteps echoed in the Dauntless compound; I miss the cool underground air. But mostly I miss the fears of the past few weeks, rendered small by my fears now.

We exit the building. The outside air presses around me like a pillow meant to suffocate me. It smells green, the way a leaf does when you tear it in half.

"Does everyone know you're Marcus's son?" Caleb says. "The Abnegation, I mean?"

"Not to my knowledge," says Tobias, glancing at Caleb. "And I would appreciate it if you didn't mention it."

"I don't need to mention it. Anyone with eyes can see it for themselves." Caleb frowns at him. "How old are you, anyway?"

"Eighteen."

"And you don't think you're too old to be with my little sister?"

Tobias lets out a short laugh. "She isn't *your little* anything."

"Stop it. Both of you," I say. A crowd of people in yellow walks ahead of us, toward a wide, squat building made entirely of glass. The sunlight reflecting off the panes feels like a pinch to my eyes. I shield my face with my hand and keep walking.

The doors to the building are wide open. Around the edge of the circular greenhouse, plants and trees grow in troughs of water or small pools. Dozens of fans positioned around the room serve only to blow the hot air around, so I am already sweating. But that fades from my mind when the crowd before me thins and I see the rest of the room.

In its center grows a huge tree. Its branches are spread over most of the greenhouse, and its roots bubble up from the ground, forming a dense web of bark. In the spaces between the roots, I see not dirt but water, and metal rods holding the roots in place. I should not be surprised—the Amity spend their lives accomplishing feats of agriculture like this one, with the help of Erudite technology.

Standing on a cluster of roots is Johanna Reyes, her hair falling over the scarred half of her face. I learned in Faction History that the Amity recognize no official leader—they vote on everything, and the result is usually close to unanimous. They are like many parts of a single mind, and Johanna is their mouthpiece.

The Amity sit on the floor, most with their legs crossed, in knots and clusters that vaguely resemble the tree roots to me. The Abnegation sit in tight rows a few yards to my left. My eyes search the crowd for a few seconds before I realize what I'm looking for: my parents.

I swallow hard, and try to forget. Tobias touches the small of my back, guiding me to the edge of the meeting space, behind the Abnegation. Before we sit down, he puts his mouth next to my ear and says, "I like your hair that way."

I find a small smile to give him, and lean into him when I sit down, my arm against his.

Johanna lifts her hands and bows her head. All conversation in the room ceases before I can draw my next breath. All around me the Amity sit in silence, some with their eyes closed, some with their lips mouthing words I can't hear, some staring at a point far away.

Every second chafes. By the time Johanna lifts her head I am worn to the bone.

"We have before us today an urgent question," she says, "which is: How will we conduct ourselves in this time of conflict as people who pursue peace?"

Every Amity in the room turns to the person next to him or her and starts talking.

"How do they get anything done?" I say, as the minutes of chatter wear on.

"They don't care about efficiency," Tobias says. "They care about agreement. Watch."

Two women in yellow dresses a few feet away rise and join a trio of men. A young man shifts so that his small circle becomes a large one with the group next to him. All around the room, the smaller crowds grow and expand, and fewer and fewer voices fill the room, until there are only three or four. I can only hear pieces of what they say: "Peace—Dauntless—Erudite—safe house—involvement—"

"This is bizarre," I say.

"I think it's beautiful," he says.

I give him a look.

"What?" He laughs a little. "They each have an equal role in government; they each feel equally responsible. And it makes them care; it makes them kind. I think that's beautiful."

"I think it's unsustainable," I say. "Sure, it works for the Amity. But what happens when not everyone wants to strum banjos and grow crops? What happens when someone does something terrible and talking about it can't solve the problem?"

He shrugs. "I guess we'll find out."

Eventually someone from each of the big groups stands and approaches Johanna, picking their way carefully over the roots of the big tree. I expect them to address the rest of us, but instead they stand in a circle with Johanna and the other spokespeople and talk quietly. I begin to get the feeling that I will never know what they're saying.

"They're not going to let us argue with them, are they," I say.

"I doubt it," he says.

We are done for.

When everyone has said his or her piece, they sit down again, leaving Johanna alone in the center of the room. She angles her body toward us and folds her hands in front of her. Where will we go when they tell us to leave? Back into the city, where nothing is safe?

"Our faction has had a close relationship with Erudite for as long as any of us can remember. We need each other to survive, and we have always cooperated with each other," says Johanna. "But we have also had a strong relationship with Abnegation in the past, and we do not think it is right to revoke the hand of friendship when it has for so long been extended."

Her voice is honey-sweet, and moves like honey too, slow and careful. I wipe the sweat from my hairline with the back of my hand.

"We feel that the only way to preserve our relationships with both factions is to remain impartial and uninvolved," she continues. "Your presence here, though welcome, complicates that."

Here it comes, I think.

"We have arrived at the conclusion that we will establish our faction headquarters as a safe house for members of all factions," she says, "under a set of conditions. The first is that no weaponry of any kind is allowed on the compound. The second is that if any serious conflict arises, whether verbal or physical, all involved parties will be asked to leave. The third is that the conflict may not be discussed, even privately, within the confines of this compound. And the fourth is that everyone who stays here must contribute to the welfare of this environment by working. We will report this to Erudite, Candor, and Dauntless as soon as we can."

Her stare drifts to Tobias and me, and stays there.

"You are welcome to stay here if and only if you can abide by our rules," she says. "That is our decision."

I think of the gun I hid under my mattress, and the tension between me and Peter, and Tobias and Marcus, and my mouth feels dry. I am not good at avoiding conflict.

"We won't be able to stay long," I say to Tobias under my breath.

A moment ago, he was still faintly smiling. Now the corners of his mouth have disappeared into a frown. "No, we won't."

CHAPTER
THREE

THAT EVENING I return to my room and slide my hand beneath my mattress to make sure the gun is still there. My fingers brush over the trigger, and my throat tightens like I am having an allergic reaction. I withdraw my hand and kneel on the edge of the bed, taking hard swallows of air until the feeling subsides.

What is wrong with you? I shake my head. *Pull it together.*

And that is what it feels like: pulling the different parts of me up and in like a shoelace. I feel suffocated, but at least I feel strong.

I see a flicker of movement in my periphery, and look out the window that faces the apple orchard. Johanna Reyes and Marcus Eaton walk side by side, pausing at the herb garden to pluck mint leaves from their stems. I am out of my room before I can evaluate why I want to follow them.

I sprint through the building so that I don't lose them. Once I am outside, I have to be more careful. I walk around the far side of the greenhouse and, after I see Johanna and Marcus disappear into one row of trees, I creep down the next row, hoping the branches will hide me if either of them looks back.

". . . been confused about is the timing of the attack," says Johanna. "Is it just that Jeanine finally finished planning it, and acted, or was there an inciting incident of some kind?"

I see Marcus's face through a divided tree trunk. He presses his lips together and says, "Hmm."

"I suppose we'll never know." Johanna raises her good eyebrow. "Will we?"

"No, perhaps not."

Johanna places her hand on his arm and turns toward him. I stiffen, afraid for a moment that she will see me, but she looks only at Marcus. I sink into a crouch and crawl toward one of the trees so that the trunk will hide me. The bark itches my spine, but I don't move.

"But you *do* know," she says. "You know why she attacked when she did. I may not be Candor anymore, but I can still tell when someone is keeping the truth from me."

"Inquisitiveness is self-serving, Johanna."

If I were Johanna, I would snap at him for a comment like that, but she says kindly, "My faction depends on me to advise them, and if you know information this crucial, it is important that I know it also so that I can share it with them. I'm sure you can understand that, Marcus."

"There is a reason you don't know all the things I know. A long time ago, the Abnegation were entrusted with some sensitive information," says Marcus. "Jeanine attacked us to steal it. And if I am not careful, she will destroy it, so that is all I can tell you."

"But surely—"

"No," Marcus cuts her off. "This information is far more important than you can imagine. Most of the leaders of this city risked their lives to protect it from Jeanine and died, and I will not jeopardize it now for the sake of sating your selfish curiosity."

Johanna is quiet for a few seconds. It's so dark now I can barely see my own hands. The air smells like dirt and apples, and I try not to breathe it too loudly.

"I'm sorry," says Johanna. "I must have done something to make you believe I am not trustworthy."

"The last time I trusted a faction representative with this information, all my friends were murdered," he replies. "I don't trust anyone anymore."

I can't help it—I lean forward so that I can see around the trunk of the tree. Both Marcus and Johanna are too preoccupied to notice the movement. They are close together, but not touching, and I've never seen Marcus look so tired or Johanna so angry. But her face softens, and she touches Marcus's arm again, this time with a light caress.

"In order to have peace, we must first have trust," says Johanna. "So I hope you change your mind. Remember that I have always been your friend, Marcus, even when you did not have many to speak of."

She leans in and kisses his cheek, then walks to the end of the orchard. Marcus stands for a few seconds, apparently stunned, and starts toward the compound.

The revelations of the past half hour buzz in my mind. I thought Jeanine attacked the Abnegation to seize power, but she attacked them to steal information—information only they knew.

Then the buzzing stops as I remember something else Marcus said: *Most of the leaders of this city risked their lives for it.* Was one of those leaders my father?

I have to know. I have to find out what could possibly be important enough for the Abnegation to die for—and the Erudite to kill for.

+ + +

I pause before knocking on Tobias's door, and listen to what's going on inside.

"No, not like *that*," Tobias says through laughter.

"What do you mean, 'not like that'? I imitated you perfectly." The second voice belongs to Caleb.

"You did not."

"Well, do it again, then."

I push open the door just as Tobias, who is sitting on the floor with one leg stretched out, hurls a butter knife at the opposite wall. It sticks, handle out, from a large hunk of cheese they positioned on top of the dresser. Caleb, standing beside him, stares in disbelief, first at the cheese and then at me.

"Tell me he's some kind of Dauntless prodigy," says Caleb. "Can you do this too?"

He looks better than he did earlier—his eyes aren't red anymore and some of the old spark of curiosity is in them, like he is interested in the world again. His brown hair is tousled, his shirt buttons in the wrong buttonholes. He is handsome in a careless way, my brother, like he has no idea what he looks like most of the time.

"With my right hand, maybe," I say. "But yes, *Four* is some kind of Dauntless prodigy. Can I ask *why* you're throwing knives at cheese?"

Tobias's eyes catch mine on the word "Four." Caleb

doesn't know that Tobias wears his excellence all the time in his own nickname.

"Caleb came by to discuss something," Tobias says, leaning his head against the wall as he looks at me. "And knife-throwing just came up somehow."

"As it so often does," I say, a small smile inching its way across my face.

He looks so relaxed, his head back, his arm slung over his knee. We stare at each other for a few more seconds than is socially acceptable. Caleb clears his throat.

"Anyway, I should be getting back to my room," Caleb says, looking from Tobias to me and back again. "I'm reading this book about the water-filtration systems. The kid who gave it to me looked at me like I was crazy for wanting to read it. I think it's supposed to be a repair manual, but it's fascinating." He pauses. "Sorry. You probably think I'm crazy too."

"Not at all," Tobias says with mock sincerity. "Maybe *you* should read that repair manual too, Tris. It sounds like something you might like."

"I can loan it to you," Caleb says.

"Maybe later," I say. When Caleb closes the door behind him, I give Tobias a dirty look.

"Thanks for that," I say. "Now he's going to talk my ear off about water filtration and how it works. Though I guess

I might prefer that to what he wants to talk to me about."

"Oh? And what's that?" Tobias quirks his eyebrows. "Aquaponics?"

"Aqua-what?"

"It's one of the ways they grow food here. You don't want to know."

"You're right, I don't," I say. "What did he come to talk to you about?"

"You," he says. "I think it was the big-brother talk. 'Don't mess around with my sister' and all that."

He gets up.

"What did you tell him?"

He comes toward me.

"I told him how we got together—that's how knife-throwing came up," he says, "and I told him I wasn't messing around."

I feel warm everywhere. He wraps his hands around my hips and presses me gently against the door. His lips find mine.

I don't remember why I came here in the first place.

And I don't care.

I wrap my uninjured arm around him, pulling him against me. My fingers find the hem of his T-shirt, and slide beneath it, spreading wide over the small of his back. He feels so strong.

He kisses me again, more insistent this time, his hands squeezing my waist. His breaths, my breaths, his body, my body, we are so close there is no difference.

He pulls back, just a few centimeters. I almost don't let him get that far.

"This isn't what you came here for," he says.

"No."

"What did you come for, then?"

"Who cares?"

I push my fingers through his hair, and draw his mouth to mine again. He doesn't resist, but after a few seconds, he mumbles, "Tris," against my cheek.

"Okay, okay." I close my eyes. I did come here for something important: to tell him the conversation I overheard.

We sit side by side on Tobias's bed, and I start from the beginning. I tell him how I followed Marcus and Johanna into the orchard. I tell him Johanna's question about the timing of the simulation attack, and Marcus's response, and the argument that followed. As I do, I watch his expression. He does not look shocked or curious. Instead, his mouth works its way into the bitter pucker that accompanies any mention of Marcus.

"Well, what do you think?" I say once I finish.

"I think," he says carefully, "that it's Marcus trying to feel more important than he is."

That was not the response I was expecting.

"So . . . what? You think he's just talking nonsense?"

"I think there probably is some information the Abnegation knew that Jeanine wanted to know, but I think he's exaggerating its importance. Trying to build up his own ego by making Johanna think he's got something she wants and he won't give it to her."

"I don't . . ." I frown. "I don't think you're right. He didn't sound like he was lying."

"You don't know him like I do. He is an excellent liar."

He is right—I don't know Marcus, and certainly not as well as he does. But my instinct was to believe Marcus, and I usually trust my instincts.

"Maybe you're right," I say, "but shouldn't we find out what's going on? Just to be sure?"

"I think it's more important that we deal with the situation at hand," says Tobias. "Go back to the city. Find out what's going on there. Find a way to take Erudite down. Then maybe we can find out what Marcus was talking about, after this is all resolved. Okay?"

I nod. It sounds like a good plan—a smart plan. But I don't believe him—I don't believe it's more important to move forward than to find out the truth. When I found out that I was Divergent . . . when I found out that Erudite would attack Abnegation . . . those revelations changed everything. The truth has a way of changing a person's plans.

But it is difficult to persuade Tobias to do something he doesn't want to do, and even more difficult to justify my feelings with no evidence except my intuition.

So I agree. But I do not change my mind.

CHAPTER
FOUR

"Biotechnology has been around for a long time, but it wasn't always very effective," Caleb says. He starts on the crust of his toast—he ate the middle first, just like he used to when we were little.

He sits across from me in the cafeteria, at the table closest to the windows. Carved into the wood along the table's edge are the letters "D" and "T" linked together by a heart, so small I almost didn't see them. I run my fingers over the carving as Caleb speaks.

"But Erudite scientists developed this highly effective mineral solution a while back. It was better for the plants than dirt," he says. "It's an earlier version of that salve they put on your shoulder—it accelerates the growth of new cells."

His eyes are wild with new information. Not all the Erudite are power hungry and devoid of conscience, like their leader, Jeanine Matthews. Some of them are like Caleb: fascinated by everything, dissatisfied until they find out how it works.

I rest my chin on my hand and smile a little at him. He seems upbeat this morning. I am glad he has found something to distract him from his grief.

"So Erudite and Amity work together, then?" I say.

"More closely than Erudite and any other faction," he says. "Don't you remember from our Faction History book? It called them the 'essential factions'—without them, we would be incapable of survival. Some of the Erudite texts called them the 'enriching factions.' And one of Erudite's missions as a faction was to become both—essential and enriching."

It doesn't sit well with me, how much our society needs Erudite to function. But they *are* essential—without them, there would be inefficient farming, insufficient medical treatments, and no technological advance.

I bite my apple.

"You aren't going to eat your toast?" he says.

"The bread tastes strange," I say. "You can have it if you want."

"I'm amazed by how they live here," he says as he

takes the toast from my plate. "They're completely self-sustaining. They have their own source of power, their own water pumps, their own water filtration, their own food sources. . . . They're independent."

"Independent," I say, "and uninvolved. Must be nice."

It *is* nice, from what I can tell. The large windows beside our table let in so much sunlight I feel like I'm sitting outside. Clusters of Amity sit at the other tables, their clothes bright against their tanned skin. On me the yellow looks dull.

"So I take it Amity wasn't one of the factions you had an aptitude for," he says, grinning.

"No." The group of Amity a few seats away from us bursts into laughter. They haven't even glanced in our direction since we sat down to eat. "Keep it down, all right? It's not something I want to broadcast."

"Sorry," he says, leaning over the table so that he can talk quieter. "So what were they?"

I feel myself tensing, straightening. "Why do you want to know?"

"Tris," he says, "I'm your brother. You can tell me anything."

His green eyes never waver. He's abandoned the useless spectacles he wore as a member of Erudite in favor of an Abnegation gray shirt and their trademark short haircut.

He looks just as he did a few months ago, when we were living across the hall from each other, both of us considering switching factions but not brave enough to tell one another. Not trusting him enough to tell him was a mistake I do not want to make again.

"Abnegation, Dauntless," I say, "and Erudite."

"*Three* factions?" His eyebrows lift.

"Yes. Why?"

"It just seems like a lot," he says. "We each had to choose a research focus in Erudite initiation, and mine was the aptitude test simulation, so I know a lot about the way it's designed. It's really difficult for a person to get two results—the program actually doesn't allow it. But to get *three* . . . I'm not even sure how that's possible."

"Well, the test administrator had to alter the test," I say. "She forced it to go to that situation on the bus so that she could rule out Erudite—except Erudite wasn't ruled out."

Caleb props his chin on a fist. "A program override," he says. "I wonder how your test administrator knew how to do that. It's not something they're taught."

I frown. Tori was a tattoo artist and an aptitude test volunteer—how *did* she know how to alter the aptitude test program? If she was good with computers, it was only as a hobby, and I doubt that a computer hobby would enable someone to fiddle with an Erudite simulation.

Then something from one of my conversations with her surfaces. *My brother and I both transferred from Erudite.*

"She was Erudite," I say. "A faction transfer. Maybe that's how."

"Maybe," he says, tapping his fingers—from left to right—against his cheek. Our breakfasts sit, almost forgotten, between us. "What does this mean about your brain chemistry? Or anatomy?"

I laugh a little. "I don't know. All I know is that I'm always aware during simulations, and sometimes I can wake myself up from them. Sometimes they don't even work. Like the attack simulation."

"How do you wake yourself up from them? What do you do?"

"I . . ." I try to remember. I feel like it has been a long time since I was in one, though it was only a few weeks. "It's hard to say, because the Dauntless simulations were supposed to end when we had calmed down. But in one of mine . . . the one where Tobias figured out what I was . . . I just did something impossible. I broke glass just by putting my hand on it."

Caleb's expression becomes distant, like he is looking into faraway places. Nothing like what I just described ever happened to him in the aptitude test simulation, I know. So maybe he is wondering what it felt like, or how it's possible. My cheeks grow warmer—he is analyzing my brain like he would analyze a computer or a machine.

"Hey," I say. "Come back."

"Sorry," he says, focusing on me again. "It's just . . ."

"Fascinating. Yeah, I know. You always look like someone's sucked the life right out of you when something fascinates you."

He laughs.

"Can we talk about something else, though?" I say. "There may not be any Erudite or Dauntless traitors around, but it still feels weird, talking about it in public like this."

"All right."

Before he can go on, the cafeteria doors open, and a group of Abnegation come in. They wear Amity clothes, like me, but also like me, it's obvious what faction they are really in. They are silent, but not somber—they smile at the Amity they pass, inclining their heads, a few of them stopping to exchange pleasantries.

Susan sits down next to Caleb with a small smile. Her hair is pulled back in its usual knot, but her blond hair shines like gold. She and Caleb sit just slightly closer than friends would, though they do not touch. She bobs her head to greet me.

"I'm sorry," she says. "Did I interrupt?"

"No," says Caleb. "How are you?"

"I'm well. How are you?"

I am just about to flee the dining hall rather than participate in careful, polite Abnegation conversation when Tobias comes in, looking harassed. He must have been working in the kitchen this morning, as part of our agreement with the Amity. I have to work in the laundry rooms tomorrow.

"What happened?" I say as he sits down next to me.

"In their enthusiasm for conflict resolution, the Amity have apparently forgotten that meddling creates *more* conflict," says Tobias. "If we stay here much longer, I am going to punch someone, and it's not going to be pretty."

Caleb and Susan both raise their eyebrows at him. A few of the Amity at the table next to ours stop talking to stare.

"You heard me," Tobias says to them. They all look away.

"As I said," I say, covering my mouth to hide my smile, "what happened?"

"I'll tell you later."

It must have to do with Marcus. Tobias doesn't like the dubious looks the Abnegation give him when he refers to Marcus's cruelty, and Susan is sitting right across from him. I clasp my hands in my lap.

The Abnegation sit at our table, but not right next to

us—a respectful distance of two seats away, though most of them still nod at us. They were my family's friends and neighbors and coworkers, and before, their presence would have encouraged me to be quiet and self-effacing. Now it makes me want to talk louder, to be as far from that old identity and the pain that accompanies it as possible.

Tobias goes completely still when a hand falls on my right shoulder, sending prickles of pain down my right arm. I clench my teeth to keep from groaning.

"She got shot in that shoulder," Tobias says without looking at the man behind me.

"My apologies." Marcus lifts his hand and sits down on my left. "Hello."

"What do *you* want?" I say.

"Beatrice," Susan says quietly. "There's no need to—"

"Susan, please," says Caleb quietly. She presses her lips into a line and looks away.

I frown at Marcus. "I asked you a question."

"I would like to discuss something with you," says Marcus. His expression is calm, but he's angry—the terseness in his voice betrays him. "The other Abnegation and myself have discussed it and decided that we should not stay here. We believe that, given the inevitability of further conflict in our city, it would be selfish of us to stay here while what remains of our faction is inside that fence. We would like to request that you escort us."

I did not expect that. Why does Marcus want to return to the city? Is it really just an Abnegation decision, or does he intend to do something there—something that has to do with whatever information the Abnegation have?

I stare at him for a few seconds and then look at Tobias. He has relaxed a little, but he keeps his eyes focused on the table. I don't know why he acts this way around his father. No one, not even Jeanine, makes Tobias cower.

"What do you think?" I say.

"I think we should leave the day after tomorrow," Tobias says.

"Okay. Thank you," says Marcus. He gets up and sits at the other end of the table with the rest of the Abnegation.

I inch closer to Tobias, not sure how to comfort him without making things worse. I pick up my apple with my left hand, and grab his hand under the table with my right.

But I can't keep my eyes away from Marcus. I want to know more about what he said to Johanna. And sometimes, if you want the truth, you have to demand it.

CHAPTER
FIVE

AFTER BREAKFAST, I tell Tobias I'm going for a walk, but instead I follow Marcus. I expect him to walk to the guests' dormitory, but he crosses the field behind the dining hall and walks into the water-filtration building. I hesitate on the bottom step. Do I really want to do this?

I walk up the steps and through the door that Marcus just closed behind him.

The filtration building is small, just one room with a few huge machines in it. As far as I can tell, some of the machines take in dirty water from the rest of the compound, a few of them purify it, others test it, and the last set pumps clean water back out to the compound. The piping systems are all buried except one, which runs along the ground to send water to the power plant, near the fence. The plant provides power to the entire city, using a combination of wind, water, and solar energy.

Marcus stands near the machines that filter the water. There the pipes are transparent. I can see brown-tinged water rushing through one pipe, disappearing into the machine, and emerging clear. Both of us watch the purification happen, and I wonder if he is thinking what I am: that it would be nice if life worked this way, stripping the dirt from our lives and sending us out into the world clean. But some dirt is destined to linger.

I stare at the back of Marcus's head. I have to do this now.

Now.

"I heard you, the other day," I blurt out.

Marcus whips his head around. "What are you doing, Beatrice?"

"I followed you here." I fold my arms over my chest. "I heard you talking to Johanna about what motivated Jeanine's attack on Abnegation."

"Did the Dauntless teach you that it's all right to invade another person's privacy, or did you teach yourself?"

"I'm a naturally curious person. Don't change the subject."

Marcus's forehead is creased, especially between the eyebrows, and there are deep lines next to his mouth. He looks like a man who has spent most of his life frowning. He might have been handsome when he was younger— perhaps he still is, to women his age, like Johanna—but all I see when I look at him are the black-pit eyes from Tobias's fear landscape.

"If you heard me talking to Johanna, then you know that I didn't even tell *her* about this. So what makes you think that I would share the information with *you*?"

I don't have an answer at first. But then it comes to me.

"My father," I say. "My father is dead." It's the first time I've said it since I told Tobias, on the train ride over, that my parents died for me. "Died" was just a fact to me then, detached from emotion. But "dead," mingling with the churning and bubbling noises in this room, strikes a blow like a hammer to my chest, and the monster of grief awakens, clawing at my eyes and throat.

I force myself to continue.

"He may not have actually died for whatever informa- tion you were referring to," I say. "But I want to know if it was something he risked his life for."

Marcus's mouth twitches.

"Yes," he says. "It was."

My eyes fill with tears. I blink them away.

"Well," I say, almost choking, "then what on earth was

it? Was it something you were trying to protect? Or steal? Or what?"

"It was . . ." Marcus shakes his head. "I'm not going to tell you that."

I step toward him. "But you want it back. And Jeanine has it."

Marcus *is* a good liar—or at least, someone who is skilled at hiding secrets. He does not react. I wish I could see like Johanna sees, like the Candor see—I wish I could read his expression. He could be close to telling me the truth. If I press just hard enough, maybe he'll crack.

"I could help you," I say.

Marcus's upper lip curls. "You have no idea how ridiculous that sounds." He spits the words at me. "You may have succeeded in shutting down the attack simulation, girl, but it was by luck alone, not skill. I would die of shock if you managed to do anything useful again for a long time."

This is the Marcus that Tobias knows. The one who knows right where to hit to cause the most damage.

My body shudders with anger. "Tobias is right about you," I say. "You're nothing but an arrogant, lying piece of garbage."

"He said that, did he?" Marcus raises his eyebrows.

"No," I say. "He doesn't mention you enough to say anything like that. I figured it out all on my own." I clench my teeth. "You're almost nothing to him, you know. And as time goes on, you become less and less."

Marcus doesn't answer me. He turns back to the water purifier. I stand for a moment in my triumph, the sound of rushing water combining with the heartbeat in my ears. Then I leave the building, and it isn't until I'm halfway across the field that I realize I didn't win. Marcus did.

Whatever the truth is, I'll have to get it from somewhere else, because I won't be asking him again.

+ + +

That night I dream that I am in a field, and I encounter a flock of crows clustered on the ground. When I swat a few of them away, I realize that they are perched on top of a man, pecking at his clothes, which are Abnegation gray. Without warning, they take flight, and I realize that the man is Will.

Then I wake up.

I turn my face into the pillow and release, instead of his name, a sob that throws my body against the mattress. I feel the monster of grief again, writhing in the empty space where my heart and stomach used to be.

I gasp, pressing both palms to my chest. Now the monstrous thing has its claws around my throat, squeezing my airway. I twist and put my head between my knees, breathing until the strangled feeling leaves me.

Even though the air is warm, I shiver. I get out of bed and creep down the hallway toward Tobias's room. My bare legs almost glow in the dark. His door creaks when I pull it open, loud enough to wake him. He stares at me for a second.

"C'mere," he says, sluggish from sleep. He shifts back on the bed to leave space for me.

I should have thought this through. I sleep in a long T-shirt one of the Amity lent me. It comes down just past my butt, and I didn't think to put on a pair of shorts before I came here. Tobias's eyes skim my bare legs, making my face warm. I lie down, facing him.

"Bad dream?" he says.

I nod.

"What happened?"

I shake my head. I can't tell him that I'm having nightmares about Will, or I would have to explain why. What would he think of me, if he knew what I had done? How would he look at me?

He keeps his hand on my cheek, moving his thumb over my cheekbone idly.

"We're all right, you know," he says. "You and me. Okay?"

My chest aches, and I nod.

"Nothing else is all right." His whisper tickles my cheek. "But we are."

"Tobias," I say. But whatever I was about to say gets lost in my head, and I press my mouth to his, because I know that kissing him will distract me from everything.

He kisses me back. His hand starts on my cheek, and then brushes over my side, fitting to the bend in my waist, curving over my hip, sliding to my bare leg, making me shiver. I press closer to him and wrap my leg around him. My head buzzes with nervousness, but the rest of me seems to know exactly what it's doing, because it all pulses to the same rhythm, all wants the same thing: to escape itself and become a part of him instead.

His mouth moves against mine, and his hand slips under the hem of the T-shirt, and I don't stop him, though I know I should. Instead a faint sigh escapes me, and heat rushes into my cheeks, embarrassment. Either he didn't hear me or he didn't care, because he presses his palm to my lower back, presses me closer. His fingers move slowly up my back, tracing my spine. My shirt creeps up my body, and I don't pull it down, even when I feel cool air on my stomach.

He kisses my neck, and I grab his shoulder to steady myself, gathering his shirt into my fist. His hand reaches the top of my back and curls around my neck. My shirt is twisted around his arm, and our kisses become desperate. I know my hands are shaking from all the nervous energy inside me, so I tighten my grip on his shoulder so he won't notice.

Then his fingers brush the bandage on my shoulder, and a dart of pain goes through me. It didn't hurt much, but it brings me back to reality. I can't be with him in *that* way if one of my reasons for wanting it is to distract myself from grief.

I lean back and carefully pull the hem of my shirt down so it covers me again. For a second we just lie there, our heavy breaths mixing. I don't mean to cry—now is not a good time to cry; no, it has to stop—but I can't get the tears out of my eyes, no matter how many times I blink.

"Sorry," I say.

He says almost sternly, "Don't apologize." He brushes the tears from my cheeks.

I know that I am birdlike, made narrow and small as if for taking flight, built straight-waisted and fragile. But when he touches me like he can't bear to take his hand away, I don't wish I was any different.

"I don't mean to be such a mess," I say, my voice

cracking. "I just feel so . . ." I shake my head.

"It's wrong," he says. "It doesn't matter if your parents are in a better place—they aren't here with you, and that's *wrong*, Tris. It shouldn't have happened. It shouldn't have happened to you. And anyone who tells you it's okay is a liar."

A sob racks my body again, and he wraps his arms around me so tightly I find it difficult to breathe, but it doesn't matter. My dignified weeping gives way to full-on ugliness, my mouth open and my face contorted and sounds like a dying animal coming from my throat. If this continues I will break apart, and maybe that would be better, maybe it would be better to shatter and bear nothing.

He doesn't speak for a long time, until I am quiet again.

"Sleep," he says. "I'll fight the bad dreams off if they come to get you."

"With what?"

"My bare hands, obviously."

I wrap my arm around his waist and take a deep breath of his shoulder. He smells like sweat and fresh air and mint, from the salve he sometimes uses to relax his sore muscles. He smells safe, too, like sunlit walks in the orchard and silent breakfasts in the dining hall. And in the moments before I drift off to sleep, I almost forget about our war-torn city and all the conflict that will come to find us soon, if we don't find it first.

In the moments before I drift off to sleep, I hear him whisper, "I love you, Tris."

And maybe I would say it back, but I am too far gone.

CHAPTER
SIX

THAT MORNING I wake up to the buzz of an electric razor. Tobias stands in front of the mirror, his head tilted so he can see the corner of his jaw.

I hug my knees, covered by the sheet, and watch him.

"Good morning," he says. "How did you sleep?"

"Okay." I get up, and as he tilts his head back to address his chin with the razor, I wrap my arms around him, pressing my forehead to his back where the Dauntless tattoo peeks out from beneath his shirt.

He sets the razor down and folds his hands over mine. Neither of us breaks the silence. I listen to him breathe, and he strokes my fingers idly, the task at hand forgotten.

"I should go get ready," I say after a while. I am reluctant to leave, but I am supposed to work in the laundry rooms, and I don't want the Amity to say I'm not fulfilling my part of the deal they offered us.

"I'll get you something to wear," he says.

I walk barefoot down the hallway a few minutes later, wearing the shirt I slept in and a pair of shorts Tobias borrowed from the Amity. When I get back to my bedroom, Peter is standing next to my bed.

Instinct makes me straighten up and search the room for a blunt object.

"Get out," I say as steadily as I can. But it's hard to keep my voice from shaking. I can't help but remember the look in his eyes as he held me over the chasm by my throat or slammed me against the wall in the Dauntless compound.

He turns to look at me. Lately when he looks at me it's without his usual malice—instead he just seems exhausted, his posture slouched, his wounded arm in a sling. But I am not fooled.

"What are you doing in my room?"

He walks closer to me. "What are you doing stalking Marcus? I saw you after breakfast yesterday."

I match his stare with my own. "That's none of your business. Get out."

"I'm here because I don't know why *you* get to keep track of that hard drive," he says. "It's not like you're particularly stable these days."

"*I'm* unstable?" I laugh. "I find that a little funny, coming from you."

Peter pinches his lips together and says nothing.

I narrow my eyes. "Why are you so interested in the hard drive anyway?"

"I'm not stupid," he says. "I know it contains more than the simulation data."

"No, you aren't stupid, are you?" I say. "You think if you deliver it to the Erudite, they'll forgive your indiscretion and let you back in their good graces."

"I don't want to be back in their good graces," he says, stepping forward again. "If I had, I wouldn't have helped you in the Dauntless compound."

I jab his sternum with my index finger, digging in my fingernail. "You helped me because you didn't want me to shoot you again."

"I may not be an Abnegation-loving faction traitor." He seizes my finger. "But no one gets to control me, especially not the Erudite."

I yank my hand back, twisting so that he won't be able to hold on. My hands are sweaty.

"I don't expect you to understand." I wipe my hands on the hem of my shirt as I inch toward the dresser. "I'm sure if it had been Candor and not Abnegation that got attacked, you would have just let your family get shot between the eyes without protest. But I'm not like that."

"Careful what you say about my family, Stiff." He moves with me, toward the dresser, but I carefully shift so that I stand between him and the drawers. I'm not going to reveal the hard drive's location by getting it out while he's in here, but I don't want to leave the path to it clear, either.

His eyes shift to the dresser behind me, to the left side, where the hard drive is hidden. I frown at him, and then notice something I didn't before: a rectangular bulge in one of his pockets.

"Give it to me," I say. "Now."

"No."

"Give it to me, or so help me, I will kill you in your sleep."

He smirks. "If only you could see how ridiculous you look when you threaten people. Like a little girl telling me she's going to strangle me with her jump rope."

I start toward him, and he shifts back, into the hallway.

"Don't call me 'little girl.'"

"I'll call you whatever I want."

I jerk into action, aiming my left fist where I know it will hurt the worst: at the bullet wound in his arm. He dodges the punch, but instead of trying again, I seize his arm as hard as I can and wrench it to the side. Peter screams at the top of his lungs, and while he's distracted by the pain, I kick him hard in the knee, and he falls to the ground.

People rush into the hallway, wearing gray and black and yellow and red. Peter surges toward me in a half crouch, and punches me in the stomach. I hunch over, but the pain doesn't stop me—I let out something between a groan and a scream, and launch myself at him, my left elbow pulled back near my mouth so that I can slam it into his face.

One of the Amity grabs me by the arms and half lifts, half pulls me away from Peter. The wound in my shoulder throbs, but I hardly feel it through the pulse of adrenaline. I strain toward him and try to ignore the stunned faces of the Amity and the Abnegation—and Tobias—around me, and the woman kneels next to Peter, whispering words in a soothing tone of voice. I try to ignore his groans of pain and the guilt stabbing at my stomach. I hate him. I don't care. I hate him.

"Tris, calm down!" Tobias says.

"He has the hard drive!" I yell. "He stole it from me! He has it!"

Tobias walks over to Peter, ignoring the woman crouched beside him, and presses his foot into Peter's rib cage to keep him in place. He then reaches into Peter's pocket and takes out the hard drive.

Tobias says to him—very quietly—"We won't be in a safe house forever, and this wasn't very smart of you." Then he turns toward me and adds, "Not very smart of you, either. Do you want to get us kicked out?"

I scowl. The Amity man with his hand on my arm starts to pull me down the hallway. I try to wrench my body out of his grasp.

"What do you think you're doing? Let go of me!"

"You violated the terms of our peace agreement," he says gently. "We must follow protocol."

"Just go," says Tobias. "You need to cool down."

I search the faces of the crowd that has gathered. No one argues with Tobias. Their eyes skirt mine. So I allow two Amity men to escort me down the hallway.

"Watch your step," one of them says. "The floorboards are uneven here."

My head pounds, a sign that I am calming down. The graying Amity man opens a door on the left. A label on the door says CONFLICT ROOM.

"Are you putting me in time-out or something?" I scowl. That is something the Amity would do: put me in time-out, and then teach me to do cleansing breaths or think positive thoughts.

The room is so bright I have to squint to see. The opposite wall has large windows that look out over the orchard.

Despite this, the room feels small, probably because the ceiling, like the walls and floor, is also covered with wooden boards.

"Please sit," the older man says, gesturing toward the stool in the middle of the room. It, like all other furniture in the Amity compound, is made of unpolished wood, and looks sturdy, like it is still attached to the earth. I do not sit.

"The fight is over," I say. "I won't do it again. Not here."

"We have to follow protocol," the younger man says. "Please sit, and we'll discuss what happened, and then we'll let you go."

All their voices are so soft. Not hushed, like the Abnegation speak, always treading holy ground and trying not to disturb. Soft, soothing, low—I wonder, then, if that is something they teach their initiates here. How best to speak, move, smile, to encourage peace.

I don't want to sit down, but I do, perched on the edge of the chair so I can get up fast, if necessary. The younger man stands in front of me. Hinges creak behind me. I look over my shoulder—the older man is fumbling with something on a counter behind me.

"What are you doing?"

"I am making tea," he says.

"I don't think tea is really the solution to this."

"Then tell us," the younger man says, drawing my

attention back to the windows. He smiles at me. "What do you believe is the solution?"

"Throwing Peter out of this compound."

"It seems to me," the man says gently, "that you are the one who attacked him—indeed, that you are the one who shot him in the arm."

"You have no idea what he did to deserve those things." My cheeks get hot again and mimic my heartbeat. "He tried to kill me. And someone else—he stabbed someone else in the eye . . . with a *butter* knife. He is evil. I had every *right* to—"

I feel a sharp pain in my neck. Dark spots cover the man in front of me, obscuring my view of his face.

"I'm sorry, dear," he says. "We are just following protocol."

The older man is holding a syringe. A few drops of whatever he injected me with are still in it. They are bright green, the color of grass. I blink rapidly, and the dark spots disappear, but the world still swims before me, like I am tilting forward and back in a rocking chair.

"How do you feel?" the younger man says.

"I feel . . ." *Angry,* I was about to say. Angry with Peter, angry with the Amity. *But that's not true, is it?* I smile. "I feel good. I feel a little like . . . like I'm floating. Or swaying. How do *you* feel?"

"Dizziness is a side effect of the serum. You may want to rest this afternoon. And I'm feeling well. Thank you for asking," he says. "You may leave now, if you would like."

"Can you tell me where to find Tobias?" I say. When I imagine his face, affection for him bubbles up inside me, and all I want to do is kiss him. "Four, I mean. He's handsome, isn't he? I don't really know why he likes me so much. I'm not very nice, am I?"

"Not most of the time, no," the man says. "But I think you could be, if you tried."

"Thank you," I say. "That's nice of you to say."

"I think you'll find him in the orchard," he says. "I saw him go outside after the fight."

I laugh a little. "The fight. What a silly thing . . ."

And it does seem like a silly thing, slamming your fist into someone else's body. Like a caress, but too hard. A caress is much nicer. Maybe I should have run my hand along Peter's arm instead. That would have felt better to both of us. My knuckles wouldn't ache right now.

I get up and steer myself toward the door. I have to lean against the wall for balance, but it's sturdy, so I don't mind. I stumble down the hallway, giggling at my inability to balance. I'm clumsy again, just like I was when I was younger. My mother used to smile at me and say, "Be careful where you put your feet, Beatrice. I don't want you to hurt yourself."

I walk outside and the green on the trees seems greener, so potent I can almost taste it. Maybe I *can* taste it, and it is like the grass I decided to chew when I was a child just to see what it was like. I almost fall down the stairs because of the swaying and burst into laughter when the grass tickles my bare feet. I wander toward the orchard.

"Four!" I call out. Why am I calling out a number? Oh yes. Because that's his name. I call out again, "Four! Where are you?"

"Tris?" says a voice from the trees on my right. It almost sounds like the tree is talking to me. I giggle, but of course it's just Tobias, ducking under a branch.

I run toward him, and the ground lurches to the side, so I almost fall. His hand touches my waist, steadies me. The touch sends a shock through my body, and all my insides burn like his fingers ignited them. I pull closer to him, pressing my body against his, and lift my head to kiss him.

"What did they—" he starts, but I stop him with my lips. He kisses me back, but too quickly, so I sigh heavily.

"That was lame," I say. "Okay, no it wasn't, but . . ."

I stand on my tiptoes to kiss him again, and he presses his finger to my lips to stop me.

"Tris," he says. "What did they do to you? You're acting like a lunatic."

"That's not very nice of you to say," I say. "They put me in a good mood, that's all. And now I really want to kiss you, so if you could just *relax*—"

"I'm not going to kiss you. I'm going to figure out what's going on," he says.

I pout my lower lip for a second, but then I grin as the pieces come together in my mind.

"*That's* why you like me!" I exclaim. "Because you're not very nice either! It makes so much more sense now."

"Come on," he says. "We're going to see Johanna."

"I like you, too."

"That's encouraging," he replies flatly. "Come *on*. Oh, for God's sake. I'll just carry you."

He swings me into his arms, one arm under my knees and the other around my back. I wrap my arms around his neck and plant a kiss on his cheek. Then I discover that the air feels nice on my feet when I kick them, so I move my feet up and down as he walks us toward the building where Johanna works.

When we reach her office, she is sitting behind a desk with a stack of paper in front of her, chewing on a pencil eraser. She looks up at us, and her mouth drifts open slightly. A hunk of dark hair covers the left side of her face.

"You really shouldn't cover up your scar," I say. "You look prettier with your hair out of your face."

Tobias sets me down too heavily. The impact is jarring and hurts my shoulder a little, but I like the sound my feet made when they hit the floor. I laugh, but neither Johanna nor Tobias laughs with me. Strange.

"What did you do to her?" Tobias says, terse. "What in God's name did you do?"

"I . . ." Johanna frowns at me. "They must have given her too much. She's very small; they probably didn't take her height and weight into account."

"They must have given her too much of *what*?" he says.

"You have a nice voice," I say.

"Tris," he says, "please be quiet."

"The peace serum," Johanna says. "In small doses, it has a mild, calming effect and improves the mood. The only side effect is some slight dizziness. We administer it to members of our community who have trouble keeping the peace."

Tobias snorts. "I'm not an idiot. *Every* member of your community has trouble keeping the peace, because they're all human. You probably dump it into the water supply."

Johanna does not respond for a few seconds. She folds her hands in front of her.

"Clearly you know that is not the case, or this conflict

would not have occurred," she says. "But whatever we agree to do here, we do together, as a faction. If I could give the serum to everyone in this city, I would. You would certainly not be in the situation you are in now if I had."

"Oh, definitely," he says. "Drugging the entire population is the best solution to our problem. Great plan."

"Sarcasm is not kind, Four," she says gently. "Now, I am sorry about the mistake in giving too much to Tris, I really am. But she violated the terms of our agreement, and I'm afraid that you might not be able to stay here much longer as a result. The conflict between her and the boy—Peter—is not something we can forget."

"Don't worry," says Tobias. "We intend to leave as soon as humanly possible."

"Good," she says with a small smile. "Peace between Amity and Dauntless can only happen when we maintain our distance from each other."

"That explains a lot."

"Excuse me?" she says. "What are you insinuating?"

"It explains," he says, gritting his teeth, "why, under a pretense of *neutrality*—as if such a thing is possible!—you have left us to die at the hands of the Erudite."

Johanna sighs quietly and looks out the window. Beyond it is a small courtyard with vines growing in it. The vines creep onto the window's corners, like they are trying to come in and join the conversation.

"The Amity wouldn't do something like that," I say. "That's *mean*."

"It is for the sake of peace that we remain uninvolved—" Johanna begins.

"Peace." Tobias almost spits the word. "Yes, I'm sure it will be very peaceful when we are all either dead or cowering in submission under the threat of mind control or stuck in an endless simulation."

Johanna's face contorts, and I mimic her, to see what it feels like to have my face that way. It doesn't feel very good. I'm not sure why she did it to begin with.

She says slowly, "The decision was not mine to make. If it was, perhaps we would be having a different conversation right now."

"Are you saying you disagree with them?"

"I am saying," she says, "that it isn't my place to disagree with my faction publicly, but I might, in the privacy of my own heart."

"Tris and I will be gone in two days," says Tobias. "I hope your faction doesn't change their decision to make this compound a safe house."

"Our decisions are not easily unmade. What about Peter?"

"You'll have to deal with him separately," he says.

"Because he won't be coming with us."

Tobias takes my hand, and his skin feels nice against mine, though it's not smooth or soft. I smile apologetically at Johanna, and her expression remains unchanged.

"Four," she says. "If you and your friends would like to remain . . . untouched by our serum, you may want to avoid the bread."

Tobias says thank you over his shoulder as we make our way down the hallway together, me skipping every other step.

CHAPTER
SEVEN

THE SERUM WEARS off five hours later, when the sun is just beginning to set. Tobias shut me in my room for the rest of the day, checking on me every hour. This time when he comes in, I am sitting on the bed, glaring at the wall.

"Thank God," he says, pressing his forehead to the door. "I was beginning to think it would never wear off and I would have to leave you here to . . . smell flowers, or whatever you wanted to do while you were on that stuff."

"I'll kill them," I say. "I will *kill* them."

"Don't bother. We're leaving soon anyway," he says, closing the door behind him. He takes the hard drive from his back pocket. "I thought we could hide this behind your dresser."

"That's where it was before."

"Yeah, and that's why Peter won't look for it here again." Tobias pulls the dresser away from the wall with one hand and wedges the hard drive behind it with the other.

"Why couldn't I fight the peace serum?" I say. "If my brain is weird enough to resist the simulation serum, why not this one?"

"I don't know, really," he says. He drops down next to me on the bed, jostling the mattress. "Maybe in order to fight off a serum, you have to *want* to."

"Well, obviously I *wanted* to," I say, frustrated, but without conviction. Did I want to? Or was it nice to forget about anger, forget about pain, forget about everything for a few hours?

"Sometimes," he says, sliding his arm across my shoulders, "people just want to be happy, even if it's not real."

He's right. Even now, this peace between us comes from not talking about things—about Will, or my parents, or me almost shooting him in the head, or Marcus. But I do not dare to disturb it with the truth, because I am too busy clinging to it for support.

"You might be right," I say quietly.

"Are you *conceding*?" he says, his mouth falling open with mock surprise. "Seems like that serum did you some good after all. . . ."

I shove him as hard as I can. "Take that back. Take it back *now*."

"Okay, okay!" He puts up his hands. "It's just . . . I'm not very nice either, you know. That's why I like you so—"

"Out!" I shout, pointing at the door.

Laughing to himself, Tobias kisses my cheek and leaves the room.

+ + +

That evening, I am too embarrassed by what happened to go to dinner, so I spend the time in the branches of an apple tree at the far end of the orchard, picking ripe apples. I climb as high as I dare to get them, muscles burning. I have discovered that sitting still leaves little spaces for the grief to get in, so I stay busy.

I am wiping my forehead with the hem of my shirt, standing on a branch, when I hear the sound. It is faint, at first, joining the buzz of cicadas. I stand still to listen, and after a moment, I realize what it is: cars.

The Amity own about a dozen trucks that they use for transporting goods, but they only do that on weekends. The back of my neck tingles. If it isn't the Amity, it's probably the Erudite. But I have to be sure.

I grab the branch above me with both hands, but pull myself up with only my left arm. I'm surprised I'm still able to do that. I stand hunched, twigs and leaves tangled in my hair. A few apples fall to the ground when I shift my weight. Apple trees aren't very tall; I may not be able to see far enough.

I use the nearby branches as steps, with my hands to steady me, twisting and leaning around the tree's maze. I remember climbing the Ferris wheel on the pier, my muscles shaking, my hands throbbing. I am wounded now, but stronger, and the climbing feels easier.

The branches get thinner, weaker. I lick my lips and look at the next one. I need to climb as high as possible, but the branch I'm aiming for is short and looks pliable. I put my foot on it, testing its strength. It bends, but holds. I start to lift myself up, to put the other foot down, and the branch snaps.

I gasp as I fall back, seizing the tree trunk at the last second. This will have to be high enough. I stand on my tiptoes and squint in the direction of the sound.

At first I see nothing but a stretch of farmland, a strip of empty ground, the fence, and the fields and beginnings of buildings that lie beyond it. But approaching the gate are a few moving specks—silver, when the light catches them. Cars with black roofs—solar panels, which means only one thing. Erudite.

A breath hisses between my teeth. I don't allow myself

to think; I just put one foot down, then the other, so fast that bark peels off the branches and drifts toward the ground. As soon as my feet touch the earth, I run.

I count the rows of trees as I pass them. *Seven, eight.* The branches dip low, and I pass just beneath them. *Nine, ten.* I hold my right arm against my chest as I sprint faster, the bullet wound in my shoulder throbbing with each footstep. *Eleven, twelve.*

When I reach the thirteenth row, I throw my body to the right, down one of the aisles. The trees are close together in the thirteenth row. Their branches grow into one another, creating a maze of leaves and twigs and apples.

My lungs sting from a lack of oxygen, but I am not far from the end of the orchard. Sweat runs into my eyebrows. I reach the dining hall and throw open the door, shoving my way through a group of Amity men, and he is there; Tobias sits at one end of the cafeteria with Peter and Caleb and Susan. I can barely see them between the spots on my vision, but Tobias touches my shoulder.

"Erudite," is all I manage to say.

"Coming here?" he says.

I nod.

"Do we have time to run?"

I am not sure about that.

By now, the Abnegation at the other end of the table are

paying attention. They gather around us.

"Why do we need to run?" says Susan. "The Amity established this place as a safe house. No conflict allowed."

"The Amity will have trouble enforcing that policy," says Marcus. "How do you stop conflict without conflict?"

Susan nods.

"But we can't leave," Peter says. "We don't have time. They'll see us."

"Tris has a gun," Tobias says. "We can try to fight our way out."

He starts toward the dormitory.

"Wait," I say. "I have an idea." I scan the crowd of Abnegation. "Disguises. The Erudite don't know for sure that we're still here. We can pretend to be Amity."

"Those of us who aren't dressed like the Amity should go to the dormitories, then," Marcus says. "The rest of you, put your hair down; try to mimic their behavior."

The Abnegation who are dressed in gray leave the dining hall in a pack and cross the courtyard to the guests' dormitory. Once inside, I run to my bedroom, get on my hands and knees, and reach under the mattress for the gun.

I feel around for a few seconds before I find it, and when I do, my throat pinches, and I can't swallow. I don't want to touch the gun. I don't want to touch it again.

Come on, Tris. I shove the gun under the waistband of

my red pants. It is lucky they are so baggy. I notice the vials of healing salve and pain medicine on the bedside table and shove them in my pocket, just in case we do manage to escape.

Then I reach behind the dresser for the hard drive.

If the Erudite catch us—which is likely—they will search us, and I don't want to just hand over the attack simulation again. But this hard drive also contains the surveillance footage from the attack. The record of our losses. Of my parents' deaths. The only piece of them I have left. And because the Abnegation don't take photographs, the only documentation I have of how they looked.

Years from now, when my memories begin to fade, what will I have to remind me of what they looked like? Their faces will change in my mind. I will never see them again.

Don't be stupid. It's not important.

I squeeze the hard drive so tightly it hurts.

Then why does it feel *so important?*

"Don't be stupid," I say aloud. I grit my teeth and grab the lamp from my bedside table. I yank the plug from the socket, throw the lampshade onto the bed, and crouch over the hard drive. Blinking tears from my eyes, I slam the base of the lamp into it, creating a dent.

I bring the lamp down again, and again, and again, until the hard drive cracks and pieces of it spread across the floor. Then I kick the shards under the dresser, put the lamp back, and walk into the hallway, wiping my eyes with the back of my hand.

A few minutes later, a small crowd of gray-clad men and women—and Peter—stand in the hallway, sorting through stacks of clothes.

"Tris," says Caleb. "You're still wearing gray."

I pinch my father's shirt, and hesitate.

"It's Dad's," I say. If I change out of it, I will have to leave it behind. I bite my lip so that the pain will steady me. I have to get rid of it. It's just a shirt. That's all it is.

"I'll put it on under mine," Caleb says. "They'll never see it."

I nod and grab a red shirt from the dwindling pile of clothes. It is large enough to conceal the bulge of the gun. I duck into a nearby room to change, and hand off the gray shirt to Caleb when I get to the hallway. The door is open, and through it I see Tobias stuffing Abnegation clothes into the trash bin.

"Do you think the Amity will lie for us?" I ask him, leaning out the open doorway.

"To prevent conflict?" Tobias nods. "Absolutely."

He wears a red collared shirt and a pair of jeans that are fraying at the knee. The combination looks ridiculous on him.

"Nice shirt," I say.

He wrinkles his nose at me. "It was the only thing that covered up the neck tattoo, okay?"

I smile nervously. I forgot about my tattoos, but the shirt hides them well enough.

The Erudite cars pull up to the compound. There are five of them, all silver with black roofs. Their engines seem to purr as the wheels bump over uneven ground. I slip just inside the building, leaving the door open behind me, and Tobias busies himself with the latch on the trash bin.

The cars all pull to a stop, and the doors pop open, revealing at least five men and women in Erudite blue.

And about fifteen in Dauntless black.

When the Dauntless come closer, I see strips of blue fabric wrapped around their arms that can only signify their allegiance to Erudite. The faction that enslaved their minds.

Tobias takes my hand and leads me into the dormitory.

"I didn't think our faction would be that stupid," he says. "You have the gun, right?"

"Yes," I say. "But there's no guarantee I can fire it with any accuracy with my left hand."

"You should work on that," he says. Always an instructor.

"I will," I say. I shake a little as I add, "If we live."

His hands skim my bare arms. "Just bounce a little when you walk," he says, kissing my forehead, "and pretend you're afraid of their guns"—another kiss between my eyebrows—"and act like the shrinking violet you could never be"—a kiss on my cheek—"and you'll be fine."

"Okay," I say. My hands tremble as I grip his shirt collar. I pull his mouth down to mine.

A bell sounds, once, twice, three times. It is a summons to the dining hall, where the Amity gather for less formal occasions than the meeting we attended. We join the crowd of Abnegation-turned-Amity.

I pull pins from Susan's hair—the hairstyle is too severe for Amity. She gives me a small, grateful smile as her hair falls on her shoulders, the first time I have ever seen it that way. It softens her square jaw.

I am supposed to be braver than the Abnegation, but they don't seem as worried as I am. They offer each other smiles and walk in silence—in too much silence. I wedge my way between them and jab one of the older women in the shoulder.

"Tell the kids to play tag," I say to her.

"Tag?" she says.

"They're acting respectful and . . . Stiff," I say, cringing as I say the word that was my nickname in Dauntless.

"And Amity kids would be causing a ruckus. Just do it, okay?"

The woman touches one Abnegation child on the shoulder and whispers something to him, and a few seconds later a small group of children run down the hallway, dodging Amity feet and yelling, "I touched you! You're *it*!" "No, that was my sleeve!"

Caleb catches on, jabbing Susan in the ribs so she shrieks with laughter. I try to relax, injecting a bounce into my step as Tobias suggested, letting my arms swing as I turn corners. It is amazing how pretending to be in a different faction changes everything—even the way I walk. That must be why it's so strange that I could easily belong in three of them.

We catch up to the Amity in front of us as we cross the courtyard to the dining hall and disperse among them. I keep Tobias in my peripheral vision, not wanting to stray too far from him. The Amity don't ask questions; they just let us dissolve into their faction.

A pair of Dauntless traitors stand by the door to the dining hall, their guns in hand, and I stiffen. It feels real to me, suddenly, that I am unarmed and being herded into a building surrounded by Erudite and Dauntless, and if they discover me, there will be nowhere to run. They will shoot me on the spot.

I consider making a break for it. But where would I go that they could not catch me? I try to breathe normally. I am almost past them—*don't look, don't look*. A few steps away—*eyes away, away.*

Susan loops her arm through mine.

"I'm telling you a joke," she says, "that you find very funny."

I cover my mouth with my hand and force a giggle that sounds high-pitched and foreign, but judging by the smile she gives me, it was believable. We hang on each other the way Amity girls do, glancing at the Dauntless and then giggling again. I am amazed by how I manage to do it, with the leaden feeling inside me.

"Thank you," I mutter once we're inside.

"You're welcome," she replies.

Tobias sits across from me at one of the long tables, and Susan sits next to me. The rest of the Abnegation spread throughout the room, and Caleb and Peter are a few seats down from me.

I tap my fingers on my knees as we wait for something to happen. For a long time we just sit there, and I pretend to be listening to an Amity girl telling a story on my left. But every so often I look at Tobias, and he looks back at me, like we're passing fear back and forth between us.

Finally Johanna walks in with an Erudite woman. Her

bright blue shirt seems to glow against her skin, which is dark brown. She searches the room as she speaks to Johanna. I hold my breath as her eyes find me—and then let it out when she moves on without a moment's hesitation. She did not recognize me.

At least, not yet.

Someone bangs on a tabletop, and the room goes quiet. This is it. This is the moment she either hands us over, or doesn't.

"Our Erudite and Dauntless friends are looking for some people," Johanna says. "Several members of Abnegation, three members of Dauntless, and a former Erudite initiate." She smiles. "In the interest of full cooperation, I told them that the people they were looking for were, in fact, here, but have since moved on. They would like permission to search the premises, which means we have to vote. Does anyone object to a search?"

The tension in her voice suggests that if anyone does object, they should keep their mouth shut. I don't know if the Amity pick up on that kind of thing, but no one says anything. Johanna nods to the Erudite woman.

"Three of you stick around," the woman says to the Dauntless guards clustered by the entrance. "The rest of you, search all the buildings and report back if you find anything. Go."

There is so much they could find. The pieces of the hard drive. Clothes I forgot to throw out. A suspicious lack of trinkets and decorations in our living spaces. I feel my pulse behind my eyes as the three Dauntless soldiers who stayed behind pace up and down the rows of tables.

The back of my neck tingles as one of them walks behind me, his footsteps loud and heavy. Not for the first time in my life, I'm glad that I'm small and plain. I don't draw people's eyes to me.

But Tobias does. He wears his pride in his posture, in the way his eyes claim everything they land on. That is not an Amity trait. It can only be a Dauntless one.

The Dauntless woman walking toward him looks at him right away. Her eyes narrow as she walks closer, and then stops directly behind him.

I wish the collar of his shirt were higher. I wish he didn't have so many tattoos. I wish . . .

"Your hair is pretty short for an Amity," she says.

. . . he did not cut his hair like the Abnegation.

"It's hot," he says.

The excuse might work if he knew how to deliver it, but he says it with a snap.

She stretches out her hand and, with her index finger, pulls back the collar of his shirt to see his tattoo.

And Tobias moves.

He grabs the woman's wrist, yanking her forward so she loses her balance. She hits her head against the edge of the table and falls. Across the room, a gun goes off, someone screams, and everyone dives under the tables or crouches next to the benches.

Everyone except me. I sit where I was before the gunshot sounded, clutching the edge of the table. I know that's where I am, but I don't see the cafeteria anymore. I see the alley I escaped down after my mother died. I stare at the gun in my hands, at the smooth skin between Will's eyebrows.

A small sound gurgles in my throat. It would have been a scream if my teeth had not been clamped shut. The flash of memory fades, but I still can't move.

Tobias grabs the Dauntless woman by the back of her neck and wrenches her to her feet. He has her gun in his hand. He uses her to shield him as he fires over her right shoulder at the Dauntless soldier across the room.

"Tris!" he shouts. "A little help here?"

I pull my shirt up just far enough to reach the handle of the gun, and my fingers meet metal. It feels so cold that it hurts my fingertips, but that can't be; it's so hot in here. A Dauntless man at the end of the aisle aims his own revolver at me. The black spot at the end of the barrel grows around me, and I can hear my heart but nothing else.

Caleb lunges forward and grabs my gun. He holds it in both hands and fires at the knees of the Dauntless man who stands just feet away from him.

The Dauntless man screams and collapses, his hands clutching his leg, which gives Tobias the opportunity to shoot him in the head. His pain is momentary.

My entire body is trembling and I can't stop it. Tobias still has the Dauntless woman by the throat, but this time, he aims his gun at the Erudite woman.

"Say another word," says Tobias, "and I'll shoot."

The Erudite woman's mouth is open, but she doesn't speak.

"Whoever's with us should start running," Tobias says, his voice filling the room.

All at once, the Abnegation rise from their places under tables and benches, and start toward the door. Caleb pulls me up from the bench. I start toward the door.

Then I see something. A twitch, a flicker of movement. The Erudite woman lifts a small gun, points it at a man in a yellow shirt in front of me. Instinct, not presence of mind, pushes me into a dive. My hands collide with the man, and the bullet hits the wall instead of him, instead of me.

"Put the gun down," says Tobias, pointing his revolver at the Erudite woman. "I have *very* good aim, and I'm betting that you don't."

I blink a few times to get the blurriness out of my eyes. Peter stares back at me. I just saved his life. He does not thank me, and I don't acknowledge him.

The Erudite woman drops her gun. Together Peter and I walk toward the door. Tobias follows us, walking backward so he can keep his gun on the Erudite woman. At the last second before he passes through the threshold, he slams the door between him and her.

And we all run.

We sprint down the center aisle of the orchard in a breathless pack. The night air is heavy as a blanket and smells like rain. Shouts follow us. Car doors slam. I run faster than I can possibly run, like I'm breathing adrenaline instead of air. The purr of engines chases me into the trees. Tobias's hand closes around mine.

We run through a cornfield in a long line. By then, the cars have caught up to us. The headlights creep through the tall stalks, illuminating a leaf here, an ear of corn there.

"Split up!" someone yells, and it sounds like Marcus.

We divide and spread through the field like spilling water. I grab Caleb's arm. I hear Susan gasping behind Caleb.

We crash over cornstalks. The heavy leaves cut my

cheeks and arms. I stare between Tobias's shoulder blades as we run. I hear a heavy thump and a scream. There are screams everywhere, to my left, to my right. Gunshots. The Abnegation are dying again, dying like they were when I pretended to be under the simulation. And all I'm doing is running.

Finally we reach the fence. Tobias runs along it, pushing it until he finds a hole. He holds the chain links back so Caleb, Susan, and I can crawl through. Before we start running again, I stop and look back at the cornfield we just left. I see headlights distantly glowing. But I don't hear anything.

"Where are the others?" whispers Susan.

I say, "Gone."

Susan sobs. Tobias pulls me to his side roughly, and starts forward. My face burns with shallow cuts from the corn leaves, but my eyes are dry. The Abnegation deaths are just another weight I am unable to set down.

We stay away from the dirt road the Erudite and Dauntless took to get to the Amity compound, following the train tracks toward the city. There is nowhere to hide out here, no trees or buildings that can shield us, but it doesn't matter. The Erudite can't drive through the fence anyway, and it will take them a while to reach the gate.

"I have to . . . stop . . ." says Susan from somewhere in

the darkness behind me.

We stop. Susan collapses to the ground, crying, and Caleb crouches next to her. Tobias and I look toward the city, which is still illuminated, because it's not midnight yet. I want to feel something. Fear, anger, grief. But I don't. All I feel is the need to keep moving.

Tobias turns toward me.

"What was that, Tris?" he says.

"What?" I say, and I am ashamed of how weak my voice sounds. I don't know whether he's talking about Peter or what came before or something else.

"You froze! Someone was about to kill you and you just *sat* there!" He is yelling now. "I thought I could rely on you at least to save your own life!"

"Hey!" says Caleb. "Give her a break, all right?"

"No," says Tobias, staring at me. "She doesn't need a break." His voice softens. "What happened?"

He still believes that I am strong. Strong enough that I don't need his sympathy. I used to think he was right, but now I am not sure. I clear my throat.

"I panicked," I say. "It won't happen again."

He raises an eyebrow.

"It won't," I say again, louder this time.

"Okay." He looks unconvinced. "We have to get somewhere safe. They'll regroup and start looking for us."

"You think they care that much about us?" I say.

"Us, yes," he says. "We were probably the only ones they were really after, apart from Marcus, who is most likely dead."

I don't know how I expected him to say it—with relief, maybe, because Marcus, his father and the menace of his life, is finally gone. Or with pain and sadness, because his father might have been killed, and sometimes grief doesn't make much sense. But he says it like it's just a fact, like the direction we're moving or the time of day.

"Tobias . . ." I start to say, but then I realize I don't know what comes after it.

"Time to go," Tobias says over his shoulder.

Caleb coaxes Susan to her feet. She moves only with the help of his arm across her back, pressing her forward.

I didn't realize until that moment that Dauntless initiation had taught me an important lesson: how to keep going.

CHAPTER
EIGHT

WE DECIDE TO follow the railroad tracks to the city, because none of us is good at navigation. I walk from tie to tie, Tobias balances on the rail, wobbling only occasionally, and Caleb and Susan shuffle behind us. I twitch at every unidentified noise, tensing until I realize it is just the wind, or the squeak of Tobias's shoes on the rail. I wish we could keep running, but it's a feat that my legs are even moving at this point.

Then I hear a low groan from the rails.

I bend down and press my palms to the rail, closing my eyes to focus on the feeling of the metal beneath my hands. The vibration feels like a sigh going through my body. I stare between Susan's knees down the tracks and see no train light, but that doesn't mean anything. The train could be running with no horns and no lamps to announce its arrival.

I see the gleam of a small train car, far away now but approaching fast.

"It's coming," I say. It is an effort to get to my feet when all I want to do is sit down, but I do, brushing my hands on my jeans. "I think we should get on."

"Even if it's run by the Erudite?" says Caleb.

"If the Erudite were running the train, they would have taken it to the Amity compound to look for us," Tobias says. "I think it's worth the risk. We'll be able to hide in the city. Here we're just waiting for them to find us."

We all get off the tracks. Caleb gives Susan step-by-step instructions for getting on a moving train, the way only a former Erudite can. I watch the first car approach; listen to the rhythmic bump of the car over the ties, the whisper of metal wheel against metal rail.

As the first car passes me, I start to run. I ignore the burning in my legs. Caleb helps Susan into a middle car first, then jumps in himself. I take a quick breath and throw my body to the right, slamming into the floor of the car with my legs dangling over the edge. Caleb grabs my left arm and pulls me in the rest of the way. Tobias uses the handle to swing himself in after me.

I look up, and stop breathing.

Eyes glitter in the darkness. Dark shapes sit in the car, more numerous than we are.

The factionless.

+ + +

The wind whistles through the car. Everyone is on their feet and armed—except Susan and me, who have no weapons. A factionless man with an eye patch has a gun pointed at Tobias. I wonder how he got it.

Next to him, an older factionless woman holds a knife—the kind I used to cut bread with. Behind him, someone else holds a large plank of wood with a nail sticking out of it.

"I've never seen the Amity armed before," the factionless woman with the knife says.

The factionless man with the gun looks familiar. He wears tattered clothes in different colors—a black T-shirt with a torn Abnegation jacket over it, blue jeans mended with red thread, brown boots. All faction clothing is represented in the group before me: black Candor pants paired with black Dauntless shirts, yellow dresses with blue sweatshirts over them. Most items are torn or smudged in some way, but some are not. Freshly stolen, I imagine.

"They aren't Amity," the man with the gun says. "They're Dauntless."

Then I recognize him: he is Edward, a fellow initiate who left Dauntless after Peter attacked him with a butter knife. That is why he wears an eye patch.

I remember steadying his head as he lay screaming on the floor, and cleaning the blood he left behind.

"Hello, Edward," I say.

He inclines his head to me, but doesn't lower his gun. "Tris."

"Whatever you are," the woman says, "you'll have to get off this train if you want to stay alive."

"Please," says Susan, her lip wobbling. Her eyes fill with tears. "We've been running . . . and the rest of them are dead and I don't . . ." She starts to sob again. "I don't think I can keep going, I . . ."

I get the strange urge to hit my head against the wall. Other people's sobs make me uncomfortable. It's selfish of me, maybe.

"We're running from the Erudite," says Caleb. "If we get off, it will be easier for them to find us. So we would appreciate it if you let us ride into the city with you."

"Yeah?" Edward tilts his head. "What have you ever done for us?"

"I helped you when no one else would," I say. "Remember?"

"You, maybe. But the others?" says Edward. "Not so much."

Tobias steps forward, so Edward's gun is almost against his throat.

"My name is Tobias Eaton," Tobias says. "I don't think you want to push me off this train."

The effect of the name on the people in the car is immediate and bewildering: they lower their weapons. They exchange meaningful looks.

"Eaton? Really?" Edward says, eyebrows raised. "I have to admit, I did not see that coming." He clears his throat. "Fine, you can come. But when we get to the city, you've got to come with us."

Then he smiles a little. "We know someone who's been looking for you, Tobias Eaton."

+ + +

Tobias and I sit on the edge of the car with our legs dangling over the edge.

"Do you know who it is?"

Tobias nods.

"Who, then?"

"It's hard to explain," he says. "I have a lot to tell you."

I lean against him.

"Yeah," I say. "So do I."

+ + +

I don't know how much time passes before they tell us to get off. But when they do, we are in the part of the city where the factionless live, about a mile from where I grew up. I recognize each building we pass as one I walked by every time I missed the bus home from school. The one with the broken bricks. The one with a fallen streetlight leaning against it.

We stand in the doorway of the train car, all four of us in a line. Susan whimpers.

"What if we get hurt?" she says.

I grab her hand. "We'll jump together. You and me. I've done this a dozen times and never got hurt."

She nods and squeezes my fingers so hard they hurt.

"On three. One," I say, "Two. *Three.*"

I jump, and pull her with me. My feet slam into the ground and continue forward, but Susan just falls to the pavement and rolls onto her side. Aside from a scraped knee, though, she seems to be all right. The others jump off without difficulty—even Caleb, who has only jumped from a train once before, as far as I know.

I'm not sure who could know Tobias among the factionless. It could be Drew or Molly, who failed Dauntless initiation—but they didn't even know Tobias's real name, and besides, Edward probably would have killed them by now, judging by how ready he was to shoot us. It must be someone from Abnegation, or from school.

Susan seems to have calmed down. She walks on her own now, next to Caleb, and her cheeks are drying with no new tears to wet them.

Tobias walks beside me, touching my shoulder lightly.

"It's been a while since I checked that shoulder," he says. "How is it?"

"Okay. I brought the pain medicine, luckily," I say. I'm glad to talk about something light—as light as a wound can be, anyway. "I don't think I'm letting it heal very well. I keep using my arm or landing on it."

"There will be plenty of time for healing once all this is over."

"Yeah." *Or it won't matter if I heal,* I add silently, *because I'll be dead.*

"Here," he says, taking a small knife from his back pocket and handing it to me. "Just in case."

I put it in my own pocket. I feel even more nervous now.

The factionless lead us down the street and left into a grimy alleyway that stinks of garbage. Rats scatter in front of us with squeaks of terror, and I see only their tails, slipping between mounds of waste, empty trash cans, soggy cardboard boxes. I breathe through my mouth so I don't throw up.

Edward stops next to one of the crumbling brick buildings and forces a steel door open. I wince, half expecting the entire building to fall down if he pulls too hard. The windows are so thick with grime that almost no light penetrates them. We follow Edward into a dank room. In the flickering glow of a lantern, I see . . . people.

People sitting next to rolls of bedding. People prying open cans of food. People sipping bottles of water. And children, weaving between the groups of adults, not confined to a particular color of clothing—factionless children.

We are in a factionless storehouse, and the factionless, who are supposed to be scattered, isolated, and without community . . . are together inside it. Are together, like a *faction*.

I don't know what I expected of them, but I am surprised by how normal they seem. They don't fight one another or avoid one another. Some of them tell jokes, others speak to each other quietly. Gradually, though, they all seem to realize that we aren't supposed to be there.

"Come on," Edward says, bending his finger to beckon

us toward him. "She's back here."

Stares and silence greet us as we follow Edward deeper into the building that is supposed to be abandoned. Finally I can't contain my questions any longer.

"What's going on here? Why are you all together like this?"

"You thought they—we—were all split up," Edward says over his shoulder. "Well, they were, for a while. Too hungry to do much of anything except look for food. But then the Stiffs started giving them food, clothes, tools, everything. And they got stronger, and waited. They were like that when I found them, and they welcomed me."

We walk into a dark hallway. I feel at home, in the dark and the quiet that are like the tunnels in Dauntless head-quarters. Tobias, however, winds a loose thread from his shirt around his finger, backward and forward, over and over. He knows who we're meeting, but I still have no idea. How is it I know this little about the boy who says he loves me—the boy whose real name is powerful enough to keep us alive in a train car full of enemies?

Edward stops at a metal door and pounds on it with his fist.

"Wait, you said they were waiting?" says Caleb. "What were they waiting *for*, exactly?"

"For the world to fall apart," Edward says. "And now it has."

The door opens, and a severe-looking woman with a lazy eye stands in the doorway. Her steady eye scans the four of us.

"Strays?" she says.

"Not hardly, Therese." He jabs his thumb over his shoulder, at Tobias. "This one's Tobias Eaton."

Therese stares at Tobias for a few seconds, then nods. "He certainly is. Hold on."

She shuts the door again. Tobias swallows hard, his Adam's apple bobbing.

"You know who she's going to get, don't you," says Caleb to Tobias.

"Caleb," Tobias says. "Please shut up."

To my surprise, my brother suppresses his Erudite curiosity.

The door opens again, and Therese steps back to let us in. We walk into an old boiler room with machinery that emerges from the darkness so suddenly I hit it with my knees and elbows. Therese leads us through the maze of metal to the back of the room, where several bulbs dangle from the ceiling over a table.

A middle-aged woman stands behind the table. She has curly black hair and olive skin. Her features are stern, so angular they almost make her unattractive, but not quite.

Tobias clutches my hand. At that moment I realize that he and the woman have the same nose—hooked, a little too big on her face but the right size on his. They also have the same strong jaw, distinct chin, spare upper lip, stick-out ears. Only her eyes are different—instead of blue, they are so dark they look black.

"Evelyn," he says, his voice shaking a little.

Evelyn was the name of Marcus's wife and Tobias's mother. My grip on Tobias's hand loosens. Just days ago I was remembering her funeral. Her *funeral*. And now she stands in front of me, her eyes colder than the eyes of any Abnegation woman I've ever seen.

"Hello." She walks around the table, surveying him. "You look older."

"Yes, well. The passage of time tends to do that to a person."

He already knew she was alive. How long ago did he find out?

She smiles. "So you've finally come—"

"Not for the reason you think," he interrupts her. "We were running from Erudite, and the only chance of escape we had required me to tell your poorly armed lackeys my name."

She must have made him angry somehow. But I can't

help but think that if I discovered my mother was alive after thinking she was dead for so long, I would never speak to her the way Tobias speaks to his mother now, no matter what she had done.

The truth of that thought makes me ache. I push it aside and focus instead on what's in front of me. On the table behind Evelyn is a large map with markers all over it. A map of the city, obviously, but I'm not sure what the markers mean. On the wall behind her is a chalkboard with a chart on it. I can't decipher the information in the chart; it's written in shorthand I don't know.

"I see." Evelyn's smile remains, but without its former touch of amusement. "Introduce me to your fellow refugees, then."

Her eyes drift down to our joined hands. Tobias's fingers spring apart. He gestures to me first. "This is Tris Prior. Her brother, Caleb. And their friend Susan Black."

"Prior," she says. "I know of several Priors, but none of them are named Tris. Beatrice, however . . ."

"Well," I say, "I know of several living Eatons, but none of them are named Evelyn."

"Evelyn Johnson is the name I prefer. Particularly among a pack of Abnegation."

"Tris is the name *I* prefer," I reply. "And we're not Abnegation. Not all of us, anyway."

Evelyn gives Tobias a look. "Interesting friends you've made."

"Those are population counts?" says Caleb from behind me. He walks forward, his mouth open. "And . . . what? Factionless safe houses?" He points to the first line on the chart, which reads 7 . . . . *Grn Hse.* "I mean, these places, on the map? They're safe houses, like this one, right?"

"That's a lot of questions," says Evelyn, arching an eyebrow. I recognize the expression. It belongs to Tobias—as does her distaste for questions. "For security purposes, I will not answer any of them. Anyway, it is time for dinner."

She gestures toward the door. Susan and Caleb start toward it, followed by me, and Tobias and his mother are last. We work our way through the maze of machinery again.

"I'm not stupid," she says in a low voice. "I know you want nothing to do with me—though I still don't quite understand why—"

Tobias snorts.

"But," she says, "I will extend my invitation again. We could use your help here, and I know you are like-minded about the faction system—"

"Evelyn," Tobias says. "I chose Dauntless."

"Choices can be made again."

"What makes you think I'm interested in spending time anywhere *near* you?" he demands. I hear his footsteps stop, and slow down so I can hear how she responds.

"Because I'm your mother," she says, and her voice almost breaks over the words, uncharacteristically vulnerable. "Because you're my son."

"You really don't get it," he says. "You don't have the vaguest conception of what you've done to me." He sounds breathless. "I don't want to join up with your little band of factionless. I want to get out of here as quickly as possible."

"My *little* band of factionless is twice the size of Dauntless," says Evelyn. "You would do well to take it seriously. Its actions may determine the future of this city."

With that, she walks ahead of him, and ahead of me. Her words echo in my mind: *Twice the size of Dauntless.* When did they become so large?

Tobias looks at me, eyebrows lowered.

"How long have you known?" I say.

"About a year." He slumps against the wall and closes his eyes. "She sent a coded message to me in Dauntless, telling me to meet her at the train yard. I did, because I was curious, and there she was. Alive. It wasn't a happy reunion, as you can probably guess."

"Why did she leave Abnegation?"

"She had an affair." He shakes his head. "And no

wonder, since my father . . ." He shakes his head again. "Well, let's just say Marcus wasn't any nicer to her than he was to me."

"Is . . . that why you're angry with her? Because she was unfaithful to him?"

"No," he says too sternly, his eyes opening. "No, that's not why I'm angry."

I walk toward him as if approaching a wild animal, each footstep careful on the cement floor. "Then why?"

"She had to leave my father, I get that," he says. "But did she think of taking me with her?"

I purse my lips. "Oh. She left you with *him*."

She left him alone with his worst nightmare. No wonder he hates her.

"Yeah." He kicks at the floor. "She did."

My fingers find his, fumbling, and he guides them into the spaces between his own. I know that's enough questions, for now, so I let the silence linger between us until he decides to break it.

"It seems to me," he says, "that the factionless are better friends than enemies."

"Maybe. But what would the cost of that friendship be?" I say.

He shakes his head. "I don't know. But we may not have any other option."

CHAPTER
NINE

ONE OF THE factionless started a fire so we could heat up our food. Those who want to eat sit in a circle around the large metal bowl that contains the fire, first heating the cans, then passing out spoons and forks, then passing cans around so everyone can have a bite of everything. I try not to think about how many diseases could spread this way as I dip my spoon into a can of soup.

Edward drops to the ground next to me and takes the can of soup from my hands.

"So you were all Abnegation, huh?" He shovels several noodles and a piece of carrot into his mouth, and passes the can to the woman on his left.

"We were," I say. "But obviously Tobias and I transferred, and . . ." Suddenly it occurs to me that I shouldn't tell anyone Caleb joined Erudite. "Caleb and Susan are still Abnegation."

"And he's your brother. Caleb," he says. "You ditched your family to become Dauntless?"

"You sound like the Candor," I say irritably. "Mind keeping your judgments to yourself?"

Therese leans over. "He was Erudite first, actually. Not Candor."

"Yeah, I know," I say, "I—"

She interrupts me. "So was I. Had to leave, though."

"What happened?"

"I wasn't smart enough." She shrugs and takes a can of beans from Edward, plunging her spoon into it. "I didn't get a high enough score on my initiation intelligence test. So they said, 'Spend your entire life cleaning up the research labs, or leave.' And I left."

She looks down and licks her spoon clean. I take the beans from her and pass them along to Tobias, who is staring at the fire.

"Are many of you from Erudite?" I say.

Therese shakes her head. "Most are from Dauntless, actually." She jerks her head toward Edward, who scowls. "Then Erudite, then Candor, then a handful of Amity. No one fails Abnegation initiation, though, so we have very few of those, except for a bunch who survived the simulation attack and came to us for refuge."

"I guess I shouldn't be surprised about Dauntless," I say.

"Well, yeah. You've got one of the worst initiations, and there's that whole old-age thing."

"Old-age thing?" I say. I glance at Tobias. He is listening now, and he looks almost normal again, his eyes thoughtful and dark in the firelight.

"Once the Dauntless reach a certain level of physical deterioration," he says, "they are asked to leave. In one way or another."

"What's the other way?" My heart pounds, like it already knows an answer I can't face without prompting.

"Let's just say," says Tobias, "that for some, death is preferable to factionlessness."

"Those people are idiots," says Edward. "I'd rather be factionless than Dauntless."

"How fortunate that you ended up where you did, then," says Tobias coldly.

"Fortunate?" Edward snorts. "Yeah. I'm so fortunate, with my one eye and all."

"I seem to recall hearing rumors that you provoked that attack," says Tobias.

"What are you talking about?" I say. "He was winning, that's all, and Peter was jealous, so he just . . ."

I see the smirk on Edward's face and stop talking. Maybe I don't know everything about what happened during initiation.

"There was an inciting incident," says Edward. "In which Peter did not come out the victor. But it certainly didn't warrant a butter knife to the eye."

"No arguments here," says Tobias. "If it makes you feel any better, he got shot in the arm from a foot away during the simulation attack."

And it does seem to make Edward feel better, because his smirk carves a deeper line into his face.

"Who did that?" he says. "You?"

Tobias shakes his head. "Tris did."

"Well done," Edward says.

I nod, but I feel a little sick to be congratulated for that. Well, not *that* sick. It was Peter, after all.

I stare at the flames wrapping around the fragments of wood that fuel them. They move and shift, like my thoughts. I remember the first time I realized I had never seen an elderly Dauntless. And when I realized my father was too old to climb the paths of the Pit. Now I understand more about that than I'd like to.

"Do you know much about how things are right now?"

Tobias asks Edward. "Did all the Dauntless side with Erudite? Has Candor done anything?"

"Dauntless is split in half," Edward says, talking around the food in his mouth. "Half at Erudite headquarters, half at Candor headquarters. What's left of Abnegation is with us. Nothing much has happened yet. Except for whatever happened to you, I guess."

Tobias nods. I feel a little relieved to know that half of the Dauntless, at least, are not traitors.

I eat spoonful after spoonful until my stomach is full. Then Tobias gets us sleeping pallets and blankets, and I find an empty corner for us to lie down in. When he bends over to untie his shoes, I see the symbol of Amity on the small of his back, the branches curling over his spine. When he straightens, I step across the blankets and put my arms around him, brushing the tattoo with my fingers.

Tobias closes his eyes. I trust the dwindling fire to disguise us as I run my hand up his back, touching each tattoo without seeing it. I imagine Erudite's staring eye, Candor's unbalanced scales, Abnegation's clasped hands, and the Dauntless flames. With my other hand I find the patch of fire tattooed over his rib cage. I feel his heavy breaths against my cheek.

"I wish we were alone," he says.

"I almost always wish that," I say.

I drift off to sleep, carried by the sound of distant conversations. These days it's easier for me to fall asleep when there is noise around me. I can focus on the sound instead of whatever thoughts would crawl into my head in silence. Noise and activity are the refuges of the bereaved and the guilty.

I wake when the fire is just a glow, and only a few of the factionless are still up. It takes me a few seconds to figure out why I woke up: I heard Evelyn's and Tobias's voices, a few feet away from me. I stay still and hope they don't discover that I'm awake.

"You'll have to tell me what's going on here if you expect me to consider helping you," he says. "Though I'm still not sure why you need me at all."

I see Evelyn's shadow on the wall, flickering with the fire. She is lean and strong, just like Tobias. Her fingers twist into her hair as she speaks.

"What would you like to know, exactly?"

"Tell me about the chart. And the map."

"Your friend was correct in thinking that the map and the chart listed all of our safe houses," she says. "He was wrong about the population counts . . . sort of. The numbers don't document all the factionless—only certain ones. And I'll bet you can guess which ones those are."

"I'm not in the mood for guessing."

She sighs. "The Divergent. We're documenting the Divergent."

"How do you know who they are?"

"Before the simulation attack, part of the Abnegation aid effort involved testing the factionless for a certain genetic anomaly," she says. "Sometimes that testing involved re-administering the aptitude test. Sometimes it was more complicated than that. But they explained to us that they suspected we might have the highest Divergent population of any group in the city."

"I don't understand. Why—"

"Why would the factionless have a high Divergent population?" It sounds like she's smirking. "Obviously those who can't confine themselves to a particular way of thinking would be most likely to leave a faction or fail its initiation, right?"

"That's not what I was going to ask," he says. "I want to know why *you* care how many Divergent there are."

"The Erudite are looking for manpower. They found it temporarily in Dauntless. Now they'll be looking for more, and we're the obvious place, unless they figure out that we've got more Divergent than any other group. Just in case they don't, I want to know how many people we've got who are resistant to simulations."

"Fair enough," he says, "but why were the Abnegation so concerned with finding the Divergent? It wasn't to help Jeanine, was it?"

"Of course not," she says. "But I'm afraid I don't know. The Abnegation were reluctant to provide information that only serves to relieve curiosity. They told us as much as they believed we should know."

"Strange," he mumbles.

"Perhaps you should ask your father about it," she says. "He was the one who told me about you."

"About me," says Tobias. "What about me?"

"That he suspected you were Divergent," she says. "He was always watching you. Noting your behavior. He was very attentive to you. That's why . . . that's why I thought you would be safe with him. Safer with him than with me."

Tobias says nothing.

"I see now that I must have been wrong."

He still says nothing.

"I wish—" she starts.

"Don't you dare try to apologize." His voice shakes. "This is not something you can bandage with a word or two and some hugging, or something."

"Okay," she says. "Okay. I won't."

"For what purpose are the factionless uniting?" he says. "What do you intend to do?"

"We want to usurp Erudite," she says. "Once we get rid of them, there's not much stopping us from controlling the government ourselves."

"That's what you expect me to help you with. Overthrowing one corrupt government and instating some kind of factionless tyranny." He snorts. "Not a chance."

"We don't want to be tyrants," she says. "We want to establish a new society. One without factions."

My mouth goes dry. No factions? A world in which no one knows who they are or where they fit? I can't even fathom it. I imagine only chaos and isolation.

Tobias lets out a laugh. "Right. So how are you going to usurp Erudite?"

"Sometimes drastic change requires drastic measures." Evelyn's shadow lifts a shoulder. "I imagine it will involve a high level of destruction."

I shiver at the word "destruction." Somewhere in the darker parts of me, I crave destruction, as long as it is Erudite being destroyed. But the word carries new meaning for me, now that I have seen what it can look like: gray-clothed bodies slung across curbs and over sidewalks, Abnegation leaders shot on their front lawns, next to their mailboxes. I press my face into the pallet I'm sleeping on, so hard it hurts my forehead, just to force the memory out, out, *out*.

"As for why we need you," Evelyn says. "In order to do this, we will need Dauntless's help. They have the weapons and the combat experience. You could bridge the gap between us and them."

"Do you think I'm important to the Dauntless? Because I'm not. I'm just someone who isn't afraid of much."

"What I am suggesting," she says, "is that you *become* important." She stands, her shadow stretching from ceiling to floor. "I am sure you can find a way, if you want to. Think about it."

She pulls back her curly hair and ties it in a knot. "The door is always open."

A few minutes later he lies next to me again. I don't want to admit that I was eavesdropping, but I want to tell him I don't trust Evelyn, or the factionless, or anyone who speaks so casually about demolishing an entire faction.

Before I can muster the courage to speak, his breaths become even, and he falls asleep.

CHAPTER
TEN

I RUN MY hand over the back of my neck to lift the hair that sticks there. My entire body aches, especially my legs, which burn with lactic acid even when I am not moving. And I don't smell very good. I need to shower.

I wander down the hall and into the bathroom. I am not the only person with bathing in mind—a group of women stand at the sinks, half of them naked, the other half completely unfazed by it. I find a free sink in the corner and stick my head under the faucet, letting cold water spill over my ears.

"Hello," Susan says. I turn my head to the side. Water courses down my cheek and into my nose. She is carrying two towels: one white, one gray, both frayed at the edges.

"Hi," I say.

"I have an idea," she says. She turns her back to me and holds up a towel, blocking my view of the rest of the bathroom. I sigh with relief. Privacy. Or as much of it as possible.

I strip quickly and grab the bar of soap next to the sink.

"How are you?" she says.

"I'm fine." I know she's only asking because faction rules dictate that she does. I wish she would just speak to me freely. "How are you, Susan?"

"Better. Therese told me there is a large group of Abnegation refugees in one of the factionless safe houses," says Susan as I lather soap into my hair.

"Oh?" I say. I shove my head under the faucet again, this time massaging my scalp with my left hand to get the soap out. "Are you going to go?"

"Yes," says Susan. "Unless you need my help."

"Thanks for the offer, but I think your faction needs you more," I say, turning off the faucet. I wish I didn't have to get dressed. It's too hot for denim pants. But I grab the other towel from the floor and dry myself in a hurry.

I put on the red shirt I was wearing before. I don't want to put on something that dirty again, but I have no other choice.

"I suspect some of the factionless women have spare clothes," says Susan.

"You're probably right. Okay, your turn."

I stand with the towel as Susan washes up. My arms start to ache after a while, but she ignored the pain for me, so I'll do the same for her. Water splashes on my ankles when she washes her hair.

"This is a situation I never thought we would be in together," I say after a while. "Bathing from the sink of an abandoned building, on the run from the Erudite."

"I thought we would live near each other," says Susan. "Go to social events together. Have our kids walk to the bus stop together."

I bite my lip at that. It is my fault, of course, that that was never a possibility, because I chose another faction.

"I'm sorry, I didn't mean to bring it up," she says. "I just regret that I didn't pay more attention. If I had, maybe I would have known what you were going through. I acted selfishly."

I laugh a little. "Susan, there's nothing wrong with the way you acted."

"I'm done," she says. "Can you hand me that towel?"

I close my eyes and turn so she can grab the towel from my hands. When Therese walks into the bathroom, smoothing her hair into a braid, Susan asks her for spare clothes.

By the time we leave the bathroom, I wear jeans and a black shirt that is so loose up top that it slips off my shoulders, and Susan wears baggy jeans and a white Candor shirt with a collar. She buttons it up to her throat. The Abnegation are modest to the point of discomfort.

When I enter the large room again, some of the factionless are walking out with buckets of paint and paintbrushes. I watch them until the door closes behind them.

"They're going to write a message to the other safe houses," says Evelyn from behind me. "On one of the billboards. Codes formed out of personal information—so-and-so's favorite color, someone else's childhood pet."

I am not sure why she would choose to tell me something about the factionless codes until I turn around. I see a familiar look in her eyes—it is the same as the one Jeanine wore when she told Tobias she had developed a serum that could control him: pride.

"Clever," I say. "Your idea?"

"It was, actually." She shrugs, but I am not fooled. She is anything but nonchalant. "I was Erudite before I was Abnegation."

"Oh," I say. "Guess you couldn't keep up with a life of academia, then?"

She doesn't take the bait. "Something like that, yes." She pauses. "I imagine your father left for the same reason."

I almost turn away to end the conversation, but her words create a kind of pressure inside my mind, like she is squeezing my brain between her hands. I stare.

"You didn't know?" She frowns. "I'm sorry; I forgot that faction members rarely discuss their old factions."

"What?" I say, my voice cracking.

"Your father was born in Erudite," she says. "His parents were friends with Jeanine Matthews's parents, before they died. Your father and Jeanine used to play together as children. I used to watch them pass books back and forth at school."

I imagine my father, a grown man, sitting next to Jeanine, a grown woman, at a lunch table in my old cafeteria, a book between them. The idea is so ridiculous to me that I half snort, half laugh. It can't be true.

Except.

Except: He never talked about his family or his childhood.

Except: He did not have the quiet demeanor of someone who grew up in Abnegation.

Except: His hatred of Erudite was so vehement it must have been *personal*.

"I'm sorry, Beatrice," Evelyn says. "I didn't mean to reopen closing wounds."

I frown. "Yes, you did."

"What do you mean—"

"Listen carefully," I say, lowering my voice. I check over her shoulder for Tobias, to make sure he isn't listening in. All I see is Caleb and Susan on the ground in the corner, passing a jar of peanut butter back and forth. No Tobias.

"I'm not stupid," I say. "I can see that you're trying to use him. And I'll tell him so, if he hasn't figured it out already."

"My dear girl," she says. "I am his family. I am permanent. You are only temporary."

"Yeah," I say. "His mom abandoned him, and his dad beat him up. How could his loyalty *not* be with his blood, with a family like that?"

I walk away, my hands shaking, and sit down next to Caleb on the floor. Susan is now across the room, helping one of the factionless clean up. He passes me the jar of peanut butter. I remember the rows of peanut plants in the Amity greenhouses. They grow peanuts because they are high in protein and fat, which is important for the factionless in particular. I scoop some of the peanut butter out with my fingers and eat it.

Should I tell him what Evelyn just told me? I don't want

to make him think that he has Erudite in his blood. I don't want to give him any reason to return to them.

I decide to keep it to myself for now.

"I wanted to talk to you about something," says Caleb.

I nod, still working the peanut butter off the roof of my mouth.

"Susan wants to go see the Abnegation," he says. "And so do I. I also want to make sure she's all right. But I don't want to leave you."

"It's okay," I say.

"Why don't you come with us?" he asks. "Abnegation would welcome you back; I'm sure of it."

So am I—the Abnegation don't hold grudges. But I am teetering on the edge of grief's mouth, and if I returned to my parents' old faction, it would swallow me.

I shake my head. "I have to go to Candor headquarters and find out what's going on," I say. "I'm going crazy, not knowing." I force a smile. "But you should go. Susan needs you. She seems better, but she still needs you."

"Okay." Caleb nods. "Well, I'll try to join you soon. Be careful, though."

"Aren't I always?"

"No, I think the word for how you usually are is 'reckless.'"

Caleb squeezes my good shoulder lightly. I eat another

fingertip's worth of peanut butter.

Tobias emerges from the men's bathroom a few minutes later, his red Amity shirt replaced by a black T-shirt, and his short hair glistening with water. Our eyes meet across the room, and I know it's time to leave.

+ + +

Candor headquarters is large enough to contain an entire world. Or so it seems to me.

It is a wide cement building that overlooks what was once the river. The sign says MERC   IS MART—it used to read "Merchandise Mart," but most people refer to it as the Merciless Mart, because the Candor are merciless, but honest. They seem to have embraced the nickname.

I don't know what to expect, because I have never been inside. Tobias and I pause outside the doors and look at each other.

"Here we go," he says.

I can't see anything beyond my reflection in the glass doors. I look tired and dirty. For the first time, it occurs to me that we don't have to do anything. We could hole up with the factionless and let the rest of them sort through this mess. We could be nobodies, safe, together.

He still hasn't told me about the conversation he had with his mother last night, and I don't think he's going to. He seemed so determined to get to Candor headquarters that I wonder if he's planning something without me.

I don't know why I walk through the doors. Maybe I decide that we've come this far, we might as well see what's going on. But I suspect it's more that I know what's true and what's not. I am Divergent, so I am not nobody, there's no such thing as "safe," and I have other things on my mind than playing house with Tobias. And so, apparently, does he.

The lobby is large and well-lit, with black marble floors that stretch back to an elevator bank. A ring of white marble tiles in the center of the room form the symbol of Candor: a set of unbalanced scales, meant to symbolize the weighing of truth against lies. The room is crawling with armed Dauntless.

A Dauntless soldier with an arm in a sling approaches us, gun held ready, barrel fixed on Tobias.

"Identify yourselves," she says. She is young, but not young enough to know Tobias.

The others gather behind her. Some of them eye us with suspicion, the rest with curiosity, but far stranger than both is the light I see in some of their eyes. Recognition. They might know Tobias, but how could they possibly recognize me?

"Four," he says. He nods toward me. "And this is Tris. Both Dauntless."

The Dauntless soldier's eyes widen, but she does not lower her gun.

"Some help here?" she asks. Some of the Dauntless step forward, but they do it cautiously, like we're dangerous.

"Is there a problem?" Tobias says.

"Are you armed?"

"Of course I'm armed. I'm Dauntless, aren't I?"

"Stand with your hands behind your head." She says it wildly, like she expects us to refuse. I glance at Tobias. Why is everyone acting like we're about to attack them?

"We walked through the front door," I say slowly. "You think we would have done that if we were here to hurt you?"

Tobias doesn't look back at me. He just touches his fingertips to the back of his head. After a moment, I do the same. Dauntless soldiers crowd around us. One of them pats down Tobias's legs while the other takes the gun tucked under his waistband. Another one, a round-faced boy with pink cheeks, looks at me apologetically.

"I have a knife in my back pocket." I say. "Put your hands on me, and I will make you regret it."

He mumbles some kind of apology. His fingers pinch the knife handle, careful not to touch me.

"What's going on?" asks Tobias.

The first soldier exchanges looks with some of the others.

"I'm sorry," she says. "But we were instructed to arrest you upon your arrival."

CHAPTER
ELEVEN

THEY SURROUND US, but don't handcuff us, and walk us to the elevator bank. No matter how many times I ask why we are under arrest, no one says anything or even looks in my direction. Eventually I give up and stay silent, like Tobias.

We go to the third level, where they take us to a small room with a white marble floor instead of a black one. There's no furniture except for a bench along the back wall. Every faction is supposed to have holding rooms for those who make trouble, but I've never been in one before.

The door closes behind us, and locks, and we're alone again.

Tobias sits down on the bench, his brow furrowed. I pace back and forth in front of him. If he had any idea why we were in here, he would tell me, so I don't ask. I walk five steps forward and five steps back, five steps forward and five steps back, at the same rhythm, hoping it will help me figure something out.

If Erudite didn't take over Candor—and Edward told us they didn't—why would the Candor arrest us? What could we have done to them?

If Erudite *didn't* take over, the only real crime left is siding with them. Did I do anything that could have been interpreted as siding with Erudite? My teeth dig into my lower lip so hard I wince. Yes, I did. I shot Will. I shot a number of other Dauntless. They were under the simulation, but maybe Candor doesn't know that or doesn't think it's a good enough reason.

"Can you please calm down?" Tobias says. "You're making me nervous."

"This is me calming down."

He leans forward, resting his elbows on his knees, and stares between his sneakers. "The wound in your lip begs to differ."

I sit next to him and hug my knees to my chest with one arm, my right arm hanging at my side. For a long time, he says nothing, and my arm wraps tighter and tighter around my legs. I feel like, the smaller I become, the safer I am.

"Sometimes," he says, "I worry that you don't trust me."

"I trust you," I say. "Of course I trust you. Why would you think otherwise?"

"Just seems like there's something you're not telling me. I told *you* things. . . ." He shakes his head. "I would never have told anyone else. Something's been going on with you, though, and you haven't told me yet."

"There's been a lot going on. You know that," I say. "And anyway, what about you? I could say the same thing to you."

He touches my cheek, his fingers pushing into my hair. Ignoring my question just like I ignored his.

"If it's just about your parents," he says softly, "tell me and I'll believe you."

His eyes should be wild with apprehension, given where we are, but they are still and dark. They transport me to familiar places. Safe places, where confessing that I shot one of my best friends would be easy, where I would not be afraid of the way that Tobias will look at me when he finds out what I did.

I cover his hand with mine. "That's all it is," I say weakly.

"Okay," he says. He touches his mouth to mine. Guilt clutches at my stomach.

The door opens. A few people file in—two Candor with guns; a dark-skinned, older Candor man; a Dauntless woman I don't recognize. And then: Jack Kang, representative of Candor.

By most faction standards, he is a young leader—only thirty-nine years old. But by Dauntless standards, that's nothing. Eric became a Dauntless leader at seventeen. But that's probably one of the reasons the other factions don't take our opinions or decisions seriously.

Jack is handsome, too, with short black hair and warm, slanted eyes, like Tori's, and high cheekbones. Despite his good looks, he isn't known for being charming, probably because he's Candor, and they see charm as deceptive. I do trust him to tell us what's going on without wasting time on pleasantries. That is something.

"They told me you seemed confused about why you were arrested," he says. His voice is deep, but strangely flat, like it could not create an echo even at the bottom of an empty cavern. "To me that means either you're falsely accused or good at pretending. The only—"

"What are we accused of?" I interrupt him.

"*He* is accused of crimes against humanity. *You* are accused of being his accomplice."

"Crimes against humanity?" Tobias finally sounds angry. He gives Jack a disgusted look. "What?"

"We saw video footage of the attack. You were *running* the attack simulation," says Jack.

"How could you have seen footage? We took the data," says Tobias.

"You took one copy of the data. All the footage of the Dauntless compound recorded during the attack was also sent to other computers throughout the city," says Jack. "All we saw was you running the simulation and *her* nearly getting punched to death before she gave up. Then you stopped, had a rather abrupt lovers' reconciliation, and stole the hard drive together. One possible reason is because the simulation was over and you didn't want us to get our hands on it."

I almost laugh. My great act of heroism, the only important thing I have ever done, and they think I was working for the Erudite when I did it.

"The simulation didn't end," I say. "We *stopped* it, you—"

Jack holds up his hand. "I am not interested in what you have to say right now. The truth will come out when you are both interrogated under the influence of truth serum."

Christina told me about truth serum once. She said the most difficult part of Candor initiation was being given truth serum and answering personal questions in front of everyone in the faction. I don't need to search myself for my deepest, darkest secrets to know that truth serum is the last thing I want in my body.

"Truth serum?" I shake my head. "No. No way."

"There's something you have to hide?" Jack says, lifting both eyebrows.

I want to tell him that anyone with an ounce of dignity wants to keep some things to herself, but I don't want to arouse his suspicions. So I shake my head.

"All right, then." He checks his watch. "It is now noon. The interrogation will be at seven. Don't bother preparing for it. You can't withhold information while under the influence of truth serum."

He turns on his heel and walks out of the room.

"What a pleasant man," says Tobias.

+ + +

A group of armed Dauntless escort me to the bathroom in the early afternoon. I take my time, letting my hands turn red in the hot-faucet water and staring at my reflection. When I was in Abnegation and wasn't allowed to look into mirrors, I used to think that a lot could change in a person's appearance in three months. But it only took a few days to change me this time.

I look older. Maybe it's the short hair or maybe it's just that I wear all that has happened like a mask. Either way, I always thought I would be happy when I stopped looking like a child. But all I feel is a lump in my throat. I am no longer the daughter my parents knew. They will never know me as I am now.

I turn away from the mirror and shove the door to the hallway open with the heels of my hands.

When the Dauntless drop me off at the holding room, I linger by the door. Tobias looks like he did when I first met him—black T-shirt, short hair, stern expression. The sight of him used to fill me with nervous excitement. I remember when I grabbed his hand outside the training room, just for a few seconds, and when we sat together on the rocks next to the chasm, and I feel a pang of longing for how things used to be.

"Hungry?" he says. He offers me a sandwich from the plate next to him.

I take it and sit down, leaning my head on his shoulder. All that's left for us to do is wait, so that's what we do. We eat until the food is gone. We sit until we get uncomfortable. Then we lie down next to each other on the floor, shoulders touching, staring at the same patch of white ceiling.

"What are you afraid of saying?" he says.

"Any of it. All of it. I don't want to relive anything."

He nods. I close my eyes and pretend to sleep. There's no clock in the room, so I can't count down the minutes until the interrogation. Time might as well not exist in this place, except I feel it pressing against me as seven o'clock inevitably draws closer, pushing me into the floor tiles.

Maybe time would not feel as heavy if I didn't have this guilt—the guilt of knowing the truth and stuffing it down where no one can see it, not even Tobias. Maybe I should not be so afraid of saying anything, because honesty will make me feel lighter.

I must fall asleep eventually, because I jerk awake at the sound of the door opening. A few Dauntless walk in as we get to our feet, and one of them says my name. Christina shoves her way past the others and throws her arms around me. Her fingers dig into the wound in my shoulder, and I cry out.

"Got shot," I say. "Shoulder. Ow."

"Oh God!" She releases me. "Sorry, Tris."

She doesn't look like the Christina I remember. Her hair is shorter, like a boy's, and her skin is grayish instead of a warm brown. She smiles at me, but the smile doesn't travel to her eyes, which still look tired. I try to smile back, but I'm too nervous. Christina will be there at my interrogation. She will hear what I did to Will. She will never forgive me.

Unless I fight the serum, swallow the truth—if I can.

But is that really what I want? To let it fester inside me forever?

"You okay? I heard you were here so I asked to escort you," she says as we leave the holding room. "I know you didn't do it. You're not a traitor."

"I'm fine," I say. "And thank you. How are you?"

"Oh, I'm . . ." Her voice trails off, and she bites her lip. "Did anyone tell you . . . I mean, maybe now isn't the time, but . . ."

"What? What is it?"

"Um . . . Will died in the attack," she says.

She gives me a worried look, and an expectant one. Expecting what?

Oh. I am not supposed to know that Will is dead. I could pretend to be emotional, but I probably wouldn't do it convincingly. It's best to admit that I already knew. But I don't know how to explain that without telling her everything.

I feel suddenly sick. Am I really evaluating how best to deceive my friend?

"I know," I say. "I saw him on the monitors when I was in the control room. I'm sorry, Christina."

"Oh." She nods. "Well, I'm . . . glad you already knew. I really didn't want to break the news to you in a hallway."

A short laugh. A flash of a smile. Neither of them like they used to be.

We file into an elevator. I can feel Tobias staring at me—he knows I didn't see Will in the monitors, and he didn't know that Will was dead. I stare straight ahead and pretend his eyes aren't setting me on fire.

"Don't worry about the truth serum," she says. "It's easy. You barely know what's happening when you're under. It's only when you resurface that you even know what you said. I went under when I was a kid. It's pretty commonplace in Candor."

The other Dauntless in the elevator give each other looks. In normal circumstances, someone would probably reprimand her for discussing her old faction, but these are not normal circumstances. At no other time in Christina's life will she escort her best friend, now a suspected traitor, to a public interrogation.

"Is everyone else all right?" I say. "Uriah, Lynn, Marlene?"

"All here," she says. "Except Uriah's brother, Zeke, who is with the other Dauntless."

"What?" Zeke, who secured my straps on the zip line, a traitor?

The elevator stops on the top floor, and the others file out.

"I know," she says. "No one saw it coming."

She takes my arm and tugs me toward the doors. We walk down a black-marble hallway—it must be easy to get lost in Candor headquarters, since everything looks the same. We walk down another hallway and through a set of double doors.

From the outside, the Merciless Mart is a squat block with a narrow raised portion in its center. From the inside, that raised portion is a hollow three-story room with empty spaces in the walls instead of windows. I see the darkening sky above me, starless.

Here the marble floors are white, with a black Candor symbol in the center of the room, and the walls are lit with rows of dim yellow lights, so the whole room glows. Every voice echoes.

Most of Candor and the remnants of Dauntless are already gathered. Some of them sit on the tiered benches that wrap around the edge of the room, but there isn't enough space for everyone, so the rest are crowded around the Candor symbol. In the center of the symbol, between the unbalanced scales, are two empty chairs.

Tobias reaches for my hand. I lace my fingers in his.

Our Dauntless guards lead us to the center of the room, where we are greeted with, at best, murmurs, and at worst, jeers. I spot Jack Kang in the front row of the tiered benches.

An old, dark-skinned man steps forward, a black box in his hands.

"My name is Niles," he says. "I will be your questioner. You—" He points at Tobias. "You will be going first. So if you will please step forward . . ."

Tobias squeezes my hand, and then releases it, and I stand with Christina at the edge of the Candor symbol. The air in the room is warm—moist, summer air, sunset air—but I feel cold.

Niles opens the black box. It contains two needles, one for Tobias and one for me. He also takes an antiseptic wipe from his pocket and offers it to Tobias. We didn't bother with that kind of thing in Dauntless.

"The injection site is in your neck," Niles says.

All I hear, as Tobias applies antiseptic to his skin, is the wind. Niles steps forward and plunges the needle into Tobias's neck, squeezing the cloudy, bluish liquid into his veins. The last time I saw someone inject Tobias with something, it was Jeanine, putting him under a new simulation, one that was effective even on the Divergent— or so she believed. I thought, then, that he was lost to me forever.

I shudder.

CHAPTER
TWELVE

"I WILL ASK you a series of simple questions so that you can grow accustomed to the serum as it takes full effect," says Niles. "Now. What is your name?"

Tobias sits with slouched shoulders and a lowered head, like his body is too heavy for him. He scowls and squirms in the chair, and through gritted teeth says, "Four."

Maybe it isn't possible to lie under the truth serum, but to select which version of the truth to tell: Four is his name, but it is not his name.

"That is a nickname," Niles says. "What is your real name?"

"Tobias," he says.

Christina elbows me. "Did you know that?"

I nod.

"What are the names of your parents, Tobias?"

Tobias opens his mouth to answer, and then clenches his jaw as if to stop the words from spilling out.

"Why is this relevant?" Tobias asks.

The Candor around me mutter to each other, some of them scowling. I raise my eyebrow at Christina.

"It's extremely difficult not to immediately answer questions while under the truth serum," she says. "It means he has a seriously strong will. And something to hide."

"Maybe it wasn't relevant before, Tobias," Niles says, "but it is now that you've resisted answering the question. The names of your parents, please."

Tobias closes his eyes. "Evelyn and Marcus Eaton."

Surnames are just an additional means of identification, useful only to prevent confusion in official records. When we marry, one spouse has to take the other's surname, or both have to take a new one. Still, while we may carry our names from family to faction, we rarely mention them.

But everyone recognizes Marcus's surname. I can tell by the clamor that rises in the room after Tobias speaks. The Candor all know Marcus is the most influential government official, and some of them must have read the article Jeanine released about his cruelty toward his son.

It was one of the only things she said that was true. And now everyone knows that Tobias is that son.

Tobias Eaton is a powerful name.

Niles waits for silence, then continues. "So you are a faction transfer, are you not?"

"Yes."

"You transferred from Abnegation to Dauntless?"

"*Yes*," snaps Tobias. "Isn't that obvious?"

I bite my lip. He should calm down; he is giving away too much. The more reluctant he is to answer a question, the more determined Niles will be to hear the answer.

"One of the purposes of this interrogation is to determine your loyalties," says Niles, "so I must ask: Why did you transfer?"

Tobias glares at Niles, and keeps his mouth shut. Seconds pass in complete silence. The longer he tries to resist the serum, the harder it seems to be for him: color fills his cheeks, and he breathes faster, heavier. My chest aches for him. The details of his childhood should stay inside him, if that's where he wants them to be. Candor is cruel for forcing them from him, for taking away his freedom.

"This is horrible," I say hotly to Christina. "Wrong."

"What?" she says. "It's a simple question."

I shake my head. "You don't understand."

Christina smiles a little at me. "You really care about him."

I am too busy watching Tobias to respond.

Niles says, "I'll ask again. It is important that we understand the extent of your loyalty to your chosen faction. So why did you transfer to Dauntless, Tobias?"

"To protect myself," says Tobias. "I transferred to protect myself."

"Protect yourself from what?"

"From my father."

All the conversations in the room stop, and the silence they leave in their wake is worse than the muttering was. I expect Niles to keep probing, but he doesn't.

"Thank you for your honesty," Niles says. The Candor repeat the phrase under their breath. All around me are the words "Thank you for your honesty" at different volumes and pitches, and my anger begins to dissolve. The whispered words seem to welcome Tobias, to embrace and then discard his darkest secret.

It's not cruelty, maybe, but a desire to understand, that motivates them. That doesn't make me any less afraid of going under truth serum.

"Is your allegiance with your current faction, Tobias?" Niles says.

"My allegiance lies with anyone who does not support

the attack on Abnegation," he says.

"Speaking of which," Niles says, "I think we should focus on what happened that day. What do you remember about being under the simulation?"

"I was not under the simulation, at first," says Tobias. "It didn't work."

Niles laughs a little. "What do you mean, it didn't *work*?"

"One of the defining characteristics of the Divergent is that their minds are resistant to simulations," says Tobias. "And I am Divergent. So no, it didn't work."

More mutters. Christina nudges me with her elbow.

"Are you too?" she says, close to my ear so she can stay quiet. "Is that why you were awake?"

I look at her. I have spent the past few months afraid of the word "Divergent," terrified that anyone would discover what I am. But I won't be able to hide it anymore. I nod.

It's like her eyes swell to fill their sockets; that's how big they get. I have trouble identifying her expression. Is it shock? Fear?

Awe?

"Do you know what it means?" I say.

"I heard about it when I was young," she says in a reverent whisper.

Definitely awe.

"Like it was a fantasy story," she says. "'There are people with special powers among us!' Like that."

"Well, it's not a fantasy, and it's not that big a deal," I say. "It's like the fear landscape simulation—you were aware while you were in it, and you could manipulate it. Except for me, it's like that in every simulation."

"But Tris," she says, setting her hand on my elbow. "That's *impossible*."

In the center of the room, Niles has his hands up and is trying to silence the crowd, but there are too many whispers—some hostile, some terrified, and some awed, like Christina's. Finally Niles stands and yells, "If you don't quiet down, you will be asked to leave!"

At last everyone quiets down. Niles sits.

"Now," he says. "When you say 'resistant to simulations,' what do you mean?"

"Usually, it means we're aware during simulations," says Tobias. He seems to have an easier time with the truth serum when he answers factual questions instead of emotional ones. He doesn't sound like he's under the truth serum at all now, though his slumped posture and wandering eyes indicate otherwise. "But the attack simulation was different, using a different kind of simulation serum, one with long-range transmitters. Evidently the long-range transmitters didn't work on the Divergent at all, because I awoke in my own mind that morning."

"You say you weren't under the simulation *at first*. Can you explain what you mean by that?"

"I mean that I was discovered and brought to Jeanine, and she injected a version of the simulation serum that specifically targeted the Divergent. I was aware during *that* simulation, but it didn't do much good."

"The video footage from the Dauntless headquarters shows you *running* the simulation," Niles says darkly. "How, exactly, do you explain that?"

"When a simulation is running, your eyes still see and process the actual world, but your brain no longer comprehends them. On some level, though, your brain still knows what you're seeing and where you are. The nature of this new simulation was that it recorded my emotional responses to outside stimuli," Tobias says, closing his eyes for a few seconds, "and responded by altering the appearance of that stimuli. The simulation made my enemies into friends, my friends into enemies. I thought I was shutting the simulation down. Really I was receiving instructions about how to keep it running."

Christina nods along to his words. I feel calmer when I see that most of the crowd is doing the same thing. This is the benefit of the truth serum, I realize. Tobias's testimony is irrefutable this way.

"We have seen footage of what ultimately happened to you in the control room," says Niles, "but it is confusing. Please describe it to us."

"Someone entered the room, and I thought it was a Dauntless soldier, trying to stop me from destroying the simulation. I was fighting her, and . . ." Tobias scowls, struggling. ". . . and then she stopped, and I got confused. Even if I had been awake, I would have been confused. Why would she surrender? Why didn't she just kill me?"

His eyes search the crowd until they find my face. My heartbeat lives in my throat; lives in my cheeks.

"I still don't understand," he says softly, "how she knew that it would work."

Lives in my fingertips.

"I think my conflicted emotions confused the simulation," he says. "And then I heard her voice. Somehow, that enabled me to fight the simulation."

My eyes burn. I have tried not to think of that moment, when I thought he was lost to me and that I would soon be dead, when all I wanted was to feel his heartbeat. I try not to think of it now; I blink the tears from my eyes.

"I recognized her, finally," he says. "We went back into the control room and stopped the simulation."

"What is the name of this person?"

"Tris," he says. "Beatrice Prior, I mean."

"Did you know her before this happened?"

"Yes."

"How did you know her?"

"I was her instructor," he says. "Now we're together."

"I have a final question," Niles says. "Among the Candor, before a person is accepted into our community, they have to completely expose themselves. Given the dire circumstances we are in, we require the same of you. So, Tobias Eaton: what are your deepest regrets?"

I look him over, from his beat-up sneakers to his long fingers to his straight eyebrows.

"I regret . . ." Tobias tilts his head, and sighs. "I regret my choice."

"What choice?"

"Dauntless," he says. "I was born for Abnegation. I was planning on leaving Dauntless, and becoming faction-less. But then I met *her*, and . . . I felt like maybe I could make something more of my decision."

Her.

For a moment, it's like I'm looking at a different person, sitting in Tobias's skin, one whose life is not as simple as I thought. He wanted to leave Dauntless, but he stayed because of me. He never told me that.

"Choosing Dauntless in order to escape my father was an act of cowardice," he says. "I regret that cowardice.

It means I am not worthy of my faction. I will always regret it."

I expect the Dauntless to let out indignant shouts, maybe to charge the chair and beat him to a pulp. They are capable of far more erratic things than that. But they don't. They stand in stony silence, with stony faces, staring at the young man who did not betray them, but never truly felt that he belonged to them.

For a moment we are all silent. I don't know who starts the whisper; it seems to originate from nothing, to come from no one. But someone whispers, "Thank you for your honesty," and the rest of the room repeats it.

"Thank you for your honesty," they whisper.

I don't join in.

I am the only thing that kept him in the faction he wanted to leave. I am not worth that.

Maybe he deserves to know.

+ + +

Niles stands in the center of the room with a needle in hand. The lights above him make it shine. All around me, the Dauntless and the Candor wait for me to step forward and spill my entire life before them.

The thought occurs to me again: *Maybe I can fight the serum.* But I don't know if I should try. It might be better for the people I love if I come clean.

I walk stiffly to the center of the room as Tobias leaves it. As we pass each other, he takes my hand and squeezes my fingers. Then he's gone, and it's just me and Niles and the needle. I wipe the side of my neck with the antiseptic, but when he reaches out with the needle, I pull back.

"I would rather do it myself," I say, holding out my hand. I will never let someone else inject me again, not after letting Eric inject me with attack simulation serum after my final test. I can't change the contents of the syringe just by doing it myself, but at least this way, I am the instrument of my own destruction.

"Do you know how?" he says, raising a bushy eyebrow.

"Yes."

Niles offers me the syringe. I position it over the vein in my neck, insert the needle, and press the plunger. I barely feel the pinch. I am too charged with adrenaline.

Someone comes forward with a trash can, and I toss the needle in. I feel the effects of the serum immediately afterward. It makes my blood feel like lead in my veins. I almost collapse on my way to the chair—Niles has to grab my arm and guide me toward it.

Seconds later my brain goes silent. *What was I thinking about?* It doesn't seem to matter. Nothing matters except the chair beneath me and the man sitting across from me.

"What is your name?" he says.

The second he asks the question, the answer pops out of my mouth. "Beatrice Prior."

"But you go by Tris?"

"I do."

"What are the names of your parents, Tris?"

"Andrew and Natalie Prior."

"You are also a faction transfer, are you not?"

"Yes," I say, but a new thought whispers at the back of my mind. *Also?* Also refers to someone else, and in this case, someone else is Tobias. I frown as I try to picture Tobias, but it is difficult to force the image of him into my mind. Not so difficult that I can't do it, though. I see him, and then I see a flash of him sitting in the same chair I'm sitting in.

"You came from Abnegation? And chose Dauntless?"

"Yes," I say again, but this time, the word sounds terse. I don't know why, exactly.

"Why did you transfer?"

That question is more complicated, but I still know the answer. *I was not good enough for Abnegation* is on the tip of my tongue, but another phrase replaces it: *I wanted to be free.* They are both true. I want to say them both. I squeeze the armrests as I try to remember where I am, what I'm doing. I see people all around me, but I don't know why they're there.

I strain, the way I used to strain when I could almost remember the answer to a test question but couldn't call it to mind. I used to close my eyes and picture the textbook page the answer was on. I struggle for a few seconds, but I can't do it; I can't remember.

"I wasn't good enough for Abnegation," I say, "and I wanted to be free. So I chose Dauntless."

"Why weren't you good enough?"

"Because I was selfish," I say.

"You *were* selfish? You aren't anymore?"

"Of course I am. My mother said that everyone is selfish," I say, "but I became less selfish in Dauntless. I discovered there were people I would fight for. Die for, even."

The answer surprises me—but why? I pinch my lips together for a moment. Because it's true. If I say it here, it must be true.

That thought gives me the missing link in the chain of thought I was trying to find. I am here for a lie-detector test. Everything I say is true. I feel a bead of sweat roll down the back of my neck.

Lie-detector test. Truth serum. I have to remind myself. It is too easy to get lost in honesty.

"Tris, would you please tell us what happened the day of the attack?"

"I woke up," I say, "and everyone was under the simulation. So I played along until I found Tobias."

"What happened after you and Tobias were separated?"

"Jeanine tried to have me killed, but my mother saved me. She used to be Dauntless, so she knew how to use a gun." My body feels even heavier now, but no longer cold. I feel something stir in my chest, something worse than sadness, worse than regret.

I know what comes next. My mother died and then I killed Will; I shot him; I killed him.

"She distracted the Dauntless soldiers so I could get away, and they killed her," I say.

Some of them ran after me, and I killed them. But there are Dauntless in the crowd around me, Dauntless, I killed some of the Dauntless, I shouldn't talk about it here.

"I kept running," I say, "And . . ." *And Will ran after me. And I killed him.* No, no. I feel sweat near my hairline.

"And I found my brother and father," I say, my voice strained. "We formed a plan to destroy the simulation."

The edge of the armrest digs into my palm. I withheld some of the truth. Surely that counts as deception.

I fought the serum. And in that short moment, I won.

I should feel triumphant. Instead I feel the weight of

what I did crush me again.

"We infiltrated the Dauntless compound, and my father and I went up to the control room. He fought off Dauntless soldiers at the expense of his life," I say. "I made it to the control room, and Tobias was there."

"Tobias said you fought him, but then stopped. Why did you do that?"

"Because I realized that one of us would have to kill the other," I say, "and I didn't want to kill him."

"You gave up?"

"No!" I snap. I shake my head. "No, not exactly. I remembered something I had done in my fear landscape in Dauntless initiation . . . in a simulation, a woman demanded that I kill my family, and I let her shoot me instead. It worked then. I thought . . ." I pinch the bridge of my nose. My head is starting to ache and my control is gone and my thoughts run into words. "I was so frantic, but all I could think was that there was something to it; there was a strength in it. And I couldn't kill him, so I had to try."

I blink tears from my eyes.

"So you were never under the simulation?"

"No." I press the heel of my hands to my eyes, pushing the tears out of them so they don't fall on my cheeks where everyone can see them.

"No," I say again. "No, I am Divergent."

"Just to clarify," says Niles. "Are you telling me that you were almost murdered by the Erudite . . . and then fought your way into the Dauntless compound . . . and destroyed the simulation?"

"Yes," I say.

"I think I speak for everyone," he says, "when I say that you have earned the title of Dauntless."

Shouts rise up from the left side of the room, and I see blurs of fists pressing into the dark air. My faction, calling to me.

But no, they're wrong, I'm not brave, I'm not brave, I shot Will and I can't admit it, I can't even admit it. . . .

"Beatrice Prior," says Niles, "what are your deepest regrets?"

What do I regret? I do not regret choosing Dauntless or leaving Abnegation. I do not even regret shooting the guards outside the control room, because it was so important that I get past them.

"I regret . . ."

My eyes leave Niles's face and drift over the room, and land on Tobias. He is expressionless, his mouth in a firm line, his stare blank. His hands, crossed over his chest, clasp his arms so hard his knuckles are white. Next to him stands Christina. My chest squeezes, and I can't breathe.

I have to tell them. I have to tell the truth.

"Will," I say. It sounds like a gasp, like it was pulled straight from my stomach. Now there is no turning back.

"I shot Will," I say, "while he was under the simulation. I killed him. He was going to kill me, but I killed him. My friend."

Will, with the crease between his eyebrows, with green eyes like celery and the ability to quote the Dauntless manifesto from memory. I feel pain in my stomach so intense that I almost groan. It hurts to remember him. It hurts every part of me.

And there is something else, something worse that I didn't realize before. I was willing to die rather than kill Tobias, but the thought never occurred to me when it came to Will. I decided to kill Will in a fraction of a second.

I feel bare. I didn't realize that I wore my secrets as armor until they were gone, and now everyone sees me as I really am.

"Thank you for your honesty," they say.

But Christina and Tobias say nothing.

CHAPTER
THIRTEEN

I RISE FROM the chair. I don't feel as dizzy as I did a moment ago; the serum is already wearing off. The crowd tilts, and I search for a door. I don't usually run away from things, but I would run from this.

Everyone starts to file out of the room except for Christina. She stands where I left her, her hands in fists that are in the process of uncurling. Her eyes meet mine and yet they do not. Tears swim in her eyes and yet she is not crying.

"Christina," I say, but the only words I can think of—*I'm sorry*—sound more like an insult than an apology. Sorry is what you are when you bump someone with your elbow, what you are when you interrupt someone. I am more than sorry.

"He had a gun," I say. "He was about to shoot me. He was under the simulation."

"You killed him," she says. Her words sound bigger than words usually do, like they expanded in her mouth before she spoke them. She looks at me as if she doesn't recognize me for a few seconds, then turns away.

A younger girl with the same skin color and the same height takes her hand—Christina's younger sister. I saw her on Visiting Day, a thousand years ago. The truth serum makes the sight of them swim before me, or that could be the tears gathering in my eyes.

"You okay?" says Uriah, emerging from the crowd to touch my shoulder. I haven't seen him since before the simulation attack, but I can't find it in me to greet him.

"Yeah."

"Hey." He squeezes my shoulder. "You did what you had to do, right? To save us from being Erudite slaves. She'll see that eventually. When the grief fades."

I can't even find it in me to nod. Uriah smiles at me and walks away. Some Dauntless brush against me and they murmur words that sound like gratitude, or compliments, or reassurance. Others give me a wide berth, look at me with narrowed, suspicious eyes.

The black-clothed bodies smear together in front of me. I am empty. Everything has spilled out of me.

Tobias stands next to me. I brace myself for his reaction.

"I got our weapons back," he says, offering me my knife.

I shove it in my back pocket without meeting his eyes.

"We can talk about it tomorrow," he says. Quietly. Quiet is dangerous, with Tobias.

"Okay."

He slides his arm across my shoulders. My hand finds his hip, and I pull him against me.

I hold on tight as we walk toward the elevators together.

+ + +

He finds us two cots at the end of a hallway somewhere. We lie with our heads inches apart, not speaking.

When I'm sure he's asleep, I slip out from beneath the blankets and walk down the hallway, past a dozen sleeping Dauntless. I find the door that leads to the stairs.

As I climb step after step, and my muscles begin to burn, and my lungs fight for air, I feel the first moments of relief I've experienced in days.

I may be good at running on flat ground, but walking up stairs is another matter. I massage a spasm from my hamstring as I march past the twelfth floor, and try to recover some of my lost air. I grin at the fierce burn in my legs, in my chest. Using pain to relieve pain. It doesn't make much sense.

By the time I reach the eighteenth floor, my legs feel like they have turned to liquid. I shuffle toward the room where I was interrogated. It's empty now, but the amphitheater benches are still there, as is the chair I sat in. The moon glows behind a haze of clouds.

I set my hands on the back of the chair. It's plain: wooden, a little creaky. How strange that something so simple could have been instrumental in my decision to ruin one of my most important relationships, and damage another.

It's bad enough that I killed Will, that I didn't think fast enough to come up with another solution. Now I have to live with everyone else's judgment as well as my own, and the fact that nothing—not even me—will ever be the same again.

The Candor sing the praises of the truth, but they never tell you how much it costs.

The edge of the chair bites into my palms. I was squeezing it harder than I thought. I stare down at it for a second and then lift it, balancing it legs-up on my good shoulder. I search the edge of the room for a ladder or a staircase that will help me climb. All I see are the amphitheater benches, rising high above the floor.

I walk up to the highest bench, and lift the chair above my head. It just barely touches the ledge beneath one of the window spaces. I jump, shoving the chair forward, and it slides onto the ledge. My shoulder aches—I shouldn't really be using my arm—but I have other things on my mind.

I jump, grab the ledge, and pull myself up, my arms shaking. I swing my leg up and drag the rest of my body onto the ledge. When I'm up, I lie there for a moment, sucking in air and heaving it back out again.

I stand on the ledge, under the arch of what used to be a window, and stare out at the city. The dead river curls around the building and disappears. The bridge, its red paint peeling, stretches over the muck. Across it are buildings, most of them empty. It is hard to believe there were ever enough people in the city to fill them.

For a second, I allow myself to reenter the memory of the interrogation. Tobias's lack of expression; his anger afterward, suppressed for the sake of my sanity. Christina's empty look. The whispers, "Thank you for your honesty." Easy to say that when what I did doesn't affect them.

I grab the chair and hurl it over the ledge. A faint cry escapes me. It grows into a yell, which transforms into a scream, and then I'm standing on the ledge of the Merciless Mart, screaming as the chair sails toward the ground, screaming until my throat burns. Then the chair hits the ground, shattering like a brittle skeleton. I sit down on the ledge, leaning into the side of the window frame, and close my eyes.

And then I think of Al.

I wonder how long Al stood at the ledge before he pitched himself over it, into the Dauntless Pit.

He must have stood there for a long time, making a list of all the terrible things he had done—almost killing me was one of those things—and another list of all the good, heroic, brave things he had not done, and then decided that he was tired. Tired, not just of living, but of existing. Tired of being Al.

I open my eyes, and stare at the pieces of chair I can faintly see on the pavement below. For the first time I feel like I understand Al. I am tired of being Tris. I have done bad things. I can't take them back, and they are part of who I am. Most of the time, they seem like the only thing I am.

I lean forward, into the air, holding on to the side of the window with one hand. Another few inches and my weight would pull me to the ground. I would not be able to stop it.

But I can't do it. My parents lost their lives out of love for me. Losing mine for no good reason would be a terrible way to repay them for that sacrifice, no matter what I've done.

"Let the guilt teach you how to behave next time," my father would say.

"I love you. No matter what," my mother would say.

Part of me wishes I could burn them from my mind, so I would never have to mourn for them. But the rest of me is afraid of who I would be without them.

My eyes blurry with tears, I lower myself back into the interrogation room.

+ + +

I return to my cot early that morning, and Tobias is already awake. He turns and walks toward the elevators, and I follow him, because I know that's what he wants. We stand in the elevator, side by side. I hear ringing in my ears.

The elevator sinks to the second floor, and I start to shake. It starts with my hands, but travels to my arms and my chest, until little shudders go through my entire body and I have no way to stop them. We stand between the elevators, right above another Candor symbol, the uneven scales. The symbol that is also drawn on the middle of his spine.

He doesn't look at me for a long time. He stands with his arms crossed and his head down until I can't stand it anymore, until I feel like I might scream. I should say something, but I don't know what to say. I can't apologize, because I only told the truth, and I can't change the truth into a lie. I can't give excuses.

"You didn't tell me," he says. "Why not?"

"Because I didn't . . ." I shake my head. "I didn't know how to."

He scowls. "It's pretty *easy*, Tris—"

"Oh yeah," I say, nodding. "It's *so* easy. All I have to do is go up to you and say, 'By the way, I shot Will, and now guilt is ripping me to shreds, but what's for breakfast?' Right? *Right?*" Suddenly it is too much, too much to contain. Tears fill my eyes, and I yell, "Why don't *you* try killing one of your best friends and then dealing with the consequences?"

I cover my face with my hands. I don't want him to see me sobbing again. He touches my shoulder.

"Tris," he says, gently this time. "I'm sorry. I shouldn't pretend that I understand. I just meant that . . ." He struggles for a moment. "I wish you trusted me enough to tell me things like that."

I do trust you, is what I want to say. But it isn't true—I didn't trust him to love me despite the terrible things I had done. I don't trust anyone to do that, but that isn't his problem; it's mine.

"I mean," he says, "I had to find out that you almost drowned in a water tank from *Caleb*. Doesn't that seem a little strange to you?"

Just when I was about to apologize.

I wipe my cheeks hard with my fingertips and stare at him.

"Other things seem stranger," I say, trying to make my voice light. "Like finding out that your boyfriend's supposedly dead mother is still alive by *seeing her in person*. Or overhearing his plans to ally with the factionless, but he never tells you about it. That seems a little strange to me."

He takes his hand from my shoulder.

"Don't pretend this is only my problem," I say. "If I don't trust you, you don't trust me either."

"I thought we would get to those things eventually," he says. "Do I have to tell you everything right away?"

I feel so frustrated I can't even speak for a few seconds. Heat fills my cheeks.

"God, *Four!*" I snap. "You don't want to have to tell me everything right away, but I have to tell *you* everything right away? Can't you see how stupid that is?"

"First of all, don't use that name like a weapon against me," he says, pointing at me. "Second, I was not making plans to ally with the factionless; I was just thinking it over. If I had made a decision, I would have said something to you. And third, it would be different if you had actually intended to tell me about Will at some point, but it's obvious that you didn't."

"I *did* tell you about Will!" I say. "That wasn't truth serum; it was me. *I* said it because I chose to."

"What are you talking about?"

"I was aware. Under the serum. I could have lied; I could have kept it from you. But I didn't, because I thought you deserved to know the truth."

"What a way to tell me!" he says, scowling. "In front of over a hundred people! How intimate!"

"Oh, so it's not enough that I told you; it has to be in the right setting?" I raise my eyebrows. "Next time should I brew some tea and make sure the lighting is right, too?"

Tobias lets out a frustrated sound and turns away from me, pacing a few steps. When he turns back, his cheeks are splotchy. I can't remember ever seeing his face change color before.

"Sometimes," he says quietly, "it isn't easy to be with you, Tris." He looks away.

I want to tell him that I know it's not easy, but I wouldn't have made it through the past week without him. But I just stare at him, my heart pounding in my ears.

I can't tell him I need him. I can't need him, period—or really, we can't need each other, because who knows how long either of us will last in this war?

"I'm sorry," I say, all my anger gone. "I should have been honest with you."

"That's it? That's all you have to say?" He frowns.

"What else do you want me to say?"

He just shakes his head. "Nothing, Tris. Nothing."

I watch him walk away. I feel like a space has opened up within me, expanding so rapidly it will break me apart.

CHAPTER
FOURTEEN

"OKAY, WHAT THE hell are you doing here?" a voice demands.

I sit on a mattress in one of the hallways. I came here to do something, but I lost my train of thought when I arrived, so I just sat down instead. I look up. Lynn—who I first met when she stomped on my toes in a Hancock building elevator—stands over me with raised eyebrows. Her hair is growing out—it's still short, but I can't see her skull anymore.

"I'm sitting," I say. "Why?"

"You're ridiculous, is what you are." She sighs. "Get your stuff together. You're Dauntless, and it's time you acted like it. You're giving us a bad reputation among the Candor."

"How exactly am I doing that?"

"By acting like you don't know us."

"I'm just doing Christina a favor."

"Christina." Lynn snorts. "She's a lovesick puppy. People die. That's what happens in war. She'll figure it out eventually."

"Yeah, people die, but it's not always your good friend who kills them."

"Whatever." Lynn sighs impatiently. "Come on."

I don't see a reason to refuse. I get up and follow her down a series of hallways. She moves at a brisk pace, and it's difficult to keep up with her.

"Where's your scary boyfriend?" she says.

My lips pucker like I just tasted something sour. "He's not scary."

"Sure he's not." She smirks.

"I don't know where he is."

She shrugs. "Well, you can grab him a bunk, too. We're trying to forget those Dauntless-Erudite bastard children. Pull together again."

I laugh. "Dauntless-Erudite bastard children, huh."

She pushes a door open, and we stand in a large, open room that reminds me of the building's lobby. Unsurprisingly, the floors are black with a huge white symbol in the center of the room, but most of it has been covered up with bunk beds. Dauntless men, women, and children are everywhere, and there isn't a single Candor in sight.

Lynn leads me to the left side of the room and between the rows of bunks. She looks at the boy sitting on one of the bottom bunks—he is a few years younger than we are, and he's trying to undo a knot in his shoelaces.

"Hec," she says, "you're going to have to find another bunk."

"What? No way," he says without looking up. "I'm not relocating *again* just because you want to have late-night pillow chats with one of your stupid friends."

"She is not my friend," snaps Lynn. I almost laugh. "Hec, this is Tris. Tris, this is my little brother, Hector."

At the sound of my name, his head jerks up, and he stares at me, openmouthed.

"Nice to meet you," I say.

"You're *Divergent*," he says. "My mom said to stay away from you because you might be dangerous."

"Yeah. She's a big scary Divergent, and she's going to make your head explode with only the power of her brain," says Lynn, jabbing him between the eyes with her index finger. "Don't tell me you actually *believe* all that kid stuff about the Divergent."

He turns bright red and snatches some of his things from a pile next to the bed. I feel bad for making him move until I see him toss his things down a few bunks over. He doesn't have to go far.

"I could have done that," I say. "Slept over there, I mean."

"Yeah, I know." Lynn grins. "He deserves it. He called Zeke a traitor right to Uriah's face. It's not like it's not true, but that's no reason to be a jerk about it. I think Candor is rubbing off on him. He feels like he can just say whatever he wants. Hey, Mar!"

Marlene pokes her head around one of the bunks and smiles toothily at me.

"Hey, Tris!" says Marlene. "Welcome. What's up, Lynn?"

"Can you get some of the smaller girls to give up a few pieces of clothing each?" Lynn says, "Not all shirts, though. Jeans, underwear, maybe a spare pair of shoes?"

"Sure," says Marlene.

I put my knife down next to the bottom bunk.

"What 'kid stuff' were you referring to?" I say.

"*The Divergent*. People with special brainpowers? Come on." She shrugs. "I know you believe in it, but I don't."

"So how do you explain me being awake during simulations?" I say. "Or resisting one entirely?"

"I think the leaders choose people at random and

change the simulations for them."

"Why would they do that?"

She waves her hand in my face. "Distraction. You're so busy worrying about the Divergent—like my mom—that you forget to worry about what the leaders are doing. It's just a different kind of mind control."

Her eyes skirt mine, and she kicks at the marble floor with the toe of her shoe. I wonder if she's remembering the last time she was on mind control. During the attack simulation.

I have been so focused on what happened to Abnegation that I almost forgot what happened to Dauntless. Hundreds of Dauntless woke to discover the black mark of murder on them, and they didn't even choose it for themselves.

I decide not to argue with her. If she wants to believe in a government conspiracy, I don't think I can dissuade her. She would have to experience it for herself.

"I come bearing clothes," says Marlene, stepping in front of our bunk. She holds a stack of black clothes the size of her torso, which she offers to me with a proud look on her face. "I even guilt-tripped your sister into handing over a dress, Lynn. She brought three."

"You have a sister?" I ask Lynn.

"Yeah," she says, "she's eighteen. She was in Four's initiate class."

"What's her name?"

"Shauna," she says. She looks at Marlene. "I *told* her none of us would need dresses anytime soon, but she didn't listen, as usual."

I remember Shauna. She was one of the people who caught me after zip lining.

"I think it would be easier to fight in a dress," says Marlene, tapping her chin. "It would give your legs freer movement. And who really cares if you flash people your underwear, as long as you're kicking the crap out of them?"

Lynn goes silent, like she recognizes that as a spark of brilliance but can't bring herself to admit it.

"What's this about flashing underwear?" says Uriah, sidestepping a bunk. "Whatever it is, I'm in."

Marlene punches him in the arm.

"Some of us are going to the Hancock building tonight," says Uriah. "You should all come. We're leaving at ten."

"Zip lining?" says Lynn.

"No. Surveillance. We've heard the Erudite keep their lights on all night, which will make it easier to look through their windows. See what they're doing."

"I'll go," I say.

"Me too," says Lynn.

"What? Oh. Me too," Marlene says, smiling at Uriah. "I'm going to get food. Want to come?"

"Sure," he says.

Marlene waves as they walk away. She used to walk with a lift in her step, like she was skipping. Now her steps are smoother—more elegant, maybe, but lacking the childish joy I associate with her. I wonder what she did when she was under the simulation.

Lynn's mouth puckers.

"What?" I say.

"Nothing," she snaps. She shakes her head. "They've just been hanging out alone all the time lately."

"He needs all the friends he can get, it sounds like," I say. "What with Zeke and all."

"Yeah. What a nightmare that was. One day he was here, and the next . . ." She sighs. "No matter how long you train someone to be brave, you never know if they are or not until something real happens."

Her eyes fix on mine. I never noticed before how strange they are, a golden brown. And now that her hair has grown in somewhat, and her baldness isn't the first thing I see, I also notice her delicate nose, her full lips— she is striking without trying to be. I am envious of her for a moment, and then I think she must hate it, and that's why she shaved her head.

"*You* are brave," she says. "You don't need me to say it, because you already know it. But I want you to know that I know."

She is complimenting me, but I still feel like she smacked me with something.

Then she adds, "Don't mess it up."

+ + +

A few hours later, after I've eaten lunch and taken a nap, I sit down on the edge of my bed to change the bandage on my shoulder. I take off my T-shirt, leaving my tank top on—there are a lot of Dauntless around, gathering between the bunks, laughing at one another's jokes. I have just finished applying more healing salve when I hear a shriek of laughter. Uriah charges down the aisle between the bunks with Marlene thrown over his shoulder. She waves at me as they pass, her face red.

Lynn, who is sitting on the next bunk, snorts. "I don't see how he can be *flirty*, with everything that's going on."

"He's supposed to shuffle around, scowling all the time?" I say, reaching over my shoulder to press the bandage to my skin. "Maybe you can learn something from him."

"You're one to talk," she says. "You're always moping. We should start calling you Beatrice Prior, Queen of Tragedy."

I stand and punch her arm, harder than if I was kidding, softer than if I was serious. "Shut up."

Without looking at me, she shoves my shoulder into the bunk. "I don't take orders from Stiffs."

I notice a slight curl in her lip and suppress a grin myself.

"Ready to go?" Lynn says.

"Where are you going?" Tobias says, slipping between his bunk and mine to stand in the aisle with us. My mouth feels dry. I haven't spoken to him all day, and I'm not sure what to expect. Will it be awkward, or will we go back to normal?

"Top of the Hancock building to spy on Erudite," Lynn says. "Want to come?"

Tobias gives me a look. "No, I've got a few things to take care of here. But be careful."

I nod. I know why he doesn't want to come—Tobias tries to avoid heights, if at all possible. He touches my arm, holding me back for just a moment. I tense up—he hasn't touched me since before our fight—and he releases me.

"I'll see you later," he mutters. "Don't do anything stupid."

"Thanks for that vote of confidence," I say, frowning.

"I didn't mean that," he says. "I meant don't let anyone else do anything stupid. They'll listen to you."

He leans toward me like he's going to kiss me, then seems to think better of it and leans back, biting his lip. It's a small act, but it still feels like rejection. I avoid his eyes and run after Lynn.

Lynn and I walk down the hallway toward the elevator bank. Some of the Dauntless have started to mark the walls with colored squares. Candor headquarters is like a maze to them, and they want to learn to navigate it. I know only how to get to the most basic places: the sleeping area, the cafeteria, the lobby, the interrogation room.

"Why did everyone leave Dauntless headquarters?" I say. "The traitors aren't there, are they?"

"No, they're at Erudite headquarters. We left because Dauntless headquarters has the most surveillance cameras of any area in the city," Lynn says. "We knew the Erudite could probably access all the footage, and that it would take forever to find all the cameras, so we thought it was best to just leave."

"Smart."

"We have our moments."

Lynn jabs her finger into the button for the first floor. I stare at our reflections in the doors. She's taller than I am by just a few inches, and though her baggy shirt and pants try to obscure it, I can tell that her body bends and curves like it's supposed to.

"What?" she says, scowling at me.

"Why did you shave your head?"

"Initiation," she says. "I love Dauntless, but Dauntless guys don't see Dauntless girls as a threat during initiation. I got sick of it. So I figured, if I don't look so much like a girl, maybe they won't look at me that way."

"I think you could have used being underestimated to your advantage."

"Yeah, and what? Acted all faint every time something scary came around?" Lynn rolls her eyes. "Do you think I have zero dignity or something?"

"I think a mistake the Dauntless make is refusing to be cunning," I say. "You don't always have to smack people in the face with how strong you are."

"Maybe you should dress in blue from now on," she says, "if you're going to act like such an Erudite. Plus, you do the same thing, but without the head shaving."

I slip out of the elevator before I say something I'll regret. Lynn is quick to forgive, but quick to ignite, like most Dauntless. Like me, except for the "quick to forgive" part.

As usual, a few Dauntless with large guns cross back and forth in front of the doors, watching for intruders. Just in front of them stands a small group of younger Dauntless, including Uriah; Marlene; Lynn's sister,

Shauna; and Lauren, who taught the Dauntless-born initiates as Four taught the faction transfers during initiation. Her ear gleams when she moves her head—it is pierced from top to bottom.

Lynn stops short, and I step on her heel. She swears.

"What a charmer you are," says Shauna, smiling at Lynn. They don't look much alike, except for their hair color, which is a medium brown, but Shauna's is chin length, like mine.

"Yes, that's my goal. To be charming," Lynn replies.

Shauna drapes an arm across Lynn's shoulders. It's strange to see Lynn with a sister—to see Lynn with a connection to someone at all. Shauna glances at me, her smile disappearing. She looks wary.

"Hi," I say, because there's nothing else to say.

"Hello," she says.

"Oh God, Mom's gotten to you, too, hasn't she." Lynn covers her face with one hand. "Shauna—"

"Lynn. Keep your mouth shut for once," says Shauna, her eyes still on me. She seems tense, like she thinks I might attack her at any moment. With my special brainpowers.

"Oh!" says Uriah, rescuing me. "Tris, do you know Lauren?"

"Yeah," Lauren says, before I can answer. Her voice is

sharp and clear, like she's scolding him, except it seems to be the way she naturally sounds. "She went through my fear landscape for practice during initiation. So she knows me better than she should, probably."

"Really? I thought the transfers would go through Four's landscape," says Uriah.

"Like he would let anyone do that," she says, snorting.

Something inside me gets warm and soft. He let *me* go through it.

I see a flicker of blue over Lauren's shoulder, and peer around her to get a better look.

Then the guns go off.

The glass doors explode into fragments. Dauntless soldiers with blue armbands stand on the sidewalk outside, carrying guns I've never seen before, guns with narrow, blue beams of light streaming from above their barrels.

"Traitors!" someone screams.

The Dauntless draw their guns, almost in unison. I do not have one to draw, so I duck behind the wall of loyal Dauntless in front of me, my shoes crunching pieces of glass beneath their soles, and pull my knife out of my back pocket.

All around me, people drop to the ground. My fellow faction members. My closest friends. All of them falling—they must be dead, or dying—as the earsplitting bang of bullets filling my ears.

Then I freeze. One of the blue beams is fixed on my chest. I dive sideways to get out of the line of fire, but I don't move fast enough.

The gun goes off. I fall.

CHAPTER
FIFTEEN

THE PAIN SUBSIDES to a dull ache. I slide my hand under my jacket and feel for the wound.

I'm not bleeding. But the force of the gunshot knocked me down, so I had to have been hit with something. I run my fingers over my shoulder, and feel a hard bump where the skin used to be smooth.

I hear a crack against the floor next to my face, and a metal cylinder about the size of my hand rolls to a stop against my head. Before I can move it, white smoke sprays out of both ends. I cough, and throw it away from me, deeper into the lobby. It isn't the only cylinder, though—they are everywhere, filling the room with smoke that does not burn or sting. In fact, it only obscures my view for a few seconds before evaporating completely.

What was the point of that?

Lying on the floor all around me are Dauntless soldiers with their eyes closed. I frown as I look Uriah up and down—he doesn't seem to be bleeding. I see no wound near his vital organs, which means he isn't dead. So what knocked him unconscious? I look over my left shoulder, where Lynn fell in a strange, half-curled position. She's also unconscious.

The Dauntless traitors walk into the lobby, their guns held up. I decide to do what I always do when I'm not sure what's going on: I act like everyone else. I let my head drop and close my eyes. My heart pounds as the Dauntless's footsteps come closer, and closer, squeaking on the marble floors. I bite my tongue to suppress a cry of pain as one of them steps on my hand.

"Not sure why we can't just shoot them all in the head," one of them says. "If there's no army, we win."

"Now, Bob, we can't just kill *everyone*," a cold voice says.

The hair on the back of my neck stands up. I would know that voice anywhere. It belongs to Eric, leader of the Dauntless.

"No people means no one left to create prosperous conditions," Eric continues. "Anyway, it's not your job to ask questions." He raises his voice. "Half in the elevators, half in the stairwells, left and right! Go!"

There's a gun a few feet to my left. If I opened my eyes, I could grab it and fire at him before he knew what hit him. But there's no guarantee I would be able to touch it without panicking again.

I wait until I hear the last footstep disappear behind an elevator door or into a stairwell before opening my eyes. Everyone in the lobby appears to be unconscious. Whatever they gassed us with, it had to be simulation-inducing or I wouldn't be the only one awake. It doesn't make any sense—it doesn't follow the simulation rules I'm familiar with—but I don't have time to think it through.

I grab my knife and get up, trying to ignore the ache in my shoulder. I run over to one of the dead Dauntless traitors near the doorway. She was middle-aged; there are hints of gray in her dark hair. I try not to look at the bullet wound in her head, but the dim light glows on what looks like bone, and I gag.

Think. I don't care who she was, or what her name was, or how old she was. I care only about the blue armband she wears. I have to focus on that. I try to hook my finger around the fabric, but it doesn't come loose. It appears to be attached to her black jacket. I will have to take that, too.

I unzip my jacket and toss it over her face so I don't have to look at her. Then I unzip her jacket and pull it, first from her left arm, and then from her right arm, gritting my teeth as I slide it from beneath her heavy body.

"Tris!" someone says. I turn around, jacket in one hand, knife in the other. I put the knife away—the invading Dauntless weren't carrying them, and I don't want to be conspicuous.

Uriah stands behind me.

"Divergent?" I ask him. There is no time to be shocked.

"Yeah," he says.

"Get a jacket," I say.

He crouches next to one of the other Dauntless traitors, this one young, not even old enough to be a Dauntless member. I flinch at the sight of his death-pale face. Someone so young shouldn't be dead; shouldn't even have been here in the first place.

My face hot with anger, I shrug the woman's jacket on. Uriah pulls his own jacket on, his mouth pinched.

"*They're* the only ones who are dead," he says quietly. "Something about that seem wrong to you?"

"They must have known we would shoot at them, but they came anyway," I say. "Questions later. We have to get up there."

"Up there? Why?" he says. "We should get out of here."

"You want to run away before you know what's going on?" I scowl at him. "Before the Dauntless upstairs know what hit them?"

"What if someone recognizes us?"

I shrug. "We just have to hope they won't."

I sprint toward the stairwell, and he follows me. As soon as my foot touches the first stair, I wonder what on earth I intend to do. There are bound to be more of the Divergent in this building, but will they know what they are? Will they know to hide? And what do I expect to gain from submerging myself in an army of Dauntless traitors?

Deep inside me I know the answer: I am being reckless. I will probably gain nothing. I will probably die.

And more disturbing still: I don't really care.

"They'll work their way upward," I say between breaths. "So you should . . . go to the third floor. Tell them to . . . evacuate. Quietly."

"Where are *you* going, then?"

"Floor two," I say. I shove my shoulder into the second-floor door. I know what to do on the second floor: look for the Divergent.

+ + +

As I walk down the hallway, stepping over unconscious people dressed in black and white, I think of a verse of the song Candor children used to sing when they thought no one could hear them:

Dauntless is the cruelest of the five
They tear each other to pieces. . . .

It has never seemed truer to me than now, watching Dauntless traitors induce a sleeping simulation that is not so different from the one that forced them to kill members of Abnegation not a month ago.

We are the only faction that could divide like this. Amity would not allow a schism; no one in Abnegation would be so selfish; Candor would argue until they found a common solution; and even Erudite would never do something so illogical. We really are the cruelest faction.

I step over a draped arm and a woman with her mouth hanging open, and hum the beginning of the next verse of the song under my breath.

Erudite is the coldest of the five
Knowledge is a costly thing. . . .

I wonder when Jeanine realized that Erudite and Dauntless would make a deadly combination. Ruthlessness and cold logic, it seems, can accomplish almost anything, including putting one and a half factions to sleep.

I scan faces and bodies as I walk, searching for irregular breaths, flickering eyelids, anything to suggest that the people lying on the ground are just pretending to be unconscious. So far, all the breathing is even and all the eyelids are still. Maybe none of the Candor are Divergent.

"Eric!" I hear someone shout from down the hall. I hold my breath as he walks right toward me. I try not to move. If I move, he'll look at me, and he'll recognize me, I know it. I look down, and tense so hard I tremble. *Don't look at me don't look at me don't look at me . . .*

Eric strides past me and down the hallway to my left. I should continue my search as quickly as possible, but curiosity urges me forward, toward whoever called for Eric. The shout sounded urgent.

When I lift my eyes, I see a Dauntless soldier standing over a kneeling woman. She wears a white blouse and a black skirt, and has her hands behind her head. Eric's smile looks greedy even in profile.

"Divergent," he says. "Well done. Bring her to the elevator bank. We'll decide which ones to kill and which ones to bring back later."

The Dauntless soldier grabs the woman by the ponytail and starts toward the elevator bank, dragging her behind him. She shrieks, and then scrambles to her feet, bent over. I try to swallow but it feels like I have a wad of cotton balls in my throat.

Eric continues down the hallway, away from me, and I try not to stare as the Candor woman stumbles past me, her hair still trapped in the fist of the Dauntless soldier. By now I know how terror works: I let it control me for a few seconds, and then force myself to act.

One . . . two . . . three . . .

I start forward with a new sense of purpose. Watching each person to see if they're awake is taking too much time. The next unconscious person I come across, I step hard on their pinkie finger. No response, not even a twitch. I step over them and find the next person's finger, pressing hard with the toe of my shoe. No response there either.

I hear someone else shout, "Got one!" from a distant hallway and start to feel frantic. I hop over fallen man after fallen woman, over children and teenagers and the elderly, stepping on fingers or stomachs or ankles, searching for signs of pain. I barely see their faces after a while, but still I get no response. I am playing hide-and-seek with the Divergent, but I'm not the only person who's "it."

And then it happens. I step on a Candor girl's pinkie, and her face twitches. Just a little—an impressive attempt at concealing the pain—but enough to catch my attention.

I look over my shoulder to see if anyone is near me, but they've all moved on from this central hallway. I check for the nearest stairwell—there's one just ten feet away, down a side hallway to my right. I crouch next to the girl's head.

"Hey, kid," I say as quietly as I can. "It's okay. I'm not one of them."

Her eyes open, just a little.

"There's a staircase about three yards away," I say. "I'll tell you when no one is watching, and then you have to run, understand?"

She nods.

I stand and turn in a slow circle. A Dauntless traitor to my left is looking away, nudging a limp Dauntless with her foot. Two Dauntless traitors behind me are laughing about something. One in front of me is spacing out in my direction, but then he lifts his head and starts down the hallway again, away from me.

"Now," I say.

The girl gets up and sprints toward the door to the stairwell. I watch her until the door clicks shut, and see my reflection in one of the windows. But I'm not standing alone in a hallway of sleeping people, like I thought. Eric is standing right behind me.

+ + +

I look at his reflection, and he looks back at me. I could make a break for it. If I move fast enough, he might not have the presence of mind to grab me. But I know, even as the idea occurs to me, that I won't be able to outrun him. And I won't be able to shoot him, because I didn't take a gun.

I spin around, bringing my elbow up as I do, and thrust it toward Eric's face. It catches the end of his chin, but not hard enough to do any damage. He grabs my left arm with one hand and presses a gun barrel to my forehead with the other, smiling down at me.

"I don't understand," he says, "how you could possibly be stupid enough to come up here with no gun."

"Well, I'm smart enough to do this," I say. I stomp hard on his foot, which I fired a bullet into less than a month ago. He screams, his face contorting, and drives the heel of the gun into my jaw. I clench my teeth to suppress a groan. Blood trickles down my neck—he broke the skin.

Through all that, his grip on my arm does not loosen once. But the fact that he didn't just shoot me in the head tells me something: He's not allowed to kill me yet.

"I was surprised to discover you were still alive," he says. "Considering I'm the one who told Jeanine to construct that water tank just for you."

I try to figure out what I can do that will be painful enough for him to release me. I've just decided on a hard kick to the groin when he slips behind me and grabs me by both arms, pressing against me so I can barely move my feet. His fingernails dig into my skin, and I grit my teeth, both from the pain and from the sickening feeling of his chest on my back.

"She thought studying one of the Divergent's reaction to a real-life version of a simulation would be fascinating," he says, and he presses me forward so I have to walk. His breath tickles my hair. "And I agreed. You see, ingenuity—one of the qualities we most value in Erudite—requires creativity."

He twists his hands so the calluses scrape against my arms. I shift my body slightly to the left as I walk, trying to position one of my feet between his advancing feet. I notice with fierce pleasure that he's limping.

"Sometimes creativity seems wasteful, illogical . . . unless it's done for a greater purpose. In this case, the accumulation of knowledge."

I stop walking just long enough to bring my heel up, hard, between his legs. A high-pitched cry hitches in his throat, stopped before it really began, and his hands go limp for just a moment. In that moment, I twist my body as hard as I can and break free. I don't know where I will run, but I have to run, I have to—

He grabs my elbow, yanking me back, and pushes his thumb into the wound in my shoulder, twisting until pain makes my vision go black at the edges, and I scream at the top of my lungs.

"I *thought* I recalled from the footage of you in that water tank that you got shot in that shoulder," he says. "It seems I was right."

My knees crumple beneath me, and he grabs my collar almost carelessly, dragging me toward the elevator bank. The fabric digs into my throat, choking me, and I stumble after him. My body throbs with lingering pain.

When we reach the elevator bank, he forces me to my knees next to the Candor woman I saw earlier. She and four others sit between the two rows of elevators, kept in place by Dauntless with guns.

"I want one gun on her at all times," says Eric. "Not just aimed at her. *On* her."

A Dauntless man pushes a gun barrel into the back of my neck. It forms a cold circle on my skin. I lift my eyes to Eric. His face is red, his eyes watering.

"What's the matter, Eric?" I say, raising my eyebrows. "Afraid of a little girl?"

"I'm not stupid," he says, pushing his hands through his hair. "That little-girl act may have worked on me before, but it won't work again. You're the best attack dog they've got." He leans closer to me. "Which is why I'm sure you'll be put down soon enough."

One of the elevator doors opens, and a Dauntless soldier shoves Uriah—whose lips are stained with blood—toward the short row of the Divergent. Uriah glances at me, but I can't read his expression well enough to know if he succeeded or failed. If he's here, he probably failed. Now they'll find all the Divergent in the building, and most of us will die.

I should probably be afraid. But instead a hysterical laugh bubbles inside me, because I just remembered something:

Maybe I can't hold a gun. But I have a knife in my back pocket.

CHAPTER
SIXTEEN

I SHIFT MY hand back, centimeter by centimeter, so the soldier pointing a gun at me doesn't notice. The elevator doors open again, bringing more of the Divergent with more Dauntless traitors. The Candor woman on my right whimpers. Strands of her hair are stuck to her lips, which are wet with spit, or tears, I can't tell.

My hand reaches the corner of my back pocket. I keep it steady, my fingers shaking with anticipation. I have to wait for the right moment, when Eric is close.

I focus on the mechanics of my breathing, imagining air filling every part of my lungs as I inhale, then remembering as I exhale how all my blood, oxygenated and unoxygenated, travels to and from the same heart.

It's easier to think of biology than the line of the

Divergent sitting between the elevators. A Candor boy who can't be older than eleven sits to my left. He's braver than the woman to my right—he stares at the Dauntless soldier in front of him, unflinching.

Air in, air out. Blood pushed all the way to my extremities—the heart is a powerful muscle, the strongest muscle in the body in terms of longevity. More Dauntless arrive, reporting successful sweeps of specific floors of the Merciless Mart. Hundreds of people unconscious on the floor, shot with something other than bullets, and I have no idea why.

But I am thinking of the heart. Not of my heart anymore, but of Eric's, and how empty his chest will sound when his heart is no longer beating. Despite how much I hate him, I don't really want to kill him, at least not with a knife, up close where I can see the life leave him. But I have one chance left to do something useful, and if I want to hit the Erudite where it hurts, I have to take one of their leaders from them.

I notice that no one ever brought the Candor girl I warned to the elevator bank, which means she must have gotten away. Good.

Eric clasps his hands behind his back and begins to pace, back and forth, before the line of Divergent.

"My orders are to take only two of you back to Erudite

headquarters for testing," says Eric. "The rest of you are to be executed. There are several ways to determine who among you will be least useful to us."

His footsteps slow when he approaches me. I tense my fingers, about to grab the knife handle, but he doesn't come close enough. He keeps walking and stops in front of the boy to my left.

"The brain finishes developing at age twenty-five," says Eric. "Therefore your Divergence is not completely developed."

He lifts his gun and fires.

A strangled scream leaps out of my body as the boy slumps to the ground, and I squeeze my eyes shut. Every muscle in my body strains toward him, but I hold myself back. *Wait, wait, wait.* I can't think of the boy. *Wait.* I force my eyes open and blink tears from them.

My scream accomplished one thing: now Eric stands in front of me, smiling. I caught his attention.

"You are also rather young," he says. "Nowhere near finished developing."

He steps toward me. My fingertips inch closer to the knife handle.

"Most of the Divergent get two results in the aptitude test. Some only get one. No one has ever gotten three, not because of aptitude, but simply because in order to get that result, you have to refuse to choose something," he says, moving closer still. I tilt my head back to look at him, at all the metal gleaming in his face, at his empty eyes.

"My superiors suspect that you got two, Tris," he says. "They don't think you're that complex—just an even blend of Abnegation and Dauntless—selfless to the point of idiocy. Or is that brave to the point of idiocy?"

I close my hand around the knife handle and squeeze. He leans closer.

"Just between you and me . . . *I* think you might have gotten three, because you're the kind of bullheaded person who would refuse to make a simple choice just because she was told to," he says. "Care to enlighten me?"

I lurch forward, pulling my hand out of my pocket. I close my eyes as I thrust the blade up and toward him. I don't want to see his blood.

I feel the knife go in and then pull it out again. My entire body throbs to the rhythm of my heart. The back of my neck is sticky with sweat. I open my eyes as Eric slumps to the ground, and then—chaos.

The Dauntless traitors aren't holding lethal guns, only ones that shoot whatever it is they shot at us before, so they all scramble for their real guns. As they do, Uriah launches himself at one of them and punches him hard in the jaw. The life goes out of the soldier's eyes and he falls, knocked out. Uriah takes the soldier's gun and starts shooting at the Dauntless closest to us.

I reach for Eric's gun, so panicked I can barely see, and when I look up, I swear the amount of Dauntless in the room has doubled. Gunshots fill my ears, and I drop to the ground as everyone starts running. My fingers brush the gun barrel, and I shudder. My hands are too weak to grasp it.

A heavy arm wraps around my shoulders and shoves me toward the wall. My right shoulder burns, and I see the Dauntless symbol tattooed on the back of a neck. Tobias turns, crouched around me to shield me from the gunfire, and shoots.

"Tell me if anyone's behind me!" he says.

I peer over his shoulder, curling my hands into fists around his shirt.

There *are* more Dauntless in the room, Dauntless without blue armbands—loyal Dauntless. My faction. My faction has come to save us. How are they awake?

The Dauntless traitors sprint away from the elevator bank. They were not prepared for an attack, not from all sides. Some of them fight back, but most run for the stairs. Tobias fires over and over again, until his gun runs out of bullets, and the trigger makes a clicking sound instead. My vision is too blurry with tears and my hands too useless to fire a gun. I scream into gritted teeth, frustrated. I can't help. I am worthless.

On the floor, Eric moans. Still alive, for now.

The gunshots gradually stop. My hand is wet. One glimpse of red tells me it's covered in blood—Eric's. I wipe it off on my pants and try to blink the tears away. My ears ring.

"Tris," Tobias says. "You can put the knife down now."

CHAPTER
SEVENTEEN

Tobias tells me this story:

When the Erudite reached the lobby stairwell, one of them didn't go up to the second floor. Instead, she ran up to one of the highest levels of the building. There she evacuated a group of loyal Dauntless—including Tobias—to a fire escape the Dauntless traitors had not sealed off. Those loyal Dauntless gathered in the lobby and split into four groups that stormed the stairwells simultaneously, surrounding the Dauntless traitors, who had clustered around the elevator banks.

The Dauntless traitors were not prepared for that much resistance. They thought everyone but the Divergent was unconscious, so they ran.

The Erudite woman was Cara. Will's older sister.

Heaving a sigh, I let the jacket slide from my arms and examine my shoulder. A metal disc about the size of my pinkie fingernail is pressed against my skin. Surrounding it is a patch of blue strands, like someone injected blue dye into the tiny veins just beneath the surface of my skin. Frowning, I try to peel the metal disc away from my arm, and feel a sharp pain.

Gritting my teeth, I wedge the flat of my knife blade under the disc and force it up. I scream into my teeth as the pain races through me, making everything go black for a moment. But I keep pushing, as hard as I can, until the disc lifts from my skin enough for me to get my fingers around it. Attached to the bottom of the disc is a needle.

I gag, grasp the disc in my fingertips, and pull one last time. This time, the needle comes free. It's as long as my littlest finger and smeared with my blood. I ignore the blood running down my arm and hold the disc and the needle up to the light above the sink.

Judging by the blue dye in my arm and the needle, they must have injected us with something. But what? Poison? An explosive?

I shake my head. If they had wanted to kill us, most of us were unconscious already, so they could have just shot us all. Whatever they injected us with isn't meant to kill us.

Someone knocks on the door. I don't know why—I'm in a public restroom, after all.

"Tris, you in there?" Uriah's muffled voice asks.

"Yeah," I call back.

Uriah looks better than he did an hour ago—he washed the blood from his mouth, and some of the color has returned to his face. I'm struck, suddenly, by how handsome he is—all his features are proportionate, his eyes dark and lively, his skin bronze-brown. And he has probably always been that handsome. Only boys who have been handsome from a young age have that arrogance in their smile.

Not like Tobias, who is almost shy when he smiles, like he is surprised you bothered to look at him in the first place.

My throat aches. I put the needle and disc on the edge of the sink.

Uriah looks from me to the needle in my hand to the line of blood running from my shoulder to my wrist.

"Gross," he says.

"Wasn't paying attention," I say. I set the needle down and grab a paper towel, mopping up the blood on my arm. "How are the others?"

"Marlene's cracking jokes, as usual." Uriah's smile grows, putting a dimple in his cheek. "Lynn's grumbling.

Wait, you yanked that out of your own arm?" He points to the needle. "God, Tris. Do you have no nerve endings or something?"

"I think I need a bandage."

"You think?" Uriah shakes his head. "You should get some ice for your face, too. So, everyone's waking up now. It's a madhouse out there."

I touch my jaw. It is tender where Eric's gun struck me—I will have to put healing salve on it so it doesn't bruise.

"Is Eric dead?" I don't know which answer I'm hoping for, yes or no.

"No. Some of the Candor decided to give him medical treatment." Uriah scowls at the sink. "Something about honorable treatment of prisoners. Kang's interrogating him in private right now. Doesn't want us there, disturbing the peace or whatever."

I snort.

"Yeah. Anyway, no one gets it," he says, perching on the edge of the sink next to mine. "Why storm in here and fire those things at us and then knock us all out? Why not just kill us?"

"No idea," I say. "The only use I see for it is that it helped them figure out who's Divergent and who's not. But that can't be the only reason they did it."

"I don't get why they have it out for us. I mean, when

they were trying to mind control themselves an army, sure, but now? Seems useless."

I frown as I press a clean paper towel to my shoulder, to stop the bleeding. He's right. Jeanine already has an army. So why kill the Divergent now?

"Jeanine doesn't want to kill everyone," I say slowly. "She knows that would be illogical. Without each faction, society doesn't function, because each faction trains its members for particular jobs. What she wants is *control*."

I glance up at my reflection. My jaw is swollen, and fingernail marks are still on my arms. Disgusting.

"She must be planning another simulation," I say. "Same thing as before, but this time, she wants to make sure that everyone is either under its influence or dead."

"But the simulation only lasts for a certain period of time," he says. "It's not useful unless you're trying to accomplish something specific."

"Right." I sigh. "I don't know. I don't get it." I pick up the needle. "I don't get what this thing is either. If it was like the other simulation-inducing injections, it was just meant for one use. So why shoot these things at us just to put us unconscious? It doesn't make any sense."

"I dunno, Tris, but right now we've got a huge building full of panicked people to deal with. Let's go get you a bandage." He pauses and then says, "Can you do me a favor?"

"What is it?"

"Don't tell anyone I'm Divergent." He bites his lip. "Shauna's my friend, and I don't want her to suddenly become afraid of me."

"Sure," I say, forcing a smile. "I'll keep it to myself."

+ + +

I am awake all night removing needles from people's arms. After a few hours I stop trying to be gentle. I just pull as hard as I can.

I find out that the Candor boy Eric shot in the head was named Bobby, and that Eric is in stable condition, and that of the hundreds of people in the Merciless Mart, only eighty don't have needles buried in their flesh, seventy of whom are Dauntless, one of whom is Christina. All night I puzzle over needles and serums and simulations, trying to inhabit the minds of my enemies.

In the morning, I run out of needles to remove and go to the cafeteria, rubbing my eyes. Jack Kang announced that we would have a meeting at noon, so maybe I can fit in a long nap after I eat.

When I walk into the cafeteria, though, I see Caleb.

Caleb runs up to me and folds me carefully into his arms. I breathe a sigh of relief. I thought I had gotten to the point where I didn't need my brother anymore, but I don't think such a point actually exists. I relax against him for a moment, and catch Tobias's eye over Caleb's shoulder.

"Are you all right?" Caleb says, pulling back. "Your jaw . . ."

"It's nothing," I say. "Just swollen."

"I heard they got a bunch of the Divergent and started shooting them. Thank God they didn't find you."

"Actually, they did. But they only killed one," I say. I pinch the bridge of my nose to relieve some of the pressure in my head. "But I'm all right. When did you get here?"

"About ten minutes ago. I came with Marcus," he says. "As our only legal political leader, he felt it was his duty to be here—we didn't hear about the attack until an hour ago. One of the factionless saw the Dauntless storming into the building, and news takes a while to travel among the factionless."

"Marcus is *alive*?" I say. We never actually saw him die when we escaped the Amity compound, but I just assumed he had—I'm not sure how I feel. Disappointed, maybe, because I hate him for how he treated Tobias? Or relieved, because the last Abnegation leader is still alive? Is it possible to feel both?

"He and Peter escaped, and walked back to the city," says Caleb.

I am not at all relieved to find out that Peter is still alive. "Where's Peter, then?"

"He is where you would expect him to be," Caleb replies.

"Erudite," I say. I shake my head. "What a—"

I can't even think of a word strong enough to describe him. Apparently I need to expand my vocabulary.

Caleb's face twists for a moment, then he nods and touches my shoulder. "Are you hungry? Want me to get you something?"

"Yes, please," I say. "I'll be back in a little while, okay? I have to talk to Tobias."

"All right." Caleb squeezes my arm and walks off, probably to get in the miles-long cafeteria line. Tobias and I stand yards away from each other for a few seconds.

He approaches me slowly.

"You okay?" he says.

"I might throw up if I have to answer that one more time," I say. "I don't have a bullet in my head, do I? So I'm good."

"Your jaw is so swollen you look like you have a wad of food in your cheek, and you just stabbed Eric," he says, frowning. "I'm not allowed to ask if you're okay?"

I sigh. I should tell him about Marcus, but I don't want to do it here, with so many people around. "Yeah. I'm okay."

His arm jerks like he was thinking of touching me but

decided against it. Then he reconsiders and slides his arm around me, pulling me to him.

Suddenly I think maybe I'll let someone else take all the risks, maybe I'll just start acting selfishly so that I can stay close to Tobias without hurting him. All I want is to bury my face in his neck and forget anything else exists.

"I'm sorry it took me so long to come get you," he whispers into my hair.

I sigh and touch his back with just my fingertips. I could stand here until I go unconscious from exhaustion, but I shouldn't; I can't. I pull back and say, "I need to talk to you. Can we go somewhere quiet?"

He nods, and we leave the cafeteria. One of the Dauntless we pass yells, "Oh, look! It's *Tobias Eaton*!"

I had almost forgotten about the interrogation, and the name it revealed to all of Dauntless.

Another one yells, "I saw your daddy here earlier, Eaton! Are you gonna go hide?"

Tobias straightens and stiffens, like someone is training a gun at his chest instead of jeering at him.

"Yeah, are you gonna hide, coward?"

A few people around us laugh. I grab Tobias's arm and steer him toward the elevators before he can react. He looked like he was about to punch someone. Or worse.

"I was going to tell you—he came with Caleb," I say. "He and Peter escaped Amity—"

"What were you waiting for, then?" he says, but not harshly. His voice sounds somehow detached from him, like it is floating between us.

"It's not the kind of news you deliver in a cafeteria," I say.

"Fair enough," he says.

We wait in silence for the elevator, Tobias chewing on his lip and staring into space. He does that all the way to the eighteenth floor, which is empty. There, the silence wraps around me like Caleb's embrace did, calming me. I sit down on one of the benches on the edge of the inter-rogation room, and Tobias pulls Niles's chair over to sit in front of me.

"Didn't there used to be two of these?" he says, frown-ing at the chair.

"Yeah," I say. "I, uh . . . it got thrown out the window."

"Strange," he says. He sits. "So what did you want to talk about? Or was that about Marcus?"

"No, that wasn't it. Are you . . . all right?" I say cautiously.

"I don't have a bullet in my head, do I?" he says, staring at his hands. "So I'm fine. I'd like to talk about something else."

"I want to talk about simulations," I say. "But first,

something else—your mother thought Jeanine would go after the factionless next. Obviously she was wrong—and I'm not sure why. It's not like the Candor are battle ready or anything—"

"Well, think about it," he says. "Think it through, like the Erudite."

I give him a look.

"What?" he says. "If you can't, the rest of us have no hope."

"Fine," I say. "Um . . . it had to be because Dauntless and Candor were the most logical targets. Because . . . the factionless are in multiple places, whereas we're all in the same place."

"Right," he says. "Also, when Jeanine attacked Abnegation, she got all the Abnegation data. My mother told me that the Abnegation had documented the faction-less Divergent populations, which means that after the attack, Jeanine must have found out that the proportion of Divergent among the factionless is higher than among the Candor. That makes them an illogical target."

"All right. Then tell me about the serum again," I say. "It has a few parts, right?"

"Two," he says, nodding. "The transmitter and the liquid that induces the simulation. The transmitter com-municates information to the brain from the computer, and vice versa, and the liquid alters the brain to put it in a simulation state."

I nod. "And the transmitter only works for one simulation, right? What happens to it after that?"

"It dissolves," he says. "As far as I know, the Erudite haven't been able to develop a transmitter that lasts for more than one simulation, although the attack simulation lasted far longer than any simulation I've seen before."

The words "as far as I know" stick in my mind. Jeanine has spent most of her adult life developing the serums. If she's still hunting down the Divergent, she's probably still obsessed with creating more advanced versions of the technology.

"What's this about, Tris?" he says.

"Have you seen this yet?" I say, pointing at the bandage covering my shoulder.

"Not up close," he says. "Uriah and I were hauling wounded Erudite up to the fourth floor all morning."

I peel away the edge of the bandage, revealing the puncture wound—no longer bleeding, thankfully—and the patch of blue dye that doesn't seem to be fading. Then I reach into my pocket and take out the needle that was buried in my arm.

"When they attacked, they weren't trying to kill us. They were shooting us with these," I say.

His hand touches the dyed skin around the puncture wound. I didn't notice it before because it was happening right in front of me, but he looks different than he used to, during initiation. He's let his facial hair grow in a little, and his hair is longer than I've ever seen it—dense enough to show me that it is brown, not black.

He takes the needle from me and taps the metal disc at the end of it. "This is probably hollow. It must have contained whatever that blue stuff in your arm is. What happened after you were shot?"

"They tossed these gas-spewing cylinders into the room, and everyone went unconscious. That is, everyone but Uriah and me and the other Divergent."

Tobias doesn't seem surprised. I narrow my eyes.

"Did you know that Uriah was Divergent?"

He shrugs. "Of course. I ran his simulations, too."

"And you never told me?"

"Privileged information," he says. "Dangerous information."

I feel a flare of anger—how many things is he going to keep from me?—and try to stifle it. Of course he couldn't tell me Uriah was Divergent. He was just respecting Uriah's privacy. It makes sense.

I clear my throat. "You saved our lives, you know," I say. "Eric was trying to hunt us down."

"I think we're past keeping track of who has saved whose life." He looks at me for a few long seconds.

"Anyway," I say to break the silence. "After we figured out that everyone was asleep, Uriah ran upstairs to warn the people who were up there, and I went to the second floor to figure out what was going on. Eric had all the Divergent by the elevators, and he was trying to figure out which of us he was going to take back with him. He said he was allowed to take two. I don't know why he was going to take any."

"Odd," he says.

"Any ideas?"

"My guess is that the needle injected you with a transmitter," he says, "and the gas was an aerosol version of the liquid that alters the brain. But why . . ." A crease appears between his eyebrows. "Oh. She put everyone to sleep to find out who the Divergent were."

"You think that's the only reason for shooting us with transmitters?"

He shakes his head, and his eyes lock on mine. Their blue is so dark and familiar that I feel like it could swallow me whole. For a moment I wish it would, so that I could escape this place and all that has happened.

"I think you've already figured it out," he says, "but you want me to contradict you. And I'm not going to."

"They've developed a long-lasting transmitter," I say.

He nods.

"So now we're all wired for multiple simulations," I add. "As many as Jeanine wants, maybe."

He nods again.

My next breath shakes on the way out of my mouth. "This is really bad, Tobias."

+ + +

In the hallway outside the interrogation room, he stops, leaning against the wall.

"So you attacked Eric," he says. "Was that during the invasion? Or when you were by the elevators?"

"By the elevators," I say.

"One thing I don't understand," he says. "You were downstairs. You could have just run away. But instead, you decided to dive into a crowd of armed Dauntless all by yourself. And I'm willing to bet you weren't carrying a gun."

I press my lips together.

"Is that true?" he demands.

"What makes you think I didn't have a gun?" I scowl.

"You haven't been able to touch a gun since the attack," he says. "I understand why, with the whole Will thing, but—"

"That has nothing to do with it."

"No?" He lifts his eyebrows.

"I did what I had to do."

"Yeah. But now you should be done," he says, pulling away from the wall to face me. Candor hallways are wide, wide enough for all the space I want to keep between us. "You should have stayed with the Amity. You should have stayed far away from all of this."

"No, I shouldn't have," I say. "You think you know what's best for me? You have no idea. I was going crazy with the Amity. Here I finally feel . . . sane again."

"Which is odd, considering you are acting like a psychopath," he says. "It's not brave, choosing the position you were in yesterday. It's beyond stupid—it's suicidal. Don't you have any regard for your own life?"

"Of course I do!" I retort. "I was trying to do something useful!"

For a few seconds he just stares at me.

"You're more than Dauntless," he says in a low voice. "But if you want to be just like them, hurling yourself into ridiculous situations for no reason and retaliating against your enemies without any regard for what's ethical, go right ahead. I thought you were better than that, but maybe I was wrong!"

I clench my hands, my jaw.

"You shouldn't insult the Dauntless," I say. "They took

you in when you had nowhere else to go. Trusted you with a good job. Gave you all your friends."

I lean against the wall, my eyes on the floor. The tiles in the Merciless Mart are always black and white, and here they are in a checkered pattern. If I unfocus my eyes, I see exactly what the Candor don't believe in—gray. Maybe Tobias and I don't believe in it either. Not really.

I weigh too much, more than my frame can support, so much I should fall right through the floor.

"Tris."

I keep staring.

"Tris."

I finally look at him.

"I just don't want to lose you."

We stand there for a few minutes. I don't say what I'm thinking, which is that he might be right. There is a part of me that wants to be lost, that struggles to join my parents and Will so that I don't have to ache for them anymore. A part of me that wants to see whatever comes next.

+ + +

"So you're her brother?" says Lynn. "I guess we know who got the good genes."

I laugh at the expression on Caleb's face, his mouth

drawn into a slight pucker and his eyes wide.

"When do you have to get back?" I say, nudging him with my elbow.

I bite into the sandwich Caleb got me from the cafeteria line. I am nervous to have him here, mixing the sad remains of my family life with the sad remains of my Dauntless life. What will he think of my friends, my faction? What will my faction think of him?

"Soon," he says. "I don't want anyone to worry."

"I didn't realize Susan had changed her name to 'Anyone,'" I say, raising an eyebrow.

"Ha-ha," he says, making a face at me.

Teasing between siblings should feel familiar, but it doesn't for us. Abnegation discouraged anything that might make someone feel uncomfortable, and teasing was included.

I can feel how cautious we are with each other, now that we're discovering a different way to relate in light of our new factions and our parents' deaths. Every time I look at him, I realize that he's the only family I have left and I feel desperate, desperate to keep him around, desperate to narrow the gap between us.

"Is Susan another Erudite defector?" says Lynn, stabbing a string bean with her fork. Uriah and Tobias are still in the lunch line, waiting behind two dozen Candor who are too busy bickering to get their food.

"No, she was our neighbor when we were kids. She's Abnegation," I say.

"And you're involved with her?" she asks Caleb. "Don't you think that's kind of a stupid move? I mean, when all this is over, you'll be in different factions, living in completely different places. . . ."

"Lynn," Marlene says, touching her shoulder, "shut up, will you?"

Across the room, something blue catches my attention. Cara just walked in. I put down my sandwich, my appetite gone, and look up at her with my head lowered. She walks to the far corner of the cafeteria, where a few tables of Erudite refugees sit. Most of them have abandoned their blue clothes in favor of black-and-white ones, but they still wear their glasses. I try to focus on Caleb instead— but Caleb is watching the Erudite, too.

"I can't go back to Erudite any more than *they* can," says Caleb. "When this is over, I won't have a faction."

For the first time I notice how sad he looks when he talks about the Erudite. I didn't realize how difficult the decision to leave them must have been for him.

"You could go sit with them," I say, nodding toward the Erudite refugees.

"I don't know them." He shrugs. "I was only there for a month, remember?"

Uriah drops his tray on the table, scowling. "I overheard someone talking about Eric's interrogation in the lunch line. Apparently he knew almost *nothing* about Jeanine's plan."

"What?" Lynn slaps her fork on the table. "How is that even possible?"

Uriah shrugs, and sits.

"I'm not surprised," Caleb says.

Everyone stares at him.

"What?" He flushes. "It would be stupid to confide your entire plan to one person. It's infinitely smarter to give little pieces of it to each person working with you. That way, if someone betrays you, the loss isn't too great."

"Oh," says Uriah.

Lynn picks up her fork and starts eating again.

"I heard the Candor made ice cream," says Marlene, twisting her head around to see the lunch line. "You know, as a kind of 'it sucks we got attacked, but at least there are desserts' thing."

"I feel better already," says Lynn dryly.

"It probably won't be as good as Dauntless cake," says Marlene mournfully. She sighs, and a strand of mousy brown hair falls in her eyes.

"We had good cake," I tell Caleb.

"We had fizzy drinks," he says.

"Ah, but did you have a ledge overlooking an underground river?" says Marlene, waggling her eyebrows. "Or a room where you faced all your nightmares at once?"

"No," says Caleb, "and to be honest, I'm kind of okay with that."

"*Si-ssy,*" sings Marlene.

"*All* your nightmares?" says Caleb, his eyes lighting up. "How does that work? I mean, are the nightmares produced by the computer or by your brain?"

"Oh God." Lynn drops her head into her hands. "Here we go."

Marlene launches into a description of the simulations, and I let her voice, and Caleb's voice, wash over me as I finish my sandwich. Then, despite the clatter of forks and the roar of hundreds of conversations all around me, I rest my head on the table and fall asleep.

CHAPTER
EIGHTEEN

"QUIET DOWN, EVERYONE!"

Jack Kang lifts his hands, and the crowd goes silent. That is a talent.

I stand among the crowd of Dauntless who got here late, when there were no seats left. A flash of light catches my eye—lightning. It's not the best time to be meeting in a room with holes in the walls instead of windows, but this is the biggest room they have.

"I know many of you are confused and shaken by what happened yesterday," Jack says. "I have heard many reports from a variety of perspectives, and have gotten a sense for what is straightforward and what requires more investigation."

I tuck my wet hair behind my ears. I woke up ten

minutes before the meeting was supposed to start and ran to the showers. Though I'm still exhausted, I feel more alert now.

"What seems to me to require more investigation," Jack says, "is the Divergent."

He looks tired—he has dark circles under his eyes, and his short hair sticks out at random, like he's been pulling it all night. Despite the stifling heat of the room, he wears a long-sleeved shirt that buttons at the wrists—he must have been distracted when he dressed this morning.

"If you are one of the Divergent, please step forward so that we can hear from you."

I look sideways at Uriah. This feels dangerous. My Divergence is something I am supposed to hide. Admitting it is supposed to mean death. But there is no sense in hiding it now—they already know about me.

Tobias is the first to move. He starts into the crowd, at first turning his body to wedge his way between people, and then, when they step back for him, moving straight toward Jack Kang with his shoulders back.

I move, too, muttering "Excuse me" to the people in front of me. They draw back like I just threatened to spit poison at them. A few others step forward, in Candor black and white, but not many. One of them is the girl I helped.

Despite the notoriety Tobias now has among the

Dauntless, and my new title as That Girl Who Stabbed Eric, we are not the real focus of everyone's attention. Marcus is.

"You, Marcus?" says Jack when Marcus reaches the middle of the room and stands on top of the lower scale in the floor.

"Yes," Marcus says. "I understand that you are concerned—that you all are concerned. You had never heard of the Divergent a week ago, and now all that you know is that they are immune to something to which you are susceptible, and that is a frightening thing. But I can assure you that there is nothing to be afraid of, as far as we are concerned."

As he speaks, his head tilts and his eyebrows lift in sympathy, and I understand at once why some people like him. He makes you feel that if you just placed everything in his hands, he would take care of it.

"It seems clear to me," says Jack, "that we were attacked so that the Erudite could find the Divergent. Do you know why that is?"

"No, I do not," says Marcus. "Perhaps their intention was merely to identify us. It seems like useful information to have, if they intend to use their simulations again."

"That was *not* their intention." The words are past my lips before I decide to speak them. My voice sounds high and weak compared to Marcus's and Jack's, but it's too late to stop. "They wanted to kill us. They've been killing us since before any of this happened."

Jack's eyebrows draw together. I hear hundreds of tiny sounds, raindrops hitting the roof. The room darkens, as if under the gloom of what I just said.

"That sounds very much like a conspiracy theory," Jack says. "What reason would the Erudite have to kill you?"

My mother said people feared the Divergent because we couldn't be controlled. That may be true, but fear of the uncontrollable is not a concrete enough reason to give Jack Kang for the Erudite wanting us dead. My heart races as I realize that I can't answer his question.

"I . . ." I start. Tobias interrupts me.

"Obviously we don't know," he says, "but there are nearly a dozen mysterious deaths recorded among the Dauntless from the past six years, and there is a correlation between those people and irregular aptitude test results or initiation simulation results."

Lightning strikes, making the room glow. Jack shakes his head. "While that is intriguing, correlation does not constitute evidence."

"A Dauntless leader shot a Candor child in the *head*," I snap. "Did you get a report of *that*? Did it seem 'worthy of investigation'?"

"In fact I did," he says. "And shooting a child in cold blood is a terrible crime that cannot go unpunished. Fortunately, we have the perpetrator in custody and will be able to put him on trial. *However*, we must keep in mind that the Dauntless soldiers did not give any evidence of wanting to harm the majority of us, or they would have killed us while we were unconscious."

I hear irritated murmurs all around me.

"Their peaceful invasion suggests to me that it may be possible to negotiate a peace treaty with the Erudite and the other Dauntless," he continues. "So I will arrange a meeting with Jeanine Matthews to discuss that possibility as soon as possible."

"Their invasion wasn't *peaceful*," I say. I can see the corner of Tobias's mouth from where I stand, and he is smiling. I take a deep breath and begin again. "Just because they didn't shoot you all in the head doesn't mean their intentions were somehow honorable. Why do you think they came here? Just to run through your hallways, knock you unconscious, and leave?"

"I assume they came here for people like you," says Jack. "And while I am concerned for your safety, I don't think we can attack them just because they wanted to kill a fraction of our population."

"Killing you is not the worst thing they can do to

you," I say. "Controlling you is."

Jack's lips curl with amusement. *Amusement.* "Oh? And how will they manage that?"

"They shot you with needles," Tobias says. "Needles full of simulation transmitters. Simulations control you. That's how."

"We know how simulations work," says Jack. "The transmitter is not a permanent implant. If they intended to control us, they would have done it right away."

"But—" I begin.

He interrupts me. "I know you have been under a lot of stress, Tris," he says quietly, "and that you have done a great service to your faction and to Abnegation. But I think your traumatic experience may have compromised your ability to be completely objective. I can't launch an attack based on a little girl's speculations."

I stand statue-still, unable to believe that he could be so stupid. My face burning. *Little girl,* he called me. A little girl who is stressed out to the point of paranoia. That is not me, but now, it's who the Candor think I am.

"*You* don't make our decisions for us, Kang," says Tobias.

All around me, the Dauntless shout their assent. Someone else yells, "You are not the leader of our faction!"

Jack waits for their shouts to die down and then says,

"That is true. If you want to, you can feel free to storm the Erudite compound by yourselves. But you will do so without our support, and may I remind you, you are greatly outnumbered and unprepared."

He's right. We can't attack Dauntless traitors and Erudite without Candor's numbers. It would be a bloodbath if we tried. Jack Kang has all the power. And now we all know it.

"I thought so," he says smugly. "Very well. I will contact Jeanine Matthews, and see if we can negotiate a peace. Any objections?"

We can't attack without Candor, I think, *unless we have the factionless.*

CHAPTER
NINETEEN

THAT AFTERNOON I join a group of Candor and Dauntless cleaning up the broken windows in the lobby. I focus on the path of the broom, keeping my eyes on the dust that collects between glass fragments. My muscles remember the movement before the rest of me does, but when I look down, instead of dark marble I see plain white tile and the bottom of a light gray wall; I see strands of blond hair that my mother trimmed, and the mirror safely tucked behind its wall panel.

My body goes weak, and I lean into the broom handle for support.

A hand touches my shoulder, and I twitch away from it. But it's just a Candor girl—a child. She looks up at me, wide-eyed.

"Are you all right?" she says, her voice high and indistinct.

"I'm fine," I say. Too sharply. I hurry to amend it. "Just tired. Thank you."

"I think you're lying," she says.

I notice a bandage peeking out from the end of her sleeve, probably covering the needle puncture. The idea of this little girl under a simulation nauseates me. I can't even look at her. I turn away.

And I see them: outside, a traitor Dauntless man, propping up a woman with a bleeding leg. I see the gray streaks in the woman's hair and the end of the man's hooked nose and the blue armband of a Dauntless traitor just beneath their shoulders, and recognize them both. Tori and Zeke.

Tori is trying to walk, but one of her legs drags behind her, useless. A wet, dark patch covers most of her thigh.

The Candor stop sweeping and stare at them. The Dauntless guards standing near the elevators rush toward the entrance with their guns lifted. My fellow sweepers back up to get out of the way, but I stay where I am, heat rushing through me as Zeke and Tori approach.

"Are they even armed?" someone says.

Tori and Zeke reach what used to be the doors, and he puts up one of his hands when he sees the row of Dauntless with guns. The other he keeps wrapped around Tori's waist.

"She needs medical attention," says Zeke. "Right now."

"Why should we give a traitor medical attention?" a Dauntless man with wispy blond hair and a double-pierced lip asks over his gun. A patch of blue dye marks his forearm.

Tori moans, and I slip between two Dauntless to reach for her. She puts her hand, which is sticky with blood, in mine. Zeke lowers her to the ground with a grunt.

"Tris," she says, sounding dazed.

"Better step back, girl," the blond Dauntless man says.

"No," I say. "Put your gun down."

"Told you the Divergent were crazy," one of the other armed Dauntless mutters to the woman next to him.

"I don't care if you bring her upstairs and tie her to a bed to keep her from going on a shooting spree!" says Zeke, scowling. "Don't let her bleed to death in the lobby of Candor headquarters!"

Finally, a few Dauntless come forward and lift Tori up.

"Where should we . . . take her?" one of them asks.

"Find Helena," Zeke says. "Dauntless nurse."

The men nod and carry her toward the elevators. Zeke and I meet eyes.

"What happened?" I ask him.

"The traitor Dauntless found out we were collecting information from them," he says. "Tori tried to get away, but they shot her as she was running. I helped her get here."

"That's a nice story," says the blond Dauntless man. "Want to tell it again under truth serum?"

Zeke shrugs. "All right." He puts his wrists together in front of him dramatically. "Haul me away, if you're so desperate to."

Then his eyes focus on something over my shoulder, and he starts walking. I turn to see Uriah jogging from the elevator bank. He is grinning.

"Heard a rumor you were a dirty traitor," Uriah says.

"Yeah, whatever," says Zeke.

They collide in an embrace that looks almost painful to me, slapping each other's backs and laughing with their fists clasped between them.

+++

"I can't believe you didn't tell us," says Lynn, shaking her head. She sits across from me at the table, her arms crossed and one of her legs propped up.

"Oh, don't get all huffy about it," says Zeke. "I wasn't even supposed to tell Shauna and Uriah. And it sort of defeats the purpose of being a spy if you tell everyone that's what you are."

We sit in a room in Candor headquarters called the Gathering Place, which the Dauntless have taken to saying in a mocking way whenever they can. It is large and open, with black-and-white cloth draped on every wall, and a circle of podiums in the center of the room. Large round tables surround the podiums. Lynn told me they host monthly debates here, for entertainment, and also hold religious services here once a week. But even when no events are scheduled, the room is usually full.

Zeke was cleared by the Candor an hour ago, in a short interrogation on the eighteenth floor. It was not as somber an occasion as Tobias's and my interrogation, partly because there was no suspicious video footage implicating Zeke, and partly because Zeke is funny even when under truth serum. Maybe especially so. In any case, we came to the Gathering Place "for a 'Hey, you're not a dirty traitor!' celebration," as Uriah put it.

"Yeah, but we've been insulting you since the simulation attack," Lynn says. "And now I feel like a jerk about it."

Zeke puts his arm around Shauna. "You *are* a jerk, Lynn. It's part of your charm."

Lynn launches a plastic cup at him, which he deflects. Water sprays over the table, hitting him in the eye.

"Anyway, as I was saying," says Zeke, rubbing his eye, "I was mostly working on getting Erudite defectors out safely. That's why there's a big group of them here, and a small group at Amity headquarters. But Tori . . . I have no idea what she was doing. She kept sneaking away for hours at a time, and whenever she was around, it was like she was about to explode. It's no wonder she gave us away."

"How'd *you* get the job?" says Lynn. "You're not that special."

"It was more because of where I was after the simulation attack. Smack-dab in a pack of Dauntless traitors. I decided to go with it," he says. "Not sure about Tori, though."

"She transferred from Erudite," I say.

What I don't say, because I'm sure she wouldn't want everyone to know, is that Tori probably seemed explosive in Erudite headquarters because they murdered her brother for being Divergent.

She told me once that she was waiting for an opportunity to get revenge.

"Oh," says Zeke. "How do you know that?"

"Well, all the faction transfers have a secret club," I say, leaning back in my chair. "We meet every third Thursday."

Zeke snorts.

"Where's Four?" says Uriah, checking his watch. "Should we start without him?"

"We can't," says Zeke. "He's getting The Info."

Uriah nods like that means something. Then he pauses and says, "What info, again?"

"The info about Kang's little peacemaking meeting with Jeanine," says Zeke. "Obviously."

Across the room, I see Christina sitting at a table with her sister. They are both reading something.

My entire body tenses. Cara, Will's older sister, is walking across the room toward Christina's table. I duck my head.

"What?" Uriah says, looking over his shoulder. I want to punch him.

"Stop it!" I say. "Could you be any more obvious?" I lean forward, folding my arms on the table. "Will's sister is over there."

"Yeah, I talked to her about getting out of Erudite once, while I was there," says Zeke. "Said she saw an Abnegation woman get killed while she was on a mission for Jeanine and couldn't stomach it anymore."

"Are we sure she's not just an Erudite spy?" Lynn says.

"Lynn, she saved half our faction from *this* stuff," says Marlene, tapping the bandage on her arm from where the Dauntless traitors shot her. "Well, half of half of our faction."

"In some circles they call that a quarter, Mar," Lynn says.

"Anyway, who cares if she is a traitor?" Zeke says. "We're not planning anything that she can inform them about. And we certainly wouldn't include her if we were."

"There is plenty of information for her to gather here," Lynn says. "How many of us there are, for example, or how many of us aren't wired for simulations."

"You didn't see her when she was telling me why she left," says Zeke. "I believe her."

Cara and Christina have gotten up, and are walking out of the room.

"I'll be right back," I say. "I have to go to the bathroom."

I wait until Cara and Christina have gone through the doors, then half walk, half jog in that direction. I open one of the doors slowly, so it doesn't make any noise, and then close it slowly behind me. I am in a dim hallway that smells like garbage—this must be where the Candor trash chute is.

I hear two female voices around the corner and creep toward the end of the hallway to hear better.

". . . just can't handle her being here," one of them sobs. Christina. "I can't stop picturing it . . . what she did. . . . I don't understand how she could have done that!"

Christina's sobs make me feel like I am about to crack open.

Cara takes her time responding.

"Well, I do," she says.

"What?" Christina says with a hiccup.

"You have to understand; we're trained to see things as logically as possible," says Cara. "So don't think that I'm callous. But that girl was probably scared out of her mind, certainly not capable of assessing situations cleverly at the time, if she was ever able to do so."

My eyes fly open. *What a—* I run through a short list of insults in my mind before listening to her continue.

"And the simulation made her incapable of reasoning with him, so when he threatened her life, she reacted as she had been trained by the Dauntless to react: Shoot to kill."

"So what are you saying?" says Christina bitterly. "We should just forget about it, because it makes perfect sense?"

"Of course not," says Cara. Her voice wobbles, just a little, and she repeats herself, quietly this time. "Of *course* not."

She clears her throat. "It's just that you have to be around her, and I want to make it easier for you. You don't have to forgive her. Actually, I'm not sure why you were friends with her in the first place; she always seemed a bit erratic to me."

I tense up as I wait for Christina to agree with her, but

to my surprise—and relief—she doesn't.

Cara continues. "Anyway. You don't have to forgive her, but you should try to understand that what she did was not out of malice; it was out of panic. That way, you can look at her without wanting to punch her in her exceptionally long nose."

My hand moves automatically to my nose. Christina laughs a little, which feels like a hard poke to the stomach. I back up through the door to the Gathering Place.

Even though Cara was rude—and the nose comment was a low blow—I am grateful for what she said.

+ + +

Tobias emerges from a door hidden behind a length of white cloth. He flicks the cloth out of the way irritably before coming toward us and sitting beside me at the table in the Gathering Place.

"Kang is going to meet with a representative of Jeanine Matthews at seven in the morning," he says.

"A representative?" Zeke says. "She's not going herself?"

"Yeah, and stand out in the open where a bunch of angry people with guns can take aim?" Uriah smirks a little. "I'd like to see her try. No, really, I would."

"Is Kang the Brilliant taking a Dauntless escort, at least?" Lynn says.

"Yes," Tobias says. "Some of the older members volunteered. Bud said he would keep his ears open and report back."

I frown at him. How does he know all this information? And why, after two years of avoiding becoming a Dauntless leader at all costs, is he suddenly acting like one?

"So I guess the real question is," says Zeke, folding his hands on the table, "if you were Erudite, what would *you* say at this meeting?"

They all look at me. Expectantly.

"What?" I say.

"You're Divergent," Zeke replies.

"So is Tobias."

"Yeah, but he doesn't have aptitude for Erudite."

"And how do you know I do?"

Zeke lifts his shoulder. "Seems likely. Doesn't it seem likely?"

Uriah and Lynn nod. Tobias's mouth twitches, as if in a smile, but if that's what it was, he suppresses it. I feel like a stone just dropped into my stomach.

"You all have functional brains, last time I checked," I say. "You can think like the Erudite, too."

"But we don't have special *Divergent* brains!" says Marlene. She touches her fingertips to my scalp and squeezes lightly. "Come on, do your magic."

"There's no such thing as Divergent magic, Mar," says Lynn.

"And if there is, we shouldn't be consulting it," says Shauna. It's the first thing she's said since we sat down. She doesn't even look at me when she says it; she just scowls at her younger sister.

"Shauna—" Zeke starts.

"Don't 'Shauna' me!" she says, focusing her scowl on him instead. "Don't you think someone with the aptitude for multiple factions might have a loyalty problem? If she's got aptitude for Erudite, how can we be sure she's not *working* for Erudite?"

"Don't be ridiculous," says Tobias, his voice low.

"I am not being ridiculous." She smacks the table. "I know I belong in Dauntless because everything I did in that aptitude test told me so. I'm loyal to my faction for that reason—because there's nowhere else I could possibly be. But her? And you?" She shakes her head. "I have no idea who you're loyal to. And I'm not going to pretend like everything's okay."

She gets up, and when Zeke reaches for her, she throws his hand aside, marching toward one of the doors. I watch her until the door closes behind her and the black fabric that hangs in front of it settles.

I feel wound up, like I might scream, only Shauna isn't

here for me to scream at.

"It's not *magic*," I say hotly. "You just have to ask yourself what the most logical response to a particular situation is."

I am greeted with blank stares.

"Seriously," I say. "If I were in this situation, staring at a group of Dauntless guards and Jack Kang, I probably wouldn't resort to violence, right?"

"Well, you might, if you had your own Dauntless guards. And then all it takes is one shot—bam, he's dead, and Erudite's better off," says Zeke.

"Whoever they send to talk to Jack Kang isn't going to be some random Erudite kid; it's going to be someone important," I say. "It would be a stupid move to fire on Jack Kang and risk losing whoever they send as Jeanine's representative."

"See? This is why we need you to analyze the situation," Zeke says. "If it was me, I would kill him; it would be worth the risk."

I pinch the bridge of my nose. I already have a headache. "Fine."

I try to put myself in Jeanine Matthews's place. I already know she won't negotiate with Jack Kang. Why would she need to? He has nothing to offer her. She will use the situation to her advantage.

"I think," I say, "that Jeanine Matthews will manipulate

him. And that he will do anything to protect his faction, even if it means sacrificing the Divergent." I pause for a moment, remembering how he held his faction's influence over our heads at the meeting. "Or sacrificing the Dauntless. So we *need* to hear what they say in that meeting."

Uriah and Zeke exchange a look. Lynn smiles, but it isn't her usual smile. It doesn't spread to her eyes, which look more like gold than ever, with that coldness in them.

"So let's listen in," she says.

CHAPTER
TWENTY

I CHECK MY watch. It is seven o'clock in the evening. Just twelve hours until we can hear what Jeanine has to say to Jack Kang. I have checked my watch at least a dozen times in the past hour, as if that will make the time go faster. I am itching to do something—*anything* except sit in the cafeteria with Lynn, Tobias, and Lauren, picking at my dinner and sneaking looks at Christina, who sits with her Candor family at one of the other tables.

"I wonder if we'll be able to return to the old way after all this is over," says Lauren. She and Tobias have been talking about Dauntless initiate training methods for at least five minutes already. It's probably the only thing they have in common.

"If there's a faction *left* after all this is over," Lynn says, piling her mashed potatoes onto a roll.

"Don't tell me you're going to eat a mashed-potato sandwich," I say to her.

"So what if I am?"

A group of Dauntless walk between our table and the one next to us. They are older than Tobias, but not by much. One of the girls has five different colors in her hair, and her arms are covered with tattoos so that I can't see even an inch of bare skin. One of the boys leans close to Tobias, whose back is to them, and whispers, "Coward," as he passes.

A few of the others do the same thing, hissing "coward" into Tobias's ears and then continuing on their way. He pauses with his knife against a piece of bread, a glob of butter waiting to be spread, and stares at the table.

I wait, tense, for him to explode.

"What idiots," says Lauren. "And the Candor, for making you spill your life story for everyone to see . . . they're idiots too."

Tobias doesn't answer. He puts down his knife and the piece of bread, and pushes back from the table. His eyes lift and focus on something across the room.

"This needs to stop," he says distantly, and starts toward whatever it is he's looking at before I figure out what it is. This can't be good.

He slips between the tables and the people like he's more liquid than solid, and I stumble after him, muttering apologies as I push people aside.

And then I see exactly who Tobias is headed toward. Marcus. He is sitting with a few of the older Candor.

Tobias reaches him and grabs him by the back of the neck, wrestling him from his seat. Marcus opens his mouth to say something, and that is a mistake, because Tobias punches him hard in the teeth. Someone shouts, but no one rushes to Marcus's aid. We are in a room full of Dauntless, after all.

Tobias shoves Marcus toward the middle of the room, where there is a space between the tables to reveal the symbol of Candor. Marcus stumbles over one of the scales, his hands covering his face so I can't see the damage Tobias did.

Tobias shoves Marcus to the ground and presses the heel of his shoe to his father's throat. Marcus smacks at Tobias's leg, blood streaming past his lips, but even if he was at his strongest, he still wouldn't be as strong as his son. Tobias undoes his belt buckle and slides it from its loops.

He lifts his foot from Marcus's throat and draws the belt back.

"This is for your own good," he says.

That, I remember, is what Marcus, and his many mani-festations, always says to Tobias in his fear landscape.

Then the belt flies through the air and hits Marcus in the arm. Marcus's face is bright red, and he covers his head as the next blow falls, this one hitting his back. All around me is laughter, coming from the Dauntless tables, but I am not laughing, I cannot possibly laugh at this.

Finally I come to my senses. I run forward and grab Tobias's shoulder.

"Stop!" I say. "Tobias, stop *right now!*"

I expect to see a wild look in his eyes, but when he looks at me, I do not. His face is not flushed and his breaths are steady. This was not an act performed in the heat of passion.

It was a calculated act.

He drops the belt and reaches into his pocket. From it he takes a silver chain with a ring dangling from it. Marcus is on his side, gasping. Tobias drops the ring onto the ground next to his father's face. It is made of tar-nished, dull metal, an Abnegation wedding band.

"My mother," says Tobias, "says hello."

Tobias walks away, and it takes a few seconds for me to breathe again. When I do, I leave Marcus cringing on the floor and run after him. It takes me until I reach the hall-way to catch up to him.

"What *was* that?" I demand.

Tobias presses the DOWN button for the elevator and doesn't look at me.

"It was necessary," he says.

"Necessary for what?" I say.

"What, you're feeling sorry for *him* now?" Tobias says, turning toward me with a scowl. "Do you know how many times he did that to me? How do you think I learned the moves?"

I feel brittle, like I might break. It did seem rehearsed, like Tobias had gone over the steps in his mind, recited the words in front of a mirror. He knew it by heart; he was just playing the other part this time.

"No," I say quietly. "No, I don't feel sorry for him, not at all."

"Then *what*, Tris?" His voice is rough; it could be the thing that breaks me. "You haven't cared about what I do or say for the past week; what's so different about this?"

I am almost afraid of him. I don't know what to say or do around the erratic part of him, and it is here, bubbling just beneath the surface of what he does, just like the cruel part of me. We both have war inside of us. Sometimes it keeps us alive. Sometimes it threatens to destroy us.

"Nothing," I say.

The elevator beeps as it arrives. He gets on, and presses

the CLOSE button so the doors shut between us. I stare at the brushed metal and try to think through the last ten minutes.

"This needs to stop," he said. "This" was the ridicule, which was a result of the interrogation, where he admitted that he joined Dauntless to escape his father. And then he beat up Marcus—publicly, where all the Dauntless could see it.

Why? To salvage his pride? It can't be. It was far too intentional for that.

+ + +

On my way back to the cafeteria, I see a Candor man walk Marcus toward the bathroom. He walks slowly, but he isn't hunched over, which makes me think Tobias didn't do him any serious damage. I watch the door close behind him.

I had all but forgotten about what I heard in the Amity compound, about the information my father risked his life for. *Supposedly,* I remind myself. It may not be wise to trust Marcus. And I promised myself I wouldn't ask him about this again.

I dawdle outside the bathroom until the Candor man walks out, and then walk in before the door has a chance to shut properly. Marcus is sitting on the floor by the sink with a wad of paper towel pressed to his mouth. He doesn't look happy to see me.

"What, here to gloat?" he says. "Get out."

"No," I say.

Why am I here, exactly?

He looks at me expectantly. "Well?"

"I thought you could use a reminder," I say. "Whatever it is you want to get from Jeanine, you won't be able to do it alone, and you won't be able to do it with only the Abnegation to help you."

"I thought we went over this." His voice is muffled by the paper towels. "The idea that *you* could help—"

"I don't know where you get this delusion that I'm useless, but that's what it is," I snap. "And I'm not interested in hearing about it. All I want to say is that when you stop being delusional and start feeling desperate because you're too inept to figure this out on your own, you know who to come to."

I leave the bathroom just as the Candor man comes back with an ice pack.

CHAPTER
TWENTY-ONE

I STAND BEFORE the sinks in the women's bathroom on the newly claimed Dauntless floor, a gun resting on my palm. Lynn put it there a few minutes ago; she seemed confused that I did not wrap my hand around it and put it somewhere, in a holster or under the waistband of my jeans. I just let it stay there, and walked to the bathroom before I started to panic.

Don't be an idiot. I can't set out to do what I'm doing without a gun. It would be crazy. So I will have to solve this problem I've been having in the next five minutes.

I curl my pinkie around the handle first, then my second finger, then the others. The weight is familiar. My index finger slips around the trigger. I release a breath.

I start to lift it, bringing my left hand to meet my right

to steady it. I hold the gun out from my body, my arms straight, just as Four taught me, when that was his only name. I used a gun like this to defend my father and brother from simulation-bound Dauntless. I used it to stop Eric from shooting Tobias in the head. It is not inherently evil. It is just a tool.

I see a flicker of movement in the mirror, and before I can stop myself, I stare at my reflection. *This is how I looked to him,* I think. *This is how I looked when I shot him.*

Moaning like a wounded animal, I let the gun fall from my hands and wrap my arms around my stomach. I want to sob because I know it will make me feel better, but I can't force the tears to come. I just crouch in the bathroom, staring at the white tiles. I can't do it. I can't take the gun with me.

I shouldn't even go; I am still going to.

"Tris?" Someone knocks. I stand and uncross my arms as the door squeaks open a few inches. Tobias steps into the room.

"Zeke and Uriah told me you were going to eavesdrop on Jack," he says.

"Oh."

"Are you?"

"Why should I tell you? You don't tell me about *your* plans."

His straight eyebrows furrow. "What are you talking about?"

"I'm talking about beating Marcus to a pulp in front of all the Dauntless for no apparent reason." I step toward him. "But there is a reason, isn't there? Because it's not like you lost control; it's not like he did something to provoke you, so there has to be a reason!"

"I needed to prove to the Dauntless that I am not a coward," he says. "That's all. That's all it was."

"Why would you need to . . ." I start.

Why would Tobias need to prove himself to the Dauntless? Only if he wanted them to hold him in high regard. Only if he wants to become a Dauntless leader. I remember Evelyn's voice, speaking in the shadows in the factionless safe house: "What I am suggesting is that you *become* important."

He wants the Dauntless to ally with the factionless, and he knows the only way he can make that happen is to do it himself.

Why he didn't feel the need to share this plan with me is another mystery entirely. Before I can ask, he says, "So are you going to eavesdrop or not?"

"What does it matter?"

"You're throwing yourself into danger for no reason again," he says. "Just like when you stormed up to fight the

Erudite with only a . . . a *pocket knife* to protect yourself."

"There is a reason. A good one. We won't know what's going on unless we eavesdrop, and we need to know what's going on."

He crosses his arms. He is not bulky, the way some Dauntless boys are. And some girls might focus on the way his ears stick out, or the way his nose hooks at the end, but to me . . .

I swallow the rest of that thought. He's here to yell at me. He's been keeping things from me. Whatever we are now, I can't indulge thoughts about how attractive he is. It will just make it harder for me to do what needs to be done. And right now, that is going to listen to what Jack Kang has to say to the Erudite.

"You're not cutting your hair like the Abnegation anymore," I say. "That because you want to look more Dauntless?"

"Don't change the subject," he says. "There are four people going to eavesdrop already. You don't need to be there."

"Why are you so insistent on me staying home?" My voice gets louder. "I am not the kind of person who just sits back and lets other people take all the risks!"

"As long as you are someone who doesn't seem to value her own life . . . someone who can't even pick up and fire a *gun . . .*" He leans toward me. "You should sit back and let other people take the risks."

His quiet voice pulses around me like a second heartbeat. I hear the words "doesn't seem to value her own life" again and again.

"What are you going to do?" I say. "Lock me in the bathroom? Because that's the only way you'll be able to keep me from going."

He touches his forehead and lets his hand drag down the side of his face. I have never seen his face sag that way before.

"I don't want to stop you. I want you to stop yourself," he says. "But if you're going to be reckless, you can't prevent me from coming along."

+ + +

It is still dark, but just barely, when we reach the bridge, which is two-tiered, with stone pillars at each corner. We descend the stairs next to one of the stone pillars and creep with silent feet at river level. Large puddles of standing water gleam as the light of day hits them. The sun is rising; we have to get into position.

Uriah and Zeke are in the buildings on either side of the bridge so they can get a better view and cover us from a distance. They have better aim than Lynn or Shauna, who came because Lynn asked her to, despite her outburst in the Gathering Place.

Lynn goes first, her back pressed to the stone as she inches along the lower lip of the bridge supports. I follow her, with Shauna and Tobias behind me. The bridge is supported by four curved metal structures that secure it to the stone wall, and by a maze of narrow girders beneath its lower tier. Lynn wedges herself under one of the metal structures and climbs quickly, keeping the narrow girders beneath her as she works her way to the middle of the bridge.

I let Shauna go in front of me because I can't climb as well. My left arm shakes as I try to balance on top of the metal structure. I feel Tobias's cool hand on my waist, steadying me.

I crouch low to fit in the space between the bottom of the bridge and the girders beneath me. I don't make it very far before I have to stop, my feet on one girder and my left arm on another. And I will have to stay that way for a long time.

Tobias slides along one of the girders and puts his leg under me. It is long enough to stretch beneath me and onto a second girder. I breathe out and smile at him as a kind of thank-you. It's the first time we have acknowledged each other since we left the Merciless Mart.

He smiles back, but grimly.

We bide our time in silence. I breathe through my mouth and try to control the shaking of my arms and legs. Shauna and Lynn seem to communicate without speaking. They make faces at each other that I can't read, and nod and smile at each other when they reach an understanding. I have never thought about what it would be like to have a sister. Would Caleb and I be closer if he were a girl?

The city is so quiet in the morning that the footsteps echo as they approach the bridge. The sound comes from behind me, which must mean it's Jack and his Dauntless escort, not the Erudite, who have arrived. The Dauntless know that we are here, though Jack Kang himself does not. If he stares down for more than a few seconds, he might see us through the metal mesh beneath his feet. I try to breathe as quietly as possible.

Tobias checks his watch, and then holds his arm out to me to show me the time. Seven o'clock exactly.

I glance up and peer through the steel web above me. Feet pass over my head. And then I hear him.

"Hello, Jack," he says.

It's Max, who appointed Eric to Dauntless leadership

at Jeanine's demand, who implemented policies of cruelty and brutality in Dauntless initiation. I have never spoken to him directly, but the sound of his voice makes me shiver.

"Max," Jack says. "Where's Jeanine? I thought she would at least have the courtesy to show up herself."

"Jeanine and I divide our responsibilities according to our strengths," he says. "That means I make all military decisions. I believe that includes what we are doing today."

I frown. I haven't heard Max speak much, but something about the words he's using, and their rhythm, sounds . . . *off.*

"Fine," says Jack. "I came to—"

"I should inform you that this will not be a negotiation," Max says. "In order to negotiate, you have to be on even footing, and you, Jack, are not."

"What do you mean?"

"I mean that you are the only disposable faction. Candor does not provide us with protection, sustenance, or technological innovation. Therefore you are expendable to us. And you have not done much to win the favor of your Dauntless guests," says Max, "so you are completely vulnerable and completely useless. I recommend, therefore, that you do exactly as I say."

"You piece of scum," says Jack through gritted teeth. "How *dare*—"

"Now let's not get testy," Max says.

I chew on my lip. I should trust my instincts, and my instincts tell me that something is wrong here. No self-respecting Dauntless man would say the word "testy." Nor would he react so calmly to an insult. He's speaking like someone else. He's speaking like Jeanine.

The back of my neck prickles. It makes perfect sense. Jeanine would not trust anyone, particularly not a volatile Dauntless, to speak on her behalf. The best solution to that problem is to give Max an earpiece. And the signal from an earpiece can stretch only a quarter of a mile at most.

I catch Tobias's eye, and slowly move my hand to point at my ear. Then I point above me, at my best approximation of where Max stands.

Tobias frowns for a moment, then nods, but I'm not sure he understands me.

"I have three requirements," says Max. "First, that you return the Dauntless leader you currently hold in captivity unharmed. Second, that you allow your compound to be searched by our soldiers so that we can extract the Divergent; and third, that you provide us with the names of those who were not injected with the simulation serum."

"Why?" Jack says bitterly. "What are you searching for? And why do you need those names? What do you intend to do with them?"

"The purpose of our search would be to locate and remove any of the Divergent from the premises. And as for the names, that is none of your concern."

"None of my concern!" I hear footsteps squeak above me and stare up through the mesh. From what I can see, Jack has the collar of Max's shirt wrapped around his fist.

"Release me," says Max. "Or I will order my guards to fire."

I frown. If Jeanine is speaking through Max, she had to be able to see him in order to know that he was grabbed. I lean forward to look at the buildings on the other side of the bridge. On my left, the river bends, and a squat glass building stands at the edge. That must be where she is.

I start to climb backward, toward the metal structure that supports the bridge, toward the staircase that will lead me to Wacker Drive. Tobias follows me immediately, and Shauna taps Lynn on the shoulder. But Lynn is doing something else.

I was too busy thinking about Jeanine. I failed to notice that Lynn took out her gun and started to climb toward the edge of the bridge. Shauna's mouth opens and her eyes go wide as Lynn swings herself forward, grabbing the lip of the bridge, and shoves her arm over it. Her finger squeezes the trigger.

Max gasps, his hand clapping over his chest, and stumbles back. When he pulls his hand away, it is dark with blood.

I don't bother to climb anymore. I drop into the mud, closely followed by Tobias, Lynn, and Shauna. My legs sink into the mire, and my feet make sucking noises as I pull them free. My shoes slip off but I keep going until I reach the concrete. Guns fire and bullets stick in the mud next to me. I throw myself against the wall under the bridge so they can't aim at me.

Tobias presses into the wall behind me, so close to me that his chin floats over my head and I can feel his chest against my shoulders. Shielding me.

I can run back to Candor headquarters, and to temporary safety. Or I can find Jeanine in what is probably the most vulnerable state she will ever be in.

It's not even a choice.

"Come on!" I say. I sprint up the stairs, the others on my heels. On the lower tier of the bridge, our Dauntless shoot at the Dauntless traitors. Jack is safe, bent over with a Dauntless arm slung across his back. I run faster. I run across the bridge and don't look behind me. I can already hear Tobias's footsteps. He is the only one who can keep up with me.

The glass building is in my sights. And then I hear more footsteps, more gunshots. I weave as I run, to make it more difficult for the Dauntless traitors to hit me.

I am close to the glass building. I am yards away. I grit my teeth and push myself harder. My legs are numb; I barely feel the ground beneath me. But before I reach the doors, I see movement in the alley to my right. I swerve and follow it with my feet.

Three figures run down the alley. One is blond. One is tall. And one is Peter.

I stumble, and almost fall.

"Peter!" I shout. He lifts his gun, and behind me, Tobias lifts his own, and we stand just yards away from each other, at a standstill. Behind him, the blond woman— Jeanine, probably—and the tall Dauntless traitor turn the corner. Though I don't have a weapon, and I don't have a plan, I want to run after them, and maybe I would if Tobias did not clamp his hand over my shoulder and hold me in place.

"You traitor," I say to Peter. "I knew it. I *knew* it."

A scream pierces the air. It is anguished and female.

"Sounds like your friends need you," Peter says with

the flash of a smile—or bared teeth, I can't tell. He keeps his gun steady. "So you have a choice. You can let us go, and help them, or you can die trying to follow us."

I almost scream. We both know what I'm going to do.

"I hope you die," I say.

I back up into Tobias, who backs up with me, until we reach the end of the alley, and then turn and run.

CHAPTER
TWENTY-TWO

S<small>HAUNA LIES ON</small> the ground, facedown, blood pooling on her shirt. Lynn crouches at her side. Staring. Doing nothing.

"It's my fault," Lynn mumbles. "I shouldn't have shot him. I shouldn't have . . ."

I stare at the patch of blood. A bullet hit her in the back. I can't tell if she's breathing or not. Tobias places two fingers on the side of her neck, and nods.

"We've got to get out of here," he says. "Lynn. Look at me. I'm going to carry her, and it's going to hurt her a lot, but it's our only option."

Lynn nods. Tobias crouches next to Shauna and puts his hands under her arms. He lifts her, and she moans. I rush forward to help him pull her limp body over his shoulder. My throat tightens, and I cough to relieve the pressure.

Tobias stands with a grunt of effort, and together we walk toward the Merciless Mart—Lynn in front, with her gun, and me in the back. I walk backward to watch behind us, but I don't see anyone. I think the Dauntless traitors retreated. But I have to make sure.

"Hey!" someone shouts. It's Uriah, jogging toward us. "Zeke had to help them get Jack . . . oh no." He stops. "Oh no. Shauna?"

"Now's not the time," says Tobias sharply. "Run back to the Merciless Mart and get a doctor."

But Uriah just stares.

"Uriah! Go, *now*!" The shout rings with nothing on the street to soften the sound of it. Uriah finally turns and sprints in the direction of the Merciless Mart.

It's only half a mile back, but with Tobias's grunts and Lynn's uneven breathing and the knowledge that Shauna is bleeding to death, it feels endless. I watch the muscles in Tobias's back expanding and contracting with each labored breath, and I don't hear our footsteps; I hear only my heartbeat. When we finally reach the doors, I feel like I might throw up, or faint, or scream at the top of my lungs.

Uriah, an Erudite man with a comb-over, and Cara meet us just inside the entrance. They set up a sheet for

Shauna to lie on. Tobias lowers her onto it, and the doctor gets to work immediately, cutting the shirt away from Shauna's back. I turn away. I don't want to see the bullet wound.

Tobias stands in front of me, his face red with exertion. I want him to fold me into his arms again, like he did after the last attack, but he doesn't, and I know better than to initiate it.

"I'm not going to pretend to know what's going on with you," he says. "But if you senselessly risk your life again—"

"I am not senselessly risking my life. I am trying to make *sacrifices*, like my parents would have, like—"

"You are *not* your parents. You are a sixteen-year-old girl—"

I grit my teeth. "How *dare* you—"

"—who doesn't understand that the value of a sacrifice lies in its *necessity*, not in throwing your life away! And if you do that again, you and I are done."

I wasn't expecting him to say that.

"You're giving me an ultimatum?" I try to keep my voice down so the others can't hear.

He shakes his head. "No, I'm telling you a fact." His lips are just a line. "If you throw yourself into danger for no reason again, you will have become nothing more than a Dauntless adrenaline junkie looking for a hit, and I'm not going to help you do it." He spits the words out bitterly. "I love Tris the Divergent, who makes decisions apart from faction loyalty, who isn't some faction archetype. But the Tris who's trying as hard as she can to destroy herself . . . I can't love her."

I want to scream. But not because I'm angry, because I'm afraid he's right. My hands shake and I grab the hem of my shirt to steady them.

He touches his forehead to mine and closes his eyes. "I believe you're still in there," he says against my mouth. "Come back."

He kisses me lightly, and I am too shocked to stop him.

He walks back to Shauna's side, and I stand over one of the Candor scales in the lobby, at a loss.

+ + +

"It's been a while."

I sink down on the bed across from Tori. She is sitting up, her leg propped on a stack of pillows.

"Yes, it has," I say. "How are you feeling?"

"Like I got shot." A smile plays over her lips. "I hear you're familiar with the feeling."

"Yeah. It's great, right?" All I can think of is the bullet in Shauna's back. At least Tori and I will recover from our wounds.

"Did you discover anything interesting at Jack's meeting?" she says.

"A few things. Do you know how we might go about calling a Dauntless meeting?"

"I can make it happen. One thing about being a tattoo artist in Dauntless is . . . you know pretty much everyone."

"Right," I say. "You also have the prestige of being a former spy."

Tori's mouth twists. "I had almost forgotten."

"Did *you* discover anything interesting? As a spy, I mean."

"My mission was primarily focused on Jeanine Matthews." She glares at her hands. "How she spends her days. And, more importantly, *where* she spends them."

"Not in her office, then?"

Tori doesn't answer at first.

"I guess I can trust you, Divergent." She looks at me from the corner of her eye. "She has a private laboratory on the top level. Insane security measures protecting it. I was trying to get up there when they figured out what I was."

"You were trying to get up there," I say. Her eyes flit away from mine. "Not to spy, I take it."

"I thought it would be more . . . *expedient* if Jeanine Matthews didn't survive much longer."

I see a kind of thirst in her expression, the same one I saw when she told me about her brother in the back room of the tattoo parlor. Before the attack simulation I might have called it a thirst for justice, or even revenge, but now I am able to identify it as a thirst for blood. And even as it frightens me, I understand it.

Which should probably frighten me even more.

Tori says, "I'll work on calling that meeting."

+ + +

The Dauntless are gathered in the space between the rows of bunk beds and the doors, which are held shut by a tightly wrapped bedsheet, the best lock the Dauntless could muster. I have no doubt that Jack Kang will agree to Jeanine's demands. We aren't safe here anymore.

"What were the terms?" Tori says. She sits in a chair between a few of the bunks, her wounded leg stuck out in front of her. She asks Tobias, but he doesn't seem to be paying attention. He is leaning against one of the bunks, his arms crossed, staring at the floor.

I clear my throat. "There were three. Return Eric to the Erudite. Report the names of all people who did not get shot with needles last time. And deliver the Divergent to Erudite headquarters."

I look at Marlene. She smiles back at me a little sadly. She is probably worried about Shauna, who is still with the Erudite doctor. Lynn, Hector, their parents, and Zeke are with her.

"If Jack Kang is making deals with the Erudite, we can't stay here," says Tori. "So where can we go?"

I think of the blood on Shauna's shirt, and long for the Amity orchards, the sound of the wind in the leaves, the feeling of bark beneath my hands. I never thought I would crave that place. I didn't think it was in me.

I close my eyes briefly, and when I open them I am in reality, and Amity is a dream.

"Home," Tobias says, lifting his head at last. Everyone is listening. "We should take back what's ours. We can break the security cameras in Dauntless headquarters so the Erudite can't see us. We should go home."

Someone assents with a shout, and someone else joins in. That is how things in Dauntless are decided: with nods and yells. In these moments we don't seem like individuals anymore. We are all a part of the same mind.

"But before we do that," says Bud, who once worked with Tori in the tattoo parlor and who now stands with his hand on the back of Tori's chair, "we need to decide what to do about Eric. To let him stay here with the Erudite, or to execute him."

"Eric is Dauntless," Lauren says, turning the ring in her lip with her fingertips. "That means *we* decide what happens to him. Not Candor."

This time a yell tears from my body of its own volition, joining with the others in agreement.

"According to Dauntless law, only Dauntless leaders can perform an execution. All five of our former leaders are Dauntless traitors," says Tori. "So I think it's time we pick new ones. The law says we need more than one, and we need an odd number. If you've got suggestions, you should shout them out now, and we'll vote if we need to."

"You!" someone calls out.

"Okay," says Tori. "Anyone else?"

Marlene cups her hands around her mouth and calls out, "Tris!"

My heart pounds. But to my surprise, no one mutters in dissent and no one laughs. Instead, a few people nod, just like they did when Tori's name was mentioned. I scan the crowd and find Christina. She stands with her arms crossed, and does not seem to react at all to my nomination.

I wonder how I seem to them. They must see someone I don't see. Someone capable and strong. Someone I can't be; someone I can be.

Tori acknowledges Marlene with a nod and scans the

crowd for another recommendation.

"Harrison," someone says. I don't know who Harrison is until someone slaps a middle-aged man with a blond ponytail on the shoulder, and he grins. I recognize him—he's the Dauntless man who called me "girl" when Zeke and Tori came back from Erudite headquarters.

The Dauntless are quiet for a moment.

"I'm going to nominate Four," says Tori.

Apart from a few angry murmurs in the back of the room, no one disagrees. No one is calling him a coward anymore, not after he beat up Marcus in the cafeteria. I wonder how they would react if they knew how calculated that move was.

Now he could get exactly what he intended to get. Unless I stand in his way.

"We only need three leaders," Tori says. "We'll have to vote."

They would never have considered me if I had not stopped the attack simulation. And maybe they wouldn't have considered me if I hadn't stabbed Eric by those elevators, or put myself under that bridge. The more reckless I get, the more popular I am with the Dauntless.

Tobias looks at me. I can't be popular with the Dauntless, because Tobias is right—I'm not Dauntless; I'm Divergent. I am whatever I choose to be. And I can't choose to be *this*.

I have to stay separate from them.

"No," I say. I clear my throat and say it louder. "No, you don't have to vote. I refuse my nomination."

Tori raises her eyebrows at me. "Are you sure, Tris?"

"Yes," I say. "I don't want it. I'm sure."

And then, without argument and without ceremony, Tobias is elected to be a leader of Dauntless. And I am not.

CHAPTER
TWENTY-THREE

NOT TEN SECONDS after we choose our new leaders, something rings—one long pulse, two short ones. I move toward the sound, my right ear toward the wall, and find a speaker suspended from the ceiling. There is another one across the room.

Then Jack Kang's voice speaks all around us.

"Attention all occupants of Candor headquarters. A few hours ago I met with a representative of Jeanine Matthews. He reminded me that we Candor are in a weak position, dependent on Erudite for our survival, and told me that if I intend to keep my faction free, I will have to meet a few demands."

I stare up at the speaker, stunned. I shouldn't be surprised that the leader of Candor is this forthright, but I wasn't expecting a public announcement.

"In order to comply with these demands, I ask that everyone make their way to the Gathering Place to report whether you have an implant or not," he says. "The Erudite have also ordered all Divergent to be turned over to Erudite. I do not know for what purpose."

He sounds listless. Defeated. *Well, he* is *defeated,* I think. *Because he was too weak to fight back.*

One thing Dauntless knows that Candor does not is how to fight even when fighting seems useless.

Sometimes I feel like I am collecting the lessons each faction has to teach me, and storing them in my mind like a guidebook for moving through the world. There is always something to learn, always something that is important to understand.

Jack Kang's announcement ends with the same three rings it started with. The Dauntless rush through the room, throwing their things into bags. A few young Dauntless men cut the sheet away from the door, screaming something about Eric. Someone's elbow presses me to a wall, and I just stand and watch the pandemonium intensify.

On the other hand, one thing Candor knows that Dauntless does not is how not to get carried away.

+ + +

The Dauntless stand in a semicircle around the inter-rogation chair, where Eric now sits. He looks more dead than alive. He is slumped in the chair, sweat shining on his pale forehead. He stares at Tobias with his head tilted down, so his eyelashes blend into his eyebrows. I try to keep my eyes on him, but his smile—how the piercings pull wide when his lips spread—is almost too awful to take.

"Would you like me to tell you your crimes?" says Tori. "Or would you like to list them yourself?"

Rain sprays against the side of the building and streams down the walls. We stand in the interrogation room, on the top floor of the Merciless Mart. The afternoon storm is louder here. Every crack of thunder and flash of light-ning makes the back of my neck prickle, as if electricity is dancing over my skin.

I like the smell of wet pavement. It is faint here, but once this is done, all the Dauntless will storm down the stairs and leave the Merciless Mart behind, and wet pave-ment will be the only thing I smell.

We have our bags with us. Mine is a sack made of a sheet and some rope. It contains my clothes and a spare pair of shoes. I wear the jacket I stole from the Dauntless traitor—I want Eric to see it if he looks at me.

Eric scans the crowd for a few seconds, and then his

eyes settle on me. He laces his fingers and sets them—gingerly—on his stomach. "I'd like *her* to list them. Since she's the one who stabbed me, clearly she is familiar with them."

I don't know what game he's playing, or what the point of rattling me is, especially now, before his execution. He seems arrogant, but I notice that his fingers tremble when he moves them. Even Eric must be afraid of death.

"Leave her out of this," says Tobias.

"Why? Because you're doing her?" Eric smirks. "Oh wait, I forgot. Stiffs don't *do* that sort of thing. They just tie each other's shoes and cut each other's hair."

Tobias's expression does not change. I think I understand: Eric doesn't really care about me. But he knows exactly where to hit Tobias, and how hard. And one of the places to hit Tobias the hardest is to hit me.

This is what I wanted most to avoid: for my rises and falls to become Tobias's rises and falls. That's why I can't let him step in to defend me now.

"I want her to list them," repeats Eric.

I say, as evenly as possible:

"You conspired with Erudite. You are responsible for the deaths of hundreds of Abnegation." As I go on, I can't keep my voice steady anymore; I start to spit out the words like venom. "You betrayed Dauntless. You shot a child in the head. You are a ridiculous plaything of Jeanine Matthews."

His smile fades.

"Do I deserve to die?" he says.

Tobias opens his mouth to interrupt. But I respond before he can.

"Yes."

"Fair enough." His dark eyes are empty, like pits, like starless nights. "But do you have the right to decide that, Beatrice Prior? Like you decided the fate of that other boy—what was his name? Will?"

I don't answer. I hear my father asking me, "What makes you think you have the right to shoot someone?" as we fought our way to the control room in Dauntless headquarters. He told me there is a right way to do something, and I needed to figure it out. I feel something in my throat, like a ball of wax, so thick I can barely swallow, barely breathe.

"You have committed every crime that warrants execution among the Dauntless," says Tobias. "*We* have the right to execute you, under the laws of Dauntless."

He crouches by the three guns on the floor near Eric's feet. One by one, he empties the chambers of bullets. They almost jingle as they hit the floor, and then roll, coming to rest against the toes of Tobias's shoes. He picks up the middle gun and puts a bullet into the first slot.

Then he moves the three guns on the floor, around and around, until my eyes can't follow the middle gun anymore. I lose track of which one holds the bullet. He picks up the guns and offers one to Tori, and another one to Harrison.

I try to think of the attack simulation, and what it did to the Abnegation. All the gray-clothed innocents lying dead on the street. There weren't even enough Abnegation left to take care of the bodies, so most of them are probably still there. And that would not have been possible without Eric.

I think of the Candor boy, shot without a second's hesitation, how stiff he was as he hit the ground next to me.

Maybe we are not the ones deciding if Eric lives or dies. Maybe he is the one who decided that, when he did all those terrible things.

But it's still hard to breathe.

I look at him without malice, without hatred, and without fear. The rings in his face shine, and a lock of dirty hair falls into his eyes.

"Wait," he says. "I have a request."

"We don't take requests from criminals," says Tori. She's standing on one leg, and has been for the past few minutes. She sounds tired—she probably wants to get this over with so she can sit down again. To her this execution is just an inconvenience.

"I am a leader of Dauntless," he says. "And all I want is for Four to be the one who fires that bullet."

"Why?" Tobias says.

"So you can live with the guilt," Eric replies. "Of knowing that you usurped me and then shot me in the head."

I think I understand. He wants to see people break—has always wanted to, ever since he set up the camera in my execution room when I nearly drowned, and probably long before then. And he believes that if Tobias has to kill him, he will see that before he dies.

Sick.

"There won't be any guilt," says Tobias.

"Then you'll have no problem doing it." Eric smiles again.

Tobias picks up one of the bullets.

"Tell me," says Eric quietly, "because I've always wondered. Is it your daddy who shows up in every fear landscape you've ever gone through?"

Tobias puts the bullet into an empty chamber without looking up.

"You didn't like that question?" Eric says. "What, afraid the Dauntless are going to change their minds about you?

Realize that even though you've only got four fears, you're still a coward?"

He straightens in the chair and puts his hands on the armrests.

Tobias holds his gun out from his left shoulder.

"Eric," he says, "be brave."

He squeezes the trigger.

I shut my eyes.

CHAPTER
TWENTY-FOUR

BLOOD IS A strange color. It's darker than you expect it to be.

I stare down at Marlene's hand, which is wrapped around my arm. Her fingernails are short and jagged—she bites them. She pushes me forward, and I must be walking, because I can feel myself moving, but in my mind I stand before Eric and he is still alive.

He died just like Will did. Slumped just like Will did.

I thought the swollen feeling in my throat would go away once he was dead, but it didn't. I have to take deep, hard breaths to get enough air. Good thing the crowd around me is so loud that no one can hear me. We march toward the doors. At the front of the pack is Harrison, carrying Tori on his back like a child. She laughs, her arms wrapped around his neck.

Tobias sets his hand on my back. I know because I see him come up behind me and do it, not because I feel it. I don't feel anything at all.

The doors open from the outside. We stop short of stampeding Jack Kang and the group of Candor that followed him here.

"What have you done?" he says. "I was just told that Eric is missing from his holding cell."

"He was under our jurisdiction," says Tori. "We gave him a trial and executed him. You should be thanking us."

"Why . . ." Jack's face turns red. Blood is darker than blush, even though one consists of the other. "Why should I be thanking you?"

"Because you wanted him to be executed, too, right? Since he murdered one of your children?" Tori tilts her head, her eyes wide, innocent. "Well, we took care of it for you. And now, if you'll excuse us, we're leaving."

"Wha— *Leaving*?" Jack splutters.

If we leave, he will be incapable of fulfilling two of the three demands Max had of him. The thought terrifies him, and it is all over his face.

"I can't let you do that," he says.

"You don't *let* us do anything," says Tobias. "If you don't step aside, we will be forced to walk over you instead of past you."

"Didn't you come here to find allies?" Jack scowls. "If you do this, we will side with Erudite, I promise you, and you will never find an ally in us again, you—"

"We don't need you as an ally," says Tori. "We're Dauntless."

Everyone shouts, and somehow their screams pierce the haze in my mind. The entire crowd presses forward at once. The Candor in the corridor yelp and dive out of the way as we spill into the hallway like a burst pipe, Dauntless water spreading to fill the empty space.

Marlene's grip on my arm breaks. I run down the stairs, chasing the heels of the Dauntless in front of me, ignoring the jostle of elbows and all the shouts around me. I feel like I am an initiate again, storming the stairs of the Hub right after the Choosing Ceremony. My legs burn, but that is all right.

We reach the lobby. A group of Candor and Erudite are waiting there, including the blond Divergent woman who got dragged to the elevators by her hair, the girl I helped escape, and Cara. They watch the Dauntless stream past them with helpless looks on their faces.

Cara spots me and grabs my arm, wrenching me back. "Where are you all going?"

"Dauntless headquarters." I try to pull my arm free, but she won't let go. I don't look at her face. I can't look at her right now.

"Go to Amity," I say. "They promised safety to anyone who wants it. You won't be safe here."

She releases me, almost pushing me away from her in the process.

Outside, the ground feels slick beneath my sneakers, and my sack of clothes thumps against my back as I slow to a jog. Rain sprinkles my head and my back. My feet splash through puddles, soaking my pant legs.

I smell wet pavement, and pretend that this is all there is.

+ + +

I stand at the railing overlooking the chasm. Water hits the wall beneath me, but it doesn't come high enough to splash my shoes.

A hundred yards away, Bud passes out paintball guns. Someone else passes out paintballs. Soon the hidden corners of Dauntless headquarters will be coated in multicolored paint, blocking the lenses of the surveillance cameras.

"Hey, Tris," Zeke says, joining me at the railing. His eyes are red and swollen, but his mouth is curled into a small smile.

"Hey. You made it."

"Yeah. We waited until Shauna was stable and then

took her here." He rubs one of his eyes with his thumb. "I didn't want to move her, but . . . wasn't safe with Candor anymore. Obviously."

"How is she?"

"Dunno. She's gonna survive it, but the nurse thinks she might be paralyzed from the waist down. And that wouldn't bother me, but . . ." He lifts a shoulder. "How can she be Dauntless if she can't walk?"

I stare across the Pit, where some Dauntless children chase each other up the path, hurling paintballs at the walls. One of them breaks and splatters the stone with yellow.

I think of what Tobias told me when we spent the night with the factionless, about the older Dauntless leaving the faction because they were no longer physically capable of staying in it. I think of Candor's rhyming song, which calls us the cruelest faction.

"She can," I say.

"Tris. She won't even be able to move around."

"Sure she will." I look up at him. "She can get a wheelchair, and someone can push her up the paths in the Pit, and there's an elevator in the building up *there*." I point above our heads. "She doesn't need to be able to walk to slide down the zip line or fire a gun."

"She won't want me to push her." His voice cracks a

little. "She won't want me to lift her, or carry her."

"She'll have to get over it, then. Are you going to let her drop out of Dauntless for a stupid reason like not being able to walk?"

Zeke is quiet for a few seconds. His eyes shift over my face, and he squints, as if weighing and measuring me.

Then he turns and bends and wraps his arms around me. It's been so long since someone hugged me that I stiffen. Then I relax, and let the gesture force warmth into my body, which is chilled by damp clothing.

"I'm gonna go shoot things," he says as he pulls away. "Want to come?"

I shrug and chase him across the Pit floor. Bud hands each of us a paintball gun, and I load mine. Its weight, shape, and material are so different from a revolver that I have no trouble holding it.

"We've mostly got the Pit and the underground covered," Bud says. "But you should tackle the Pire."

"The Pire?"

Bud points up at the glass building above us. The sight pierces me like a needle. The last time I stood in this spot and stared up at this ceiling, I was on a mission to destroy the simulation. I was with my father.

Zeke is already on his way up the path. I force myself to follow him, one foot and then the other. It's difficult to walk because it's difficult to breathe, but somehow I manage. By the time I reach the stairs, the pressure on my chest is almost gone.

Once we're in the Pire, Zeke lifts up his gun and aims at one of the cameras near the ceiling. He fires, and green paint sprays across one of the windows, missing the camera lens.

"Ooh," I say, wincing. "Ouch."

"Yeah? I'd like to see you do it perfectly the first time."

"Would you?" I lift my own gun, propping it up on my left shoulder instead of my right. The gun feels unfamiliar in my left hand, but I can't bear its weight with my right yet. Through the scope I find the camera, and then squint to stare at the lens. A voice whispers in my head. *Inhale. Aim. Exhale. Fire.* It takes me a few seconds to realize it's Tobias's voice, because he's the one who taught me to shoot. I squeeze the trigger and the paintball hits the camera, spraying blue paint across the lens. "There. Now you have. With the wrong hand, too."

Zeke mutters something under his breath that doesn't sound pleasant.

"Hey!" shouts a cheerful voice. Marlene pokes her head above the glass floor. Paint is smeared across her forehead, giving her a purple eyebrow. With a wicked smile, she aims at Zeke, hitting his leg, and then at me. The paintball hits my arm, stinging.

Marlene laughs and ducks under the glass. Zeke and I look at each other, and then run after Marlene. She laughs as she sprints down the path, weaving through a crowd of kids. I shoot at her, and hit the wall instead. Marlene fires at a boy near the railing—Hector, Lynn's little brother. He looks shocked at first, but then fires back, hitting the person next to Marlene.

Popping sounds fill the air as everyone in the Pit starts to fire at one another, young and old, the cameras momentarily forgotten. I charge down the path, surrounded by laughter and shouting. We cluster together to form teams, and then turn against one another.

By the time the fight dies down, my clothes are more paint-colored than black. I decide to keep the shirt to remind me why I chose Dauntless in the first place: not because they are perfect, but because they are alive. Because they are free.

CHAPTER
TWENTY-FIVE

SOMEONE RAIDS THE Dauntless kitchens and heats up the imperishables kept there, so we have a warm dinner that night. I sit at the same table I used to claim with Christina, Al, and Will. From the moment I sit down, I feel a lump in my throat. How is it that only half of us are left?

I feel responsible for that. My forgiveness could have saved Al, but I withheld it. My clearheadedness could have spared Will, but I could not summon it.

Before I can sink too far into my guilt, Uriah drops his tray next to me. It is loaded with beef stew and chocolate cake. I stare at the cake pile.

"There was cake?" I say, looking at my own plate, which is more sensibly stocked than Uriah's.

"Yeah, someone just brought it out. Found a couple

boxes of the mix in the back and baked it," he says. "You can have a few bites of mine."

"A *few* bites? So you're planning on eating that mountain of cake by yourself?"

"Yes." He looks confused. "Why?"

"Never mind."

Christina sits across the table, as far away from me as she can get. Zeke puts his tray down next to her. We are soon joined by Lynn, Hector, and Marlene. I see a flash of movement under the table, and see Marlene's hand meet Uriah's over his knee. Their fingers twist together. They are both clearly trying to look casual, but they sneak looks at each other.

To Marlene's left, Lynn looks like she just tasted something sour. She shovels food into her mouth.

"Where's the fire?" Uriah asks her. "You're going to hurl if you keep eating that fast."

Lynn scowls at him. "I'm going to hurl anyway, with you two making eyes at each other all the time."

Uriah's ears turn red. "What are you talking about?"

"I am not an idiot, and neither is anyone else. So why don't you just make out with her and get it over with?"

Uriah looks stunned. Marlene, however, glares at Lynn, leans over, and kisses Uriah firmly on the mouth, her fingers sliding around his neck, under the collar of his shirt.

I notice that all the peas have fallen off my fork, which was on its way to my mouth.

Lynn grabs her tray and storms away from the table.

"What was that all about?" says Zeke.

"Don't ask me," says Hector. "She's always angry about something. I've stopped trying to keep track."

Uriah's and Marlene's faces are still close together. And they are still smiling.

I force myself to stare at my plate. It is so strange to see two people you have known separately join together, though I have watched it happen before. I hear a squeak as Christina scratches her plate with her fork idly.

"Four!" Zeke calls out, beckoning. He looks relieved. "C'mere, there's room."

Tobias rests his hand on my good shoulder. A few of his knuckles are split, and the blood looks fresh. "Sorry, I can't stay."

He leans down and says, "Can I borrow you for a while?"

I get up, waving a good-bye to everyone at the table who is paying attention—which is just Zeke, really, because Christina and Hector are staring at their plates, and Uriah and Marlene are talking quietly. Tobias and I walk out of the cafeteria.

"Where are we going?"

"The train," he says. "I have a meeting, and I want you

there to help me read the situation."

We walk up one of the paths that lines the Pit walls, toward the stairs that lead us to the Pire.

"Why do you need *me* to—"

"Because you're better at it than I am."

I don't have a response to that. We ascend the stairs and cross the glass floor. On our way out, we walk through the dank room in which I faced my fear landscape. Judging by the syringe on the floor, someone has been there recently.

"Did you go through your fear landscape today?" I say.

"What makes you say that?" His dark eyes skirt mine. He pushes the front door open, and the summer air swims around me. There is no wind.

"Your knuckles are cut up and someone's been using that room."

"This is exactly what I mean. You're far more perceptive than most." He checks his watch. "They told me to catch the one leaving at 8:05. Come on."

I feel a surge of hope. Maybe we won't argue this time. Maybe things will finally get better between us.

We walk to the tracks. The last time we did this, he wanted to show me that the lights were on in the Erudite compound, wanted to tell me that Erudite was planning an attack on Abnegation. Now I get the sense we are about to meet with the factionless.

"Perceptive enough to know you're evading the question," I say.

He sighs. "Yes, I went through my fear landscape. I wanted to see if it had changed."

"And it has. Hasn't it?"

He brushes a stray hair away from his face and avoids my eyes. I didn't know his hair was so thick—it was hard to tell when it was buzzed short, Abnegation hair, but now it's two inches long and almost hangs over his forehead. It makes him look less threatening, more like the person I've come to know in private.

"Yes," he says. "But the number is still the same."

I hear the train horn blasting to my left, but the light fixed to the first car is not on. Instead it slides over the rails like some hidden, creeping thing.

"Fifth car back!" he shouts.

We both break into a sprint. I find the fifth car and grab the handle on the side with my left hand, pulling as hard as I can. I try to swing my legs inside, but they don't quite make it; they are dangerously close to the wheels— I shriek, and scrape my knee against the floor as I yank myself inside.

Tobias gets in after me and crouches by my side. I clutch my knee and grit my teeth.

"Here, let me see," he says. He pushes my jeans up my

leg and over my knee. His fingers leave streaks of cold on my skin, invisible to the eye, and I think about wrapping his shirt around my fist and pulling him in to kiss me; I think about pressing myself against him, but I can't, because all our secrets would keep a space between us.

My knee is red with blood. "It's shallow. It'll heal quickly," he says.

I nod. The pain is already subsiding. He rolls my jeans so they will stay up. I lie back, staring at the ceiling.

"So is *he* still in your fear landscape?" I say.

It looks like someone lit a match behind his eyes. "Yes. But not in the same way."

He told me, once, that his fear landscape hadn't changed since he first went through it, during his initiation. So if it has, even in a small way, that's something.

"You're in it, though." He frowns at his hands. "Instead of having to shoot that woman, like I used to, I have to watch you die. And there's nothing I can do to stop it."

His hands shake. I try to think of something helpful to say. *I'm not going to die*—but I don't know that. We live in a dangerous world, and I am not so attached to life that I will do anything to survive. I can't reassure him.

He checks his watch. "They'll be here any minute."

I get up, and see Evelyn and Edward standing next to the tracks. They run before the train passes them, and jump in with almost as little trouble as Tobias. They must have been practicing.

Edward smirks at me. Today his eye patch has a big blue "X" stitched over it.

"Hello," Evelyn says. She looks only at Tobias as she says it, like I'm not even there.

"Nice meeting location," says Tobias. It is almost dark now, so I see only shadows of buildings against a dark blue sky, and a few glowing lights near the lake that must belong to Erudite headquarters.

The train takes a turn it doesn't usually take—left, away from the glow of Erudite and into the abandoned part of the city. I can tell by the growing quiet in the car that it is slowing down.

"It seemed safest," says Evelyn. "So you wanted to meet."

"Yes. I'd like to discuss an alliance."

"An alliance," repeats Edward. "And who gave you the authority to do that?"

"He's a Dauntless leader," I say. "He has the authority."

Edward raises his eyebrows, looking impressed. Evelyn's eyes finally shift to me, but only for a second before she smiles at Tobias again.

"Interesting," she says. "And is *she* also a Dauntless leader?"

"No," he says. "She's here to help me decide whether or not to trust you."

Evelyn purses her lips. Part of me wants to thumb my nose at her and say, "Ha!" But I settle for a small smile.

"We will, of course, agree to an alliance . . . under a certain set of conditions," Evelyn says. "A guaranteed—and equal—place in whatever government forms after Erudite is destroyed, and full control over Erudite data after the attack. Clearly—"

"What are you going to do with the Erudite data?" I interrupt her.

"Obviously we will destroy it. The only way to deprive the Erudite of power is to deprive them of knowledge."

My first instinct is to tell her she's a fool. But something stops me. Without the simulation technology, without the data they had about all the other factions, without their focus on technological advancement, the attack on Abnegation would not have happened. My parents would be alive.

Even if we manage to kill Jeanine, could the Erudite be trusted not to attack and control us again? I am not sure.

"What would we receive in return, under those terms?" Tobias says.

"Our much-needed manpower, in order to take Erudite headquarters, and an equal place in government, with us."

"I am sure that Tori would also request the right to rid the world of Jeanine Matthews," he says in a low voice.

I raise my eyebrows. I didn't know that Tori's hatred of Jeanine was common knowledge—or maybe it isn't. He must know things about her that others don't, now that he and Tori are leaders.

"I'm sure that could be arranged," Evelyn replies. "I don't care who kills her; I just want her dead."

Tobias glances at me. I wish I could tell him why I feel so conflicted . . . explain to him why I, of all people, have reservations about burning Erudite to the ground, so to speak. But I would not know how to say it even if I had the time to. He turns toward Evelyn.

"Then we are agreed," he says.

He extends his hand, and she shakes it.

"We should convene in a week's time," she says. "In neutral territory. Most of the Abnegation have graciously agreed to let us stay in their sector of the city to plan as they clean up the aftermath of the attack."

"Most of them," he says.

Evelyn's expression turns flat. "I'm afraid your father still commands the loyalty of many of them, and he advised them to avoid us when he came to visit a few days ago." She smiles bitterly. "And they agreed, just as they did when he persuaded them to exile me."

"They exiled you?" says Tobias. "I thought you *left*."

"No, the Abnegation were inclined toward forgiveness and reconciliation, as you might expect. But your father has a lot of influence over the Abnegation, and he always has. I decided to leave rather than face the indignity of public exile."

Tobias looks stunned.

Edward, who has been leaning out the side of the car for a few seconds, says, "It's time!"

"See you in a week," Evelyn says.

As the train dips down to street level, Edward leaps. A few seconds later, Evelyn follows. Tobias and I remain on the train, listening to it hiss against the rails, without speaking.

"Why did you even bring me along, if you were just going to make an alliance anyway?" I say flatly.

"You didn't stop me."

"What was I supposed to do, wave my hands in the air?" I scowl at him. "I don't like it."

"It has to be done."

"I don't think it does," I say. "There has to be another way—"

"What other way?" he says, folding his arms. "You just

don't like her. You haven't since you first met her."

"Obviously I don't like her! She abandoned you!"

"They *exiled* her. And if I decide to forgive her, you had better try to do it too! I'm the one who got left behind, not you."

"This is about more than that. I don't trust her. I think she's trying to use you."

"Well, it isn't for you to decide."

"Why did you bring me, again?" I say, mirroring him by folding my arms. "Oh yeah—so that I could read the situation for you. Well, I read it, and just because you don't like what I decided doesn't mean—"

"I forgot about how your biases cloud your judgment. If I had remembered, I might not have brought you."

"*My* biases. What about *your* biases? What about thinking everyone who hates your father as much as you do is an ally?"

"This is not about him!"

"Of course it is! He knows things, Tobias. And we should be trying to find out what they are."

"This again? I thought we resolved this. He is a *liar*, Tris."

"Yeah?" I raise my eyebrows. "Well, so is your mother. You think the Abnegation would really exile someone? Because I don't."

"Don't talk about my mother that way."

I see light up ahead. It belongs to the Pire.

"Fine." I walk to the edge of the car door. "I won't."

I jump out, running a few steps to keep my balance. Tobias jumps out after me, but I don't give him a chance to catch up—I walk straight into the building, down the stairs, and back into the Pit to find a place to sleep.

CHAPTER
TWENTY-SIX

SOMETHING SHAKES ME awake.

"Tris! Get up!"

A shout. I don't question it. I throw my legs over the edge of the bed and let a hand pull me toward the door. My feet are bare, and the ground is uneven here. It scrapes at my toes and the edges of my heels. I squint ahead of me to figure out who's dragging me. Christina. She's almost pulling my left arm from its socket.

"What happened?" I say. "What's going on?"

"Shut up and run!"

We run to the Pit, and the roar of the river follows me up the paths. The last time Christina pulled me out of bed, it was to see Al's body lifted out of the chasm. I grit my teeth and try not to think about that. It can't have happened again. It can't.

I gasp—she runs faster than I do—as we sprint across the glass floor of the Pire. Christina slams her palm into an elevator button and slips inside before the doors are fully open, dragging me behind her. She jabs the DOOR CLOSE button, and then the button for the top floor.

"Simulation," she says. "There's a simulation. It's not everyone, it's just . . . just a few."

She puts her hands on her knees and takes deep breaths.

"One of them said something about the Divergent," she says.

"Said that?" I say. "While under a simulation?"

She nods. "Marlene. Didn't sound like her, though. Too . . . monotone."

The doors open, and I follow her down the hallway to the door marked ROOF ACCESS.

"Christina," I say, "why are we going to the roof?"

She doesn't answer me. The stairs to the roof smell like old paint. Dauntless graffiti is scrawled on the cement-block walls in black paint. The symbol of Dauntless. Initials paired together with plus signs: RG + NT, BR + FH. Couples who are probably old now, maybe broken up. I touch my chest to feel my heartbeat. It's so fast, it's a wonder I'm still breathing at all.

The night air is cool; it gives me goose bumps on my

arms. My eyes have adjusted to the darkness by now, and across the roof I see three figures standing on the ledge, facing me. One is Marlene. One is Hector. One is someone I don't recognize—a young Dauntless, barely eight years old, with a green streak in her hair.

They stand still on the ledge, though the wind is blowing hard, tossing their hair over their foreheads, into their eyes, into their mouths. Their clothes snap in the wind, but still they stand motionless.

"Just come down off the ledge now," Christina says. "Don't do anything stupid. Come on, now . . ."

"They can't hear you," I say quietly as I walk toward them. "Or see you."

"We should all jump at them at once. I'll take Hec, you—"

"We'll risk shoving them off the roof if we do that. Stand by the girl, just in case."

She is too young for this, I think, but I don't have the heart to say it, because it means Marlene is old enough.

I stare at Marlene, whose eyes are blank like painted stones, like spheres of glass. I feel as if those stones are slipping down my throat and settling in my stomach, pulling me toward the ground. There is no way to get her off that ledge.

Finally she opens her mouth and speaks.

"I have a message for the Divergent." Her voice sounds flat. The simulation is using her vocal cords, but robs them of the natural fluctuations of human emotion.

I look from Marlene to Hector. Hector, who was so afraid of what I am because his mother told him to be. Lynn is probably still at Shauna's bedside, hoping Shauna can move her legs when she wakes up again. Lynn can't lose Hector.

I step forward to receive the message.

"This is not a negotiation. It is a warning," says the simulation through Marlene, moving her lips and vibrating in her throat. "Every two days until one of you delivers yourself to Erudite headquarters, this will happen again."

This.

Marlene steps back, and I throw myself forward, but not at her. Not at Marlene, who once let Uriah shoot a muffin off her head on a dare. Who gathered a stack of clothing for me to wear. Who always, always greeted me with a smile. No, not at Marlene.

As Marlene and the other Dauntless girl step off the edge of the roof, I dive at Hector.

I grab whatever my hands can find. An arm. A fistful of shirt. The rough rooftop scrapes my knees as his weight drags me forward. I am not strong enough to lift him. I whisper, "Help," because I can't speak any louder than that.

Christina is already at my shoulder. She helps me haul Hector's limp body onto the roof. His arm flops to the side, lifeless. A few feet away, the little girl lies on her back on the rooftop.

Then the simulation ends. Hector opens his eyes, and they are no longer empty.

"Ow," he says. "What's going on?"

The little girl whimpers, and Christina walks over to her, mumbling something in a reassuring voice.

I stand, my entire body shaking. I inch toward the edge of the roof and stare at the ground. The street below isn't lit very well, but I can see Marlene's faint outline on the pavement.

Breathing—who cares about breathing?

I turn from the sight, listening to my heart beat in my ears. Christina's mouth moves. I ignore her, and walk to the door and down the stairs and down the hallway and into the elevator.

The doors close and as I drop to the earth, just as Marlene did after I decided not to save her, I scream, my hands tearing at my clothes. My throat is raw after just a few seconds, and there are scratches on my arms where I missed the fabric, but I keep screaming.

The elevator stops with a *ding*. The doors open.

I straighten my shirt, smooth my hair down, and walk out.

+ + +

I have a message for the Divergent.

I am Divergent.

This is not a negotiation.

No, it is not.

It is a warning.

I understand.

Every two days until one of you delivers yourself to Erudite headquarters . . .

I will.

. . . this will happen again.

It will never happen again.

CHAPTER
TWENTY-SEVEN

I WEAVE THROUGH the crowd next to the chasm. It's loud in the Pit, and not just because of the river's roar. I want to find some silence, so I escape into the hallway that leads to the dormitories. I don't want to hear the speech Tori will make on Marlene's behalf or be around for the toasting and the shouting as the Dauntless celebrate her life and her bravery.

This morning Lauren reported that we missed some of the cameras in the initiate dormitories, where Christina, Zeke, Lauren, Marlene, Hector, and Kee, the girl with the green hair, were sleeping. That's how Jeanine figured out who the simulation was controlling. I do not doubt that Jeanine chose young Dauntless because she knew their deaths would affect us more.

I stop in an unfamiliar hallway and press my forehead to the wall. The stone feels rough and cool on my skin. I can hear the Dauntless shouting behind me, their voices muffled by layers of rock.

I hear someone approaching, and look to the side. Christina, still wearing the same clothes she wore last night, stands a few feet away.

"Hey," she says.

"I'm not really in the mood to feel more guilt right now. So go away, please."

"I just want to say one thing, and then I will."

Her eyes are puffy and her voice sounds a little sleepy, which is either due to exhaustion or a little alcohol, or both. But her stare is direct enough that she must know what she's saying. I pull away from the wall.

"I'd never seen that kind of simulation before. You know, from the outside. But yesterday . . ." She shakes her head. "You were right. They couldn't hear you, couldn't see you. Just like Will . . ."

She chokes on his name. Stops, takes a breath, swallows hard. Blinks a few times. Then looks at me again.

"You told me you had to do it, or he would have shot you, and I didn't believe you. I believe you now, and . . . I'm going to try to forgive you. That's . . . all I wanted to say."

There's a part of me that feels relief. She believes me,

she's trying to forgive me, even though it won't be easy.

But a larger part of me feels anger. What did she think, before now? That I *wanted* to shoot Will, one of my best friends? She should have trusted me from the beginning, should have *known* that I wouldn't have done it if I had been able to see another option at the time.

"How fortunate for me that you finally got *proof* that I'm not a cold-blooded murderer. You know, other than my word. I mean, what reason would you have to trust that?" I force a laugh, trying to stay nonchalant. She opens her mouth, but I keep talking, unable to stop myself. "You'd better hurry on that forgiving-me thing, because there isn't much time—"

My voice cracks, and I can't hold myself together anymore. I start sobbing. I lean against the wall for support and feel myself sliding down as my legs get weak.

My eyes are too blurry to see her, but I feel her when she wraps her arms around me and squeezes so hard it hurts. She smells like coconut oil and she feels strong, exactly like she was during initiation into Dauntless, when she hung over the chasm by her fingertips. Back then—which was not so long ago—she made me feel weak, but now her strength makes me feel like I could be stronger too.

We kneel together on the stone floor, and I clutch her as tightly as she clutches me.

"It's already done," she says. "That's what I meant to say. That the forgiving was already done."

+ + +

All the Dauntless go quiet when I walk into the cafeteria that night. I don't blame them. As one of the Divergent, I have the power to let Jeanine kill one of them. Most of them probably want me to sacrifice myself. Or they are terrified that I won't.

If this were Abnegation, no Divergent would be sitting here right now.

For a moment I don't know where to go or how to get there. But then Zeke waves me over to his table, looking grim, and I guide my feet in that direction. But before I make it there, Lynn approaches me.

She is a different Lynn from the one I have always known. She doesn't have a fierce look in her eyes. Instead she is pale and biting her lip to hide its wobble.

"Um . . ." she says. She looks to the left, to the right, anywhere but at my face. "I really . . . I miss Marlene. I've known her for a long time, and I . . ." She shakes her head. "The point is, don't think that my saying this means *anything* about Marlene," she says, like she's scolding me, "but . . . thank you for saving Hec."

Lynn shifts her weight from one foot to the other, her

eyes flicking around the room. Then she hugs me with one arm, her hand gripping my shirt. Pain shoots through my shoulder. I don't say anything about it.

She lets go, sniffs, and walks back to her table like nothing happened. I stare at her retreating back for a few seconds, and then sit down.

Zeke and Uriah sit side by side at the otherwise empty table. Uriah's face is slack, like he's not completely awake. He has a dark brown bottle in front of him that he sips from every few seconds.

I feel cautious around him. I saved Hec—which means I failed to save Marlene. But Uriah doesn't look at me. I pull out the chair across from him and sit on the edge of it.

"Where's Shauna?" I say. "Still in the hospital?"

"No, she's over there," says Zeke, nodding to the table Lynn walked back to. I see her there, so pale she might as well be translucent, sitting in a wheelchair. "Shauna shouldn't be up, but Lynn's pretty messed up, so she's keeping her company."

"But if you're wondering why they're all the way over there . . . Shauna found out I'm Divergent," says Uriah sluggishly. "And she doesn't want to catch it."

"Oh."

"She got all weird with me, too," says Zeke, sighing. "'How do you know your brother isn't working against us?

Have you been watching him?' What I wouldn't give to punch whoever poisoned her mind."

"You don't have to give anything," says Uriah. "Her mother's sitting right there. Go ahead and hit her."

I follow his gaze to a middle-aged woman with blue streaks in her hair and earrings all the way down her earlobe. She is pretty, just like Lynn.

Tobias enters the room a moment later, followed by Tori and Harrison. I have been avoiding him. I haven't spoken to him since that fight we had, before Marlene . . .

"Hello, Tris," Tobias says when I'm close enough to hear him. His voice is low, rough. It transports me to quiet places.

"Hi," I say in a tight little voice that does not belong to me.

He sits next to me and puts his arm on the back of my chair, leaning close. I don't stare back—I *refuse* to stare back.

I stare back.

Dark eyes—a peculiar shade of blue, somehow capable of shutting the rest of the cafeteria out, of comforting me and also of reminding me that we are farther away from each other than I want us to be.

"Aren't you going to ask me if I'm all right?" I say.

"No, I'm pretty sure you're not all right." He shakes his

head. "I'm going to ask you not to make any decisions until we've talked about it."

It's too late, I think. *The decision's made.*

"Until we've all talked about it, you mean, since it involves all of us," says Uriah. "I don't think anyone should turn themselves in."

"No one?" I say.

"No!" Uriah scowls. "I think we should attack back."

"Yeah," I say hollowly, "let's provoke the woman who can force half of this compound to kill themselves. That sounds like a great idea."

I was too harsh. Uriah tips the contents of his bottle down his throat. He brings the bottle down on the table so hard I'm afraid it will shatter.

"Don't talk about it like that," he says in a growl.

"I'm sorry," I say. "But you know I'm right. The best way to ensure that half our faction doesn't die is to sacrifice one life."

I don't know what I expected. Maybe that Uriah, who knows too well what will happen if one of us does not go, would volunteer himself. But he looks down. Unwilling.

"Tori and Harrison and I decided to increase security. Hopefully if everyone is more aware of these attacks, we will be able to stop them," Tobias says. "If it doesn't work, then we will think of another solution. End of discussion.

But no one is going to do anything yet. Okay?"

He looks at me when he asks and raises his eyebrows.

"Okay," I say, not quite meeting his eyes.

+ + +

After dinner, I try to go back to the dormitory where I've been sleeping, but I can't quite walk through the door. Instead I walk through the corridors, brushing the stone walls with my fingers, listening to the echoes of my footsteps.

Without meaning to, I pass the water fountain where Peter, Drew, and Al attacked me. I knew it was Al by the way he smelled—I can still call the scent of lemongrass to mind. Now I associate it not with my friend but with the powerlessness I felt as they dragged me to the chasm.

I walk faster, keeping my eyes wide open so it will be harder to picture the attack in my mind. I have to get away from here, far from the places where my friend attacked me, where Peter stabbed Edward, where a sightless army of my friends began its march toward the Abnegation sector and all this insanity began.

I go straight toward the last place where I felt safe: Tobias's small apartment. The second I reach the door, I feel calmer.

The door is not completely closed. I nudge it open with

my foot. He isn't there, but I don't leave. I sit on his bed and gather the quilt in my arms, burying my face in the fabric and taking deep breaths of it through my nose. The smell it used to have is almost gone, it's been so long since he slept on it.

The door opens and Tobias slips in. My arms go limp, and the quilt falls into my lap. How will I explain my presence here? I'm supposed to be angry with him.

He doesn't scowl, but his mouth is so tense that I know he's angry with *me*.

"Don't be an idiot," he says.

"An idiot?"

"You were lying. You said you wouldn't go to Erudite, and you were lying, and going to Erudite would make you an idiot. So don't."

I set the blanket down and get up.

"Don't try to make this simple," I say. "It's not. You know as well as I do that this is the right thing to do."

"You choose *this* moment to act like the Abnegation?" His voice fills the room and makes fear prickle in my chest. His anger seems too sudden. Too strange. "All that time you spent insisting that you were too selfish for them, and now, when your *life* is on the line, you've got to be a hero? What's wrong with you?"

"What's wrong with *you*? People died. They walked

right off the edge of a building! And I can stop it from happening again!"

"You're too important to just . . . die." He shakes his head. He won't even look at me—his eyes keep shifting across my face, to the wall behind me or the ceiling above me, to everything but me. I am too stunned to be angry.

"I'm not important. Everyone will do just fine without me," I say.

"Who cares about everyone? What about *me*?"

He lowers his head into his hand, covering his eyes. His fingers are trembling.

Then he crosses the room in two long strides and touches his lips to mine. Their gentle pressure erases the past few months, and I am the girl who sat on the rocks next to the chasm, with river spray on her ankles, and kissed him for the first time. I am the girl who grabbed his hand in the hallway just because I wanted to.

I pull back, my hand on his chest to keep him away. The problem is, I am also the girl who shot Will and lied about it, and chose between Hector and Marlene, and now a thousand other things besides. And I can't erase those things.

"You *would* be fine." I don't look at him. I stare at his T-shirt between my fingers and the black ink curling around his neck, but I don't look at his face. "Not at first.

But you would move on, and do what you have to."

He wraps an arm around my waist and pulls me against him. "That's a *lie*," he says, before he kisses me again.

This is wrong. It's wrong to forget who I have become, and to let him kiss me when I know what I'm about to do.

But I want to. Oh, I want to.

I stand on my tiptoes and wrap my arms around him. I press one hand between his shoulder blades and curl the other one around the back of his neck. I can feel his breaths against my palm, his body expanding and contracting, and I know he's strong, steady, unstoppable. All things I need to be, but I am not, I am not.

He walks backward, pulling me with him so I stumble. I stumble right out of my shoes. He sits on the edge of the bed and I stand in front of him, and we're finally eye to eye.

He touches my face, covering my cheeks with his hands, sliding his fingertips down my neck, fitting his fingers to the slight curve of my hips.

I can't stop.

I fit my mouth to his, and he tastes like water and smells like fresh air. I drag my hand from his neck to the small of his back, and put it under his shirt. He kisses me harder.

I knew he was strong; I didn't know how strong until I

felt it myself, the muscles in his back tightening beneath my fingers.

Stop, I tell myself.

Suddenly it's as if we're in a hurry, his fingertips brushing my side under my shirt, my hands clutching at him, struggling closer but there is no closer. I have never longed for someone this way, or this much.

He pulls back just enough to look into my eyes, his eyelids lowered.

"Promise me," he whispers, "that you won't go. For me. Do this one thing for me."

Could I do that? Could I stay here, fix things with him, let someone else die in my place? Looking up at him, I believe for a moment that I could. And then I see Will. The crease between his eyebrows. The empty, simulation-bound eyes. The slumped body.

Do this one thing for me. Tobias's dark eyes plead with me.

But if I don't go to Erudite, who will? Tobias? It's the kind of thing he would do.

I feel a stab of pain in my chest as I lie to him. "Okay."

"Promise," he says, frowning.

The pain becomes an ache, spreads everywhere—all mixed together, guilt and terror and longing. "I promise."

CHAPTER
TWENTY-EIGHT

WHEN HE STARTS to fall asleep, he keeps his arms around me fiercely, a life-preserving prison. But I wait, kept awake by the thought of bodies hitting pavement, until his grip loosens and his breathing steadies.

I will not let Tobias go to Erudite when it happens again, when someone else dies. I will not.

I slip out of his arms. I shrug on one of his sweatshirts so I can carry the smell of him with me. I slip my feet into my shoes. I don't take any weapons or keepsakes.

I pause by the doorway and look at him, half buried under the quilt, peaceful and strong.

"I love you," I say quietly, trying out the words. I let the door close behind me.

It's time to put everything in order.

I walk to the dormitory where the Dauntless-born initiates once slept. The room looks just like the one I slept in when I was an initiate: it is long and narrow, with bunk beds on either side and a chalkboard on one wall. I see by a blue light in the corner that no one bothered to erase the rankings that are written there—Uriah's name is still at the top.

Christina sleeps in the bottom bunk, beneath Lynn. I don't want to startle her, but there's no way to wake her otherwise, so I cover her mouth with my hand. She wakes with a start, her eyes wide until they find me. I touch my finger to my lips and beckon for her to follow me.

I walk to the end of the hallway and turn a corner. The corridor is lit by a paint-spattered emergency lamp that hangs over one of the exits. Christina isn't wearing shoes; she curls her toes under to protect them from the cold.

"What is it?" she says. "Are you going somewhere?"

"Yeah, I'm . . ." I have to lie, or she'll try to stop me. "I'm going to see my brother. He's with the Abnegation, remember?"

She narrows her eyes.

"I'm sorry to wake you," I say. "But there's something I need you to do. It's really important."

"Okay. Tris, you're acting really strange. Are you sure you're not—"

"I'm not. Listen to me. The timing of the simulation attack wasn't random. The reason it happened when it did is because the Abnegation were about to do something—I don't know what it was, but it had to do with some important information, and now Jeanine *has* that information. . . ."

"What?" She frowns. "You don't know what they were about to do? Do you know what the information is?"

"No." I must sound crazy. "The thing is, I haven't been able to find out very much about this, because Marcus Eaton is the only person who knows everything, and he won't tell me. I just . . . it's the reason for the attack. It's the *reason*. And we need to know it."

I don't know what else to say. But Christina is already nodding.

"The reason Jeanine forced us to attack innocent people," she says bitterly. "Yeah. We need to know it."

I had almost forgotten—*she* was under the simulation. How many Abnegation did she kill, guided by the simulation? How did she feel when she awoke from that dream a murderer? I have never asked, and I never will.

"I want your help, and soon. I need someone to persuade Marcus to cooperate, and I think you can do it."

She tilts her head and stares at me for a few seconds.

"Tris. Don't do anything stupid."

I force a smile. "Why do people keep saying that to me?"

She grabs my arm. "I'm not kidding around."

"I told you, I'm going to visit Caleb. I'll be back in a few days, and we can make a strategy then. I just thought it would be better if someone else knew about all this before I left. Just in case. Okay?"

She holds my arm for a few seconds, and then releases me. "Okay," she says.

I walk toward the exit. I hold myself together until I'm through the door, and then I feel the tears come.

The last conversation I'll ever have with her, and it was full of lies.

+ + +

Once I'm outside, I put up the hood of Tobias's sweatshirt. When I reach the end of the street, I glance up and down, searching for signs of life. There is nothing.

The cool air prickles in my lungs on the way in, and on the way out unfurls in a cloud of vapor. Winter will be here soon. I wonder if Erudite and Dauntless will still be at a standstill then, waiting for one group to obliterate the other. I'm glad I won't have to see it.

Before I chose Dauntless, thoughts like that never

occurred to me. I felt assured of my long lifespan, if nothing else. Now there are no reassurances, except that where I go, I go because I choose to.

I walk in the shadows of buildings, hoping my footsteps won't attract any attention. None of the city lights are on in this area, but the moon is bright enough that I can walk by it without too much trouble.

I walk beneath the elevated tracks. They shudder with the movement of an oncoming train. I have to walk fast if I want to get there before anyone notices that I'm gone. I sidestep a large crack in the street, and jump over a fallen streetlight.

I didn't think about how far I would have to walk when I set out. It isn't long before my body warms with the exertion of walking and checking over my shoulder and dodging hazards in the road. I pick up the pace, half walking and half jogging.

Soon I reach a part of the city that I recognize. The streets are better kept here, swept clean, with few holes. Far away I see the glow of Erudite headquarters, their lights violating our energy conservation laws. I don't know what I will do when I get there. Demand to see Jeanine? Or just stand there until someone notices me?

My fingertips skim a window in the building beside

me. Not long now. Tremors go through my body now that I am close, making it difficult to walk. Breathing is tricky too; I stop trying to be quiet, and let air wheeze in and out of my lungs. What will they do with me when I get there? What plans do they have for me before I outlive my usefulness, and they kill me? I don't doubt that they will kill me eventually. I concentrate on forward motion, on moving my legs even though they seem to be unwilling to support my weight.

And then I'm standing in front of Erudite headquarters.

Inside, crowds of blue-shirted people sit around tables, typing on computers or bent over books or passing sheets of paper back and forth. Some of them are decent people who do not understand what their faction has done, but if their entire building collapsed in on them before my eyes, I might not find it in myself to care.

This is the last moment I will be able to turn back. The cold air stings my cheeks and my hands as I hesitate. I can walk away now. Take refuge in the Dauntless compound. Hope and pray and wish that no one else dies because of my selfishness.

But I can't walk away, or the guilt, the weight of Will's life, and my parents' lives, and now Marlene's life, will break my bones, will make it impossible to breathe.

I slowly walk toward the building and push open the doors.

This is the only way to keep from suffocating.

+ + +

For a second after my feet touch the wood floors, and I stand before the giant portrait of Jeanine Matthews hung on the opposite wall, no one notices me, not even the two Dauntless traitor guards milling around near the entryway. I walk up to the front desk, where a middle-aged man with a bald patch on the crown of his head sits, sorting through a stack of paper. I set my hands on the desk.

"Excuse me," I say.

"Give me a moment," he says without looking up.

"No."

At *that* he looks up, his glasses askew, scowling like he's about to chastise me. Whatever words he was about to use seem to stick in his throat. He stares at me with an open mouth, his eyes skipping from my face to the black sweatshirt I wear.

In my terror, his expression seems amusing. I smile a little and conceal my hands, which are trembling.

"I believe Jeanine Matthews wanted to see me," I say. "So I would appreciate it if you would contact her."

He signals to the Dauntless traitors by the door, but

there is no need. The guards have finally caught on. Dauntless soldiers from the other parts of the room have also started forward, and they all surround me, but don't touch me, and don't speak to me. I scan their faces, trying to look as placid as possible.

"Divergent?" one of them finally asks as the man behind the desk picks up the receiver of the building's communication system.

If I close my hands into fists, I can stop them from shaking. I nod.

My eyes shift to the Dauntless coming out of the elevator on the left side of the room, and the muscles in my face go slack. Peter is coming toward us.

A thousand potential reactions, ranging from launching myself at Peter's throat to crying to making some kind of joke, rush through my mind at once. I can't decide on one. So I stand still and watch him. Jeanine must have known that I would come, she must have chosen Peter on purpose to collect me, she must have.

"We've been instructed to take you upstairs," says Peter.

I mean to say something sharp, or nonchalant, but the only sound that escapes me is an assenting noise, squeezed tight by my swollen throat. Peter starts toward the elevators, and I follow him.

We walk down a series of sleek corridors. Despite the

fact that we climb a few flights of stairs, I still feel like I am plunging into the earth.

I expect them to take me to Jeanine, but they don't. They stop walking in a short hallway with a series of metal doors on each side. Peter types in a code to open one of the doors, and the traitor Dauntless surround me, shoulder to shoulder, forming a narrow tunnel for me to pass through on my way into the room.

The room is small, maybe six feet long by six feet wide. The floor, the walls, and the ceiling are all made of the same light panels, dim now, that glowed in the aptitude test room. In each corner is a tiny black camera.

I finally let myself panic.

I look from corner to corner, at the cameras, and fight the scream building in my stomach, chest, and throat, the scream that fills every part of me. Again I feel guilt and grief clawing inside me, warring with each other for dominance, but terror is stronger than both. I breathe in, and don't breathe out. My father once told me it was a cure for hiccups. I asked him if I could die from holding my breath.

"No," he said. "Your body's instincts will take over, and force you to breathe."

A shame, really. I could use a way out. The thought makes me want to laugh. And then scream.

I curl up so I can press my face to my knees. I have to make a plan. If I can make a plan, I won't be so afraid.

But there is no plan. No escape from deep in Erudite headquarters, no escape from Jeanine, and no other escape from what I've done.

CHAPTER
TWENTY-NINE

I FORGOT MY watch.

Minutes or hours later, when the panic subsides, that is what I most regret. Not coming here in the first place—that seemed like an obvious choice—but my bare wrist, which makes it impossible for me to know how long I have been sitting in this room. My back aches, which is some indication, but it is not definite enough.

After a while I get up and pace, stretching my arms above my head. I hesitate to do anything while the cameras are there, but they can't learn anything by watching me touch my toes.

The thought makes my hands tremble, but I don't try to push it from my mind. Instead I tell myself that I am Dauntless and I am no stranger to fear. I will die in this place. Perhaps soon. Those are the facts.

But there are other ways to think of it. Soon I will honor my parents by dying as they died. And if all they believed about death was true, soon I will join them in whatever comes next.

I shake my hands as I pace. They're still trembling. I want to know what time it is. I arrived a little after midnight. It must be early in the morning by now, maybe 4:00, or 5:00. Or maybe it hasn't been that long, and only seems that way because I haven't been doing anything.

The door opens, and at last I stand face-to-face with my enemy and her Dauntless guards.

"Hello, Beatrice," Jeanine says. She wears Erudite blue and Erudite spectacles and an Erudite look of superiority that I was taught by my father to hate. "I thought you might be the one who came."

But I don't feel hate when I look at her. I don't feel anything at all, even though I know she's responsible for countless deaths, including Marlene's. The deaths exist in my mind as a string of meaningless equations, and I stand frozen, unable to solve them.

"Hello, Jeanine," I say, because it is the only thing that comes to mind.

I look from Jeanine's watery gray eyes to the Dauntless who flank her. Peter stands at her right shoulder, and a woman with lines on either side of her mouth stands at her left. Behind her is a bald man with sharp planes in his skull. I frown.

How does Peter find himself in such a prestigious position, as Jeanine Matthews's bodyguard? Where is the logic in that?

"I'd like to know what time it is," I say.

"Would you," she says. "That's interesting."

I should have known she wouldn't tell me. Every piece of information she receives factors into her strategy, and she won't tell me what time it is unless she decides that providing the information is more useful than withholding it.

"I'm sure my Dauntless companions are disappointed," she says, "that you have not tried to claw my eyes out yet."

"That would be stupid."

"True. But in keeping with your 'act first, think second' behavioral trend."

"I'm sixteen." I purse my lips. "I change."

"How refreshing." She has a way of flattening even those phrases that should have inflection built into them. "Let's go on a little tour, shall we?"

She steps back and gestures toward the doorway. The last thing I want to do is walk out of this room and toward an uncertain destination, but I don't hesitate. I walk out, the severe-looking Dauntless woman in front of me. Peter follows me soon afterward.

The hallway is long and pale. We turn a corner and walk down a second one exactly like the first.

Two more hallways follow. I am so disoriented I could never find my way back. But then my surroundings change—the white tunnel opens to a large room where Erudite men and women in long blue jackets stand behind tables, some holding tools, some mixing multicolored liquids, some staring at computer screens. If I had to guess, I would say they are mixing simulation serum, but I hesitate to confine Erudite's work to simulations alone.

Most of them stop to watch us as we walk down the center aisle. Or rather, they watch *me*. Some of them whisper, but most remain silent. It is so quiet here.

I follow the Dauntless traitor woman through a doorway, and stop so abruptly Peter runs into me.

This room is just as large as the last one, but there is only one thing in it: a large metal table with a machine next to it. A machine I vaguely recognize as a heart monitor. And dangling above it, a camera. I shudder without meaning to. Because I know what this is.

"I am very pleased that *you*, in particular, are here," says Jeanine. She walks past me and perches on the table, her fingers curled around the edge.

"I am pleased, of course, because of your aptitude test results." Her blond hair, pulled tight to her skull, reflects the light, catches my attention.

"Even among the Divergent, you are somewhat of an oddity, because you have aptitude for three factions. Abnegation, Dauntless, and Erudite."

"How . . ." My voice croaks. I push the question out. "How do you know that?"

"All in good time," she says. "From your results I have determined that you are one of the strongest Divergent, which I say not to compliment you but to explain my purpose. If I am to develop a simulation that cannot be thwarted by the Divergent mind, I must study the strongest Divergent mind in order to shore up all weaknesses in the technology. Understand?"

I don't respond. I am still staring at the heart monitor next to the table.

"Therefore, for as long as possible, my fellow scientists and I will be studying you." She smiles a little. "And then, at the conclusion of my study, you will be executed."

I knew that. I knew it, so why do my knees feel weak, why is my stomach writhing, why?

"That execution will take place here." She runs her fingertips over the table beneath her. "On this table. I thought it would be interesting to show it to you."

She wants to study my response. I barely breathe. I used to think that cruelty required malice, but that is not true. Jeanine has no reason to act out of malice. But she is cruel because she doesn't care what she does, as long as it fascinates her. I may as well be a puzzle or a broken machine she wants to fix. She will break open my skull just to see the inner workings of my brain; I will die here, and that will be the merciful thing.

"I knew what would happen when I came here," I say. "It's just a table. And I'd like to go back to my room now."

+ + +

I don't really comprehend time's passing, at least not in the way that I used to, when time was available to me. So when the door opens again and Peter walks into my cell, I don't know how much time has gone by, only that I am exhausted.

"Let's go, Stiff," he says.

"I'm not Abnegation." I stretch my arms above my head so they brush against the wall. "And now that you're an Erudite lackey, you can't call me 'Stiff.' It's inaccurate."

"I said, let's go."

"What, no snide comments?" I look up at him with mock surprise. "No 'You're an idiot for coming here; your brain must be deficient as well as Divergent'?"

"That really goes without saying, doesn't it?" he says. "You can either get up or I can drag you down the hallway. Your choice."

I feel calmer. Peter is always mean to me; this is familiar.

I stand and walk out of the room. I notice as I walk that Peter's arm, the one I shot, is no longer in a sling.

"Did they fix up your bullet wound?"

"Yeah," he says. "Now you'll need to find a different weakness to exploit. Too bad I'm fresh out of them." He grabs my good arm and walks faster, pulling me along beside him. "We're late."

Despite the length and emptiness of the hallway, our footsteps don't echo much. I feel like someone put their hands over my ears and I only just noticed it. I try to keep track of the hallways we walk down, but I lose count after a while. We reach the end of one and turn left, into a dim room that reminds me of an aquarium. One of the walls is made of one-way glass—reflective on my side, but I'm sure it's transparent on the other side.

A large machine stands on the other side, with a man-sized tray coming out of it. I recognize it from my Faction History textbook, the unit on Erudite and medicine. An MRI machine. It will take pictures of my brain.

Something sparks inside me. It's been so long since I

felt it that I barely recognize it at first. Curiosity.

A voice—Jeanine's voice—speaks over an intercom.

"Lie down, Beatrice."

I look at the man-sized tray that will slide me into the machine.

"No."

She sighs. "If you don't do it yourself, we have ways of making you."

Peter is standing behind me. Even with an injured arm, he was stronger than me. I imagine his hands on me, wrestling me toward the tray, shoving me against the metal, pulling the straps that dangle from the tray across my body, too tightly.

"Let's make a deal," I say. "If I cooperate, I get to see the scan."

"You will cooperate whether you want to or not."

I hold up a finger. "That's not true."

I look at the mirror. It's not so difficult to pretend that I'm speaking to Jeanine when I speak to my own reflection. My hair is blond like hers; we are both pale and stern-looking. The thought is so disturbing to me that I lose my train of thought for a few seconds, and instead stand with my finger in the air in silence.

I am pale-skinned, pale-haired, and cold. I am curious about the pictures of my brain. I am like Jeanine. And I can either despise it, attack it, eradicate it . . . or I can use it.

"That's not true," I repeat. "No matter how many restraints you use, you can't keep me as still as I need to be for the pictures to be clear." I clear my throat. "I want to see the scans. You're going to kill me anyway, so does it really matter how much I know about my own brain before you do?"

Silence.

"Why do you want to see them so badly?" she says.

"Surely you, of all people, understand. I have equal aptitude for Erudite as I do for Dauntless and Abnegation, after all."

"All right. You can see them. Lie down."

I walk over to the tray and lie down. The metal feels like ice. The tray slides back, and I am inside the machine. I stare up at whiteness. When I was young, I thought that was what heaven would be like, all white light and nothing else. Now I know that can't be true, because white light is menacing.

I hear thumping, and I close my eyes as I remember one of the obstacles in my fear landscape, the fists pounding against my windows and the sightless men trying to kidnap me. I pretend the pounding is a heartbeat, a drumbeat. The river crashing against the walls of the chasm in the Dauntless compound. Feet stamping at the end-of-initiation ceremony. Feet pounding on the staircase after the Choosing Ceremony.

I don't know how much time has passed when the thumping stops and the tray slides back. I sit up and rub my neck with my fingertips.

The door opens, revealing Peter in the hallway. He beckons to me. "Come on. You can go see the scans now."

I hop down from the tray and walk toward him. When we're in the hallway, he shakes his head at me.

"What?"

"I don't know how you manage to always get what you want."

"Yeah, because I wanted to get myself into a cell in Erudite headquarters. I wanted to be executed."

I sound cavalier, like executions are something I face on a regular basis. But forming my lips around the word "executed" makes me shudder. I pretend I'm cold, squeezing my arms with my hands.

"Didn't you, though?" he says. "I mean, you did come here of your own free will. That's not what I call a good survival instinct."

He types in a series of numbers on a keypad outside the next door, and it opens. I enter the room on the other side of the mirror. It's full of screens and light, reflecting off the glass in the Erudites' spectacles. Across the room, another door clicks shut. There is an empty chair behind one of the screens, still turning. Someone just left.

Peter stands too close behind me—ready to grab me if I decide to attack anyone. But I won't attack anyone. How far could I get if I did? Down one hallway, or two? And then I would be lost. I couldn't get out of here even if there weren't guards stopping me from leaving.

"Put them up there," says Jeanine, pointing toward the large screen on the left wall. One of the Erudite scientists taps his own computer screen, and an image appears on the left wall. An image of my brain.

I don't know what I'm looking at, exactly. I know what a brain looks like, and generally what each region of it does, but I don't know how mine compares to others. Jeanine taps her chin and stares for what feels like a long time.

Finally she says, "Someone instruct Ms. Prior as to what the prefrontal cortex does."

"It's the region of the brain behind the forehead, so to speak," one of the scientists says. She doesn't look much older than I am, and wears large round glasses that make her eyes look bigger. "It's responsible for organizing your thoughts and actions to attain your goals."

"Correct," Jeanine says. "Now someone tell me what they observe about Ms. Prior's lateral prefrontal cortex."

"It's large," another scientist—this one a man with thinning hair—says.

"Specificity," says Jeanine. Like she's chastising him.

I am in a classroom, I realize, because every room with more than one Erudite in it is a classroom. And among them, Jeanine is their most valued teacher. They all stare at her with wide eyes and eager, open mouths, waiting to impress her.

"It's much larger than average," the man with thinning hair corrects himself.

"Better." Jeanine tilts her head. "In fact, it is one of the largest lateral prefrontal cortexes I've ever seen. Yet the orbitofrontal cortex is remarkably small. What do these two facts indicate?"

"The orbitofrontal cortex is the reward center of the brain. Those who exhibit reward-seeking behavior have a large orbitofrontal cortex," someone says. "That means that Ms. Prior engages in very little reward-seeking behavior."

"Not just that." Jeanine smiles a little. Blue light from the screens makes her cheekbones and forehead brighter but casts shadows in her eye sockets. "It does not merely indicate something about her behavior, but about her desires. She is not reward motivated. Yet she is extremely good at directing her thoughts and actions toward her goals. This explains both her tendency toward harmful-but-selfless behavior and, perhaps, her ability to wriggle out of simulations. How does this change our approach to the new simulation serum?"

"It should suppress some, but not all, of the activity in the prefrontal cortex," the scientist with the round glasses says.

"Precisely," says Jeanine. She finally looks at me, her eyes gleaming with delight. "Then that is how we will proceed. Did this satisfy my end of our agreement, Ms. Prior?"

My mouth is dry, so it's difficult to swallow.

And what happens if they suppress the activity in my prefrontal cortex—if they damage my ability to make decisions? What if this serum works, and I become a slave to the simulations like everyone else? What if I forget reality entirely?

I did not know that my entire personality, my entire being, could be discarded as the byproduct of my anatomy. What if I really am just someone with a large prefrontal cortex . . . and nothing more?

"Yes," I say. "It did."

+ + +

In silence Peter and I make our way back to my room. We turn left, and a group of people stands at the other end of the hallway. It is the longest of the corridors we will travel through, but that distance shrinks when I see him.

Held at either arm by a Dauntless traitor, a gun aimed at the back of his skull.

Tobias, blood trailing down the side of his face and marking his white shirt with red; Tobias, fellow Divergent, standing in the mouth of this furnace in which I will burn.

Peter's hands clamp around my shoulders, holding me in place.

"Tobias," I say, and it sounds like a gasp.

The Dauntless traitor with the gun presses Tobias toward me. Peter tries to push me forward too, but my feet remain planted. I came here so that no one else would die. I came here to protect as many people as I could. And I care more about Tobias's safety than anyone else's. So why am I here, if he's here? What's the point?

"What did you do?" I mumble. He is just a few feet away from me now, but not close enough to hear me. As he passes me he stretches out his hand. He wraps it around my palm and squeezes. Squeezes, then lets go. His eyes are bloodshot; he is pale.

"What did you do?" This time the question tears from my throat like a growl.

I throw myself toward him, struggling against Peter's grip, though his hands chafe.

"What did you do?" I scream.

"You die, I die too." Tobias looks over his shoulder at me. "I asked you not to do this. You made your decision. These are the repercussions."

He disappears around the corner. The last I see of him and the Dauntless traitors leading him is the gleam of the gun barrel and blood on the back of his earlobe from an injury I didn't see before.

All the life goes out of me as soon as he's gone. I stop struggling and let Peter's hands push me toward my cell. I slump to the ground as soon as I walk in, waiting for the door to slide shut to signify Peter's departure, but it doesn't.

"Why did he come here?" Peter says.

I glance at him.

"Because he's an idiot."

"Well, yeah."

I rest my head against the wall.

"Did he think he could rescue you?" Peter snorts a little. "Sounds like a Stiff-born thing to do."

"I don't think so," I say. If Tobias intended to rescue me, he would have thought it through; he would have brought others. He would not have burst into Erudite headquarters alone.

Tears well up in my eyes, and I don't try to blink them away. Instead I stare through them and watch my surroundings smear together. A few days ago I would never have cried in front of Peter, but I don't care anymore. He is the least of all my enemies.

"I think he came to die with me," I say. I clamp my hand over my mouth to stifle a sob. If I can keep breathing, I can stop crying. I didn't need or want him to die with me. I wanted to keep him safe. *What an idiot,* I think, but my heart isn't in it.

"That's ridiculous," he says. "That doesn't make any sense. He's eighteen; he'll find another girlfriend once you're dead. And he's stupid if he doesn't know that."

Tears run down my cheeks, hot at first and then cold. I close my eyes. "If you think that's what it's about . . ." I swallow another sob. ". . . you're the stupid one."

"Yeah. Whatever."

His shoes squeak as he turns away. About to leave.

"Wait!" I look up at his blurry silhouette, unable to make out his face. "What will they do to him? The same thing they're doing to me?"

"I don't know."

"Can you find out?" I wipe my cheeks with the heels of my hands, frustrated. "Can you at least find out if he's all right?"

He says, "Why would I do that? Why would I do anything for you?"

A moment later I hear the door slide shut.

CHAPTER
THIRTY

I READ SOMEWHERE, once, that crying defies scientific explanation. Tears are only meant to lubricate the eyes. There is no real reason for tear glands to overproduce tears at the behest of emotion.

I think we cry to release the animal parts of us without losing our humanity. Because inside me is a beast that snarls, and growls, and strains toward freedom, toward Tobias, and, above all, toward life. And as hard as I try, I cannot kill it.

So I sob into my hands instead.

+ + +

Left, right, right. Left, right, left. Right, right. Our turns, in order, from our point of origin—my cell—to our destination.

It is a new room. In it is a partially reclined chair, like a dentist's chair. In one corner is a screen and a desk. Jeanine sits at the desk.

"Where is he?" I say.

I have been waiting for hours to ask that question. I fell asleep and dreamed that I was chasing Tobias through Dauntless headquarters. No matter how fast I ran he was always just far enough ahead of me that I watched him disappear around corners, catching sight of a sleeve or the heel of a shoe.

Jeanine gives me a puzzled look. But she is not puzzled. She is playing with me.

"Tobias," I say anyway. My hands shake, but not from fear this time—from anger. "Where is he? What are you doing to him?"

"I see no reason to provide that information," says Jeanine. "And since you are all out of leverage, I see no way for you to give me a reason, unless you would like to change the terms of our agreement."

I want to scream at her that of course, of *course* I would rather know about Tobias than about my Divergence, but I don't. I can't make hasty decisions. She will do what she intends to do to Tobias whether I know about it or not. It is more important that I fully understand what is happening to me.

I breathe in through my nose, and out through my nose. I shake my hands. I sit down in the chair.

"Interesting," she says.

"Aren't you supposed to be running a faction and planning a war?" I say. "What are you doing here, running tests on a sixteen-year-old girl?"

"You choose different ways of referring to yourself depending on what is convenient," she says, leaning back in her chair. "Sometimes you insist that you are not a little girl, and sometimes you insist that you are. What I am curious to know is: How do you really view yourself? As one or the other? As both? As neither?"

I make my voice flat and factual, like hers. "I see no reason to provide that information."

I hear a faint snort. Peter is covering his mouth. Jeanine glares at him, and his laughter effortlessly transforms into a coughing fit.

"Mockery is childish, Beatrice," she says. "It does not become you."

"Mockery is childish, Beatrice," I repeat in my best imitation of her voice. *"It does not become you."*

"The serum," Jeanine says, eyeing Peter. He steps forward and fumbles with a black box on the desk, taking out a syringe with a needle already attached to it.

Peter starts toward me, and I hold out my hand.

"Allow me," I say.

He looks at Jeanine for permission, and she says, "All right, then." He hands me the syringe and I shove the needle into the side of my neck, pressing down on the plunger. Jeanine jabs one of the buttons with her finger, and everything goes dark.

+ + +

My mother stands in the aisle with her arm stretched above her head so she can hold the bar. Her face is turned, not toward the people sitting around me, but toward the city we pass as the bus lurches forward. I see wrinkles in her forehead and around her mouth when she frowns.

"What is it?" I ask her.

"There is so much to be done," she says with a small gesture toward the bus windows. "And so few of us left to do it."

It is clear what she's referring to. Beyond the bus is rubble as far as I can see. Across the street, a building lies in ruins. Fragments of glass litter the alleyways. I wonder what caused so much destruction.

"Where are we going?" I say.

She smiles at me, and I see different wrinkles than before, at the corners of her eyes. "We're going to Erudite headquarters."

I frown. Most of my life has been spent avoiding Erudite headquarters. My father used to say that he didn't even like to breathe the air in there. "Why are we going there?"

"They're going to help us."

Why do I feel a pang in my stomach when I think of my father? I picture his face, weathered by a lifetime of frustration with the world around him, and his hair, kept short by Abnegation standard practice, and feel the same kind of pain in my stomach that I get when I have not eaten in too long—a hollow pain.

"Did something happen to Dad?" I say.

She shakes her head. "Why would you ask that?"

"I don't know."

I don't feel the pain when I look at my mother. But I do feel like every second we spend standing these inches apart is one that I must impress upon my mind until my entire memory conforms to its shape. But if she is not permanent, what is she?

The bus stops, and the doors creak open. My mother starts down the aisle, and I follow her. She is taller than I am, so I stare between her shoulders, at the top of her spine. She looks fragile, but she is not.

I step down onto the pavement. Pieces of glass crinkle beneath my feet. They are blue and, judging by the holes in the building to my right, used to be windows.

"What happened?"

"War," my mother says. "This is what we've been trying so hard to avoid."

"And the Erudite will help us . . . by doing what?"

"I worry that all your father's blustering about Erudite has been to your detriment," she says gently. "They've made mistakes, of course, but they, like everyone else, are a blend of good and bad, not one or the other. What would we do without our doctors, our scientists, our teachers?"

She smooths down my hair.

"Take care to remember that, Beatrice."

"I will," I promise.

We keep walking. But something about what she said bothers me. Is it what she said about my father? No—my father is always complaining about Erudite. Is it what she said about Erudite? I hop over a large shard of glass. No, that can't be it. She was right about Erudite. All my teachers were Erudite, and so was the doctor who set my mother's arm when she broke it several years ago.

It's the last part. "Take care to remember." As if she won't have the opportunity to remind me later.

I feel something shift in my mind, like something that was closed has just opened.

"Mom?" I say.

She looks back at me. A lock of blond hair falls from

its knot and touches her cheek.

"I love you."

I point at a window to my left, and it explodes. Particles of glass rain over us.

I don't want to wake up in a room in Erudite headquarters, so I don't open my eyes right away, not even when the simulation fades. I try to preserve the image of my mother and the hair sticking to her cheekbone for as long as I can. But when all I see is the redness of my own eyelids, I open them.

"You'll have to do better than that," I say to Jeanine.

She says, "That was only the beginning."

CHAPTER
THIRTY-ONE

THAT NIGHT I dream, not of Tobias, and not of Will, but of my mother. We stand in the Amity orchards, where the apples are ripe and dangle just inches above our heads. Leaf shadows pattern her face, and she wears black, though I never saw her in black when she was alive. She is teaching me to braid hair, demonstrating on a lock of her own, laughing when my fingers fumble.

I wake wondering how I did not notice, every day I sat across from her at the breakfast table, that she was full to bursting with Dauntless energy. Was it because she hid it well? Or was it because I wasn't looking?

I bury my face in the thin mattress I slept on. I will never know her. But at least she will never know what I did to Will, either. At this point I don't think I could bear it if she did.

I am still blinking the haze of sleep from my eyes when I follow Peter down the corridor, seconds or minutes later, I can't tell.

"Peter." My throat aches; I must have screamed while I slept. "What time is it?"

He wears a watch, but the face is covered, so I can't see it. He doesn't even bother to look at it.

"Why are you constantly escorting me places?" I say. "Isn't there a depraved activity you're supposed to be taking part in? Kicking puppies or spying on girls while they change, or something?"

"I know what you did to Will, you know. Don't pretend that you're better than I am, because you and I, we're exactly the same."

The only thing that distinguishes one hallway from another, here, is their length. I decide to label them according to how many steps I take before I turn. Ten. Forty-seven. Twenty-nine.

"You're wrong," I say. "We may both be bad, but there's a huge difference between us—I'm not content with being this way."

Peter snorts a little, and we walk between the Erudite lab tables. That's when I realize where I am, and where we're going: back to the room Jeanine showed me. The room where I will be executed. I shudder so hard my teeth chatter, and it's difficult to keep walking, hard to keep my thoughts straight. *It's just a room,* I tell myself. *Just a room like any other room.*

I am such a liar.

This time the execution chamber is not empty. Four Dauntless traitors mill around in one corner, and two of the Erudite, one a dark-skinned woman, one an older man, both wearing lab coats, stand with Jeanine near the metal table in the center. Several machines are set up around it, and there are wires everywhere.

I don't know what most of those machines do, but among them is a heart monitor. What does Jeanine plan to do that requires a heart monitor?

"Get her on the table," says Jeanine, sounding bored. I stare for a second at the sheet of steel that awaits me. What if she changed her mind about waiting to execute me? What if this is when I die? Peter's hands clamp around my arms and I writhe, throwing all my strength into the struggle.

But he just lifts me up, dodging my kicking feet, and slams me down on the metal slab, knocking the wind out of me. I gasp, and fling a fist out at whatever I can hit, which just happens to be Peter's wrist. He winces, but by now the other Dauntless traitors have come forward to help.

One of them holds down my ankles, and the other holds down my shoulders as Peter pulls black straps across my body to keep me pinned. I flinch at the pain in my wounded shoulder and stop struggling.

"What the hell is going on?" I demand, craning my neck to look at Jeanine. "We agreed—cooperation in exchange for results! We *agreed*—"

"This is entirely separate from our agreement," says Jeanine, glancing at her watch. "This is not about you, Beatrice."

The door opens again.

Tobias walks in—*limps* in—flanked by Dauntless traitors. His face is bruised and there's a cut above his eyebrow. He does not move with his usual care; he's holding himself perfectly straight. He must be injured. I try not to think about how he got that way.

"What is this?" he says, his voice rough and creaky.

From screaming, probably.

My throat feels swollen.

"Tris," he says, and he lurches toward me, but the Dauntless traitors are too quick. They grab him before he can move more than a few steps. "Tris, are you okay?"

"Yeah," I say. "Are you?"

He nods. I don't believe him.

"Rather than waste any more time, Mr. Eaton, I thought

I would take the most logical approach. Truth serum would be preferable, of course, but it would take days to coerce Jack Kang into handing some over, as it is jealously guarded by the Candor, and I'd rather not waste a few days." She steps forward, a syringe in hand. This serum is tinted gray. It could be a new version of the simulation serum, but I doubt it.

I wonder what it does. It can't be good, if she looks this pleased with herself.

"In a few seconds, I will inject Tris with this liquid. At that point, I trust, your selfless instincts will take over and you will tell me exactly what I need to know."

"What does she need to know?" I say, interrupting her.

"Information about the factionless safe houses," he replies without looking at me.

My eyes widen. The factionless are the last hope any of us has, now that half the loyal Dauntless and all the Candor are simulation-ready, and half the Abnegation are dead.

"Don't give it to her. I'm going to die anyway. Don't give her anything."

"Remind me, Mr. Eaton," says Jeanine. "What do Dauntless simulations do?"

"This isn't a classroom," he replies through gritted teeth. "Tell me what you're going to do."

"I will if you answer my very simple question."

"Fine." Tobias's eyes shift to me. "The simulations stimulate the amygdala, which is responsible for processing fear, induce a hallucination based on that fear, and then transmit the data to a computer to be processed and observed."

It sounds like he's had that memorized for a long time. Maybe he has—he did spend a lot of time running simulations.

"Very good," she says. "When I was developing the Dauntless simulations, years ago, we discovered that certain levels of potency overwhelmed the brain and made it too insensible with terror to invent new surroundings, which was when we diluted the solution so that the simulations would be more instructive. But I still remember how to make it."

She taps the syringe with her fingernail.

"Fear," she says, "is more powerful than pain. So is there anything you'd like to say, before I inject Ms. Prior?"

Tobias presses his lips together.

And Jeanine inserts the needle.

+ + +

It begins quietly, with the pounding of a heart. I am not sure, at first, whose heartbeat I'm hearing, because it's far too loud to be my own. But then I realize that it is my own, and it's getting faster and faster.

Sweat collects in my palms and behind my knees.

And then I have to gasp in order to breathe.

That's when the screaming starts

And I

Can't

Think.

+ + +

Tobias is fighting the Dauntless traitors by the door.

I hear what sounds like a child's scream beside me, and wrench my head around to see where it's coming from, but there is only a heart monitor. Above me the lines between the ceiling tiles warp and twist into monstrous creatures. The scent of rotting flesh fills the air and I gag. The monstrous creatures take on a more definite shape—they are birds, crows, with beaks as long as my forearm and wings so dark they seem to swallow all the light.

"Tris," says Tobias. I look away from the crows.

He stands by the door, where he was before I was injected, but now he has a knife. He holds it out from his body and turns it so the blade points in, at his stomach. Then he brings it toward himself, touching the tip of the blade to his stomach.

"What are you doing? Stop!"

He smiles a little and says, "I'm doing this for you."

He pushes the knife in farther, slow, and blood stains the hem of his shirt. I gag, and throw myself against the bonds holding me to the table. "No, stop!" I thrash and in a simulation I would have pulled free by now so this must mean that this is real, it's real. I scream and he sticks the knife in to the handle. He collapses to the floor and his blood spills fast and surrounds him. The shadow-birds turn their beady eyes on him and swarm in a tornado of wings and talons, pecking at his skin. I see his eyes through the whirling feathers and he is still awake.

A bird lands on the fingers that hold the knife. He draws it out again and it clatters to the ground and I should hope that he is dead but I'm selfish so I can't. My back lifts from the table and all my muscles clench and my throat aches from this scream that no longer shapes itself into words and will not stop.

+ + +

"Sedative," a stern voice commands.

Another needle in my neck, and my heart begins to slow down. I sob with relief. For seconds all I can do is sob with relief.

That was not fear. That was something else; an emotion that should not exist.

"Let me go," Tobias says, and he sounds scratchier than before. I blink fast so I can see him through my tears. There are red marks on his arms from where the Dauntless traitors held him back, but he is not dying; he is all right. "That's the only way I'll tell you, is if you let me go."

Jeanine nods, and he runs to me. He wraps one hand around mine and touches my hair with the other. His fingertips come away wet with tears. He doesn't wipe them off. He leans over and presses his forehead to mine.

"The factionless safe houses," he says dully, right against my cheek. "Get me a map and I'll mark them for you."

His forehead feels cool and dry against mine. My muscles ache, probably from being clenched for however long Jeanine left me with that serum pulsing through me.

He pulls back, his fingers wrapped around my fingers for as long as they can be until the Dauntless traitors pull him from my grasp to escort him elsewhere. My hand falls heavy on the table. I don't want to struggle against the restraints anymore. All I want to do is sleep.

"While you're here . . ." Jeanine says once Tobias and his escorts are gone. She looks up and focuses her watery eyes on one of the Erudite. "Get him and bring him in here. It's time."

She looks back down at me.

"While you sleep, we will be performing a short procedure to observe a few things about your brain. It will not be invasive. But before that . . . I promised you full transparency with these procedures. So I feel it's only fair that you know exactly who has been assisting me in my endeavors." She smiles a little. "Who told me what three factions you had an aptitude for, and what our best chance was to get you to come here, and to put your mother in the last simulation to make it more effective."

She looks toward the doorway as the sedative sets in, making everything blur at the edges. I look over my shoulder, and through the haze of drugs I see him.

Caleb.

CHAPTER
THIRTY-TWO

I WAKE TO a headache. I try to go back to sleep—at least when I'm asleep, I'm calm—but the image of Caleb standing in the doorway runs through my mind over and over again, accompanied by the sound of squawking crows.

Why did I never wonder how Eric and Jeanine knew that I had aptitude for three factions?

Why did it never occur to me that only three people in the world knew that particular fact: Tori, Caleb, and Tobias?

My head pounds. I can't make sense of it. I don't know why Caleb would betray me. I wonder when it happened—after the attack simulation? After the escape from Amity? Or was it earlier than that—was it back when my father was still alive? Caleb told us he left Erudite when he found out what they were planning—was he lying?

He must have been. I press the heel of my hand to my forehead. My brother chose faction over blood. There has to be a reason. She must have threatened him. Or coerced him in some way.

The door opens. I don't lift my head or open my eyes.

"Stiff." It's Peter. Of course.

"Yes." When I let my hand fall from my face, a lock of hair falls with it. I look at it from the corner of my eye. My hair has never been this greasy before.

Peter sets a bottle of water next to the bed, and a sandwich. The thought of eating it nauseates me.

"You brain-dead?" he asks.

"Don't think so."

"Don't be so sure."

"Ha-ha," I say. "How long have I been asleep?"

"About a day. I'm supposed to escort you to the showers."

"If you say something about how badly I need one," I say tiredly, "I *will* poke you in the eye."

The room spins when I lift my head, but I manage to put my legs over the edge of the bed and stand. Peter and I start down the hallway. When we turn the corner to get to the bathroom, though, there are people at the end of the hallway.

One of them is Tobias. I can see where our paths will

intersect, between where I stand now and my cell door. I stare, not at him but at where he will be when he reaches for my hand, as he did the last time we passed each other. My skin tingles with anticipation. For just a moment, I will touch him again.

Six steps until we pass each other. Five steps.

At four steps, though, Tobias stops. His entire body goes limp, catching his Dauntless traitor escort off guard. The guard loses his grip on him for just a second, and Tobias crumples to the floor.

Then he twists around. Lurches forward. And grabs a gun from the shorter Dauntless traitor's holster.

The gun goes off. Peter dives to the right, dragging me with him. My head skims the wall. The Dauntless guard's mouth is open—he must be screaming. I can't hear him.

Tobias kicks him hard in the stomach. The Dauntless in me admires his form—perfect—and his speed—incredible. Then he turns, training the gun on Peter. But Peter has already released me.

Tobias reaches for my left arm, helps me to my feet, and starts running. I stumble after him. Each time my foot hits the ground, pain slices into my head, but I can't stop. I blink tears from my eyes. *Run*, I tell myself, as if that will make it easier. Tobias's hand is rough and strong. I let it guide me around a corner.

"Tobias," I wheeze.

He stops, and looks back at me. "Oh no," he says, brushing my cheek with his fingers. "Come on. On my back."

He bends, and I put my arms around his neck, burying my face between his shoulder blades. He lifts me without difficulty and holds on to my leg with his left hand. His right hand still holds the gun.

He runs, and even with my weight, he is fast. Idly I think, *How could he ever have been Abnegation?* He seems designed specifically for speed and deadly accuracy. But not strength, not particularly—he is smart, but not strong. Only strong enough to carry me.

The hallways are empty now, but not for long. Soon every Dauntless in the building will rush toward us from every angle, and we will be trapped in this pale maze. I wonder how Tobias plans to get past them.

I lift my head long enough to see that he just ran past an exit.

"Tobias, you missed it."

"Missed . . . what?" he says between breaths.

"An exit."

"Not trying to escape. We'd get shot if we did," he says. "Trying to . . . find something."

I would suspect that I'm dreaming if the pain in my head wasn't so intense. Usually only my dreams make this little sense. Why, if he was not trying to escape, did he take me with him? And what is he doing, if not escaping?

He stops abruptly, almost dropping me, as he reaches a wide hallway with panes of glass on either side, revealing offices. The Erudite sit frozen at their desks, staring at us. Tobias pays no attention to them; his eyes, as far as I can tell, are fixed on the door at the end of the corridor. A sign outside the door says CONTROL-A.

Tobias searches every corner of the room, and then shoots at the camera attached to the ceiling on our right. The camera drops. He shoots at the camera attached to the ceiling on our left. Its lens shatters.

"Time to get down," he says. "No more running, I promise."

I slide off his back and take his hand instead. He walks toward a closed door that we passed already, and into a supply closet. He shuts the door and wedges a busted chair under the doorknob. I face him, a shelf stacked with paper at my back. Above us, the blue light flickers. His eyes roam over my face almost hungrily.

"I don't have much time, so I'm going to be direct," he says.

I nod.

"I didn't come here on some suicide mission," he says. "I came for two reasons. The first was to find Erudite's two central control rooms so that when we invade, we'll know what to destroy first to get rid of all the simulation data, so she can't activate the Dauntless's transmitters."

That explains the running without escaping. And we found a control room, at the end of that hallway.

I stare at him, still dazed from the past few minutes.

"The second," he says, clearing his throat, "is to make sure you hold on, because we have a plan."

"What plan?"

"According to one of our insiders, your execution is tentatively scheduled for two weeks from today," he says. "At least, that's Jeanine's target date for the new, Divergent-proof simulation. So fourteen days from now, the factionless, the loyal Dauntless, and the Abnegation who are willing to fight will storm the Erudite compound and take out their best weapon—their computer system. That means we'll outnumber the traitor Dauntless, and therefore the Erudite."

"But you told Jeanine where the factionless safe houses were."

"Yeah." He frowns a little. "That is problematic. But as you and I know, a lot of the factionless are Divergent, and many of them were already moving toward the Abnegation sector when I left, so only some of the safe houses will be affected. So they will still have a huge population to contribute to the invasion."

Two weeks. Will I be able to make it through two weeks of this? I am already so tired I'm finding it difficult to stand on my own. Even the rescue that Tobias is proposing barely appeals to me. I don't want freedom. I want sleep. I want this to end.

"I don't . . ." I choke on the words and start to cry. "I can't . . . make it . . . that long."

"Tris," he says sternly. He never coddles me. I wish that, just this once, he would coddle me. "You have to. You have to survive this."

"Why?" The question forms in my stomach and launches from my throat like a moan. I feel like thumping my fists against his chest, like a child throwing a tantrum. Tears cover my cheeks, and I know I'm acting ridiculous but I can't stop. "Why do I have to? Why can't someone else do something for once? What if I don't want to do this anymore?"

And what *this* is, I realize, is life. I don't want it. I want my parents and I have for weeks. I've been trying to claw my way back to them, and now I am so close and he is telling me not to.

"I know." I have never heard his voice sound so soft. "I know it's hard. The hardest thing you've had to do."

I shake my head.

"I can't force you. I can't make you want to survive this." He pulls me against him and runs his hand over my hair, tucking it behind my ear. His fingers trail down my neck and over my shoulder, and he says, "But you will do it. It doesn't matter if you believe you can or not. You will, because that's who you are."

I pull back and fit my mouth to his, not gently, not hesitantly. I kiss him like I used to, when I felt sure of us, and run my hands over his back, down his arms, like I used to.

I don't want to tell him the truth: that he is wrong, and I do not want to survive this.

The door opens. Dauntless traitors crowd into the supply closet. Tobias steps back, turns the gun in his hand, and offers it, handle first, to the nearest Dauntless traitor.

CHAPTER
THIRTY-THREE

"Beatrice."

I jerk awake. The room I am in now—for whatever experiment they want to run on me—is large, with screens along the back wall and blue lights glowing just above the floor and rows of padded benches across the middle. I'm sitting on the farthest bench back with Peter at my left shoulder, my head leaning against the wall. I still can't seem to get enough sleep.

Now I wish I hadn't woken up. Caleb stands a few feet away, his weight on one foot, an uncertain posture.

"Did you *ever* leave Erudite?" I say.

"It's not that simple," he starts. "I—"

"It is that simple." I want to yell, but instead my voice comes out flat. "At what point did you betray our family?

Before our parents died, or after?"

"I did what I had to do. You think you understand this, Beatrice, but you don't. This whole situation . . . it's much bigger than you think it is." His eyes plead with me to understand, but I recognize his tone—it's the one he employed when we were younger, to scold me. It is condescending.

Arrogance is one of the flaws in the Erudite heart—I know. It is often in mine.

But greed is the other. And I do not have that. So I am halfway in and halfway out, as always.

I push myself to my feet. "You still haven't answered my question."

Caleb steps back.

"This isn't about Erudite; it's about everyone. All the factions," he says, "and the city. And what's outside the fence."

"I don't care," I say, but that isn't true. The phrase "outside the fence" prickles in my brain. Outside? How could any of this have to do with what's outside?

Something itches at the back of my mind. Marcus said that information the Abnegation possessed motivated Jeanine's attack on Abnegation. Does that information have to do with what's outside, too?

I push the thought away for the time being.

"I thought you were all about facts. About freedom of information? Well, how about *this* fact, Caleb? When—" My voice quakes. "*When* did you betray our parents?"

"I have always been Erudite," he says softly. "Even when I was supposed to be Abnegation."

"If you're with Jeanine, then I hate you. Just like our father would have."

"Our father." Caleb snorts a little. "Our father *was* Erudite, Beatrice. Jeanine told me—he was in her year at school."

"He wasn't Erudite," I say after a few seconds. "He chose to leave them. He chose a different identity, just like you, and became something else. Only you chose this . . . this *evil*."

"Spoken like a true Dauntless," says Caleb sharply. "It's either one way or the other way. No nuances. The world doesn't *work* like that, Beatrice. Evil depends on where you're standing."

"No matter where I stand, I'll still think mind controlling an entire city of people is evil." I feel my lip wobble. "I'll still think delivering your sister to be prodded and executed is evil!"

He is my brother, but I want to tear him to pieces.

Instead of trying to, though, I find myself sitting down again. I could never hurt him enough to make his betrayal stop hurting. And it *hurts*, in every part of my body. I press my fingers to my chest to massage some of the smarting tension away.

Jeanine and her army of Erudite scientists and Dauntless traitors walk in just as I wipe tears from my cheeks. I blink rapidly so she won't see. She barely even gives me a glance.

"Let us view the results, shall we?" she announces. Caleb, now standing by the screens, presses something at the front of the room, and the screens turn on. Words and numbers I don't understand fill them.

"We discovered something extremely interesting, Ms. Prior." I have never seen her so cheerful before. She almost smiles—but not quite. "You have an abundance of a particular kind of neuron, called, quite simply, a mirror neuron. Would someone like to explain to Ms. Prior exactly what mirror neurons do?"

The Erudite scientists raise their hands in unison. She points to an older woman in the front.

"Mirror neurons fire both when one performs an action and when one sees another person performing that action. They allow us to imitate behavior."

"What else are they responsible for?" Jeanine scans her "class" the same way my teachers did in Upper Levels. Another Erudite raises his hand.

"Learning language, understanding other people's intentions based on their behavior, um . . ." He frowns. "And empathy."

"More specifically," Jeanine says, and this time she does smile at me, broadly, forcing creases into her cheeks, "someone with many, strong mirror neurons could have a flexible personality—capable of mimicking others as the situation calls for it rather than remaining constant."

I understand why she smiles. I feel like my mind is cracked open, its secrets spilling over the floor for me to finally see.

"A flexible personality," she says, "would probably have aptitude for more than one faction, don't you agree, Ms. Prior?"

"Probably," I say. "Now if only you could get a simulation to suppress that particular ability, we could be done with this."

"One thing at a time." She pauses. "I must admit, it confuses me that you are so eager for your own execution."

"No, it doesn't." I close my eyes. "It doesn't confuse you at all." I sigh. "Can I go back to my cell now?"

I must seem nonchalant, but I'm not. I want to go back to my room so that I can cry in peace. But I don't want her to know that.

"Don't get too comfortable," she chirps. "We'll have

a simulation serum to try out soon."

"Yeah," I say. "Whatever."

+ + +

Someone shakes my shoulder. I jerk awake, my eyes wide and searching, and I see Tobias kneeling over me. He wears a Dauntless traitor jacket, and one side of his head is coated with blood. The blood streams from a wound on his ear—the top of his ear is gone. I wince.

"What happened?" I say.

"Get up. We have to run."

"It's too soon. It hasn't been two weeks."

"I don't have time to explain. Come on."

"Oh God. Tobias."

I sit up and wrap my arms around him, pressing my face into his neck. His arms tighten around me and squeeze. Warmth courses through me, and comfort. If he is here, that means I'm safe. My tears make his skin slippery.

He stands and pulls me to my feet, which makes my wounded shoulder throb.

"Reinforcements will be here soon. Come on."

I let him lead me out of the room. We make it down the first hallway without difficulty, but in the second hallway, we encounter two Dauntless guards, one a young man and one a middle-aged woman. Tobias fires twice in a matter of seconds, both hits, one in the head and one in the chest. The woman, who was hit in the chest, slumps against the wall but doesn't die.

We keep moving. One hallway, then another, all of them look the same. Tobias's grip on my hand never falters. I know that if he can throw a knife so that it hits just the tip of my ear, he can fire accurately at the Dauntless soldiers who ambush us. We step over fallen bodies—the people Tobias killed on the way in, probably—and finally reach a fire exit.

Tobias lets go of my hand to open the door, and the fire alarm screeches in my ears, but we keep running. I am gasping for air but I don't care, not when I'm finally escaping, not when this nightmare is finally over. My vision starts to go black at the edges, so I grab Tobias's arm and hold on tight, trusting him to lead me safely to the bottom of the stairs.

I run out of steps to run down, and I open my eyes. Tobias is about to open the exit door, but I hold him back. "Got to . . . catch my breath. . . ."

He pauses, and I put my hands on my knees, leaning over. My shoulder still throbs. I frown, and look up at him.

"Come on, let's get out of here," he says insistently.

My stomach sinks. I stare into his eyes. They are dark blue, with a patch of light blue on his right iris.

I take his chin in hand and pull his lips down to mine, kissing him slowly, sighing as I pull back.

"We can't get out of here," I say. "Because this is a simulation."

He pulled me to my feet with my right hand. The real Tobias would have remembered the wound in my shoulder.

"What?" He scowls at me. "Don't you think I would know if I was under a simulation?"

"You aren't under a simulation. You *are* the simulation." I look up and say in a loud voice, "You'll have to do better than that, Jeanine."

All I have to do now is wake up, and I know how—I have done it before, in my fear landscape, when I broke a glass tank just by touching my palm to it, or when I made a gun appear in the grass to shoot descending birds. I take a knife from my pocket—a knife that wasn't there a moment ago—and will my leg to be hard as diamond.

I thrust the knife toward my thigh, and the blade bends.

+ + +

I wake with tears in my eyes. I wake to Jeanine's scream of frustration.

"What is it?" She grabs Peter's gun out of his hand and stalks across the room, pressing the barrel to my forehead. My body stiffens, goes cold. She won't shoot me. I am a problem she can't solve. She won't shoot me.

"What is it that clues you in? Tell me. Tell me or I will kill you."

I slowly push myself up from the chair, coming to my feet, pushing my skin harder into the cold barrel.

"You think I'm going to tell you?" I say. "You think I believe that you would kill me without figuring out the answer to this question?"

"You stupid girl," she says. "You think this is about you, and your abnormal brain? This is not about you. It is not about me. It is about keeping this city safe from the people who intend to plunge it into hell!"

I summon the last of my strength and launch myself at her, clawing at whatever skin my fingernails find, digging in as hard as I can. She screams at the top of her lungs, a sound that turns my blood into fire. I punch her hard in the face.

A pair of arms wrap around me, pulling me off her, and a fist meets my side. I groan, and lunge toward her, held at bay by Peter.

"Pain can't make me tell you. Truth serum can't make me tell you. Simulations can't make me tell you. I'm immune to all three."

Her nose is bleeding, and I see lines of fingernail scrapes in her cheeks, on the side of her throat, turning

374

red with blossoming blood. She glares at me, pinching her nose closed, her hair disheveled, her free hand trembling.

"You have *failed*. You can't control me!" I scream, so loud it hurts my throat. I stop struggling and sag against Peter's chest. "You will *never* be able to control me."

I laugh, mirthless, a mad laugh. I savor the scowl on her face, the hate in her eyes. She was like a machine; she was cold and emotionless, bound by logic alone. And I broke her.

I broke her.

CHAPTER
THIRTY-FOUR

ONCE I'M IN the hallway, I stop struggling toward Jeanine. My side throbs from where Peter punched me, but it's nothing compared to the pulse of triumph in my cheeks.

Peter walks me back to my cell without a word. I stand in the middle of the room for a long time, staring at the camera in the back-left corner. Who is watching me all the time? Is it Dauntless traitors, guarding me, or the Erudite, observing me?

Once the heat leaves my face and my side stops hurting, I lie down.

A picture of my parents floats into my head the moment I close my eyes. Once, when I was about eleven, I stopped at the doorway to my parents' bedroom to watch them make the bed together. My father smiled at my mother as they pulled the sheets back and smoothed them down in perfect synchronicity. I knew by the way he looked at her that he held her in a higher regard than he held even himself.

No selfishness or insecurity kept him from seeing the full extent of her goodness, as it so often does with the rest of us. That kind of love may only be possible in Abnegation. I do not know.

My father: Erudite-born, Abnegation-grown. He often found it difficult to live up to the demands of his chosen faction, just as I did. But he tried, and he knew true self-lessness when he saw it.

I clutch my pillow to my chest and bury my face in it. I don't cry. I just ache.

Grief is not as heavy as guilt, but it takes more away from you.

+ + +

"Stiff."

I wake with a start, my hands still clutching the pillow. There is a wet patch on the mattress under my face. I sit up, wiping my eyes with my fingertips.

Peter's eyebrows, which usually turn up in the middle, are furrowed.

"What happened?" Whatever it is, it can't be good.

"Your execution has been scheduled for tomorrow morning at eight o'clock."

"My execution? But she . . . she hasn't developed the right simulation yet; she couldn't *possibly* . . ."

"She said that she will continue the experiments on Tobias instead of you," he says.

All I can say is: "Oh."

I clutch the mattress and rock forward and back, forward and back. Tomorrow my life will be over. Tobias may survive long enough to escape in the factionless invasion. The Dauntless will elect a new leader. All the loose ends I will leave will be easily tied up.

I nod. No family left, no loose ends, no great loss.

"I could have forgiven you, you know," I say. "For trying to kill me during initiation. I probably could have."

We are both quiet for a while. I don't know why I told him that. Maybe just because it's true, and tonight, of all nights, is the time for honesty. Tonight I will be honest, and selfless, and brave. Divergent.

"I never asked you to," he says, and turns to leave. But then he stops at the door frame and says, "It's 9:24."

Telling me the time is a small act of betrayal—and therefore an ordinary act of bravery. It is maybe the first time I've seen Peter be truly Dauntless.

I'm going to die tomorrow. It has been a long time since I felt certainty about anything, so this feels like a gift. Tonight, nothing. Tomorrow, whatever comes after life. And Jeanine still doesn't know how to control the Divergent.

When I start to cry, I clutch the pillow to my chest and let it happen. I cry hard, like a child cries, until my face is hot and I feel like I might be sick. I can pretend to be brave, but I'm not.

I suppose that now would be the time to ask for forgiveness for all the things I've done, but I'm sure my list would never be complete. I also don't believe that whatever comes after life depends on my correctly reciting a list of my transgressions—that sounds too much like an Erudite afterlife to me, all accuracy and no feeling. I don't believe that what comes after depends on anything I do at all.

I am better off doing as Abnegation taught me: turning away from myself, projecting always outward, and hoping that in whatever is next, I will be better than I am now.

I smile a little. I wish I could tell my parents that I will die like the Abnegation. They would be proud, I think.

CHAPTER
THIRTY-FIVE

THIS MORNING I put on the clean clothes I am given: black pants—too loose, but who cares?—and a long-sleeved black shirt. No shoes.

It is not time yet. I find myself lacing my fingers together and bowing my head. Sometimes my father did this in the morning before sitting down at the breakfast table, but I never asked him what he was doing. Still, I would like to feel like I belong to my father again before I . . . well, before it's over.

A few silent moments later, Peter tells me it's time to go. He barely looks at me, scowls at the back wall instead. I suppose it would have been too much to ask, to see a friendly face this morning. I stand, and together we walk down the hallway.

My toes are cold. My feet stick to the tiles. We turn a corner, and I hear muffled shouts. At first I can't tell what the voice is saying, but as we draw closer, it takes shape.

"I want to . . . her!" Tobias. "I . . . *see* her!"

I glance at Peter. "I can't speak to him one last time, can I?"

Peter shakes his head. "There's a window, though. Maybe if he sees you he'll finally shut up."

He takes me down a dead-end corridor that's only six feet long. At the end is a door, and Peter is right, there's a small window near the top, about a foot above my head.

"Tris!" Tobias's voice is even clearer here. "I want to see her!"

I reach up and press my palm to the glass. The shouts stop, and his face appears behind the glass. His eyes are red; his face, blotchy. Handsome. He stares down at me for a few seconds and then presses his hand to the glass so it lines up with mine. I pretend I can feel the warmth of it through the window.

He leans his forehead against the door and squeezes his eyes shut.

I take my hand down and turn away before he can open his eyes. I feel pain in my chest, worse than when I got shot in the shoulder. I clutch the front of my shirt, blink away tears, and rejoin Peter in the main hallway.

"Thank you," I say quietly. I meant to say it louder.

"Whatever." Peter scowls again. "Let's just go."

I hear rumbling somewhere ahead of us—the sound of a crowd. The next hallway is packed with Dauntless traitors, tall and short, young and old, armed and unarmed. They all wear the blue armband of betrayal.

"Hey!" Peter shouts. "Clear a path!"

The Dauntless traitors closest to us hear him, and press against the walls to make way for us. The other Dauntless traitors follow suit soon after, and everyone is quiet. Peter steps back to let me go ahead of him. I know the way from here.

I don't know where the pounding starts, but someone drums their fists against the wall, and someone else joins in, and I walk down the aisle between solemn-but-raucous Dauntless traitors, their hands in motion at their sides. The pounding is so fast my heart races to keep up with it.

Some of the Dauntless traitors incline their heads to me—I'm not sure why. It doesn't matter.

I reach the end of the hallway and open the door to my execution chamber.

I open it.

Dauntless traitors crowded the hallway; the Erudite crowd the execution room, but there, they have made a path for me already. Silently they study me as I walk to the metal table in the center of the room. Jeanine stands a few steps away. The scratches on her face show through hastily applied makeup. She doesn't look at me.

Four cameras dangle from the ceiling, one at each corner of the table. I sit down first, wipe my hands off on my pants, and then lie down.

The table is cold. Frigid, seeping into my skin, into my bones. Appropriate, perhaps, because that is what will happen to my body when all the life leaves it; it will become cold and heavy, heavier than I have ever been. As for the rest of me, I am not sure. Some people believe that I will go nowhere, and maybe they're right, but maybe they're not. Such speculations are no longer useful to me anyway.

Peter slips an electrode beneath the collar of my shirt and presses it to my chest, right over my heart. He then attaches a wire to the electrode and switches on the heart monitor. I hear my heartbeat, fast and strong. Soon, where that steady rhythm was, there will be nothing.

And then rising from within me is a single thought:

I don't want to die.

All those times Tobias scolded me for risking my life, I never took him seriously. I believed that I wanted to be with my parents and for all of this to be over. I was sure I wanted to emulate their self-sacrifice. But no. No, no.

Burning and boiling inside me is the desire to live.

I don't want to die I don't want to die I don't want to!

Jeanine steps forward with a syringe full of purple serum. Her glasses reflect the fluorescent light above us, so I can barely see her eyes.

Every part of my body chants it in unison. *Live, live, live.* I thought that in order to give my life in exchange for Will's, in exchange for my parents', that I needed to die, but I was wrong; I need to live my life in the light of their deaths. I need to live.

Jeanine holds my head steady with one hand and inserts the needle into my neck with the other.

I'm not done! I shout in my head, and not at Jeanine. *I am not done here!*

She presses the plunger down. Peter leans forward and looks into my eyes.

"The serum will go into effect in one minute," he says. "Be brave, Tris."

The words startle me, because that is exactly what Tobias said when he put me under my first simulation.

My heart begins to race.

Why would Peter tell me to be brave? Why would he offer any kind words at all?

All the muscles in my body relax at once. A heavy, liquid

feeling fills my limbs. If this is death, it isn't so bad. My eyes stay open, but my head drops to the side. I try to close my eyes, but I can't—I can't move.

Then the heart monitor stops beeping.

CHAPTER
THIRTY-SIX

BUT I'M STILL breathing. Not deeply; not enough to satisfy, but *breathing*. Peter pushes my eyelids over my eyes. Does he know I'm not dead? Does Jeanine? Can she see me breathing?

"Take the body to the lab," Jeanine says. "The autopsy is scheduled for this afternoon."

"All right," Peter replies.

Peter pushes the table forward. I hear mutters all around me as we pass the group of Erudite bystanders. My hand falls off the edge of the table as we turn a corner, and smacks into the wall. I feel a prickle of pain in my fingertips, but I can't move my hand, as hard as I try.

This time, when we go down the hallway of Dauntless traitors, it is silent. Peter walks slowly at first, then turns another corner and picks up the pace. He almost sprints down the next corridor, and stops abruptly. *Where am I? I can't be in the lab already. Why did he stop?*

Peter's arms slide under my knees and shoulders, and he lifts me. My head falls against his shoulder.

"For someone so small, you're *heavy*, Stiff," he mutters.

He knows I'm awake. He *knows*.

I hear a series of beeps, and a slide—a locked door, opening.

"What do—" Tobias's voice. *Tobias!* "Oh my God. Oh—"

"Spare me your blubbering, okay?" Peter says. "She's not dead; she's just paralyzed. It'll only last for about a minute. Now get ready to run."

I don't understand.

How does Peter know?

"Let me carry her," Tobias says.

"No. You're a better shot than I am. Take my gun. I'll carry her."

I hear the gun slide out of its holster. Tobias brushes a hand over my forehead. They both start running.

At first all I hear is the pounding of their feet, and my head snaps back painfully. I feel tingling in my hands and feet. Peter shouts, "Left!" at Tobias.

Then a shout from down the hallway. "Hey, what—!"

A bang. And nothing.

More running. Peter shouts, "Right!" I hear another bang, and another. "Whoa," he mumbles. "Wait, stop here!"

Tingling down my spine. I open my eyes as Peter opens another door. He charges through it, and just before I smack my head against the door frame, I stick my arm out and stop us.

"Careful!" I say, my voice strained. My throat still feels as tight as it did when he first injected me and I found it difficult to breathe. Peter turns sideways to bring me through the door, then nudges it shut with his heel and drops me on the floor.

The room is almost empty, except for a row of empty trash cans along one wall and a square metal door large enough for one of the cans to fit through it along the other wall.

"Tris," Tobias says, crouching next to me. His face is pale, almost yellow.

There is too much I want to say. The first thing that comes out is, "Beatrice."

He laughs weakly.

"Beatrice," he amends, and touches his lips to mine. I curl my fingers into his shirt.

"Unless you want me to throw up all over you guys, you might want to save it for later."

"Where are we?" I ask.

"This is the trash incinerator," says Peter, slapping the square door. "I turned it off. It'll take us to the alley. And then your aim had better be perfect, Four, if you want to get out of the Erudite sector alive."

"Don't concern yourself with my aim," Tobias retorts. He, like me, is barefoot.

Peter opens the door to the incinerator. "Tris, you first."

The trash chute is about three feet wide and four feet high. I slide one leg down the chute and, with Tobias's help, swing the other leg in. My stomach drops as I slide down a short metal tube. Then a series of rollers pound against my back as I slip over them.

I smell fire and ash, but I am not burned. Then I drop, and my arm smacks into a metal wall, making me groan. I land on a cement floor, hard, and pain from the impact prickles up my shins.

"Ow." I limp away from the opening and shout, "Go ahead!"

My legs have recovered by the time Peter lands, on his side instead of his feet. He groans, and drags himself away from the opening to recover.

I look around. We are inside the incinerator, which would be completely dark if not for the lines of light glowing in the shape of a small door on the other side.

The floor is solid metal in some places and metal grating in others. Everything smells like rotting garbage and fire.

"Don't say I never took you anywhere nice," Peter says.

"Wouldn't dream of it," I say.

Tobias drops to the floor, landing first on his feet and then tilting forward to his knees, wincing. I pull him to his feet and then draw close to his side. All the smells and sights and feelings of the world feel magnified. I was almost dead, but instead I am alive. Because of Peter.

Of all people.

Peter walks across the grate and opens the small door. Light streams into the incinerator. Tobias walks with me away from the fire smell, away from the metal furnace, into the cement-walled room that contains it.

"Got that gun?" Peter says to Tobias.

"No," says Tobias, "I figured I would shoot the bullets out of my nostrils, so I left it upstairs."

"Oh, shut up."

Peter holds another gun in front of him and leaves the incinerator room. A dank hallway with exposed pipes in the ceiling greets us, but it's only ten feet long. The sign next to the door at the end says EXIT. I am alive, and I am leaving.

+ + +

The stretch of land between Dauntless headquarters and Erudite headquarters does not look the same in reverse. I suppose everything is bound to look different when you aren't on your way to die.

When we reach the end of the alley, Tobias presses his shoulder to one wall and leans forward just enough to see around the corner. His face blank, he puts one arm around the corner, steadying it with the building wall, and fires twice. I shove my fingers in my ears and try not to pay attention to the gunshots and what they make me remember.

"Hurry," Tobias says.

We sprint, Peter first, me second, and Tobias last, down Wabash Avenue. I look over my shoulder to see what Tobias shot at, and see two men on the ground behind Erudite headquarters. One isn't moving, and the other is clutching his arm and running toward the door. They will send others after us.

My head feels muddled, probably from exhaustion, but the adrenaline keeps me running.

"Take the least logical route!" shouts Tobias.

"What?" Peter says.

"The least logical route," Tobias says. "So they won't find us!"

Peter swerves to the left, down another alley, this one

full of cardboard boxes that contain frayed blankets and stained pillows—old factionless dwellings, I assume. He jumps over a box that I go crashing through, kicking it behind me.

At the end of the alley he turns left, toward the marsh. We are back on Michigan Avenue. In plain sight of Erudite headquarters, if anyone cares to glance down the street.

"Bad idea!" I shout.

Peter takes the next right. At least all the streets here are clear—no fallen street signs to dodge or holes to jump over. My lungs burn like I inhaled poison. My legs, which ached at first, are now numb, which is better. Somewhere far away, I hear shouts.

Then it occurs to me: The least logical thing to do is stop running.

I grab Peter's sleeve and drag him toward the nearest building. It is six stories high, with wide windows arranged into a grid, divided by pillars of brick. The first door I try is locked, but Tobias fires at the window next to it until it breaks, and unlocks the door from the inside.

The building is completely empty. Not a single chair or table. And there are too many windows. We walk toward the emergency stairwell, and I crawl beneath the first flight so that we are hidden by the staircase. Tobias sits next to me, and Peter across from us both, his knees drawn to his chest.

I try to catch my breath and calm myself down, but it isn't easy. I was dead. I was *dead*, and then I wasn't, and why? Because of Peter? *Peter?*

I stare at him. He still looks so innocent, despite all that he has done to prove that he is not. His hair lies smooth against his head, shiny and dark, like we didn't just run for a mile at full speed. His round eyes scan the stairwell and then rest on my face.

"What?" he says. "Why are you looking at me like that?"

"How did you do it?" I say.

"It wasn't that hard," he says. "I dyed a paralytic serum purple and switched it out with the death serum. Replaced the wire that was supposed to read your heartbeat with a dead one. The bit with the heart monitor was harder; I had to get some Erudite help with a remote and stuff—you wouldn't understand it if I explained it to you."

"*Why* did you do it?" I say. "You *want* me dead. You were willing to do it yourself! What changed?"

He presses his lips together and doesn't look away, not for a long time. Then he opens his mouth, hesitates, and finally says, "I can't be in anyone's debt. Okay? The idea that I owed you something made me sick. I would wake up in the middle of the night feeling like I was going to vomit.

Indebted to a Stiff? It's ridiculous. Absolutely ridiculous. And I couldn't have it."

"What are you talking about? You owed me something?"

He rolls his eyes. "The Amity compound. Someone shot me—the bullet was at head level; it would have hit me right between the eyes. And you shoved me out of the way. We were even before that—I almost killed you during initiation, you almost killed me during the attack simulation; we're square, right? But after that . . ."

"You're insane," says Tobias. "That's not the way the world works . . . with everyone keeping score."

"It's not?" Peter raises his eyebrows. "I don't know what world *you* live in, but in mine, people only do things for you for one of two reasons. The first is if they want something in return. And the second is if they feel like they owe you something."

"Those aren't the only reasons people do things for you," I say. "Sometimes they do them because they love you. Well, maybe not *you*, but . . ."

Peter snorts. "That's exactly the kind of garbage I expect a delusional Stiff to say."

"I guess we just have to make sure you owe us," says Tobias. "Or you'll go running to whoever offers you the best deal."

"Yeah," Peter says. "That's pretty much how it is."

I shake my head. I can't imagine living the way he does—always keeping track of who gave me what and what I should give them in return, incapable of love or loyalty or forgiveness, a one-eyed man with a knife in hand, looking for someone else's eye to poke out. That isn't life. It's some paler version of life. I wonder where he learned it from.

"So when can we get out of here, you think?" Peter says.

"Couple hours," says Tobias. "We should go to the Abnegation sector. That's where the factionless and the Dauntless who aren't wired for simulations will be by now."

"Fantastic," says Peter.

Tobias puts his arm around me. I press my cheek into his shoulder, and close my eyes so I don't have to look at Peter. I know there is a lot to say, though I'm not sure exactly what it is, but we can't say it here, or now.

+ + +

As we walk the streets I once called home, conversations sputter and die, and eyes cling to my face and body. As far as they knew—and I'm sure they knew, because Jeanine knows how to spread news—I died less than six hours ago. I notice that some of the factionless I pass are marked with patches of blue dye. They are simulation-ready.

Now that we're here, and safe, I realize that there are cuts all over the bottoms of my feet from running over rough pavement and bits of glass from broken windows. Every step stings. I focus on that instead of all the stares.

"Tris?" someone calls out ahead of us. I lift my head, and see Uriah and Christina on the sidewalk, comparing revolvers. Uriah drops his gun in the grass and sprints toward me. Christina follows him, but at a slower pace.

Uriah reaches for me, but Tobias sets a hand on his shoulder to stop him. I feel a surge of gratitude. I don't think I can handle Uriah's embrace, or his questions, or his surprise, right now.

"She's been through a lot," Tobias says. "She just needs to sleep. She'll be down the street—number thirty-seven. Come visit tomorrow."

Uriah frowns at me. The Dauntless don't usually understand restraint, and Uriah has only ever known the Dauntless. But he must respect Tobias's assessment of me, because he nods and says, "Okay. Tomorrow."

Christina reaches out as I pass her and squeezes my shoulder lightly. I try to stand up straighter, but my muscles feel like a cage, holding my shoulders hunched. The eyes follow me down the street, pinching the back of my neck. I am relieved when Tobias leads us up the front walk of the gray house that belonged to Marcus Eaton.

I don't know by what strength Tobias marches through the doorway. For him this house must contain echoes of screaming parents and belt snaps and hours spent in small, dark closets, yet he doesn't look troubled as he leads Peter and me into the kitchen. If anything he stands taller. But maybe that is Tobias—when he's supposed to be weak, he's strong.

Tori, Harrison, and Evelyn stand in the kitchen. The sight overwhelms me. I lean my shoulder into the wall and squeeze my eyes shut. The outline of the execution table is printed on my eyelids. I open my eyes. I try to breathe. They are talking but I can't hear what they're saying. Why is Evelyn here, in Marcus's house? Where is Marcus?

Evelyn puts one arm around Tobias and touches his face with the other, pressing her cheek to his. She says something to him. He smiles at her when he pulls away. Mother and son, reconciled. I am not sure it's wise.

Tobias turns me around and, keeping one hand on my arm and one on my waist, to avoid my shoulder wound, presses me toward the staircase. We climb the steps together.

Upstairs are his parents' old bedroom and his old bedroom, with a bathroom between them, and that's it. He takes me into his bedroom, and I stand for a moment, looking around at the room where he spent most of his life.

He keeps his hand on my arm. He has been touching me in some way since we left the stairwell of that building, like he thinks I might break apart if he doesn't hold me together.

"Marcus didn't go into this room after I left, I'm pretty sure," says Tobias. "Because nothing was moved when I came back here."

Members of Abnegation don't own many decorations, since they are viewed as self-indulgent, but what few things we were allowed, he has. A stack of school papers. A small bookshelf. And, strangely, a sculpture made of blue glass on his dresser.

"My mother smuggled that to me when I was young. Told me to hide it," he says. "The day of the ceremony, I put it on my dresser before I left. So he would see it. A small act of defiance."

I nod. It is strange to be in a place that carries one single memory so completely. This room is sixteen-year-old Tobias, about to choose Dauntless to escape his father.

"Let's take care of your feet," he says. But he doesn't move, just shifts his fingers to the inside of my elbow.

"Okay," I say.

We walk into the adjoined bathroom, and I sit on the edge of the tub. He sits next to me, a hand on my knee as he turns on the faucet and plugs the drain. Water spills into the tub, covering my toenails. My blood turns the water pink.

He crouches in the tub and puts my foot in his lap, dabbing at the deeper cuts with a washcloth. I don't feel it. Even when he smears soap lather over them, I don't feel anything. The bathwater turns gray.

I pick up the bar of soap and turn it in my hands until my skin is coated with white lather. I reach for him and run my fingers over his hands, careful to get the lines in his palms and the spaces between his fingers. It feels good to do something, to clean something, and to have my hands on him again.

We get water all over the bathroom floor as we both splash it on ourselves to get the soap off. The water makes me cold, but I shiver and I don't care. He gets a towel and starts to dry my hands.

"I don't . . ." I sound like I am being strangled. "My family is all *dead*, or traitors; how can I . . ."

I am not making any sense. The sobs take over my body, my mind, everything. He gathers me to him, and bathwater soaks my legs. His hold is tight. I listen to his heartbeat and, after a while, find a way to let the rhythm calm me.

"I'll be your family now," he says.

"I love you," I say.

I said that once, before I went to Erudite headquarters, but he was asleep then. I don't know why I didn't say it when he could hear it. Maybe I was afraid to trust him with something so personal as my devotion. Or afraid that I did not know what it was to love someone. But now I think the scary thing was not saying it before it was almost too late. Not saying it before it was almost too late for me.

I am his, and he is mine, and it has been that way all along.

He stares at me. I wait with my hands clutching his arms for stability as he considers his response.

He frowns at me. "Say it again."

"Tobias," I say, "I love you."

His skin is slippery with water and he smells like sweat and my shirt sticks to his arms when he slides them around me. He presses his face to my neck and kisses me right above the collarbone, kisses my cheek, kisses my lips.

"I love you, too," he says.

CHAPTER
THIRTY-SEVEN

HE LIES NEXT to me as I fall asleep. I expect to have night-mares, but I must be too tired, because my mind stays empty. When I open my eyes next, he's gone, but there's a stack of clothes on the bed beside me.

I get up and walk into the bathroom and I feel raw, like my skin was scraped clean and every breath of air stings it a little, but stable. I don't turn on the lights in the bathroom because I know they will be pale and bright, just like the lights in the Erudite compound. I shower in the dark, barely able to tell soap from condi-tioner, and tell myself that I will emerge new and strong, that the water will heal me.

Before I leave the bathroom, I pinch my cheeks hard to bring blood to the surface of my skin. It's stupid, but I don't want to look weak and exhausted in front of everyone.

When I walk back into Tobias's room, Uriah is sprawled across the bed facedown; Christina is holding the blue sculpture above Tobias's desk, examining it; and Lynn is poised above Uriah with a pillow, a wicked grin creeping across her face.

Lynn smacks Uriah hard in the back of the head, Christina says, "Hey Tris!" and Uriah cries, "Ow! How on earth do you make a *pillow* hurt, Lynn?"

"My exceptional strength," she says. "Did you get smacked, Tris? One of your cheeks is bright red."

I must not have pinched the other one hard enough. "No, it's just . . . my morning glow."

I try the joke out on my tongue like it's a new language. Christina laughs, maybe a little harder than my comment warrants, but I appreciate the effort. Uriah bounces on the bed a few times when he moves to the edge.

"So, the thing we're all not talking about," he says. He gestures to me. "You almost died, a sadistic pansycake saved you, and now we're all waging some serious war with the factionless as allies."

"Pansycake?" says Christina.

"Dauntless slang." Lynn smirks. "Supposed to be a huge insult, only no one uses it anymore."

"Because it's so offensive," says Uriah, nodding.

"No. Because it's so stupid no Dauntless with any sense would speak it, let alone think it. Pansycake. What are you, twelve?"

"And a half," he says.

I get the feeling their banter is for my benefit, so that I don't have to say anything; I can just laugh. And I do, enough to warm the stone that has formed in my stomach.

"There's food downstairs," says Christina. "Tobias made scrambled eggs, which, as it turns out, is a disgusting food."

"Hey," I say. "I *like* scrambled eggs."

"Must be a Stiff breakfast, then." She grabs my arm. "C'mon."

Together we go down the stairs, our footsteps thundering as they never would have been allowed to in my parents' house. My father used to scold me for running down the stairs. "Do not call attention to yourself," he said. "It is not courteous to the people around you."

I hear voices in the living room—a chorus of them, in fact, joined by occasional bursts of laughter and a faint melody plucked on an instrument, a banjo or a guitar. It is not what I expect in an Abnegation house, where everything is always quiet, no matter how many people are gathered within. The voices and the laughter and the music breathe life into the sullen walls. I feel even warmer.

I stand in the doorway to the living room. Five people are crowded onto the three-person couch, playing a card game I recognize from Candor headquarters. A man sits in the armchair with a woman balanced on his lap, and someone else perches on the arm, a can of soup in hand. Tobias sits on the floor, his back against the coffee table. Every part of his posture suggests ease—one leg bent, the other straight, an arm slung across his knee, his head tilted to listen. I have never seen him look so comfortable without a gun. I didn't think it was possible.

I get the same sinking feeling in my stomach that I always get when I know I've been lied to, but I don't know who it was that lied to me this time, or about what, exactly. But this is not what I was taught to expect of factionlessness. I was taught that it was worse than death.

I stand there for just a few seconds before people realize that I'm there. Their conversation peters out. I wipe my palms off on the hem of my shirt. Too many eyes, and too much silence.

Evelyn clears her throat. "Everyone, this is Tris Prior. I believe you may have heard a lot about her yesterday."

"And Christina, Uriah, and Lynn," supplies Tobias. I'm grateful for his attempt to divert everyone's attention from me, but it doesn't work.

I stand glued to the door frame for a few seconds, and then one of the factionless men—older, his wrinkled skin patterned with tattoos—speaks up.

"Aren't you supposed to be dead?"

Some of the others laugh, and I try a smile. It emerges crooked and small.

"Supposed to be," I say.

"We don't like to give Jeanine Matthews what she wants, though," Tobias says. He gets up and hands me a can of peas—but it isn't full of peas; it's full of scrambled eggs. The aluminum warms my fingers.

He sits, so I sit next to him, and scoop some of the eggs into my mouth. I am not hungry, but I know I need to eat, so I chew and swallow anyway. I am familiar with the way the factionless eat, so I pass the eggs to Christina, and take a can of peaches from Tobias.

"Why is everyone camped out in Marcus's house?" I ask him.

"Evelyn kicked him out. Said it was her house, too, and he'd gotten to use it for years, and it was her turn." Tobias grins. "It caused a huge blowup on the front lawn, but eventually Evelyn won."

I glance at Tobias's mother. She is in the far corner of the room, talking to Peter and eating more eggs from another can. My stomach churns. Tobias talks about her almost reverently. But I still remember what she said to me about my transience in Tobias's life.

"There's bread somewhere." He picks up a basket from the coffee table and hands it to me. "Take two pieces. You need it."

As I chew on the bread crust, I look at Peter and Evelyn again.

"I think she's trying to recruit him," Tobias says. "She has a way of making the factionless life sound extraordinarily appealing."

"Anything to get him out of Dauntless. I don't care if he saved my life, I still don't like him."

"Hopefully we won't have to worry about faction distinctions anymore by the time this is over. It'll be nice, I think."

I don't say anything. I don't feel like picking a fight with him here. Or reminding him that it won't be so easy to persuade Dauntless and Candor to join the factionless in their crusade against the faction system. It may take another war.

The front door opens, and Edward enters. Today he wears a patch with a blue eye painted on it, complete with a half-lowered eyelid. The effect of the overlarge eye against his otherwise handsome face is both grotesque and amusing.

"Eddie!" someone calls out in greeting. But Edward's good eye has already fallen on Peter. He starts across the room, nearly kicking a can of food out of someone's hand. Peter presses into the shadow of the door frame like he is trying to disappear into it.

Edward stops inches from Peter's feet, and then jerks toward him like he is about to throw a punch. Peter jolts back so hard he slams his head into the wall. Edward grins, and all around us, the factionless laugh.

"Not so brave in broad daylight," Edward says. And then, to Evelyn, "Make sure you don't give him any utensils. Never know what he might do with them."

As he speaks, he plucks the fork from Peter's hand.

"Give that back," says Peter.

Edward slams his free hand into Peter's throat, and presses the tines of the fork between his fingers, right against Peter's Adam's apple. Peter stiffens, blood rushing into his face.

"Keep your mouth shut around me," he says, his voice low, "or I will do this again, only next time, I'll shove it right through your esophagus."

"That's enough," Evelyn says. Edward drops the fork

and releases Peter. Then he walks across the room and sits next to the person who called him "Eddie" a moment before.

"I don't know if you know this," Tobias says, "but Edward is a little unstable."

"I'm getting that," I say.

"That Drew guy, who helped Peter perform that butter-knife maneuver," Tobias says. "Apparently when he got kicked out of Dauntless, he tried to join the same group of factionless Edward was a part of. Notice that you haven't seen Drew anywhere."

"Did Edward kill him?" I say.

"Nearly," Tobias says. "Evidently that's why that other transfer—Myra, I think her name was?—left Edward. Too gentle to bear it."

I feel hollow at the thought of Drew, almost dead at the hands of Edward. Drew attacked me, too.

"I don't want to talk about this," I say.

"Okay," Tobias says. He touches my shoulder. "Is it hard for you to be in an Abnegation house again? I meant to ask before. We can go somewhere else, if it is."

I finish my second piece of bread. All Abnegation houses are the same, so this living room is exactly the same as my own, and it does bring back memories, if I look at it carefully. Light glowing through the blinds every morning, enough for my father to read by. The click of my mother's knitting needles every evening. But I don't feel like I'm choking. It's a start.

"Yes," I say. "But not as hard as you might think."

He raises an eyebrow.

"Really. The simulations in Erudite headquarters . . . helped me, somehow. To hold on, maybe." I frown. "Or maybe not. Maybe they helped me to stop holding on so tightly." That sounds right. "Someday I'll tell you about it." My voice sounds far away.

He touches my cheek and, even though we're in a room full of people, crowded by laughter and conversation, slowly kisses me.

"Whoa there, Tobias," says the man to my left. "Weren't you raised a Stiff? I thought the most you people did was . . . graze hands or something."

"Then how do you explain all the Abnegation children?" Tobias raises his eyebrows.

"They're brought into being by sheer force of will," the woman on the arm of the chair interjects. "Didn't you know that, Tobias?"

"No, I wasn't aware." He grins. "My apologies."

They all laugh. *We* all laugh. And it occurs to me that I might be meeting Tobias's true faction. They are not characterized by a particular virtue. They claim all colors, all activities, all virtues, and all flaws as their own.

I don't know what binds them together. The only common ground they have, as far as I know, is failure. Whatever it is, it seems to be enough.

I feel, as I look at him, that I am finally seeing him as he is, instead of how he is in relation to me. So how well do I really know him, if I have not seen this before?

+ + +

The sun is beginning to set. The Abnegation sector is far from quiet. The Dauntless and factionless wander the streets, some with bottles in their hands, some with guns in their other hands.

Ahead of me, Zeke pushes Shauna in her wheelchair past the house of Alice Brewster, former Abnegation leader. They don't see me.

"Do it again!" she says.

"Are you sure?"

"Yes!"

"Okay . . ." Zeke starts to jog behind the wheelchair. Then, when he's almost too far away for me to see, he pushes himself up with the handles so that his feet aren't touching the ground, and together they fly down the middle of the street, Shauna shrieking, Zeke laughing.

I turn left at the next intersection and start down the

cracked sidewalk toward the building where Abnegation had its monthly faction-wide meetings. Though it feels like it has been a long time since I last went there, I still remember where it is. One block south, two blocks west.

The sun inches toward the horizon as I walk. The color drains from the surrounding buildings in the evening light, so that they all appear to be gray.

The face of Abnegation headquarters is just a cement rectangle, like all the other buildings in the Abnegation sector. But when I shove the front door open, familiar wood floors and rows of wooden benches arranged in a square greet me. In the center of the room is a skylight that lets in a square of orange sunlight. It is the room's only adornment.

I sit on my family's old bench. I used to sit next to my father, and Caleb, next to my mother. Now I feel like the only one left. The last Prior.

"It's nice, isn't it?" Marcus walks in and sits down across from me, his hands folded in his lap. The sunlight is between us.

He has a large bruise on his jaw from where Tobias hit him, and his hair is freshly buzzed.

"It's fine," I say, straightening. "What are you doing here?"

"I saw you come in." He examines his fingernails

carefully. "And I want to have a word with you about the information Jeanine Matthews stole."

"What if you're too late? What if I already know what it is?"

Marcus looks up from his fingernails, and his dark eyes narrow. The look is far more poisonous than any Tobias could muster, though he has his father's eyes. "You can't possibly."

"You don't know that."

"I do, actually. Because I have seen what happens to people when they hear the truth. They look like they have forgotten what they were searching for, and are just wandering around trying to remember."

A chill makes its way up my spine and spreads down my arms, giving me goose bumps.

"I know that Jeanine decided to murder half a faction to steal it, so it must be incredibly important," I say. I pause. I know something else, too, but I only just realized it.

Right before I attacked Jeanine, she said, "This is not about you! It's not about me!"

And *this* meant what she was doing to me—trying to find a simulation that worked on me. On the Divergent.

"I know it has something to do with the Divergent," I blurt out. "I know the information is about what's outside the fence."

"That is not the same thing as knowing what's outside the fence."

"Well, are you going to tell me or are you going to dangle it over my head and make me jump for it?"

"I did not come here for self-indulgent arguing. And no, I am not going to tell you, but not because I don't want to. It's because I have no idea how to describe it to you. You have to see it for yourself."

As he speaks, I notice the sunlight turning more orange than yellow, and casting darker shadows over his face.

"I think Tobias might be right," I say. "You *like* to be the only one who knows. You like that I don't know. It makes you feel important. That's why you won't tell me, not because it's indescribable."

"That's not true."

"How am I supposed to know that?"

Marcus stares, and I stare back.

"A week before the simulation attack, the Abnegation leaders decided it was time to reveal the information in the file to everyone. *Everyone*, in the entire city. The day we intended to reveal it was approximately seven days after the simulation attack. Obviously we were unable to do so."

"She didn't want you to reveal what was outside the fence? Why not? How did she even know about it in the first place? I thought you said only the Abnegation leaders knew."

"We are not *from* here, Beatrice. We were all placed here, for a specific purpose. A while ago, the Abnegation were forced to enlist the help of Erudite in order to achieve that purpose, but eventually everything went awry because of Jeanine. Because she doesn't want to do what we are supposed to do. She would rather resort to murder."

Placed here.

My brain feels like it is buzzing with information. I clutch the edge of the bench beneath me.

"What are we supposed to do?" I say, my voice barely more than a whisper.

"I have told you enough to convince you that I am not a liar. As for the rest, I truly find myself unequal to the task of explaining it to you. I only told you as much as I did because the situation has become dire."

Dire. Suddenly I understand the problem. The factionless plan to destroy, not only the important figures in Erudite, but all the data they have. They will level everything.

I have never thought that plan was a good idea, but I knew that we could come back from it, because the Erudite still *know* the relevant information, even if they don't have their data. But this is something even the most intelligent Erudite do not know; something that, if every-thing is destroyed, we cannot replicate.

"If I help you, I betray Tobias. I will lose him." I swallow hard. "So you have to give me a good reason."

"Aside from the good of everyone in our society?" Marcus wrinkles his nose in disgust. "That isn't enough for you?"

"Our society is in pieces. So no, it's not."

Marcus sighs.

"Your parents died for *you*, it's true. But the reason your mother was in Abnegation headquarters the night you were almost executed was not to save you. She didn't know you were there. She was trying to rescue the file from Jeanine. And when she heard that you were about to die, she rushed to save you, and left the file in Jeanine's hands."

"That's not what she told me," I say hotly.

"She was lying. Because she had to. But Beatrice, the point is . . . the point is, your mother knew she probably would not get out of Abnegation headquarters alive, but she had to try. This file, it was something she was willing to die for. Understand?"

The Abnegation are willing to die for any person, friend or enemy, if the situation calls for it. That is, perhaps, why they find it difficult to survive in life-threatening situations. But there are few *things* they are willing to die for. They don't value many things in the physical world.

So if he's telling me the truth, and my mother really was willing to die for this information to become public . . . I would do just about anything to accomplish the goal she failed to achieve.

"You're trying to manipulate me. Aren't you."

"I suppose," he says as shadows slip into his eye sockets like dark water, "that is something you must decide for yourself."

CHAPTER
THIRTY-EIGHT

I TAKE MY time on my walk back to the Eaton house, and try to remember what my mother told me when she saved me from the tank during the simulation attack. Something about having watched the trains since the attack started. *I didn't know what I would do when I found you. But it was always my intention to save you.*

But when I go over the memory of her voice in my mind, it sounds different. *I didn't know what I would do, when I found you.* Meaning: I didn't know how to save both you and the file. *But it was always my intention to save you.*

I shake my head. Is that how she said it, or am I manipulating my own memory because of what Marcus told me? There is no way to know. All I can do is decide if I trust Marcus or not.

And while he has done cruel, evil things, our society is not divided into "good" and "bad." Cruelty does not make a person dishonest, the same way bravery does not make a person kind. Marcus is not good or bad, but both.

Well, he is probably more bad than good.

But that doesn't mean he's lying.

On the street ahead of me, I see the orange glow of fire. Alarmed, I walk faster, and see that the fire rises from large, man-sized metal bowls set up on the sidewalks. The Dauntless and the factionless have gathered between them, a narrow divide separating one group from the other. And before them stand Evelyn, Harrison, Tori, and Tobias.

I spot Christina, Uriah, Lynn, Zeke, and Shauna on the right side of the cluster of Dauntless, and stand with them.

"Where've you been?" Christina says. "We looked all over for you."

"I went for a walk. What's going on?"

"They're finally going to tell us the attack plan," says Uriah, looking eager.

"Oh," I say.

Evelyn lifts her hands, palms out, and the factionless fall silent. They are better trained than the Dauntless, whose voices take thirty seconds to peter out.

"The past few weeks, we have been developing a plan to fight the Erudite," Evelyn says, her low voice carrying easily. "And now that we have finished, we would like to share it with you."

Evelyn nods at Tori, who takes over. "Our strategy is not pointed, but broad. There is no way to know who among the Erudite supports Jeanine and who does not. It is therefore safer to assume that all those who do not support her have already vacated Erudite headquarters."

"We all know that Erudite's power lies not in its people but in its information," says Evelyn. "As long as they still possess that information, we will never be free of them, especially while large numbers of us are wired for simulations. They have used information to control us and keep us under their thumb for far too long."

A shout, beginning among the factionless and spreading to the Dauntless, rises up from the crowd like we are all parts of one organism, following the commands of a single brain. But I am not sure what I think, or how I feel. There is a part of me that is shouting, too—clamoring for the destruction of every single Erudite and all that they hold dear.

I look at Tobias. His expression is neutral, and he stands behind the glow of firelight, where he is difficult to see. I wonder what he thinks of this.

"I am sorry to tell you that those of you who were shot with simulation transmitters will have to remain here," says Tori, "or you can be activated as a weapon of Erudite at any time."

There are a few cries of protest, but no one seems all that surprised. They know too well what Jeanine can do with simulations, maybe.

Lynn groans and looks at Uriah. "We have to *stay*?"

"*You* have to stay," he says.

"You got shot too," she says. "I saw it."

"Divergent, remember?" he says. Lynn rolls her eyes, and he hurries on, probably to avoid hearing Lynn's Divergent conspiracy theory again. "Anyway, I bet you no one checks, and what are the odds she'll activate you, specifically, if she knows everyone else with simulation transmitters is staying behind?"

Lynn frowns, considering this. But she looks more cheerful—as cheerful as Lynn gets, anyway—as Tori begins speaking again.

"The rest of us will divide into groups of mixed factionless and Dauntless," says Tori. "A single, large group will attempt to penetrate Erudite headquarters and work its way up through the building, cleansing it of Erudite's influence. Several other, smaller groups will proceed

420

immediately to the higher levels of the building to dispense with certain key Erudite officials. You will receive your group assignments later this evening."

"The attack will occur in three days' time," says Evelyn. "Prepare yourselves. This will be dangerous and difficult. But the factionless are familiar with difficulty—"

At this the factionless cheer, and I am reminded that we, the Dauntless, are the same people who, just a few weeks ago, were criticizing Abnegation for giving the factionless food and other necessary items. How was that so easy to forget?

"And the Dauntless are familiar with danger—"

Everyone around me punches the air with their fists and screams. I feel their voices inside my head, and the burn of triumph in my chest that makes me want to join them.

Evelyn's expression is too empty for someone giving an impassioned speech. Her face looks like a mask.

"Down with Erudite!" Tori yells, and everyone repeats her, all voices joining together, regardless of faction. We share a common enemy, but does that make us friends?

I notice that Tobias does not join in the chant, and neither does Christina.

"This doesn't feel right," she says.

"What do you mean?" Lynn says as the voices rise around us. "Don't you remember what they did to us? Put our minds under a simulation and forced us to shoot people without even knowing it? Murdered every single Abnegation leader?"

"Yeah," says Christina. "It's just . . . Invading a faction's headquarters and killing everyone, isn't that what the Erudite just did to Abnegation?"

"This is different. *This* is not an attack out of nowhere, unprovoked," says Lynn, scowling at her.

"Yeah," Christina says. "Yeah, I know."

She looks at me. I don't say anything. She has a point—it doesn't feel right.

I walk toward the Eaton house in search of silence.

I open the front door and climb the stairs. When I reach Tobias's old room, I sit on the bed and look out the window, where factionless and Dauntless are gathered around the fires, laughing and talking. But they aren't mixed together; there is still an uneasy divide between them, factionless on one side and Dauntless on the other.

I watch Lynn, Uriah, and Christina by one of the fires. Uriah snatches at the flames, too quickly to be burned. His smile looks more like a grimace, twisted as it is by grief.

After a few minutes I hear footsteps on the stairs, and Tobias comes into the room, slipping off his shoes by the doorway.

"What's wrong?" he says.

"Nothing, really," I say. "I was just thinking, I'm surprised the factionless agreed to work with Dauntless so easily. It's not like the Dauntless were ever kind to them."

He stands beside me at the window and leans into the frame.

"It's not a natural alliance, is it," he says. "But we have the same goal."

"Right now. But what happens when the goals change? The factionless want to get rid of factions, and the Dauntless don't."

Tobias presses his mouth into a line. I suddenly remember Marcus and Johanna, walking together through the orchard—Marcus wore the same expression when he was keeping something from her.

Did Tobias get that expression from his father? Or does it mean something different?

"You're in my group," he says. "During the attack. I hope you don't mind. We're supposed to lead the way to the control rooms."

The attack. If I participate in the attack, I can't go after the information Jeanine stole from Abnegation. I have to choose one or the other.

Tobias said that dealing with Erudite was more important than finding out the truth. And if he had not promised the factionless control over all of Erudite's data, he might have been right. But he left me no choice. I have to help Marcus, if there is even a chance that he is telling the truth. I have to work against the people I love best.

And right now, I have to lie.

I twist my fingers together.

"What is it?" he says.

"I still can't fire a gun." I look up at him. "And after what happened in Erudite headquarters . . ." I clear my throat. "Risking my life doesn't seem so appealing anymore."

"Tris." He brushes my cheek with his fingertips. "You don't have to go."

"I don't want to seem like a coward."

"Hey." His fingers fit beneath my jaw. They are cool against my skin. He looks sternly at me. "You have done more for this faction than any other person. You . . ."

He sighs, and touches his forehead to mine.

"You're the bravest person I've ever met. Stay here. Let yourself mend."

He kisses me, and I feel like I am crumbling again,

beginning with the deepest parts of me. He thinks I will be here, but I will be working against him, working with the father he despises. This lie—this lie is the worst I have ever told. I will never be able to take it back.

When we part, I am afraid he will hear my breaths shake, so I turn toward the window.

CHAPTER
THIRTY-NINE

"OH YEAH. YOU totally look like a banjo-strumming softie," says Christina.

"Really?"

"No. Not at all, actually. Just . . . let me fix it, okay?"

She rummages in her bag for a few seconds and pulls out a small box. In it are different-sized tubes and containers that I recognize as makeup, but wouldn't know what to do with.

We are in my parents' house. It was the only place I could think of to go to get ready. Christina has no reservations about poking around—she already discovered two textbooks wedged between the dresser and the wall, evidence of Caleb's Erudite leanings.

"Let me get this straight. So you left the Dauntless

compound to get ready for war . . . and took your makeup bag with you?"

"Yep. Figured it would be harder for anyone to shoot me if they saw how devastatingly attractive I was," she says, arching an eyebrow. "Hold still."

She takes the cap off a black tube about the size of one of my fingers, revealing a red stick. Lipstick, obviously. She touches it to my mouth and dabs it until my lips are covered in color. I can see it when I purse them.

"Has anyone ever talked to you about the miracle of eyebrow tweezing?" she says, holding up a pair of tweezers.

"Get those away from me."

"Fine." She sighs. "I would take out the blush, but I'm pretty sure it's not the right color for you."

"Shocking, considering we're so similar in skin tone."

"Ha-ha," she says.

By the time we leave, I have red lips and curled eyelashes, and I'm wearing a bright red dress. And there's a knife strapped to the inside of my knee. This all makes perfect sense.

"Where's Marcus, Destroyer of Lives, going to meet us?" Christina says. She wears Amity yellow instead of red, and it glows against her skin.

I laugh. "Behind Abnegation headquarters."

We walk down the sidewalk in the dark. All the others

should be eating dinner now—I made sure of that—but in case we run into someone, we wear black jackets to conceal most of our Amity clothing. I hop over a crack in the cement out of habit.

"Where are you two going?" Peter's voice says. I look over my shoulder. He's standing on the sidewalk behind us. I wonder how long he's been there.

"Why aren't you with your attack group, eating dinner?" I say.

"I don't have one." He taps the arm I shot. "I'm injured."

"Yeah right, you are!" says Christina.

"Well, I don't want to go to battle with a bunch of factionless," he says, his green eyes glinting. "So I'm going to stay here."

"Like a coward," says Christina, her lip curled in disgust. "Let everyone else clean up the mess for you."

"Yep!" he says with a kind of malicious cheer. He claps his hands. "Have fun dying."

He crosses the street, whistling, and walks in the other direction.

"Well, we distracted him," she says. "He didn't ask where we were going again."

"Yeah. Good." I clear my throat. "So, this plan. It's kind of stupid, right?"

"It's not . . . *stupid*."

"Oh, come on. Trusting Marcus is stupid. Trying to get past the Dauntless at the fence is stupid. Going against the Dauntless and factionless is stupid. All three combined is . . . a different kind of stupid formerly unheard of by humankind."

"Unfortunately it's also the best plan we have," she points out. "If we want everyone to know the truth."

I trusted Christina to take up this mission when I thought I would die, so it seemed stupid not to trust her now. I was worried she wouldn't want to come with me, but I forgot where Christina came from: Candor, where the pursuit of truth is more important than anything else. She may be Dauntless now, but if there's one thing I've learned through all this, it's that we never leave our old factions behind.

"So this is where you grew up. Did you like it here?" She frowns. "I guess you couldn't have, if you wanted to leave."

The sun inches toward the horizon as we walk. I never used to like evening light because it made everything in the Abnegation sector look more monochromatic than it already is, but now I find the unchanging gray comforting.

"I liked some things and hated some things," I say. "And there were some things I didn't know I had until I lost them."

We reach Abnegation headquarters, and its face is just a cement square like everything else in the Abnegation sector. I would love to walk into the meeting room and breathe the smell of old wood, but we don't have time. We slip into the alley next to the building and walk to the back, where Marcus told me he would be waiting.

A powder-blue pickup truck waits there, its engine running. Marcus is behind the wheel. I let Christina walk ahead of me so that she can be the one to slide into the middle. I don't want to sit close to him if I can help it. I feel like hating him while I work with him lessens my betrayal of Tobias somehow.

You have no other choice, I tell myself. *There is no other way.*

With that in mind, I pull the door shut and look for a seat belt to buckle. I find only the frayed end of a seat belt and a broken buckle.

"Where did you find this piece of junk?" says Christina.

"I stole it from the factionless. They fix them up. It wasn't easy to get it to start. Better ditch those jackets, girls."

I ball up our jackets and toss them out the half-open window. Marcus shifts the truck into drive, and it groans.

I half expect it to stay still when he presses the gas pedal, but it moves.

From what I remember, it takes about an hour to drive from the Abnegation sector to Amity headquarters, and the trip requires a skilled driver. Marcus pulls onto one of the main thoroughfares and pushes his foot into the gas pedal. We lurch forward, narrowly avoiding a gaping hole in the road. I grab the dashboard to steady myself.

"Relax, Beatrice," says Marcus. "I've driven a car before."

"I've done a lot of things before, but that doesn't mean I'm any good at them!"

Marcus smiles and jerks the truck to the left so that we don't hit a fallen stoplight. Christina whoops as we bump over another piece of debris, like she's having the time of her life.

"A different kind of stupid, right?" she says, her voice loud enough to be heard over the rush of wind through the cab.

I clutch the seat beneath me and try not to think of what I ate for dinner.

+ + +

When we reach the fence, we see the Dauntless standing in our headlight beams, blocking the gate. Their blue armbands stand out against the rest of their clothing. I try to keep my expression pleasant. I will not be able to fool them into thinking I'm Amity with a scowl on my face.

A dark-skinned man with a gun in hand approaches Marcus's window. He shines a flashlight at Marcus first, then Christina, then me. I squint into the beam, and force a smile at the man like I don't mind bright lights in the eyes and guns pointed at my head in the slightest.

The Amity must be deranged if this is how they really think. Or they've been eating too much of that bread.

"So tell me," the man says. "What's an Abnegation member doing in a truck with two Amity?"

"These two girls volunteered to bring provisions to the city," Marcus says, "and I volunteered to escort them so that they would be safe."

"Also, we don't know how to drive," says Christina, grinning. "My dad tried to teach me years ago but I kept confusing the gas pedal for the brake pedal, and you can imagine what a disaster that was! Anyway, it was *really* nice of Joshua to volunteer to take us, because it would have taken us forever otherwise, and the boxes were *so* heavy—"

The Dauntless man holds up his hand. "Okay, I get it."

"Oh, of course. Sorry." Christina giggles. "I just thought I would explain, because you seemed so confused, and no wonder, because how many times do you encounter this—"

"Right," the man says. "And do you intend to return to the city?"

"Not anytime soon," Marcus says.

"All right. Go ahead, then." He nods to the other Dauntless by the gate. One of them types a series of numbers on the keypad, and the gate slides open to admit us. Marcus nods to the guard who let us through and drives over the worn path to Amity headquarters. The truck's headlights catch tire tracks and prairie grass and insects weaving back and forth. In the darkness to my right I see fireflies lighting up to a rhythm that is like a heartbeat.

After a few seconds, Marcus glances at Christina. "What on earth was *that*?"

"There's nothing the Dauntless hate more than cheerful Amity babble," says Christina, lifting a shoulder. "I figured if he got annoyed it would distract him and he would let us through."

I smile with all my teeth. "You are a *genius*."

"I know." She tosses her head like she's throwing her hair over one shoulder, only she doesn't have enough to throw.

"Except," says Marcus, "Joshua is not an Abnegation name."

"Whatever. As if anyone knows the difference."

I see the glow of Amity headquarters ahead, the familiar cluster of wooden buildings with the greenhouse in their center. We drive through the apple orchard. The air smells like warm earth.

Again I remember my mother stretching to pick an apple in this orchard, years ago when we came to help the Amity with the harvest. A pang hurts my chest, but the memory doesn't overwhelm me as it did a few weeks ago. Maybe it's because I am on a mission to honor her. Or maybe I am too apprehensive about what's coming to grieve properly. But something has changed.

Marcus parks the truck behind one of the sleeping cabins. For the first time I notice that there are no keys in the ignition.

"How did you get it to start?" I ask him.

"My father taught me a lot about mechanics and computers," he says. "Knowledge that I passed to my own son. You didn't think he figured it all out on his own, did you?"

"Actually yes, I did." I push the door open and climb out of the truck. Grass brushes my toes and the back of my calves. Christina stands at my right shoulder and tilts her head back.

"It's so different out here," she says. "You could almost forget what's going on in *there*." She points her thumb toward the city.

"And they often do," I say.

"They know what's beyond the city, though, right?" she asks.

"They know about as much as the Dauntless patrols," says Marcus. "Which is that the outside world is unknown and potentially dangerous."

"How do you know what they know?" I say.

"Because that's what we told them," he says, and he walks toward the greenhouse.

I exchange a look with Christina. Then we jog to catch up to him.

"What does *that* mean?"

"When you are entrusted with all the information, you have to decide how much other people should know," says Marcus. "The Abnegation leaders told them what we had to tell them. Now, let's hope Johanna is keeping up her normal habits. She is usually in the greenhouse this early in the evening."

He opens the greenhouse door. The air is just as dense as the last time I was in here, but now it is misty, too. The moisture cools my cheeks.

"Wow," Christina says.

The room is lit by moonlight, so it is hard to distinguish plant from tree from man-made structure. Leaves brush my face as I make my way around the outer edge of the room. And then I see Johanna, crouched beside a bush with a bowl in her hands, picking what appear to be raspberries. Her hair is pulled back, so I can see her scar.

"I didn't think I would see you here again, Ms. Prior," she says.

"Is that because I'm supposed to be dead?" I say.

"I always expect those who live by the gun to die by it. I am often pleasantly surprised." She balances the bowl on her knees and looks up at me. "Although I also know better than to think you came back because you like it here."

"No," I say. "We came for something else."

"All right," she says, standing. "Let's go talk about it, then."

She carries the bowl toward the middle of the room, where the Amity meetings are held. We follow her onto the tree roots, where she sits and offers me the bowl of raspberries. I take a small handful of berries and pass the bowl to Christina.

"Johanna, this is Christina," Marcus says. "Candor-born Dauntless."

"Welcome to Amity headquarters, Christina." Johanna smiles knowingly. It seems so strange, that two people born in Candor could end up in such different places: Dauntless, and Amity.

"Tell me, Marcus," says Johanna. "Why have you come to visit?"

"I think Beatrice should handle that," he says. "I am merely the transportation."

She shifts her focus to me without question, but I can tell by the wary look in her eyes that she would rather talk to Marcus. She would deny it if I asked her, but I am almost certain Johanna Reyes hates me.

"Um . . ." I say. Not my most brilliant opening. I wipe my palms on my skirt. "Things have gotten bad."

The words start to spill out, without finesse or sophistication. I explain that the Dauntless have allied with the factionless, and they plan to destroy all of Erudite, leaving us without one of the two essential factions. I tell her that there is important information in the Erudite compound, in addition to all the knowledge they possess, that especially needs to be recovered. When I finish, I realize I haven't told her why that has anything to do with her or her faction, but I don't know how to say it.

"I'm confused, Beatrice," she says. "What exactly do you want us to do?"

"I didn't come here to ask you for help," I say. "I thought you should know that a lot of people are going to die, very soon. And I know you don't want to stay here doing nothing while that happens, even if some of your faction does."

She looks down, her crooked mouth betraying just how right I am.

"I also wanted to ask you if we can talk to the Erudite you're keeping safe here," I say. "I know they're hidden, but I need access to them."

"And what do you intend to do?" she says.

"Shoot them," I say, rolling my eyes.

"That isn't funny."

I sigh. "Sorry. I need information. That's all."

"Well, you'll have to wait until tomorrow," Johanna says. "You can sleep here."

+ + +

I sleep as soon as my head touches the pillow, but wake earlier than I planned. I can tell by the glow near the horizon that the sun is about to rise.

Across the narrow aisle between two beds is Christina, her face pressed to the mattress with her pillow over her head. A dresser with a lamp on top of it stands between us. The wooden floorboards creak no matter where you step on them. And on the left wall is a mirror, casually placed. Everyone but the Abnegation takes mirrors for granted. I still feel a prickle of shock whenever I see one in the open.

I get dressed, not bothering to be quiet—five hundred stomping Dauntless can't wake Christina when she's deeply asleep, though an Erudite whisper might be able to. She is odd that way.

I walk outside as the sun peeks through the tree branches, and see a small group of Amity gathered near the orchard. I move closer to see what they are doing.

They stand in a circle, hands clasped. Half of them are in their early teens, and the other half are adults. The oldest one, a woman with braided gray hair, speaks.

"We believe in a God who gives peace and cherishes it," she says. "So we give peace to each other, and cherish it."

I would not hear that as a cue, but the Amity seem to. They all begin to move at once, finding someone across the circle and clasping hands with them. When everyone is paired off, they stand for several seconds, looking at each other. Some of them mutter a phrase, some smile, some remain silent and still. Then they break apart and move to someone else, performing the same series of actions again.

I have never seen an Amity religious ceremony before.

I am only familiar with the religion of my parents' faction, which part of me still holds to and the other rejects as foolishness—the prayers before dinner, the weekly meetings, the acts of service, the poems about a selfless God. This is something different, something mysterious.

"Come and join us," the gray-haired woman says. It takes me a few seconds to realize she's talking to me. She beckons to me, smiling.

"Oh no," I say. "I'm just—"

"Come," she says again, and I feel like I have no choice but to walk forward and stand among them.

She approaches me first, clasping my hand. Her fingers are dry and rough and her eyes seek mine, persistent, though I feel strange meeting her gaze.

Once I do, the effect is immediate and peculiar. I stand still, and every part of me is still, like it weighs more than it used to, only the weight is not unpleasant. Her eyes are brown, the same shade throughout, and unmoving.

"May the peace of God be with you," she says, her voice low, "even in the midst of trouble."

"Why would it?" I say softly, so no one else can hear. "After all I've done . . ."

"It isn't about you," she says. "It is a gift. You cannot earn it, or it ceases to be a gift."

She releases me and moves to someone else, but I stand

with my hand outstretched, alone. Someone moves to take my hand, but I withdraw from the group, first at a walk, and then at a run.

I sprint into the trees as fast as I can, and only when my lungs feel like they are on fire do I stop.

I press my forehead to the nearest tree trunk, though it scrapes my skin, and fight off tears.

+ + +

Later that morning I walk through light rain to the main greenhouse. Johanna has called an emergency meeting.

I stay as hidden as possible at the edge of the room, between two large plants that are suspended in mineral solution. It takes me a few minutes to find Christina, dressed in Amity yellow on the right side of the room, but it is easy to spot Marcus, who stands on the roots of the giant tree with Johanna.

Johanna has her hands clasped in front of her and her hair pulled back. The injury that gave her the scar also damaged her eye—her pupil is so dilated it overwhelms her iris, and her left eye doesn't move with the right one as she scans the Amity in front of her.

But there are not just Amity. There are people with close-cropped hair and tightly twisted buns who must belong to Abnegation, and a few rows of people in glasses who must be Erudite. Cara is among them.

"I have received a message from the city," says Johanna when everyone quiets down. "And I would like to communicate it to you."

She tugs at the hem of her shirt, then clasps her hands in front of her. She seems nervous.

"The Dauntless have allied with the factionless," she says. "They intend to attack Erudite in two days' time. Their battle will be waged not against the Erudite-Dauntless army but against Erudite innocents and the knowledge they have worked so hard to acquire."

She looks down, breathes deeply, and continues: "I know that we recognize no leader, so I have no right to address you as if that is what I am," she says. "But I am hoping that you will forgive me, just this once, for asking if we can reconsider our previous decision to remain uninvolved."

There are murmurs. They are nothing like Dauntless murmurs—they are gentler, like birds launching from branches.

"Our relationship with Erudite notwithstanding, we know better than any faction how essential their role in this society is," she says. "They must be protected from needless slaughter, if not because they are human beings, then because we cannot survive without them. I propose that we enter the city as nonviolent, impartial peacekeepers in order to curb in whatever way possible the extreme violence that will undoubtedly occur. Please discuss this."

Rain dusts the glass panels above our heads. Johanna sits on a tree root to wait, but the Amity do not burst into conversation as they did the last time I was here. Whispers, almost indistinguishable from the rain, turn to normal speech, and I hear some voices lift above others, almost yelling, but not quite.

Every lifted voice sends a jolt through me. I've sat through plenty of arguments in my life, mostly in the last two months, but none of them ever scared me like this. The Amity aren't supposed to argue.

I decide not to wait any longer. I walk along the edge of the meeting area, squeezing past the Amity who are on their feet and hopping over hands and outstretched legs. Some of them stare at me—I may be wearing a red shirt, but the tattoos along my collarbone are clear as ever, even from a distance.

I pause near the row of Erudite. Cara stands when I get close, her arms folded.

"What are you doing here?" she says.

"I came to tell Johanna what was going on," I say. "And to ask you for help."

"Me?" she says. "Why—"

"Not *you*," I say. I try to forget what she said about my nose, but it's hard. "All of you. I have a plan to save some of your faction's data, but I need your help."

"Actually," Christina says, appearing at my left shoulder, "*we* have a plan."

Cara looks from me to Christina and back to me again.

"*You* want to help Erudite?" she says. "I'm confused."

"You wanted to help Dauntless," I say. "You think you're the only one who doesn't just blindly do what your faction tells you to?"

"It is in keeping with your pattern of behavior," says Cara. "Shooting people who get in your way is a Dauntless trait, after all."

I feel a pinch at the back of my throat. She looks so much like her brother, down to the crease between her eyebrows and the dark streaks in her otherwise blond hair.

"Cara," says Christina. "Will you help us, or not?"

Cara sighs. "Obviously I will. I'm sure the others will, too. Meet us in the Erudite dormitory at the end of the meeting, and tell us the plan."

+ + +

The meeting lasts for another hour. By then the rain has stopped, though water still sprinkles the wall and ceiling panels. Christina and I have been sitting against one of the walls, playing a game in which each of us tries to pin down the other's thumb. She always wins.

Finally Johanna and the others who emerged as discussion leaders stand in a line on the tree roots. Johanna's hair now hangs over her lowered face. She is supposed to tell us the outcome of the conversation, but she just stands with her arms folded, her fingers tapping against her elbow.

"What's going on?" Christina says.

Finally Johanna looks up.

"Obviously it was difficult to find agreement," she says. "But the majority of you wish to uphold our policy of uninvolvement."

It does not matter to me whether the Amity decide to go into the city or not. But I had begun to hope they were not all cowards, and to me, this decision sounds very much like cowardice. I sink back against the window.

"It is not my wish to encourage division in this community, which has given so much to me," says Johanna. "But my conscience forces me to go against this decision. Anyone else whose conscience drives them toward the city is welcome to come with me."

At first I, like everyone else, am not sure what she's saying. Johanna tilts her head so that her scar is again visible, and adds, "I understand if this means I can't be a part of Amity anymore." She sniffs. "But please know that if I have to leave you, I leave you with love, rather than malice."

Johanna bows in the general direction of the crowd, tucks her hair behind her ears, and walks toward the exit. A few of the Amity scramble to their feet, then a few more, and soon the entire crowd is on their feet, and some of them—not many, but some—are walking out behind her.

"That," says Christina, "is not what I was expecting."

CHAPTER
FORTY

THE ERUDITE DORMITORY is one of the larger sleeping rooms in Amity headquarters. There are twelve beds total: a row of eight crammed together along the far wall, and two pressed together on each side, leaving a huge space in the middle of the room. A large table occupies that space, covered with tools and scraps of metal and gears and old computer parts and wires.

Christina and I just finished explaining our plan, which sounded a lot dumber with more than a dozen Erudite staring us down as we talked.

"Your plan is flawed," Cara says. She is the first to respond.

"That's why we came to you," I say. "So you could tell us how to fix it."

"Well, first of all, this important data you want to rescue," she says. "Putting it on a disc is a ridiculous idea. Discs just end up breaking or in the wrong person's hands, like all other physical objects. I suggest you make use of the data network."

"The . . . what?"

She glances at the other Erudite. One of the others—a brown-skinned young man in glasses—says, "Go on. Tell them. There's no reason to keep secrets anymore."

Cara looks back at me. "Many of the computers in the Erudite compound are set up to access data from the computers in other factions. That's how it was so easy for Jeanine to run the attack simulation from a Dauntless computer instead of an Erudite one."

"What?" says Christina. "You mean you can just take a stroll through every faction's data whenever you want?"

"You can't 'take a stroll' through data," the young man says. "That's illogical."

"It's a metaphor," says Christina. She frowns. "Right?"

"A metaphor, or simply a figure of speech?" he says, also frowning. "Or is a metaphor a definite category beneath the heading of 'figure of speech'?"

"Fernando," says Cara. "Focus."

He nods.

"The fact is," Cara continues, "the data network exists,

and that is ethically questionable, but I believe it can work to our advantage here. Just as the computers can access data from other factions, they can *send* data to other factions. If we sent the data you wished to rescue to every other faction, destroying it all would be impossible."

"When you say 'we,'" I say, "are you implying that—"

"That we would be going with you?" she says. "Obviously not all of us would go, but some of us must. How do you expect to navigate Erudite headquarters on your own?"

"You do realize that if you come with us, you might get shot," says Christina. She smiles. "And no hiding behind us because you don't want to break your glasses, or whatever."

Cara removes her glasses and snaps them in half at the bridge.

"We risked our lives by defecting from our faction," says Cara, "and we will risk them again to save our faction from itself."

"Also," pipes up a small voice behind Cara. A girl no older than ten or eleven peers around Cara's elbow. Her black hair is short, like mine, and a halo of frizz surrounds her head. "We have useful gadgets."

Christina and I exchange a look.

I say, "What kinds of gadgets?"

"They're just prototypes," Fernando says, "so there's no need to scrutinize them."

"Scrutiny's not really our thing," says Christina.

"Then how do you make things better?" the little girl asks.

"We don't, really," Christina says, sighing. "They kind of just keep getting worse."

The little girl nods. "Entropy."

"What?"

"Entropy," she chirps. "It's the theory that all matter in the universe is gradually moving toward the same temperature. Also known as 'heat death.'"

"Elia," Cara says, "that is a gross oversimplification."

Elia sticks out her tongue at Cara. I can't help but laugh. I have never seen one of the Erudite stick out her tongue before. But then again, I haven't interacted with many young Erudite. Only Jeanine and the people who work for her. Including my brother.

Fernando crouches next to one of the beds and takes out a box. He digs inside it for a few seconds, then picks up a small, round disc. It is made of a pale metal that I saw often in Erudite headquarters but have never seen anywhere else. He carries it toward me on his palm. When I reach for it, he jerks it away from me.

"Careful!" he says. "I brought this from headquarters. It's not something we invented here. Were you there when they attacked Candor?"

"Yes," I say. "*Right* there."

"Remember when the glass shattered?"

"Were *you* there?" I say, narrowing my eyes.

"No. They recorded it and showed the footage at Erudite headquarters," he says. "Well, it looked like the glass shattered because they shot at it, but that's not really true. One of the Dauntless soldiers tossed one of *these* near the windows. It emits a signal that you can't hear, but that will cause glass to shatter."

"Okay," I say. "And how will that be useful to us?"

"You may find that it's rather distracting for people when all their windows shatter at once," he says with a small smile. "Especially in Erudite headquarters, where there are a lot of windows."

"Right," I say.

"What else have you got?" says Christina.

"The Amity will like this," Cara says. "Where is it? Ah. Here."

She picks up a black box made of plastic, small enough for her to wrap her fingers around it. At the top of the box are two pieces of metal that look like teeth. She flips a switch at the bottom of the box, and a thread of blue light stretches across the gap between the teeth.

"Fernando," says Cara. "Want to demonstrate?"

"Are you joking?" he says, his eyes wide. "I'm never doing that again. You're dangerous with that thing."

Cara grins at him, and explains, "If I touched you with this stunner right now, it would be extremely painful, and then it would disable you. Fernando found that out the hard way yesterday. I made it so that the Amity would have a way of defending themselves without shooting anyone."

"That's . . ." I frown. "Understanding of you."

"Well, technology is supposed to make life better," she says. "No matter what you believe, there's a technology out there for you."

What did my mother say, in that simulation? "I worry that your father's blustering about Erudite has been to your detriment." What if she was right, even if she was just a part of a simulation? My father taught me to see Erudite a particular way. He never taught me that they made no judgments about what people believed, but designed things for them within the confines of those beliefs. He never told me that they could be funny, or that they could critique their own faction from the inside.

Cara lunges toward Fernando with the stunner,

laughing when he jumps back.

He never told me that an Erudite could offer to help me even after I killed her brother.

+ + +

The attack will begin in the afternoon, before it is too dark to see the blue armbands that mark some of the Dauntless as traitors. As soon as our plans are finalized, we walk through the orchard to the clearing where the trucks are kept. When I emerge from the trees, I see that Johanna Reyes is perched on the hood of one of the trucks, the keys dangling from her fingers.

Behind her waits a small convoy of vehicles packed with Amity—but not just Amity, because Abnegation, with their severe hairstyles and still mouths, are among them. Robert, Susan's older brother, is with them.

Johanna hops down from the hood. In the back of the truck she was just sitting on is a stack of crates marked APPLES and FLOUR and CORN. It's a good thing we only have to fit two people in the back.

"Hello, Johanna," says Marcus.

"Marcus," she says. "I hope you don't mind if we accompany you to the city."

"Of course not," he says. "Lead the way."

Johanna gives Marcus the keys and climbs into the

bed of one of the other trucks. Christina starts toward the truck cab, and I go for the truck bed, with Fernando behind me.

"You don't want to sit up front?" says Christina. "And you call yourself a Dauntless. . . ."

"I went for the part of the truck in which I was least likely to vomit," I say.

"Puking is a part of life."

I am about to ask her exactly how often she intends to throw up in the future when the truck surges forward. I grab the side with both hands so that I don't fall out, but after a few minutes, when I get used to the bumping and jostling, I let go. The other trucks trundle along in front of us, behind Johanna's, which leads the way.

I feel calm until we reach the fence. I expect to encounter the same guards who tried to stop us on the way in, but the gate is abandoned, left open. A tremor starts in my chest and spreads to my hands. In the midst of meeting new people and making plans, I forgot that my plan is to walk straight into a battle that could claim my life. Right after I realized that my life was worth living.

The convoy slows down as we pass through the fence, like they expect someone to jump out and stop us. Everything is silent apart from the cicadas in the distant trees and the truck engines.

"Do you think it's already started?" I say to Fernando.

"Perhaps. Perhaps not," he says. "Jeanine has many informants. Someone probably told her that something was going to happen, so she called all the Dauntless forces back to Erudite headquarters."

I nod, but I am really thinking of Caleb. He was one of those informants. I wonder why he believed so strongly that the outside world should be hidden from us that he would betray everyone he supposedly cared about for Jeanine, who cares about no one.

"Did you ever meet someone named Caleb?" I say.

"Caleb," Fernando says. "Yes, there was a Caleb in my initiate class. Brilliant, but he was . . . what's the colloquial term for it? A suck-up." He smirks. "There was a bit of a division between initiates. Those who embraced everything Jeanine said and those who didn't. Obviously I was a member of the latter group. Caleb was a member of the former. Why do you ask?"

"I met him while I was imprisoned," I say, and my voice sounds far away even to me. "I was just curious."

"I wouldn't judge him too harshly," says Fernando. "Jeanine can be extraordinarily persuasive to those who aren't naturally suspicious. I have always been naturally suspicious."

I stare over his left shoulder, at the skyline that gets

clearer the closer we get to the city. I search for the two prongs at the top of the Hub, and when I find them, I feel better and worse at the same time—better, because the building is so familiar, and worse, because seeing the prongs means that we are getting closer.

"Yeah," I say. "So have I."

CHAPTER
FORTY-ONE

BY THE TIME we reach the city, all conversation has halted in the truck, replaced by pressed lips and pale faces. Marcus steers around potholes the size of a person and parts from broken-down buses. The ride is smoother when we get out of factionless territory and into the clean parts of the city.

Then I hear gunshots. From this distance they sound like popping.

For a moment I am disoriented, and all I can see are the leaders of Abnegation on their knees on the pavement and the slack-faced Dauntless with guns in hand; all I can see is my mother turning to embrace the bullets, and Will dropping to the ground. I bite my fist to keep from crying out, and the pain brings me back to the present.

My mother told me to be brave. But if she had known

that her death would make me so afraid, would she have sacrificed herself so willingly?

Breaking away from the convoy of trucks, Marcus turns on Madison Avenue and, when we are just two blocks away from Michigan Avenue, where the fighting is, he pulls the truck into an alley and turns off the engine.

Fernando hops out of the truck bed and offers me his arm.

"Come on, Insurgent," he says with a wink.

"What?" I say. I take his arm and slide down the side of the truck.

He opens the bag he was sitting with. It is full of blue clothes. He sorts through them, tossing garments to Christina and me. I get a bright blue T-shirt and a pair of blue jeans.

"Insurgent," he says. "Noun. A person who acts in opposition to the established authority, who is not necessarily regarded as a belligerent."

"Do you need to give *everything* a name?" says Cara, running her hands over her dull blond hair to tuck the stray pieces back. "We're just doing something and it happens to be in a group. No need for a new title."

"I happen to enjoy categorization," Fernando replies, arching a dark eyebrow.

I look at Fernando. The last time I broke into a faction's

headquarters, I did it with a gun in my hand, and I left bodies behind me. I want this time to be different. I *need* this time to be different. "I like it," I say. "Insurgent. It's perfect."

"See?" Fernando says to Cara. "I'm not the only one."

"Congratulations," she says wryly.

I stare at my Erudite clothes while the others strip off their outer layers of clothing.

"No time for modesty, Stiff!" Christina says, giving me a pointed look.

I know she's right, so I pull off the red shirt I was wearing and put on the blue one instead. I glance at Fernando and Marcus to make sure they aren't watching, and change out of my pants too. I have to roll up the jeans four times, and when I belt them, they bunch at the top like the neck of a crushed paper bag.

"Did she just call you 'Stiff'?" Fernando says.

"Yeah," I say. "I transferred into Dauntless from Abnegation."

"Huh." He frowns. "That's quite a shift. That kind of leap in personality between generations is almost genetically impossible these days."

"Sometimes personality has nothing to do with a person's choice of faction," I say, thinking of my mother. She left Dauntless not because she was ill-suited for it but because it was safer to be Divergent in Abnegation. And then there's Tobias, who switched to Dauntless to escape his father. "There are many factors to consider."

To escape the man I have made my ally. I feel a twinge of guilt.

"Keep talking like that and they'll never discover you're not really Erudite," Fernando says.

I run a comb through my hair to smooth it down and then tuck it behind my ears.

"Here," says Cara. She lifts a piece of hair from my face and pins it back with a silver hair clip, the way Erudite girls do.

Christina takes out the guns we brought with us and looks at me.

"Do you want one?" she says. "Or would you rather carry the stunner?"

I stare at the gun in her hand. If I don't take the stunner, I leave myself completely undefended against people who will gladly shoot me. If I do, I admit to weakness in front of Fernando, Cara, and Marcus.

"You know what Will would say?" says Christina.

"What?" I say, my voice breaking.

"He would tell you to get over it," she says. "To stop being so irrational and take the stupid gun."

Will had little patience for the irrational. Christina

must be right; she knew him better than I did.

And she—who lost someone dear to her that day, just as I did—was able to forgive me, an act that must have been nearly impossible. It would have been impossible for me, if the situation were reversed. So why is it so difficult for me to forgive myself?

I close my hand around the gun Christina offered me. The metal is warm from where she touched it. I feel the memory of shooting him poking at the back of my mind, and try to stifle it. But it won't be stifled. I let go of the gun.

"The stunner is a perfectly good option," Cara says as she plucks a hair from her shirtsleeve. "If you ask me, the Dauntless are too gun-happy anyway."

Fernando offers me the stunner. I wish I could communicate my gratitude to Cara, but she isn't looking at me.

"How am I going to conceal this thing?" I say.

"Don't bother," Fernando says.

"Right."

"We'd better go," says Marcus, glancing at his watch.

My heart beats so hard it marks each second for me, but the rest of me is numb. I can barely feel the ground. I have never been this afraid before, and considering all that I have seen in simulations, and all that I did during the attack simulation, that doesn't make any sense.

Or maybe it does. Whatever the Abnegation were about to show everyone before the attack, it was enough to make Jeanine take drastic and terrible measures to stop them. And now I am about to finish their work, the work my old faction died for. So much more than my life is at stake now.

Christina and I lead the way. We run down the clean, even sidewalks on Madison Avenue, passing State Street, toward Michigan Avenue.

Half a block from Erudite headquarters, I come to a sudden stop.

Standing in four rows in front of us are a group of people, mostly dressed in black and white, spaced two feet apart, guns held up and ready. I blink and they become simulation-controlled Dauntless in the Abnegation sector, during the simulation attack. *Get a grip! Get a grip get a grip get a grip. . . .* I blink again and they are the Candor again—though some of them, dressed all in black, do look like Dauntless. If I'm not careful I'll lose touch with where, and when, I am.

"Oh my God," Christina says. "My sister, my *parents* . . . what if they . . ."

She looks at me, and I think I know her thoughts, because I have experienced them before. *Where are my parents? I have to find them.* But if her parents are like these Candor, simulation controlled and armed, there is nothing she can do for them.

I wonder if Lynn stands in one of these rows, somewhere else.

"What do we do?" Fernando asks.

I step toward the Candor. Maybe they aren't programmed to shoot. I stare into the glazed eyes of a woman in a white blouse and black slacks. She looks like she just came from work. I take another step.

Bang. By instinct I drop to the ground, covering my head with my arms, and scramble backward, toward Fernando's shoes. He helps me to my feet.

"How about let's not do *that*?" he says.

I lean forward—not too far—and peer into the alley between the building next to us and Erudite headquarters. The Candor are in the alley too. I wouldn't be surprised if there was a dense layer of Candor surrounding the entire complex of Erudite buildings.

"Is there any other way to Erudite headquarters?" I say.

"Not that I know of," says Cara. "Unless you want to jump from one roof to another."

She laughs a little as she says it, like it's a joke. I raise my eyebrows at her.

"Wait," she says. "You aren't considering—"

"The roof?" I say. "No. Windows."

I walk to the left, careful not to advance even an inch

toward the Candor. The building on my left overlaps with Erudite headquarters on its far left side. There have to be a few windows that face each other.

Cara mutters something about crazy Dauntless stunts, but runs after me, and Fernando, Marcus, and Christina follow. I try to open the back door of the building, but it's locked.

Christina steps forward and says, "Stand back." She points her gun at the lock. I shield my face with an arm as she fires. We hear a loud bang, and then a high ringing, the aftereffects of firing a gun in such a close space. The lock is broken.

I pull the door open and walk inside. A long hallway with a tile floor greets me, doors on either side, some open, some closed. When I look into the open rooms, I see rows of old desks, and chalkboards on the walls like the ones in Dauntless headquarters. The air smells musty, like the pages of a library book mixed with cleaning solution.

"This used to be a commercial building," says Fernando, "but Erudite converted it into a school, for post-Choosing education. After the major renovations in Erudite headquarters about a decade ago—you know, when all the buildings across from Millennium were connected?—they stopped teaching there. Too old, hard to update."

"Thanks for the history lesson," says Christina.

When I reach the end of the hallway, I walk into one of the classrooms to see where I am. I see the back of Erudite headquarters, but there are no windows across the alley at street level.

Right outside the window, so close I could touch her if I stretched my hand through the window, is a Candor child, a girl, holding a gun that is as long as her forearm. She stands so still I wonder if she is even breathing.

I crane my neck to see the windows above street level. Over my head in the school building there are plenty of windows. At the back of Erudite headquarters, there is only one that lines up. And it's on the third story.

"Good news," I say. "I found a way across."

CHAPTER
FORTY-TWO

EVERYONE SPREADS THROUGHOUT the building in search of janitor's closets, per my instruction to find a ladder. I hear sneakers squeaking on the tile and shouts of "I found one—no, wait, it's just got buckets in it, never mind" and "How long does the ladder have to be? A stepladder won't work, right?"

While they search, I find the third-floor classroom that looks into the Erudite window. It takes me three tries to open the right window.

I lean out, over the alley, and shout, "Hey!" Then I duck as fast as I can. But I don't hear gunshots—*Good,* I think. *They don't respond to noise.*

Christina marches into the classroom with a ladder under her arm, the others behind her. "Got one! I think it'll be long enough once we stretch it out."

She tries to turn too soon, and the ladder smacks into Fernando's shoulder.

"Oh! Sorry, Nando."

The jolt knocked his glasses askew. He smiles at Christina and takes the glasses off, shoving them into his pocket.

"Nando?" I say to him. "I thought the Erudite didn't like nicknames?"

"When a pretty girl calls you by a nickname," he says, "it is only logical to respond to it."

Christina looks away, and at first I think she is bashful, but then I see her face contort like he slapped her instead of complimented her. It is too soon after Will's death for her to be flirted with.

I help her guide the end of the ladder through the classroom window and across the gap between buildings. Marcus helps us steady it. Fernando whoops when the ladder hits the Erudite window across the alley.

"Time to break the glass," I say.

Fernando takes the glass-breaking device from his pocket and offers it to me. "You probably have the best aim."

"I wouldn't count on it," I say. "My right arm is out of commission. I'd have to throw with my left."

"I'll do it," says Christina.

She presses the button on the side of the device and tosses it across the alley, underhand. I clench my hands as I wait for it to land. It bounces onto the windowsill and rolls into the glass. An orange light flashes, and all at once the window—and the windows above, below, and next to it—shatters into hundreds of tiny pebbles that shower over the Candor below.

At the same time, the Candor twist and fire up into the sky. Everyone else drops to the ground, but I stay on my feet, part of me marveling at the perfect synchronicity of it, and the other part disgusted at how Jeanine Matthews has turned yet another faction from human beings into parts of a machine. None of the bullets even hit the classroom windows, let alone penetrate the room.

When the Candor do not fire another round, I peer down at them. They have returned to their original position, half facing Madison Avenue and half facing Washington Street.

"They respond to movement only, so . . . don't fall off the ladder," I say. "Whoever goes first will secure the ladder on the other side."

I notice that Marcus, who is supposed to selflessly offer himself up for every task, does not volunteer.

"Not feeling very Stiff today, Marcus?" says Christina.

"If I were you, I would be careful who you insult," he says. "I am still the only person here who can find what we're looking for."

"Is that a *threat*?"

"I'll go," I say, before Marcus can answer. "I'm part Stiff too, right?"

I shove the stunner under the waistband of my jeans and climb onto a desk to get a better angle on the window. Christina holds the ladder from the side as I clamber on top of it and start forward.

Once I'm through the window, I position my feet on the narrow edges of the ladder and my hands on the rungs. The ladder feels about as solid and stable as an aluminum can. It creaks and sags beneath my weight. I try not to look down at the Candor; try not to think about their guns lifting and firing at me.

Taking quick breaths, I stare at my destination, the Erudite window. Just a few rungs left.

A breeze blows through the alley, pushing me to one side, and I think of scaling the Ferris wheel with Tobias. He kept me steady then. There is no one left to keep me steady now.

I catch a glimpse of the ground, three stories down, the bricks smaller than they should be, the lines of Candor Jeanine enslaved. My arms—especially my right arm—ache as I inch my way across the gap.

The ladder shifts, moving closer to the edge of the window frame on the other side. Christina is holding one side steady, but she can't keep the ladder from slipping off the other windowsill. I grit my teeth and try not to move it too much, but I can't move both legs at the same time. I have to let the ladder sway a little. Just four more rungs to go.

The ladder jerks to the left, and then, as I move my right foot forward, I miss the edge of the rung.

I yell as my body shifts to the side, my arms wrapping around the ladder and my leg dangling in space.

"Are you okay?" Christina calls from behind me.

I don't answer. I bring my leg up and wedge it beneath my body. My fall made the ladder slip even farther off the windowsill. It is now supported by just a millimeter of concrete.

I decide to move fast. I lurch toward the opposite windowsill just as the ladder slips off. My hands catch the sill and concrete scrapes my fingertips as they bear my body weight. Several voices behind me scream.

I grit my teeth as I pull myself up, my right shoulder shrieking with pain. I kick at the brick building, hoping it will give me traction, but it doesn't help. I scream into my teeth as I pull myself up and over the windowsill, half my body in the building and the other half still dangling. Thankfully Christina didn't let the ladder drop too far.

None of the Candor shoot me.

I pull myself into the Erudite room across the alley. It is a bathroom. I collapse to the floor on my left shoulder, and try to breathe through the pain. Sweat trickles down my forehead.

An Erudite woman comes out of a stall, and I scramble to my feet, draw the stunner, and point it at her, all without thinking.

She freezes, her arms up, toilet paper stuck to her shoe.

"Don't shoot!" Her eyes bulge from her head.

I remember, then, that I am dressed like the Erudite. I set the stunner on the edge of a sink.

"My apologies," I say. I try to adopt the formal speech common to the Erudite. "I am slightly edgy, with everything that's occurring. We are reentering in order to retrieve some of our test results from . . . Laboratory 4-A."

"Oh," the woman says. "That seems rather unwise."

"The data is of the utmost importance," I say, trying to sound as arrogant as some of the Erudite I've met. "I would rather not leave it to get riddled with bullets."

"It's hardly my place to prevent you from trying to recover it," she says. "Now if you'll excuse me, I'm going to wash my hands and take cover."

"Sounds good," I say. I decide not to tell her she has toilet paper on her shoe.

I turn back to the window. Across the alley, Christina and Fernando are trying to lift the ladder back onto the windowsill. Though my arms and hands ache, I lean out the window and grab the other end of the ladder, lifting it back onto the windowsill. Then I hold it in place as Christina crawls across.

This time the ladder is more stable, and Christina makes it across the gap without trouble. She takes my place holding it as I shove the trash can in front of the door so no one else can come in. I then run my fingers under cool water to soothe them.

"This is pretty smart, Tris," she says.

"You don't have to sound so surprised."

"It's just . . ." She pauses. "You had aptitude for Erudite, didn't you?"

"Does it matter?" I say too sharply. "The factions are destroyed, and it was all stupid to begin with."

I have never said anything like that before. I have never even thought it. But I'm surprised to find that I believe it—surprised to find that I agree with Tobias.

"I wasn't trying to insult you," says Christina. "Having aptitude for Erudite isn't a bad thing. Especially right now."

"Sorry. I'm just . . . tense. That's all."

Marcus comes through the window and drops to the tile floor. Cara is surprisingly nimble—she moves over the rungs like she's plucking banjo strings, touching each one only briefly before she moves to the next one.

Fernando will be last, and he will be in the same position I was in, with the ladder secured from only one side. I move closer to the window so I can tell him to stop if I see the ladder slip.

Fernando, who I didn't think would have trouble, moves more awkwardly than anyone else. He has probably spent his entire life behind a computer or a book. He shuffles forward, his face bright red, and holds the rungs so tightly that his hands turn blotchy and purple.

Halfway across the alley, I see something slip out of his pocket. It is his spectacles.

I scream, "Fernan—"

But I am too late.

The spectacles fall, hit the edge of the ladder, and topple to the pavement.

In a wave, the Candor below twist and fire upward. Fernando yells, and collapses against the ladder. One bullet hit his leg. I didn't see where the others went, but I know when I see blood drip between the rungs of the ladder that it was not a good place.

CHAPTER
FORTY-THREE

CHRISTINA STEPS BACK into the room. We are all still.

"I don't mean to be insensitive," says Marcus, "but we have to go before the Dauntless and factionless enter this building. If they haven't already."

I hear tapping against the window and jerk my head to the side, for a split second believing that it is Fernando, trying to get in. But it's just rain.

We follow Cara out of the bathroom. She is our leader now. She knows Erudite headquarters best. Christina follows, then Marcus, then me. We leave the bathroom, and we are in an Erudite hallway like every other Erudite hallway: pale, bright, sterile.

But this hallway is more active than I have ever seen it. People in Erudite blue sprint back and forth, in groups and alone, shouting things at each other like, "They're at the front doors! Go as high as you can!" and "They've disabled the elevators! Run for the stairs!" It's only there, in the midst of chaos, that I realize I forgot the stunner in the bathroom. I am unarmed again.

Dauntless traitors also run past us, though they are less frantic than the Erudite. I wonder what Johanna, the Amity, and the Abnegation are doing in this chaos. Are they tending to the wounded? Or are they standing between Dauntless guns and Erudite innocents, taking bullets for the sake of peace?

I shudder. Cara leads us to a back staircase, and we join a group of terrified Erudite as we run up one, two, three flights of stairs. Then Cara shoves her shoulder into a door next to the landing, holding her gun close to her chest.

I recognize this floor.

It is my floor.

My thoughts become sluggish. I almost died here. I craved death here.

I slow down and fall behind. I can't break out of the daze, though people keep rushing past me, and Marcus shouts something at me, but his voice is muffled. Christina doubles back and grabs me, dragging me toward Control-A.

Inside the control room, I see rows of computers but I don't really see them; there is a film covering my eyes. I try to blink it away. Marcus sits at one of the computers, and Cara sits at another. They will send all the data from the Erudite computers to the other faction computers.

Behind me, the door opens.

And I hear Caleb say, "What are you doing here?"

+ + +

His voice wakes me. I turn and stare right at his gun.

His eyes are my mother's eyes—a dull green, almost gray, though his blue shirt makes their color appear more potent.

"Caleb," I say. "What do you think you're doing?"

"I'm here to stop whatever you're doing!" His voice trembles. The gun wavers in his hands.

"We're here to save the Erudite data that the faction-less want to destroy," I say. "I don't think you want to stop us."

"That's not true," he says. He jerks his head toward Marcus. "Why would you bring him if you weren't trying to find something else? Something more important to him than all the Erudite data combined?"

"She told *you* about it?" Marcus says. "*You*, a child?"

"She didn't tell me at first," Caleb says. "But she didn't want me to choose a side without knowing the facts!"

"The facts," says Marcus, "are that she is terrified of

reality, and the Abnegation were not. Are not. And neither is your sister. To her credit."

I scowl. Even when he is complimenting me, I want to smack him.

"My sister," says Caleb gently, looking at me again, "doesn't know what she's getting into. Doesn't know what it is that you want to show everyone . . . doesn't know it will ruin *everything*!"

"We are here to serve a purpose!" Marcus is almost yelling now. "We have completed our mission, and it is time for us to do what we were sent here to do!"

I don't know the purpose or the mission that Marcus is referring to, but Caleb doesn't look confused.

"*We* were not sent here," Caleb says. "We have no responsibility to anyone but ourselves."

"That kind of self-interested thinking is what I have come to expect from those who have spent too much time with Jeanine Matthews. You are so unwilling to relinquish your comfort that your selfishness drains you of humanity!"

I don't care to hear more. While Caleb stares down Marcus, I turn and kick hard at Caleb's wrist. The impact shocks him, and his gun topples from his hands. I slide it across the floor with my toes.

"You need to trust me, Beatrice," he says, chin wobbling.

"After you helped her torture me? After you let her almost *kill* me?"

"I didn't help her tort—"

"You certainly didn't stop her! You were right there, and you just *watched*—"

"What could I have done? What—"

"You could have *tried*, you coward!" I scream so loud my face gets hot and tears jump into my eyes. "Tried, and failed, because you love me!"

I gasp, just to take in enough air. All I hear is the click of keys as Cara works on the task at hand. Caleb doesn't seem to have a response. His pleading look slowly disappears, replaced by a blank stare.

"You won't find what you're looking for here," he says. "She wouldn't keep such important files on public computers. That would be illogical."

"So she hasn't destroyed it?" Marcus says.

Caleb shakes his head. "She does not believe in the destruction of information. Only its containment."

"Well, thank God for that," says Marcus. "Where is she keeping it?"

"I'm not going to tell you," Caleb says.

"I think I know," I say. Caleb said she wouldn't keep

the information on a public computer. So he must mean she is keeping it on a private one: either the one in her office or the one in the laboratory Tori told me about.

Caleb doesn't look at me.

Marcus picks up Caleb's revolver and turns it in his hand so the butt of the gun protrudes from his fist. Then he swings, striking Caleb under the jaw. Caleb's eyes roll back, and he falls to the floor.

I don't want to know how Marcus perfected that maneuver.

"We can't have him running off to tell someone what we're doing," says Marcus. "Let's go. Cara can take care of the rest, right?"

Cara nods without looking up from her computer. A sick feeling in my stomach, I follow Marcus and Christina out of the control room and toward the stairs.

+ + +

The hallway outside is now empty. There are scraps of paper and footprints on the tile. Marcus, Christina, and I jog in a line to the stairwell. I stare at the back of his head, where the shape of his skull shows through his buzzed hair.

All I can see when I look at him is a belt swinging toward Tobias, and the butt of a gun slamming into

Caleb's jaw. I don't care that he hurt Caleb—I would have done it, too—but that he is simultaneously a man who knows how to hurt people and a man who parades around as the self-effacing leader of Abnegation, suddenly makes me so angry I can't see straight.

Especially because I chose him. I chose *him* over Tobias.

"Your brother is a traitor," says Marcus as we turn a corner. "He deserved worse. There's no need to look at me that way."

"Shut up!" I shout, shoving him hard into the wall. He is too surprised to push back. "I hate you, you know that! I hate you for what you did to him, and I am *not* talking about Caleb." I lean close to his face and whisper, "And while I may not shoot you myself, I will definitely not help you if someone tries to kill you, so you'd better hope to God we don't get into that situation."

He stares at me, apparently indifferent. I release him and start toward the stairs again, Christina on my heels, Marcus a few steps behind.

"Where are we going?" she says.

"Caleb said what we're looking for won't be on a public computer, so it has to be on a private one. As far as I know, Jeanine only has two private computers, one in her office, and one in her laboratory," I say.

"So which one do we go to?"

"Tori told me there were insane security measures protecting Jeanine's laboratory," I say. "And I've been to her office; it's just another room."

"So . . . laboratory, then."

"Top floor."

We reach the door to the stairwell, and when I throw it open, a group of Erudite, including children, are sprinting down the stairs. I cling to the railing and force my way through them with my elbow, not looking at their faces, like they are not human, just a wall of mass to push aside.

I expect the stream to stop, but more come from the next landing, a steady flow of blue-clad people in dim blue light, the whites of their eyes bright as lamps by contrast to everything else. Their terrified sobs echo in the cement chamber a hundred times, the shrieks of the demons with glowing eyes.

When we reach the seventh-floor landing, the crowd thins, and then disappears. I run my hands along my arms to get rid of the ghosts of hair, sleeves, and skin that brushed against me on the way up. I can see the top of the stairs from where we stand.

I also see the body of a guard, his arm dangling over the edge of a stair, and standing over him, a factionless man with an eye patch.

Edward.

"Look who it is," Edward says. He stands at the top of a short flight, only seven steps long, and I stand at the bottom. The Dauntless traitor guard lies between us, his eyes glazed, a dark patch on his chest from where someone—Edward, probably—shot him.

"That's a strange outfit for someone who is supposed to despise Erudite," he says. "I thought you were supposed to be at home, waiting for your boyfriend to come back a hero?"

"As you may have gathered," I say, walking up a step, "that was never going to happen."

The blue light casts shadows into the faint hollows beneath Edward's cheekbones. He reaches behind him.

If he is here, that means Tori is already up here. Which means that Jeanine might already be dead.

I feel Christina close behind me; I hear her breaths.

"We are going to get past you," I say, walking up another step.

"I doubt that," he replies. He grabs his gun. I launch myself forward, over the fallen guard. He fires, but my hands are wrapped around his wrist, so he doesn't fire straight.

My ears ring, and my feet scramble for stability on the dead guard's back.

Christina punches over my head. Her knuckles connect with Edward's nose. I can't balance on top of the body; I fall to my knees, digging my fingernails into his wrist. He wrenches me to the side and fires again, hitting Christina in the leg.

Gasping, Christina draws her gun and shoots. The bullet hits him in the side. Edward screams and drops the gun, pitching forward. He falls on top of me, and I smack my head against one of the cement steps. The dead guard's arm is jammed into my spine.

Marcus picks up Edward's gun and trains it on both of us.

"Get up, Tris," he says. And to Edward: "You. Don't move."

My hand searches for the corner of a step, and I squeeze from between Edward and the dead guard. Edward pushes himself to a sitting position on top of the guard—like he's some kind of *cushion*—clutching his side with both hands.

"You okay?" I ask Christina.

Her face contorts. "*Ahh*. Yeah. It hit the side, not the bone."

I reach for her, to help her up.

"Beatrice," Marcus says. "We have to leave her."

"What do you mean *leave*?" I demand. "We can't leave! Something terrible could happen!"

Marcus presses his index finger to my sternum, in the gap between my collarbones, and leans over me.

"Listen to me," he says. "Jeanine Matthews will have retreated to her laboratory at the first sign of attack, because it is the safest room in this building. And at any moment, she will decide that Erudite is lost and it is better to delete the data than risk anyone else finding it, and this mission of ours will be useless."

And I will have lost everyone: my parents, Caleb, and finally, Tobias, who will never forgive me for working with his father, especially if I have no way to prove that it was worthwhile.

"We are going to leave your friend here." His breath smells stale. "And move on, unless you would rather me go on alone."

"He's right," says Christina. "There's no time. I'll stay here and keep Ed from coming after you."

I nod. Marcus removes his finger, leaving an aching circle behind. I rub the pain away and open the door at the top of the landing. I look back before I walk through it, and Christina gives me a pained smile, her hand pressed to her thigh.

CHAPTER
FORTY-FOUR

THE NEXT ROOM is more like a hallway: it is wide, but not
deep, with blue tile, blue walls, and a blue ceiling, all the
same shade. Everything glows, but I can't tell where the
light is coming from.

At first I don't see any doors, but once my eyes adjust to
the shock of color, I see a rectangle in the wall to my left,
and another one in the wall to my right. Just two doors.

"We have to split up," I say. "We don't have time to try
each one together."

"Which one do you want?" Marcus says.

"Right," I say. "Wait, no. Left."

"Fine. I will go right."

"If I'm the one who finds the computer," I say, "what
should I look for?"

"If you find the computer, you will find Jeanine. I assume you know a few ways to coerce her into doing what you want. She is not, after all, accustomed to pain," he says.

I nod. We walk at the same pace toward our respective doors. A moment ago I would have said that separating from Marcus would be a relief. But going on alone is its own burden. What if I can't get through the security measures Jeanine undoubtedly has in place to keep out intruders? What if, if I somehow manage to get through them, I can't find the right file?

I put my hand on the door handle. There doesn't seem to be a lock. When Tori said there were insane security measures, I thought she meant eye scanners and passwords and locks, but so far, everything has been open.

Why does that worry me?

I open my door, and Marcus opens his. We share a look. I walk into the next room.

+++

The room, like the hallway outside, is blue, though here it is clear where the light is coming from. It glows from the center of every panel, ceiling, floor, and walls.

Once the door closes behind me, I hear a thud like a dead bolt shifting into place. I grab the door handle again and push down as hard as I can, but it doesn't budge. I am trapped.

Small, piercing lights come at me from all angles. My eyelids aren't enough to block them, so I have to press my palms over my eye sockets.

I hear a calm, feminine voice:

"Beatrice Prior, second generation. Faction of origin: Abnegation. Selected faction: Dauntless. Confirmed Divergent."

How does this room know who I am?

And what does "second generation" mean?

"Status: Intruder."

I hear a click, and pull my fingers apart just enough to see if the lights are gone. They aren't, but fixtures in the ceiling spray tinted vapor. Instinctively I clap my hand over my mouth. In seconds I stare through a blue fog. And then I stare at nothing.

I now stand in darkness so complete that when I hold my hand in front of my nose, I can't even see its silhouette. I should walk forward and search for a door on the other side of the room, but I am afraid to move—who knows what would happen to me here if I did?

Then the lights lift, and I stand in the Dauntless training room, in the circle in which we used to spar. I have so many mixed memories of this circle, some triumphant, like beating Molly, and some haunting—Peter punching me until I fell unconscious. I sniff, and the air smells the same, like sweat and dust.

Across the circle is a blue door that doesn't belong there. I frown at it.

"Intruder," the voice says, and now it sounds like Jeanine, but that could be my imagination. "You have five minutes to reach the blue door before the poison will kick in."

"What?"

But I know what she said. Poison. Five minutes. I shouldn't be surprised; this is Jeanine's work, just as empty of conscience as she is. My body shudders, and I wonder if that is the poison, if the poison is already shutting down my brain.

Focus. I can't get out; I have to move forward, or . . .

Or nothing. I have to move forward.

I start toward the door, and someone appears in my path. She is short, thin, and blond, with dark circles under her eyes. She is me.

A reflection? I wave at her to see if she will mirror me. She doesn't.

"Hello," I say. She doesn't answer. I didn't really think she would.

What is this? I swallow hard to pop my ears, which feel

like they are stuffed with cotton. If Jeanine designed this, it is probably a test of intelligence or logic, which means I will have to think clearly, which means I will have to calm down. I clasp my hands over my chest and press down, hoping the pressure will make me feel safe, like an embrace.

It doesn't.

I step to the right to get a better angle on the door, and my double hops to the side, her shoes scraping the dirt, to block my way again.

I think I know what will happen if I start toward the door, but I have to try. I break into a run, intending to swerve around her, but she is ready for me: she grabs my wounded shoulder and wrenches me to the side. I scream so loud it scrapes my throat; I feel like knives are stabbing deeper and deeper into my right side. As I begin to sink to my knees, she kicks me in the stomach and I sprawl across the floor, inhaling dust.

That, I realize as I clutch my stomach, is exactly what I would have done if I had been in her position. Which means that in order to defeat her, I have to think of a way to defeat myself. And how can I be a better fighter than myself, if she knows the same strategies I know, and is exactly as resourceful and clever as I am?

She starts toward me again, so I scramble to my feet

and try to put aside the pain in my shoulder. My heart beats faster. I want to punch her, but she gets there first. I duck at the last second, and her fist hits my ear, knocking me off balance.

I back up a few steps, hoping that she won't pursue me, but she does. She comes at me again, this time seizing my shoulders and pulling me down, toward her bent knee.

I put my hands up, between my stomach and her knee, and push as hard as I can. She was not expecting that; she stumbles back, but doesn't fall.

I run at her, and as the desire to kick her slips into my mind, I realize that it is also *her* desire. I twist away from her foot.

The second I want something, she also wants it. She and I can only be, at best, at a standstill—but I need to *beat* her to get through the door. To survive.

I try to think it through, but she is coming at me again, her forehead tightened into a scowl of concentration. She grabs my arm, and I grab hers, so that we are clutched forearm to forearm.

At the same time, we yank our elbows back and thrust them forward. I lean in at the last second, and my elbow smashes into her teeth.

Both of us cry out. Blood spills over her lip, and runs down my forearm. She grits her teeth and yells, diving at me, stronger than I anticipated.

Her weight knocks me down. She pins me to the floor with her knees and tries to punch my face, but I cross my arms in front of me. Her fists hit my arms instead, each one like a stone striking my skin.

With a heavy exhale, I grab at one of her wrists, and I notice that spots are dancing at the corners of my eyes. *Poison.*

Focus.

As she struggles to free herself, I bring my knee up to my chest. Then I push her back, grunting with effort, until I can press my foot to her stomach. I kick her, my face boiling hot.

The logical puzzle: In a fight between two perfect equals, how can one win?

The answer: One can't.

She pushes herself to her feet and wipes the blood from her lip.

Therefore: we must not be perfectly equal. So what is different about us?

She walks toward me again, but I need more time to think, so for every step she takes forward, I take back. The room sways, and then twists, and I lurch to the side, brushing my fingertips on the ground to steady myself.

What is different about us? We have the same mass,

skill level, patterns of thinking . . .

I see the door over her shoulder, and I realize: We have different goals. I *have* to get through that door. She has to protect it. But even in a simulation, there is no way she is as desperate as I am.

I sprint toward the edge of the circle, where there is a table. A moment ago, it was empty, but I know the rules of simulations and how to control them. A gun appears on it as soon as I think it.

I slam into the table, the spots crowding my view of it. I don't even feel pain when I collide with it. I feel my heartbeat in my face, like my heart has detached from its moorings in my chest and begun to migrate to my brain.

Across the room, a gun appears on the ground before my double. We both reach for our weapons.

I feel the weight of the gun, and its smoothness, and I forget about her; I forget about the poison; I forget about everything.

My throat constricts, and I feel like there is a hand around it, tightening. My head throbs from the sudden loss of air, and I feel my heartbeat everywhere, everywhere.

Across the room, it's no longer my double who stands between me and my goal; it's Will. *No, no.* It can't be Will. I force myself to breathe in. The poison is cutting off oxygen to my brain. He is just a hallucination within a simulation. I exhale in a sob.

For a moment I see my double again, holding the gun but visibly shuddering, the weapon as far out from her body as she can possibly hold it. She is as weak as I am. No, not as weak, because she is not going blind and losing air, but almost as weak, almost.

Then Will is back, his eyes simulation-dead, his hair a yellow halo around his head. Brick buildings loom from each side, but behind him is the door, the door that separates me from my father and brother.

No, no, it is the door that separates me from Jeanine and my goal.

I have to get through that door. I *have to.*

I lift the gun, though it hurts my shoulder to do it, and wrap one hand around the other to steady it.

"I . . ." I choke, and tears smear my cheeks, run into my mouth. I taste salt. "I'm sorry."

And I do the one thing my double is unable to do, because she is not desperate enough:

I fire.

CHAPTER
FORTY-FIVE

I DON'T SEE him die again.

I close my eyes at the moment the trigger presses back, and when I open them, it is the other Tris who lies on the ground between the dark patches in my vision; it is me.

I drop the gun and sprint toward the door, almost tripping over her. I throw my body against the door, twist the handle, and fall through. My hands numb, I press it closed behind me, and shake them to regain feeling.

The next room is twice as big as the first one, and it, too, is blue-lit, but paler. A large table stands in the middle, and taped to the walls are photographs, diagrams, and lists.

I take deep breaths, and my vision begins to clear, my heart rate returning to normal. Among the photographs on the walls, I recognize my own face, and Tobias's, and Marcus's, and Uriah's. A long list of what appear to be chemicals is posted on the wall beside our pictures. Each one is crossed out with red marker. This must be where Jeanine develops the simulation serums.

I hear voices somewhere ahead of me, and scold myself. *What are you doing? Hurry!*

"My brother's name," I hear. "I want to hear you say it." Tori's voice.

How did she get through that simulation? Is she Divergent too?

"I didn't kill him." Jeanine's voice.

"Do you think that exonerates you? Do you think that means you don't deserve to die?"

Tori is not screaming, but wailing, the whole of her grief escaping through her mouth. I start toward the door. Too quickly, though, because my hip slams into the corner of the table in the middle of the room, and I have to stop, wincing.

"The reasons for my actions are beyond your understanding," Jeanine says. "I was willing to make a sacrifice for the greater good, something you have never understood, not even when we were classmates!"

I limp toward the door, which is a pane of frosted glass. It slides back to admit me, and I see Jeanine, pressed against a wall, with Tori standing a few feet away, her gun high.

Behind them is a glass table with a silver box on it—a computer—and a keyboard. The entire far wall is covered with a computer screen.

Jeanine stares at me, but Tori doesn't move an inch; doesn't seem to hear me. Her face is red and tear-streaked, her hand shaking.

I have no confidence that I can find the video file on my own. If Jeanine is here, I can get her to find it for me, but if she's dead . . .

"No!" I scream. "Tori, don't!"

But her finger is already over the trigger. I launch myself at her as hard as I can, my arms slamming into her side. The gun goes off, and I hear a scream.

My head hits the tile. I ignore the stars in my eyes and throw myself across Tori. I shove the gun forward and it slides away from us.

Why didn't you grab it, you idiot?!

Tori's fist connects with the side of my throat. I choke, and she uses the opportunity to throw me off, to crawl toward the gun.

Jeanine is slumped against the wall, blood soaking her leg. *Leg!* I remember, and punch Tori hard near the bullet wound in her thigh. She yells, and I find my feet.

I step toward the fallen weapon, but Tori is too quick. She wraps her arms around my legs and pulls them out from under me. My knees slam into the ground, but I am still above her; I punch down, at her rib cage.

She groans, but it doesn't stop her; as I drag myself toward the gun, she sinks her teeth into my hand. It is a different pain than any blow I've ever received, different even from a bullet wound. I scream louder than I thought possible, tears blurring my vision.

I have not come this far to let Tori shoot Jeanine before I've gotten what I need.

I yank my hand from between her teeth, my vision going black at the edges, and with a lurch, smack my hand around the handle of the gun. I twist, and point it at Tori.

My hand. My hand is covered in blood, and so is Tori's chin. I hide my hand from view so that it's easier to ignore the pain and get up, still pointing the gun at her.

"I didn't take you for a traitor, Tris," she says, and it sounds like a snarl, not a sound any human can make.

"I'm not," I say. I blink the tears down my cheeks so that I can see her better. "I can't explain it right now, but . . . all I'm asking is for you to trust me, please. There's something important, something only she knows the location of—"

"That's right!" says Jeanine. "It is on *that* computer,

498

Beatrice, and only I can locate it. If you don't help me survive this, it will die with me."

"She is a liar," says Tori. "A *liar*, and if you believe her, you are both an idiot and a traitor, Tris!"

"I do believe her," I say. "I believe her because it makes perfect sense! The most sensitive information that exists and it's hidden on *that computer*, Tori!" I take a deep breath, and lower my voice. "Please listen to me. I hate her as much as you do. I have no reason to defend her. I'm telling you the truth. This is important."

Tori is silent. I think, for a moment, that I've won, that I've persuaded her. But then she says, "Nothing is more important than her death."

"If that's what you insist upon believing," I say, "I can't help you. But I'm also not going to let you kill her."

Tori pushes herself to her knees, and wipes my blood from her chin. She looks up into my eyes.

"I am a Dauntless leader," she says. "You don't get to decide what I do."

And before I can think—

Before I can even think about firing the gun I'm holding—

She draws a long knife from the side of her boot, lunges, and stabs Jeanine in the stomach.

I yell. Jeanine releases a horrible sound—a gurgling,

screaming, dying sound. I see Tori's gritted teeth, I hear her murmur her brother's name—"George Wu"—and then I watch the knife go in again.

And Jeanine's eyes turn into glass.

CHAPTER
FORTY-SIX

TORI STANDS, A wild look in her eyes, and turns toward me.

I feel numb.

All the risks I took to get here—conspiring with Marcus, asking the Erudite for help, crawling across a ladder three stories up, shooting myself in a simulation—and all the sacrifices I made—my relationship with Tobias, Fernando's life, my standing among the Dauntless—were for nothing.

Nothing.

A moment later, the glass door opens again. Tobias and Uriah storm in as if to fight a battle—Uriah coughing, probably from the poison—but the battle is done. Jeanine is dead, Tori is triumphant, and I am a Dauntless traitor.

Tobias stops in the middle of a step, almost stumbling

over his feet, when he sees me. His eyes open wider.

"She is a traitor," says Tori. "She just almost shot me to defend Jeanine."

"What?" says Uriah. "Tris, what's going on? Is she right? Why are you even here?"

But I look only at Tobias. A sliver of hope pierces me, strangely painful, when combined with the guilt I feel for how I deceived him. Tobias is stubborn and proud, but he is mine—maybe he will listen, maybe there's a chance that all I did was not in vain—

"You know why I'm here," I say quietly. "Don't you?"

I hold out Tori's gun. He walks forward, a little unsteady on his feet, and takes it.

"We found Marcus in the next room, caught in a simulation," Tobias says. "You came up here with him."

"Yes, I did," I say, blood from Tori's bite trickling down my arm.

"I trusted you," he says, his body shaking with rage. "I *trusted* you and you abandoned me to work with *him*?"

"No." I shake my head. "He told me something, and everything my brother said, everything Jeanine said while I was in Erudite headquarters, fit perfectly with what he told me. And I wanted—I *needed* to know the truth."

"The truth." He snorts. "You think you learned the

truth from a liar, a traitor, and a sociopath?"

"The truth?" says Tori. "What are you talking about?"

Tobias and I stare at each other. His blue eyes, usually so thoughtful, are now hard and critical, like they are peeling back layer after layer of me and searching each one.

"I think," I say. I have to pause and take a breath, because I have not convinced him; I have failed, and this is probably the last thing they will let me say before they arrest me.

"I think that *you* are the liar!" I say, my voice quaking. "You tell me you love me, you trust me, you think I'm more perceptive than the average person. And the first second that belief in my perceptiveness, that trust, that *love* is put to the test, it all falls apart." I am crying now, but I am not ashamed of the tears shining on my cheeks or the thickness of my voice. "So you must have lied when you told me all those things . . . you must have, because I can't believe your love is really that feeble."

I step closer to him, so that there are only inches between us, and none of the others can hear me.

"I am still the person who would have died rather than kill you," I say, remembering the attack simulation and the feel of his heartbeat under my hand. "I am exactly who you think I am. And right now, I'm telling you that I know . . . I *know* this information will change everything. Everything we have done, and everything we are about to do."

I stare at him like I can communicate the truth with my eyes, but that is impossible. He looks away, and I'm not sure he even heard what I said.

"Enough of this," says Tori. "Take her downstairs. She will be tried along with all the other war criminals."

Tobias doesn't move. Uriah takes my arm and leads me away from him, through the laboratory, through the room of light, through the blue hallway. Therese of the faction-less joins us there, eyeing me curiously.

Once we're in the stairwell, I feel something nudge my side. When I look back, I see a wad of gauze in Uriah's hand. I take it, trying to give him a grateful smile and failing.

As we descend the stairs, I wrap the gauze tightly around my hand, sidestepping bodies without looking at their faces. Uriah takes my elbow to keep me from falling. The gauze wrapping doesn't help with the pain of the bite, but it makes me feel a little better, and so does the fact that Uriah, at least, doesn't seem to hate me.

For the first time the Dauntless's disregard for age does not seem like an opportunity. It seems like the thing that will condemn me. They will not say, *But she's young; she must have been confused.* They will say, *She is an adult, and she made her choice.*

Of course, I agree with them. I did make my choice. I chose my mother and father, and what they fought for.

+ + +

Walking down the stairs is easier than going up. We reach the fifth level before I realize that we're going down to the lobby.

"Give me your gun, Uriah," says Therese. "Someone needs to be able to shoot potential belligerents, and you can't do it if you're keeping her from falling down the stairs."

Uriah surrenders his gun without question. I frown— Therese already *has* a gun, so why did it matter for him to give his? But I don't ask. I am in enough trouble as it is.

We reach the bottom floor and walk past a large meeting room full of people dressed in black and white. I pause for a moment to watch them. Some of them are huddled in small groups, leaning on one another, tears streaking their faces. Others are alone, leaning against walls or sitting in corners, their eyes hollow or staring at something that is far away.

"We had to shoot so many," Uriah mutters, squeezing my arm. "Just to get into the building, we had to."

"I know," I say.

I see Christina's sister and mother clutched together on the right side of the room. And on the left side, a young man with dark hair that gleams in the fluorescent light—Peter. His hand is on the shoulder of a middle-aged woman I recognize as his mother.

"What is he doing here?" I say.

"Little coward came in the aftermath, after all the work was done," Uriah says. "I heard his dad's dead. Looks like his mother's okay, though."

Peter looks over his shoulder, and his gaze meets mine, just for a second. In that second I try to summon some pity for the person who saved my life. But while the hatred I once had for him is gone, I still feel nothing.

"What's the holdup?" demands Therese. "Let's get going."

We walk past the meeting room to the main lobby, where I once embraced Caleb. The giant portrait of Jeanine is in pieces on the floor. The smoke that hovers in the air is condensed around the bookshelves, which are burned to cinders. All the computers are in pieces, strewn across the floor.

Sitting in rows in the center of the room are some of the Erudite who didn't get away, and the Dauntless traitors who survived. I search the faces for anything familiar. I find Caleb near the back, looking dazed. I look away.

"Tris!" I hear. Christina sits near the front, next to Cara, her leg wrapped tightly with fabric. She beckons to me, and I sit down next to her.

"No success?" she says quietly.

I shake my head.

She sighs, and puts her arm around me. The gesture is so comforting I almost start to cry. But Christina and I are not people who cry together; we're people who fight together. So I hold my tears in.

"I saw your mom and your sister in the next room," I say.

"Yeah, me too," she says. "My family is okay."

"Good," I say. "How's your leg?"

"Fine. Cara said it'll be fine; it's not bleeding too much. One of the Erudite nurses stuffed some pain meds and antiseptic and gauze into her pockets before they took her down here, so it doesn't hurt too bad either," she says. Beside her, Cara is examining another Erudite's arm. "Where's Marcus?"

"Dunno," I say. "We had to split up. He should be down here. Unless they killed him or something."

"I wouldn't be that surprised, honestly," she says.

The room is chaotic for a while—people rushing in and rushing out again, our factionless guards trading places, new people in Erudite blue brought to sit among us—but gradually everything gets quieter, and then I see him: Tobias, walking through the stairwell door.

I bite my lip, hard, and try not to think, try not to dwell on the cold feeling that surrounds my chest and the weight that hangs over my head. He hates me. He does not believe me.

Christina clutches me tighter as he walks past us, without even looking at me. I watch him over my shoulder. He stops next to Caleb, grabs his arm, and wrenches him to his feet. Caleb wriggles for a second, but he is not half as strong as Tobias and can't break away.

"What?" Caleb says, panicking. "What do you want?"

"I want you to disarm the security system for Jeanine's laboratory," says Tobias without looking back. "So that the factionless can access her computer."

And destroy it, I think, and if possible, my heart becomes even heavier. Tobias and Caleb disappear into the stairwell again.

Christina slumps against me, and I slump against her, so we hold each other up.

"Jeanine activated all the Dauntless transmitters, you know," Christina says. "One of the factionless groups got ambushed by simulation-controlled Dauntless, coming late from the Abnegation sector about ten minutes ago. I guess the factionless won, though I don't know how you call shooting a bunch of brain-dead people winning."

"Yeah." There isn't much more to say. She seems to realize that.

"What happened after I got shot?" she says.

I describe the blue hallway with two doors, and the simulation that followed, from the moment I recognized the Dauntless training room to the moment I shot myself. I do not tell her about hallucinating Will.

"Wait," she says. "It was a simulation? Without a transmitter?"

I frown. I hadn't bothered to wonder about that. Especially not at the time. "If the laboratory recognizes people, maybe it also knows data about everyone, and can present a corresponding simulated environment depending on your faction."

It doesn't matter, now, to figure out how Jeanine set up the security on her laboratory, of all things. But it feels good to put myself to some use, to think of a new problem to solve now that I have failed to solve the most important one.

Christina sits up straighter. Maybe she feels the same way.

"Or the poison somehow contains a transmitter."

I hadn't thought of that.

"But how did Tori get past it? She's not Divergent."

I tilt my head. "I don't know."

Maybe she is, I think. Her brother was, and after what happened to him, she might never admit it, no matter how accepted it becomes.

People, I have discovered, are layers and layers of secrets. You believe you know them, that you understand them, but their motives are always hidden from you, buried in their own hearts. You will never know them, but sometimes you decide to trust them.

"What do you think they're going to do to us when they find us guilty?" she says after a few minutes of silence have passed.

"Honestly?"

"Does now seem like the time for honesty?"

I look at her from the corner of my eye. "I think they're going to force us to eat lots of cake and then take an unreasonably long nap."

She laughs. I try not to—if I let myself laugh, I'll start to cry, too.

+ + +

I hear a yell, and peer around the crowd to see where it came from.

"Lynn!" The yell came from Uriah. He runs toward

the door, where two Dauntless are carrying Lynn in on a makeshift stretcher, made of what looks like a shelf from a bookcase. She is pale—too pale—and her hands are folded over her stomach.

I jump to my feet and start toward her, but a few factionless guns stop me from going much farther. I put up my hands and stand still, watching.

Uriah walks around the crowd of war criminals and points to a severe-looking Erudite woman with gray hair. "You. Come here."

The woman gets to her feet and brushes off her pants. She walks, light-footed, to the edge of the seated crowd and looks expectantly at Uriah.

"You're a doctor, right?" he says.

"I am, yes," she says.

"Then fix her!" He scowls. "She's hurt."

The doctor approaches Lynn and asks the two Dauntless to set her down. They do, and she crouches over the stretcher.

"My dear," she says. "Please remove your hands from your wound."

"I can't," moans Lynn. "It hurts."

"I am aware that it hurts," the doctor says. "But I won't be able to assess your wound if you do not reveal it to me."

Uriah kneels across from the doctor and helps her shift Lynn's hands away from her stomach. The doctor peels Lynn's shirt back from her stomach. The bullet wound itself is just a round, red circle in Lynn's skin, but surrounding it is what looks like a bruise. I have never seen a bruise that dark.

The doctor purses her lips, and I know that Lynn is as good as dead.

"Fix her!" says Uriah. "You can fix her, so do it!"

"On the contrary," the doctor says, looking up at him. "Because you set the hospital floors of this building on fire, I cannot fix her."

"There are other hospitals!" he says, almost shouting. "You can get stuff from there and heal her!"

"Her condition is far too advanced," the doctor says, her voice quiet. "If you had not insisted upon burning everything that came into your path, I could have tried, but as the situation stands, trying would be worthless."

"You shut up!" he says, pointing at the doctor's chest. "I'm not the one who burned your hospital! She's my friend, and I . . . I just . . ."

"Uri," says Lynn. "Shut up. It's too late."

Uriah lets his arms fall to his sides, then reaches for Lynn's hand, his lip quivering.

"I'm her friend too," I say to the factionless pointing guns at me. "Can you at least point guns at me from over there?"

They let me pass, and I run to Lynn's side, holding her free hand, which is sticky with blood. I ignore the gun barrels pointed at my head and focus on Lynn's face, which is now yellowish instead of white.

She doesn't seem to notice me. She focuses on Uriah.

"I'm just glad I didn't die while under the simulation," she says weakly.

"You're not gonna die now," he says.

"Don't be stupid," she says. "Uri, listen. I loved her too. I did."

"You loved who?" he says, his voice breaking.

"Marlene," says Lynn.

"Yeah, we all loved Marlene," he says.

"No, that's not what I mean." She shakes her head. She closes her eyes.

Still, it takes a few minutes before her hand goes limp in mine. I guide it across her stomach, and then take her other hand from Uriah and do the same to it. He wipes his eyes before his tears can fall. Our eyes meet across her body.

"You should tell Shauna," I say. "And Hector."

"Right." He sniffs and presses his palm to Lynn's face. I wonder if her cheek is still warm. I don't want to touch her and find that it's not.

I rise and walk back to Christina.

CHAPTER
FORTY-SEVEN

MY MIND KEEPS tugging me toward my memories of Lynn, in an attempt to persuade me that she is actually gone, but I push away the short flashes as they come. Someday I will stop doing that, if I'm not executed as a traitor, or whatever our new leaders have planned. But right now I fight to keep my mind blank, to pretend that this room is all that has ever existed and all that will ever exist. It should not be easy, but it is. I have learned how to fend off grief.

Tori and Harrison come to the lobby after a while, Tori limping toward a chair—I almost forgot about her bullet wound again; she was so nimble when she killed Jeanine—and Harrison following her.

Behind both of them is one of the Dauntless with Jeanine's body slung over his shoulder. He heaves it like a stone on a table in front of the rows of Erudite and Dauntless traitors.

Behind me I hear gasps and mutters, but no sobs. Jeanine was not the kind of leader people cry for.

I stare up at her body, which seems so much smaller in death than it did in life. She is only a few inches taller than I am, her hair only a few shades darker. She looks calm now, almost peaceful. I have trouble connecting this body with the woman I knew, the woman without a conscience.

And even she was more complicated than I thought, keeping a secret that she thought was too terrible to reveal, out of a heinously twisted protective instinct.

Johanna Reyes steps into the lobby, soaked to the bone from all the rain, her red clothes smeared with a darker red. The factionless flank her, but she doesn't appear to notice them or the guns they carry.

"Hello," she says to Harrison and Tori. "What is it that you want?"

"I didn't know the leader of Amity would be so curt," says Tori with a wry smile. "Isn't that against your manifesto?"

"If you were actually familiar with Amity's customs, you would know that they don't have a formal leader," says Johanna, her voice simultaneously gentle and firm. "But I'm not the representative of Amity anymore. I stepped down in order to come here."

"Yeah, I saw you and your little band of peacekeepers, getting in everyone's way," says Tori.

"Yes, that was intentional," Johanna replies. "Since getting in the way meant standing between guns and innocents, and saved a great number of lives."

Color fills her cheeks, and I think it again: that Johanna Reyes might still be beautiful. Except now I think that she isn't just beautiful in spite of the scar, she's somehow beautiful *with* it, like Lynn with her buzzed hair, like Tobias with the memories of his father's cruelty that he wears like armor, like my mother in her plain gray clothing.

"Since you are still so very generous," says Tori, "I wonder if you might carry a message back to the Amity."

"I don't feel comfortable leaving you and your army to dole out justice as you see fit," says Johanna, "but I will certainly send someone else to Amity with a message."

"Fine," says Tori. "Tell them that a new political system will soon be formed that will exclude them from representation. This, we believe, is their just punishment for failing to choose a side in this conflict. They will, of course, be obligated to continue to produce and deliver food to the city, but they will be under supervision by one of the leading factions."

For a second, I think that Johanna might launch herself

at Tori and strangle her. But she draws herself up taller and says, "Is that all?"

"Yes."

"Fine," she says. "I'm going to go do something useful. I don't suppose you would allow some of us to come in here and tend to *these* wounded?"

Tori gives her a look.

"I didn't think so," says Johanna. "Do remember, though, that sometimes the people you oppress become mightier than you would like."

She turns and walks out of the lobby.

Something about her words hits me. I am sure she meant them as a threat, and a feeble one, but it rings in my head like it was something more—like she could easily have been talking not about the Amity, but about another oppressed group. The factionless.

And as I look around the room, at every Dauntless soldier and every factionless soldier, I begin to see a pattern.

"Christina," I say. "The factionless have all the guns."

She looks around, and then back at me, frowning.

In my mind I see Therese, taking Uriah's gun when she already had one herself. I see Tobias's mouth pressed into a line when I asked him about the uneasy Dauntless-factionless alliance, holding something back.

Then Evelyn emerges into the lobby, her posture regal,

like a queen returning to her kingdom. Tobias does not follow her. *Where is he?*

Evelyn stands behind the table where Jeanine Matthews's body lies. Edward limps into the lobby behind her. Evelyn takes out a gun, points it at the fallen portrait of Jeanine, and fires.

A hush falls over the room. Evelyn drops the gun on the table, next to Jeanine's head.

"Thank you," she says. "I know that you are all wondering what will happen next, so I am here to tell you."

Tori sits up straighter in her chair and leans toward Evelyn, like she wants to say something. But Evelyn pays no attention.

"The faction system that has long supported itself on the backs of discarded human beings will be disbanded at once," says Evelyn. "We know this transition will be difficult for you, but—"

"*We?*" Tori breaks in, looking scandalized. "What are you talking about, disbanded?"

"What I am talking about," says Evelyn, looking at Tori for the first time, "is that your faction, which up until a few weeks ago was clamoring along with the Erudite for the restriction of food and goods to the factionless, a clamor that resulted in the destruction of the Abnegation, will no longer exist."

Evelyn smiles a little.

"And if you decide to take up arms against us," she says, "you will be hard pressed to find any arms to take up."

I watch, then, as each factionless soldier holds up a gun. Factionless are evenly spaced around the edge of the room, and they disappear into one of the stairwells. They have us all surrounded.

It is so elegant, so clever, that I almost laugh.

"I instructed my half of the army to relieve your half of the army of their weapons as soon as their missions were completed," says Evelyn. "I see now that they were successful. I regret the duplicity, but we knew that you have been conditioned to cling to the faction system like it is your own mother, and that we would have to help ease you into this new era."

"Ease us?" Tori demands. She pushes herself to her feet and limps toward Evelyn, who calmly takes her gun in hand and points it at Tori.

"I have not been starving for more than a decade just to give in to a Dauntless woman with a leg injury," Evelyn says. "So unless you want me to shoot you, take a seat with your fellow ex-faction members."

I see all the muscles in Evelyn's arm standing at attention, her eyes not cold, not quite like Jeanine's, but calculating, assessing, planning. I don't know how this woman could have ever bent to Marcus's will. She must not have been this woman then, all steel, tested in fire.

Tori stands before Evelyn for a few seconds. She then limps backward, away from the gun and toward the edge of the room.

"Those of you who assisted us in the effort to take down Erudite will be rewarded," says Evelyn. "Those of you who resisted us will be tried and punished according to your crimes." She raises her voice for the last sentence, and I am surprised by how well it carries over the space.

Behind her, the door to the stairwell opens, and Tobias steps out with Marcus and Caleb behind him, almost unnoticed. Almost, except I notice him, because I have trained myself to notice him. I watch his shoes as he comes closer. They are black sneakers with chrome eyelets for the laces. They stop right next to me, and he crouches by my shoulder.

I look at him, expecting to find his eyes cold and unyielding.

But I don't.

Evelyn is still talking, but her voice fades for me.

"You were right," Tobias says quietly, balancing on the balls of his feet. He smiles a little. "I do know who you are. I just needed to be reminded."

I open my mouth, but I don't have anything to say.

Then all the screens in the Erudite lobby—at least those that weren't destroyed in the attack—flicker on, including a projector positioned over the wall where Jeanine's portrait used to be.

Evelyn stops in the middle of whatever sentence she was speaking. Tobias takes my hand and helps me to my feet.

"What is this?" Evelyn demands.

"This," he says, only to me, "is the information that will change everything."

My legs shake with relief and apprehension.

"You did it?" I say.

"*You* did it," he says. "All I did was force Caleb to cooperate."

I throw my arm around his neck, and press my lips to his. He holds my face in both hands and kisses me back. I press into the distance between us until it is gone, crushing the secrets we have kept and the suspicions we have harbored—for good, I hope.

And then I hear a voice.

We pull apart and turn toward the wall, where a woman with short brown hair is projected. She sits at a metal desk with her hands folded, in a location I don't recognize. The background is too dim.

"Hello," she says. "My name is Amanda Ritter. In this

file I will tell you only what you need to know. I am the leader of an organization fighting for justice and peace. This fight has become increasingly more important—and consequently, nearly impossible—in the past few decades. That is because of this."

Images flash across the wall, almost too fast for me to see. A man on his knees with a gun pressed to his forehead. The woman pointing it at him, her face emotionless.

From a distance, a small person hanging by the neck from a telephone pole.

A hole in the ground the size of a house, full of bodies.

And there are other images too, but they move faster, so I get only impressions of blood and bone and death and cruelty, empty faces, soulless eyes, terrified eyes.

Just when I have had enough, when I feel like I am going to scream if I see any more, the woman reappears on the screen, behind her desk.

"You do not remember any of that," she says. "But if you are thinking these are the actions of a terrorist group or a tyrannical government regime, you are only partially correct. Half of the people in those pictures, committing those terrible acts, were your neighbors. Your relatives. Your coworkers. The battle we are fighting is not against a particular group. It is against human nature itself—or at least what it has become."

This is what Jeanine was willing to enslave minds and murder people for—to keep us all from knowing. To keep us all ignorant and safe and *inside the fence*.

There is a part of me that understands.

"That is why you are so important," Amanda says. "Our struggle against violence and cruelty is only treating the symptoms of a disease, not curing it. *You* are the cure.

"In order to keep you safe, we devised a way for you to be separated from us. From our water supply. From our technology. From our societal structure. We have formed your society in a particular way in the hope that you will rediscover the moral sense most of us have lost. Over time, we hope that you will begin to change as most of us cannot.

"The reason I am leaving this footage for you is so that you will know when it's time to help us. You will know that it is time when there are many among you whose minds appear to be more flexible than the others. The name you should give those people is Divergent. Once they become abundant among you, your leaders should give the command for Amity to unlock the gate forever, so that you may emerge from your isolation."

And that is what my parents wanted to do: to take what we had learned and use it to help others. Abnegation to the end.

"The information in this video is to be restricted to

those in government only," Amanda says. "You are to be a clean slate. But do not forget us."

She smiles a little.

"I am about to join your number," she says. "Like the rest of you, I will voluntarily forget my name, my family, and my home. I will take on a new identity, with false memories and a false history. But so that you know the information I have provided you with is accurate, I will tell you the name I am about to take as my own."

Her smile broadens, and for a moment, I feel that I recognize her.

"My name will be Edith Prior," she says. "And there is much I am happy to forget."

Prior.

The video stops. The projector glows blue against the wall. I clutch Tobias's hand, and there is a moment of silence like a withheld breath.

Then the shouting begins.

ACKNOWLEDGMENTS

Thank you, God, for keeping your promises.

Thank you:

Nelson, beta reader, tireless supporter, photographer, best friend, and most importantly, husband. . . . I think the Beach Boys said it best: God only knows what I'd be without you.

Joanna Volpe, I could not ask for a better agent or friend. Molly O'Neill, my editor of wonder, for your tireless work on this book in all arenas. Katherine Tegen, for being kind and discerning, and the whole KT Books crew, for your support.

Susan Jeffers, Andrea Curley, and the illustrious Brenna Franzitta, for watching my words; Joel Tippie and Amy Ryan, for making this book so beautiful; and Jean McGinley and Alpha Wong, for extending the reach of these books farther than I ever expected. Jessica Berg, Suzanne Daghlian, Barb Fitzsimmons, Lauren Flower, Kate Jackson, Susan Katz, Alison Lisnow, Casey McIntyre, Diane Naughton, Colleen O'Connell, Aubrey Parks-Fried, Andrea Pappenheimer, Shayna Ramos, Patty Rosati, Sandee Roston, Jenny Sheridan, Megan Sugrue, Molly Thomas, and Allison Verost, as well as everyone in audio, design, finance, international sales, inventory, legal, managing editorial, marketing, online marketing, publicity, production, sales, school and library marketing, special sales, and subrights at HarperCollins, for doing such fantastic work in the world of books as well as *my* world of books.

All the teachers, librarians, and booksellers who have supported my books with so much enthusiasm. Book bloggers, reviewers, and readers of all ages and varieties and countries of origin. I'm probably biased, but I think I have the best readers ever.

Lara Ehrlich, for much writing wisdom. My writer friends—listing all of the people in the writer community who have been kind to me would take multiple pages, but I could not ask for better peers. Alice, Mary Katherine, Mallory, and Danielle—what fantastic friends I have.

Nancy Coffey, for your eyes and your wisdom. Pouya Shahbazian and Steve Younger, my fantastic film team; and Summit Entertainment, Red Wagon, and Evan Daugherty, for wanting to live in this world I made.

My family: My incredible mother-slash-psychologist-slash-cheerleader, Frank Sr., Karl, Ingrid, Frank Jr., Candice, McCall, and Dave. You are incredible people and I am so glad I have you.

Beth and Darby, who have won me more readers than I can possibly count through charm and sheer determination; and Chase-baci and Sha-neni, who took such good care of us in Romania. Also Roger, Trevor, Tyler, Rachel, Fred, Billie, and Granny, for so effortlessly embracing me as one of you.

Mulțumesc/Köszönöm to Cluj-Napoca/Kolozsvár, for all the inspiration and the dear friends I left there—but not forever.

INSURGENT

BONUS MATERIALS

BONUS MATERIALS

INSURGENT Alternate Beginning   1

Evelyn's Speech to the Factionless   5

The Reality of Grief   9

Veronica Roth's Faction Playlists   15

INSURGENT Discussion Questions   18

An Excerpt from ALLEGIANT   21

INSURGENT ALTERNATE BEGINNING

I WENT THROUGH *four beginnings* in Insurgent *before I found the right one. This was probably my favorite, taking place a little while after the Dauntless attack simulation, when Tobias and Tris are starting to get restless in the Amity compound. Ultimately I decided I didn't want a break in time between the end of* Divergent *and the beginning of* Insurgent; *I wanted the stories to be continuous, which is how they felt in my mind, so I started the book with our heroes jumping off a train (a far more appropriate beginning for them, I think). But there is something about this quiet start that I still like, because it feels like Amity does: peaceful, but with the sense that this is just the eye of the storm, and something bad is still on its way.*

I wake with his name in my mouth.

Will.

There are so many faces that I should see in my nightmares, but for the past few weeks, it has only been him. I watch him crumple to the pavement every night. Dead. My doing.

It is not night now, though. It is midafternoon. I hear insects buzzing in the distant trees. Warm metal touches the back of my skull and my knees, the rails of the train tracks.

The trains haven't run since the simulation attack. I take that as a good sign. If the trains were running, that would mean that some order has returned to the city behind us, and the only order that is possible right now is the kind we would find under Erudite control. As long as the trains are still, everyone's minds are their own. It is consolation enough.

On my right are Tobias's denim-covered legs. He lies with his head on the other rail, his eyes closed. He wears Abnegation gray, because we didn't bring any clothes with us when we escaped the Dauntless compound. I barely notice it most of the time. The color looks right on him.

I think he's asleep, but he takes my wrist and sits up, looking down at me. Sweat runs down the side of his face, making it shine.

"You okay?" he says.

I sit up too, massaging my aching neck. "Yeah. Why?" I sound too defensive. He'll know I'm trying to hide something.

Or maybe he's gotten so used to deceit in my voice that he won't notice. I lie to him all the time now.

"You cried out," he says. "If you're screaming in your sleep, Tris, you aren't okay."

I have two dead parents, I killed one of my best friends, and Tobias, one of the only people I have left, has barely touched me since he told me he loved me and I didn't say it back. If okay exists, it is not this.

"I'm fine," I say. "All right?"

He nods, and releases my wrist.

"We should go back soon," he says, standing. He wipes his face with the hem of his shirt. I catch a glimpse of the patch of Dauntless flames tattooed on his side, over his rib cage. He may wear Abnegation clothing now, but he will always be Dauntless; it's written on his skin, like it's written on mine.

"Trains are still out of commission," he adds. "That's good."

We talk this way a lot now—short sentences, nothing deep or profound. It isn't because there's nothing to talk about. It's just the opposite. There is too much to talk about, so we don't. We spend hours together without conversation.

I twist around to see the skyline. All the buildings are covered with the haze of too much distance, but I can still see the Hub's two prongs stabbing the sky. I feel a pang of something—sadness, maybe, or longing—in my stomach. I want to go back. I *have* to go back.

"I won't be able to stand it here for much longer," I say.

"I won't either."

I know that. We were both built for war. The worse things are, the stronger we are. Hiding in the peace of the Amity compound, we are both weak. Useless.

He offers me his hand. "Come on. Time to go."

I put one hand on the rail and grab his hand with the other. But before I let him pull me up, I pause, frowning. The rail hums beneath my hand. I hold it tightly, my lips moving in a prayer with words I don't know. *Please*, is all I can think. I don't know who I'm begging, or what exactly I'm begging them for.

Trains mean order. Order means Erudite. Maybe I am asking for chaos.

I turn so I'm on my knees, and press my ear to the rail, closing my eyes. I hear a low groan in the metal, like a beast waking after hibernation. It is unmistakable.

The trains are running again.

Evelyn's Speech to the Factionless
Factionless gathering, five years before the events of DIVERGENT

"Welcome. Welcome, everyone.

"I must ask you to look around you. No, I mean it—go ahead and look.

"Standing to your left is someone an Erudite would call an aberration. Standing to your right is someone an Abnegation would call a charity case. Behind you is someone an Amity would look at with pity. In front of you is someone a Candor or a Dauntless would ignore completely.

"All around you there are people who couldn't cut it in a faction's initiation, couldn't cut it as a faction member—people who failed, in one way or another, to meet the expectations of their society. This is a room full of failures.

"Right? Isn't that what we've been told?

"They tell us, in this city, that those who live outside of the factions are weaker than those who live inside them. They tell us that their society is a well-oiled machine that runs perfectly as long as everyone participates. They tell us that the system will help us to grow into morally superior people, to become who we need to be. And they also tell us—most heinously of all—that they have given us a choice.

"I am here today to tell you that they are liars. They have been lying to you all your lives. If you are so weak, why does this city make you its backbone? Why does it depend on you to drive its trains and its buses, to maintain its facilities and equipment, to create the very fabric—the *literal fabric*—of its existence? If you are such failures, then why does the system *depend* on your failure in order to function? A system that cannot survive without the exclusion of some of its members is not a well-oiled machine; it is broken.

"It is broken, and the illusion of choice that it offers you is no choice at all. Choosing a faction is like choosing death by knife, gun, or hanging—the result is the same no matter what method you use.

"But in this case, the result isn't death of the body; it's death of the soul—death of the individual's richness and complexity, the very things that make people worth loving, worth *being*. When you were asked to choose a faction, you were asked to disappear, piece by piece, until only a shadow of you was left. That shadow may have worn your clothes and kissed your spouse good-bye and performed the work to which you were assigned, but it was not you; it could never have been you.

"When they look at you, they may see someone who has faded away, but that is a lie. Let me tell you the truth: You are the ones who were unwilling to fade away. You are the ones who were brave, honest, kind, selfless, or smart, and more than any of those things, more than any words can describe.

"And the people who keep that pathetic, broken machine running know this. On some level they sense that you are far greater, far larger, far more powerful than they can possibly imagine. That is why they starve you, deprive you of homes and clean clothing and representation in government. They want you to be silent, and weak, and desperate. Since they can't control you with the system, they want to control you with distraction. They want you to be so busy thinking of your next meal that you aren't thinking about what has been done to you. They want you to feel that you are utterly and completely alone.

"But you are not failures, and you are not alone. Those who are gathered in this room are not your fellow faction members, wasting away in self-denial—they are your brothers and sisters, your dearest friends, your fellow soldiers. Let us be knit together, not by commitment to empty ideals, to a narrow existence, but by our thirst for a better life.

"It is time to fight. If we are desperate, let it be for an end to this broken system, no matter the cost. If we hunger, let it be for freedom from the factions. And if we are silent, let it be for only a moment as we draw breath for our battle cry."

THE REALITY OF GRIEF
VERONICA ROTH

AFTER THE RELEASE of *Divergent*, I read a comment from a reader somewhere expressing dissatisfaction with the way the book had ended. The reader was older, someone who had lost his or her mother and felt Tris had been a little too cavalier about the death of her parents, a little too capable of moving forward after such trauma. My feeling had been that Tris's adrenaline alone had carried her to the end of the book, that the grief would catch up to her in the moments afterward, but obviously this reader could not have known that (and arguably, should not have had to read the next installment to see at least hints of what was to come in the first one).

Seeing this reader's personal reaction to the end of the story, though negative, sparked in me a determination to make some changes in the rough draft of *Insurgent*. I had never lost anyone I was close to—certainly not someone I was as close to as my mother—and it had not occurred to me that I would need more than a few nightmares and crying fits to capture Tris's grief until I saw that comment about the end of *Divergent*. I had not been thinking, as I began to draft the sequel, of Tris's loss as *real*, or as something that should feel real, even in a futuristic context.

The common wisdom for writers is to "write what you know," but then writers are left to wonder: What happens when your characters experience something you don't know? What happens when your inexperience begins to show? The answer is research. A lot of research, and different kinds of research. You don't need to have lost someone yourself to write about grief, but you do need to treat the issue with care, to do justice to the real experiences that people have had (particularly if they are your readers).

I began my research by consulting with my own mother. My grandmother passed away before I was born, which meant my mother knew what it was like to lose a parent. I asked her how she had felt in the months following her mother's passing, and she gave me a memorable description—that even when she wasn't thinking directly about the loss, she felt like there was a lump in her throat that she just couldn't swallow. It was as if the grief had taken physical form and lodged itself inside her, present even when she tried to distract herself.

I was intrigued by the idea of grief becoming physical, becoming a force that you can't understand or control. But I wanted more feedback, so I asked a group of writer friends, too, and they gave me a few ideas: that grief can make a person wild, turning them to impulsive, self-destructive behavior; that certain touchstones in memory can trigger strong emotions.

I also researched post-traumatic stress disorder, since the violent loss of both parents certainly qualifies as a trauma, and not a small one. I took notes about survivor's guilt, re-experiencing through dreams or memories, angry outbursts, avoidance of anything associated with the traumatic event, and anything else I could find that might apply in Tris's situation. I read articles about PTSD specifically as it related to soldiers, since Tris's losses had occurred in a kind of battle and were not just limited to losing her parents—she had also, in a panic, fired at a friend (Will) and killed him while he was unable to stop himself from attacking her, and that needed to be incorporated into her psychology in *Insurgent* as well.

Eventually I had too many notes and wasn't making enough decisions. I knew Tris didn't need to have every

PTSD symptom I had read about—that would have been overwhelming—and that since she was continuing to charge forward through a chaotic situation without slowing down, the manifestations of her grief might make more sense if they were a little peculiar, and if she wasn't quite aware of them. She hadn't been able to process it all.

I was determined to intertwine Tris's grief and her guilt, since the two seemed necessarily tied—her parents had lost their lives *for her*, after all, which meant she felt responsible, and she had been the one to pull the trigger on Will, even if it had been to save her own life. I settled on two specific elements that I wanted to work into the text: Tris would not be able to touch a gun without remembering the attack (this incorporated both the re-experiencing and the avoidance mentioned earlier), and she would become even more impulsive than she was already. The inability to touch weapons felt more guilt-focused to me, since it was related to her actions with Will, and the self-destructive behavior felt more grief-focused, since it meant, in a roundabout way, that she was trying to find her way back to her parents, who believed in an afterlife. Occasionally the two would come together, the gun avoidance making her impulsivity even more self-destructive.

Tris also suffers from nightmares, fits of anger, and

other, more common signs of grief (periods of strong emotion, periods of numbness, etc.), but those were smaller and could be woven into the text without too much difficulty. Figuring out how to keep Tris alive until the end of the book when she wouldn't touch a gun was much trickier! Tobias's intervention became crucial, since he was determined to protect her, as much as I didn't want to dabble *too* much in the "boyfriend saves the day" trope. I wanted Tris to be active, to continue to be useful with her mind and her instincts even if she wasn't terribly useful in a fighting capacity.

Ultimately the answers came from the limitations I had placed on myself. Tris couldn't be useful through violence, so how else could she be useful? What else could she find herself committed to, if not overcoming the Erudite and traitor Dauntless with an attack? What, even in the midst of all her guilt and grief, could she discover that was worth seeking?

In *Insurgent*, I let Tris travel as far down the dark paths of grief and guilt as she would go. I let her be angry and in denial and self-destructive and stubborn; I let her be deceitful and naive and confused. It resulted in a far less likable Tris than I had seen in *Divergent*, but I loved how real her emotions felt to me, and I knew she would come out of that dark maze alive and changed, so I was

Veronica Roth's Faction Playlists

Dauntless

Dauntless songs capture both the faction's bravado (and occasional cockiness!) as well as their commitment to taking chances, facing difficulty, and living without regret.

"Glory and Gore" by Lorde
"Hysteria" by Muse
"Help I'm Alive" by Metric

Amity

These songs approach the Amity lifestyle from a few different angles—their compassion for each other, for one; their love of group decision-making and harmony, for another; and finally, their strong belief in pacifism.

"No Envy, No Fear" by Joshua Radin
"One Voice" by The Wailin' Jennys
"Charlie Boy" by The Lumineers

Abnegation

Abnegation is the trickiest faction to create a playlist for, probably because they would consider recreational music-listening to be self-indulgent! But these songs assert the smallness of the self and praise ordinariness.

"Holocene" by Bon Iver
"My Hero" by Foo Fighters
"Goodbye, I!" by mewithoutYou

Candor

The Candor embrace honesty even when it's abrasive—they love the hard truth rather than the easy lie. These songs present Candor self-awareness, revelations about life, and harsh but clear communication with others, in turn.

"Madder Red" by Yeasayer
"Wake Up" by Arcade Fire
"Two Points for Honesty" by Guster

Erudite

There are many facets to the Erudite life: a love of order (as expressed in the first song); an understanding that the individual is both essential to a group's functioning yet not more important than that group (the second song); and a sense of wonder about all that is to be known about the universe, and how that wonder creates a thirst for knowledge (the third song, and parts of the second).

"Everything in Its Right Place" by Radiohead
"Helplessness Blues" by Fleet Foxes
"2-1" by Imogen Heap

FACTIONLESS

The factionless come from diverse backgrounds, but one thing unifies them above all: rebellion. These are people who don't want to be controlled anymore, who want to be more than their label, and who desire freedom above all else.

"Uprising" by Muse
"I Want to Break Free" by Queen
"Escape" by Thirty Seconds to Mars

INSURGENT DISCUSSION QUESTIONS

1. Tris often relies heavily on her instincts to guide her. Find at least two examples of this in *Insurgent*. What do you think are the benefits and drawbacks of following one's instincts? Do you follow your own instincts to make decisions in your life?

2. In deciding between gathering information and taking action, Tris says, "I don't believe it's more important to move forward than to find out the truth. . . . The truth has a way of changing a person's plans" (pp. 31–32). What do you think she means by this? Do you agree with her?

3. Caleb tells Tris that, according to the Faction History book, Erudite and Amity are the "essential factions" (p. 34). Do you agree? What character traits do you think are most necessary for people's survival? Why?

4. While under the influence of the Amity peace serum, Tris says to Tobias, "*That's* why you like me! Because you're not very nice either! It makes so much more sense now" (p. 62). As a reader, how important do you feel that it is for a story's main characters to be likable or nice? Are other attributes equal to or more important

than likability? What character traits are most appealing to you about your favorite book characters?

5. Tobias says, "Sometimes people just want to be happy, even if it's not real" (p. 68). Relate this statement to the expression "Ignorance is bliss." Do you think bliss is possible in Tris's world, or in the real world? What do you think of "Ignorance is bliss" as a way of life?

6. Tris prefers to fall asleep surrounded by sounds, saying that "noise and activity are the refuges of the bereaved and the guilty" (p. 107). What other ways does she find to cope with her guilt? Do you have similar or different ways of coping with guilt and other strong emotions?

7. The people of Candor are "merciless, but honest" (p. 119). Do you think the truth is always merciless? Does it have to be?

8. The Candor faction also sees charm as deceptive. Do you agree? Is it possible for a person to be charming and candid at the same time?

9. Would the factionless have a symbol? If you think they

would, what would it look like? What about for the Divergent?

10. Was Tris's decision to surrender herself to the Erudite—without warning any of the people who love her—brave or selfish? Discuss.

11. What do you think happens after the last page of *Insurgent*? From the point of view of any character in the story, write a bonus chapter that describes what you think might happen next.

12. Put yourself in Tris's shoes, having the opportunity to interact with all of the factions and collect life lessons from each of them. What are the main lessons you'd take away?

ONE CHOICE CAN TRANSFORM YOU
ONE CHOICE CAN DESTROY YOU
ONE CHOICE WILL DEFINE YOU

DIVE INTO THIS EXCERPT FROM

ALLEGIANT

THE POWERFUL CONCLUSION TO THE
DIVERGENT TRILOGY

CHAPTER
ONE

TRIS

I PACE IN our cell in Erudite headquarters, her words echoing in my mind: *My name will be Edith Prior, and there is much I am happy to forget.*

"So you've *never* seen her before? Not even in pictures?" Christina says, her wounded leg propped up on a pillow. She was shot during our desperate attempt to reveal the Edith Prior video to our city. At the time we had no idea what it would say, or that it would shatter the foundation we stand on, the factions, our identities. "Is she a grandmother or an aunt or something?"

"I told you, no," I say, turning when I reach the wall. "Prior is—was—my father's name, so it would have to be on his side of the family. But Edith is an Abnegation name, and my father's relatives must have been Erudite, so . . ."

"So she must be older," Cara says, leaning her head against the wall. From this angle she looks just like her brother, Will, my friend, the one I shot. Then she straightens, and the ghost of him is gone. "A few generations back. An ancestor."

"Ancestor." The word feels old inside me, like crumbling brick. I touch one wall of the cell as I turn around. The panel is cold and white.

My ancestor, and this is the inheritance she passed to me: freedom from the factions, and the knowledge that my Divergent identity is more important than I could have known. My existence is a signal that we need to leave this city and offer our help to whoever is outside it.

"I want to know," Cara says, running her hand over her face. "I need to know how long we've been here. Would you stop pacing for *one minute*?"

I stop in the middle of the cell and raise my eyebrows at her.

"Sorry," she mumbles.

"It's okay," Christina says. "We've been in here way too long."

It's been days since Evelyn mastered the chaos in the lobby of Erudite headquarters with a few short commands and had all the prisoners hustled away to cells on the third floor. A factionless woman came to doctor our wounds and distribute painkillers, and we've eaten and showered several times, but no one has told us what's going on outside. No matter how forcefully I've asked them.

"I thought Tobias would come by now," I say, dropping to the edge of my cot. "Where *is* he?"

"Maybe he's still angry that you lied to him and went behind his back to work with his father," Cara says.

I glare at her.

"Four wouldn't be that petty," Christina says, either to chastise Cara or to reassure me, I'm not sure. "Something's probably going on that's keeping him away. He told you to trust him."

In the chaos, when everyone was shouting and the factionless were trying to push us toward the staircase, I curled my fingers in the hem of his shirt so I wouldn't lose him. He took my wrists in his hands and pushed me away, and those were the words he said. *Trust me. Go where they tell you.*

"I'm trying," I say, and it's true. I'm trying to trust him. But every part of me, every fiber and every nerve, is straining toward freedom, not just from this cell but from the prison of the city beyond it.

I need to see what's outside the fence.

CHAPTER
TWO

TOBIAS

I CAN'T WALK these hallways without remembering the days I spent as a prisoner here, barefoot, pain pulsing inside me every time I moved. And with that memory is another one, one of waiting for Beatrice Prior to go to her death, of my fists against the door, of her legs slung across Peter's arms when he told me she was just drugged.

I hate this place.

It isn't as clean as it was when it was the Erudite compound; now it is ravaged by war, bullet holes in the walls and the broken glass of shattered lightbulbs everywhere. I walk over dirty footprints and beneath flickering lights to her cell and I am admitted without question, because I bear the factionless symbol—an empty circle—on a black band around my arm and Evelyn's features on my face. Tobias Eaton was a shameful name, and now it is a powerful one.

Tris crouches on the ground inside, shoulder to shoulder with Christina and diagonal from Cara. My Tris should look pale and small—she *is* pale and small, after all—but instead the room is full of her.

Her round eyes find mine and she is on her feet, her arms wound tightly around my waist and her face against my chest.

I squeeze her shoulder with one hand and run my other hand over her hair, still surprised when her hair stops above her neck instead of below it. I was happy when she cut it, because it was hair for a warrior and not a girl, and I knew that was what she would need.

"How'd you get in?" she says in her low, clear voice.

"I'm Tobias Eaton," I say, and she laughs.

"Right. I keep forgetting." She pulls away just far enough to look at me. There is a wavering expression in her eyes, like she is a heap of leaves about to be scattered by the wind. "What's happening? What took you so long?"

She sounds desperate, pleading. For all the horrible memories this place carries for me, it carries more for her, the walk to her execution, her brother's betrayal, the fear serum. I have to get her out.

Cara looks up with interest. I feel uncomfortable, like I have shifted in my skin and it doesn't quite fit anymore. I hate having an audience.

"Evelyn has the city under lockdown," I say. "No one goes a step in any direction without her say-so. A few days ago she gave a speech about uniting against our oppressors, the people outside."

"Oppressors?" Christina says. She takes a vial from her pocket and dumps the contents into her mouth—painkillers for the bullet wound in her leg, I assume.

I slide my hands into my pockets. "Evelyn—and a lot of people, actually—think we shouldn't leave the city just to help a bunch of people who shoved us in here so they could use us later. They want to try to heal the city and solve our own problems instead of leaving to solve other people's. I'm paraphrasing, of course," I say. "I suspect that opinion is very convenient for my mother, because as long as we're all contained, she's in charge. The second we leave, she loses her hold."

"Great." Tris rolls her eyes. "Of course she would choose the most selfish route possible."

"She has a point." Christina wraps her fingers around the vial. "I'm not saying I don't want to leave the city and see what's out there, but we've got enough going on here. How are we supposed to help a bunch of people we've never met?"

Tris considers this, chewing on the inside of her cheek. "I don't know," she admits.

My watch reads three o'clock. I've been here too long—long enough to make Evelyn suspicious. I told her I came to break things off with Tris, that it wouldn't take much time. I'm not sure she believed me.

I say, "Listen, I mostly came to warn you—they're starting the trials for all the prisoners. They're going to put you all under truth serum, and if it works, you'll be convicted as traitors. I think we would all like to avoid that."

"Convicted as *traitors*?" Tris scowls. "How is revealing the truth to our entire city an act of betrayal?"

"It was an act of defiance against your leaders," I say. "Evelyn and her followers don't want to leave the city. They won't thank you for showing that video."

"They're just like Jeanine!" She makes a fitful gesture, like she wants to hit something but there's nothing available. "Ready to do anything to stifle the truth, and for what? To be kings of their tiny little world? It's ridiculous."

I don't want to say so, but part of me agrees with my mother. I don't owe the people outside this city anything, whether I am Divergent or not. I'm not sure I want to offer myself to them to solve humanity's problems, whatever that means.

But I do want to leave, in the desperate way that an

animal wants to escape a trap. Wild and rabid. Ready to gnaw through bone.

"Be that as it may," I say carefully, "if the truth serum works on you, you will be convicted."

"*If* it works?" says Cara, narrowing her eyes.

"Divergent," Tris says to her, pointing at her own head. "Remember?"

"That's fascinating." Cara tucks a stray hair back into the knot just above her neck. "But atypical. In my experience, most Divergent can't resist the truth serum. I wonder why you can."

"You and every other Erudite who ever stuck a needle in me," Tris snaps.

"Can we focus, please? I would like to avoid having to break you out of prison," I say. Suddenly desperate for comfort, I reach for Tris's hand, and she brings her fingers up to meet mine. We are not people who touch each other carelessly; every point of contact between us feels important, a rush of energy and relief.

"All right, all right," she says, gently now. "What did you have in mind?"

"I'll get Evelyn to let you testify first, of the three of you," I say. "All you have to do is come up with a lie that will exonerate both Christina and Cara, and then tell it under truth serum."

"What kind of lie would do that?"

"I thought I would leave that to you," I say. "Since you're the better liar."

I know as I'm saying the words that they hit a sore spot in both of us. She lied to me so many times. She promised me she wouldn't go to her death in the Erudite compound when Jeanine demanded the sacrifice of a Divergent, and then she did it anyway. She told me she would stay home during the Erudite attack, and then I found her in Erudite headquarters, working with my father. I understand why she did all those things, but that doesn't mean we aren't still broken.

"Yeah." She looks at her shoes. "Okay, I'll think of something."

I set my hand on her arm. "I'll talk to Evelyn about your trial. I'll try to make it soon."

"Thank you."

I feel the urge, familiar now, to wrench myself from my body and speak directly into her mind. It is the same urge, I realize, that makes me want to kiss her every time I see her, because even a sliver of distance between us is infuriating. Our fingers, loosely woven a moment ago, now clutch together, her palm tacky with moisture, mine rough in places where I have grabbed too many handles on too many moving trains. Now she looks pale and small, but her eyes make me think of wide-open skies that I have never actually seen, only dreamed of.

"If you're going to kiss, do me a favor and tell me so I can look away," says Christina.

"We are," Tris says. And we do.

I touch her cheek to slow the kiss down, holding her mouth on mine so I can feel every place where our lips touch and every place where they pull away. I savor the air we share in the second afterward and the slip of her nose across mine. I think of something to say, but it is too intimate, so I swallow it. A moment later I decide I don't care.

"I wish we were alone," I say as I back out of the cell.

She smiles. "I almost always wish that."

As I shut the door, I see Christina pretending to vomit, and Cara laughing, and Tris's hands hanging at her sides.

CHAPTER
THREE

TRIS

"I THINK YOU'RE all idiots." My hands are curled in my lap like a sleeping child's. My body is heavy with truth serum. Sweat collects on my eyelids. "You should be thanking me, not questioning me."

"We should thank you for defying the instructions of your faction leaders? Thank you for trying to prevent one of your faction leaders from killing Jeanine Matthews? You behaved like a traitor." Evelyn Johnson spits the word like a snake. We are in the conference room in Erudite headquarters, where the trials have been taking place. I have now been a prisoner for at least a week.

I see Tobias, half-hidden in the shadows behind his mother. He has kept his eyes averted since I sat in the chair and they cut the strip of plastic binding my wrists together. For just for a moment, his eyes touch mine, and I know it's time to start lying.

It's easier now that I know I can do it. As easy as pushing the weight of the truth serum aside in my mind.

"I am not a traitor," I say. "At the time I believed that Marcus was working under Dauntless-factionless orders. Since I couldn't join the fight as a soldier, I was happy to help with something else."

"Why couldn't you be a soldier?" Fluorescent light glows behind Evelyn's hair. I can't see her face, and I can't focus on anything for more than a second before the truth serum threatens to pull me down again.

"Because." I bite my lip, as if trying to stop the words from rushing out. I don't know when I became so good at acting, but I guess it's not that different from lying, which I have always had a talent for. "Because I couldn't hold a gun, okay? Not after shooting . . . him. My friend Will. I couldn't hold a gun without panicking."

Evelyn's eyes pinch tighter. I suspect that even in the softest parts of her, there is no sympathy for me.

"So Marcus told you he was working under my orders," she says, "and even knowing what you do about his rather tense relationship with both the Dauntless and the factionless, you believed him?"

"Yes."

"I can see why you didn't choose Erudite." She laughs.

My cheeks tingle. I would like to slap her, as I'm sure many of the people in this room would, though they wouldn't dare to admit it. Evelyn has us all trapped in the city, controlled by armed factionless patrolling the streets. She knows that whoever holds the guns holds the power. And with Jeanine Matthews dead, there is no one left to challenge her for it.

From one tyrant to another. That is the world we know, now.

"Why didn't you tell anyone about this?" she says.

"I didn't want to have to admit to any weakness," I say. "And I didn't want Four to know I was working with his father. I knew he wouldn't like it." I feel new words rising in my throat, prompted by the truth serum. "I brought you the truth about our city and the reason we are in it. If you aren't thanking me for it, you should at least *do* something about it instead of sitting here on this mess you made, pretending it's a throne!"

Evelyn's mocking smile twists like she has just tasted something unpleasant. She leans in close to my face, and I see for the first time how old she is; I see the lines that frame her eyes and mouth, and the unhealthy pallor she wears from years of eating far too little. Still, she is handsome like her son. Near-starvation could not take that.

"I am doing something about it. I am making a new world," she says, and her voice gets even quieter, so that I can barely hear her. "I was Abnegation. I have known the truth far longer than you have, Beatrice Prior. I don't know how you're getting away with this, but I promise you, you will not have a place in my new world, especially not with my son."

I smile a little. I shouldn't, but it's harder to suppress gestures and expressions than words, with this weight in my veins. She believes that Tobias belongs to her now. She doesn't know the truth, that he belongs to himself.

Evelyn straightens, folding her arms.

"The truth serum has revealed that while you may be a fool, you are no traitor. This interrogation is over. You may leave."

"What about my friends?" I say sluggishly. "Christina, Cara. They didn't do anything wrong either."

"We will deal with them soon," Evelyn says.

I stand, though I'm weak and dizzy from the serum. The room is packed with people, shoulder to shoulder, and I can't find the exit for a few long seconds, until someone takes my arm, a boy with warm brown skin and a wide smile—Uriah. He guides me to the door. Everyone starts talking.

Uriah leads me down the hallway to the elevator bank. The elevator doors spring open when he touches the button, and I follow him in, still not steady on my feet. When the doors close, I say, "You don't think the part about the mess and the throne was too much?"

"No. She expects you to be hotheaded. She might have been suspicious if you hadn't been."

I feel like everything inside me is vibrating with energy, in anticipation of what is to come. I am free. We're going to find a way out of the city. No more waiting, pacing a cell, demanding answers that I won't get from the guards.

The guards did tell me a few things about the new factionless order this morning. Former faction members are required to move closer to Erudite headquarters and mix, no more than four members of a particular faction in each dwelling. We have to mix our clothing, too. I was given a yellow Amity shirt and black Candor pants earlier as a result of that particular edict.

"All right, we're this way. . . ." Uriah leads me out of the elevator. This floor of Erudite headquarters is all glass, even the walls. Sunlight refracts through it and casts slivers of rainbows across the floor. I shield my eyes with one hand and follow Uriah to a long, narrow room with beds on either side. Next to each bed is a glass cabinet for clothes and books, and a small table.

"It used to be the Erudite initiate dormitory," Uriah says. "I reserved beds for Christina and Cara already."

Sitting on a bed near the door are three girls in red shirts—Amity girls, I would guess—and on the left side of the room, an older woman lies on one of the beds, her spectacles dangling from one ear—possibly one of the Erudite. I know I should try to stop putting people in factions when I see them, but it's an old habit, hard to break.

Uriah falls on one of the beds in the back corner. I sit on the one next to his, glad to be free and at rest, finally.

"Zeke says it sometimes takes a little while for the factionless to process exonerations, so they should be out later," Uriah says.

For a moment I feel relieved that everyone I care about will be out of prison by tonight. But then I remember that Caleb is still there, because he was a well-known lackey of Jeanine Matthews, and the factionless will never exonerate him. But just how far they will go to destroy the mark Jeanine Matthews left on this city, I don't know.

I don't care, I think. But even as I think it, I know it's a lie. He's still my brother.

"Good," I say. "Thanks, Uriah."

He nods, and leans his head against the wall to prop it up.

"How are you?" I say. "I mean . . . Lynn . . ."

Uriah had been friends with Lynn and Marlene as long as I'd known them, and now both of them are dead. I feel like I might be able to understand—after all, I've lost two friends too, Al to the pressures of initiation and Will to the attack simulation and my own hasty actions. But I don't want to pretend that our suffering is the same. For one thing, Uriah knew his friends better than I did.

"I don't want to talk about it." Uriah shakes his head. "Or think about it. I just want to keep moving."

"Okay. I understand. Just . . . let me know if you need . . ."

"Yeah." He smiles at me and gets up. "You're okay here, right? I told my mom I'd visit tonight, so I have to go soon. Oh—almost forgot to tell you—Four said he wants to meet you later."

I pull up straighter. "Really? When? Where?"

"A little after ten, at Millennium Park. On the lawn." He smirks. "Don't get too excited, your head will explode."

CHAPTER FOUR

TOBIAS

MY MOTHER ALWAYS sits on the edges of things—chairs, ledges, tables—as if she suspects she will have to flee in an instant. This time it's Jeanine's old desk in Erudite headquarters that she sits on the edge of, her toes balanced on the floor and the cloudy light of the city glowing behind her. She is a woman of muscle twisted around bone.

"I think we have to talk about your loyalty," she says, but she doesn't sound like she's accusing me of something, she just sounds tired. For a moment she seems so worn that I feel like I can see right through her, but then she straightens, and the feeling is gone.

"Ultimately, it was you who helped Tris and got that video released," she says. "No one else knows that, but *I* know it."

"Listen." I lean forward to prop my elbows on my knees. "I didn't know what was in that file. I trusted Tris's judgment more than my own. That's all that happened."

I thought telling Evelyn that I broke up with Tris would make it easier for my mother to trust me, and I was right—she has been warmer, more open, ever since I told that lie.

"And now that you've seen the footage?" Evelyn says. "What do you think now? Do you think we should leave the city?"

I know what she wants me to say—that I see no reason to join the outside world—but I'm not a good liar, so instead I select a part of the truth.

"I'm afraid of it," I say. "I'm not sure it's smart to leave the city knowing the dangers that might be out there."

She considers me for a moment, biting the inside of her cheek. I learned that habit from her—I used to chew my skin raw as I waited for my father to come home, unsure which version of him I would encounter, the one the Abnegation trusted and revered, or the one whose hands struck me.

I run my tongue along the bite scars and swallow the memory like it's bile.

She slides off the desk and moves to the window. "I've been receiving disturbing reports of a rebel organization among us." She looks up, raising an eyebrow. "People always organize into groups. That's a fact of our existence. I just didn't expect it to happen this quickly."

"What kind of organization?"

"The kind that wants to leave the city," she says. "They released some kind of manifesto this morning. They call themselves the Allegiant." When she sees my confused look, she adds, "Because they're *allied* with the original purpose of our city, see?"

"The original purpose—you mean, what was in the Edith Prior video? That we should send people outside when the city has a large Divergent population?"

"That, yes. But also living in factions. The Allegiant claim that we're meant to be in factions because we've been in them since the beginning." She shakes her head. "Some people will always fear change. But we can't indulge them."

With the factions dismantled, part of me has felt like a man released from a long imprisonment. I don't have to evaluate whether every thought I have or choice I make fits into a narrow ideology. I don't want the factions back.

But Evelyn hasn't liberated us like she thinks—she's just made us all factionless. She's afraid of what we would choose, if we were given actual freedom. And that means that no matter what I believe about the factions, I'm relieved that someone, somewhere, is defying her.

I arrange my face into an empty expression, but my heart is beating faster than before. I have had to be careful, to stay in Evelyn's good graces. It's easy for me to lie to everyone else, but it's more difficult to lie to her, the only person who knew all the secrets of our Abnegation house, the violence contained within its walls.

"What are you going to do about them?" I say.

"I am going to get them under control, what else?"

The word "control" makes me sit up straight, as rigid as the chair beneath me. In this city, "control" means needles and serums and seeing without seeing; it means simulations, like the one that almost made me kill Tris, or the one that made the Dauntless into an army.

"With simulations?" I say slowly.

She scowls. "Of course not! I am not Jeanine Matthews!"

Her flare of anger sets me off. I say, "Don't forget that I barely know you, Evelyn."

She winces at the reminder. "Then let me tell you that I will never resort to simulations to get my way. Death would be better."

It's possible that death is what she will use—killing people would certainly keep them quiet, stifle their revolution before it begins. Whoever the Allegiant are, they need to be warned, and quickly.

"I can find out who they are," I say.

"I'm sure that you can. Why else would I have told you about them?"

There are plenty of reasons she would tell me. To test me. To catch me. To feed me false information. I know what my mother is—she is someone for whom the end of a thing justifies the means of getting there, the same as my father, and the same, sometimes, as me.

"I'll do it, then. I'll find them."

I rise, and her fingers, brittle as branches, close around my arm. "Thank you."

I force myself to look at her. Her eyes are close above her nose, which is hooked at the end, like my own. Her skin is a middling color, darker than mine. For a moment I see her in Abnegation gray, her thick hair bound back with a dozen pins, sitting across the dinner table from me. I see her crouched in front of me, fixing my mismatched shirt buttons before I go to school, and standing at the window, watching the uniform street for my father's car, her hands clasped—no, clenched, her tan knuckles white with tension. We were united in fear then, and now that she isn't afraid anymore, part of me wants to see what it would be like to unite with her in strength.

I feel an ache, like I betrayed her, the woman who used to be my only ally, and I turn away before I can take it all back and apologize.

VERONICA ROTH

is the #1 *New York Times* bestselling author of **DIVERGENT**, **INSURGENT**, **ALLEGIANT**, and **FOUR: A DIVERGENT COLLECTION**. Now a full-time writer, Ms. Roth and her husband live near Chicago. You can visit her online at www.veronicarothbooks.com.

FOLLOW VERONICA ROTH ON

FOLLOW THE SERIES

/DivergentSeries

DivergentOfficial.com

For exclusive information on your favorite authors and artists, visit www.authortracker.com.

Also available as an ebook, CDs, and downloadable audio.

A CHOICE
BECOMES A SACRIFICE

A SACRIFICE
BECOMES A LOSS

A LOSS
BECOMES A BURDEN

A BURDEN
BECOMES A BATTLE

ONE CHOICE
CAN DESTROY YOU

New York Times bestselling author Veronica Roth's much-anticipated second book of the dystopian DIVERGENT series is another intoxicating thrill ride of a story, rich with hallmark twists, heartbreaks, romance, and powerful insights about human nature.

BONUS MATERIALS INCLUDE:

Alternate Beginning ♦ Evelyn's Speech to the Factionless "The Reality of Grief" by Veronica Roth ♦ Faction Playlist Insurgent Discussion Guide ♦ and an Excerpt from ALLEGIANT

KATHERINE TEGEN BOOKS
An Imprint of HarperCollins Publishers

Cover art ™ & © Veronica Roth 2012
Cover art and landscape design by Joel Tippie

FIND US ON
WWW.EPICREADS.COM

CAN $15.99
ISBN 978-0-06-238774-5

$1.79

Cyberspace and the Law:

Your Rights and Duties in the On-line World

Edward A. Cavazos
Gavino Morin

The MIT Press
Cambridge, Massachusetts
London, England

This book was set in Palatino by The MIT Press and was printed and bound in the United States of America.

Library of Congress Cataloging-in-Publication Data

Cavazos, Edward A.
   Cyberspace and the law: your rights and duties in the on-line word / Edward A.
   Cavazos, Gavino Morin.
      p.   cm.
   Includes bibliographical references and index.
   ISBN 0-262-53123-2
   1. Telematics—Law and Legislation—United States.   I. Morin, Gavino.   II. Title.
KF2765. C38 1994
343. 7309′944—dc20   94-12356
[347. 3039944]   CIP

To our parents

Contents

Preface   ix

1 **Defining Cyberspace**   1
A Quick Tour of Cyberspace   2
Activities in Cyberspace   5
The Dimensions of Cyberspace   9
The Future of Cyberspace   10

2 **Electronic Privacy**   13
Anonymity   14
The Privacy of Electronic Communications and the ECPA   16
State Privacy Law   26
Common Law Actions for Invasion of Privacy   26
The Great Cryptography Debate   28

3 **The Virtual Marketplace: Business Transactions on the Net**   33
Electronic Contracts   34
Acceptable Use Policies and Caller Contracts   44
Credit Card Transactions in Cyberspace   45

4 **Intellectual Property in Cyberspace: Copyright Law in a New World**   47
A Copyright Primer   48
Copyright in Cyberspace   56
Software   62
Other Copyright Issues   64

5 **Harmful and Dangerous Words and the First Amendment**   67
The First Amendment in Cyberspace   67

Freedom of Speech   69
Freedom of the Press   85

6 **Adult Material: Drawing the Line between the Legal and Illegal**   89
An Overview of Adult Materials and Activities Available in Cyberspace   90
Indecency vs. Obscenity: Classifying On-line Adult Materials and Activities   93
Significance of Being Deemed Obscene   97
Laws Governing Adult Material   97
Possession of Obscene Material   98
Child Pornography   99
What Does All This Mean?   102

7 **Cyber-Crimes: Pitfalls for the Unwary Traveler**   105
The Computer Fraud and Abuse Act   107
Credit Card Abuse Laws   109
Wire Fraud   110
The National Stolen Property Act   110
Software Piracy   111
Obscenity and Child Pornography   114
Computer Viruses and Other Harmful Software   114
Electronic Communications Privacy Act   116
State Computer Crime Laws   116
Are the Authorities Overzealous?   120

Notes   123
Appendix A: Where to Go for More Help   129
Appendix B: The Electronic Communications Privacy Act   143
Appendix C: 18 U.S.C. § 1465: Transportation of Obscene Matter for Sale or Distribution   177
Appendix D: 7 U.S.C. § 223: Obscene or Harrassing Telephone Calls   179
Appendix E : Federal Child Pornography Statute   183
Appendix F: State Child Pornography Statutes   187
Appendix G: The Computer Fraud and Abuse Act   191
Appendix H: The Texas Computer Crime Law   197
Appendix I: State Computer Crime Laws   201
Index   207

Preface

Our involvement with cyberspace and the law started long before this book was conceived. While it is hard to pinpoint when our interest involving legal issues in cyberspace actually began, we can say with confidence that this interest was piqued by the time we entered law school. As we continued our study of the law, we found more and more pieces of e-mail addressed to us that began with a variation of the phrase "I know you're a law student; could you give me your thoughts on the following issue?" Quite often, the e-mail would go on to describe an interesting hypothetical situation involving computer-mediated communication, and would conclude with a request for legal analysis. Much to our dismay, our response too often included the phrase "I'll have to research that."

From these exchanges came two realizations. First, there was a strong need for analysis of the legal issues of cyberspace. Second, there was no single source to which a user in cyberspace could turn for this analysis. This book is our response to these realizations.

The greatest challenge we faced in writing this book was to present the law in a concise and accurate manner, and to do so without resorting to legalese. John Page, author of PFS: FILE, once observed that "complicated programs are far easier to write than straightforward programs." The same is true about writing a book such as this one. As attorneys, we would have found it easier to write a book using legal terms and assume that our readers were also attorneys or had immediate access to a legal dictionary. We chose to write a more straightforward book, and we hope we succeeded in meeting that goal.

About This Book

Who Should Read This Book?

A complex legal system is one of the characteristics (some may call it the price) of a large and highly structured society. In our society, the law is a prevalent part of daily life. Although the law plays a large role in everyone's life, few people go to the trouble of consulting attorneys for their day-to-day affairs. This is so for a variety of reasons. First, and most important, consulting an attorney can be expensive. Most people contact one only when they feel it is absolutely necessary: when obtaining a divorce, responding to a lawsuit or ciminal charges, or devising a will. A second reason is that most of the laws encountered on a daily basis tend to be fairly intuitive. Nobody needs to refer to the penal code to know that shoplifting is a crime. Finally, many legal questions are simple ones, which are easily answered by referring to legal material aimed at, and available to, the general public.

It is somewhat surprising that, despite the wealth of general legal materials available, there is little out there that covers the topic of computer telecommunications from the user's perspective. While some excellent treatises and articles on the subject of computer telecommunications do exist, they are often too technical to be of real value to the lay person, or they address the issues from a different perspective (that of the system operator, or the government, for example). This work attempts to fill some of this void.

This book is written primarily for the members of the on-line world who have little or no legal training. It attempts to answer some of the more frequently encountered legal questions: What legal recourse do I have if someone has intercepted and read my private electronic mail without my consent? What sort of trouble can I get into for having downloaded a risqué computer graphic file? Who owns the copyright to the message I just posted on a bulletin board?

This book may also prove useful to the legal community. It is not a legal treatise, nor was it our intent to write one. It does, however, provide an overview of some of the more common legal issues created by the on-line world. An attorney who is handling a case involving computer communications might find this overview helpful. Where we thought it useful, we included case citations and references to statutes. The notes and appendixes will act as a good starting point for conducting more specific legal research.

Topics Addressed

This book covers a wide range of legal issues that a user is likely to encounter on-line. Chapter two discusses the issue of electronic privacy. The chapter deals with a wide range of topics, including the use of "handles," encryption, and lawsuits that arise when privacy is infringed. The bulk of the chapter is dedicated to a discussion of the Electronic Communications Privacy Act (ECPA)—a statute of great importance to the on-line world. The ECPA was at the heart of one of the most celebrated cyberspace cases, *Steve Jackson Games v. The United States Secret Service*.

Chapter three, focusing on business transactions in the on-line world, is organized around the traditional principles of contract law. These principles are discussed and then applied to a telecommunications setting. The chapter ends with a brief discussion of acceptable use policies, caller contracts, and the use of credit cards over the network.

Copyright law is addressed in chapter four. The chapter gives the reader a basic overview of copyright law and then applies the law discussed to cyberspace. For example, the chapter explores issues such as who owns electronic mail, the legality of reposting messages on bulletin boards, and the transfer of software through cyberspace.

Chapter five deals with the application of the First Amendment to on-line activities. It addresses such topics as censorship by system operators, defamation, and freedom of the press.

Closely related to chapter five is chapter six, which concerns itself with sexually explicit material. The chapter classifies this material into one of three legal categories and offers advice on the legality of transactions involving each. It includes a flow-chart to assist the reader in determining which activities are protected.

Finally, chapter seven covers "cyber-crimes." The chapter outlines the most important federal and state criminal laws which regulate on-line activities. The chapter explores topics from credit card fraud to computer viruses.

Because of the wide variety of potential legal issues posed by cyberspace, this book only covers those topics that are likely to be most useful to on-line users. For example, the discussion of electronic commerce does not attempt to explain every doctrine of traditional contract law and apply it to the on-line world. The result is a lighter, more practical manual for the on-line user.

Getting the Most from This Book

Regardless of whether you are reading this book straight through or using it as a reference guide, one important note about style should be mentioned. For most chapters, this book follows a simple paradigm. First, the area of law being addressed is defined in its traditional context, that is, outside of cyberspace. Next, that area of law is applied to cyberspace and the resulting problems are examined. Thus, for example, the chapter on sexually explicit material discusses historical approaches developed for dealing with this issue in a noncomputer environment. The chapter then examines computerized adult material in light of the earlier discussion. Resulting problems are then examined, and solutions are suggested.

As a result, most chapters are organized in a fashion that allows readers to locate quickly those sections that are most important to them and to avoid those that provide them with little, if any, insight. Consequently, a reader with legal training in intellectual property will probably want to gloss over, or skip entirely, the section that serves as a copyright primer, and jump straight into the section dealing with the application of copyright law in cyberspace. Likewise, those readers who are familiar with the topic will want to skip over those sections that deal with the basic workings of cyberspace. Those sections are provided only for explanatory purposes and the sake of completeness and offer no new technical information to those who are already veterans of cyberspace.

With this in mind, it should be noted that chapter one deals with the history and basic functions of the on-line world, not only to provide background into this area, but also to identify the many different systems that comprise cyberspace. This is necessary because many users, even the most sophisticated ones, define "cyberspace" by the systems they have explored, and the tools they have used. Consequently, many users of large commercial systems may not be aware of local bulletin board systems, and many users of single-line bulletin board systems may have no idea that "chatting" is a popular on-line activity. Chapter one, therefore, helps to define the scope of this book by providing a working definition of cyberspace.

Electronic Pocket Parts

A book such as this is a snapshot of the law as it existed when the manuscript was written. The law, especially as it relates to computer-mediated communication, is constantly changing. Existing statutes are amended, reinterpreted, and repealed and new statutes are enacted. Likewise, precedents set by cases are expanded, redefined, reversed, and overruled. The problems that result from attempts to define a dynamic system using a static medium are obvious—the solutions less so. One popular solution is to give those who purchase legal texts the option of subscribing to an updating service. The subscription service will occasionally publish and distribute a "pocket part."

A pocket part is an addendum to the main text of a book. It is designed to fit snugly into a slit or pocket at the back of a bound volume. While traditional pocket parts are an effective remedy to the problems posed by outdated texts, they suffer from some inherent limitations. First, there is always a delay from the time a pocket part is written and the time it reaches the reader. This delay is caused by the mechanics of printing and distributing. Another drawback of pocket parts is that they tend to be expensive. Usually the cost of keeping a law book up to date far exceeds the price of the original text.

In an effort to maintain the benefits of pocket parts and to minimize their limitations, updates to this book will be provided in the form of "electronic pocket parts." From time to time, significant legal developments related to the contents of the book will be compiled and made available in cyberspace. Readers who wish to stay abreast of such developments will find the electronic parts of this book archived at mitpress.mit.edu, ftp.eff.org, and various other locations on the Internet, BBSs, and on-line services.

Acknowledgments

We would like to acknowledge the many people who helped us make this a better book. Special thanks go out to Smoot Carl-Mitchell, Mike Godwin, Steve Jackson, Tom Moynihan, Jim Owens, John Quarterman, Jesus Ramirez, David Smith, Shari Steele, Bruce Sterling, and Mark Whitworth. Pete Kennedy of George, Donaldson & Ford deserves a special mention for his careful reading of early drafts and his valuable comments and rewrites of several parts of this text. We would further like to thank Elaine Hansen, Bryan Newcombe, and Aaron Pickell, for providing us with support and inspiration during those hectic times when we struggled to meet our deadlines.

We would especially like to extend our gratitude to our editor, Bob Prior, whose foresight and enthusiasm created this project. Without

1   Defining Cyberspace

In the early 1980s, William Gibson, then a relatively unknown author, wrote an award-winning science fiction novel set in a not-too-distant future. The novel, *Neuromancer*, involved large corporations that replaced governments and computer hackers who waged war against secure data. *Neuromancer* set the stage for an entire genre of science fiction that would have a profound influence on the computer and telecommunications community. What made this such an influential and somewhat prophetic work was that a large part of the plot unfolded in a setting that had no physical existence. Gibson named this setting *cyberspace*.

As described in *Neuromancer*, Cyberspace was a consensual hallucination that felt and looked like a physical space but actually was a computer-generated construct representing abstract data. People could plug into data systems and networks and have the sense they were actually entering a place that had no correlation in physical reality. In this setting, people carried out business transactions, communicated with one another, worked, played, and, as they have done in every other place they had occupied, broke the law.

Scarcely ten years later, social commentators have awakened to the fact that Gibson's vision was much closer to reality than anyone previously realized. While Gibsonian cyberspace was first seen as science fiction, in the real world a system of computer networks and bulletin boards was emerging in which people recognized the beginning of a true cyberspace. At an ever-increasing rate, mass computer connectivity was becoming possible. More and more people and systems were going on-line either by connecting their computers over the phone system or by establishing direct connections using the networks created by universities and government agencies. The term *cyberspace* quickly caught on as a shorthand way to describe this matrix of interconnected computers. While purists debate the exact scope and definition of the term, millions of Americans find themselves interacting every day in a world they call by that name.

The mechanics of this interaction are fairly simple. Typically, a user with a personal computer makes a connection with another computer through standard telephone lines. When the connection is established, the user's computer and the remote host system become linked in a way to create the perception that there is no physical distance between the two machines. This is the case even if the two machines are hundreds of miles or even continents apart from one another. In this simple example of cyberspace communication, the mechanics are no more complex than those involved in a standard voice telephone call.

Unlike the common telephone call, however, where there is one simple stream of data being transmitted, when computers communicate there can be immense amounts of data transferred simultaneously. This entire book can be sent across the globe in just a few seconds, as can financial data, digitized audio and video, and computer software. In short, if it can be stored in a computer-readable format, it can be transmitted in cyberspace. Instead of waiting days for a letter to make its way through the conventional postal system, a user can have electronic mail delivered instantly to distant locations. If two users are connected to the same system at the same time, they can "chat" in real-time through their monitors and keyboards. In fact, several different users separated by vast distances can interact in the computer equivalent of a conference call. These are just a few examples to illustrate uses of a completely new medium of communication, a medium that brings with it not only an immense potential for productivity, but also a wide range of novel problems and unique twists on old ones.

A Quick Tour of Cyberspace

Cyberspace now represents a vast array of computer systems accessible from remote physical locations. It also embodies the so-called *data highways* and networks that connect them. The following four categories describe the major components of today's cyberspace.

Commercial On-line Services

Perhaps the remote systems most familiar to Americans are the commercial on-line services. These are large computers that often have the capacity to host thousands of users simultaneously. Some of the more popular services include Prodigy (operated by Sears and IBM), CompuServe, GEnie, America Online, and Delphi. A person with a computer and the proper access equipment can purchase a personalized account. Each time users log on to the service, they enter a unique name and password combination that identifies them to the host system. The use of a unique name and password, in theory, allows users to restrict who may access their personalized account.

Once the account is established, the user can traverse the host system selecting activities from a series of available menus. The number and nature of activities available to the user varies from system to system, but there are several features and services that most systems offer. These include electronic mail (e-mail), recreational activities, comprehensive databases, and libraries of electronic publications. Also available are vast collections of software, on-going conversations consisting of messages posted by users, and current news and financial information. On many systems, the user can make airline and hotel reservations or shop in on-line stores. Finally, most on-line services allow the user to communicate in real-time "chats" with other people who are also logged in to the system.

The large variety of activities available has contributed to the popularity of on-line services. A sense of community can develop among system subscribers, who sometimes spend hours interacting with the service and each other. Sometimes, users make the on-line service an integral part of their daily routine where they can socialize, catch up on current events, and retrieve useful information.

Computer Bulletin Board Systems (BBSs)

Like their larger cousins, the on-line services, BBSs allow users to set up accounts on remote systems and access some basic system features. The distinction between large BBSs and the on-line services is often hard to see. The vast majority of BBSs in existence, however, are operated on small personal computers with a single phone line, and have a relatively small number of users. More often than not, there are no access charges since the system operator, or *sysop*, is running the board as a hobby. BBSs tend to emphasize electronic mail, message bases, and software trading. Many systems also host games, and some of the larger multiline systems offer user chat.

Because of the large number of bulletin boards in existence and the ease of setting them up, bulletin boards tend to cater to a wide range of specialized interests. Boards focus on everything from ornithology to neo-Nazi white supremacist dogma. City, state, and federal government agencies run bulletin boards as public services. In short, as consumer advocate Ralph Nader pointed out, "the personal computer bulletin board is the lowest-entry-barrier mass communications system in history."[1]

Sysops have wide discretion in shaping their boards, in limiting membership, and in establishing rules for participation. Because of this, BBSs can be dynamic and volatile testing grounds for social and legal policy issues.

Private Systems

Many computers in cyberspace are meant to be used only by a small group of users. These systems may be run by companies or organizations who do not wish to open them to the public. Along with the traditional bulletin board functions, private systems sometimes allow users to perform specialized computing operations or access specific applications and data. A company's *local area network* (LAN), for instance, might become part of cyberspace if made accessible to remote computers.

Computer Networks

Computer *networks* are collections of interconnected systems that have the ability to exchange information between one another. Systems from each of the previously discussed categories might be part of a network. The most important computer network in the world is the Internet, which has been called a "network of networks."[2]

The Internet evolved out of defense department networks that linked large government computers. As more and more systems became interconnected, tools were developed to facilitate working between them. For example, the *Telnet* program allows anyone on any computer connected to the Internet (an Internet *node*) to access any other Internet node as if he were sitting at a terminal attached to the distant host. A program called *file transfer protocol* (FTP) allows files to be transferred back and forth between Internet systems. E-mail programs send packets containing personal and business correspondence from and to accounts on any Internet machine. *WAIS* and *Gopher* are programs that allow users to tunnel through information set up and indexed by distributed host systems. These tools make the Internet a vital conduit for information in cyberspace.

Another notable network is Fidonet, which is a network of BBSs using the Fidonet standard. Unlike the Internet, Fidonet does not work in a real-time mode. That is, Fidonet nodes do not maintain a continuous connection with other systems, but instead establish connections when needed. Although Fidonet tends to be slower than real-time networks, it accomplishes the goal of distributing data over wide areas at low costs.

The larger networks are decentralized in both a technical sense and in their governance. They are decentralized in the technical sense in that on the Internet, Fidonet, and similar networks, there is no central hub through which all messages must be routed. Likewise, there is no central governing body on many large networks, and they are governed through a surprisingly effective yet anarchic autonomy.

Activities in Cyberspace

The number of potential uses for cyberspace is inestimable. Of these, some activities are so essential that they are offered by almost all systems. These basic functions comprise the core of on-line activity. These core activities are listed and described below, and it is these activities that will be the focus of our analysis in the following chapters.

E-mail

Of these core on-line activities, the transmission of *electronic mail*, or *e-mail*, is the most common. E-mail is similar to its conventional paper counterpart in that it allows individuals to correspond with one another. Armed with the intended recipient's unique user name and address, the sender of e-mail can compose a message that will be deposited into the recipient's mailbox. The message becomes available to the recipient when he or she next comes on-line.

E-mail is generally more convenient than regular postal mail. Usually, for example, a piece of e-mail can be responded to, stored, forwarded, or simply deleted, all automatically. E-mail may also be distributed to multiple users with little effort; creating large mailing lists is a simple task.

On an on-line service or BBS, you might be restricted to mailing only those users with accounts on that system. In other words, as long as the person to whom you want to send e-mail has an account on the same system you do, there is no problem. If the system is part of a network, or "gated" into a network, the potential number of people with whom you can correspond is greatly increased. Using a more complex address, you can direct your e-mail to a certain user on a specific system, and the computers handle the rest. For example, on the Internet, addressing a message to joe@bigcomputer.com tells the mail software to send the message to a system called "bigcomputer.com" and deposit the message into Joe's private mailbox.

Public Messaging Systems

Public messaging systems, like e-mail, involve users communicating with one another through written text. Unlike private correspondence, however, a message posted on a *message base* is publicly accessible. The public can read and respond to the message, and an on-line conversation develops. Message bases are analogous to graffiti discussions on public restroom walls. Each message becomes part of a *thread* of messages that relate to a particular topic. Some systems that offer public message bases are networked to other similar systems. With networking, distributed message bases (sometimes called *newsgroups* or *Echomail*) bring together users from widely dispersed systems.

With some messaging systems, all messages are sent to a centralized location where they can be scanned by a moderator before they are made available for public viewing. This allows the moderator to screen messages that are not topical or are otherwise unacceptable. In essence, moderators act like hosts of call-in radio shows, helping to steer and control the discussion. Not all message bases are moderated in this way. *Usenet*, for example, is a distributed messaging system that works primarily over the Internet and is often unmoderated. Any contribution to an unmoderated Usenet newsgroup will appear on any system subscribing to that newsgroup. This ungoverned approach tends to put the fate of the newsgroup in the users' hands. While sometimes chaotic, the ungoverned approach is nonetheless very popular.

Software Exchange

All computers need software to operate. Cyberspace offers an extremely large amount of software for every imaginable computer system. Sometimes it is free for the taking; other times it must be purchased or traded. Large programs can quickly be transferred between two computers.

On BBSs, software is often traded like a currency, with strict ratios enforced for the amount a user must contribute to a collection in order to continue taking from it. Public bulletin boards featuring hundreds of megabytes of software made freely available by its authors are common. On the Internet, large libraries of software are available free of charge. Special programs (such as *Archie*) index software repositories and help users locate the software for which they are looking.

Electronic Publishing

At one time, in order to become a publisher, an individual needed not only a printing press but also a method of distribution so that the printed word could reach its audience. With the advent of cyberspace, the nature of publishing changed dramatically. On-line systems and networks make distribution of electronic publications feasible even to individuals with limited resources. There are now countless electronic periodicals (often called *zines*) distributed to residents of cyberspace. One can subscribe to these periodicals by sending e-mail over a network to the publisher so that each issue is sent directly to the subscriber's mailbox. Zines are frequently archived by BBSs and on-line services so that every back issue is available upon demand. Such systems are similar to traditional newsstands where a multitude of titles is made available to the public. Usually, no fee is attached to acquiring zines, although commercial zines are becoming more prevalent.

Besides the zines, which usually are not found in paper format at all, there are many electronic versions of conventional paper periodicals. These are sometimes distributed at the same time or even before their paper counterparts hit the stands. Most of the major newspapers and magazines can be found in digital form somewhere in cyberspace. For example, Mead Data Corporation's *NEXIS* database archives countless newspapers, magazines, and journals that are accessible using a powerful search system.

Entertainment

Recreational activities are abundant in cyberspace. Without leaving home, a user can interact and play games with people from all over the globe. These games range from the electronic version of multiplayer board games to complex fantasy role playing. This aspect of cyberspace is so popular that an entire on-line service (*The Sierra Network*) has been developed simply for entertainment purposes. It is also not unusual to find BBSs that cater specifically to game players and provide low-cost or free entertainment services to computer owners. On the Internet, *multiuser dungeons* (MUDs) allow for real-time interactions in various imaginary settings. MUDs began as on-line versions of fantasy role playing games, but many have evolved into a more unusual social forum.[3]

Chat

The most direct form of communication is real-time dialogue between users. This is often called *chat* and takes many forms. On the Internet, for example, the *Internet Relay Chat* (IRC) offers channels where Internet users can find live discussions relating to different topics at any time. Many multiline BBSs have devout communities of users who participate daily in chat with people they may never meet face to face. The more advanced systems allow for private *rooms* where users can have intimate conversations with a select group of fellow users. On the larger on-line services, guest speakers or lecturers are often featured in live chat sessions where users can engage in dialogue with the guest.

Educational and Research Services

Because of the huge amount of data that can be accessed in cyberspace, it is only natural that some systems make educational resources such as encyclopedias, dictionaries, and large databases available to students and scholars. System operators of these information services often provide free trial subscription periods for students. This is done in the hope that the students will recognize the value of these services and eventually become paying customers. Not all on-line educational resources charge for access. Many public libraries are making their card catalogs available electronically, and many government agencies are putting public documents on-line at no charge.

Research is not the only educational use for cyberspace. On-line tutors exist for one-on-one assistance, and automated computer-aided instruction programs help users master a variety of disciplines; some colleges now offer courses via modem.[4] The wealth of information available makes cyberspace an educational tool more powerful than any tool that has come before it.

Commercial Applications

As the power and scope of cyberspace become more and more obvious, its commercial potential grows. The market has not ignored cyberspace. Electronic catalogs and product listings are increasingly becoming available on on-line systems and networks. Electronic shopping is now possible, allowing consumers to place orders to remote systems. Some commercial on-line transactions involve only cyberspace, with few ramifications for the physical world. For example, orders for on-line time with a subscription service might be placed via e-mail using credit card information for payment.

The business community has been quick to recognize the power of cyberspace as a communication tool and is carrying out much of its correspondence through the networks. BBSs are sometimes used for customer support and as a means of distributing product information and updates. Securities and market information is available instantaneously to even the most distant systems. The power to move large amounts of data quickly makes cyberspace a valuable business resource.

The Dimensions of Cyberspace

With all of the applications listed above, it is not surprising that cyberspace has become expansive. By all accounts, the size of cyberspace is astounding.[5] No one is sure of the size because of the rate at which new systems go on-line daily. The most recent estimates show that millions of people are interacting in this medium at any given time.

Approximately ten million computer owners also own modems.[6] Although not all use their modems to interact with other systems, the number is significant because it indicates the potential number of participants cyberspace has.

The number of public BBSs has been estimated at 60,000 systems in the United States. Another 60,000 or more private and commercial boards are thought to exist. Because of the ease of setting up a BBS, exact figures are difficult to estimate. Most likely, these estimates are conservative, and by the time that you read this the numbers will be even higher.[7]

The on-line services have massive user bases. CompuServe, the largest of the major systems, has approximately 1.4 million subscribers. Prodigy has somewhere in the range of 1 million. GEnie, the service operated by General Electric, hosts 400,000 users. America Online has 350,000.[8]

Another indicator of the dimensions of cyberspace is the size of the major computer networks. The Internet has somewhere between 10 and 15 million users using the 1,313,000 host systems (computers that connect directly to the network via the *Internet Protocol* or "IP"). Approximately 10,000 smaller networks are linked by the Internet in roughly 50 countries.

The largest BBS network, Fidonet, has over 22,000 nodes. A slew of other bulletin board networks of varying sizes exists. *WWIVnet*, for example, a relatively unknown network, links over 1,500 mostly single-line hobby bulletin boards. Becoming a node on Fidonet or WWIVnet is free to anyone with the software.

The Future of Cyberspace

Cyberspace has grown at an almost incredible rate over the last few years, and indications are that this rate will continue. The bulletin board phenomenon clearly indicates this growth. The first bulletin board software, written by Ward Christensen and called "CBBS," was put on line in 1978.[9] If Christensen's board is still running, it is by no means alone, as 60,000 other systems have come on-line since then.

Networks are also growing explosively. An indication of this trend is the Internet's growth since its beginnings in 1981. At that time, the number of host systems was 213 machines. At the time of this writing, twelve years later, the number has jumped to 1,313,000 systems connecting directly to the Internet. The dramatic rate of growth becomes evident when the numbers of hosts in 1992—727,000—is compared to the 1.3 million figure of 1993.

The growth of the Internet will be further boosted by recently passed federal legislation designed to bolster the development of a digital "information infrastructure." The law, called the High Performance Computing Act, was passed in 1991. It calls for a government and industry coalition working to research the hardware and software needs for the digital equivalent of the federal highway system with computer connections linking millions of Americans.

Like the Internet, Fidonet has experienced startling growth. The original Fido BBS was released in June of 1984, and within a year 160 nodes had signed on. Today with over 22,000 nodes, Fidonet is one of the fastest growing computer networks in the world.

2   Electronic Privacy

Privacy plays a unique role in American law. Although considered a core value by most citizens, it is not explicitly delineated as a protected right by the U.S. Constitution. The privacy rights recognized by today's courts find their authority in state constitutions, federal and state statutes, a variety of related provisions of the U.S. Constitution, and judicial interpretations that form a body of common law guaranteeing an individual's right to a private life. Some have argued that the reason privacy is not explicitly mentioned in the U.S. Constitution is that at the time of its drafting there were only a small number of ways that one's privacy could be invaded. The biggest privacy fears were that the government might search one's home or demand that troops be sheltered there during wartime. The framers of the Constitution addressed these problems with amendments specifically prohibiting unreasonable search and seizure and the unwarranted quartering of troops.

What the framers of the Constitution could not address was the myriad of privacy concerns that developed as new technologies were introduced into society. Electronic eavesdropping devices, video and sound recording instruments, and large databases of personal information are all now a part of life in this country. Our legal system has had to react constantly to these new developments as they emerge, striving to maintain the proper balance between civil liberties and the needs of society.

Computers and digital communication technologies present a serious challenge to legislators and judges who try to meet the demands of economic and social change while protecting this most basic and fundamental personal freedom. Computer networks make it possible for prying eyes to peek instantly at data located across the globe. Gigabytes of private personal communications are transferred on a daily basis. Confidential records and data are kept on easily accessible systems, which sometimes are protected by inadequate security. The potential for privacy invasions of a magnitude never before seen exists in today's computerized world. In this chapter, we examine the role of privacy in cyberspace from a legal perspective in an attempt to map out the function it plays in the on-line society. We begin with a discussion of the notion of anonymity on-line, and follow that with an analysis of the Electronic Communications Privacy Act and the *Steve Jackson Games v. United States Secret Service* case. State and common law privacy issues are also explored. Finally, the interesting legal ramifications of cryptography technology are contemplated.

Anonymity

Handles and Pseudonyms

Anyone who is familiar with cyberspace knows that a large percentage of the activities that take place there occur under assumed names, or *handles*. The use of handles in cyberspace most likely was influenced by the popular practice of using handles on CB radio channels. The ability to assume a pseudonym is viewed as a cherished right by many BBS and network participants, who feel more comfortable interacting under a fictitious name. Unfortunately, handles often can seem mysterious and threatening to those unfamiliar with on-line culture. In fact, hackers facing criminal charges often regret using ominous-sounding nicknames when they see them in print on court documents.

Still, on most systems or networks, there is nothing illegal about using a handle in cyberspace. It is perfectly legitimate to conduct your affairs as "John Doe," "Keyboard Kreature," or any other imaginative nickname you might fancy. Usually, the system on which you have an account established will require you to provide some valid identification data in case a sysop needs to contact you by non-electronic means. Depending on the agreement governing use of the system, this information may or may not be kept confidential by your system operator. On systems connected to the Internet, executing the *finger* command often can display account information about other Internet users. Other systems make user *registries* containing detailed personal information about each user on the system available for public perusal. If you wish to keep personal information private, talk to your system administrator and find out how confidential your account information is.

The right to conduct at least some forms of speech activity anonymously has been upheld by the U.S. Supreme Court. In a 1960 decision, the Court invalidated an ordinance requiring all publicly distributed pamphlets to include the name and address of the person who prepared, distributed, or published them.[1] This is not surprising. Alexander Hamilton, James Madison, and John Jay published the controversial *Federalist Papers* under the pseudonym "Publius." The right to express oneself under conditions of anonymity has also been frequently exercised by authors publishing books and articles under pen names.

Right to Associate

In certain situations sysops might effectively be able to block the government's access to the information contained in their user records. This is the result of an interesting and often overlooked portion of the First Amendment that prohibits the government from abridging the right of people to associate with one another. This right is implied by the rights of free speech and assembly found in the text of the amendment. Although still under development, the right to associate protects the privacy of organizations and other groups, which can be crucial to the proper functioning of a democracy.

It is interesting to speculate about the way this unique right might one day become relevant to cyberspace and the important associational activities that occur there. In some ways, mailing lists and bulletin board user lists are the on-line equivalent of organizations' membership lists. The Supreme Court upheld the right of the NAACP to keep its membership list out of government hands on the basis of this right of association.[2] It may be that this precedent can be applied by a system operator or someone else who wishes to keep private the names of subscribers or users involved in certain associational conduct. This becomes even more interesting when one considers the fact that many users prefer to conduct their affairs in cyberspace under handles. Will law enforcement attempts to reveal the true identity of these users (usually supplied only to the system operator) be judged to be a violation of the First Amendment? Surely, the sense of community that develops in some on-line situations resembles an association for purposes of constitutional law analysis. Only time will tell if this doctrine will cross the line from traditional situations into the world of computer-mediated communications.

Anonymous Remailers

On the larger computer networks, users have clamored for even more anonymity than is provided by using a handle or pseudonym. What they demanded was the freedom to send e-mail messages without any possibility that the messages could be traced back to them. This demand was met with *anonymous remailers,* programs that receive mail, strip it of any traceable identifying information, and forward it to the addressee. Some systems assign a random identification code, which allows a recipient to respond to the sender. Thus, the remailer acts as a filter that keeps the person receiving the mail from knowing who sent it. This type of system is called an *anonymous server.* On the Internet, there are now several servers and remailers available for public use, and they have proven to be quite popular. They are, however, still somewhat unstable operations, often carried out without the knowledge of the system administrators or host system operators.

Even remailers and anonymous servers do not guarantee absolute anonymity, as their traffic might be monitored, or the individuals operating the service might keep system logs that compromise the confidential nature of the service. People using these services should keep in mind that they are only as effective as their operators are trustworthy. It is best to investigate the entity operating such a system if you are interested in sending or receiving truly sensitive anonymous messages.

Anonymous Internet FTP

File transfer protocol (FTP) makes it possible to transfer Internet files from one machine to another at high speed. Many sites have publicly accessible *anonymous FTP* capabilities that allow users to log-in anonymously and transfer files to and from the site. The name of this service can be deceptive. Many such anonymous FTP sites routinely monitor and log system activity including the e-mail addresses of those using the system. Users should be aware that these systems are not, then, truly anonymous, and care should be taken to avoid sensitive FTP transactions under the assumption of anonymity.

The Privacy of Electronic Communications and the ECPA

Worried that newly developed means of electronic eavesdropping posed a serious threat to privacy rights, in 1968 the U.S. Congress enacted an expansive law governing the privacy of electronic communications. Originally, the act, entitled the Omnibus Crime Control and Safe Streets Act, focused on telephone wiretaps. In 1986 it was broadened to include digital electronic communications.[3] Computer bulletin boards were specifically mentioned in the legislative sessions as being one of the new media that would be addressed under the terms of the law. Today the Electronic Communications Privacy Act (ECPA) makes it illegal to intercept or disclose private communications and provides victims of such conduct a right to sue anyone violating its mandate. The ECPA is clearly the most important statute dealing with privacy in cyberspace.

In this section we will examine what the ECPA does, when it applies, and how one court has applied it in the context of protecting BBS e-mail. A lay person's explanation of this complicated statute is provided in the text below, but readers may wish refer to appendix B, where the full text of the law is included for reference.

The important provisions of the ECPA are divided into two chapters of Title 18 (Crimes and Criminal Procedures) of the United States Code. The first chapter (119) is entitled "Wire and Electronic Communications Interceptions and Interceptions of Oral Communications"; the second chapter (121) is entitled "Stored Wire and Electronic Communications and Transactional Records Access."

Interception of Electronic Communications

Chapter 119 focuses on the act of intercepting a private electronic communication. As far as computer communications are concerned, under the ECPA, any government agent, business, or individual who does or tries to do any of the following is acting in violation of the law:

1. intentionally intercepts any electronic communication;

2. intentionally uses or discloses the contents of any electronic communication, knowing or having reason to know that the information was obtained through the interception of an electronic communication in violation of the ECPA.[4]

These violations all rely on an *interception* having taken place. "Interception" is defined (as are most of the important terms in the ECPA) in the text of the statute. As with many legal terms, the word has a definition different from the one ordinarily associated with it. The statute defines it as meaning "the aural or other acquisition of the contents of any wire, electronic, or oral communication through the use of any electronic, mechanical, or other device." As we will see later, the exact meaning of words such as "interception" are still being fine-tuned by the courts. Sometimes these judicial interpretations add important meaning to the statutory definitions. For instance, according to one court, it appears that to qualify as an interception under the law, the act of interception must be contemporaneous with the transmission of the communication.[5]

Although the notion of an illegal real-time interception was originally framed in the context of telephone wiretaps and other electronic surveillance, there are situations in cyberspace where this type of interception might be relevant. Many systems monitor every keystroke entered by a user. Such keystroke monitoring may very well constitute an interception for purposes of the ECPA. Of course, a more obvious interception would be a physical tap into a data line that allowed for all data transmission to be rerouted or logged. Any means of intercepting the communication in question potentially violates the ECPA.

System operators and other providers of communication services cannot intentionally divulge the contents of any communication on their service unless the communication is sent to them or to their agents. Under this provision of the act, it is illegal to disclose the contents of a message to anyone other than the addressee or intended recipient of such communication. This prohibition does not hold true in four situations: (1) if the system operator is authorized to do so by other parts of the ECPA; (2) if the system operator has the lawful consent of the originator or any addressee or intended recipient of such communication; (3) if such divulgence is necessary to forward the communication properly; or (4) if a communication that was inadvertently obtained by the service provider appears to pertain to the commission of a crime.[6] In the last scenario, the only lawful disclosure is to law enforcement officials.

The ECPA also provides some general exceptions to violations resulting from an illicit interception. The most notable exceptions are summarized below. It is not unlawful for:

1. a provider of electronic communication service to intercept, disclose, or use that communication in the normal course of employment while engaged in any activity that is necessary to the rendition of service or to the protection of the rights or property of the provider of that service, not including random monitoring;

2. providers of an electronic communication service (or their employees, agents, cosysops, landlords, or other persons) to provide assistance to persons authorized by law to intercept electronic communications or to conduct electronic surveillance, if such provider has been provided with a signed court order, a proper certification in writing (see 18 U.S.C. § 2518), or a signed writing from the Attorney General of the United States that no warrant or court order is required by law, that all statutory requirements have been met, and that the specified assistance is required;

3. a person acting under color of law to intercept an electronic communication, where such person is a party to the communication or one of the parties to the communication has given prior consent to such interception;

4. a person not acting under color of law to intercept an electronic communication where such person is a party to the communication or where one of the parties to the communication has given prior consent to such interception unless such communication is intercepted for the purpose of committing any criminal or tortious act;

5. any person to intercept or access an electronic communication made through an electronic communication system that is configured so that such electronic communication is readily accessible to the public;

6. a provider of electronic communication service to record the fact that an electronic communication was initiated or completed in order to protect such provider, another provider furnishing service toward the completion of the electronic communication, or a user of that service, from fraudulent, unlawful or abusive use of such service.[7]

Not only must one be aware of the possible violations that can result from illegally intercepting electronic messages, but also one must keep in mind all of the exceptions. Your system operator legally can act in ways that initially appear to violate the ECPA if he or she does so for debugging or system maintenance purposes, or has been required to do so by the proper authorities. A sysop also legally can intercept your communications if he or she is a party to the communication (i.e., you are sending mail or other messages to the sysop), or if you or the person you are communicating with consents. You may have consented and thereby waived your rights under the ECPA by means of a user contract or system use agreement. Being asked to give up your ECPA rights is not as uncommon as you might think; many sysops explicitly request that you do so, or may post a message putting you on notice that their system should not be considered private for purposes of the ECPA.

A system operator can also lawfully intercept your private messages if you are using the messaging capabilities to damage the system or harm another user. Finally, it is not illegal for anyone to intercept messages intended for publicly accessible destinations (like posts to the public message bases or USENET newsgroups), as those systems are configured so as to be accessible to the general public.

There are also restrictions on what a system operator can do when a valid interception or surveillance is being conducted on his or her system.[8] The sysop cannot expose the monitoring to anyone unless required to by the legal process, and then only after prior notification to the Attorney General or the relevant prosecuting attorney, as may be appropriate. Any such disclosure exposes a person to both civil and criminal damages. Do not expect your system operator to inform you if for some reason the communication channels you use to conduct private correspondence in cyberspace are tapped by law enforcement agents. The sysop is probably prohibited by law from telling you.

Violation of these provisions of the ECPA can result in fines, imprisonment of not more than five years, or both. The court may also use any means within its authority to enforce an *injunction* (a court order to cease the activity), and must impose a civil fine of not less than $500 for each violation of such an injunction.[9] Finally, anyone who feels that he or she has been harmed by a violation of this part of the ECPA can sue the responsible party for civil damages. If successful, the injured party will be awarded monetary damages (based on actual harm or set statutory amounts), punitive damages (in appropriate situations) and will be compensated for any attorney's fees.[10]

Access to and Disclosure of Stored Communications

Chapter 121 of the ECPA deals with stored electronic communications. The first activity addressed involves *unauthorized access*. These sections further criminalize some of the same "hacking" activity already made illegal by the laws discussed in chapter seven. Under this section it is illegal intentionally to:

1. access without authorization a facility through which an electronic communication service is provided; or

2. exceed an authorization to access a facility; and thereby obtain, alter, or prevent authorized access to an electronic communication while it is in electronic storage in such system.[11]

Anyone who exceeds his or her access on a system or intentionally accesses a system without authorization is in violation of the law. If it turns out that you have accidentally acquired more privileges on a system than you are authorized to have, intentionally using those privileges to alter, obtain, or obstruct electronic communications is illegal. If you find yourself in this situation, be sure to notify your sysop. Of course, it is also illegal for you to acquire access to a system in the first place if you are not authorized to do so. The access provisions of the ECPA are, in essence, a special antihacking law covering systems that provide private electronic communications.

If committed for purposes of commercial advantage, malicious destruction or damage, or private commercial gain, the punishment for a first offense under this section includes a fine of not more than $250,000 or imprisonment for not more than one year, or both. Subsequent offenses can result in imprisonment for not more than two years, and similar fines. Any other case (i.e., one not involving malicious destruction or commercial motives) can be punished by a fine of not more than $5,000 or imprisonment for not more than six months, or both.[12] A violator might also be sued by anyone harmed by his or her activities, as discussed below.

Once again, there are some exceptions to the prohibitions banning unauthorized access.[13] If the person or entity providing the electronic communications service, or a user of that service (with respect to a communication of or intended for that user) authorizes such access, then the access is not illegal. Of course, it is not illegal if the access occurs pursuant to a validly issued court order or warrant. Also, there are special situations in which the government may request that a system operator back up or archive records of communication for purposes of a law enforcement investigation.[14]

Along with unauthorized access, the ECPA proscribes *disclosure* of the contents of private communications.[15] Under this section of the act, a person or entity providing an electronic communication service to the public shall not knowingly divulge to anyone the contents of a communication while in electronic storage on that service. In other words, if the system operator is not authorized to access material you have stored on the system, it is illegal for him or her to divulge its contents to others.

These rules do not apply if the party disclosing the communication does so to an addressee or intended recipient of such communication, or under authority of other parts of the ECPA. Moreover, it is not illegal to divulge the content of communications when there is lawful consent granted by the originator or an addressee or intended recipient of such communication. It is also legal to divulge such messages to a person whose facilities are used to forward the message to its final destination, or to divulge the contents for system administration and debugging purposes, or to protect the property rights of the system. As could be expected, it is not illegal to divulge to a law enforcement agency if such contents were inadvertently obtained by the service provider and appear to pertain to the commission of a crime.

The victim of a violation of access or improper disclosure of a private communication can sue those responsible.[16] Along with attorney's fees and court costs, a successful plaintiff can be awarded actual damages based on the injury suffered or any profits made by the violating party. There are minimum damages of $1,000 under the law, and in no case will the award be less than that. Such a lawsuit needs to be brought no later than two years after the date upon which the claimant first discovered or had a reasonable opportunity to discover the violation.

Throughout the ECPA, there are references to the "intent" of the party committing the acts in question. As is often the case with laws that are designed to punish intentional conduct, determining whether an act was intentional or not can be difficult. At least one court has specifically addressed this problem as it applies to the ECPA. In 1989, a federal court from the Eastern District of Pennsylvania held that, while not necessary, the use of surreptitious means is strong evidence of intent for purposes of the ECPA.[17] This tidbit of judicial guidance in an otherwise ambiguous area should help those trying to determine whether a specific act constitutes an ECPA violation.

Steve Jackson Games v. United States Secret Service

On the morning of March 1, 1990, the Secret Service raided an Austin, Texas, role-playing games publisher called Steve Jackson Games. The Secret Service thought it was hot on the trail of the Legion of Doom (an informal yet notorious group of computer hackers) and a "stolen" document detailing the rather arcane bureaucracy surrounding the operation of Bell South's Emergency 911 (E911) telephone system. In fact, the Secret Service's imagined connection between the company and the Legion of Doom (LOD) or the E911 document was essentially inaccurate. Although an employee of the company had at one time claimed membership in the LOD, and he was, at the time of the raid, authoring a role-playing game called *GURPS Cyberpunk* concerning fanciful futuristic computer hacking, there was no evidence of anything remotely illegal going on at the company. Steve Jackson Games was no haven for evil hackers. The Secret Service had made a mistake.

Although several computers were seized, the primary target of the raid was the company's BBS that provided customers and game writers a forum to discuss and test new games and publications. The BBS, named Illuminati after one of the company's most successful products, had an active user base of hundreds of users when it was shut down by the Secret Service and transported to Chicago for the investigation. According to Wayne Bell, the author of the WWIV BBS software used by Illuminati, in the course of the Secret Service review of the BBS computer someone individually accessed and deleted all of the electronic mail stored on the system.

Steve Jackson, his company, and three of his bulletin board users filed suit against the Secret Service alleging violations of the ECPA and

ECPA prohibitions	Examples of violations
Interception of electronic communication	• keystroke monitoring; • tapping a data line; • rerouting an electronic communication to provide contemporaneous acquisition.
Unauthorized access to electronic communication service	• obtaining an account through "hacking"; • using inadvertently granted authority to read or alter other people's e-mail; • using a bug or other system flaw to read other user's private messages; • preventing others from accessing their stored private messages.
Disclosure of electronic communications	• Divulging the contents of e-mail to which you were not a party.

Figure 2.1
ECPA violations

the Privacy Protection Act (see chapter five for a discussion of the PPA claim). These plaintiffs claimed that by seizing the Illuminati BBS and accessing the electronic mail stored on its hard drive, the Secret Service violated the ECPA's provisions prohibiting interception and disclosure of private electronic communications. The case, which was tried before a federal judge in January 1993, was apparently the first chance for a court to interpret the ECPA in a case involving electronic mail and computer bulletin board systems.[18]

The trial featured testimony from Jackson and other Illuminati users, Secret Service agents, Wayne Bell, and a phone company expert. Part of Jackson's testimony took place while he was sitting at a working replica of the Illuminati BBS, with federal judge Sam Sparks observing over his shoulder. It may have been the first time a BBS was operated in a U.S. courtroom.

There were several significant hurdles to overcome before the plaintiffs were entitled to win a money judgment from the government for the seizure and interception of the electronic mail. The plaintiffs had to prove that their private electronic mail was (a) seized and disclosed or (b) intercepted, and that the Secret Service did not rely in good faith on the warrant authorizing the search of Steve Jackson Games. The search warrant and supporting affidavit revealed a lack of preraid investigation (the judge found it was "sloppy"), contained numerous misstatements and exaggerations, and did not mention that private electronic mail messages were targeted or suspected to contain evidence of a crime. The plaintiffs also had to prove that the electronic mail was in fact private; that is, that the system was not configured to allow general public access to the e-mail.

After three days of testimony and argument, the trial ended. A few weeks later, Judge Sparks issued a written opinion finding that the Secret Service had violated the ECPA and the Privacy Protection Act of 1980 and had not relied in good faith on the search warrant. He ruled that Steve Jackson's company was entitled to over $50,000 for lost sales under the Privacy Protection Act. In an important part of the decision for sysops and users, Judge Sparks found that each individual plaintiff was entitled to $1,000 statutory damages for the Secret Service's violation of the ECPA, and their attorneys' fees and court costs in bringing suit.

The victory was not absolute. Although he ruled that the Secret Service's reading of the electronic mail was an unauthorized disclosure, the judge rejected the argument that the act of seizing the BBS resulted in an "interception" of electronic mail. The plaintiffs argued that common sense dictated that any electronic mail messages that had been sent, but not yet received by its addressee when the Secret Service took the BBS computer were "intercepted." Judge Sparks disagreed, basing his decision on an analogy to the seizure of a tape recording. He concluded that there is no "interception" of a communication unless the seizure is contemporaneous with its transmission.

As anyone familiar with the technology can attest, there are some serious problems with Judge Sparks's analogy. In the case of a seized tape recording, the communication is completed, and the government has merely seized a record of that communication. The seizure of undelivered e-mail is more like a wiretap, because the government acquires the communication before it is completed, and may well prevent the communication from ever being delivered. As the ECPA itself recognizes, that type of interception is much more intrusive to privacy interests than the seizure of stored completed communications.

The distinction is not academic. The ECPA requires that the government obtain a court order to wiretap, rather than the relatively simple process of obtaining search warrant to seize stored communications. Further, the ECPA provides a $10,000 civil penalty for each unlawful "interception"—a far larger deterrent to government overreaching. Steve Jackson and the other plaintiffs have elected to appeal this decision. The government is also appealing the money judgments against the Secret Service.

Technically, Judge Sparks's decision in *Steve Jackson Games v. United States Secret Service* is precedent only in the federal court where it was tried—the Western District of Texas. Federal trial court decisions are not given as much weight as opinions handed down by appellate courts, and fewer judges are bound by the reasoning in the decision. Many experts following the case, however, believe it will have an important influence in similar cases that might arise. Judges referring to the decision will no longer need to be convinced that private BBS e-mail is deserving of protection. Instead, they can get right to the question of whether the ECPA was violated in a particular case.

Depending upon the situation, users of an electronic messaging system who find that their private communications have been intercepted, used, or disclosed by someone not authorized to do so will very likely have a valid ECPA lawsuit to assert.

State Privacy Law

Many states protect privacy with statutes similar to those adopted at the federal level. There is quite a bit of variance in the statutory language and nuances of state privacy laws. Some, for instance, track pre-ECPA thinking, which limited liability to the interception of oral communications, never bothering to update the laws to take electronic messaging into account. The only way to know for certain if there are state-based privacy statutes in any particular case is to consult an attorney or carefully research the laws of the state.

For more general privacy concerns, ten states have specific provisions in their constitution that explicitly refer to the right of privacy, or the right to be left alone.[19] Even more of them have interpreted their constitutions to create an implied right of privacy, such as the one implied by the U.S. Constitution. Whatever the basis, a state constitutional privacy right might be more expansive than the one guaranteed by the U.S. Constitution, as the U.S. Constitution only mandates a "baseline" below which rights may not fall. For this reason, something that is not a violation of the federal right of privacy may very well give rise to state-based complaints. A complete survey of state privacy issues is beyond the scope of this chapter; those interested in more specific and detailed information about a particular state's laws should consult an attorney.

Common Law Actions for Invasion of Privacy

State common law provides for civil remedies based on violating privacy rights under one of several doctrines. Each state has taken a different approach in interpreting and developing the right to sue for privacy violations, but the following guidelines provide some indication of the scope and nature of common law privacy.

Public Disclosure of Private Facts

The widespread disclosure of facts about a person, even if those facts are true, may be deemed harmful enough to justify a lawsuit. The test in these cases is whether the disclosure would be highly objectionable to an average person. An example of a fact that has been determined to be highly offensive by a court is the disclosure that a person has undergone a sex-change operation.[20] Communicating such information to the public (or to enough individuals that it is likely to reach the general public) might be grounds for a lawsuit.

Keep in mind that the facts disclosed must be private in nature. In order to be deemed private, they must not have been the subject of previous publicity and may not already be common knowledge. Consequently, public activities cannot form the basis for this type of lawsuit.

Finally, there is a special exception if the disclosure of facts is in the public interest, or if the person to whom the facts relate is a public figure. Such "newsworthy" private facts must be of such a nature that there is a legitimate and current public interest in the subject matter that could justify the publication.

Given the potential for widespread disclosure through such activities as posting on a distributed message base or posting to a heavily trafficked BBS, this area of the law seems especially applicable on line. Remember, this type of privacy breach might involve not only text (as in a case where someone posts the private facts to a public forum) but could also involve digitized images (as in a case where a compromising photo is distributed through a BBS).

One final note about the public disclosure of private facts claim: If the person to whom the private facts relate has given consent to their revelation, there is no cause of action. This holds true even if the person passed along the information in the strictest confidence, only to find that the confidant breached a promise of secrecy. Once the private facts are volunteered, there can be no cause of action for making them known to the public.

False Light

A similar cause of action arises when a person wrongfully attributes views or characteristics to a person in ways that damage that person's reputation. This is to be distinguished from libel and slander, discussed in chapter five, in that the statements that constitute *false light* need not be defamatory. For example, inaccurately attributing certain political affiliations to an individual might not be defamatory, but could form the basis of a false light claim. The wrongfully attributed facts must be highly offensive to a reasonable person in order to form the basis of a lawsuit. Most of the defenses discussed earlier (newsworthiness and consent, for instance) also apply to false light lawsuits.

Once again, cyberspace is a natural forum for the commission of this type of wrongful act, especially considering that widespread distribution of false material must be established to support this claim.

Wrongful Intrusion

The law often protects those areas of a person's life in which he can reasonably expect he will not be intruded upon. For instance, a person's home is usually considered a private place, and wrongfully wiretapping or photographing in the confines of his home might form the basis of an intrusion lawsuit. The intrusion must also be highly offensive but, unlike the other common law privacy claims, no publication to others is necessary; the intrusion is enough.

In cyberspace, it is easy to imagine situations where the wrongful intrusion tort might be applicable. For instance, reading another's private correspondence might be actionable. Likewise, surreptitiously gaining access to someone's data or files might be considered a wrongful intrusion for purposes of this type of lawsuit.

Sysops or system administrators might also face potential liability if they negligently make it possible for someone to intrude wrongfully in private affairs of a user or account holder on a system. In an analogous situation, Ohio Bell Telephone Company was successfully sued by a woman for giving her estranged husband an extension to her private phone line.[21] Sysops who give third parties access levels that facilitate illicit prying into private areas might be found liable for similar reasons.

The Great Cryptography Debate

So far in this chapter, we have looked at ways in which private communications and information are protected by legal doctrines that punish those who wrongfully delve into or manipulate them. Obviously, there has been quite a bit of effort on the part of legislators, judges, and others to attempt to address this problem with a system that meets everyone's needs. Still, technology has a way of staying well ahead of the law. In the case of privacy, the whole legal battle may be quickly becoming moot.

We need laws to protect confidential information only when people who should not be accessing it have the ability to do so. With the advent of powerful and virtually insurmountable techniques to guarantee that private communications remain secret, the ability to intercept private communications is significantly, if not completely, reduced. High-powered *cryptography* is such a technique, and the debate over cryptography in cyberspace seems to be heading toward a boiling point.

With strong cryptography algorithms, users can rely on the computational prowess of their computer system to encode messages, files, and any other digital information in such a way that only the author and the intended recipient of the message can decipher it. Since all information on-line is digital, cryptography offers the ability to encrypt nearly everything that comprises cyberspace. Even with mammoth computers and vast amounts of resources, no one (including the government) can easily decrypt messages encrypted with today's more advanced cryptographic tools. One can reasonably assume that more advanced techniques will be developed, making the prospect for absolutely indecipherable messages highly likely. With cryptographic technology, individuals seeking absolute privacy no longer need to depend on the legal system for their protection. Rather, the technology itself provides all the protection needed.

The Constitutionality of Encryption

There are many misconceptions about the right to engage in encrypted communications. Writing a letter in code or sending e-mail using computerized encryption methods both appear to be obvious examples of protected activities under the First Amendment's guarantees of freedom of speech; however, there is no real legal precedent to establish this seemingly obvious point. Banning encrypted communications would be tantamount to declaring that it is suddenly illegal to speak in languages unfamiliar to investigators. Any government attempt to force an individual to communicate only in ways decipherable to the authorities would result in a devastatingly chilling effect on protected speech. Luckily, no laws currently restrict such encoded communications. Any that may be proposed would have to pass serious scrutiny under the First Amendment.

There are also strong restraints on the government's power to pry into what you are saying. These restraints are derived from other parts of the U.S. Constitution. The most notable is the restraint that stems from the "right of the people to be secure in their persons, papers, and effects, against unreasonable searches and seizures," which is guaranteed by the Fourth Amendment.

Public Key Encryption

Recently, a cryptography system based on the *public key* algorithm has become the focus of attention in cyberspace.[22] In a public key system, each message requires two keys that usually comprise lengthy strings of text. An individual distributes his or her public key to anyone who wants it. Using the recipient's public key, the sender encodes the message in a way that cannot be deciphered without the recipient's private key. Therefore, only the holder of the private key can decrypt it. In theory, this is among the most secure of all techniques, since no one ever has to give anyone one's private key in order to communicate securely. This reduces the chance that anyone but the receiving party will ever have the ability to decrypt the message.

The public key method has been implemented into a freely distributed (public domain) software package called *Pretty Good Privacy* (PGP), which is available for a variety of computer systems. PGP, written by privacy advocate Phil Zimmermann, has been surrounded by controversy since its initial distribution in 1991. The main problem is that a patent covering the public key algorithm is owned by a California company intent on guarding its property rights in the method. According to the company, distribution of PGP is a violation of its patent. Proponents of PGP argue that it should not be proper to own the algorithm, just as it is not proper to own basic rules of physics and math. Until the issue is resolved (talks are underway as of August 1993), many system operators are refraining from distributing PGP. The company maintains that any use or distribution of public key-based encryption software is a violation of its patent, entitling it to take legal action against users, sysops, and others involved. When a version of PGP becomes available that is properly sanctioned by the owners of the algorithm it will be perfectly legitimate to own or use it.

Another complication with PGP involves export restrictions that limit the transport of encryption tools. Under federal law, data encryption hardware and software are *munitions* subject to government regulation. The U.S. State Department actively controls the export of such technology with a licensing system. If a high-tech product such as PGP is not properly licensed by the State Department, it cannot be transferred out of the country. The algorithm upon which PGP is based currently does not meet this test. Until it does, transferring it across the border, or allowing someone outside of the United States to download it from your system, is a violation of the law.

Because of these legal problems, PGP, while enticing, should be avoided by users wishing to steer clear of potential legal problems. Remember, however, that events in this arena are occurring at a breakneck pace. It may well be that by the time you read this, PGP or another product like it will be fully legitimate. Users would be well advised to keep up to date on the legal status of cryptographic tools such as PGP by following official announcements, available on USENET, in the print media and other sources.

Is Widespread Cryptography a Good Thing?

The power of generally accessible, strong cryptography has some people fairly concerned. Law enforcement advocates are quick to describe a nightmarish future where terrorists, mobsters, and other "bad guys" run amok because of the secrecy afforded by cryptography. This scenario, often referred to as crypto-anarchy, threatens the long term stability of our social order. On the other hand, civil libertarians and *cypherpunks* (the name given to radical cryptography activists) maintain that the only way to guarantee privacy in an increasingly digitized world is through unfettered distribution of the most powerful cryptography techniques and tools. In the middle are average citizens, who recognize the value of privacy yet want to rest assured that the authorities have some ways to protect them from harm.

The federal government has recently entered the cryptography debate on several fronts. The FBI has circulated its *Digital Telephony Proposal*, which would mandate that communication systems (possibly including bulletin boards, networks, phone systems, and on-line services) be designed with the ability to facilitate government investigations. In layman's terms, the F.B.I. wants back doors built into systems in case it has to gain access for law enforcement purposes. The initiative has met resounding resistance from industry and concerned public interest groups. In a similar development, the Clinton administration has endorsed an encryption scheme based on a microchip called the Clipper Chip, which it hopes will become a national standard for voice encryption. The Clipper initiative makes it possible for government agents, if necessary, to decrypt encoded private communications. Both the Digital Telephony and Clipper Chip proposals, while controversial, do have supporters.

The Virtual Marketplace: Business Transactions on the Net

The most successful capitalists are those who efficiently manage to exploit the resources available to them. Technology is one of the most important resources available in the market. Indeed, it can be said that the business person who does not take advantage of the newest technological innovations is not only failing to stay ahead of the competition, but is falling behind as well. Technological advances and a free market are necessary partners. A business seeking to outperform its competitors will invest its resources to create new technologies. Likewise, a new technology will often create a market that previously did not exist.

It comes as no surprise that the market has not overlooked cyberspace as an important business resource. The number and variety of business transactions that transpire in cyberspace is growing, and will continue to grow as more businesses begin to discover the potential benefits of computerized commerce.

While business and technology do tend to be partners that drive each other, the partnership is sometimes an uneasy one. No one denies that huge portions of cyberspace are commercial in nature. The on-line services, for example, are run by huge corporations whose main objective is to make a profit. But some areas of cyberspace have avoided commercialization. In these realms, cyberspace purists are wary of business people in their domain. Much of the architecture of noncommercial cyberspace was created by these same people. Business in cyberspace, especially big corporate business, represents a fundamental change of the *status quo*.

Still, business transactions on the net are already too numerous to be ignored. This mixture of business and cyberspace has generated many legal questions, and it is these questions that we address in this chapter. We focus exclusively on consumer-oriented commercial transactions and do not address issues that arise between merchants. Consequently, topics such as electronic data interchange (EDI) are not addressed.[1] Instead we will discuss issues that may crop up when a user engages in simple business transactions over the net.

Electronic Contracts

Almost every question posed by business dealings in cyberspace can be reduced to a question involving contract law. This is because contracts form the basis of almost all business transactions. They create security in commercial transactions so that consumers have something to rely on other than the good faith of the parties with whom they deal. Although many oral contracts are valid, the majority of contracts used in daily business dealings are written. Many of the contract issues that arise in cyberspace involve e-mail or public messages.

What Are Electronic Contracts?

A contract is "a promise or a set of promises for the breach of which the law gives a remedy, or the performance of which the law in some way recognizes as a duty."[2] *Electronic contracts*, as we use the term in this chapter, are contracts that were formed primarily in cyberspace. They are simply contracts under the standard definition created in a medium that was unanticipated when traditional contract law was being developed and that bring with them new issues and problems. The standard definition is a helpful start to understanding electronic contracts, but it is not useful unless you understand what it is that makes a promise (or sets of promises) enforceable.

A transaction can usually be said to constitute a contract if three basic elements are present. These elements are *offer, acceptance,* and *consideration.* You can think of each element as representing a leg on a stool. Just as a missing leg will cause the stool to fall, if one of the elements is missing there will usually be no contract.

Offer

When someone makes an offer he or she communicates a special message that creates the power of acceptance in the person to whom the offer is being made. When a valid offer is made, the person making the offer (the *offeror*) cannot change it after it has been accepted. In order to be valid, an offer must create a reasonable expectation in the person to whom the offer is being made (the *offeree*) that the offeror is actually willing to enter into a contract. Although sometimes the phrases "I promise" or "I offer" are used to indicate that the communication represents an offer, these words are not necessary. Sending someone e-mail that reads, "I will sell my 200-megabyte hard drive for $120" constitutes a valid offer.

Some types of communications that may appear to be offers are often deemed to be merely *invitations* for offers. For example, catalogs are usually held to be invitations for offers and not actual offers. So, if you receive personal e-mail that was directed exclusively to you and it contained what could be reasonably interpreted as an offer to form a contract, then it more likely than not is an offer. If, on the other hand, you read a general post in a newsgroup or message base, and that post offers an item for sale, it is likely to be construed not as an offer, but rather as an invitation for offers. Thus, if the same e-mail discussed above ("I will sell my 200-megabyte hard drive for $120") had been posted in a message base that was publicly accessible, it would likely be held not to be an offer, but rather simply an invitation for an offer. There is an exception to this rule if the message clearly identifies the offeree and contains terms that are certain and definite. For example, a post in a message base that reads "I will sell my 200-megabyte hard drive for $120 to the first person who sends me e-mail" will likely be construed as an offer even though it is made to the public in general. The same words can have different legal consequences depending upon to whom they are directed. Anyone attempting to make an offer in cyberspace should keep these subtle rules in mind.

Revoking an Offer
The offeror may terminate an offer by revoking it. The communication that revokes the offer, however, must be made before the offer is accepted. Direct communication to the offeree is the best way of revoking an offer. If you sent an offer to someone via e-mail and you wish to revoke that offer, you should send that person e-mail explicitly indicating your revocation. Indirect communication can sometimes serve to revoke an offer, but it is obviously much better for the offeror to communicate directly with the offeree. Generally, a revocation becomes effective the moment it is received. If the offer was one made through mass distribution (as in the public message base example) then the revocation should be made in the same form that the offer

took. In other words, if the offer was communicated in a post in a message base on a local BBS, the communication revoking that offer should be made in that same message base, and on that same local BBS. A communication attempting to revoke the offer that is posted on a different BBS would probably not serve as a proper revocation. Revocations made by general publication become effective when they are published.

There are times when the offeror is prevented by law from revoking an offer. One such time is when the offer is a *firm* offer. A firm offer is a *signed* written offer made by a merchant to either buy or sell goods that indicates that the offer will remain open for a period of time. A firm offer need not specify how long it will remain open. If no time is specified a reasonable time will be assumed. (The issue of signatures in cyberspace is treated later in this chapter.) Another instance when an offer is not revocable by the offeror is when the offeree relies on the offer to his or her detriment. In order for this doctrine to apply, the offeror must have reasonably expected that the offeree would rely on the offer.

An offer is also terminated when the offeree rejects it. Rejection of an offer should be distinguished from mere *inquiry* about it. The following reply, for example, would be considered an inquiry and not a rejection: "$120 seems high, would you be willing to take less?" A *counteroffer* coupled with an expressed rejection serves as a rejection. Thus "$120 is too much for a used hard drive. I will not pay it. I will give you $100 instead." acts as a rejection. Finally, acceptance based on conditional terms can also serve as a rejection. Thus the reply, "I will take the hard drive for $120, but only if you include the controller card," serves as a rejection of the original offer. Rejections become effective when received by the offeror.

People involved in negotiating an offer and acceptance should be aware of the Uniform Commercial Code (U.C.C.), which modifies some of the common law rules discussed above. Article 2 of the U.C.C. (which has been adopted by every state except Louisiana) deals solely with the sale of goods. Under the U.C.C., what may have constituted a rejection under the common law might still be viewed as an acceptance. For example, the addition of new terms by an offeree is not necessarily fatal to the formation of a contract under the U.C.C. If any party to the contract is a nonmerchant, then the different terms are considered to be proposals to modify the contract and do not become part of the contract unless the offeror agrees. On the other hand, if both parties are merchants, the new terms will become part of the contract unless: (1) they materially alter the original terms of the offer; (2) the offeror has already objected to the particular terms or objects within a reasonable time after notice of the terms is received; or (3) the original offer expressly limited acceptance to the terms of the offer. If your electronic contracts involve these tricky issues, you will want to consult an attorney.

Termination of Offers
Offers expire after a specified time or, if no specified time is mentioned, after a reasonable time. Consequently, a user cannot force an offeror to keep her offer to sell her hard drive open ten months after it was received since that would be unreasonable.

Acceptance

Acceptance is the offeree's assent to an offer. Acceptance cannot exist without an offer first having been communicated. Generally, the acceptance of an offer must be communicated to the offeror. The U.C.C. states that an acceptance may be communicated by any "medium reasonable in the circumstances."[3] An offeror may restrict the form that the communication indicating acceptance may take (e.g., "If you accept, reply to this offer via e-mail to the address listed above"). Note that limitations as to how the acceptance is to be made must be unambiguous; otherwise the offeree will be allowed to use any reasonable means of communicating acceptance.

Who May Accept an Offer
Ordinarily, only the person to whom an offer is addressed has the power to accept and thus bind both parties into a contract. In a case where the offer is one that is posted to a general audience, anyone may accept. In a case where the offeror makes a general post but intends for only one person to be able to accept, no one can accept once someone else does. Thus, in our example of the user who makes a general post about her hard drive and states that she will sell that drive to the first person who replies to her via e-mail, the first person to respond to the offeror will preclude others from accepting the offer.

As was noted earlier, under the U.C.C., an acceptance need not be the mirror image of what was originally offered. An acceptance may be accompanied by terms new or different from those that appeared in the original offer. The effect of an acceptance that contains new or different terms depends on the status of the parties to the contract. Whether the additional terms become part of the contract depends mostly on whether or not the parties to the contract are all merchants. The section on revoking offers found earlier in this chapter provides further detail on the function of this rule.

When Acceptance Becomes Effective: The Mailbox Rule

Acceptance of an offer by mail (or similar services) creates a contract at the moment of dispatch, provided that it is properly addressed and stamped. If the letter is improperly sent, then the acceptance becomes effective when the letter is received by the offeror. This is known as the *mailbox rule*, and it applies only to acceptances. How this traditional rule is treated in cyberspace is discussed later in the chapter.

There are some limitations to the mailbox rule. For example, the offeror can explicitly state in the offer that acceptance will not become effective until it is received. Also, in the event that the offeree sends a rejection first and then sends an acceptance, whichever arrives first is controlling. If the offeree sends an acceptance first and then a rejection, the acceptance is effective *unless* the offeror receives the rejection first and detrimentally relies on it.

If two offers containing identical terms cross in the mail, there is no acceptance. In order for acceptance to take place there must be knowledge of an offer.

Consideration

The third element necessary to form a valid contract is *consideration*. This term has a special meaning in contract law. Consideration consists of two elements, a bargained-for-exchange, and legal value. A bargained-for-exchange is simply an exchange of one thing for another. The exchange could take the form of promises (e.g., "I promise to give you my hard drive if you promise to paint my house") or there could be an exchange of a promise for an act (e.g., "I promise to give you my hard drive if you paint my house"). When no bargained-for-exchange exists, there is no consideration, and the transaction is a gift (e.g., "I promise to give you my hard drive, and you don't have to give me anything."). Economic benefit is not a requirement for valid consideration. For example, giving someone peace of mind is sufficient. Generally, past consideration is not enough. Thus, a promise to give a good Samaritan money for having saved your life is not a contract because there is no consideration (assuming, of course, that the promise is made after the person saved your life).

The second element, legal value, is one into which courts generally do not inquire. If the consideration given is something with no value, courts often will consider the transaction to be a gift and not a contract. Also, sham transactions (sometimes used to avoid tax liability) where the consideration is minimal are often deemed not to be contracts.

When a Contract Must Be in Writing: The Statute of Frauds

There is a common misconception that in order for a contract to be enforceable it must be in writing. This is only partially true. Many oral contracts are valid. But, there are some types of contracts that must be written (or mentioned in a writing) in order for them to be enforceable. Each state has enacted a statute (called a *statute of frauds*) that lists specific transactions that must be backed up by a writing to be enforceable. If the law requires a writing, then the transaction in question is said to "fall within the statute." The writing must be *signed* by the party against whom you are trying to enforce the agreement. Although there are several types of agreements that fall within the statute, the most common are those dealing with land (with the exception of leases that are for less than one year), those dealing with the sale of goods priced at $500 or more, and promises that by their own terms cannot be performed within one year.

Promises that by their own term cannot be performed within one year can be confusing and thus deserve further explanation. A contract that in theory is possible to complete within one year does not fall within the statute. So, for example, a contract between NASA and a programmer to reprogram the entire NASA tracking system would not need to be evidenced in writing even though the actual performance may take much longer than one year. Likewise, a life-time contract of employment does not fall within the statute since it is possible that the person contracting to work may die within one year. The fact that the person lives for several years does not change the writing requirement; the only question asked is whether there is any possibility that at the time the contract was formed it could be completed in one year or less. A contract that calls for a person to work for two years must be in writing, as it would be impossible, by the terms of the contract, for it to be completed in one year or less.

Contract Issues Peculiar to the On-line World

The law of contracts is rich with issues and treatises that discuss them. It would be a mistake to attempt to cover such a large body of law in this sort of book. Instead, it is much more productive to attack those issues and problems that tend to plague contracts in the on-line world. The following is not intended to be a complete analysis of the law of electronic contracts. It is, instead, an examination of some of the more interesting and troubling issues in this new field.

The Mailbox Rule Revisited: The E-mailbox Rule?
Recall that the under the mailbox rule the moment that an acceptance was posted by the offeree was the precise moment that the offer was deemed accepted, even if a revocation of the offer was already in the mail. At first blush the mailbox rule may seem to be a quirky little rule set up by attorneys to ensure that their services are needed. If the reasons behind the rule are examined, however, it seems to be a logical method of regulating these sorts of activities. Various justifications for this rule have been propounded. One reason that has often been cited is that

the rule curtails the offeror's freedom to revoke by ending it at the earliest feasible time. Ending the offeror's powers to revoke at the time of dispatch of the acceptance binds the offeror while the acceptance is in transit, even though he does not know that the offer has been accepted and even though the offeree may not yet have relied on the contract. But allowing the offeror to revoke until the acceptance is received would aggravate the already vulnerable situation of the offeree, who may have relied, even though he may not be able to prove it (for example, if his reliance is by inaction).[4]

In other words, the mailbox rule is just a method for allocating risk. The offeree who accepts is deemed to be in a more vulnerable position and is thus given an additional degree of protection by the mailbox rule. While the rule applies to messages in any public service instrumentality similar to mail or telegram, it does not apply to a medium where the communication is instantaneous (such as telephones).[5] This, of course, makes sense when viewed in light of the purpose of the rule. An offeree who accepts via an instantaneous medium will know immediately of any revocation on the part of the offeror; he will not have a chance to rely to his detriment on the presumption that the bargain is still open.

The question of whether the mailbox rule applies to e-mail is one that courts have not yet answered. The applicability of the rule seems to depend on whether the e-mail is deemed to be more like an instantaneous communication than like traditional mail services. Unlike real-time chat (which resembles a telephone conversation) e-mail, though very quick, is probably not instantaneous for the purpose of this rule. Since questions about the applicability of the mailbox rule to e-mail remain, it is not a bad idea for an offeror to spell out the terms of acceptance in her offer. The offeror can specify when an acceptance becomes effective in the original proposal. The offeror is thus said to be "the master of the bargain," since he or she can modify the mailbox rule.

Unauthorized Modification of a Written Contract by One Party
A major problem facing the use of electronic contracts involves forgery. To illustrate the point, suppose you send another user an e-mail offer that reads "I will sell you my hard drive for $90 to be paid now, and $30 to be paid within one month." Suppose she accepts your offer and remits the $90. You ship the drive. Once she is in possession of the drive she refuses to pay you the additional $30 claiming that it was never part of the bargain. When you sue her for breach of contract, you introduce as evidence your copy of the offer with the original terms. But further suppose that your not-so-honest fellow user, wishing to avoid paying you the additional $30, introduces as evidence a copy of the offer, which she has modified to read "I will sell you my hard drive for $90." Ignoring, for the moment, the ethical implications of what she has done, what can a court do in a situation like this? All other things being equal, it is just as likely that the document was modified by the seller as by the buyer. While forgery is also a problem with "paper contracts," modifications made to paper tend to leave physical traces of the forgery. In a purely electronic contract, however, no eraser marks, no ink smudges, and no blacked out portions stand out to alert the court of the possibility of fraud.

The forgery issue is really mostly an evidentiary one. How can you protect yourself from an unscrupulous party when dealing with electronic contracts? How can you create a contract that leaves legal proof of fraud if it is modified? One way of solving the problem is to reproduce the agreement on paper and have the other party sign off on the paper copy. While this solution does reduce the chance that the terms of the contract will be modified by a dishonest party, it also cuts against the benefits of creating contracts on-line. Two advantages of doing business in cyberspace are that transactions can be entered into quickly, and there is a reduction in the amount of paperwork required to keep track of these transactions. Having to create hard copies of contracts and then submitting these hard copies to all parties for their signatures nullifies those advantages.

Another solution to the fraud problem is to assign a noninterested third party (such as a sysop) as custodian of the records. The custodian can then keep a copy of the message stored on disk or backup tape away from anyone who may wish to modify the contents. This is somewhat like having the original documents put in escrow, with neither party having access to them unless a dispute arises. While this system virtually eliminates the possibility of fraud, it does necessitate the use of a third party and, consequently, may incur additional fees for this service. Furthermore, this system presupposes some form of agreement between the offeror and the offeree as to which third party will be used. For many small transactions this sort of agreement may seem overly burdensome.

Another possible approach involves the use of an encryption routine. The sender of the message attaches an encrypted summary of the material terms to the original document. Should the terms later be modified by the recipient, the sender can simply decrypt the summary and show the terms as they were originally written. The encryption/decryption key should be given to a neutral third party who can be trusted to protect it from outsiders. This system overlooks the possibility of fraud at the onset of the contract; the sender can just as easily attach an encrypted summary that does not reflect the true terms of the document.

One final authentication system worth mentioning is one now being employed by some companies. This system uses a mathematical function known as a *hash function* to produce a numerical representation for the entire document. The hash value is appended to the end of the contract by an independent source in charge of generating the hash value. To illustrate how a hash function works, imagine taking every single character of a contract and assigning a numeric value to it. For example, suppose we give the letter A the value of 1, B the value of 2, C the value of 3, and so on. In an extremely simplistic hash function, you would then take the message you wanted to create a hash value for and substitute the value for the character. You could then perform some math function on the values, for example adding all the values, to come up with a final numeric representation of the message. So, for example, the message ABBA would be first changed into its value (1 2 2 1) and then those values would be added to give the sum of 6. If someone later altered the message to read ABBC, the hash value would change to 8 (1 + 2 + 2 + 3) and the modification could be detected immediately. The net result is that if a single character is changed by either party the hash number associated with the document will alert the parties that a change has been made. The above example of a hash function is extremely simplistic, and is not the same function used by industry; the systems currently in use are much more powerful, and are virtually impossible to defeat.

Each user is left with a choice of systems to use for protection against this form of forgery. Factors such as the value of the transaction, the previous trading history of the parties, and the reputation of the parties should be considered in deciding which system, if any, is to be used.

Meeting the Requirements for the Statute of Frauds
The statute of frauds requires that certain transactions be evidenced in writing in order to be legally enforceable. As with the mailbox rule, an understanding of the statute of frauds and its application in the on-line world is difficult without an understanding of the underlying policy behind the rule. It seems that the main function of statute of frauds in the United States is to provide evidence of the terms of a contract should they ever become an issue. A perhaps less obvious function is to stress to the signing parties the importance of the promises they are making. The formalities imposed by the statute alert the parties that their promises are legally binding, and that they should give thought before entering into the agreement.[6]

For a contract that falls within the statute, two requirements must be met before the statute can be satisfied. First, there must be some writing evidencing the agreement, and second, that writing must be signed. The first requirement does not seem difficult to meet since virtually all communications sent in cyberspace are written. Courts have found the written requirement to have been met by telegrams[7] and telexes.[8] Although there appears to be no case law regarding the issue, it seems likely that e-mail would meet the writing requirement of the statute. The two main objectives of the statute are met when using e-mail: evidence is created showing the existence and terms of the contract, and the formality of having the contract written and posted alert the parties of the legally binding effect. It is not so clear, however, whether real-time chat constitutes writing. While the communication certainly is in a fixed form (it can be printed onto a hard copy, or it can be retrieved from a drive or tape), the parties are generally acting in a more informal environment and thus the policy goal of alerting the parties of the seriousness of their actions may not be satisfied. Real-time chat tends to be more akin to a telephone conversation than to written correspondence. Real-time chat would likely satisfy the writing requirements, but because there is some uncertainty, it is clearly in the parties best interest to record their agreements and transmit them in e-mail or some other form of writing that will likely be acceptable to a court.

The second requirement, that the writing be signed, likewise does not appear to have been litigated in the area of on-line services. In general, however, the signature requirement is one that has been subject to very liberal interpretation. Courts do not seem to be as interested in an actual handwritten mark as much as in "whether the other party reasonably believes that the asserted signer's intention is to authenticate the writing as his own."[9] A mark constituting a signature may take many means. It may, for example, be typed.[10] A letterhead may be adopted as a signature.[11] Furthermore, telegrams that bear a typewritten name have been held to satisfy the statute of frauds.[12] Thus, transmissions sent in e-mail that indicate the intent of the sender to authenticate the writing as her own will likely satisfy the signature requirement for purpose of the statute of frauds.

Acceptable Use Policies and Caller Contracts

A common form of electronic contract encountered in the on-line world is frequently referred to as *acceptable use policies* (AUPs) or *caller contracts*. These agreements purport to restrict the types of activities allowed on a particular network or system. One notable AUP governs the National Science Foundation Internet backbone by limiting the nature of network traffic over the backbone to noncommercial material. Users who sign on to a system, whether it be a small BBS or a on-line service such as CompuServe, are probably familiar with caller contracts. Often a user new to a system will have to acknowledge having read the system policies and assent to abide by the terms of the contract before he or she is allowed to use any of the system functions. The user accepts the conditions in the contract in consideration for permission to access the system. The same rules governing all other electronic contracts apply to AUPs and caller contracts. If, for example, there is no exchange of consideration, the contract fails.

If the contract is valid, it is generally binding and should be read carefully by the user. A typical caller contract may attempt to limit sysop liability in case of data loss or some form of tortious conduct by a sysop or other user.[13] The law does not always allow a sysop to limit liability in this way, but barring this, such a caller contract is enforceable. Caller contracts will also often spell out who maintains the property rights to items that are posted in message bases. (Refer to chapter four for more information on intellectual property rights of users.) Fees are also often discussed in these contracts, and for some of the more expensive systems, this may be the most important part of the contract. It is also not unusual to see privacy issues discussed in caller contracts. If you are concerned about the integrity of the system you call, and if you are transmitting material that is sensitive, you will want to examine any terms that deal with privacy very carefully. (Refer to chapter two for a discussion of privacy issues.) In short, a caller contract or AUP is an important type of electronic contract that, ironically, often does not receive more than a second glance by a user. Because a user's rights can be so drastically affected by them, every user should carefully consider the terms of these contracts before entering into them.

Credit Card Transactions in Cyberspace

As commerce becomes more and more prevalent in the on-line community, credit card transactions become more common. The exchange of goods or services in return for payment by credit card is perfectly legal in cyberspace. The user who intends to pay for an item or service by credit card, however, should always be cautious. Valid credit card information is a valuable commodity traded in the computer underworld. Users should take precautions to ensure that the persons to whom they are sending their credit card information are legitimate providers of goods and services. Furthermore, every user should be careful to make sure that the information being transmitted is not vulnerable to interception by other users. For the most part, common sense precautions will keep users from falling prey to credit card thieves.

4   Intellectual Property in Cyberspace: Copyright Law in a New World

Few computer communication issues have received more attention and caused more confusion than those dealing with questions of intellectual property. Copyright law, in particular, can seem especially difficult. Some legal issues in cyberspace require a great deal of attention because of the novel problems they present. With copyright law, however, the issues raised in cyberspace are readily addressed by well-established principles.

Nonetheless, people prematurely conclude that the traditional copyright law simply cannot deal effectively with computer mediated communication. Several arguments are raised in support of this conclusion. One such argument is that cyberspace is so different from the physical world that copyright law cannot possibly cope with the differences.

In support of this argument, people note that with the vast powers of digital connectivity, instantaneous duplication and distribution of someone else's work is easier today than ever before. Those same people also point out that never before has an individual been able to distribute his or her own work more readily to such a wide audience. Today a user on a network or large messaging system can do this with a simple keystroke or click of a mouse button. Those who highlight the differences between cyberspace and noncomputer communications correctly state that when the copyright system was originally developed, this type of powerful manipulation of intellectual property was unthinkable.

Another argument involves attaching significance to the idea that the words, sounds, and images of cyberspace are nothing more than a collection of ones and zeros. These digits are meaningless until they are rearranged or processed by a computer. Those who challenge copyright law's applicability in cyberspace sometimes contend that duplicating or transferring this raw data is not the same as duplicating or transferring the image that is represented by the data. To many, this proves that copyright law simply cannot be imposed on new technology.

At first blush, these arguments based on perplexing twists on traditional intellectual property scenarios seem to pose tough obstacles for lawyers and judges wrestling with the idea of ownership in the matrix. But, when carefully examined, the existing copyright system seems to hold up rather well. The trick to analyzing intellectual property in cyberspace lies in recognizing the way traditional notions of copyright law apply when dealing with novel technologies. It is best to begin by examining the fundamentals of copyright law as they have developed with regard to the more conventional media. Only then can we tackle copyright problems in cyberspace.

A Copyright Primer

The copyright system developed as a means of promoting and advancing knowledge. It was clear to the founding fathers that the best way to do this was to protect the property rights authors or creators have in the products of their creative work. That is why the Constitution grants Congress the authority to *"promote the Progress of Science and useful Art, by securing for limited Times to Authors and Inventors the exclusive Right to their respective Writings and Discoveries."*[1] By granting authors or creators a special property right (the copyright) in the fruits of their labor, the government protects the economic incentive to be creative.

The legislative power found in the Constitution has been exercised by the Congress through the enactment of the Copyright Act.[2] This federal law has been substantially rewritten several times, most dramatically in 1976. That version of the law applies to works created or published after January 1, 1978. U.S. copyright law was also significantly changed in March 1989, when the United States signed the *Berne Convention,* an international copyright treaty. It should be noted that slightly different rules govern materials written, created, or published before these dates. As most on-line materials were created and published after the 1976 revisions and the adoption of the *Berne Convention,* this chapter will focus on the newest version of the Copyright Act.

With the recent revisions, the legal hurdles an author or creator has to jump in order to establish a valid copyright have become less cumbersome. Today the act provides automatic protection for just about any original expression that can be *fixed* in tangible form, as soon as it is expressed. This protection is secured even if the creator or owner of the work takes no further steps to establish ownership.

This means that the moment a person composes an original text, draws an image, records some sound, takes a photograph, or otherwise fixes an idea in a tangible form, a copyright covering the resulting work is owned by the creator. The act spells this out by stating that a work is "fixed" in a tangible medium of expression when its embodiment in a copy or phonorecord, by or under the authority of the author, is sufficiently permanent or stable to permit it to be perceived, reproduced, or otherwise communicated for a period of more than transitory duration.[3]

If anyone copies, distributes, sells, or uses such a work in any way inconsistent with the owner's property rights, that person violates the owner's copyright interest. The owner can sue the violator for damages computed by looking at the actual harm incurred as a result of the infringement or, in some cases, statutorily imposed minimums. The owner may also have the illicit use of the work stopped by a court-issued injunction. Copyright violation is also a federal crime, which means that violating a copyright could make the infringing party subject to fines, jail sentences, or both.

What It Takes to Create a Copyright

Expression and Originality

Before a valid copyright can be asserted, the person making that assertion must show that the work in question consists of an original *expression*. An idea or fact cannot be owned, but the unique description of the idea or fact in original terms can be. An author could not claim ownership to the idea of three pigs attempting to outsmart a big, bad wolf, but if the author writes her version of the story, it becomes her property, protected by a copyright. Several different versions of the same story can each be the subject of separate valid copyrights. Similarly, a calendar design can be protected under a copyright (e.g., because of the layout or accompanying photographs), but the actual arrangement of months and dates cannot be; otherwise, the first person to "create" a calendar for the year could argue that all other calendars infringe on his right. This absurd result is prevented by the requirement that a work must be the product of the author's expression before a copyright can be asserted.

An expression must also be *original*.[4] That means it must emanate and originate from the author who created it, and not someone else. The exact meaning of originality has often been litigated, but there are some well-settled principles to keep in mind. One is that in order to be deemed original, a work must be the product of the creator's own creative labor. Merely copying the work of someone else is not an original enough expression on which to justify asserting a copyright in the finished product. Some reproductions can be copyrighted, but there must be a showing that there is more than a trivial distinction between the original and the copy. Another is that a collective work can warrant copyright protection distinct from the copyrights of the individual works of which it is composed. An anthology, for example, might consist of several stories, each with its own copyright. The editor of the anthology might successfully defend a copyright on the complete collection as well, under the premise that the process of collecting the individual works is a substantial original creative contribution that deserves protection. *Compilations* of facts can also be protected, even if the underlying facts themselves are not subject to copyright protection. The manner in which the facts are arranged and presented can be sufficient original expression for the law to recognize it as protected by a property right.

Formalities

Under earlier versions of the act, an author had to take certain steps to guarantee protection of his or her work. These steps are called *formalities* because they were formally required before a copyright could be said to exist. The recent revisions of the law have done away with most of the formalities or decreased their significance dramatically. As the law stands, an author or creator needs to do very little to ensure ownership over a work.

The most misunderstood formality is the *notice* requirement. At one time it was necessary to put the world on notice of a copyright interest in a work by affixing some type of notification regarding the copyright ownership. Usually, a statement of the owner's name, the year, and either the word "Copyright" or the symbol © would constitute proper notice. Under the old regime, failure to affix such notice, or an error in the notice information, could be fatal to the assertion of a copyright.

Today, contrary to popular belief, no such formal notice is required. A copyright is automatically created when an original expression is fixed in a tangible medium. Failure to affix notice is not a critical error in the way it once was. Distribution without notice can be cured if the copyright is formally registered within a five-year period and a reasonable effort is made to attach a notice to copies that have been distributed without it. The most important remaining effect of omitting a copyright notice is that it raises the possibility that a defendant might successfully rely on an *innocent infringement* defense to avoid certain types of liability. Innocent infringement is not a defense against the claim of infringement itself, but it can be used to show the infringement was not willful. This could affect the amount of damages collected by the copyright owner in an infringement suit.

Although notice is no longer a requirement, it is still good practice to affix notice to any work in which an author plans to maintain a copyright interest. There are still countries that do not recognize a copyright unless there is notice on the work. With the international scope of computer networks, this makes it prudent to attach notice to valuable digital work. Also, attaching notice to your work alerts others that you intend on protecting your interests in it.

The registration requirement has also been relaxed by the recent revisions of the act. It is no longer necessary to register the copyright or to send in an official copy for the collection at the Library of Congress. Registration is required to assert a claim in court against an infringing party. In other words, if you plan to sue someone for violating your copyright, you must first register it. This can be done at any time before the litigation. Also, some statutory remedies are not available if registration occurs after the date of the infringement. Nonetheless, the failure to register does not affect the validity of the ownership right itself, and, for practical purposes, registration is not nearly as important as it once was.

What Types of Work Can Be Copyrighted?

With the new copyright law in place, almost all forms of expression that are fixed in a tangible medium are subject to copyright protection. This includes, but is not limited to: written text, recorded sound, visual images (drawings, photographs and video); and computer software. Of the works listed, the most recent to be recognized as being subject to copyright law is computer software. A special section of the law deals directly with software, and this rapidly developing area is often subject to revision. Special attention is given to software copyright later in this chapter.

The Author or Creator's Rights

Once a work has been created, certain basic rights are granted exclusively to the author.[5] The first of these is the right to *reproduce* the work. Only the copyright holder can make a copy of the work, regardless of the duplication method. Making a photocopy, digitally scanning, or using any other means of duplicating a work would be the sole right of the copyright holder. No one else can exercise this right without the copyright holder's authorization.

Another exclusive right is the ability to create a *derivative* work based on the original. This includes translating the work into a different medium (from print to television, for example) or translating it into a another language. Whenever the work of an author is taken and transformed into another work, the result is a derivative work. Creation of a derivative work can be legally accomplished only by the owner of the copyright.

The rights to *distribute, display,* or *conduct* a performance of the work also belong exclusively to the copyright holder. Only *public* distribution, performance, or display is considered the copyright holder's exclusive right.

The *attribution right* (sometimes called the paternity right) is the right of artists or creators to claim the work and to prevent the use of their name as the author of works they did not create. A similar right is the *integrity right*, which is the right of artists or creators to prevent the use of their name as the creators of distorted versions of the work, and to prevent intentional distortion or destruction of them. Both of these rights apply also to visual works.

Duration

A copyright lasts for fifty years past the death of the author if the work was created after 1977.[6] The attribution and integrity rights only last for the lifetime of the artist or creator.[7]

Infringement

If someone other than the owner of the copyright tries to exercise any one of the owner's exclusive rights, that person is said to *infringe* the copyright. As noted earlier, both the civil and criminal penalties for infringement can be serious. Determining if an infringement occurred is not always an easy task for a court or jury.

When looking at infringement, the most important consideration is whether the allegedly infringing work is *substantially similar* to a work covered by a valid copyright. The intent of the person accused of infringing the copyright is not relevant, except with regard to the punishment. Not intending to violate the copyright, or not knowing that a copied work was protected, does not excuse illegal exploitation of someone else's work. Independently creating a work without knowledge of a previously existing copyright, however, can be a defense. A plaintiff wishing to collect damages must show that the defendant had access to the original in order to prove that it was copied.

Although it may be easy for a judge or jury to recognize a complete and identical copy of a work as an infringement, it becomes much more difficult when only parts of a work are at issue. Several legal formulas have developed to aid a fact finder in assessing whether one work is too similar to another and therefore violates a copyright. All of these tests emphasize substantial similarity as a threshold issue in determining whether a copyright has been violated.

If a plaintiff successfully establishes that an infringement has taken place, there are several types of damages that might be awarded. *Actual* damages are meant to compensate the plaintiff for the harm caused by the infringement. Recovering actual damages requires the plaintiff to prove the particular damages caused by the wrongful use of his or her work. If a work was registered prior to infringement, a plaintiff need not show actual damages in order to recover. *Statutory* damages are set out in the act that alleviate this burden. Depending on what a judge decides, these damages can range from $500 to $20,000. If the infringer proves that he or she was not aware and had no reason to believe that the act constituted an illegal infringement, the court may lower damages to as low as $200. If the plaintiff proves that the defendant's infringement was "committed willfully," the judge may, at his or her discretion, award damages of up to $100,000 per infringement.[8]

Fair Use

Not every use of a copyrighted work is a violation of the law. Congress and the courts have recognized that sometimes reproducing someone else's work is not harmful to that person, and the ability to quote or sample the work of another is an important part of public discourse. Without an exception of this type, book reviews and academic commentary that do not constitute an infringement would be difficult to create. The doctrine of *fair use* has developed to cover situations such as these and provides a shield against copyright liability in certain limited instances.

There are four basic statutory concerns that should be examined in determining whether a use is legitimate under the fair-use doctrine:[9]

1. the purpose and character of the use (including whether the use is commercial or noncommercial in nature);

2. the nature of the copyrighted (original) work;

3. the amount or proportion that was taken or copied; and

4. the economic impact of the use on the copyright owner of the original work.

As will become evident, these four interests do not lend themselves to clear-cut decision making. There is often quite a bit of overlap between them, and different courts have interpreted them to imply different things.

When a fair-use defense is asserted, a judge or jury will examine each of the four concerns and balance them against the right of the author or creator. The perfect fair-use case involves a noncommercial use of a small bit of a work that lends itself to incorporation or quotation, and the use of which in no way could be said to impair the copyright owner's ability to profit from his or her property. Quoting a song lyric in a school essay, for example, would undoubtedly be a legitimate use under the defense. Unfortunately, very few cases are so simple. Sometimes, taking even a small amount of a copyrighted work and using it in a seemingly harmless way might lead to liability.

The difficulty facing litigants, judges, and juries is that many of the factors require qualitative as well as quantitative analysis. For example, if an author is claiming that parts of his book were illegally used by a magazine article, how should the courts determine the amount and proportion taken? Is it enough to count the words from the original that can be found in the article that incorporates them? Or should some small bits of the author's work be viewed as more "proportionate" than others because of their content? Despite the obvious difficulties posed by problems like these, many copyright claims turn on exactly this type of issue.

A good rule of thumb is that those who use someone else's work for commercial purposes will have a harder time establishing fair use than those who use the work for nonprofit or academic purposes. Although the commercial element is but one part of the test, it has assumed a prominent role, and is arguably the closest thing to a litmus test as exists in fair-use analysis.[10]

Several major court cases have scrutinized the nuances of the fair-use doctrine. J. D. Salinger successfully banned the use of his unpublished letters when he learned that a biographer intended to quote them in an upcoming book.[11] This was accomplished even though (and partially because) Salinger had no plans to publish the letters. The biographer's claim that using the letters was a fair use was rejected. Sony used the fair use doctrine in defending its marketing of videotapes against Universal Picture's claim that doing so facilitated copyright infringement by people who taped television shows for private use.[12] The Supreme Court held that because of the nature of personal use recordings, such duplication was protected as a fair use.

Licensing

When authors transfer away part of their rights in a work, they are said to *license* the copyright. To license a work, the licensing agreement must be in writing, and authors can give away no more than what they actually own. Also, in order for the licensing agreement to be enforceable, there must be an exchange of consideration. This means that each party gets something as inducement to enter into a binding contract. Without consideration, a license (and any other contract) is not enforceable.

A license might also be implied from the circumstances surrounding the distribution or publication of the work. Sometimes the way an author presents the work will grant certain rights to the public by implication.

Copyright in Cyberspace

Copyright issues are pervasive in cyberspace. This is largely because almost everything communicated on a BBS, an on-line service, or a network is subject to copyright protection. The nature of the medium is such that virtually all on-line discourse is an expression that has been fixed in a tangible medium as defined by copyright law. Whereas a short telephone call does not implicate copyright, the electronic equivalents (a live user-to-user chat session, a short note in e-mail, or a post on a messaging system) often do. The following is a survey of the copyright implications of several computer telecommunication activities.

E-mail

Like J. D. Salinger, authors of e-mail automatically hold a copyright in their words. The moment your e-mail is fixed on a storage device somewhere, you own it, even if you have not attached a copyright notice declaring your ownership. Anyone who copies, republishes, or otherwise uses your words without your consent is violating your copyright.

Being the recipient of a particular piece of e-mail does not excuse you from potential copyright related liability if you use the mail in a way inconsistent with the sender's rights. If you were to send an electronic fan letter to a famous poet and it so inspired her that she replied by sending her response in poetry, that does not give you the right to copy, sell, or publicly recite the poetry without consulting her first. You can usually make fair use of the e-mail, however, by quoting small portions of it or summarizing its content without worrying about copyright problems.

Just as any mail you receive belongs to the sender, any e-mail you send to someone else is your property, and the recipient can only use it in ways consistent with your wishes. If the recipient copies and distributes it to the entire network, he or she has clearly violated your copyright, and could be subject to liability. As with many such violations, though, determining whether the infringement is serious enough to warrant legal action is a decision only you and your attorney can make.

The fact that the sender of e-mail owns the e-mail does not mean that he or she cannot be held liable for violating someone else's copyright in the first place. You cannot send the full text of a book in e-mail and expect to be exempt from copyright prosecution simply because it is e-mail. The act of typing or scanning the original is an illegal duplication, and the act of distributing it is also illegal. In this respect, as in most others, e-mail communications get no special treatment because they are made possible by a new technology.

One should remember that certain systems might force you to waive your rights to e-mail ownership as part of a contract you enter into in exchange for access to the system. A standard log-in contract requiring users to agree that all e-mail sent through the system is going to be owned by the sysop might effectively waive the user's ownership rights in the e-mail. (Contract issues such as this are more generally discussed in chapter three.) Also, if you are composing your e-mail communications on the job, the work-for-hire doctrine might make the e-mail the property of your employer. This doctrine applies to almost any copyrightable material produced in the scope of your employment, or any work specially commissioned under a work-for-hire agreement.

Message Bases and Newsgroups

Posting a message to a message base or newsgroup is very similar to sending e-mail as far as copyright law is concerned. Once composed, the message is subject to a copyright that belongs to the author. Although it is fairly common, reposting the message to another forum is almost always a copyright violation (illicit distribution and duplication). This practice of capturing an interesting post and re-posting it elsewhere may seem tempting and harmless, but if you want to abide by the letter of the law, you should refrain from doing so without the consent of the author.

In some cases, however, the person posting the message will relinquish all claims on it and explicitly note that the message can be distributed or circulated without permission. In this case, the message can be safely copied and posted to other message bases, mailing lists, or newsgroups without fear of copyright liability. Sometimes, this is exactly what the person posting the message wants you to do, so that the message can be widely disseminated with a minimal amount of work.

In other situations, the author requests that, if circulated, the message be treated only in certain ways. Perhaps the author requests that it only be circulated in its entirety, or that full credit to the author be included on any copies. In this case, the author is attempting to establish a *licensing agreement* with those who circulate the post. The necessary elements that comprise a valid license seem to be present. The license is in writing and the author is giving away no more than she has a legal right to. The author is granting the permission to duplicate and redistribute the work to the public in exchange for abiding by her special request. This exchange is arguably the necessary exchange of consideration that the law requires. If a licensing agreement is formed, then anyone distributing the work has to follow the author's special requests.

Unlike e-mail, a message on a newsgroup or message base is part of a collection of individual texts written by different people. A single newsgroup or message base is really a *compilation* or *collective work* consisting of many messages. While the copyright that protects any particular message is retained by the author, someone else might have a claim to a compilation or collective work copyright over the entire group of messages. A collective work copyright probably exists only where someone actively serves as a *moderator* (someone who controls or edits the content of the collection/discussion). The moderator, or the owner of the host system, might argue that her work in screening certain messages and allowing others to remain as part of the message base gives her a valid copyright in the collection as a whole. CompuServe, one of the largest on-line services, actively asserts a compilation copyright on user messages as do other on-line services and some bulletin boards. This means that capturing an entire discussion off of CompuServe or another system and reposting it somewhere else violates the host system's copyright. Remember, this right is separate from the author's individual copyright in a particular message. The moderator's compilation or collective work copyright protects the collection as a whole. If someone reproduces a series of messages from the message base, the moderator can assert a claim against them, but she cannot assert a claim if someone only infringes the copyright covering an individual message.

What about someone copying a post from one forum to another similar forum in the same bulletin board or system? A system operator or conference moderator might see a message and feel it would be better placed in a different discussion area. Perhaps the author mistakenly posted about dogs in the "Cats" discussion. While at first glance this duplication seems like a violation, it might be helpful to recall the notion of implied license here. It is likely that, by posting to a particular forum, an author has granted an implied license permitting certain insignificant excursions into her exclusive power to control the use of her words. Copying from one message area to another on the same system seems likely to be a legitimate use under this implied license. Just how far this power stretches is not clear. It probably only covers very similar forums in the same conferencing system. Users should be wary of taking a message from one system and copying it to another system with different audiences and distribution methods. For example, taking a message posted on a private system and posting it to a USENET newsgroup almost certainly constitutes a clear violation. Taking a message from USENET and posting it to a smaller forum, might arguably be less problematic, since users posting to USENET cannot reasonably be thought to maintain much control of their words. But, nonetheless, such copying is probably a violation and should be avoided.

Newspaper and Magazine Articles and Fair Use

Anyone familiar with USENET, Fidonet, and other networked and non-networked messaging systems knows that a familiar sight in many discussions is the posting of the complete text of a newspaper or magazine article. These are often typed or copied (with a digital scanner and Optical Character Reader software) by a user wishing to share the contents of the article with the readers of the message base. Often, the person posting the article will defend this blatant copyright violation with a claim that the practice is protected by the fair-use doctrine. Unfortunately, this argument does not hold up under scrutiny.

With more publishers of traditional print media exploring the commercial potential of electronic distribution, the economic impact of widely distributing someone else's article in cyberspace is obvious. Many publishers, however, will consent to electronic distribution of a single article if approached. Without such authorization (preferably in writing) it is not wise to expose oneself to civil and criminal liability that could result from posting a copyrighted article on a BBS or the networks.

What should you do if you feel it is important to let everyone on your favorite newsgroup know about a story you just read in the newspaper? The answer is to summarize, paraphrase, and quote the story within the scope of the fair-use doctrine. Tell people what the story was about, and use specific facts from the story to make sure they get the full picture. But do not copy the whole article word for word; doing so could get you and the system you are using into trouble with the owner of the story's copyright.

Incidentally, according to the Copyright Act, the federal government cannot own a copyright in official government documents or publications. So, if you run across a law or statute, a pamphlet from a federal agency, or any other government publication, you are probably free to distribute it in any way you want. These works should be considered to be part of the public domain. But, be careful. Many on-line services that distribute government documents claim a copyright on the format, synopses, comments, or other parts of such documents. Thus, unless the copy is clearly ASCII (plain text) with no such non–public domain portions, you might not be able to copy it.

Digital Images

Digital images have become popular on computer bulletin board systems and the on-line services, and are actively traded and distributed through the networks. These images take the form of computer files that can be transferred to and from host systems and viewed with special software. Some of these images can have very high resolution and depict anything from flowers to pornography.

Every image file is protected by a copyright held by the creator of the image unless it has been specifically waived. Unless individuals copying or creating the image with a digital scanner actually own the copyright, they are duplicating the work of someone else. If they do not have permission, they are also violating copyright law by duplicating and distributing the image.

A large percentage—probably a majority—of the image files available on bulletin boards and other systems represent a violation of someone's copyright. Especially prevalent are sexual images scanned from adult magazines or captured from pornographic movies. Many of these even bear a reference to the original source, in blatant disregard of the owner's exclusive rights. Many people feel that there is no harm in scanning an image from a magazine or book and trading it with other users through their favorite bulletin board. The owner of the copyright may often feel differently, as might the system operator of the system being used as a conduit for the illegal images.

Recently, the consequences of distributing illicit image files in cyberspace were dramatically illustrated. *Playboy* magazine became aware of a large number of its images being distributed from a commercial BBS called Events Horizons. Recognizing the profit potential in distributing its images, *Playboy* sued the bulletin board in March 1992 for copyright infringement along with an alleged trademark violation stemming from the BBS using the *Playboy* name on some of the images. In October 1992, Playboy collected $500,000 based on the alleged copyright infringement. Clearly, the potential liability associated with distributing copyrighted image files is huge and should not be taken lightly.

Live Chat

When two people speak to each other, whether face to face or over the telephone, copyright law does not govern the words spoken unless there is some process whereby the words are fixed in a tangible medium. For instance, if someone turns on a tape recorder, the speaker's words become protected by a copyright the moment they are captured. The same would be true if someone was actively transcribing the conversation onto paper.

On-line chat systems are an interesting evolution of the standard face-to-face conversation. Users on any chat system have the ability to carry on real-time conversations by typing their messages to each other. Sometimes, several users at once can be parties to the conversation in the on-line equivalent of a conference call. Do these sessions end up being covered by copyright law? No one is sure. As with many legal issues in cyberspace, there is no precedent on which to back up any conclusions in this regard. Nonetheless, applying established law gives us some ideas as to how the courts might handle such a situation.

Clearly, an on-line chat session can be fixed in a tangible medium in some situations. If the system is buffering the discussion (saving it to a storage device somewhere or echoing it to a printer), then the answer seems easy: The copyright law applies. Also, if a chat participant is capturing the chat transcript, he or she is satisfying the fixing in a tangible medium required by the Copyright Act. There are probably several copyrights created, one for each speaker (typist) and possibly a compilation or collective work copyright, especially if there is a moderator.

Often, however, the text is held in memory just long enough for the users to read it, after which it is allowed to evaporate from computer memory leaving no trace. This poses a more difficult scenario. Are the expressions of the participants being fixed in a tangible medium, as described by the Copyright Act? Although there is not much authority to which to turn, the answer is that they probably are not. The fleeting moments during which the typed conversation is stored would most likely be deemed insufficient to qualify it as having been fixed in a tangible medium. A contrary finding would open a Pandora's box for other media (such as the telephone system) that use technologies that store live communications for a brief period of time and then forward them along the communication chain. Certainly, a court would be hard-pressed to defend a position claiming that all telephone conversations are protected by copyrights.

Users actively involved in on-line chat sessions probably should not consider their expressions protected unless those expressions are being transcribed, buffered, or captured to disk. This may all be moot, however, as any infringement will most likely occur by someone writing, typing, or copying the text of a chat session. The moment the writing, typing, or copying occurs, the copyright law covers the situation, giving the speakers immediate protection.

Software

Making a copy of a piece of software is so easy to do that many people are amazed that this simple act can amount to a violation of the law. As the old adage advises, however, ignorance of the law is no excuse. Recently, the possible consequences for violating software copyright have become more severe. Anyone involved in copying or transferring software in cyberspace should pay special attention to the rules of the game so as to stay out of trouble.

Although software is covered by many of the same basic rules as other works, in some instances the copyright law pays special attention to computer software. For example, the act provides special rules governing the creation of archival copies or copies necessary for program execution. These copies are not considered an infringement of the owner's exclusive right of duplication. There are also specialized ways of looking at whether a programmer infringes on a software copyright when he or she writes software that is similar to some already protected. These issues are beyond the scope of this discussion. The remainder of this section focuses on software copyright issues that are particular to cyberspace.

Specialized licensing agreements almost always govern the rights a user acquires from the owner of the software copyright. It is possible to group programs one might encounter in cyberspace into different classes based on the licensing rights their authors or publishers decide should accompany them.

Commercial Software

Most of the software in existence is written, marketed, and distributed with the intention that it be used only by individuals who pay to use it under a strict licensing agreement. This agreement usually forbids making duplicates for anything other than archival purposes. This type of software cannot be traded or transferred on bulletin boards or on-line services without violating the copyright law, although it often is. Users and system operators should be aware of the intentions of the author when they encounter a new piece of software. Barring reason to think otherwise, it is safe to assume that a particular program is covered by a copyright. If it is governed by a typical commercial licensing agreement, the only legal way to acquire a copy is to purchase it directly from the author or from an authorized reseller. Criminal penalties for violating commercial software copyrights are discussed in chapter seven.

Shareware

Perhaps the most common legal licensing arrangement found in cyberspace is that which accompanies software marketed as shareware. The shareware method has become increasingly popular as a means of marketing software written by independent authors and small publishing houses. When a piece of software is distributed as shareware, users usually have the right to make copies for trial use. If they decide to continue using the software beyond the trial period, the licensing agreement requires them to register with the author, usually by sending the author a registration fee.

Shareware authors actively take advantage of cyberspace as a distribution method. As copies disseminate through the bulletin boards and on-line services, the chance increases that they will fall into the hands of users who value them enough to register them. With this in mind, shareware authors often spend large amounts of time uploading their products to various systems and encouraging others to copy and redistribute them.

Accordingly, making copies of shareware and distributing them or trading them with others is almost always a legitimate use of the files. Care should be taken to read the licensing agreement carefully, however, as it may put restrictions on the manner of distribution. Sometimes, authors will request that the several files that make up their product not be distributed separately. Or, they may request that only certain systems be used for product distribution. Whatever the restrictions, it is safest to abide by authors' express wishes when treading on ground that otherwise would be considered their exclusive right.

Public Domain

If authors explicitly state that they intend for their work to enter the public domain, there are no restrictions whatsoever on the distribution, duplication, or any other manipulation of the software. Many hobbyists and beginning programmers will write a useful utility and find great pleasure in making it available free of charge to others as public domain software. If you encounter public domain software, you can rest assured that any use you make of it (such as duplication, modification, or redistribution) is legitimate.

Be wary, however, of harboring the mistaken assumption that the lack of copyright notice means that a piece of software is in the public domain. While at one time this may have been true, this is no longer the case under the new version of the law. The only way for a piece of software to enter the public domain is for the author explicitly to waive all rights in it, or for the copyright to expire. If you do not see language to that effect in the documentation or on the opening screens of the software when it is executed, you should assume that it is protected under a standard commercial copyright and refrain from using it in ways that would infringe upon the author's rights.

Other Copyright Issues

There is a wide variety of other copyright problems that could crop up when dealing with on-line computer communications. For instance, allowing users to access and use an application or game program through a BBS may well represent a breach of the licensing agreement entered into by the software's licensee. Also, there are some tricky issues relating to the ownership of information in a database. Although the person who created and designed the database may hold a copyright over it, the U.S. Supreme Court recently held that the data itself does not warrant as much protection.[13]

With the advent of multimedia systems that digitize audio and video, new copyright issues inevitably will arise. Selling a digital recording of your favorite band's hit single is clearly a copyright violation. Barring fair use, so would be distributing a snippet from a television show or movie. Like digitized image files, sound files are often sampled from copyrighted material and users who exchange them should be careful to respect the ownership of the sampled audio.[14] As these and other issues develop, they will help to determine the parameters of copyright law in cyberspace.

Supreme Court has determined that the First Amendment speech and press clause covers a wide range of traditional communicative activities beyond the spoken word. Artistic expression, writing, and many other activities that convey meaningful ideas fall under the umbrella of First Amendment protection. Most of the activities in which a user can engage while spending time in cyberspace appear to qualify as protected First Amendment activities of one type or another. One would think that they should be given the same protection from government interference as the more traditional means of communication.

Unfortunately, our legal system is sometimes slow to recognize how the First Amendment applies to the new media that are the inevitable product of technological advances. When electronic broadcast technologies first surfaced, for example, lawmakers and judges wrestled with First Amendment questions as if the expressions at issue were somehow different because of the manner in which they were delivered to the audience. As noted constitutional scholar Laurence Tribe points out, "These [court] decisions reveal a curious judicial blindness, as if the Constitution had to be reinvented with the birth of each technology."[1] The result was a system of regulation for television and radio that would be viewed as intolerable if imposed on print media.[2] Tribe, a Harvard Law School professor recognized as one of the nation's leading constitutional law scholars, feels that this start-from-scratch approach compromises the free speech ideal that is so important to our society. He recently proposed a 27th Amendment, which would guarantee that all freedoms in the Bill of Rights be construed as equally applicable without regard to the technological method or medium through which information is generated or stored.[3] Few commentators expect the Tribe Amendment to become law. Tribe himself later recognized it as more of a "thought experiment than as a practical suggestion."[4] Nonetheless, the mere proposal of such an amendment highlights a growing realization that civil liberties might suffer without a constitutional recognition of new technology.

Even in the face of the troubling gap between the law and technology, there are some fundamental notions of First Amendment law that provide guidance for citizens testing the boundaries of the "electronic frontier." It is important to note that, like other areas of constitutional law, our judicial understanding of the First Amendment is constantly evolving. The courts often provide contradictory or vague guidance in their attempts to balance the rights of the individual against the public good. For the most part, however, the issues with which people are

most often concerned are governed by some well-established principles that offer fairly clear guidance in all but the most difficult of cases.

If a law criminalizes speech-related activities in a way inconsistent
with the First Amendment, then it is said to be *unconstitutional*. As is
the case with any criminal conviction, someone found guilty of violating a law abridging speech has a right to appeal to a higher court. On
appeal, if the law is found to be constitutionally invalid because it violates the First Amendment, then the conviction will not hold up. Even
in cases where there is no criminal indictment involved, if the government violates the victim's First Amendment rights by acting in a particular way, the victim might have the right to sue for damages. With
this much riding on whether government activity unconstitutionally
abridges speech rights, it is important to understand exactly what the
First Amendment does and does not do.

Freedom of Speech

Can a System Operator Violate the First Amendment?

The first step in First Amendment analysis is determining if it applies.
Every citizen has First Amendment rights. It makes no difference who
you are, what you do, or what you believe. With the exception of a
limited set of situations (described below), it also makes no difference
what you say. According to the Constitution, these rights cannot be
abridged. But the Constitution only provides this protection where the
government is the one infringing on your rights.

It is not unusual to hear users in cyberspace complain that their
First Amendment rights have been violated by a system operator or
moderator who has censored them in one way or another. Usually, the
user claims that by deleting a message from a discussion area or newsgroup, the sysop has acted in an unconstitutional manner. Those
familiar with basic constitutional law realize that this analysis is faulty.
The First Amendment protects citizens from the federal government.
The Fourteenth Amendment extends this protection to cover acts of
state and local governments. Some state constitutions also extend First
Amendment–type speech protection to state citizens. Nowhere in the
federal Constitution is there a prohibition on private acts that might
abridge the right of free speech. Your employer, neighbor, sysop, or
any other private citizen is not part of the class of actors governed by
the First Amendment. The First Amendment prohibits government
officials or agents, and no one else, from violating speech freedoms.

This means that claims that a private party violated the First Amendment are doomed to fail. This is not to say that ignoring free speech rights in the on-line world is prudent. Generally, sysops or system administrators who put harsh restraints on expression find themselves to be quite lonely. Users, like most citizens, are not normally very comfortable with excessive or unfair censorship and often avoid the areas of cyberspace where reasonable expression is not tolerated. Finding the right balance of editorial control and tolerance has proven to be a difficult task for sysops.

Prodigy, the mammoth on-line service, has found its policies in this regard hotly debated in the national media more than once. In 1990, after it changed its rate structure by increasing the charges assessed on users with high levels of e-mail activity, some subscribers began an on-line dissent. They began posting angry messages to some of Prodigy's public message bases declaring their dissatisfaction with the policy shift. The messages were screened by Prodigy personnel, making them unavailable for public viewing. This prompted cries of censorship and talk of First Amendment violations. Geoffrey Moore, Prodigy's director of market programs and communications, felt compelled to respond to the claims on the Op/Ed page of the *New York Times*. In his rebuttal, Moore clarified Prodigy's view that the First Amendment does not apply to it. "Some authors have made the bizarre suggestion that Prodigy is required to publish whatever is submitted and the failure to do so is censorship," he wrote. "The Constitution bestows no rights on readers to have their views published in someone else's private medium. . . . It's called editorial discretion," the piece continued. Moore summed up Prodigy's position by writing "[editorial control] does not limit speech in any constitutional sense." Although not popular, Prodigy's stance on the issue was obviously formed after careful analysis of what the First Amendment actually protects.

Prodigy found itself faced with censorship problems of another sort the next year. In another controversial decision that drew national attention, the on-line service decided to censor some strongly worded responses in a discussion with anti-Semitic undertones. The responses were prompted by user posts that talked in generally offensive terms about the Holocaust. According to Prodigy policy at the time, no censorship would occur if the postings were not specifically aimed at particular individuals. So, pointed comments aimed at a group (in this case, Jews) were allowed to be distributed. When some angry users responded by attacking the parties originally responsible for the offensive material, Prodigy stepped in. It exercised its editorial control to keep the responses off of subscriber's monitors. B'nai B'rith's Anti-Defamation League quickly responded in the press by chastising the Prodigy decision to tolerate the original posts and censor the responses. Prodigy and the Anti-Defamation league eventually reached a truce of sorts. Prodigy decided to "amplify" its definition of what was offensive so as to not allow comments that were "grossly repugnant to community standards." Presumably, this new policy would have kept the original posts off line. Clearly, though, the problem of defining a private system's obligation to free expression is a troubling one.

A commercial system such as Prodigy that depends on consumer satisfaction should be wary of stifling its users' ability to express themselves. Nonetheless, as Prodigy maintains, the First Amendment generally does not come into play when a private party is the one controlling or censoring the expression.

Isn't Cyberspace a Public Forum?

Modern First Amendment theory includes an exception to the general rule that the First Amendment only prohibits government agents, and no one else, from infringing on speech rights. In a very small number of situations, the courts have ruled that a private place so resembles a *public forum* that the Constitution will not allow anyone to restrict speech activities there. Because state constitutions can provide more extensive constitutional protection than the federal constitution does, it is also possible that under state law an otherwise private place can be viewed as a public forum for free speech purposes. This means that the owner of that particular forum no longer has the right to control and censor speech activities there.

Several commentators have recently called for the application of the public forum doctrine to cyberspace.[5] The notion is that cyberspace has so many of the traits normally associated with public places that it should be a forum where speech is given protection against private oppression.

Is Prodigy or CompuServe any more of a public forum than a call-in radio show or the eagerly awaited interactive television media? Only the courts can answer this question definitively. For now, most of cyberspace is still considered nonpublic and is privately owned; the owners are free to exercise editorial control over speech in just about any manner they want.

The Difference between Speech and Conduct

While the government is prohibited by the First Amendment from infringing on speech activity, it is not prohibited from punishing conduct. Sometimes, the line between conduct and speech is hard to recognize. Wearing a jacket with an obscene commentary about the draft has been protected as speech. So has burning a flag in public. Of course, certain speech so clearly constitutes illegal conduct that there is no constitutional protection for it. For instance, a criminal conspirator cannot claim First Amendment protection against prosecution for the speech involved in planning a crime. Computer crime laws like the Computer Fraud and Abuse Act (more thoroughly discussed in chapter seven) make it illegal to disseminate or traffic in "passwords or similar information" that make it possible to access a system without authorization. This is obviously a restriction on speech in furtherance of the goal of decreasing illegal hacking activity. Nonetheless, the number of situations where speech activities are actually illegal is fairly low. Most of the time, if it feels as if the conduct involved is primarily intended to communicate ideas and does not in and of itself constitute a crime, it qualifies as speech, and warrants First Amendment protection.

Even so, the government can place restrictions on pure speech activities if the restrictions are content neutral and are aimed at the time, place, or manner of the activity. Such laws must serve an important governmental interest and be narrowly tailored to do so. The laws in question must also leave open other channels of communication. So, it is not unconstitutional to ban the dissemination of leaflets at certain times or at certain places, as long as the ban does not focus on the content of the leaflets; the law must also serve an important purpose and allow dissemination of leaflets at other, more appropriate times or places. A public university, then, might limit the use of its computer facilities in ways that hinder speech activity if it can show an appropriate reason. If it directs the restrictive rules at certain viewpoints, however, only then does it run the risk of acting outside the scope of the law.

In cyberspace, the speech/conduct distinction can prove important in many different situations. A user defending software piracy on First Amendment grounds will not escape trouble by arguing that distribution of illegal copies of software is speech activity. Nor will the publisher of a newsletter that contains illegally obtained proprietary information be safe from criminal or civil punishment. Posting credit card numbers is not a constitutionally protected right, regardless of what techno-thieves might tell you. These activities all violate the law, even though they might be construed as speech. The key to this analysis is understanding when an act is truly protected speech and when it becomes criminal conduct. Even if you determine that the act is purely speech related, it might still fall into one of the few categories of speech outside of the scope of the First Amendment.

Speech That Warrants No First Amendment Protection

It should be evident that the First Amendment provides fairly broad coverage for all types of speech activities in cyberspace. Usually, it is safe to assume that the government cannot criminalize your ability to express your views and ideas while on-line. There are only a few exceptions to this rule that users should keep in mind.

Sometimes the law holds that the harm caused by the speech outweighs the value of allowing the speaker to go unpunished. These instances are fairly limited. Aside from the restrictions on conduct discussed above, the following categories represent the only situations where the government can punish someone for the things he or she writes, says, or otherwise expresses in cyberspace.

Clear and Present Danger
Sometimes people use the powerful communication potential of cyberspace to advocate illegal, dangerous, or violent activity. For instance, a post on a message base devoted to radical political discussions might advocate violent or illegal resistance to government policies. Many so called *computer underground* or *elite* bulletin boards offer a large selection of text files that provide detailed information about such crimes as computer hacking, *phreaking* (hacking the phone system), and other rebellious activities. In chat, or while participating in a MUD, a user might declare that he or she will no longer obey the laws and urge others to do so as well. There are very active USENET newsgroups devoted to the discussion of illegal substances that provide details on using and buying drugs. Does the law tolerate such speech?

The answer is almost always a resounding "yes." The Supreme Court has provided us with some special rules governing when speech that advocates violence and illegal activities can be forbidden. Unless the situation meets a special test, this type of speech is protected by the Constitution.

The Supreme Court decision that formulated the present test was the 1969 case of *Brandenburg v. Ohio*.[6] Brandenburg was a Ku Klux Klan leader who delivered a speech declaring that white people should take "revenge" on the president, the Congress, and the Supreme Court. He was convicted of violating an Ohio law that forbade "advocacy of the duty, necessity or propriety of crime, sabotage, violence or unlawful methods of terrorism as a means of accomplishing industrial or political reform." Ironically, it was the very Supreme Court that was the subject of Brandenburg's call to revenge that eventually overturned his conviction.

The Court held that a law cannot forbid speech advocating illegal or violent action unless the following two-part test is met:

1. the speech in question must be directed to inciting or producing imminent lawless action; and

2. the speech must be likely to incite or produce such action.

This test is the synthesis of several previous Supreme Court decisions that collectively developed a precedent commonly referred to as the *clear and present danger* doctrine. Under the test, most speech activities described at the beginning of this section would probably be exempt from prosecution. Detailing the newest hacking or phreaking techniques would be unlikely to meet either of the two parts of the *Brandenburg* test. Nor would advocating illegal or violent resistance to government activity, or discussing drug use on a message base or newsgroup.

In fact, it is hard to imagine an on-line activity that could meet the *Brandenburg* test of illegality. The test was designed to allow authorities to criminalize situations such as a volatile rally, where a speaker takes the podium and incites a riot. But a volatile rally is probably not possible on a bulletin board or chat system. Only if the on-line speech activity in question designates a particular target for illegal activity and is shown to have enough force to be likely to cause imminent (present) action might it lose constitutional protection from criminal prosecution. If a statute forbidding the speech exists, and the government decides to prosecute, the user responsible (and possibly the system that allowed the message to be disseminated) could be in trouble. The nature of the medium, however, makes it highly unlikely that such a prosecution would ever be successful.

With this in mind, it should be pointed out that there are some clear-cut cases where the clear and present danger test as laid out in

Brandenburg does not provide protection. One such case involves speech that poses an immediate threat to an important governmental interest. For instance, a user would be hard pressed to claim First Amendment protection if he or she somehow acquired detailed military strategies regarding an upcoming military conflict and published it through the networks. The Supreme Court has allowed sanctions against the publishers of information regarding U.S. intelligence operations and personnel. Threatening the president is also a federal crime if the threat is a serious statement that would cause apprehension to a reasonable person, and is not just idle talk, exaggeration, or a comment made in a joking manner.

Here, as in all other areas of First Amendment law, the speech/conduct distinction needs to be kept in mind. As discussed earlier, all kinds of communicative activity can be suppressed if they constitute illegal conduct. So, passing illegally obtained passwords or phone codes through the network is not exempt from criminal prosecution on First Amendment grounds. Likewise, messages, zines, or text files that contain stolen material or copyright infringements are still illegal.

Law enforcement agents might not be the only people upset about the messages passed along in cyberspace. It is conceivable that someone harmed by the types of material in question here might sue for damages based on an allegation of negligence. The system operator, moderator, or person originally responsible for authoring the text might all be named in the lawsuit. If they are found to have violated a duty of care by causing harm with the material or allowing the material to cause harm, they might be forced to compensate the victim. Since the imposition of civil penalties is a function of the court (a branch of the government), the First Amendment also limits the civil penalties that can be assessed against someone for First Amendment–protected activities.

In order to assert a civil suit successfully, then, plaintiffs have to prove the elements of the *tort* (wrongful act) alleged. Usually, the tort involved would be negligence. This means they have to show that damages were caused by the defendant breaching some duty derived from an applicable standard of care. Moreover, the plaintiffs have to demonstrate that the speech involved unprotected material pursuant to the *Brandenburg test*.

Cases such as this have been litigated with television and print media, but never with computer-mediated communication. *Hustler* magazine was sued after publishing an article on a sexual practice called autoerotic asphyxiation. The article described how some people heighten the intensity of their sexual experiences by asphyxiating themselves in order to deprive oxygen to the brain during orgasm. A copy of the magazine article found its way into the hands of a young boy who, tragically, decided to experiment with the method. He was found dead with the magazine open to the pages containing the article. The Fifth Circuit Court of Appeals denied recovery (the claim was brought by the boy's family) on the grounds that the article, albeit packed with details on how the deadly sexual practice could be accomplished, was not incitement of the type contemplated by *Brandenburg*.[7]

This does not mean that civil liability could never be imposed. There have been cases where a party transmitting a dangerous message to the public found itself successfully sued. For instance, a radio station was held liable for announcing a contest that incited listeners to rush across town in a reckless manner, leading to traffic accidents.[8] But it is easy to see how this situation was the exception, rather than the rule. If your on-line activities look as if they might meet the *Brandenburg* clear and present danger test, you should consult an attorney for more specific legal advice. Lawsuits can be expensive, even if you have a solid case.

Fighting Words

Another category of speech that can be criminalized without violating the First Amendment is the category consisting of what are commonly called *fighting words*. Under this doctrine, states can pass special laws outlawing speech that is so offensive and abusive that it is likely to cause or incite immediate physical retaliation by the audience. Under the current Supreme Court analysis, however, the laws involved must be very narrowly tailored. In fact, although this category is still recognized, it is very rare for the Supreme Court to uphold a fighting words conviction.

Because this category is so limited, it is unlikely that anything communicated through a computer could be constitutionally punished as fighting words. This may come as a surprise to people familiar with the volatile abusive *flames* that can be found on many bulletin boards and USENET newsgroups. Flames are confrontational messages that often seem like the type of speech that should qualify for some sort of regulation. But, in this case, cyberspace acts as a buffer between the speaker and the intended audience. The likelihood of immediate physical retaliation is almost nonexistent. This takes the otherwise criminally offensive speech outside of the fighting words category and back into the realm of the First Amendment.

In discussions of the fighting words doctrine, you may often hear references to hate crimes or hate speech. Recent legislative initiatives targeting speech and violence aimed at particular groups of people because of their race, religion, gender, or sexual orientation have attempted to criminalize words that insult or provoke violence. Although present legislation does not specifically address computerized hate speech, future laws might. There are many bulletin boards run by groups committed to controversial causes and ideas. The Ku Klux Klan, neo-Nazis, and the various "skinhead" groups have all made their appearance in cyberspace. It is fairly common to encounter highly offensive and divisive messages in many of the unmoderated USENET newsgroups, BBS networked message bases, and other areas.

The courts tend to restrict government efforts to curtail speech based on its content. This includes laws aimed at punishing certain viewpoints. Still, hate speech and crimes get quite a bit of media attention, and one gets the sense that the last word has not been spoken about the legitimacy of government regulation in this arena. At least one federal agency has begun looking into the issue as it relates to cyberspace. In 1993, the National Telecommunications and Information Administration (NTIA) requested public comments on the role the mass media and computer communications play in promoting hate crimes. The NTIA is a federal agency that advises Congress and the executive branch, including the FCC. It specifically sought information regarding bulletin boards, and language in the request for comments indicated that one option being investigated was some sort of regulatory scheme aimed at bulletin boards and on-line services. The inquiry prompted immediate concern from several civil-liberties organizations and others monitoring digital free-speech issues. Most notably, the Electronic Frontier Foundation[9] formally responded to the request for comments by arguing that the unique communicative power of cyberspace allows for a real marketplace of ideas where the remedy for offensive speech is more speech. At this writing, the NTIA has not come to any official conclusions regarding this issue but is expected to report to Congress when it does.

Defamation

The struggle to balance the rights of a speaker against the rights of his or her audience is perhaps best exemplified by defamation law. This area of the law exists to protect a person's reputation from harm caused by false and damaging statements. If the defamatory message is spoken, it is called *slander*; if it is written, it is called *libel*. In cyberspace, defamation will probably always be classified as libel.

Defamation law has garnered quite a bit of attention in cyberspace. The potential for causing significant damage to someone's reputation is huge when a message can be quickly spread across the country with so little effort. A single post calling into question someone's character might reach thousands of people and do irreparable harm to his or her reputation. Defamation can also occur in private e-mail, on a chat system, in a MUD, on IRC channels, or through the distribution of text files or zines. Each of these methods of spreading damaging allegations can be extremely harmful. For these reasons, legal scholars who normally pay little attention to cyberspace have spent more time analyzing and debating on-line libel and slander than most other legal issues posed by computer communications and networks.[10]

A defamation claim must establish several points before a plaintiff can recover damages from a defendant in court. First, the plaintiff must show that there is *defamatory* language involved that is discernibly aimed at or refers to the plaintiff with some degree of specificity. Defamatory language can be recognized by its tendency to harm one's reputation by attacking honesty, integrity, or sanity. It must do so in a manner that makes the identity of the defamed party clear to the audience. Defamatory language not aimed at anyone in particular, or so vague that the defamed party is not clear, is not sufficient grounds for a defamation suit. The practice of using handles in cyberspace may make the specificity requirement burdensome for some plaintiffs. Nonetheless, if a particular plaintiff can show that he was the subject of the defamatory message, he can meet this burden.

Next, the plaintiff must show that the language was *published* to an audience composed of people other than just the plaintiff. There are no damages if the speaker communicated the defamatory message only to the plaintiff. Therefore, receiving defamatory private e-mail is not grounds for a defamation lawsuit. Conversely, when there are many people in the potential audience, the claim is strengthened. Thus, if copies of the e-mail are sent to more than the person defamed therein, or if the message is publicly distributed in some other way, the requisite publication has occurred. With millions of people using cyber-space, it is easy to imagine a single, short message having a huge audience, especially if it is posted to a larger on-line service or a distributed newsgroup or message base.

After showing that publication has occurred, the plaintiff must usually establish damages resulting from the defamatory communication. These might be in the form of general damages to reputation, or they might be specific *pecuniary* (economic) harms suffered as the result of the libel. Especially damaging might be false statements regarding businesses or professionals who rely on their good reputation to maintain consumer confidence. It is important to note that if it is unlikely that anyone believes the claims made in the message, damages may not have been suffered. Some of the more obnoxious flames are not actionable libel because no one would ever believe the disparaging claims that they make. In some cases, however (those involving private figures, as discussed below), *presumed* damages are allowed, which alleviate the harmed person's burden of establishing damages.

Even if the plaintiff can prove all of the elements discussed above, there are some things a defendant can prove to avoid being held liable. The most important of these is establishing the *truth* of the matter asserted. Defamatory language must be untrue in order for a plaintiff to recover. Declaring that "Joe is a con artist" when, in fact, Joe has been found guilty of fraudulent activities, will not get you in trouble. There is also a defense based on *consent*. If the party claiming damages gave either express or implied consent to the publication of the message in question, there will be no liability. Finally, there are also some narrowly drawn exceptions called *privileges* that can be invoked by someone accused of libel or slander. These include, among others, a privilege for judicial proceedings (usually anything said in court is protected) and communications between spouses.

Something that looks defamatory might not be sufficient grounds for a lawsuit. Statements of the speaker's *opinion* are one such example. Opinions will only get the speaker in trouble if they are based on particular facts and those facts, if represented as true, would be defamatory. So, saying "It is my opinion that Joe cannot be trusted" is not a problem, but saying "Joe cannot be trusted to keep your password secret" might be, as it implicates specific factual allegations. Determining whether a statement is fact or opinion is not easy, and one should be careful not to come too close to the line when publishing damaging opinions about someone.

Because a judgment is enforced by the government, there are First Amendment concerns whenever someone is sued for libel or slander. This is a fairly recent development, the result of a series of Supreme Court cases following the important 1964 decision of *New York Times v. Sullivan.*[11] In that case, the Court recognized that there should be some constitutional restraints on the ability to punish people for the things they say, even if they prove to be defamatory. Although the facts in this celebrated case dealt with a traditional print publication, the precedent established applies equally to all different media, including computer-mediated communication.

From *New York Times* and subsequent decisions, a basic framework for analyzing the constitutionality of a defamation claim has emerged. It is based on the degree of fault that can be shown in the defendant. Different degrees of fault are needed depending on who the plaintiff is. If the plaintiff is a public figure, the degree of fault that must be shown on the part of the defendant is quite high. The public figure must prove that the statements were disseminated with *actual malice.* That means that the defendant had knowledge that the statements were false, or had a high degree of awareness of their probable falsity. Public figures are people who are involved in public debate, or have thrust themselves into the public eye. Some people may be public figures for all purposes (e.g., celebrities or politicians); others may be public figures for limited purposes only (where they are involved in a particular special issue). The president, Michael Jackson, and Michael Jordan are all public figures. They can only win a defamation suit against someone if the defendant knew his or her statements were false, or if the defendant had actual, substantial doubts about the veracity of the defamatory message. To hold otherwise would stifle public discussion because of a *chilling effect* caused by the fear of being held liable in a court of law for things said or printed.

Citizens who are not public figures, on the other hand, do not need to establish actual malice in order to recover from someone who defames them as long as they are not involved in issues of *public concern.* This is partly because the Court recognized that private citizens often do not have the means of access to mass media where they can rebut or disprove the damaging comments. Interestingly, this is no longer the case with cyberspace, where everyone has a similar ability to communicate with large numbers of people. If a nonpublic figure is involved in an issue of public concern, another standard comes into play. In these cases, actual malice need not be established to show lia-

Defamed party	Standard	Damages
Public figure	Actual malice	• Actual • Punitive
Private figure in public concerns	Negligence	• Actual • Punitive[*]
Private figure in private concerns	No fault	• Actual • Punitive
* But only if actual malice is established		

Figure 5.1

bility, but a plaintiff must show at least *negligence* on the part of the defendant as to the truth or falsity of the statements at issue. Also, in cases such as these, only damages based on *actual injuries* can be awarded. No *punitive damages* are allowed unless there is a showing of actual malice.

Obviously, defamation law involves some fairly complicated legal rules. Most people simply are not aware of what it takes to establish libel or slander in the courtroom. This leads to all kinds of misstatements of the law and empty threats of legal action in cyberspace. As anyone involved in electronic messaging will attest, open discussions on networks and bulletin boards can turn quite abrasive. Often when this happens someone who feels slighted will threaten to sue someone involved in the discussion. Only if all of the conditions laid out above are met does this threat have any teeth. Most of the time, for one reason or another, when someone threatens legal action based on comments made in cyberspace, the threats are empty. With the communicative power of the networks and bulletin boards being what it is, however, there is always the chance that a legitimate plaintiff might recover large sums of money from someone based on a libel or slander suit.

A case involving on-line defamation is working its way through the legal system as of this writing. The defamation suit stems from comments made by a user of the Prodigy on-line service about a New Jersey company called MEDphone. It seems that the user in question was responsible for some on-line comments that were critical of

MEDphone. MEDphone claims that these comments made their stock value tumble. According to MEDphone, the company was in good financial health until criticized on Prodigy. After the comments were posted, however, things started to go downhill for the maker of high-tech medical equipment. MEDphone is suing the user who posted the comments. Although Prodigy is not named in the lawsuit, the case remains notable because it highlights the possibility for an on-line discussion to lead to legal trouble for the participants. It is too early to tell, however, whether the fact that the alleged defamation took place in cyberspace will have any real bearing on the case.

What about the liability of a bulletin board or on-line service that facilitates the distribution of the defamatory language? One of the few bits of judicial guidance on this point emerged from a situation involving CompuServe. Among other things, CompuServe distributes electronic newsletters (zines). One such newsletter made available to the hundreds of thousands of CompuServe subscribers was called Rumorville USA. Rumorville USA, which could be found in the "Journalism" forum, was written and published by a company called DFA. DFA provided it to another company, CCI, that was in charge of getting the text of the daily newsletter and placing it on CompuServe. CCI's contract with CompuServe put the responsibility for editing and controlling the zine's content on CCI.

Cubby, Inc., is a company that competes with DBA in the journalism newsletter business. When an article in Rumorville USA allegedly defamed Cubby, Cubby sued both DBA and CompuServe for damages arising out of the resulting harm to Cubby's professional reputation. The suit of *Cubby v. CompuServe* was brought in federal court in New York. Even before the merits of the defamation claim were decided, however, the presiding judge dismissed the part of the lawsuit implicating CompuServe.[12]

The basis for dismissing the suit against CompuServe was an established First Amendment precedent that protects libraries and bookstores. It has long been established that these *secondary publishers* (those who take the work of primary publishers and disseminate them to a larger audience) can only be responsible for the content of a book or magazine they distribute if they know, or should have known, about the questionable nature of the material. In a landmark case dealing with obscene materials, the Supreme Court noted "If the bookseller is criminally liable without knowledge of the contents . . . he will tend to restrict the books he sells to those inspected; and thus the State will have imposed a restriction upon the distribution of constitutionally protected as well as obscene literature."[13] The judge in *Cubby v. CompuServe* took this rule and extended it to cover on-line services and bulletin boards. Under the holding, as long as the operator of a BBS or on-line service is not familiar with the content of the publications he offers to the public, he is protected from libel suits arising from them. The justification for such a rule is simple. Holding a secondary publisher responsible for the contents of its collection puts a huge burden on the librarian or sysop to review everything distributed to the public. This is an unreasonable burden that, if enforced, would hamper the ability to supply a large amount of diverse information to the public.

Although widely heralded by system operators as a step in the right direction, the decision in *CompuServe v. Cubby* leaves some important questions unanswered. Most notably, no one is sure what happens when a sysop or moderator *is* aware of the contents and allows distribution anyway. It may be, as might be inferred from the decision, that the sysop becomes liable, just like the primary publisher. If this is the case, there is a strong disincentive against becoming familiar with the contents of materials a sysop offers on his or her own bulletin board. Also, the case does not deal with a message base or newsgroup, which is where many experts feel much of the on-line defamation will occur. Finally, the court took special notice of the fact that CCI had entered into a contractual agreement with CompuServe to be responsible for the content of Rumorville USA. It is not exactly clear how this relationship affected the outcome of the case. It may be that without this type of contractual relationship there will be different results.

Often sysops will be heard voicing the view that they are immune from defamation suits on the basis of some special legal theory that acts a shield against liability. Sometimes they invoke the phrase *common carrier* in this regard. Common carriers are entities that hold themselves out to the public as a service that will transfer people, property, or information indiscriminately, as long as there is no legal reason to refuse such service. Historically, the telephone and telegraph systems, as well as trains, airlines, or even hotels and inns have qualified for common carrier status. Because of the public good it serves, a common carrier gets special treatment by the law. It is usually exempt from certain types of claims, including (for telephone and telegraph companies) defamation. If someone defames you during the course of a conference call, you have no claim against the phone company because of its common carrier status. Some sysops argue that bulletin boards, networks, or on-line services are common carriers as well and are therefore similarly protected.

The problem with this argument is that it is unlikely that many of the systems that comprise cyberspace are true common carriers under the current legal definition. Few systems offer unlimited access to anyone who wants it. Moreover, to maintain common carrier status, the system operator would be forced to give up any editorial control over the contents of his or her system. Once a sysop becomes involved in editorial decisions, he or she no longer qualifies for protection. Most sysops are not willing to sacrifice these freedoms for the hope that some court might apply the common carrier doctrine to shield them from a defamation lawsuit. The lack of judicial guidance on which judges can rely concerning bulletin boards and common carrier status makes assuming that BBSs will qualify as common carriers an unsafe bet. The common carrier doctrine, while interesting, probably will not play a role in on-line defamation cases.

Sysops might have a more compelling defense against defamation liability because they offer the defamed party an inherent right to reply to the damaging statements posted by others in a public forum.[14] Although the right of reply as a defamation remedy is not widely recognized in the United States, there is some indication that plaintiffs who have been given a chance to vindicate their reputation through reply have suffered less reputational damage and might not be entitled to a monetary award. Given that most users have a right to reply to libel with an equally prominent message placed in the same forum, it is possible that some court in the future will release a sysop from responsibility for the defamatory messages. Otherwise, barring a situation where *CompuServe v. Cubby* governs (where the sysop has no knowledge of the libel or slander), a sysop might be held responsible for damages resulting from the republication.

Obscenity and Child Pornography
Material deemed legally obscene and child pornography get no First Amendment protection at all and can be regulated by state and federal laws. Refer to chapter six for a complete discussion of this type of material.

False or Deceptive Advertising
Although at one time commercial speech got almost no protection, most commercial speech activities are now deemed to have most of

the same First Amendment rights as noncommercial speech. The government can and does regulate false and deceptive advertisements, however, because of the potential harm they can do to the public through their misrepresentations. Individuals using the power of cyberspace for commercial purposes should be wary of misleading the public or promising too much.

For instance, many states have consumer protection laws. These often impose stiff penalties on businesses involved in misleading or deceptive trade practices. Consumers who fall victim to such illegal methods need not worry that the perpetrator can hide behind a First Amendment defense and argue that the deception is a protected speech activity.

Freedom of the Press

With the communicative potential of cyberspace, everyone who owns a computer and modem and is connected to the networks owns a press with built-in distribution capabilities. Never before has such a high level of First Amendment press activity taken place in this country as has happened with cyberspace.

There is much academic debate about what First Amendment freedom of the press actually accomplishes. Some maintain that the right of "the press" is no different than the right of free speech, and that the extra verbiage was used by the founding fathers just to ensure that the press was included in the First Amendment. Others argue that the press should get special rights because it acts as a conduit to the people and serves an important democratic function. Regardless, there can be no mistaking that the legal system recognizes the importance of protecting the process of writing, editing, publishing, and distributing information.

Early in the development of cyberspace, people realized that zines could be low-cost alternatives to traditional publishing. The underground hacker community was one of the first to catch on. Such hackers began spewing forth information about the phone system and computer security in informal, imaginative periodicals widely circulated in digital form. Soon, others saw the power of on-line publications. Today, thousands of zines dealing with every imaginative subject are regularly being distributed. Users can have them delivered directly to their e-mailbox, can download them from a BBS or on-line service, or can get copies through USENET news or Internet FTP. With Gopher and WAIS services, finding archived zines on the Internet is getting easier every day.

People involved in the publication of digital zines should recognize that most of the First Amendment principles laid out earlier in this chapter apply to them as well. Still, the information printed in a computer newsletter can get its publisher in trouble if a watchful eye is not kept on the relevant laws.

PHRACK Newsletter

Perhaps the most notable instance of an on-line publication finding itself confronted with legal problems involved a hacker publication called Phrack.[15] Phrack contained articles on computer and network security issues written by hackers for hackers. Although almost everything in Phrack warrants First Amendment protection, a certain article in one issue caught the attention of federal authorities and led to years of legal trouble for the college student who edited and published Phrack out of his fraternity dorm room in Missouri.

The obtuse article, which detailed some obscure bureaucratic procedures governing the emergency 911 (E911) system employed by the telephone companies, was a shortened and edited version of a text file that had been acquired through unauthorized access to phone company computers. The hackers who made the illegal copy of the document were eventually convicted.[16] Bill Cook, a prosecutor in the U.S. Attorney's Chicago office, became interested in prosecuting Phrack's editor, Craig Neidorf, for publishing the document in his newsletter. The government claimed that the text was "highly proprietary" and valued it at over $23,000. If convicted, Neidorf could have been sentenced to several years in federal prison.

At the trial, the government's claims regarding the value and sensitivity of the document were shown to be exaggerated.[17] The charges against Neidorf were dropped, although he was left with substantial legal fees. The proceedings highlight the fact that publishing activities in cyberspace can and do attract the attention of the legal system.

The Privacy Protection Act of 1980

Along with potential liabilities, publishers also have rights based on their status as participants in protected publishing activity. For instance, a federal statute called the Privacy Protection Act of 1980 (PPA) limits the right of government agents to search for or seize documents that are related to the dissemination of information to the public—even when they have a valid search warrant.[18] Because law enforcement agents often use sweeping evidentiary searches in the investigation of suspected computer crimes, this statute has special importance when it comes to the electronic press.

The PPA requires that law enforcement agents use a subpoena, rather than a search warrant, when looking for documents or materials that are intended to be published. Subpoenas give the publisher an opportunity to cooperate in an investigation with a minimum of disruption to the publication, and the chance to challenge the request for documents in court *before* the government takes them. When a search warrant is used, documents are taken without asking. The PPA's "subpoena first" rule is limited, however, to publishers who are not themselves the target of a criminal investigation, *unless* the criminal investigation relates to the illegal receipt of information. In that case, the "subpoena first" rule again kicks in, protecting the material from seizure. If the government violates the PPA, it must pay for the damages it caused.

The PPA was enacted in reaction to a disruptive search of a college newspaper office.[19] Does it also protect the publisher of an electronic newsletter? How about a bulletin board operator whose system routinely distributes large amounts of information to the public?

These issues were raised in a lawsuit filed against the Secret Service based on the search and seizure of a computer bulletin board run by Steve Jackson Games, which publishes role playing games. (The *Steve Jackson Games v. United States Secret Service* case is more fully addressed in chapter two). The judge decided that the Secret Service's seizure of drafts of role-playing game books published by the company violated the PPA, because the company was not the target of the investigation, and because the materials seized were intended to be published. The company was awarded over $50,000 in damages.

The judge was not faced with the question of whether the PPA was violated by the seizure of the BBS alone because the company published its games in traditional paperback book form as well as through its BBS; however, he did list the contents of the BBS in a list of the material that was illegally seized. This language, plus the PPA's specific inclusion of computer files as protected documents, strongly suggests

6   Adult Material: Drawing the Line between the Legal and Illegal

"Sex," someone once observed, "is the beat of the universe." Sexually explicit and erotic materials are present in every category of media. There are adult videotapes, movies, television channels, magazines, and books. Sex is also present in cyberspace. In fact, the role of sex in cyberspace is evidenced by the amount of adult material that can be found there. This is not to say that cyberspace is simply the electronic equivalent of a giant adult book store; it quite clearly is not. At the same time, however, it must be noted that most of the inhabitants of cyberspace who want to obtain electronic adult material will find no problem procuring it.

For many people, the availability of digital sexually explicit material is a double-edged sword. It brings with it the pleasure and security of anonymous involvement with the explicit material, but at the same time it creates a sense of anxiety. The sources of this anxiety are many. One is the fear that the anonymity associated with cyberspace is illusory, and that the public will eventually discover the user's adult-oriented activities. Another, and more serious, anxiety may be caused by the uncertainty of the legal status of the acts that the user is engaged in. Having one's adult-oriented activities in cyberspace discovered may be embarrassing, but having those activities become the object of a criminal investigation will have long-lasting effects that go well beyond embarrassment.

Until recently, the legality of the different forms of sexually explicit material available in cyberspace was a topic of interest only to the sysops of bulletin board systems that specialized in providing adult-oriented services, and to the most paranoid of users. This is no longer the case. Recent activity by both federal and state law enforcement agencies has caused a much broader audience to become interested in these issues.

The number of reports about users and sysops finding themselves facing legal problems because of their involvement with sexually explicit on-line materials has grown dramatically in recent years. One such incident involves a sysop in Georgia who was charged with, among other things, distributing obscene material through his BBS. The sysop was arrested and his hardware was confiscated. The sysop was later convicted on a related charge, and was imprisoned.

Because these cases tend to have a high profile, there will undoubtedly be similar criminal investigations involving adult material in cyberspace in the future. Incidents such as the one described above have helped generate the feeling that users who seek to obtain adult material through cyberspace should be aware of their potential liability. The problem is, of course, that very few people know what that potential liability might be. This chapter attempts to answer that question by examining the most recent legal precedents and applying them to the various forms of adult materials and activities available in cyberspace.

An Overview of Adult Materials and Activities Available in Cyberspace

Before attempting to analyze some of the legal questions posed by the different adult materials and activities available through computer communications, it is important to note what some of these activities are. While the following is not an exhaustive list of cyberspace's sexually explicit material, it does address the more common examples.

Digitized Images

Perhaps the most popular, and certainly among the most readily available, form of adult materials are digitized images. The types of digitized images we deal with in this section are either created with graphics software (i.e., someone "paints" the picture using a "paint program") or by scanning an existing image (usually a photograph) and storing it as a computer file. The most common file formats for these digitized images have the file extensions .gif or .jpg. Thus, if you encounter a file named "sexy.gif" or "beefcake.jpg" it more likely than not is a digitized image file. These digitized images can be displayed on computers with programs called *viewers*. The resolution of the images depends on the type of hardware the user is using to view them, and how they were created. Generally, very high resolution images with near photographic detail are easy to find for almost every hardware and software platform.

Many of the digitized images available in cyberspace are not sexually oriented. This discussion deals exclusively with those images that are sexually explicit or "adult" in nature. These adult images range in content from pictures of models in swimsuits to the most hard-core pornography. Every taste, every fetish, every sexual variation is represented. It is not, for example, unusual to encounter digitized images depicting homosexual acts. Nor is it unheard of to find images of bondage or sadomasochism scenes. Some of the images depicting more unusual preferences or fetishes are more difficult to find, but are nonetheless available.

These images can be obtained from several sources. They can be downloaded from a BBS or an on-line service that caters to people looking for them. It is also possible to send them through electronic mail or through a message base. On USENET, several newsgroups are in place that allow users to post and receive image files of all types, including sexually explicit ones.

Some of the images are scanned photographs that obviously have been retouched. For example, one series of digitized images shows a woman engaging in sexual activities with a space alien. The issue of retouching scanned images presents interesting legal questions, some of which we examine later in this chapter.

Animated Sequences

Animated sequences are the kissing cousins of digitized images. Like their digitized image counterparts, animated sequences are created by the use of graphics software or by scanning in a sequence of existing images and storing the final product as a single file. The most common file formats for these digitized images have the file extensions .dl and .gl. As with digitized images, most of the animated sequences must be viewed with viewer software. Others come in the form of executable programs that automate the viewing process.

As their name implies, animated sequences are a series of images that are repeatedly projected onto a computer monitor, giving the illusion of movement. The result is analogous to a very short movie. The sequences are usually looped, so that the same series of frames is repeated over and over again. There does not yet appear to be as much variety in the content of the animated sequences as there is in the digitized images. For the most part, the content of the animated sequences often resemble (and in fact often are) short clips from pornographic videos. Animated sequences are not as popular as digitized images, although their popularity appears to be on the rise.

Sexually Explicit Text

The sexually explicit text found on-line does not differ in content from forms of sexually explicit text found elsewhere. The only difference is the medium used to convey the text. Sexually explicit text normally takes the form of messages posted on messaging systems (e.g., a "true confessions" message base on a bulletin board system) but it also frequently takes the form of text files available for downloading by users. E-mail communications can also be the vehicle for explicit sexual text sent from one user to another.

The sexually explicit text posted on a message base or news group tends to take the form of very short erotic stories. It is not unusual to see the message base forums divided by sexual preference or fetishes. It would not be hard to find a BBS, for example, that had an area set up for users to read and post stories about homosexual fantasies.

Sexually explicit text files downloaded by users are almost always straight ASCII files (pure text) and thus can be viewed with any available text editor or word processor. Because of this, the sexually explicit text files are extremely easy to modify. Sexually explicit text files do not enjoy the same popularity as the other forms of sexually explicit files (such as digitized images and animated sequences) that are available for downloading, although some bulletin boards specialize in such texts, providing thousands of files in their file libraries.

Hot Chat

Hot chat is sexually explicit text communicated in real time. Like a telephone conversation or conference call, real-time communications are transmitted live from one party to another. It is this real-time characteristic that distinguishes hot chat from sexually explicit text files or messages. A user who reads sexually explicit text could be reading text that was posted or uploaded days, weeks, or months before. In hot chat, however, the users are engaged in a contemporaneous communication.

Hot chat involves two or more users and is analogous to a steamy phone conversation. The conversations are usually conducted privately between the parties, and usually can be conducted discreetly so that other users on-line are unaware of any hot chat taking place between the users involved.

Indecency vs. Obscenity: Classifying On-line Adult Materials and Activities

The First Amendment to the U.S. Constitution protects many forms of expression. The scope of the First Amendment is broad enough to encompass written and spoken words, films, and photographs. Consequently most of the communications that occur through cyberspace enjoy some First Amendment protection. This protection amounts to the right to be free from government interference.

While most other materials in the on-line world are given full First Amendment protection, certain exceptions and limitations apply to adult materials and activities. While most people are not surprised to learn that obscene material enjoys no First Amendment protection, most *are* surprised to learn that indecent material does.[1] The source of the surprise comes from the terms *indecency* and *obscenity* themselves. For many people, the two terms are interchangeable and no distinction between the two exists. The law treats obscene and indecent materials very differently, however, and it is important to understand how to classify an activity as one or the other.

The definition of obscenity has been difficult even for the U.S. Supreme Court to formulate. The difficulty in creating such a definition was perhaps best expressed by Justice Stewart when he stated, "Perhaps I could never succeed in intelligibly [defining hard-core pornography]. But I know it when I see it. . . ."[2] The last U.S. Supreme Court case to provide a rule in determining what constituted obscene material was *Miller v. California*.[3] The *Miller* definition of obscenity is based on a three-part test. In order for an item to be deemed obscene, and therefore undeserving of First Amendment protection, all parts of the test must be met. The three-part test asks:

1. would "the average person, applying contemporary community standards" find that the work, taken as a whole, appeals to the prurient interest?;

2. does the work depict or describe, in a patently offensive way, sexual conduct specifically defined by the applicable state law?; and,

3. does the work, taken as a whole, lack serious literary, artistic, political, or scientific value?

If the answer to all three questions above is "yes," the work is considered obscene, and is stripped of free-speech protection.

Community Standards

The *Miller* court rejected the idea that a national standard should be applied to determine whether material is obscene. As the court put it, "the people of Maine or Mississippi [should not be required to] accept the public depiction of conduct found tolerable in Las Vegas, or in New York City."[4] The community standard is designed to "permit the juror in an obscenity case to draw on his own knowledge of the community from which he comes in deciding what conclusion an 'average person' would reach in a given case."[5] The community standard requirement of this part of the test is to be taken seriously by the legislature. The U.S. Supreme Court rejected the notion that a state statute created conclusive evidence of community standards.[6]

The community standard approach to defining obscenity carries with it a special burden for members of the on-line world. Cyberspace is, after all, a global community that often pays little attention to the boundaries and borders of the physical world. Adult-oriented material can travel from one end of the country to the other via any one of the vast networks that span the country. Also, even small hobby bulletin boards have callers from outside the community where the host system sits. With bigger systems, which attract users from all parts of the globe, the problem of applying a "local" community standard starts to become clear. The relevant question, then, is, "Which community's standards should we apply?" Should the standards of the community where the host computer exists be the ones used? What about the standards of the community where the user resides?

This problem is analogous to the cases where a pornography distributor is charged with having violated an antiobscenity law through the U.S. mail. The question of whether the standards of the community where the pornography distributor is located or whether those of the community of the final destination of the pornography should be used arises in these cases. The answer is that the government can choose the community from which the standards will be selected.[7] Thus, in prosecuting a user under an antiobscenity statute, the government is free to select the community that it feels has the more restrictive standards.

The community chosen must, of course, somehow be involved in the facts of the case.

If you are uploading material that may not be deemed obscene by your local community standards to a community where the material is considered obscene, you stand the risk of violating a law. Likewise, if you make material available on your system that is not considered obscene in your community, and that is later downloaded by someone from a community where that same material is considered obscene, you may have violated a law.

Prurient Interests

Prurient has been defined by the U.S. Supreme Court as "having a tendency to excite lustful thoughts."[8] Prurient interest "beckons to a shameful, morbid, degrading, unhealthy, or unwholesome interest in sex."[9] But this definition has been interpreted to exclude materials that provoke "only normal healthy sexual desires."[10] The Supreme Court has not, however, provided a definition for "normal healthy sexual desires."

Whether material appeals to prurient interests should be determined by how it affects a normal person. The fact that certain groups may react differently to the material should not be considered. For example, in determining whether material appeals to prurient interests, the fact that minors may be more easily influenced by that material should not be considered by a jury.[11] This rule is followed by a major exception, however. If the material in question was designed for, and marketed to, a specific well-defined deviant audience, then the question of prurient interests is framed around how the material affects a member of that targeted audience.[12] Consequently, material aimed at sadomasochists is not to be judged by how a "normal" person would react to it, but rather by how a sadomasochist would react to it.

One final consideration that can be used in determining whether material appeals primarily to the prurient interest involves advertising. The fashion in which an article is advertised can be used as evidence that the work appeals primarily to the prurient interest. In one case, the fact that the distributor of the material in question had sought mailing privileges from Middlesex, New Jersey, and Intercourse, Pennsylvania, was admissible evidence to show that the material was designed to appeal primarily to the prurient interests of the consumers.[13] In that same case, evidence of the nature of the defendant's

advertisements was also admitted. Keep in mind that the advertisement or self-description of the material in question is not determina-
tive to the issue of whether the article appeals primarily to the prurient
interest; it is only one factor that can be considered.[14]

Sexually oriented files such as digitized images and animated
sequence often have a brief description provided with them. This
description is used to aid users in determining whether they should
download the file. It is likely that such a description could be used in a
court as a factor to determine whether the file is obscene. As a practical
matter, then, users who are worried about downloading a file that
may cross the line between indecency and obscenity should strongly
consider the description provided with the file. They should also
assume that if the issue ever went to court, that description would be
admitted into evidence against them.

Patently Offensive

Under the second part of the *Miller* test, a work must be *patently offensive* in order for it to be deemed obscene. As was the case with prurient
interest, however, the phrase "patently offensive" is difficult to define.
The U.S. Supreme Court has given us some guidance, however, in
determining what types of materials correspond to this description.

The Court acknowledged that only hard-core pornography can be
considered patently offensive.[15] This means that digitized images of
nudes not engaging in hard-core activity are not obscene. Users can
thus feel secure that when they are downloading or uploading files
that are not hard core, they are not in violation of any obscenity
statute.

Notice, also, that under the second part of the *Miller* test, the
Supreme Court requires a state that enacts an obscenity statute to be
specific about what conduct is being banned. The Supreme Court in
Miller attempted to provide further guidance as to what sort of obscenity statute a state could adopt. The Court provided the following
examples of material that could be banned:

1. Patently offensive representations or descriptions of ultimate sexual
acts, normal or perverted, actual or simulated.

2. Patently offensive representations or descriptions of masturbation
or excretory functions, and lewd exhibition of the genitals.

Several states have enacted legislation that use this language as a base for obscenity statutes.[16] Note that these were meant to be examples, and are not exhaustive. Thus a state can add other material to the list of prohibited obscene articles, such as material depicting sadomasochism.[17]

Value of the Work

The third part of the *Miller* test asks whether the work "lacks any serious literary, artistic, political, or scientific value." The government has the burden of proving that the work has none of these values. If the prosecution does not meet its burden, the work cannot be deemed obscene. In determining whether the work lacks the values listed, the entire work, and not just a part of it, should be considered. So, for example, if a state wishes to prove that a sexually explicit text file is obscene, it cannot simply pick out the steamy parts and not bother to present the rest of the text. Unlike the first part of the test, this part is based on a national standard, not a local community standard.

The *Miller* test can be applied to all of the activities in cyberspace listed earlier in this chapter. Just because an item is composed of nothing but text does not make it immune from prosecution. The Court has declared that a book without pictures in which sexual acts are verbally described can be declared obscene, just as images can be.[18]

Significance of Being Deemed Obscene

As was noted earlier in the chapter, obscenity is not a protected form of speech under the First Amendment, but indecency is. With the exception of Oregon,[19] states do not provide obscenity with any real form of protection. In practical terms, this means that states and the federal government are free to ban obscene material altogether. Material that is merely indecent, on the other hand, can be regulated but cannot be done away with.

Laws Governing Adult Material

State Laws

As a general matter most states have legislation prohibiting the promoting of obscene material. These statutes tend to define "promoting" in a broad manner, and this includes manufacturing, selling, transferring, distributing, mailing, giving, lending, exhibiting, and advertising. The statutes are usually applied against adult bookstores and peep-show parlors, but they could be applied to on-line activities. It seems reasonable to assume that a user who uploads, downloads, or makes available for downloading obscene material is violating state law.

Nonobscene adult material is normally regulated through laws that prohibit the distribution or exhibition to minors.[20] These laws will sometimes refer to the nonobscene adult material as *material harmful to minors*.[21] As a result, sexually explicit files that are not obscene should not be uploaded, or made available for downloading to minors. Furthermore, minors should be prohibited from taking part in any adult message bases.

Federal Laws

There are two important federal laws aimed at obscenity that are significant to cyberspace. The first law is 18 USC § 1465 (which is reproduced in appendix C). This statute prohibits *interstate* transportation of obscene material for sale or distribution. Users who dial up out-of-state BBSs should be aware of this statute (as should the sysops of these systems). The second law that is important to this discussion is 47 USC § 223 (which is reproduced in appendix D). This law was enacted to deal primarily with the 1-900 adult services, but has such broad language that it could encompass cyberspace activities. The statute prohibits obscene communications through the telephone lines.

Possession of Obscene Material

Given that obscenity is not protected by the First Amendment, and that promotion of obscene material is a crime in most states, must you purge your hard drive of any obscene material? The answer, quite surprisingly, is no. The U.S. Supreme Court has held that an individual is free to possess obscene material in his or her own home. As the Court put it "if the First Amendment means anything, it means that a State has no business telling a man, sitting alone in his own house, what books he may read or what films he may watch."[22] But note that this is about all you can do with obscene material. Any other conduct involving obscene material is not protected. A state can still outlaw transportation of obscene material for private use,[23] receipt of obscene material,[24] and importation of obscene material.[25]

Child Pornography

A final area of sexually oriented materials available on-line that needs to be addressed is child pornography. Child pornography is material that depicts minors in sexually explicit ways. The exact age varies from state to state, but under the federal child-pornography statute, anyone under 18 is a minor. The sexual conduct in which the child is involved does not have to be legally obscene in order for the material to be classified as child pornography.[26] The material must, however, involve the visual depiction of children, so written text is not enough.

Accordingly, digitized images and animated sequences are the only materials available in cyberspace that are capable of qualifying for the category of child pornography. Any other form of sexually oriented material, such as sexually explicit text, should be analyzed under the *Miller* test to determine if it is obscene or merely indecent. This is the case *even if* the nonvisual material describes children engaging in sexual conduct. The reasoning behind this is that taking photographic images of children engaging in sexual conduct harms the children who participate in the activity, whereas with textual descriptions of children and sex there are no participants to be harmed.

Child Pornography without Children?

As mentioned earlier in the chapter, digitized images and animated sequences can be digitally modified. If a digitized image can be modified to give the appearance that a woman is engaging in sexual activities with a space alien, it is easy to imagine that images that are not child pornography can be modified to appear to be of children engaging in sexual conduct. Images of adults, for example, can be modified so that the adults appear to be minors. A skilled computer artist might create "paintings" of what appear to be minors engaging in sexual activities. These paintings might easily pass for photographs. Technology has, in essence, given us the ability to create visual depictions of children engaging in sexual activity without having to use actual children as models.

This poses a troubling question. Does material made to look like child pornography but not created with the use of minors qualify as such? As the federal and most of the state child-pornography statutes are currently written, the answer is no. Most child-pornography statutes require that the subjects be below a specified age, and it is up to the prosecution to prove that the subjects involved actually were underage. Given the current state of technology, this burden of proof may be difficult for the government to meet.

The issue of whether the subject of alleged child pornography was indeed a minor has been litigated in at least one case.[27] In *U.S. v. Nolan*, the defendant asserted that the prosecution had failed to present sufficient evidence to show that the pictures it claimed to be child pornography were of actual children. The defendant asserted that the photographs in question could have been of wax figures or mannequins, or could have been computer generated. The prosecution presented expert evidence that the photographs were of minors. The defendant failed to introduce any expert evidence to support his contention that the photographs were not of minors. The appellate court reviewing the case concluded that in the absence of any evidence to the contrary by the defendant, it was reasonable for the judge who presided over the case to find that the photographs were of minors. The court went on to say that on the basis of the quantity and quality of the photographs it was very unlikely that the subjects were anything but minors. The material that was the subject of the dispute in the *Nolan* case was printed on paper. The court did not have before it the same type of material available in cyberspace—material that is easy to modify.

The lesson to be learned from this case is that a defendant who possesses altered digitized images of adults and is accused of violating child-pornography laws should introduce expert evidence that the images may not be of minors. The introduction of such evidence does not ensure that the defendant will be acquitted, but it puts the government to its task of having to prove its case beyond a reasonable doubt.

The thought of simulated child pornography is, no doubt, a disturbing one to some people. Is it possible to change the current child-pornography statutes to prohibit simulated child pornography? At least one state, Arizona, has a statute that may accomplish this. Although it does not look as though it was created with cyberspace in mind, the statute does apply to the topic at hand. The statute criminalizes the visual depiction of adults who engage in sexual conduct and who "masquerade" as minors.[28] It is possible, however, that this statute may not pass constitutional muster.

The U.S. Supreme Court, in an important child-pornography case stated, "if [the visual depiction of a minor engaging in sexual performance] were necessary for literary or artistic value, a person over the statutory age who perhaps looked younger could be utilized."[29] Keep in mind, also, that the compelling interest that the U.S. Supreme Court cited for allowing the ban of child pornography was the welfare of the children who were used to create the child pornography. With simulated child pornography, there are no child actors to protect. Thus, the Arizona law is not a true child-pornography law, and it probably does not qualify as covering obscenity as defined by the *Miller* test. So far, it appears that no constitutional challenges to the Arizona law have been asserted. The main question in determining whether this law will withstand constitutional scrutiny will likely center around the state's interests in proscribing those acts.

Possession of Child Pornography

Unlike obscene material, a person has no right to possess child pornography, even if it remains in the privacy of his or her own home and is used solely for private and personal purposes.[30] If your disk drive contains child pornography, you may be violating a state statute, and if you have more than three copies of child pornography you are in violation of a federal law.

Child Pornography Laws

The federal statute banning child pornography is found in 18 USC § 2252 (the pertinent parts of which are reproduced in appendix E). The law specifically proscribes the use of computers to transmit child pornography. Knowingly uploading or downloading child pornography is a federal offense. Knowingly making child pornography available for downloading is likewise a federal offense. A closely related statute, 18 USC § 2251, makes it illegal to advertise child pornography. This statute makes advertising that offers or seeks the sale, exchange, reproduction, or distribution, of child pornography illegal.

A listing of all state child-pornography legislation is included in appendix F. If you have doubts whether an on-line service you are engaging in involves child pornography, you will want to consult the state statute that applies to you.

Child pornography is dangerous business. Enforcement agencies attack known peddlers of child pornography with vigor. Sometimes the mere suspicion of possession of child pornography is enough to trigger a police raid.

The largest law enforcement crackdown on child pornography to date has been Operation Longarm. The investigation focused on such material that was being distributed from three BBSs in Denmark. Officials in Denmark found records of callers from the U.S. and provided the names to the Customs Service, which then launched raids on those suspected of obtaining the material. A large amount of hardware was seized as a result of the raids. Several persons pleaded guilty to charges of possession of child pornography and at least one person was tried and found guilty.

Courts have been very much in favor of prosecution in cases involving child pornography. For example, in *Osborne v. Ohio* the U.S. Supreme Court upheld an Ohio statute that on its face criminalized the possession of *any* nude photo of a minor by a nonparent, except for medical, scientific, or other "proper purposes." It should be noted that the Ohio law has been narrowly construed by courts so that it only applies to images where the minors are engaged in sexual conduct.

What Does All This Mean?

Digitized Images and Animated Sequences

If the digitized images or animated sequences involve child pornography, there is nothing you can do with it. You cannot knowingly upload this material, download it, or make it available for downloading. You cannot post any advertisements seeking or offering child pornography. You may also be violating a law by simply possessing this material. Graphics files that contain pictures of children engaging in sexual conduct constitute child pornography. You should also be wary of any graphic file that contains images of naked children since lewd exhibition of genitals can constitute sexual conduct.

If the material is obscene under *Miller* analysis, you are probably violating a law by uploading or downloading, or by making it available for downloading. Remember that only hard-core material is deemed obscene. If the images are "soft porn," such as those found in *Playboy* or *Penthouse* magazines, it most likely is not obscene. More explicit material, however, may be deemed obscene. When you upload to a community other than your own you are subjecting yourself to that other community's standards for determining whether the material appeals to the prurient interest. If you are uploading material to sources outside of your own state, you may be in violation of 18 USC § 1465, which proscribes transportation of obscene material across state lines for sale or distribution. You have a right to possess material that is obscene in the privacy of your own home, but this is a very limited protection. As long as your graphic files stay in your home, and you use them for your personal enjoyment, you are protected by the Constitution.

If the material is only indecent, you will have to stay within the bounds of laws that regulate indecent materials. All states prohibit you from transferring or exhibiting the indecent material to minors, for example.

Sexually Explicit Text

Sexually explicit text cannot, by itself, be considered child pornography. The text, however, can be deemed obscene. The same analysis used above for digitized images and animated sequences applies to sexually explicit text.

If the sexually explicit material is obscene it is probably a violation of a law to upload or download the text, to make the material available for downloading, to post the text on a message base, and to make the material available for reading from a message base. In considering whether the text is obscene, the entire text, and not just particularly explicit sections, should be considered. As with the graphics files, keep in mind that when you transfer sexually explicit text to a community other than your own, you are subjecting yourself to that other community's standards for determining whether the material appeals to the prurient interest. Also keep in mind that uploading material into other states may be in violation of 18 USC § 1465. If you already possess obscene text, you do have the right to possess that material in the privacy of your own home.

Again, as with graphics files, if the material is only indecent, you will have to stay within the bounds of laws that regulate indecent material. If you are uploading indecent material you will want to make sure that it is not accessible to minors. If you are making material available for downloading you will want to take precautions to ensure that only adults have access to this material.[31]

A simple flow chart that can be used to determine criminal liability based on different activities with files is provided in figure 6.1.

Hot Chat

Although 47 USC § 223 prohibits the use of obscene language through telephone lines, there is no report of a computer user being prosecuted under this statute. It may be that prosecutors simply do not put consenting adults who engage in steamy conversations through the phone lines at the top of their list of candidates for prosecution.

There is, however, one story about a sysop in California who engaged in hot chat with an undercover law enforcement agent, and consequently ran into trouble with the law. The undercover agent alleges that he informed the sysop that he was a minor, and that the two engaged in hot chat. When the sysop agreed to meet the undercover agent, he was arrested and charged with attempted child molestation, and attempted use of a minor for an illicit purpose. So far, this appears to be an isolated incident, but it should be enough to put users on notice that hot chat with minors can lead to legal problems.

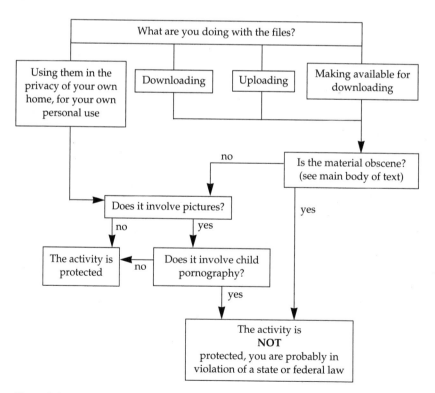

Figure 6.1
Determining criminal liability with regard to sexually explicit files

Cyber-Crimes: Pitfalls
for the Unwary Traveler

The word *hacker* conjures up a vivid image in the popular media. The term was once used to describe any computer user who spent endless hours developing unorthodox solutions to difficult hardware and software problems. Since then, the term has been twisted by the media and the general public to refer to those who engage in rebellious and often illegal computer activities. While an alternative term (some prefer *cracker*) would be more appropriate, common usage is such that one cannot refer to a "hacker" without implying illegality. The popular image of hackers has them armed with dangerous computer viruses and describes them as prone to leaving a trail of destruction and damage in their wake. Wielding stolen credit card numbers and pirated software, the evil hackers of legend seem impervious to law enforcement, which struggles to keep up with the technology that comprises the tools of their trade. This image has been bolstered by film characterizations of hackers bringing the world to the brink of nuclear Armageddon or using their knowledge to advance high tech crimes of epic proportion.

Not surprisingly, the legal system has reacted to the specter of these cyberpunks and techno-terrorists, which threatens an establishment dependent on secure and uncompromised data. There are now tough laws aimed especially at computer crime. There are federal statutes addressing computer fraud and abuse, credit card fraud, the transfer of stolen property, and wire and phone fraud. All but three states have passed computer crime statutes that outlaw computer trespass, unauthorized use of or tampering with computer equipment, and other harmful conduct. Violation of these laws can result in stiff criminal and civil penalties.

Sometimes, the laws are enforced only against the truly malicious hackers who act immorally and irresponsibly with their computers. In these situations, it is apparent that there is a need for penalties that deter lawless action; however, there are fewer of these cases than one might believe. After separating the folklore from fact, it turns out that sometimes, because of media hyperbole, harmless recreational computer use gets painted with the same brush as illegal hacking. Unfortunately, sometimes the law, like the media, cannot distinguish between the two.

The result is that it is quite possible to get in trouble for seemingly innocent activity in cyberspace. Most users are surprised to learn that it is possible to commit serious crimes (with serious penalties) while sitting at a computer keyboard in the comfort of their homes or offices, engaging in what seems like harmless modeming. Whether the laws are too harsh, unfair, or wrongly applied makes little or no difference if a prosecutor decides to enforce them. People with no intent to cause harm have been sentenced to prison time under the current laws and, until the laws are changed, there is nothing to prevent them from being enforced again.

For these reasons, it is important to understand those activities that are crimes in cyberspace and how to avoid them. This chapter will look at the most important federal statutes and some of the more common state laws that specifically govern cyber-crimes. Because laws change, it is important to remain aware of legislative action that might amend or revoke some of the statutes described here.

It is also crucial to recognize that many crimes covered by traditional criminal laws can be committed in cyberspace. In fact, computer crimes were not specifically addressed by the legislatures until the late 1970s. Before then, prosecutors molded the common law and criminal statutes to cover crimes committed with computers. For instance, theft is outlawed regardless of whether the stolen property is obtained through a computer or by breaking into someone's home. While some statutes do address computer crimes specifically, the absence of a statute that proscribes a computer activity does not make that activity legal. A rule of thumb is: if it is illegal to do without a computer, it is probably illegal to do with a computer. The special computer crime statutes and related laws that exist simply define the crimes with more precision and specifically outlaw high-tech criminal conduct.

Our legal system allows the federal and state governments to have concurrent jurisdiction over many of the crimes detailed below. A person who commits computer trespass, for instance, may be in violation of both federal and state computer crime statutes. Both federal and state prosecutors may independently prosecute a defendant for the same activity. The doctrine of *double jeopardy* (the idea that you cannot be tried twice for the same offense) does not apply to these situations. This chapter will review the federal statutes and then summarize the most common provisions of state law.

The Computer Fraud and Abuse Act

In 1986, Congress passed a comprehensive federal law outlawing many of the activities commonly referred to as "hacking."[1] Any federal government agency can investigate offenses under the act. This law also authorizes the Secret Service (as the branch of the Treasury Department traditionally involved in tracking counterfeiters) to investigate illicit use of computers as defined by the act. The law, known as the *Computer Fraud and Abuse Act* (CFAA), has been the basis of successful law prosecutions of malicious hackers, and will undoubtedly be used for such cases in the future. The full text of this law is reproduced in appendix G.

Under this comprehensive law, it is illegal to do any of the following:

1. knowingly access without authorization (or in excess of authorization) any computer system, and in doing so obtain restricted or classified government information;

2. knowingly access without authorization (or in excess of authorization) any computer system, and in doing so obtain financial information held by a financial institution, credit information held by a consumer reporting agency, or credit card information held by the issuer of credit cards;

3. intentionally and without authorization access any computer of a department or agency of the United States if the computer is exclusively for their use, or if not exclusively for their use, in a way that affects the government's use of the computer; or

4. knowingly, and with intent to defraud, traffic in any password or similar information through which a computer can be accessed without authorization if such trafficking affects interstate or foreign commerce or such computer is used by the government of the United States.

There are also prohibitions against unauthorized access of *federal interest computers*, as defined by the statute. Certain key phrases ("unauthorized" and "access") are not defined by the act, and have yet to be interpreted by the courts. The act gets its authority by referencing interstate commerce, an area specifically delineated in the Constitution as a concern of the federal government.

As is apparent from this list of offenses, many on-line activities can result in a violation of the CFAA. Although the most obvious offenses seem as if they require malicious intent, the law has also been applied in situations where the perpetrator's criminal intent was not clear.

The most notorious case of prosecution under this law involved Robert T. Morris and his infamous *Internet Worm*.[2] Morris, a 23-year-old Harvard graduate doing postgraduate work at Cornell, was far from the archetypal evil hacker of popular myth. In fact, his father, Robert Morris, is a noted computer security expert who was, at that time, the chief scientist at the National Computer Security Center, a government agency concerned with keeping computers safe from unauthorized use. Still, the younger Morris's brush with the CFAA landed him with a sentence of three years probation, a $10,000 fine, and 400 hours of community service. Yet Morris did not hack his way into any computer, or steal or fraudulently obtain any money or anything else of value.

The crime Morris was found guilty of involved unleashing a program intended to explore the Internet, gathering information about the machines on the network and their security. The program, called a *worm*, was released in 1988 and was supposed to be a harmless experiment in computer science. Unbeknown to Morris, a programming error caused the program to reproduce itself in a way that clogged computer processing time all over the network. Within hours of being released onto the Internet, the program had infected approximately 2,000 computers and caused an estimated $150,000 of down-time on machines across the country.[3] It also received international media attention and focused the country on the vulnerable state of the world's most important computer network.

The problem of Morris's criminal *intent* troubled many people following his conviction. Morris had not intended for the program to get out of control, and had not intended to do any harm. The only intent present was to access the remote systems. Although Morris's attorneys appealed the conviction on this ground, the U.S. Supreme Court refused to hear the arguments and let the conviction stand. This decision means that under the statute, the mere intent to access another system without proper authorization is sufficient grounds on which to base a finding of guilt. Users should be wary of exploratory log-in attempts or anything else that may be interpreted as unauthorized access to a computer governed by this act. Once the intent to access the computer can be established, the CFAA might be brought into play.

Credit Card Abuse Laws

One of the more troubling crimes committed in cyberspace is the illicit trafficking in credit card and other account information. With these account numbers, thieves can illegally acquire goods and services at someone else's expense. Millions of dollars are lost each year by consumers, credit card companies, merchants, and phone companies as a result of the trading and distribution of such access information. Not surprisingly, there are federal laws prohibiting this activity.[4]

The statute involved makes it a crime to produce, use, or traffic, knowingly and with intent to defraud, in one or more counterfeit *access devices*. Under the law, a counterfeit access device is defined as any card, plate, code, or account number that can be used to obtain money, goods, services, or anything of value.

One common method of acquiring access codes (especially for long distance service) is through the use of special software designed to try large numbers of randomly generated codes over the phone lines. The software keeps a log of failures and successes, providing the user with a list of illegally obtained codes at the end of the session. As might be expected, any involvement with this type of software or its use is a violation of federal law. Using the software results in the production of an access code, which is strictly prohibited. Possessing the software is prohibited under a section of the law that makes it a crime to possess any mechanism for making a code or account number. Also, possession of 15 or more codes, even without using or trafficking them, is a violation of the law.

Users should steer clear of anyone offering or soliciting credit card or long distance service account numbers. If you see this type of information posted on a bulletin board or on-line service, it is probably best to inform the sysop. Voice your dissent to the exchange so that a record of your nonparticipation will be created. If all else fails, simply avoid the area of cyberspace where you find such activities. It is better to disassociate yourself than to allow your mere presence to lead to suspicion of criminal activity.

As with the Computer Fraud and Abuse Act, the Secret Service is given jurisdiction over credit card and access device crimes.

Wire Fraud

Another potent weapon in the war on computer crime is the federal Wire Fraud Act.[5] This broad law makes it illegal for anyone to use any wire, radio, or television communication in interstate or foreign commerce to further a scheme to defraud people of money or goods. This has been interpreted by the courts to include telephone communications and electronic money transfers.[6] Although not specifically aimed at computer crime, the Wire Fraud Act has been used (especially before widespread use of the CFAA) against digital wrongdoers.[7]

In fact, the Wire Fraud Law has been interpreted so broadly that many acts that do not seem to meet its requirements are now considered illegal. In one case, a defendant used local phone calls to check on the validity of stolen credit cards. These calls, in turn, caused the credit checking entity to engage in interstate computer communications that were deemed to bring the Wire Fraud Act into play.[8] Computer users involved in illegal schemes may want to consider cases such as this when carrying out their crimes. It is likely that what appears to be a local criminal scheme has interstate ramifications if cyberspace is involved. If the scheme involves e-mailing someone out of state, for instance, the federal authorities probably have jurisdiction under the Wire Fraud Act.

The National Stolen Property Act

An important federal law aimed at the interstate transport of stolen property has recently been used in the struggle against computer criminals. The National Stolen Property Act prohibits individuals from "transport[ing] in interstate or foreign commerce any goods, wares, securities or money of the value of over $5,000 or more, knowing the same to have been stolen, converted, or taken by fraud."[9]

This law was at issue in the prosecution of the Atlanta computer hackers involved in the E911 case, discussed in chapters two and five. In a published decision, the U.S. District Court for the Northern District of Illinois was faced with the issue of whether the pilfered text file involved constituted "goods," "wares," or "merchandise" under the act. Despite the arguments of the defendants, the court held that the proprietary business information involved did indeed qualify.[10] This issue is still being developed by other courts, however, with inconsistent decisions in different jurisdictions.[11]

Another interesting situation arises if the owner of the property retains his or her copy of it. Does the law make it illegal to transport a physical copy across state lines? In a case involving the theft of a secret chemical formula, the Second Circuit Court of Appeals explained that transferring intangible information into a different physical object, and transporting that object over state lines, was illegal.[12] In a later case, however, the Supreme Court would not uphold a prosecution involving bootlegged phonograph records. In that case, the Court held that, even though it was clearly a copyright violation (see chapter four), the subject goods (the copyrighted recording) were not "physically taken" in the way contemplated by the act.[13] The latter case seems more likely to be considered as persuasive precedent by courts faced with the theft of computer data or software.[14]

Software Piracy

As detailed in chapter four, unauthorized duplication, distribution and use of someone else's intellectual property is subject to civil and criminal penalties under the U.S. Copyright Act. In this section, the laws governing illegal duplication and distribution of computer software will be discussed with more specificity.

Illegally copying and distributing computer software (commonly referred to as *software piracy*) is common in cyberspace. The ease of transmitting software through the networks or between modems, coupled with the sometimes restrictive high price of commercial software, makes software swapping a tempting proposition. Many users feel it is a harmless extension of the legitimate practice of swapping shareware and public domain software. Others do not even recognize the difference between the two activities.

Many bulletin boards boast of having large collections of *warez* or *elite files* (terms often used to describe pirate software) on line and accessible to anyone willing to trade similar files. Witnessing such bravado makes the act seem much less risky to those unfamiliar with the legal ramifications of software piracy.

Software piracy is a serious crime with stiff penalties. The software industry claims it loses billions annually to pirates, and much of the piracy takes place or is advanced in cyberspace. Law enforcement is not blind to this phenomenon, and the FBI has begun cracking down on pirate bulletin boards across the country. Software companies have begun to take action in court to protect their rights through lawsuits aimed at those who ignore the law and continue to create and distribute illicit copies of software. The *Software Publisher's Association* (SPA), an industry trade association involved in monitoring, tracking, and aiding in the prevention of software piracy, has been increasingly active, garnering much media attention in the process.

Recent changes in the law make it a felony to reproduce or distribute (during a 180-day period) ten illegal copies of copyrighted software with a total value of as little as $2,500.[15] Previously, the law required 1,000 copies. Thanks to industry pressure, Congress has determined it is time to get tough. Those found guilty of felony software copyright violations are subject to up to ten years in prison and fines up to $250,000 for first-time violations, with stiffer penalties attaching to subsequent offenses.

There are, thankfully, simple rules to follow regarding what you can and cannot do with copyrighted software in cyberspace. Most obviously, one cannot make copies of any software (unless doing so is explicitly authorized, as in the case of shareware and public domain software) and cannot transfer any copies to others in cyberspace. If you are not sure, chances are that the software is protected by the copyright law. Also, one cannot download copies of software that normally would have to be purchased from a software store or dealer. Although it may be tempting to get expensive software at no cost, the risk involved far outweighs the benefits. If you encounter pirated software on a BBS or on-line service, notify the system operator, and distance yourself from the illicit activities if possible.

System operators must be vigilant in monitoring software as it is uploaded to their system. Each file should be checked to verify that it is a legal copy. If it is not, the user uploading the file should be warned and the file should be removed. Sysops should carefully screen and verify files; it is possible to run into problems without any intent to do harm if your inactivity is deemed to promote a situation where the trafficking of illegal copies is common. It is not wise to allow pirates to use your BBS or network site as a convenient place to swap their "warez." Doing so can land you in trouble with the law and lead to expensive legal proceedings.

It is not hard to find examples where system operators suffered serious legal difficulties because of the presence of pirated software on their bulletin boards. In early 1993, the FBI served a search warrant on *Rusty & Edie's BBS*, a large for-profit system touting 124 lines and playing host to 14,000 users. The agents seized the whole system, effectively shutting down the board and the business it supported. All this happened before any charges were brought against the sysops and before a jury was allowed to decide their guilt or innocence. While this case is pending, commentators are quick to point out that allowing the suspicion that you provide commercial software to your users might invite a similar fate. There is no doubt that large bulletin boards can, an often do, cater to software piracy. But many of them do so unintentionally. Larger systems often have many megabytes of uploads on a daily basis, making it difficult to screen out the illegal software. Even the large corporate on-line services occasionally are notified that an innocuous-looking file is actually being distributed through their download areas in violation of copyright law.

This being the case, it is important for users to help sysops in spotting and removing pirated software that ends up on a bulletin board or on-line service. Most sysops want to stay within the guidelines of the law and will be appreciative of attempts to aid them in doing so. A quick note pointing out inadvertently overlooked pirate software will help protect the BBS from trouble and keep you, as a user, on the right side of the law.

Aside from pirated software itself, users might encounter programs commonly called *cracks*, which work to defeat copy protection schemes on popular commercial programs. While such cracks are legal to possess and distribute, modifying the source code of copyrighted software might amount to a violation of the licensing agreement that governs the use of the software. It is also legal to own and possess programs that circumvent copy protection methods and make duplicate copies of protected software; however, these copies can only serve as archival back-up copies for purchasers of the original program. It is still illegal to distribute these copies through cyberspace (or in person, for that matter), and care should be taken not to send or receive illicitly copied files.

Regardless of the arguments often advanced justifying piracy, it is a dangerous business that can get participants into a great deal of trouble. It is true that large corporations, bulletin board operators, and other serious offenders will be the first to draw the attention of law enforcement, but anyone engaged in piracy should realize that the potential for legal trouble is always lurking around the corner. In cyberspace, where it is hard to be sure about the intentions of those with whom you are dealing, a conservative "clean hands" approach is the safest policy.   •

Obscenity and Child Pornography

Because of the prevalence of sexually explicit materials in·cyberspace, much of the attention given to the on-line world by law enforcement officers has involved obscene materials and child pornography. A full discussion of these crimes is found in chapter six.

Computer Viruses and Other Harmful Software

In October 1987, officials at the University of Delaware's Academic Computer Center found themselves faced with a strange problem. A rogue computer program was "infecting" diskettes by hiding in the a part of the disk called the *boot sector*. Worse, the program was duplicating itself whenever it had the chance. Although not as damaging as it could have been, the epidemic was the first documented account of a computer virus in this country.[16] It was not long before other virus attacks were observed all over the world, and the computer community realized that viruses were here to stay. By 1992, over 2,000 viruses had been identified and documented by people who keep track of such things.[17] The antivirus software industry is now selling millions of dollars worth of software aimed at immunizing systems from viruses, or curing them when infected. Yet, with new viruses appearing every day, it seems as if the antivirus programs are always a step or two behind the problem.

A virus program is the result of someone developing a mischievous program that replicates itself, much like the living organism for which it is named. Cyberspace allows for transmission of software over vast geographic areas, and many viruses make their way from one place to another in this medium. Viruses might be attached to software as it is traded between bulletin board users, or the virus code or programs themselves might be transferred from place to place by hackers or security experts intent on learning how to combat the threat. Even the government has been known to distribute virus source code intentionally in order to further the ability to immunize target systems. A government-sponsored BBS came under fire recently when it was discovered that it offered such files (which could, in theory, actually be used to cause damage) in its file transfer area. Whatever the mechanism, there can be no doubt that virus software can be readily found in cyberspace.

With the recent Michelangelo virus scare (which was heavily reported by the media) and the onslaught of new, more devious viruses being identified, the legal system has taken notice of virus software and the potential for damage that it poses. Although possession of virus software and source code is not illegal, many of the existing state and federal computer intrusion and unauthorized access laws already make it illegal to introduce a virus into someone's system intentionally. Robert Morris's conviction for the viruslike Internet worm shows how the existing laws might be used to punish those involved with disseminating viruses.

Many of the computer crime laws that cover unauthorized access (and virus infection) also provide for civil remedies that can be imposed on violators by the victims of the crime. In other words, people who find their system has been infected by a virus might be able to sue for damages if they can identify the perpetrator. Texas law, for example, explicitly names the introduction of a computer virus into a program, system, or network as a crime (punishable as a misdemeanor or felony, depending on the damage suffered) and also authorizes civil suits against the person responsible.[18]

The same types of penalties might be applied to people who knowingly or intentionally introduce other dangerous programs into a remote system. *Trojans* (innocuous looking software with hidden purposes), *ANSI Bombs* (PC software that uses ANSI codes to remap a keyboard, with disastrous consequences), *logic bombs* (programs designed to damage data at a set time or under specific circumstances), and other devious code can all lead to trouble with the law if improperly used.[19]

A sysop who offers viruses or other harmful software for download on his or her BBS or network site needs to be aware that there may be civil liability if someone uses software acquired from the BBS to cause damage. It does not matter if the possession of the virus code or programs is legal in and of itself. Negligently allowing it to fall into the wrong hands might be grounds for civil liability, if someone decides to sue.

Recent calls for stiffer penalties and more stringent regulation on writing, possessing, and distributing viruses are certain to lead to tougher legislation in the future.[20] Many experts expect that new laws targeting the authors and distributors of virus programs are inevitable and, if passed, will give rise to a whole new dimension of criminal investigation and prosecution in cyberspace.

If you encounter virus software in cyberspace, treat it with caution. Do not haphazardly trade virus code with others, and certainly avoid anything that might infect another system with an active virus. If you are not sure, it is best to stay away from anything that looks like it might be a virus or other harmful piece of software. If you suspect that you may have inadvertently helped to spread a virus, take steps to notify anyone who might be infected. Provide as much detail as possible, so that they can try to stop any damage from spreading or becoming worse. This could help you get a reduced sentence if you are ever prosecuted. While possessing virus software is not illegal, using it to cause damage is. Like Robert T. Morris, you might find that what you thought was an innocent experiment could cause unforeseen damage and land you in court.

Electronic Communications Privacy Act

Although it is intended to protect private communications, the ECPA also serves as a powerful weapon for prosecutors intent on prosecuting malicious computer hackers. A thorough analysis of the ECPA and its criminal provisions can be found in chapter two.

State Computer Crime Laws

Florida passed the first state computer crime law in 1978. Almost all fifty states have passed specific legislation addressing the problem of computer crime.[21] The Texas computer crime statute is a good example of these laws and is included in appendix H. Each state imposes a slightly different system for assessing the proper punishment, but all computer crime statutes look at the amount of damage caused by the illegal computer activity. If the damage is small, the crime is most often a misdemeanor. More serious injuries can result in felony convictions. Although the statutes vary, most of them focus on one or more of the following types of conduct.

Computer Trespass or Unauthorized Access

Prohibitions on unauthorized access or computer trespass are at the heart of computer crime statutes. Almost every state bases its computer crime law on such provisions. These laws make it a crime to access a computer without the permission of the owner or someone authorized to give permission. They also often include prohibitions against accessing a system beyond the authority originally granted. If you have a valid account on a BBS or on-line service, but have found a way to exceed the access you are supposed to have, it is possible that you are violating a state computer crime law.

Those interested in the way a particular state treats unauthorized access and computer trespass should consult the relevant statute. Some states add interesting twists to common definitions, or highlight certain types of conduct as more illegal than others. For instance, it is not unusual for a state to outlaw interfering with someone's legitimate access on a given system to the same extent it outlaws actual trespass.[22]

Although the computer trespass or harmful access that is of concern here involves accessing remote systems, it is also possible to violate these laws by using someone else's computer while sitting in front of it. Hacking an account on a local area network is just as illegal as hacking an account on CompuServe or a Fidonet BBS and, depending on the circumstance, might draw more attention.

Tampering with or Manipulating Computer Data

Many state statutes have provisions that specifically outlaw the wrongful alteration, destruction, modification, or duplication of computer data found in someone else's system. In cyberspace, it is possible to change the data in a system through a vast array of different means. Fortunately, as system security gets more attention from sysops, it becomes less likely that someone could violate these types of proscriptions without meaning to. If, however, you feel that you may have inadvertently altered the data on a host system, it is best to notify a system administrator with as much detail about what happened as possible. This will ensure that your intentions are clear, and that your conduct is not mistakenly viewed as sinister.

Theft of Computer Services

It is illegal in most states to steal computer services. Commercial on-line systems and network access providers make their money by selling such services. If you are not paying for an account that normally requires payment for authorized use, you should take steps to resolve the situation. If you let the proper parties know about any oversights in billing or any mistakes in the amount of access you have, you usually will not be prosecuted. If you are knowingly using an account without paying for it, however, your state's theft of computer services statute might apply. If there is no specific statute, you still might find yourself in trouble under more general theft laws.

Computer Fraud

Using cyberspace to defraud, extort, or otherwise obtain money, property, or services with fraudulent or false intent is specifically made illegal in many states. This could encompass all sorts of scams and schemes designed to cheat people out of their money. Examples of fraudulent activities that might implicate this sort of law are pyramid schemes and similar get rich-quick-plans. These scams tend to work by convincing people that by sending a few dollars to a few people, untold riches will magically appear in their mailbox. Unfortunately, if it sounds too good to be true, it probably is, and usually the only ones who make any money are the few individuals who started the plan. Because such plans necessitate wide-scale recruiting of participants, a pyramid scheme is perfectly tailored for the vast communicative power of cyberspace, and, in a state with this kind of statute, could prove to be illegal computer fraud. There also often are specific laws outlawing pyramid schemes, whether or not they involve computers.

Any other fraudulent conduct, scheme, or artifice designed to cheat people out of something valuable might qualify as computer fraud in states that have adopted computer fraud statutes. Once again, if it is illegal to do face to face, on the telephone, or through the mails, it is almost assuredly illegal to do through cyberspace.

Possession of Illicit Computer Information

Some states make it illegal simply to possess stolen or wrongfully obtained passwords, account information, or other computer-related material. This allows law enforcement agents to prosecute malicious hackers without having to establish actual illegal access, tampering, or duplication of material. This type of statute seriously reduces the evidentiary burden on prosecutors who need only establish the possession of the illegally obtained material.

Duty to Report Violations

Two states (Georgia and Utah) impose a duty on persons, businesses, and other entities having knowledge of computer crime to report it to the proper authorities. In Georgia, if this is done in good faith, the reporting party will be immune from any civil liability resulting from the report. No specific punishments are mentioned in either statute, and it is not clear whether the duty to report computer crimes in these states is any greater because of the specific language in the law. Still, it is not hard to imagine a judge or jury reacting more harshly because of the explicit statutory duty if people suspected of other computer crimes also failed to report crimes of which they had knowledge.

Attempt, Complicity, and Conspiracy

In most jurisdictions, it is possible to be found guilty of attempting a crime as well as actually committing it. This is equally true with computer crimes. Although there are some differences between jurisdictions, generally, in order to be found guilty of an attempted crime, the government must prove two things. First, it must prove that there was some substantial step taken toward fulfilling the elements of the crime. Next, it must show that there was an intent to commit the acts constituting the crime, and that there was the necessary intent required for the specific criminal act. Some statutes (such as the CFAA) explicitly outlaw attempts as well as completed crimes.

Users should remember, then, that an illegal hacking attempt might be penalized just as harshly as a successful unauthorized access. If a user knowingly tries to "hack" into a system (with the intent required by the law of the relevant state), and the steps taken are substantial, the user can be prosecuted for an attempted computer crime. It usually does not matter that the defendant can show that it would have, in fact, been impossible to commit the crime employing the methods used, or even that the circumstances were such that no actual crime could have been successfully completed. If the user thought that the crime was possible, then a mistake about the factual circumstances is not a valid defense. If the defendant thinks the attempted conduct is illegal, however, but it actually is not, the defendant cannot be held guilty of the attempted crime. Thus, a user who misunderstands copyright law cannot be prosecuted for attempting to download a shareware program, since it is quite legal to do so, even if the user believes the activity to be illegal.

It is also often illegal to solicit criminal conduct or aid someone in his criminal activity. Although both of the above can be punished independently, they are often prosecuted under the crime of conspiracy, which is a crime under state and federal law. The rule of thumb for conspiracy is that there must be an agreement that has as its object the commission of a crime, and there has to be some kind of overt act by a member of the group in furtherance of that crime. Under conspiracy or similar theories, you need not be the one actually at the keyboard to be guilty of computer crimes. If you are involved in the planning or commission of the prohibited acts or any acts in furtherance of the crime, you might be just as guilty as the person most directly involved.

Are the Authorities Overzealous?

There is no doubt that computer crime can pose a serious threat to the integrity of sensitive data on the nation's computer systems. The potential for tragedy is always present. Many computers play a crucial role in life or death situations. The 911 system employed by phone companies, for instance, is vital to maintaining swift responses by medical and law enforcement agents in case of emergencies. Hospital databases often store medical records that must be available instantly in a medical crisis. Many of the world's most important financial transactions occur in cyberspace, with millions of dollars being transferred from one virtual account to another every day.

With so much on the line, it is easy to see why prosecutors and others who are given the task of preventing computer crime can take an aggressive stance when faced with wily hackers armed with high tech tools. But do they go too far?

Some people feel they do. Sometimes, mere association with people suspected of computer crime can make innocent people suspects. One of the few weapons law enforcement has used effectively in computer crime investigation is the evidentiary search and seizure of complete computer systems suspected of illegal use. Many suspected hackers have their computers seized by local or federal agents who argue that they cannot properly investigate the systems on site and must take them back to their crime labs for thorough review. In one particular sweep, the now infamous Operation Sundevil, computer law enforcement agents from across the country raided dozens of suspected hackers, looking for signs of criminal evidence. Over 40 computer systems and more than 20,000 disks were seized in the raids, but few indictments resulted. More often than not, the systems are never returned, even though no indictments are handed down. The fear of indictment is all that is needed to discourage suspects from demanding their property back.

Even when real crimes are found (as in the case with the illegal access into telephone company computer by members of the Legion of Doom) the damages alleged are often blown out of proportion. The E911 document copied by the LOD members and distributed in the *Phrack* newsletter (see chapter five) was initially valued at close to $80,000 by the authorities. It took a full-blown trial before the judge and prosecutors were made to understand that the same information was available from Bellcore catalogs for under $20. The process of placing a value on the damage caused by hackers is fairly controversial. In the E911 case, the cost of the computers and word processors on which the text file was written by telephone company employees was figured in to the initial estimates. Sometimes the cost of modifying existing security measures to fix gaps exposed by the exploratory hackers are included in the damage estimates. It is as if a trespasser were held responsible for the cost of building a better fence around someone's property, so that future trespassers would have less luck getting in.

Although abusive tactics and tough laws clearly are involved, this means very little if you are suspected of a computer crime. The only way to protect yourself is to stay as clean as possible until the legal system and law enforcement officers can put the ominous-sounding computer "crimes" into perspective. It is also important to monitor legislative developments, to make sure you know what is legal and what is not. The law is still developing in this area, and anyone even considering playing it close to the edge should take precautions.

Notes

Chapter 1

1. T. R. Reid and Brit Hume, "Bulletin Boards Make for Cut-rate Media Moguls," *Chicago Tribune,* December 8, 1991, p. C8.

2. For more information on the Internet and other major computer networks, refer to John Quarterman, *The Matrix: Computer Networks and Conferencing Systems Worldwide.* Bedford, Mass.: Digital Press, 1990.

3. See "Multi-User Dungeons and Alternate Identities," in Howard Rheingold, *The Virtual Community: Homesteading on the Electronic Frontier.* Reading. Mass.: Addison-Wesley, 1993.

4. The Houston Community College System, for example, has a program called "College Without Walls," which allows students to take classes by computer.

5. John Quarterman, "How Big Is the Matrix?" *Matrix News* 2, no. 2. Matrix Information and Directory Services, 1992.

6. Jack Rickard, "More Modem Numbers," *Boardwatch,* December 1991, p. 16.

7. Judith Berck, "All About/Electronic Bulletin Boards," *New York Times,* July 19, 1992, § 3, p. 12. Jack Rickard, see *supra* note 6, contends that close to 100,000 bulletin boards are projected to be in operation by 1995 and the number of individuals owning modems will be close to 23.8 million.

8. John J. Keller, "Net Assets," *Wall Street Journal,* November 15, 1993, p. R20.

9. Ward Christensen and Randy Suess, "Hobbyist Computerized Bulletin Boards," *Byte,* November 1978, p. 150.

Chapter 2

1. *Talley v. California,* 362 U.S. 60 (1960).

2. *Gibson v. Florida Legislative Investigation Committee,* 372 U.S. 539 (1963).

3. 18 U.S.C. §§ 2510-2520.

4. 18 U.S.C. § 2511.

5. See discussion of *Steve Jackson Games v. United States Secret Service, supra.*

6. 18 U.S.C. § 2511 3(b).

7. 18 U.S.C. § 2511(2)(a).

8. 18 U.S.C. § 2511(2)(a)(ii)(B).

9. 18 U.S.C. § 2511(4).

10. 18 U.S.C. 2520.

11. 18 U.S.C. § 2701(a).

12. 18 U.S.C. § 2701(b).

13. 18 U.S.C. § 2701(c).

14. 18 U.S.C. § 2704.

15. 18 U.S.C. § 2702.

16. 18 U.S.C. § 2707.

17. *Shubert v. Metrophone, Inc.*, No. 89-1966 (E.D. Pa July 13, 1989).

18. *Steve Jackson Games Inc. v. United States Secret Service*, 816 F.Sup 432 (W.D. Tex. 1993).

19. These states are Alaska, Arizona, California, Florida, Hawaii, Illinois, Louisiana, Montana, South Carolina, and Washington.

20. *Diaz v. Oakland Tribune, Inc.*, 139 Cal. App. 3d 118 (1983).

21. *LeCrone v. Ohio Bell Telephone Co.*, 201 N.E.2d 533 (Ohio 1963).

22. For a more detailed discussion of many of the issues surrounding public key encryption, see Steven Levy, "Crypto Rebels," *Wired*, May/June 1993, p. 54.

Chapter 3

1. A complete discussion of the legal issues involved in EDI can be found in Benjamin Wright, *The Law of Electronic Commerce: EDI, Fax, and E-mail Technology, Proof, and Liability* (Boston: Little, Brown, 1991).

2. Restatement, Second, Contracts §1.

3. U.C.C. §2-206

4. Farnsworth, E. Allan, *Contracts* §3.2.

5. See Restatement, second, of contracts, §§63 & 64.

6. Farnsworth, E. Allan, *Contracts* §6.1.

7. *Hillstorm v. Gosnay*, 614 P.2d 466 (1980).

8. *Ore & Chem. Corp. v. Howard Butcher Trading Corp.*, 455 F. Supp. 1150 (E.D. Pa. 1978).

9. Farnsworth, E. Allan, *Contracts* §6.8.

10. *A & G Constr. Co. v. Reid Bros. Logging Co.*, 547 P.2d 1207 (Alaska 1976).

11. *Associated Hardware Supply Co. v. Big Wheel Distrib. Co.*, 355 F.2d 114 (3d Cir.1966).

12. *Hillstrom v. Gosnay*, 614 P.2d 466 (1980).

13. For a more detailed discussion of caller contracts from the sysop perspective, see Lance Rose and Jonathan Wallace, *SYSLAW* (Winona, Minn.: LOL Productions, 1992). This informative text includes a sample caller contract.

Chapter 4

1. U.S. Constitution, art. 1, § 8, cl. 8.

2. The U.S. Copyright Act is found at title 17 U.S. Code.

3. 17 U.S.C. § 101.

4. 17 U.S.C. § 102(b), 103.

5. 17 U.S.C. § 106, 106A.

6. 17 U.S.C. § 302(a).

7. 17 U.S.C. § 106A(d).

8. 17 U.S.C. § 504(a), (c).

9. 17 U.S.C. § 107.

10. The Supreme Court held that the effect of the use on the marketability of the work is "undoubtedly the single most important element of fair use." *Harper and Row v. Nation Enterprises*, 471 U.S. 539 (1985).

11. *Salinger v. Random House, Inc.*, 811 F.2d 90 (2nd Cir. 1987).

12. *Sony Corp. of America v. Universal City Studios*, 464 U.S. 417 (1984).

13. *Feist Publications, Inc. v. Rural Telephone Service Company, Inc.*, 111 S.Ct. 1282 (1991).

14. Fair use analysis is different for musical recordings. Recent changes in the law make allowances for noncommercial, private recordings. See 17 U.S.C. 1001, *et seq.*

Chapter 5

1. Address to the Computers, Freedom and Privacy Conference, San Francisco, California, 1991.

2. For a complete discussion of how newer forms of electronic broadcast media find themselves under a unique body of law compared to print media, see Lucas A. Powe, Jr., *American Broadcasting and the First Amendment* (Berkeley: University of California Press, 1987).

3. For more about Tribe's proposal, see Don Clark, *27th Amendment Proposed for High-Tech, San Francisco Chronicle,* March 27, 1991, p. C1.

4. *Wall Street Journal,* Tech Talk, April 6, 1992, p. R13.

5. See Edward J. Naughton, "Is Cyberspace a Public Forum? Computer Bulletin Boards, Free Speech, and State Action," 81 *Georgetown Law Journal* 409, December 1992;

Michael L. Taviss, "Dueling Forums: The Public Forum Doctrine's Failure to Protect the Electronic Forum," 60 *University of Cincinnatti Law Review* 757, Winter 1992.

6. 395 U.S. 444 (1969).

7. *Herceg v. Hustler Magazine*, 814 F.2d 1017 (5th Cir. 1987).

8. *Weirum v. RKO General, Inc.*, 539 P.2d 36 (Cal. 1975).

9. More information about the Electronic Frontier Foundation can be found in Appendix A.

10. See Loftus E. Becker, Jr., "The Liability of Computer Bulletin Board Operators for Defamation Posted by Others," 22 *Connecticut Law Review* 203, fall 1989.

11. 376 U.S. 254 (1964).

12. *Cubby v. CompuServe*, 776 F. Supp. 135 (S.D.N.Y. 1991).

13. *Smith v. California*, 361 U.S. 147, 153 (1959).

14. Edward A. Cavazos, "Computer Bulletin Board Systems and the Right of Reply: Redefining Defamation Liability for a New Technology," 12 *Review of Litigation* 231, fall 1992.

15. The best discussion of the facts leading up to and surrounding the Phrack incident can be found in Bruce Sterling, *The Hacker Crackdown: Law and Disorder on the Electronic Frontier* (New York: Bantam Books, 1992).

16. *United States v. Riggs*, 739 F. Supp. 414 (N.D. Ill. 1990). See discussion in chapter seven.

17. Schatz, "Enforcement Questions Raised after Hacker Case Dismissed; Leahy Proposes Amendment to Computer Fraud Bill," *Washington Post*, August 2, 1990, p. C13.

18. 42 U.S.C. § 2000aa, et seq.

19. *Zurcher v. Stanford Daily*, 436 U.S. 547 (1978).

Chapter 6

1. *Chaplinsky v. New Hampshire*, 315 U.S. 568 (1942) was the first case to list obscenity as a type of speech that enjoyed no First Amendment protection. *FCC v. Pacifica Found.*, 438 U.S. 726 (1978), listed indecent speech as a form of expression protected by the First Amendment.

2. *Jacobellis v. Ohio*, 378 U.S. 184, 197 (1964).

3. 413 U.S. 15 (1973).

4. *Miller v. California*, 413 U.S. 15 (1973).

5. *Hamling v. United States*, 418 U.S. 87, 105–06 (1974).

6. *Smith v. United States*, 431 U.S. 291 (1977).

7. *U.S. v. Sandy*, 605 F.2d 210 (6th Cir. 1979).

8. *Roth v. U.S.*, 354 U.S. 476 (1957).

9. *Id.*

10. *Brockett v. Spokane Arcades, Inc.*, 472 U.S. 491 (1985).

11. *Butler v. Michigan*, 352 U.S. 380 (1957).

12. *Hamling v. United States*, 418 U.S. 87 (1974); *Ward v. Illinois*, 431 U.S. 767 (1977).

13. *Ginzburg v. United States*, 383 U.S. 463, 468 (1966).

14. *Hamling v. United States*, 418 U.S. 87 (1974).

15. *Miller v. California*, 413 U.S. 15, 27 (1973).

16. See, for example, Texas Penal Code §43.21.

17. *Ward v. Illinois*, 431 U.S. 767 (1977).

18. *Kaplan v. California*, 413 U.S. 115 (1973).

19. *State v. Henry*, 302 Or. 510, 732 P.2d 9 (1987). Under the Oregon Constitution, obscene material is afforded protection but can still be regulated. Thus, obscene material under Oregon law is treated the way indecent material is treated in other states.

20. See *Ginzburg v. United States*, 383 U.S. 463, 468 (1966).

21. See, for example, Texas Penal Code §43.24.

22. *Stanley v. Georgia*, 394 U.S. 557 (1969).

23. *United States v. Orita*, 413 U.S. 139 (1973).

24. *United States v. Reidel*, 402 U.S. 351 (1971).

25. *United States v. 12 200 Ft. Reels of Film*, 413 U.S. 123 (1973).

26. *New York v. Ferber*, 458 U.S. 747 (1982).

27. *U.S. v. Nolan*, 818 F.2d 1015 (1st Cir. 1987).

28. Arizona Rev. Stat.Ann. Section 13-3554 (West 1978 & Supp. 1987).

29. *New York v. Ferber*, 458 U.S. 747, 763 (1982).

30. *Osborne v. Ohio*, 493 U.S. 813 (1990).

31. For a valuable set of guidelines for sysops who carry adult material on their systems, see Lance Rose and Jonathan Wallace, *SYSLAW* (Winona, Minn.: LOL Productions, 1992).

Chapter 7

1. 18 U.S.C. § 1030.

2. For a detailed discussion of the Robert Morris Internet Worm case, see Katie Hafner and John Markoff, *Cyberpunk: Outlaws and Hackers on the Computer Frontier* (New York: Simon & Schuster, 1991).

3. These estimates are conservatively realistic. Early reports greatly exaggerated the extent of the damage. John McAfee, chairman of the Computer Virus Association, is

quoted as estimating that the Morris program caused $96 million of expenses/damage. New York Times, *Prospects: Curing a Computer Virus*, November 13, 1988, Business Section, p. 1.

4. 18 U.S.C. § 1029.

5. 18 U.S.C. §§ 1343.

6. See, *inter alia*, *United States v. Bohr*, 581 F.2d 1294 (8th Cir.), *cert. denied*, 439 U.S. 958 (1978) (telephones); *United States v. Davila*, 592 F.2d 1261 (5th Cir.), *cert. denied*, 444 U.S. 843 (1979).

7. See, *inter alia*, *United States v. De Biasi*, 712 F.2d 785 (2d Cir.), *cert. denied*, 464 U.S. 962 (1983).

8. *Id.*

9. 18 U.S.C. § 2314.

10. *United States v. Riggs*, 743 F. Supp. 556 (N.D. Ill 1990).

11. *United States v. Brown*, 925 F.2d 1801 (10th Cir. 1991) (holding that transporting software did not constitute transporting physical goods as required).

12. *United States v. Bottone*, 365 F.2d 389 (2nd Cir.), *cert. denied*, 385 U.S. 974 (1966).

13. *Downling v. United States*, 473 U.S. 207 (1985).

14. Stanley C. Arkin, Barry A. Bohrer, et al., *Prevention and Prosecution of Computer and High Tech Crime* (New York: Matthew Binder, 1992).

15. 18 U.S.C. § 2319(b).

16. Paul Mungo Bryan Clough, *Approaching Zero: The Extraordinary Underworld of Hackers, Phreakers, Virus Writers, and Keyboard Criminals* (New York: Random House, 1992).

17. In *Approaching Zero*, Mungo and Clough report that the number of catalogued viruses has grown exponentially, with only a hundred known viruses at the end of 1989, five hundred in 1990, and over two thousand by 1992.

18. Vernon's Tex. Code Ann. § 33.03 (a)(6) (reprinted in appendix H).

19. A Texas man was convicted for "harmful access to a computer" under the Texas Computer Crime Statute, after it was proven that he loaded into his company's computer system a logic bomb that deleted hundreds of thousands of records two days after the man was fired. *State v. Burleson* (Tex. Crim. Dist. Ct. Tarrant County Ind. No. 85–0274102R).

20. A "Computer Virus Eradication Act" was introduced in the House of Representatives in 1988, but was not passed.

21. Only Arkansas, Vermont and West Virginia have not passed legislation aimed specifically at computer crime. A complete listing of all state computer laws is included in appendix I.

22. Florida's Computer Crimes Act makes a criminal out of anyone who "willfully, knowingly, and without authorization denies or causes the denial of computer system services to an authorized user of such computer services." Fla. Stat. § 815.06.

Appendix A: Where
to Go for More Help

I. LEGAL RESEARCH

Where appropriate, we have included citations to cases, statutes, law review articles, and legal treatises that are intended to act as a starting point for extended legal research. For those unfamiliar with legal research, here are some quick pointers that should prove helpful:

Statutes

The standard legal citation for a statute consists of a volume or title number, followed by the name of the statute and a chapter or section number. The U.S. Code, which is the main source for federal laws, is abbreviated as "U.S.C." and an annotated version is cited as "U.S.C.A."

State statutes are usually cited in a similar form, but sometimes vary. Generally, if the citation for a state statute varies from the standard, it is because it provides more detailed information regarding the source of the law.

Example:

17 U.S.C. §§ 100 - 105.

This cite refers to Title 17 of the U.S. Code, sections 100 through 105. The double section symbol indicates that more than one section is being cited.

Cases

The case citations are similar in form to those used for statutes, but usually provide more information. The first part of the citation is the name of the case (which is composed of the names of the parties involved in the litigation) followed by a volume number, the name of the "reporter" in which the opinion was published, and a page number. In parentheses, you can find information about which court handed down the opinion and when.

Case reporters are identified with somewhat cryptic abbreviations. Figure A.1 depicts some of the most common abbreviations for reporters containing opinions issued by federal courts. State court opinions can be found in regional reporters (with names like S.W. for Southwest Reporter or P.2d for Pacific Reporter, Second Series).

Examples:

Salinger v. Random House, Inc., 811 F.2d 90 (2nd Cir. 1987).

This case involved a lawsuit brought by J.D. Salinger against Random House, Inc. The text of the court's opinion (which gives the legal rationale for its decision) can be found in volume 811 of the Federal Reporter, 2d series on page 90. From the parenthetical information, you can tell that the opinion was handed down by the Court of Appeals for the Second Circuit in 1987.

Miller v. California, 413 U.S. 15 (1973).

This case is an appeal by Miller against the state of California. The Supreme Court's opinion (note the parenthetical only contains the year, and no court abbreviation) can be found in volume 413 of the U.S. Reporter on page 15. The opinion was delivered in 1973.

Law Review Articles and Legal Treatises

Generally, law review articles and legal treatises follow a citation format that provides the author's name, a volume number, the name of the law review or treatise, a page number, and the year of publication (in that order).

F., F.2d, *or* F.3d	Federal Reporter, Federal Reporter, Second or Federal Reporter, Third Series. Contains opinions from the various Courts of Appeals
F. Supp.	Federal Supplement. Contains opinions from the various federal district courts.
U.S.	United States Reporter. Contains opinions of the U.S. Supreme Court. Supreme Court citations do not identify the Court in the parenthetical, which contains only the year of the opinion
S. Ct.	Supreme Court Reporter. Also contains opinions of the Supreme Court. The Supreme Court Report is an alternate source for the opinions found in the United States Reporter.

Figure A.1

Example:

Lynn Becker, Electronic Publishing: First Amendment Issues in the Twenty-First Century, 13 FORDHAM L.J. 801 (1985)

This citation refers to a 1985 article by Lynn Becker in volume 13 of the *Fordham Law Journal*, which can be found on page 801.

II. PUBLIC INTEREST GROUPS

In recent years, several organizations focusing on legal issues in cyberspace and related issues have emerged. Stanton McCandlish of the Electronic Frontier Foundation has compiled an up-to-date list of such groups and their contact information. The information below is but a part of his list. Although this list is by no means exhaustive, with new grass-root organizations forming regularly, it is a good starting place for anyone interested in becoming involved in on-line activism, or anyone needing specific assistance with legal issues involving computer-mediated communications.

Stanton McCandlish is interested in hearing from anyone with corrections, updates or new group information. His Internet address is mech@eff.org. We would like to give special thanks to Stanton for granting his permission to print parts of his compilation. The most current version of his list is archived at ftp.eff.org/pub/Groups/outposts.faq, and is available for anonymous ftp.

A. GROUPS ON THE NATIONAL LEVEL

Electronic Frontier Foundation

A nonprofit public interest membership organization working to protect individual rights in the emerging information age, EFF supports legal and legislative action to protect the civil liberties of online users; hosts and participates in related conferences and projects, including Big Dummy's Guide to the Internet, and Computers and Academic Freedom; and works to educate the on-line community about its legal rights and responsibilities. EFF members receive on-line bulletins about the critical issues and debates affecting computer-mediated communications and participate in online political activism. Donations are welcome and are tax deductible. EFF is a 501(c)(3) tax-exempt organization.

Contact Information

Electronic Frontier Foundation
1001 G St. NW, Suite 950 E
Washington, DC 20001, USA
voice: +1 202 347 5400
fax: +1 202 393 5509

Internet E-mail Addresses:

GENERAL: info@eff.org or ask@eff.org

LEGAL: Shari Steele (ssteele@eff.org), Dir. of Legal Services;
Mike Godwin (mnemonic@eff.org), On-line Counsel

POLICY/OPEN PLATFORM/NII: Daniel J. Weitzner (djw@eff.org), Senior Staff
Counsel

TECH: Dan Brown (brown@eff.org), Systems Administrator

MAILING LIST REQUESTS: eff@eff.org

ON-LINE NEWSLETTER: Stanton McCandlish (mech@eff.org)

HARD COPY PUBLICATIONS: pubs@eff.org

MEMBERSHIP: membership@eff.org

Net Services:

FTP: ftp.eff.org

GOPHER: gopher.eff.org

WAIS: wais.eff.org

WORLD WIDE WEB URL: http://www.eff.org/

USENET: comp.org.eff.talk, comp.org.eff.news, alt.politics.datahighway

WELL: g eff

AOL: keyword EFF

CIS: GO EFFSIG

Americans Communicating Electronically (ACE)

ACE membership is diverse and represents private and government organizations and individuals who wish to promote interactive communications among federal, state, and local governments, private businesses, public libraries, and schools, rural cooperatives, public and private universities, community-based arts and theater groups, voluntary associations, job training services, and health care organizations. The members of ACE are particularly concerned that access and participation be made possible and convenient for Americans who do not own modem-equipped computers. To support the development of interactive communications between governments and communities, ACE is recommending that all government agencies establish information access programs to help create and foster an "interactive citizen-government communications system." Many government agencies, from the White House to the NSF and the Dept. of Labor, are already participating in the ACE project. Unlike everything else on this list, ACE is actually a government-sponsored project.

Contact Information

BASIC INFORMATION: info@ace.esusda.gov

GENERAL: letters@ace.esusda.gov

MAILING LIST SUBSCRIPTIONS: almanac@ace.esusda.gov [message body: subscribe <list> <your name>]

Center for Civic Networking (CCN/CivicNet)

The Center for Civic Networking is a nonprofit organization based in Boston and Washington, D.C., that promotes broad public benefits of the emerging national information infrastructure. The center brings together expertise in large-scale computer and network systems, community-based applications of computing, nonprofit management, community development, architecture, public policy, and democratic participation. The center's programs focus on framing a national vision for civic networking, developing a policy framework that supports civic networking, developing and supporting model civic networking projects, and assisting in the technology transfer needed to achieve the broad-based benefits of civic networking. CCN is involved with SDIN network, the Cambridge Civic Forum, and the "From Townhalls to Local Civic Networks" conference.

Contact Information

VOICE: +1 202 362 3831 (R. Civille, Washington, DC, office)

Internet Addresses:

Miles Fidelman (mfidelman@world.std.com) or (mfidelman@civicnet.org), Exec. Dir. Richard Civille (rciville@civicnet.org), Dir., DC office

Net Services:

FTP: ftp.eff.org, pub/Groups/CCN; world.std.com, ftp/amo/civicnet

Computer Professionals for Social Responsibility (CPSR)

CPSR is a national membership organization, based in Palo Alto, California. CPSR conducts many activities to protect privacy and civil liberties. Membership is open to the public and support is welcome. CPSR maintains local chapters in Austin, TX; Berkeley, CA; Boston, MA; Chicago, IL; Washington, DC; Los Angeles, CA; Madison, WI; Palo Alto, CA; Portland, OR; Denver-Boulder, CO; Seattle, WA; and elsewhere. Where information is available, these chapters are listed separately under "Groups on the Regional Level."

Contact Information

CPSR National Office
P.O. Box 717
Palo Alto, CA 94302 USA
Voice: +1 415 322 3778
Fax: +1 415 322 3798

CPSR Washington Office
666 Pennsylvania Ave. SE, Ste. 303
Washington, DC 20003 USA
Voice: +1 202 544 9240
Fax: +1 202 547 5482

Internet E-Mail Addresses:

GENERAL (NATIONAL HEADQUARTERS): cpsr@csli.stanford.edu

GENERAL (WASHINGTON OFFICE): Marc Rotenberg (rotenberg@washofc.cpsr.org)

Net Services:

INTERNET MAILING LIST: listserv@gwuvm.gwu.edu (message body of: subscribe cpsr [your first and last name])

TELECOM POLICY ROUNDTABLE: Jeff Chester (cme@access.digex.net)

National Online Media Association (NOMA)

NOMA is a trade association for BBSs, Internet service providers, and other on-line services and public networks. NOMA's mission is to act for the BBS and on-line service industry on matters of national importance by creating an industry presence in Washington, D.C., and other means; assist its members at the state and local levels; educate the public on the unique social, business, and legal roles of BBSs and other on-line services; establish appropriate industry standards and guidelines; promote business development in the industry; and maintain and provide access to resources and industry information for use by the public and the industry.

Contact Information

NOMA
c/o Phill Liggett
Solutions, Inc.
89 Seymore Ave.
West Hartford, CT 06119 USA

Internet Addresses:

GENERAL: Phill Liggett (liggett@delphi.com); Lance Rose (elrose@echonyc. com); (Steve Barber sbarber@echonyc.com)

MAILING LIST REQUESTS: listproc@echonyc.com (subscribe natbbs <name>)

FIDONET: Jim Taylor, 1:310/5 (jim.taylor@f5.n310.z1.fidonet.org)

National Public Telecomputing Networking (NPTN)—Free-Net

The National Public Telecomputing Network exists to make free public access to computerized communications and information services a reality; to help people in cities throughout the U.S. and the world to establish free, open access, community computer systems (Free-Nets); to link those systems together into a common network similar to National Public Radio or PBS on TV; and to help supplement what the local systems are able to produce with high quality network-wide services and features. NPTN is a 501(c)(3) non-profit corporation.

Contact Information

National Public Telecomputing Network
P.O. Box 1987
Cleveland, OH 44106
Voice: 216-247-5800
FAX: 216-247-3328

GENERAL: info@nptn.org [Note: this is not an automailer, but a person]

COMMUNITY FREE-NET AFFILIATE SYSTEMS MODEM NUMBERS:

Big Sky Telegraph	Dillon, Montana	+1 406 683 7680
Buffalo Free-Net	Buffalo, New York	+1 716 645 6128
Cleveland Free-Net	Cleveland, Ohio	+1 216 368 3888
COIN	Columbia, Missouri	+1 314 884 7000
Denver Free-Net	Denver, Colorado	+1 303 270 4865
Heartland Free-Net	Peoria, Illinois	+1 309 674 1100
Lorain County Free-Net	Elyria, Ohio	+1 216 366 9721
Medina County Free-Net	Medina, Ohio	+1 216 723 6732
National Capital Free-Net	Ottawa, Ont., Canada	+1 613 780 3733
Tallahassee Free-Net	Tallahassee, Florida	+1 904 576 6330
Tristate Online	Cincinnati, Ohio	+1 513 579 1990
Victoria Free-Net	Victoria, BC, Canada	+1 604 595 2300
Wellington Citynet	Wellington, New Zealand	+64 4 801 3060
Youngstown Free-Net	Youngstown, Ohio	+1 216 742 3072

For more detailed information, including internet addresses and login instructions, see ftp.eff.org, pub/Groups/NPTN-Freenet/login.info

B. GROUPS ON THE STATE LEVEL

CALIFORNIA

Los Angeles Metro Area

CPSR/Los Angeles (CPSR/LA)

[See C.P.S.R. above for more information]

Palo Alto

CPSR/Palo Alto

[See C.P.S.R. above for more information]

San Francisco Bay/Berkeley Area

BAWiT (Bay Area Women in Telecom)

Hosted by CPSR/B (see below).

BAWiT is a group of women working with telecom to make the on-line community inclusive rather than exclusive of women and other minorities. The working group's activities include outreach and mentoring, and providing speakers for events and informal on-line discussions.

INFORMATION: Judi Clark (judic@sunnyside.com, judic@netcom.com)

ON-LINE CONFERENCES: listserv@cpsr.org (message body containing: subscribe bawit-announce [first and last name])

San Francisco

CPSR/Berkeley

CPSR/B P.O. Box 40361
Berkeley, CA 94704

[See C.P.S.R. above for more information]

COLORADO

Denver/Boulder Metro Area

CPSR/Denver-Boulder (CPSR/DB)

[See C.P.S.R. above for more information]

DISTRICT OF COLUMBIA/WASHINGTON, D.C.

Metro Area

CPSR/DC

[See C.P.S.R. above for more information]

ILLINOIS

Chicago

CPSR/Chicago

[See C.P.S.R. above for more information]

MASSACHUSETTS

Cambridge-Boston Metro Area

CPSR/BOSTON

[See C.P.S.R. above for more information]

EF128 (Electronic Frontier Route 128)

GENERAL: Lar Kaufman (lark@ora.com)

MISSOURI

Kansas City Area

Greater Kansas City Sysop Association

P.O. Box 14480
Parkville, MO 64152

GENERAL: Scott Lent (slent@vax1.umkc.edu)

NEW HAMPSHIRE

Statewide

Electronic Frontiers New Hampshire (EFNH)

A state/local group founded to work with federal and state legislators and media on issues of electronic democracy, freedom of speech in the on-line world, privacy of e-mail and other electronic communication, access to government information, and access issues surrounding the Nat'l. Information Infrastructure debate. Goals include airing important networking ideas, attracting media and government attention to the issues, focusing on civil rights on-line and providing a forum for discussion of same, protect against, draw attention to, and provide a voice to speak against government encroachments on individual liberties in networking, especially from a grass-roots level, and improving public access to government information.

GENERAL: efnh@mv.com, efnh@mv.mv.com

NEW YORK

New York City Metro Area

Society for Electronic Access (SEA)

Post Office Box 3131
Church Street Station
New York, NY 10008-3131
Voice: +1 212 592 3801

SEA is a membership organization focusing on civil liberties and access issues that affect theon-line world. SEA is based in New York City, so many of its activities are focused toward the New York metropolitan area, although issues of national concern are addressed.

QUERIES: sea@sea.org

GENERAL: sea-info@panix.com

Western New York State

Genesee Community College Group

Thomas J. Klotzbach
Genesee Community College
Batavia, NY 14020

GENERAL: Thomas J. Klotzbach (3751365@mcimail.com)

OREGON

Portland

CPSR/Portland

[See C.P.S.R. above for more information]

NEWSLETTER AND GENERAL:

Erik Nilsson (erikn@goldfish.mitron.tek.com)

TEXAS

Austin

CPSR/Austin

[See C.P.S.R. above for more information]

EFF-Austin

P.O. Box 18957
Austin, TX 78760
Voice: +1 512 465 7871

EFF-Austin was formed to protect constitutional guarantees of free speech and freedom from unreasonable search and seizure for users of computer networks. According to the group: "Experience has taught us that these freedoms must be fought for if they are to survive in the on-line world." EFF-Austin was created as an experimental local chapter of the national EFF but became independent in 1993 while retaining contacts with the parent organization. They are heavily involved in public speaking, education, and advocacy of constitutional rights in cyberspace.

GENERAL: eff-austin-moderator@tic.com

MAILING LIST SUBSCRIPTIONS: eff-austin-request@tic.com

DIRECTORS: eff-austin-directors@tic.com

USENET: austin.eff

FTP: ftp.tic.com, eff-austin directory

GOPHER: gopher.tic.com

Houston

Electronic Frontiers Houston (EFH)

2476 Bolsover #145
Houston, TX 77005

EFH is nonprofit corporation devoted to working with and for the Houston computer and telecommunications community. Working in alliance with the Electronic Frontier Foundation, EFF-Austin, and other national and regional organizations, EFH acts as a focal point for the diverse set of individuals who find themselves involved in computer communications. Included on EFH's agenda are: advocating civil liberty issues in cyberspace, promoting wider public access to computer networks, exploring artistic and social implications of new digital media, and educating the public about the increasingly important on-line world.

GENERAL: efh@blkbox.com

WWIVNET: efh@7385

BOARD OF DIRECTORS: efh-directors@blkbox.com (efh-directors@7385 on WWIVnet)

USENET: houston.efh.talk

FTP: ftp.tic.com, EFH directory

GOPHER: gopher.tic.com, Electronic Frontiers Houston

WASHINGTON

Seattle

CPSR/Seattle

[See C.P.S.R. above for more information]

WISCONSIN

Madison

CPSR/Madison

[See C.P.S.R. above for more information]

Appendix B:
The Electronic
Communications
Privacy Act

United States Code

Title 18 Crimes and Criminal Procedure

Part I—Crimes

Chapter 119. Wire and Electronic Communications Interception and Interception of Oral Communications

§ 2510. Definitions

As used in this chapter—

(1) "wire communication" means any aural transfer made in whole or in part through the use of facilities for the transmission of communications by the aid of wire, cable, or other like connection between the point of origin and the point of reception (including the use of such connection in a switching station) furnished or operated by any person engaged in providing or operating such facilities for the transmission of interstate or foreign communications or communications affecting interstate or foreign commerce and such term includes any electronic storage of such communication, but such term does not include the radio portion of a cordless telephone communication that is transmitted between the cordless telephone handset and the base unit;

(2) "oral communication" means any oral communication uttered by a person exhibiting an expectation that such communication is not subject to interception under circumstances justifying such expectation, but such term does not include any electronic communication;

(3) "State" means any State of the United States, the District of Columbia, the Commonwealth of Puerto Rico, and any territory or possession of the United States;

(4)   "intercept" means the aural or other acquisition of the contents of any wire, electronic, or oral communication through the use of any electronic, mechanical, or other device.

(5)   "electronic, mechanical, or other device" means any device or apparatus which can be used to intercept a wire, oral, or electronic communication other than—

   (a)   any telephone or telegraph instrument, equipment or facility, or any component thereof, (i) furnished to the subscriber or user by a provider of wire or electronic communication service in the ordinary course of its business and being used by the subscriber or user in the ordinary course of its business or furnished by such subscriber or user for connection to the facilities of such service and used in the ordinary course of its business; or (ii) being used by a provider of wire or electronic communication service in the ordinary course of its business, or by an investigative or law enforcement officer in the ordinary course of his duties;

   (b)   a hearing aid or similar device being used to correct subnormal hearing to not better than normal;

(6)   "person" means any employee, or agent of the United States or any State or political subdivision thereof, and any individual, partnership, association, joint stock company, trust, or corporation;

(7)   "Investigative or law enforcement officer" means any officer of the United States or of a State or political subdivision thereof, who is empowered by law to conduct investigations of or to make arrests for offenses enumerated in this chapter, and any attorney authorized by law to prosecute or participate in the prosecution of such offenses;

(8)   "contents," when used with respect to any wire, oral, or electronic communication, includes any information concerning the substance, purport, or meaning of that communication;

(9)   "Judge of competent jurisdiction" means—

   (a)   a judge of a United States district court or a United States court of appeals; and

   (b)   a judge of any court of general criminal jurisdiction of a State who is authorized by a statute of that State to enter orders authorizing interceptions of wire, oral, or electronic communications;

(10)   "communication common carrier" shall have the same meaning which is given the term "common carrier" by section 153(h) of title 47 of the United States Code;

(11)   "aggrieved person" means a person who was a party to any intercepted wire, oral, or electronic communication or a person against whom the interception was directed;

(12) "electronic communication" means any transfer of signs, signals, writing, images, sounds, data, or intelligence of any nature transmitted in whole or in part by a wire, radio, electromagnetic, photoelectronic or photooptical system that affects interstate or foreign commerce, but does not include—

    (a)   the radio portion of a cordless telephone communication that is transmitted between the cordless telephone handset and the base unit;

    (b)   any wire or oral communication;

    (c)   any communication made through a tone-only paging device; or

    (d)   any communication from a tracking device (as defined in section 3117 of this title);

(13) "user" means any person or entity who—

    (a)   uses an electronic communication service; and

    (b)   is duly authorized by the provider of such service to engage in such use;

(14) "electronic communications system" means any wire, radio, electromagnetic, photo-optical or photoelectronic facilities for the transmission of electronic communications, and any computer facilities or related electronic equipment for the electronic storage of such communications;

(15) "electronic communication service" means any service which provides to users thereof the ability to send or receive wire or electronic communications;

(16) "readily accessible to the general public" means, with respect to a radio communication, that such communication is not—

    (a)   scrambled or encrypted;

    (b)   transmitted using modulation techniques whose essential parameters have been withheld from the public with the intention of preserving the privacy of such communication;

    (c)   carried on a subcarrier or other signal subsidiary to a radio transmission;

    (d)   transmitted over a communication system provided by a common carrier, unless the communication is a tone only paging system communication; or

    (e)   transmitted on frequencies allocated under part 25, subpart D, E, or F of part 74, or part 94 of the Rules of the Federal Communications Commission, unless, in the case of a communication transmitted on a frequency allocated under part 74 that is not exclusively allocated to broadcast auxiliary services, the communication is a two-way voice communication by radio;

(17)   "electronic storage" means—

    (a)   any temporary, intermediate storage of a wire or electronic communication incidental to the electronic transmission thereof; and

    (b)   any storage of such communication by an electronic communication service for purposes of backup protection of such communication; and

(18)   "aural transfer" means a transfer containing the human voice at any point between and including the point of origin and the point of reception.

§ 2511. Interception and disclosure of wire, oral, or electronic communications prohibited

(1)   Except as otherwise specifically provided in this chapter any person who—

    (a)   intentionally intercepts, endeavors to intercept, or procures any other person to intercept or endeavor to intercept, any wire, oral, or electronic communication;

    (b)   intentionally uses, endeavors to use, or procures any other person to use or endeavor to use any electronic, mechanical, or other device to intercept any oral communication when—

        (i)   such device is affixed to, or otherwise transmits a signal through, a wire, cable, or other like connection used in wire communication; or

        (ii)   such device transmits communications by radio, or interferes with the transmission of such communication; or

        (iii)   such person knows, or has reason to know, that such device or any component thereof has been sent through the mail or transported in interstate or foreign commerce; or

        (iv)   such use or endeavor to use (A) takes place on the premises of any business or other commercial establishment the operations of which affect interstate or foreign commerce; or (B) obtains or is for the purpose of obtaining information relating to the operations of any business or other commercial establishment the operations of which affect interstate or foreign commerce; or

        (v)   such person acts in the District of Columbia, the Commonwealth of Puerto Rico, or any territory or possession of the United States;

(c)   intentionally discloses, or endeavors to disclose, to any other person the contents of any wire, oral, or electronic communication, knowing or having reason to know that the information was obtained through the interception of a wire, oral, or electronic communication in violation of this subsection; or

(d)   intentionally uses, or endeavors to use, the contents of any wire, oral, or electronic communication, knowing or having reason to know that the information was obtained through the interception of a wire, oral, or electronic communication in violation of this subsection;

shall be punished as provided in subsection (4) or shall be subject to suit as provided in subsection (5).

(2)   (a)   (i)   It shall not be unlawful under this chapter for an operator of a switchboard, or an officer, employee, or agent of a provider of wire or electronic communication service, whose facilities are used in the transmission of a wire communication, to intercept, disclose, or use that communication in the normal course of his employment while engaged in any activity which is a necessary incident to the rendition of his service or to the protection of the rights or property of the provider of that service, except that a provider of wire communication service to the public shall not utilize service observing or random monitoring except for mechanical or service quality control checks.

(ii)   Notwithstanding any other law, providers of wire or electronic communication service, their officers, employees, and agents, landlords, custodians, or other persons, are authorized to provide information, facilities, or technical assistance to persons authorized by law to intercept wire, oral, or electronic communications or to conduct electronic surveillance, as defined in section 101 of the Foreign Intelligence Surveillance Act of 1978 if such provider, its officers, employees, or agents, landlord, custodian, or other specified person, has been provided with—

(A)   a court order directing such assistance signed by the authorizing judge, or

(B)   a certification in writing by a person specified in section 2518(7) of this title or the Attorney General of the United States that no warrant or court order is required by law, that all statutory requirements have been met, and that the specified assistance is required, setting forth the period of time during which the provision of the information, facilities, or technical assistance is authorized and specifying the information, facilities, or technical assistance required. No provider of wire or electronic communication service, officer, employee, or agent thereof, or landlord, custodian, or other specified person shall disclose the existence of any interception or surveillance or the device used to accomplish the interception or surveillance with respect to which the person has been furnished an order or certification under this subparagraph, except as may otherwise be required by legal process and then only after prior notification to the Attorney General or to the principal prosecuting attorney of a State or any political subdivision of a State, as may be appropriate. Any such disclosure, shall render such person liable for the civil damages provided for in section 2520. No cause of action shall lie in any court against any provider of wire or electronic communication service, its officers, employees, or agents, landlord, custodian, or other specified person for providing information, facilities, or assistance in accordance with the terms of a court order or certification under this chapter.

(b)   It shall not be unlawful under this chapter for an officer, employee, or agent of the Federal Communications Commission, in the normal course of his employment and in discharge of the monitoring responsibilities exercised by the Commission in the enforcement of chapter 5 of title 47 of the United States Code, to intercept a wire or electronic communication, or oral communication transmitted by radio, or to disclose or use the information thereby obtained.

(c)   It shall not be unlawful under this chapter for a person acting under color of law to intercept a wire, oral, or electronic communication, where such person is a party to the communication or one of the parties to the communication has given prior consent to such interception.

(d)   It shall not be unlawful under this chapter for a person not acting under color of law to intercept a wire or oral communication where such person is a party to the communication or where one of the parties to the communication has given prior consent to such interception unless such communication is intercepted for the purpose of committing any criminal or tortious act in violation of the Constitution or laws of the United States or of any State.

(e)   Notwithstanding any other provision of this title or section 705 or 706 of the Communications Act of 1934 , it shall not be unlawful for an officer, employee, or agent of the United States in the normal course of his official duty to conduct electronic surveillance, as defined in section 101 of the Foreign Intelligence Surveillance Act of 1978, as authorized by that Act.

(f)   Nothing contained in this chapter or chapter 121, or section 705 of the Communications Act of 1934, shall be deemed to affect the acquisition by the United States Government of foreign intelligence information from international or foreign communications, or foreign intelligence activities conducted in accordance with otherwise applicable Federal law involving a foreign electronic communications system, utilizing a means other than electronic surveillance as defined in section 101 of the Foreign Intelligence Surveillance Act of 1978, and procedures in this chapter and the Foreign Intelligence Surveillance Act of 1978 shall be the exclusive means by which electronic surveillance, as defined in section 101 of such Act, and the interception of domestic wire, oral, or electronic communications may be conducted.

(g)   It shall not be unlawful under this chapter or chapter 121 of this title for any person—

   (i)   to intercept or access an electronic communication made through an electronic communication system that is configured so that such electronic communication is readily accessible to the general public;

   (ii)   to intercept any radio communication which is transmitted—

     (I)   by any station for the use of the general public, or that relates to ships, aircraft, vehicles, or persons in distress;

     (II)   by any governmental, law enforcement, civil defense, private land mobile, or public safety communications system, including police and fire, readily accessible to the general public;

     (III)   by a station operating on an authorized frequency within the bands allocated to the amateur, citizens band, or general mobile radio services; or

     (IV)   by any marine or aeronautical communications system;

   (iii)   to engage in any conduct which—

     (I)   is prohibited by section 633 of the Communications Act of 1934; or

(II)   is excepted from the application of section 705(a) of the Communications Act of 1934 by section 705(b) of that Act;

(iv)   to intercept any wire or electronic communication the transmission of which is causing harmful interference to any lawfully operating station or consumer electronic equipment, to the extent necessary to identify the source of such interference; or

(v)   for other users of the same frequency to intercept any radio communication made through a system that utilizes frequencies monitored by individuals engaged in the provision or the use of such system, if such communication is not scrambled or encrypted.

(h)   It shall not be unlawful under this chapter—

(i)   to use a pen register or a trap and trace device (as those terms are defined for the purposes of chapter 206 [relating to pen registers and trap and trace devices] of this title); or

(ii)   for a provider of electronic communication service to record the fact that a wire or electronic communication was initiated or completed in order to protect such provider, another provider furnishing service toward the completion of the wire or electronic communication, or a user of that service, from fraudulent, unlawful or abusive use of such service.

(3)   (a)   Except as provided in paragraph (b) of this subsection, a person or entity providing an electronic communication service to the public shall not intentionally divulge the contents of any communication (other than one to such person or entity, or an agent thereof) while in transmission on that service to any person or entity other than an addressee or intended recipient of such communication or an agent of such addressee or intended recipient.

(b)   A person or entity providing electronic communication service to the public may divulge the contents of any such communication—

(i)   as otherwise authorized in section 2511(2)(a) or 2517 of this title;

(ii)   with the lawful consent of the originator or any addressee or intended recipient of such communication;

(iii)   to a person employed or authorized, or whose facilities are

(iv)   which were inadvertently obtained by the service provider and which appear to pertain to the commission of a crime, if such divulgence is made to a law enforcement agency.

(4)   (a)   Except as provided in paragraph (b) of this subsection or in subsection (5), whoever violates subsection (1) of this section shall be fined under this title or imprisoned not more than five years, or both.

(b)   If the offense is a first offense under paragraph (a) of this subsection and is not for a tortious or illegal purpose or for purposes of direct or indirect commercial advantage or private commercial gain, and the wire or electronic communication with respect to which the offense under paragraph (a) is a radio communication that is not scrambled or encrypted, then—

(i)   if the communication is not the radio portion of a cellular telephone communication, a public land mobile radio service communication or a paging service communication, and the conduct is not that described in subsection (5), the offender shall be fined under this title or imprisoned not more than one year, or both; and

(ii)   if the communication is the radio portion of a cellular telephone communication, a public land mobile radio service communication or a paging service communication, the offender shall be fined not more than $ 500.

(c)   Conduct otherwise an offense under this subsection that consists of or relates to the interception of a satellite transmission that is not encrypted or scrambled and that is transmitted—

(i)   to a broadcasting station for purposes of retransmission to the general public; or

(ii)   as an audio subcarrier intended for redistribution to facilities open to the public, but not including data transmissions or telephone calls,

is not an offense under this subsection unless the conduct is for the purposes of direct or indirect commercial advantage or private financial gain.

(5)   (a)   (i)   If the communication is—

(A)   a private satellite video communication that is not scrambled or encrypted and the conduct in violation of this chapter is the private viewing of that communication and is not for a tortious or illegal purpose or for purposes of direct or indirect commercial advantage or private commercial gain; or

(B)   a radio communication that is transmitted on frequencies allocated under subpart D of part 74 of the
rules of the Federal Communications Commission
that is not scrambled or encrypted and the conduct in
violation of this chapter is not for a tortious or illegal
purpose or for purposes of direct or indirect commercial advantage or private commercial gain, then the
person who engages in such conduct shall be subject
to suit by the Federal Government in a court of competent jurisdiction.

(ii)   In an action under this subsection—

(A)   if the violation of this chapter is a first offense for the
person under paragraph (a) of subsection (4) and
such person has not been found liable in a civil action
under section 2520 of this title, the Federal
Government shall be entitled to appropriate injunc-
tive relief; and

(B)   if the violation of this chapter is a second or subsequent offense under paragraph (a) of subsection (4)
or such person has been found liable in any prior
civil action under section 2520, the person shall be
subject to a mandatory $ 500 civil fine.

(b)   The court may use any means within its authority to enforce an
injunction issued under paragraph (ii)(A), and shall impose a
civil fine of not less than $ 500 for each violation of such an
injunction.

§ 2512. Manufacture, distribution, possession, and advertising of wire,
oral, or electronic communication intercepting devices prohibited

(1)   Except as otherwise specifically provided in this chapter, any person
who intentionally—

(a)   sends through the mail, or sends or carries in interstate or foreign
commerce, any electronic, mechanical, or other device, knowing
or having reason to know that the design of such device renders
it primarily useful for the purpose of the surreptitious interception of wire, oral, or electronic communications;

(b)   manufactures, assembles, possesses, or sells any electronic,
mechanical, or other device, knowing or having reason to know
that the design of such device renders it primarily useful for the
purpose of the surreptitious interception of wire, oral, or electronic communications, and that such device or any component
thereof has been or will be sent through the mail or transported
in interstate or foreign commerce; or

(c)   places in any newspaper, magazine, handbill, or other publication any advertisement of—

    (i)   any electronic, mechanical, or other device knowing or having reason to know that the design of such device renders it primarily useful for the purpose of the surreptitious interception of wire, oral, or electronic communications; or

    (ii)   any other electronic, mechanical, or other device, where such advertisement promotes the use of such device for the purpose of the surreptitious interception of wire, oral, or electronic communications,

knowing or having reason to know that such advertisement will be sent through the mail or transported in interstate or foreign commerce,

shall be fined not more than $ 10,000 or imprisoned not more than five years, or both.

(2)   It shall not be unlawful under this section for—

(a)   a provider of wire or electronic communication service or an officer, agent, or employee of, or a person under contract with, such a provider, in the normal course of the business of providing that wire or electronic communication service, or

(b)   an officer, agent, or employee of, or a person under contract with, the United States, a State, or a political subdivision thereof, in the normal course of the activities of the United States, a State, or a political subdivision thereof, to send through the mail, send or carry in interstate or foreign commerce, or manufacture, assemble, possess, or sell any electronic, mechanical, or other device knowing or having reason to know that the design of such device renders it primarily useful for the purpose of the surreptitious interception of wire, oral, or electronic communications.

§ 2513. Confiscation of wire, oral, or electronic communication intercepting devices

Any electronic, mechanical, or other device used, sent, carried, manufactured, assembled, possessed, sold, or advertised in violation of section 2511 or section 2512 of this chapter may be seized and forfeited to the United States. All provisions of law relating to (1) the seizure, summary and judicial forfeiture, and condemnation of vessels, vehicles, merchandise, and baggage for violations of the customs laws contained in title 19 of the United States Code, (2) the disposition of such vessels, vehicles, merchandise, and baggage or the proceeds from the sale thereof, (3) the remission or mitigation of such forfeiture, (4) the compromise of claims, and (5) the award of compensation to informers in respect of such forfeitures, shall apply to seizures and forfeitures incurred, or alleged to have been incurred, under the provisions of this section, insofar as applicable and not inconsistent with the provisions of this section; except that such duties as are imposed upon the collector of customs or any other person with respect to the seizure and forfeiture of vessels, vehicles, merchandise, and baggage under the provisions of the customs laws contained in title 19 of the United States Code shall be performed with respect to seizure and forfeiture of electronic, mechanical, or other intercepting devices under this section by such officers, agents, or other persons as may be authorized or designated for that purpose by the Attorney General.

§ 2515. Prohibition of use as evidence of intercepted wire or oral communications

Whenever any wire or oral communication has been intercepted, no part of the contents of such communication and no evidence derived therefrom may be received in evidence in any trial, hearing, or other proceeding in or before any court, grand jury, department, officer, agency, regulatory body, legislative committee, or other authority of the United States, a State, or a political subdivision thereof if the disclosure of that information would be in violation of this chapter.

§ 2516. Authorization for interception of wire, oral, or electronic communications

(1)   The Attorney General, Deputy Attorney General, Associate Attorney General, or any Assistant Attorney General, any acting Assistant Attorney General, or any Deputy Assistant Attorney General in the Criminal Division specially designated by the Attorney General, may authorize an application to a Federal judge of competent jurisdiction for, and such judge may grant in conformity with section 2518 of this chapter an order authorizing or approving the interception of wire or oral communications by the Federal Bureau of Investigation, or a Federal agency having responsibility for the investigation of the offense as to which the application is made, when such interception may provide or has provided evidence of—

    (a)   any offense punishable by death or by imprisonment for more than one year under sections 2274 through 2277 of title 42 of the United States Code (relating to the enforcement of the Atomic Energy Act of 1954), section 2284 of title 42 of the United States Code (relating to sabotage of nuclear facilities or fuel), or under the following chapters of this title: chapter 37 (relating to espionage), chapter 105 (relating to sabotage), chapter 115 (relating to treason), chapter 102 (relating to riots), chapter 65 (relating to malicious mischief), chapter 111 (relating to destruction of vessels), or chapter 81 (relating to piracy);

    (b)   a violation of section 186 or section 501(c) of title 29, United States Code (dealing with restrictions on payments and loans to labor organizations), or any offense which involves murder, kidnapping, robbery, or extortion, and which is punishable under this title;

(c)   any offense which is punishable under the following sections of this title: section 201 (bribery of public officials and witnesses), section 215 (relating to bribery of bank officials), section 224 (bribery in sporting contests), subsection (d), (e), (f), (g), (h), or (i) of section 844 (unlawful use of explosives), section 1032 (relating to concealment of assets), section 1084 (transmission of wagering information), section 751 (relating to escape), section 1014 (relating to loans and credit applications generally; renewals and discounts), sections 1503, 1512, and 1513 (influencing or injuring an officer, juror, or witness generally), section 1510 (obstruction of criminal investigations), section 1511 (obstruction of State or local law enforcement), section 1751 (Presidential and Presidential staff assassination, kidnaping, and assault), section 1951 (interference with commerce by threats or violence), section 1952 (interstate and foreign travel or transportation in aid of racketeering enterprises), section 1958 (relating to use of interstate commerce facilities in the commission of murder for hire), section 1959 (relating to violent crimes in aid of racketeering activity), section 1954 (offer, acceptance, or solicitation to influence operations of employee benefit plan), section 1955 (prohibition of business enterprises of gambling), section 1956 (laundering of monetary instruments), section 1957 (relating to engaging in monetary transactions in property derived from specified unlawful activity), section 659 (theft from interstate shipment), section 664 (embezzlement from pension and welfare funds), section 1343 (fraud by wire, radio, or television), section 1344 (relating to bank fraud), sections 2251 and 2252 (sexual exploitation of children), sections 2312, 2313, 2314, and 2315 (interstate transportation of stolen property), section 2321 (relating to trafficking in certain motor vehicles or motor vehicle parts), section 1203 (relating to hostage taking), section 1029 (relating to fraud and related activity in connection with access devices), section 3146 (relating to penalty for failure to appear), section 3521(b)(3) (relating to witness relocation and assistance), section 32 (relating to destruction of aircraft or aircraft facilities), section 1963 (violations with respect to racketeer influenced and corrupt organizations), section 115 (relating to threatening or retaliating against a Federal official), and section 1341 (relating to mail fraud), or section 351 (violations with respect to congressional, Cabinet, or Supreme Court assassinations, kidnaping, and assault), section 831 (relating to prohibited transactions involving nuclear materials), section 33 (relating to destruction of motor vehicles or motor vehicle facilities), section 175 (relating to biological weapons), or section 1992 (relating to wrecking trains);

(d)   any offense involving counterfeiting punishable under section 471, 472, or 473 of this title;

(e)   any offense involving fraud connected with a case under title 11 or the manufacture, importation, receiving, concealment, buying, selling, or otherwise dealing in narcotic drugs, marihuana, or other dangerous drugs, punishable under any law of the United States;

(f)   any offense including extortionate credit transactions under sections 892, 893, or 894 of this title;

(g)   a violation of section 5322 of title 31, United States Code (dealing with the reporting of currency transactions);

(h)   any felony violation of sections 2511 and 2512 (relating to interception and disclosure of certain communications and to certain intercepting devices) of this title;

(i)   any felony violation of chapter 71 (relating to obscenity) of this title;

(j)   any violation of section 11(c)(2) of the Natural Gas Pipeline Safety Act of 1968 (relating to destruction of a natural gas pipeline) or subsection (i) or (n) of section 902 of the Federal Aviation Act of 1958 (relating to aircraft piracy);

(k)   any criminal violation of section 2778 of title 22 (relating to the Arms Export Control Act);

(l)   the location of any fugitive from justice from an offense described in this section;

(m)   any felony violation of sections 922 and 924 of title 18, United States Code (relating to firearms);

(n)   any violation of section 5861 of the Internal Revenue Code of 1986 (relating to firearms); and

(o)   any conspiracy to commit any offense described in any subparagraph of this paragraph.

(2)   The principal prosecuting attorney of any State, or the principal prosecuting attorney of any political subdivision thereof, if such attorney is authorized by a statute of that State to make application to a State court judge of competent jurisdiction for an order authorizing or approving the interception of wire or oral communications, may apply to such judge for, and such judge may grant in conformity with section 2518 of this chapter and with the applicable State statute an order authorizing, or approving the interception of wire or oral communications by investigative or law enforcement officers having responsibility for the investigation of the offense as to which the application is made, when such

interception may provide or has provided evidence of the commission of the offense of murder, kidnapping, gambling, robbery, bribery, extortion, or dealing in narcotic drugs, marihuana or other dangerous drugs, or other crime dangerous to life, limb, or property, and punishable by imprisonment for more than one year, designated in any applicable State statute authorizing such interception, or any conspiracy to commit any of the foregoing offenses.

(3)   Any attorney for the Government (as such term is defined for the purposes of the Federal Rules of Criminal Procedure) may authorize an application to a Federal judge of competent jurisdiction for, and such judge may grant, in conformity with section 2518 of this title, an order authorizing or approving the interception of electronic communications by an investigative or law enforcement officer having responsibility for the investigation of the offense as to which the application is made, when such interception may provide or has provided evidence of any Federal felony.

§ 2517. Authorization for disclosure and use of intercepted wire, oral, or electronic communications

(1)   Any investigative or law enforcement officer who, by any means authorized by this chapter, has obtained knowledge of the contents of any wire, oral, or electronic communication, or evidence derived therefrom, may disclose such contents to another investigative or law enforcement officer to the extent that such disclosure is appropriate to the proper performance of the official duties of the officer making or receiving the disclosure.

(2)   Any investigative or law enforcement officer who, by any means authorized by this chapter, has obtained knowledge of the contents of any wire, oral, or electronic communication or evidence derived therefrom may use such contents to the extent such use is appropriate to the proper performance of his official duties.

(3)   Any person who has received, by any means authorized by this chapter, any information concerning a wire, oral, or electronic communication, or evidence derived therefrom intercepted in accordance with the provisions of this chapter may disclose the contents of that communication or such derivative evidence while giving testimony under oath or affirmation in any proceeding held under the authority of the United States or of any State or political subdivision thereof.

(4)   No otherwise privileged wire, oral, or electronic communication intercepted in accordance with, or in violation of, the provisions of this chapter shall lose its privileged character.

(5)   When an investigative or law enforcement officer, while engaged in intercepting wire, oral, or electronic communications in the manner

authorized herein, intercepts wire, oral, or electronic communications relating to offenses other than those specified in the order of authorization or approval, the contents thereof, and evidence derived therefrom, may be disclosed or used as provided in subsections (1) and (2) of this section. Such contents and any evidence derived therefrom may be used under subsection (3) of this section when authorized or approved by a judge of competent jurisdiction where such judge finds on subsequent application that the contents were otherwise intercepted in accordance with the provisions of this chapter. Such application shall be made as soon as practicable.

§ 2518. Procedure for interception of wire, oral, or electronic communications

(1)   Each application for an order authorizing or approving the interception of a wire, oral, or electronic communication under this chapter shall be made in writing upon oath or affirmation to a judge of competent jurisdiction and shall state the applicant's authority to make such application. Each application shall include the following information:

   (a)   the identity of the investigative or law enforcement officer making the application, and the officer authorizing the application;

   (b)   a full and complete statement of the facts and circumstances relied upon by the applicant, to justify his belief that an order should be issued, including (i) details as to the particular offense that has been, is being, or is about to be committed, (ii) except as provided in subsection (11), a particular description of the nature and location of the facilities from which or the place where the communication is to be intercepted, (iii) a particular description of the type of communications sought to be intercepted, (iv) the identity of the person, if known, committing the offense and whose communications are to be intercepted;

   (c)   a full and complete statement as to whether or not other investigative procedures have been tried and failed or why they reasonably appear to be unlikely to succeed if tried or to be too dangerous;

   (d)   a statement of the period of time for which the interception is required to be maintained. If the nature of the investigation is such that the authorization for interception should not automatically terminate when the described type of communication has been first obtained, a particular description of facts establishing probable cause to believe that additional communications of the same type will occur thereafter;

   (e)   a full and complete statement of the facts concerning all previous applications known to the individual authorizing and making the application, made to any judge for authorization to intercept, or for approval of interceptions of, wire, oral, or electronic communications involving any of the same persons, facilities or places specified in the application, and the action taken by the judge on each such application; and

(f) where the application is for the extension of an order, a statement setting forth the results thus far obtained from the interception, or a reasonable explanation of the failure to obtain such results.

(2) The judge may require the applicant to furnish additional testimony or documentary evidence in support of the application.

(3) Upon such application the judge may enter an ex parte order, as requested or as modified, authorizing or approving interception of wire, oral, or electronic communications within the territorial jurisdiction of the court in which the judge is sitting (and outside that jurisdiction but within the United States in the case of a mobile interception device authorized by a Federal court within such jurisdiction), if the judge determines on the basis of the facts submitted by the applicant that—

(a) there is probable cause for belief that an individual is committing, has committed, or is about to commit a particular offense enumerated in section 2516 of this chapter;

(b) there is probable cause for belief that particular communications concerning that offense will be obtained through such interception;

(c) normal investigative procedures have been tried and have failed or reasonably appear to be unlikely to succeed if tried or to be too dangerous;

(d) except as provided in subsection (11), there is probable cause for belief that the facilities from which, or the place where, the wire, oral, or electronic communications are to be intercepted are being used, or are about to be used, in connection with the commission of such offense, or are leased to, listed in the name of, or commonly used by such person.

(4) Each order authorizing or approving the interception of any wire, oral, or electronic communication under this chapter shall specify—

(a) the identity of the person, if known, whose communications are to be intercepted;

(b) the nature and location of the communications facilities as to which, or the place where, authority to intercept is granted;

(c) a particular description of the type of communication sought to be intercepted, and a statement of the particular offense to which it relates;

(d)   the identity of the agency authorized to intercept the communications, and of the person authorizing the application; and

(e)   the period of time during which such interception is authorized, including a statement as to whether or not the interception shall automatically terminate when the described communication has been first obtained.

An order authorizing the interception of a wire, oral, or electronic communication under this chapter shall, upon request of the applicant, direct that a provider of wire or electronic communication service, landlord, custodian or other person shall furnish the applicant forthwith all information, facilities, and technical assistance necessary to accomplish the interception unobtrusively and with a minimum of interference with the services that such service provider, landlord, custodian, or person is according the person whose communications are to be intercepted. Any provider of wire or electronic communication service, landlord, custodian or other person furnishing such facilities or technical assistance shall be compensated therefor by the applicant for reasonable expenses incurred in providing such facilities or assistance.

(5)   No order entered under this section may authorize or approve the interception of any wire, oral, or electronic communication for any period longer than is necessary to achieve the objective of the authorization, nor in any event longer than thirty days. Such thirty-day period begins on the earlier of the day on which the investigative or law enforcement officer first begins to conduct an interception under the order or ten days after the order is entered. Extensions of an order may be granted, but only upon application for an extension made in accordance with subsection (1) of this section and the court making the findings required by subsection (3) of this section. The period of extension shall be no longer than the authorizing judge deems necessary to achieve the purposes for which it was granted and in no event for longer than thirty days. Every order and extension thereof shall contain a provision that the authorization to intercept shall be executed as soon as practicable, shall be conducted in such a way as to minimize the interception of communications not otherwise subject to interception under this chapter, and must terminate upon attainment of the authorized objective, or in any event in thirty days. In the event the intercepted communication is in a code or foreign language, and an expert in that foreign language or code is not reasonably available during the interception period, minimization may be accomplished as soon as practicable after such interception. An interception under this chapter may be conducted in whole or in part by Government personnel, or by an individual operating under a contract with the Government, acting under the supervision of an investigative or law enforcement officer authorized to conduct the interception.

(6)   Whenever an order authorizing interception is entered pursuant to this chapter, the order may require reports to be made to the judge who issued the order showing what progress has been made toward achievement of the authorized objective and the need for continued interception. Such reports shall be made at such intervals as the judge may require.

(7)   Notwithstanding any other provision of this chapter, any investigative or law enforcement officer, specially designated by the Attorney General, the Deputy Attorney General, the Associate Attorney General, or by the principal prosecuting attorney of any State or subdivision thereof acting pursuant to a statute of that State, who reasonably determines that—

(a)   an emergency situation exists that involves—

(i)   immediate danger of death or serious physical injury to any person,

(ii)   conspiratorial activities threatening the national security interest, or

(iii)   conspiratorial activities characteristic of organized crime,

that requires a wire, oral, or electronic communication to be intercepted before an order authorizing such interception can, with due diligence, be obtained, and

(b)   there are grounds upon which an order could be entered under this chapter to authorize such interception,

may intercept such wire, oral, or electronic communication if an application for an order approving the interception is made in accordance with this section within forty-eight hours after the interception has occurred, or begins to occur. In the absence of an order, such interception shall immediately terminate when the communication sought is obtained or when the application for the order is denied, whichever is earlier. In the event such application for approval is denied, or in any other case where the interception is terminated without an order having been issued, the contents of any wire, oral, or electronic communication intercepted shall be treated as having been obtained in violation of this chapter, and an inventory shall be served as provided for in subsection (d) of this section on the person named in the application.

(8)   (a)   The contents of any wire, oral, or electronic communication intercepted by any means authorized by this chapter shall, if possible, be recorded on tape or wire or other comparable device. The recording of the contents of any wire, oral, or electronic communication under this subsection shall be done in such way as will protect the recording from editing or other alterations.

Immediately upon the expiration of the period of the order, or extensions thereof, such recordings shall be made available to the judge issuing such order and sealed under his directions. Custody of the recordings shall be wherever the judge orders. They shall not be destroyed except upon an order of the issuing or denying judge and in any event shall be kept for ten years. Duplicate recordings may be made for use or disclosure pursuant to the provisions of subsections (1) and (2) of section 2517 of this chapter for investigations. The presence of the seal provided for by this subsection, or a satisfactory explanation for the absence thereof, shall be a prerequisite for the use or disclosure of the contents of any wire, oral, or electronic communication or evidence derived therefrom under subsection (3) of section 2517.

(b)   Applications made and orders granted under this chapter shall be sealed by the judge. Custody of the applications and orders shall be wherever the judge directs. Such applications and orders shall be disclosed only upon a showing of good cause before a judge of competent jurisdiction and shall not be destroyed except on order of the issuing or denying judge, and in any event shall be kept for ten years.

(c)   Any violation of the provisions of this subsection may be punished as contempt of the issuing or denying judge.

(d)   Within a reasonable time but not later than ninety days after the filing of an application for an order of approval under section 2518(7)(b) which is denied or the termination of the period of an order or extensions thereof, the issuing or denying judge shall cause to be served, on the persons named in the order or the application, and such other parties to intercepted communications as the judge may determine in his discretion that is in the interest of justice, an inventory which shall include notice of—

(i)   the fact of the entry of the order or the application;

(ii)   the date of the entry and the period of authorized, approved or disapproved interception, or the denial of the application; and

(iii)   the fact that during the period wire, oral, or electronic communications were or were not intercepted.

The judge, upon the filing of a motion, may in his discretion make available to such person or his counsel for inspection such portions of the intercepted communications, applications and orders as the judge determines to be in the interest of justice. On an ex parte showing of good cause to a judge of competent jurisdiction the serving of the inventory required by this subsection may be postponed.

(9)   The contents of any wire, oral, or electronic communication intercepted pursuant to this chapter or evidence derived therefrom shall not be received in evidence or otherwise disclosed in any trial, hearing, or other proceeding in a Federal or State court unless each party, not less than ten days before the trial, hearing, or proceeding, has been furnished with a copy of the court order, and accompanying application, under which the interception was authorized or approved. This ten-day period may be waived by the judge if he finds that it was not possible to furnish the party with the above information ten days before the trial, hearing, or proceeding and that the party will not be prejudiced by the delay in receiving such information.

(10)   (a)   Any aggrieved person in any trial, hearing, or proceeding in or before any court, department, officer, agency, regulatory body, or other authority of the United States, a State, or a political subdivision thereof, may move to suppress the contents of any wire or oral communication intercepted pursuant to this chapter, or evidence derived therefrom, on the grounds that—

(i)   the communication was unlawfully intercepted;

(ii)   the order of authorization or approval under which it was intercepted is insufficient on its face; or

(iii)   the interception was not made in conformity with the order of authorization or approval.

Such motion shall be made before the trial, hearing, or proceeding unless there was no opportunity to make such motion or the person was not aware of the grounds of the motion. If the motion is granted, the contents of the intercepted wire or oral communication, or evidence derived therefrom, shall be treated as having been obtained in violation of this chapter. The judge, upon the filing of such motion by the aggrieved person, may in his discretion make available to the aggrieved person or his counsel for inspection such portions of the intercepted communication or evidence derived therefrom as the judge determines to be in the interests of justice.

(b)   In addition to any other right to appeal, the United States shall have the right to appeal from an order granting a motion to suppress made under paragraph (a) of this subsection, or the denial of an application for an order of approval, if the United States attorney shall certify to the judge or other official granting such motion or denying such application that the appeal is not taken for purposes of delay. Such appeal shall be taken within thirty days after the date the order was entered and shall be diligently prosecuted.

(c)   The remedies and sanctions described in this chapter with respect to the interception of electronic communications are the only judicial remedies and sanctions for nonconstitutional violations of this chapter involving such communications.

(11)   The requirements of subsections (1)(b)(ii) and (3)(d) of this section relating to the specification of the facilities from which, or the place where, the communication is to be intercepted do not apply if—

(a)   in the case of an application with respect to the interception of an oral communication—

(i)   the application is by a Federal investigative or law enforcement officer and is approved by the Attorney General, the Deputy Attorney General, the Associate Attorney General, an Assistant Attorney General, or an acting Assistant Attorney General;

(ii)   the application contains a full and complete statement as to why such specification is not practical and identifies the person committing the offense and whose communications are to be intercepted; and

(iii)   the judge finds that such specification is not practical; and

(b)   in the case of an application with respect to a wire or electronic communication—

(i)   the application is by a Federal investigative or law enforcement officer and is approved by the Attorney General, the Deputy Attorney General, the Associate Attorney General, an Assistant Attorney General, or an acting Assistant Attorney General;

(ii)   the application identifies the person believed to be committing the offense and whose communications are to be intercepted and the applicant makes a showing of a purpose, on the part of that person, to thwart interception by changing facilities; and

(iii)   the judge finds that such purpose has been adequately shown.

(12)   An interception of a communication under an order with respect to which the requirements of subsections (1)(b)(ii) and (3)(d) of this section do not apply by reason of subsection (11) shall not begin until the facilities from which, or the place where, the communication is to be intercepted is ascertained by the person implementing the interception order. A provider of wire or electronic communications service that has received an order as provided for in subsection (11)(b) may move the court to modify or quash the order on the ground that its assistance

with respect to the interception cannot be performed in a timely or reasonable fashion. The court, upon notice to the government, shall decide such a motion expeditiously.

§ 2519. Reports concerning intercepted wire, oral, or electronic communications

(1)   Within thirty days after the expiration of an order (or each extension thereof) entered under section 2518, or the denial of an order approving an interception, the issuing or denying judge shall report to the Administrative Office of the United States Courts—

    (a)   the fact that an order or extension was applied for;

    (b)   the kind of order or extension applied for (including whether or not the order was an order with respect to which the requirements of sections 2518(1)(b)(ii) and 2518(3)(d) of this title did not apply by reason of section 2518(11) of this title);

    (c)   the fact that the order or extension was granted as applied for, was modified, or was denied;

    (d)   the period of interceptions authorized by the order, and the number and duration of any extensions of the order;

    (e)   the offense specified in the order or application, or extension of an order;

    (f)   the identity of the applying investigative or law enforcement officer and agency making the application and the person authorizing the application; and

    (g)   the nature of the facilities from which or the place where communications were to be intercepted.

(2)   In January of each year the Attorney General, an Assistant Attorney General specially designated by the Attorney General, or the principal prosecuting attorney of a State, or the principal prosecuting attorney for any political subdivision of a State, shall report to the Administrative Office of the United States Courts—

    (a)   the information required by paragraphs (a) through (g) of subsection (1) of this section with respect to each application for an order or extension made during the preceding calendar year;

    (b)   a general description of the interceptions made under such order or extension, including (i) the approximate nature and frequency of incriminating communications intercepted, (ii) the approximate nature and frequency of other communications intercepted, (iii) the approximate number of persons whose communications were intercepted, and (iv) the approximate nature, amount, and cost of the manpower and other resources used in the interceptions;

(c)   the number of arrests resulting from interceptions made under such order or extension, and the offenses for which arrests were made;

(d)   the number of trials resulting from such interceptions;

(e)   the number of motions to suppress made with respect to such interceptions, and the number granted or denied;

(f)   the number of convictions resulting from such interceptions and the offenses for which the convictions were obtained and a general assessment of the importance of the interceptions; and

(g)   the information required by paragraphs (b) through (f) of this subsection with respect to orders or extensions obtained in a preceding calendar year.

(3)   In April of each year the Director of the Administrative Office of the United States Courts shall transmit to the Congress a full and complete report concerning the number of applications for orders authorizing or approving the interception of wire, oral, or electronic communications pursuant to this chapter and the number of orders and extensions granted or denied pursuant to this chapter during the preceding calendar year. Such report shall include a summary and analysis of the data required to be filed with the Administrative Office by subsections (1) and (2) of this section. The Director of the Administrative Office of the United States Courts is authorized to issue binding regulations dealing with the content and form of the reports required to be filed by subsections (1) and (2) of this section.

§ 2520. Recovery of civil damages authorized

(a)   In general. Except as provided in section 2511(2)(a)(ii), any person whose wire, oral, or electronic communication is intercepted, disclosed, or intentionally used in violation of this chapter may in a civil action recover from the person or entity which engaged in that violation such relief as may be appropriate.

(b)   Relief. In an action under this section, appropriate relief includes—

(1)   such preliminary and other equitable or declaratory relief as may be appropriate;

(2)   damages under subsection (c) and punitive damages in appropriate cases; and

(3)   a reasonable attorney's fee and other litigation costs reasonably incurred.

(c)   Computation of damages.

   (1)   In an action under this section, if the conduct in violation of this chapter, is the private viewing of a private satellite video communication that is not scrambled or encrypted or if the communication is a radio communication that is transmitted on frequencies allocated under subpart D of part 74 of the rules of the Federal Communications Commission that is not scrambled or encrypted and the conduct is not for a tortious or illegal purpose or for purposes of direct or indirect commercial advantage or private commercial gain, then the court shall assess damages as follows:

      (A)   If the person who engaged in that conduct has not previously been enjoined under section 2511(5) and has not been found liable in a prior civil action under this section, the court shall assess the greater of the sum of actual damages suffered by the plaintiff, or statutory damages of not less than $ 50 and not more than $ 500.

      (B)   If, on one prior occasion, the person who engaged in that conduct has been enjoined under section 2511(5) or has been found liable in a civil action under this section, the court shall assess the greater of the sum of actual damages suffered by the plaintiff, or statutory damages of not less than $ 100 and not more than $ 1000.

   (2)   In any other action under this section, the court may assess as damages whichever is the greater of—

      (A)   the sum of the actual damages suffered by the plaintiff and any profits made by the violator as a result of the violation; or

      (B)   statutory damages of whichever is the greater of $ 100 a day for each day of violation or $ 10,000.

(d)   Defense. A good faith reliance on—

   (1)   a court warrant or order, a grand jury subpoena, a legislative authorization, or a statutory authorization;

   (2)   a request of an investigative or law enforcement officer under section 2518(7) of this title; or

   (3)   a good faith determination that section 2511(3) of this title permitted the conduct complained of; is a complete defense against any civil or criminal action brought under this chapter or any other law.

(e)   Limitation. A civil action under this section may not be commenced later than two years after the date upon which the claimant first has a reasonable opportunity to discover the violation.

§ 2521. Injunction against illegal interception

Whenever it shall appear that any person is engaged or is about to engage in any act which constitutes or will constitute a felony violation of this chapter, the Attorney General may initiate a civil action in a district court of the United States to enjoin such violation. The court shall proceed as soon as practicable to the hearing and determination of such an action, and may, at any time before final determination, enter such a restraining order or prohibition, or take such other action, as is warranted to prevent a continuing and substantial injury to the United States or to any person or class of persons for whose protection the action is brought. A proceeding under this section is governed by the Federal Rules of Civil Procedure, except that, if an indictment has been returned against the respondent, discovery is governed by the Federal Rules of Criminal Procedure.

Chapter 121. Stored Wire and Electronic Communications and Transactional Records Access

§ 2701. Unlawful access to stored communications

(a)   Offense. Except as provided in subsection (c) of this section whoever—

   (1)   intentionally accesses without authorization a facility through which an electronic communication service is provided; or

   (2)   intentionally exceeds an authorization to access that facility; and thereby obtains, alters, or prevents authorized access to a wire or electronic communication while it is in electronic storage in such system shall be punished as provided in subsection (b) of this section.

(b)   Punishment. The punishment for an offense under subsection (a) of this section is—

   (1)   if the offense is committed for purposes of commercial advantage, malicious destruction or damage, or private commercial gain—

      (A)   a fine of not more than $ 250,000 or imprisonment for not more than one year, or both, in the case of a first offense under this subparagraph; and

      (B)   a fine under this title or imprisonment for not more than two years, or both, for any subsequent offense under this subparagraph; and

   (2)   a fine of not more than $ 5,000 or imprisonment for not more than six months, or both, in any other case.

(c)   Exceptions. Subsection (a) of this section does not apply with respect to conduct authorized—

    (1)   by the person or entity providing a wire or electronic communications service;

    (2)   by a user of that service with respect to a communication of or intended for that user; or

    (3)   in section 2703, 2704 or 2518 of this title.

§ 2702. Disclosure of contents

(a)   Prohibitions. Except as provided in subsection (b)—

    (1)   a person or entity providing an electronic communication service to the public shall not knowingly divulge to any person or entity the contents of a communication while in electronic storage by that service; and

    (2)   a person or entity providing remote computing service to the public shall not knowingly divulge to any person or entity the contents of any communication which is carried or maintained on that service—

        (A)   on behalf of, and received by means of electronic transmission from (or created by means of computer processing of communications received by means of electronic transmission from), a subscriber or customer of such service; and

        (B)   solely for the purpose of providing storage or computer processing services to such subscriber or customer, if the provider is not authorized to access the contents of any such communications for purposes of providing any services other than storage or computer processing.

(b)   Exceptions. A person or entity may divulge the contents of a communication—

    (1)   to an addressee or intended recipient of such communication or an agent of such addressee or intended recipient;

    (2)   as otherwise authorized in section 2517, 2511(2)(a), or 2703 of this title;

    (3)   with the lawful consent of the originator or an addressee or intended recipient of such communication, or the subscriber in the case of remote computing service;

    (4)   to a person employed or authorized or whose facilities are used to forward such communication to its destination;

(5)   as may be necessarily incident to the rendition of the service or to the protection of the rights or property of the provider of that service; or

(6)   to a law enforcement agency, if such contents—

  (A)   were inadvertently obtained by the service provider; and

  (B)   appear to pertain to the commission of a crime.

§ 2704. Backup preservation

(a)   Backup preservation.

  (1)   A governmental entity acting under section 2703(b)(2) may include in its subpoena or court order a requirement that the service provider to whom the request is directed create a backup copy of the contents of the electronic communications sought in order to preserve those communications. Without notifying the subscriber or customer of such subpoena or court order, such service provider shall create such backup copy as soon as practicable consistent with its regular business practices and shall confirm to the governmental entity that such backup copy has been made. Such backup copy shall be created within two business days after receipt by the service provider of the subpoena or court order.

  (2)   Notice to the subscriber or customer shall be made by the governmental entity within three days after receipt of such confirmation, unless such notice is delayed pursuant to section 2705(a).

  (3)   The service provider shall not destroy such backup copy until the later of—

    (A)   the delivery of the information; or

    (B)   the resolution of any proceedings (including appeals of any proceeding) concerning the government's subpoena or court order.

  (4)   The service provider shall release such backup copy to the requesting governmental entity no sooner than fourteen days after the governmental entity's notice to the subscriber or customer if such service provider—

    (A)   has not received notice from the subscriber or customer that the subscriber or customer has challenged the governmental entity's request; and

    (B)   has not initiated proceedings to challenge the request of the governmental entity.

(5) A governmental entity may seek to require the creation of a back-up copy under subsection (a)(1) of this section if in its sole discretion such entity determines that there is reason to believe that notification under section 2703 of this title of the existence of the subpoena or court order may result in destruction of or tampering with evidence. This determination is not subject to challenge by the subscriber or customer or service provider.

(b) Customer challenges.

(1) Within fourteen days after notice by the governmental entity to the subscriber or customer under subsection (a)(2) of this section, such subscriber or customer may file a motion to quash such subpoena or vacate such court order, with copies served upon the governmental entity and with written notice of such challenge to the service provider. A motion to vacate a court order shall be filed in the court which issued such order. A motion to quash a subpoena shall be filed in the appropriate United States district court or State court. Such motion or application shall contain an affidavit or sworn statement—

(A) stating that the applicant is a customer or subscriber to the service from which the contents of electronic communications maintained for him have been sought; and

(B) stating the applicant's reasons for believing that the records sought are not relevant to a legitimate law enforcement inquiry or that there has not been substantial compliance with the provisions of this chapter in some other respect.

(2) Service shall be made under this section upon a governmental entity by delivering or mailing by registered or certified mail a copy of the papers to the person, office, or department specified in the notice which the customer has received pursuant to this chapter. For the purposes of this section, the term "delivery" has the meaning given that term in the Federal Rules of Civil Procedure.

(3) If the court finds that the customer has complied with paragraphs (1) and (2) of this subsection, the court shall order the governmental entity to file a sworn response, which may be filed in camera if the governmental entity includes in its response the reasons which make in camera review appropriate. If the court is unable to determine the motion or application on the basis of the parties' initial allegations and response, the court may conduct such additional proceedings as it deems appropriate. All such proceedings shall be completed and the motion or application decided as soon as practicable after the filing of the governmental entity's response.

(4)   If the court finds that the applicant is not the subscriber or customer for whom the communications sought by the governmental entity are maintained, or that there is a reason to believe that the law enforcement inquiry is legitimate and that the communications sought are relevant to that inquiry, it shall deny the motion or application and order such process enforced. If the court finds that the applicant is the subscriber or customer for whom the communications sought by the governmental entity are maintained, and that there is not a reason to believe that the communications sought are relevant to a legitimate law enforcement inquiry, or that there has not been substantial compliance with the provisions of this chapter, it shall order the process quashed.

(5)   A court order denying a motion or application under this section shall not be deemed a final order and no interlocutory appeal may be taken therefrom by the customer.

§ 2705. Delayed notice

(a)   Delay of notification.

(1)   A governmental entity acting under section 2703(b) of this title may—

(A)   where a court order is sought, include in the application a request, which the court shall grant, for an order delaying the notification required under section 2703(b) of this title for a period not to exceed ninety days, if the court determines that there is reason to believe that notification of the existence of the court order may have an adverse result described in paragraph (2) of this subsection; or

(B)   where an administrative subpoena authorized by a Federal or State statute or a Federal or State grand jury subpoena is obtained, delay the notification required under section 2703(b) of this title for a period not to exceed ninety days upon the execution of a written certification of a supervisory official that there is reason to believe that notification of the existence of the subpoena may have an adverse result described in paragraph (2) of this subsection.

(2)   An adverse result for the purposes of paragraph (1) of this subsection is—

(A)   endangering the life or physical safety of an individual;

(B)   flight from prosecution;

(C)   destruction of or tampering with evidence;

(D)   intimidation of potential witnesses; or

(E)   otherwise seriously jeopardizing an investigation or unduly delaying a trial.

(3)   The governmental entity shall maintain a true copy of certification under paragraph (1)(B).

(4)   Extensions of the delay of notification provided in section 2703 of up to ninety days each may be granted by the court upon application, or by certification by a governmental entity, but only in accordance with subsection (b) of this section.

(5)   Upon expiration of the period of delay of notification under paragraph (1) or (4) of this subsection, the governmental entity shall serve upon, or deliver by registered or first-class mail to, the customer or subscriber a copy of the process or request together with notice that—

(A)   states with reasonable specificity the nature of the law enforcement inquiry; and

(B)   informs such customer or subscriber—

(i)   that information maintained for such customer or subscriber by the service provider named in such process or request was supplied to or requested by that governmental authority and the date on which the supplying or request took place;

(ii)   that notification of such customer or subscriber was delayed;

(iii) what governmental entity or court made the certification or determination pursuant to which that delay was made; and

(iv)   which provision of this chapter allowed such delay.

(6)   As used in this subsection, the term "supervisory official" means the investigative agent in charge or assistant investigative agent in charge or an equivalent of an investigating agency's headquarters or regional office, or the chief prosecuting attorney or the first assistant prosecuting attorney or an equivalent of a prosecuting attorney's headquarters or regional office.

(b)   Preclusion of notice to subject of governmental access. A governmental entity acting under section 2703, when it is not required to notify the subscriber or customer under section 2703(b)(1), or to the extent that it may delay such notice pursuant to subsection (a) of this section, may apply to a court for an order commanding a provider of electronic communications service or remote computing service to whom a warrant, subpoena, or court order is directed, for such period as the court deems appropriate, not to notify any other person of the existence of the warrant, subpoena, or court order. The court shall enter such an order if it determines that there is reason to believe that notification of the existence of the warrant, subpoena, or court order will result in—

(1)   endangering the life or physical safety of an individual;

(2)   flight from prosecution;

(3)   destruction of or tampering with evidence;

(4)   intimidation of potential witnesses; or

(5)   otherwise seriously jeopardizing an investigation or unduly delaying a trial.

§ 2706. Cost reimbursement

(a)   Payment. Except as otherwise provided in subsection (c), a governmental entity obtaining the contents of communications, records, or other information under section 2702, 2703, or 2704 of this title shall pay to the person or entity assembling or providing such information a fee for reimbursement for such costs as are reasonably necessary and which have been directly incurred in searching for, assembling, reproducing, or otherwise providing such information. Such reimbursable costs shall include any costs due to necessary disruption of normal operations of any electronic communication service or remote computing service in which such information may be stored.

(b)   Amount. The amount of the fee provided by subsection (a) shall be as mutually agreed by the governmental entity and the person or entity providing the information, or, in the absence of agreement, shall be as determined by the court which issued the order for production of such information (or the court before which a criminal prosecution relating to such information would be brought, if no court order was issued for production of the information).

(c)   Exception. The requirement of subsection (a) of this section does not apply with respect to records or other information maintained by a communications common carrier that relate to telephone toll records and telephone listings obtained under section 2703 of this title. The court may, however, order a payment as described in subsection (a) if the court determines the information required is unusually voluminous in nature or otherwise caused an undue burden on the provider.

§ 2707. Civil action

(a)   Cause of action. Except as provided in section 2703(e), any provider of electronic communication service, subscriber, or customer aggrieved by any violation of this chapter in which the conduct constituting the violation is engaged in with a knowing or intentional state of mind may, in a civil action, recover from the person or entity which engaged in that violation such relief as may be appropriate.

(b)   Relief. In a civil action under this section, appropriate relief includes—

(1)   such preliminary and other equitable or declaratory relief as may be appropriate;

(2)   damages under subsection (c); and

(3)   a reasonable attorney's fee and other litigation costs reasonably incurred.

(c)   Damages. The court may assess as damages in a civil action under this section the sum of the actual damages suffered by the plaintiff and any profits made by the violator as a result of the violation, but in no case shall a person entitled to recover receive less than the sum of $ 1,000.

(d)   Defense. A good faith reliance on—

(1)   a court warrant or order, a grand jury subpoena, a legislative authorization, or a statutory authorization;

(2)   a request of an investigative or law enforcement officer under section 2518(7) of this title; or

(3)   a good faith determination that section 2511(3) of this title permitted the conduct complained of; is a complete defense to any civil or criminal action brought under this chapter or any other law.

(e)   Limitation. A civil action under this section may not be commenced later than two years after the date upon which the claimant first discovered or had a reasonable opportunity to discover the violation.

§ 2708. Exclusivity of remedies

The remedies and sanctions described in this chapter are the only judicial remedies and sanctions for nonconstitutional violations of this chapter.

§ 2711. Definitions for chapter

As used in this chapter—

(1)   the terms defined in section 2510 of this title have, respectively, the definitions given such terms in that section; and

(2)   the term "remote computing service" means the provision to the public of computer storage or processing services by means of an electronic communications system.

Appendix C: 18 U.S.C. § 1465: Transportation of Obscene Matter for Sale or Distribution

United States Code

Title 18. Crimes and Criminal Procedure

Part I—Crimes

§ 1465. Transportation of obscene matter for sale or distribution

Whoever knowingly transports in interstate or foreign commerce for the purpose of sale or distribution, or knowingly travels in interstate commerce, or uses a facility or means of interstate commerce for the purpose of transporting obscene material in interstate or foreign commerce, any obscene, lewd, lascivious, or filthy book, pamphlet, picture, film, paper, letter, writing, print, silhouette, drawing, figure, image, cast, phonograph recording, electrical transcription or other article capable of producing sound or any other matter of indecent or immoral character, shall be fined not more than $5,000 or imprisoned not more than five years, or both.

The transportation as aforesaid of two or more copies of any publication or two or more of any article of the character described above, or a combined total of five such publications and articles, shall create a presumption that such publications or articles are intended for sale or distribution, but such presumption shall be rebuttable.

Appendix D: 47 U.S.C. § 223: Obscene or Harrassing Telephone Calls

United States Code

Title 47. Telegraphs, Telephones, and Radiotelegraphs

Chapter 5. Wire or Radio Communication

Subchapter II—Common Carriers

§ 223. Obscene or harassing telephone calls in the District of Columbia or in interstate or foreign communications

(a)   Prohibited general purposes

Whoever—

    (1)   in the District of Columbia or in interstate or foreign communication by means of telephone—

        (A)   makes any comment, request, suggestion or proposal which is obscene, lewd, lascivious, filthy, or indecent;

        (B)   makes a telephone call, whether or not conversation ensues, without disclosing his identity and with intent to annoy, abuse, threaten, or harass any person at the called number;

        (C)   makes or causes the telephone of another repeatedly or continuously to ring, with intent to harass any person at the called number; or

        (D)   makes repeated telephone calls, during which conversation ensues, solely to harass any person at the called number; or

    (2)   knowingly permits any telephone facility under his control to be used for any purpose prohibited by this section, shall be fined not

more than $50,000 or imprisoned not more than six months, or both.

(b) Prohibited commercial purposes; defense to prosecution

    (1) Whoever knowingly—

        (A) within the United States, by means of telephone, makes (directly or by recording device) any obscene communication for commercial purposes to any person, regardless of whether the maker of such communication placed the call; or

        (B) permits any telephone facility under such person's control to be used for an activity prohibited by subparagraph (A),

    shall be fined in accordance with Title 18, or imprisoned not more than two years, or both.

    (2) Whoever knowingly—

        (A) within the United States, by means of telephone, makes (directly or by recording device) any indecent communication for commercial purposes which is available to any person under 18 years of age or to any other person without that person's consent, regardless of whether the maker of such communication placed the call; or

        (B) permits any telephone facility under such person's control to be used for an activity prohibited by subparagraph (A),

    shall be fined not more than $50,000 or imprisoned not more than six months, or both.

(3) It is a defense to prosecution under paragraph (2) of this subsection that the defendant restrict access to the prohibited communication to persons 18 years of age or older in accordance with subsection (c) of this section and with such procedures as the Commission may prescribe by regulation.

(4) In addition to the penalties under paragraph (1), whoever, within the United States, intentionally violates paragraph (1) or (2) shall be subject to a fine of not more than $50,000 for each violation. For purposes of this paragraph, each day of violation shall constitute a separate violation.

(5) (A) In addition to the penalties under paragraphs (1), (2), and (5), whoever, within the United States, violates paragraph (1) or (2) shall be subject to a civil fine of not more than $50,000 for each violation. For purposes of this paragraph, each day of violation shall constitute a separate violation.

(B)   A fine under this paragraph may be assessed either—

    (i)   by a court, pursuant to civil action by the Commission or any attorney employed by the Commission who is designated by the Commission for such purposes, or

    (ii)   by the Commission after appropriate administrative proceedings.

(6)   The Attorney General may bring a suit in the appropriate district court of the United States to enjoin any act or practice which violates paragraph (1) or (2). An injunction may be granted in accordance with the Federal Rules of Civil Procedure.

. . .

Appendix E: Federal
Child Pornography Statute

United States Code

Title 18. Crimes and Criminal Procedure

Part I—Crimes

Chapter 110. Sexual Exploitation and Other Abuse of Children

§ 2252. Certain activities relating to material involving the sexual exploitation of minors

(a)   Any person who—

    (1)   knowingly transports or ships in interstate or foreign commerce by any means including by computer or mails any visual depiction, if—

        (A)   the producing of such visual depiction involves the use of a minor engaging in sexually explicit conduct; and

        (B)   such visual depiction is of such conduct;

    (2)   knowingly receives, or distributes any visual depiction that has been mailed, or has been shipped or transported in interstate or foreign commerce, or which contains materials which have been mailed or so shipped or transported, by any means including by computer, or knowingly reproduces any visual depiction for distribution in interstate or foreign commerce by.any means including by computer or through the mails, if—

        (A)   the producing of such visual depiction involves the use of a minor engaging in sexually explicit conduct; and

        (B)   such visual depiction is of such conduct;

(3)   either—

 (A) in the special maritime and territorial jurisdiction of the United States, or on any land or building owned by, leased to, or otherwise used by or under the control of the Government of the United States, or in the Indian country as defined in section 1151 of this title, knowingly sells or possesses with intent to sell any visual depiction; or

 (B) knowingly sells or possesses with intent to sell any visual depiction that has been mailed, or has been shipped or transported in interstate or foreign commerce, or which was produced using materials which have been mailed or so shipped or transported, by any means, including by computer, if—

  (i) the producing of such visual depiction involves the use of a minor engaging in sexually explicit conduct; and

  (ii) such visual depiction is of such conduct; or

(4)   either—

 (A) in the special maritime and territorial jurisdiction of the United States, or on any land or building owned by, leased to, or otherwise used by or under the control of the Government of the United States, or in the Indian country as defined in section 1151 of this title, knowingly possesses 3 or more books, magazines, periodicals, films, video tapes, or other matter which contain any visual depiction; or

 (B) knowingly possesses 3 or more books, magazines, periodicals, films, video tapes, or other matter which contain any visual depiction that has been mailed, or has been shipped or transported in interstate or foreign commerce, or which was produced using materials which have been mailed or so shipped or transported, by any means including by computer, if—

  (i) the producing of such visual depiction involves the use of a minor engaging in sexually explicit conduct; and

  (ii) such visual depiction is of such conduct; shall be punished as provided in subsection (b) of this section.

(b)   (1)   Whoever violates paragraph (1), (2), or (3) of subsection (a) shall be fined under this title or imprisoned not more than ten years, or both, but, if such person has a prior conviction under this section, such person shall be fined under this title and imprisoned for not less than five years nor more than fifteen years.

(2)   Whoever violates paragraph (4) of subsection (a) shall be fined under this title or imprisoned for not more than five years, or both.

Appendix F: State Child Pornography Statutes

Alabama
Code 1975, §§ 13A-12-190 to 13A-12-198.

Alaska
AS 11.41.455.

Arizona
A.R.S. §13-3553, 13-3555

Arkansas
A.C.A. §§ 5-27-301 to 5-27-305.

California
West's Ann. Cal. Penal Code §§ 311 to 311.4.

Colorado
C.R.S. 18-6-403.

Connecticut
C.G.S.A. §§ 53a-196 to 53a-196b.

Delaware
11 Del.C. §§ 1108, 1109.

Florida
West's F.S.A. § 827.071

Georgia
O.G.S.A. § 16-12-100

Hawaii
HRS §§ 707-750, 707-751

Idaho
I.C. § 44-1306.

Illinois
S.H.A. ch. 38, ¶ 11-20a

Indiana
West's A.I.C. 35-49-1-1 to 35-49-1-10.

Iowa
I.C.A. § 728.12

Kansas
K.S.A. 12-3516.

Kentucky
KRS 531.320, 531.340 to 531.360.

Louisiana
LSA-R.S. 14:81.1.

Maine
17 M.R.S.A. §§ 2921 to 2923.

Maryland
Code 1957, art. 27, § 419A.

Massachusetts
M.G.L.A. c. 272, §§ 29A, 29B.

Michigan
M.C.L.A. § 750.145c.

Minnesota
M.S.A. § 617.246.

Mississippi
Code 1972, § 97-5-33.

Missouri
V.A.M.S. § 568.060.

Montana
CA 45-5-625.

Nebraska
R.R.S. 1943, § 28-1463.

Nevada
N.R.S. 200.509.

New Hampshire
RSA 650:2.

New Jersey
N.J.S.A. 2C:24-4(b)(5).

New Mexico
NMSA 1978, § 30-6-1.

North Carolina
G.S. § 14-190.6.

North Dakota
NDCC 12.1-27.1-01.

Ohio
R.C. § 2907.321.

Oklahoma
21 Okl.St.Ann. § 1021.2.

Oregon
ORS 163.485.

Pennsylvania
18 Pa.C.S.A. § 6312(c).

Rhode Island
Gen. Laws 1956, §11-9-1.1.

South Carolina
Code 1976, § 16-15-380.

South Dakota
SDCL 22-22-24, 22-22-25.

Tennessee
T.C.A. § 39-6-1137.

Texas
V.T.C.A., Penal Code § 43.25.

Utah
U.C.A. 1953, 76-10-1206.5(3).

Virginia
Code 1950, § 18.2-374.1.

Washington
West's RCWA 9.68A.060.

West Virginia
Code, 61-8C-3.

Wisconsin
W.S.A. 940.203(4).

Wyoming
W.S. 1977, § 14-3-102

Appendix G: The Computer Fraud and Abuse Act

United States Code

Title 18. Crimes and Criminal Procedure

Part I—Crimes

Chapter 47. Fraud and False Statements

1030. Fraud and related activity in connection with computers

(a)   Whoever—

    (1)   knowingly accesses a computer without authorization or exceeds authorized access, and by means of such conduct obtains information that has been determined by the United States Government pursuant to an Executive order or statute to require protection against unauthorized disclosure for reasons of national defense or foreign relations, or any restricted data, as defined in paragraph y of section 11 of the Atomic Energy Act of 1954, with the intent or reason to believe that such information so obtained is to be used to the injury of the United States, or to the advantage of any foreign nation;

    (2)   intentionally accesses a computer without authorization or exceeds authorized access, and thereby obtains information contained in a financial record of a financial institution, or of a card issuer as defined in section 1602(n) of title 15, or contained in a file of a consumer reporting agency on a consumer, as such terms are defined in the Fair Credit Reporting Act (15 U.S.C. 1681 et seq.);

    (3)   intentionally, without authorization to access any computer of a department or agency of the United States, accesses such a computer of that department or agency that is exclusively for the use

of the Government of the United States or, in the case of a computer not exclusively for such use, is used by or for the Government of the United States and such conduct affects the use of the Government's operation of such computer;

(4)   knowingly and with intent to defraud, accesses a Federal interest computer without authorization, or exceeds authorized access, and by means of such conduct furthers the intended fraud and obtains anything of value, unless the object of the fraud and the thing obtained consists only of the use of the computer;

(5)   intentionally accesses a Federal interest computer without authorization, and by means of one or more instances of such conduct alters, damages, or destroys information in any such Federal interest computer, or prevents authorized use of any such computer or information, and thereby—

    (A)   causes loss to one or more others of a value aggregating $1,000 or more during any one year period; or

    (B)   modifies or impairs, or potentially modifies or impairs, the medical examination, medical diagnosis, medical treatment, or medical care of one or more individuals; or

(6)   knowingly and with intent to defraud traffics (as defined in section 1029) in any password or similar information through which a computer may be accessed without authorization, if—

    (A)   such trafficking affects interstate or foreign commerce; or 18 USCA § 1030

    (B)   such computer is used by or for the Government of the United States; shall be punished as provided in subsection (c) of this section.

(b)   Whoever attempts to commit an offense under subsection (a) of this section shall be punished as provided in subsection (c) of this section.

(c)   The punishment for an offense under subsection (a) or (b) of this section is—

    (1)   (A)   a fine under this title or imprisonment for not more than ten years, or both, in the case of an offense under subsection (a)(1) of this section which does not occur after a conviction for another offense under such subsection, or an attempt to commit an offense punishable under this subparagraph; and

        (B)   a fine under this title or imprisonment for not more than twenty years, or both, in the case of an offense under subsection (a)(1) of this section which occurs after a conviction for another offense under such subsection, or an attempt to commit an offense punishable under this subparagraph; and

(2) (A) a fine under this title or imprisonment for not more than one year, or both, in the case of an offense under subsection (a)(2), (a)(3) or (a)(6) of this section which does not occur after a conviction for another offense under such subsection, or an attempt to commit an offense punishable under this subparagraph; and

(B) a fine under this title or imprisonment for not more than ten years, or both, in the case of an offense under subsection (a)(2), (a)(3) or (a)(6) of this section which occurs after a conviction for another offense under such subsection, or an attempt to commit an offense punishable under this subparagraph; and

(3) (A) a fine under this title or imprisonment for not more than five years, or both, in the case of an offense under subsection (a)(4) or (a)(5) of this section which does not occur after a conviction for another offense under such subsection, or an attempt to commit an offense punishable under this subparagraph; and

(B) a fine under this title or imprisonment for not more than ten years, or both, in the case of an offense under subsection (a)(4) or (a)(5) of this section which occurs after a conviction for another offense under such subsection, or an attempt to commit an offense punishable under this subparagraph.

(d) The United States Secret Service shall, in addition to any other agency having such authority, have the authority to investigate offenses under this section. Such authority of the United States Secret Service shall be exercised in accordance with an agreement which shall be entered into by the Secretary of the Treasury and the Attorney General.

(e) As used in this section—

(1) the term "computer" means an electronic, magnetic, optical, electrochemical, or other high speed data processing device performing logical, arithmetic, or storage functions, and includes any data storage facility or communications facility directly related to or operating in conjunction with such device, but such term does not include an automated typewriter or typesetter, a portable hand held calculator, or other similar device;

(2) the term "Federal interest computer" means a computer—

(A)   exclusively for the use of a financial institution or the United States Government, or, in the case of a computer not exclusively for such use, used by or for a financial institution or the United States Government and the conduct constituting the offense affects the use of the financial institution's operation or the Government's operation of such computer; or

(B)   which is one of two or more computers used in committing the offense, not all of which are located in the same State;

(3)   the term "State" includes the District of Columbia, the Commonwealth of Puerto Rico, and any other commonwealth, possession or territory of the United States;

(4)   the term "financial institution" means—

(A)   an institution with deposits insured by the Federal Deposit Insurance Corporation;

(B)   the Federal Reserve or a member of the Federal Reserve including any Federal Reserve Bank;

(C)   a credit union with accounts insured by the National Credit Union Administration;

(D)   a member of the Federal home loan bank system and any home loan bank;

(E)   any institution of the Farm Credit System under the Farm Credit Act of 1971;

(F)   a broker-dealer registered with the Securities and Exchange Commission pursuant to section 15 of the Securities Exchange Act of 1934;

(G)   the Securities Investor Protection Corporation;

(H)   a branch or agency of a foreign bank (as such terms are defined in paragraphs (1) and (3) of section 1(b) of the International Banking Act of 1978); and

(I)   an organization operating under section 25 or section 25(a) of the Federal Reserve Act.

(5)   the term "financial record" means information derived from any record held by a financial institution pertaining to a customer's relationship with the financial institution;

(6)   the term "exceeds authorized access" means to access a computer with authorization and to use such access to obtain or alter infor-

mation in the computer that the accesser is not entitled so to obtain or alter; and

(7)   the term "department of the United States" means the legislative or judicial branch of the Government or one of the executive departments enumerated in section 101 of title 5.

(f)   This section does not prohibit any lawfully authorized investigative, protective, or intelligence activity of a law enforcement agency of the United States, a State, or a political subdivision of a State, or of an intelligence agency of the United States.

Appendix H: The Texas Computer Crime Law

Texas Penal Code

Title 7. Offenses against Property

Chapter 33. Computer Crimes

§ 33.01. Definitions

In this chapter:

(1) "Communications common carrier" means a person who owns or operates a telephone system in this state that includes equipment or facilities for the conveyance, transmission, or reception of communications and who receives compensation from persons who use that system.

(2) "Computer" means an electronic, magnetic, optical, electrochemical, or other high-speed data processing device that performs logical, arithmetic, or memory functions by the manipulations of electronic or magnetic impulses and includes all input, output, processing, storage, or communication facilities that are connected or related to the device.

(3) "Computer network" means the interconnection of two or more computer systems by satellite, microwave, line, or other communication medium with the capability to transmit information among the computers.

(4) "Computer program" means an ordered set of data representing coded instructions or statements that when executed by a computer cause the computer to process data or perform specific functions.

(5) "Computer security system" means the design, procedures, or other measures that the person responsible for the operation and use of a computer employs to restrict the use of the computer to particular persons or uses or that the owner or licensee of data stored or maintained by a computer in which the owner or licensee is entitled to store or maintain the data employs to restrict access to the data.

(6)   "Computer services" means the product of the use of a computer, the information stored in the computer, or the personnel supporting the computer, including computer time, data processing, and storage functions.

(7)   "Computer system" means any combination of a computer or computers with the documentation, computer software, or physical facilities supporting the computer.

(8)   "Computer software" means a set of computer programs, procedures, and associated documentation related to the operation of a computer, computer system, or computer network.

(9)   "Computer virus" means an unwanted computer program or other set of instructions inserted into a computer's memory, operating system, or program that is specifically constructed with the ability to replicate itself and to affect the other programs or files in the computer by attaching a copy of the unwanted program or other set of instructions to one or more computer programs or files.

(10)   "Damage" includes partial or total alteration, damage, or erasure of stored data, or interruption of computer services.

(11)   "Data" means a representation of information, knowledge, facts, concepts, or instructions that is being prepared or has been prepared in a formalized manner and is intended to be stored or processed, is being stored or processed, or has been stored or processed in a computer. Data may be embodied in any form, including but not limited to computer printouts, magnetic storage media, and punchcards, or may be stored internally in the memory of the computer.

(12)   "Electric utility" has the meaning assigned by Subsection (c), Section 3, Public Utility Regulatory Act (Article 1446c, Vernon's Texas Civil Statutes).

§ 33.02. Breach of Computer Security

(a)   A person commits an offense if the person:

(1)   uses a computer without the effective consent of the owner of the computer or a person authorized to license access to the computer and the actor knows that there exists a computer security system intended to prevent him from making that use of the computer; or

(2)   gains access to data stored or maintained by a computer without the effective consent of the owner or licensee of the data and the actor knows that there exists a computer security system intended to prevent him from gaining access to that data.

(b)   A person commits an offense if the person intentionally or knowingly gives a password, identifying code, personal identification number, debit card number, bank account number, or other confidential information about a computer security system to another person without the effective consent of the person employing the computer security system to restrict the use of a computer or to restrict access to data stored or maintained by a computer.

(c)   An offense under this section is a Class A misdemeanor.

§ 33.03. Harmful Access

(a)   A person commits an offense if the person intentionally or knowingly and without authorization from the owner of the computer or a person authorized to license access to the computer:

(1)   damages, alters, or destroys a computer, computer program or software, computer system, data, or computer network;

(2)   causes a computer to interrupt or impair a government operation, public communication, public transportation, or public service providing water or gas;

(3)   uses a computer to:

(A)   tamper with government, medical, or educational records; or

(B)   receive or use records that were not intended for public dissemination to gain an advantage over business competitors;

(4)   obtains information from or introduces false information into a computer system to damage or enhance the data or credit records of a person;

(5)   causes a computer to remove, alter, erase, or copy a negotiable instrument; or

(6)   inserts or introduces a computer virus into a computer program, computer network, or computer system.

(b)   An offense under this section is a:

(1)   felony of the second degree if the value of the loss or damage caused by the conduct is $20,000 or more;

(2)   felony of the third degree if the value of the loss or damage caused by the conduct is $750 or more but less than $20,000; or

(3)   Class A misdemeanor if the value of the loss or damage caused by the conduct is $200 or more but less than $750.

§ 33.04. Defenses

It is an affirmative defense to prosecution under Sections 33.02 and 33.03 of this code that the actor was an officer, employee, or agent of a communications common carrier or electric utility and committed the proscribed act or acts in the course of employment while engaged in an activity that is a necessary incident to the rendition of service or to the protection of the rights or property of the communications common carrier or electric utility.

§ 33.05. Assistance by Attorney General

The attorney general, if requested to do so by a prosecuting attorney, may assist the prosecuting attorney in the investigation or prosecution of an offense under this chapter or of any other offense involving the use of a computer.

Appendix I: State Computer Crime Laws

Alabama
Computer Crime Act, Code of Alabama,
Sections 13A-8-100 to 13A-8-103

Alaska
Statutes,
Sections 11.46.200(a)(3), 11.46.484(a)(5),
11.46.740, 11.46.985, 11.46.990

Arizona
Revised Statues Annotated,
Sections 13-2301(E), 13-2316

Arkansas
No specific computer crime law.

California
Penal Code,
Section 502 Section 1203.047,1203.048

Colorado
Revised Statutes,
Sections 18-5.5-101, 18-5.5-102

Connecticut
General Statutes,
Sections 53a-250 to 53a-261, 52-570b

Delaware
Code Annotated,
Title 11, Sections 931-939

Florida
Computer Crimes Act, Florida Statutes Annotated,
Sections 815.01 to 815.07 and 934.01 to 934.43

Georgia
Computer Systems Protection Act, Georgia Codes Annotated,
Sections 16-9-90 to 16-9-95

Hawaii
Revised Statutes,
Sections 708-890 to 780-896

Idaho
Code, Title 18, Chapter 22,
Sections 18-2201, 18-2202

Illinois
Annotated Statutes (Criminal Code),
Sections 15-1, 16-9

Indiana
Code,
Sections 35-43-1-4, 35-43-2-3

Iowa
Statutes,
Sections 716A.1 to 716A.16

Kansas
Statutes Annotated,
Section 21-3755

Kentucky
Revised Statutes,
Sections 434.840 to 434.860

Louisiana
Revised Statutes, Title 14, Subpart D. Computer Related Crimes,
Sections 73.1 to 73.5

Maine
Revised Statutes Annotated, Chapter 15, Title 17-A,
Section 357

Maryland
Annotated Code, Article 27,
Sections 45A and 146

Massachusetts
General Laws, Chapter 266,
Section 30

Michigan
Statutes Annotated,
Section 752.791 to 752.797

Minnesota
Statutes (Criminal Code),
Sections 609.87 to 609.89

Mississippi
Code Annotated,
Sections 97-45-1 to 97-45-13

Missouri
Revised Statutes,
Sections 569.093 to 569.099

Montana
Code Annotated,
Sections 45-2-101, 45-6-310, 45-6-311

Nebraska
Revised Statutes, Article 13(p) Computers,
Sections 28-1343 to 28-1348

Nevada
Revised Statutes,
Sections 205.473 to 205.477, 205.480

New Hampshire
Revised Statutes Annotated,
Sections 638:16 to 638:19

New Jersey
Statutes,
Title 2C, Chapter 20, Sections 2C:20-1, 2C:20-23 to 2C:20-34,
Title 2A, Sections 2A:38A-1 to 2A:38A-3

New Mexico
Statutes Annotated, Criminal Offenses, Computer Crimes Act,
Sections 30-16A-1k to 30-16A-4 and 30-45-1 to 30-45-7

New York
Penal Law,
Sections 155.00, 156.00 to 156.50, 165.15 subdiv. 10,
170.00, 175.00

North Carolina
General Statutes,
Sections 14-453 to 14-457

North Dakota
Century Code,
Sections 12.1-06.1-01 subsection 3, 12.1-06.1-08

Ohio
Revised Code Annotated,
Sections 2901.01, 2913.01, 2913.04

Oklahoma
Computer Crimes Act, Oklahoma Session Laws, Title 21,
Section 1124
Sections 1951-1956

Oregon
Revised Statutes,
Sections 164.125, 164.345 to 164.365, 164.377

Pennsylvania
Consolidated Statutes Annotated,
Section 3933

Rhode Island
General Laws (Criminal Offenses),
Sections 11-52-1 to 11-52-5

South Carolina
Code of Laws,
Sections 16-16-10 to 16-16-40

South Dakota
Codified Laws,
Sections 43-43B-1 to 43-43B-8

Tennessee
Code Annotated, Computer Crimes Act,
Sections 39-3-1401 to 39-3-1406

Texas
Codes Annotated, Title 7, Chapter 33,
Sections 33.01 to 33.05

Utah
Utah Code Annotated, Computer Fraud Act
Sections 76-6-701 to 76-6-705, 97-45-7

Vermont
No specific computer crime law.

Virginia
Computer Crime Act, Code of Virginia,
Sections 18.2-152.1 to 18.2-152.14

Washington
Revised Code Annotated,
Sections 9A.48.100, 9A.52.010, 9A.52.110 to
9A.52.130

West Virginia
No Specific computer crime law.

Wisconsin
Statutes Annotated, Section 943.70

Wyoming
Statutes, Sections 6-3-501 to 6-3-505

Index

Acceptable use policies (AUPs), 44–45
Acceptance
  contracts and, 34
  offers and, 37–38
Access
  devices, counterfeit, 109
  intent, 108–109
ACE (Americans Communicating
    Electronically), 133–134
Actual damages, for copyright infringe-
    ment, 53
Actual malice, in defamation cases, 80
Adult material, 89. *See also* Child pornog-
    raphy
  advertising, prurient interests and,
    95–96
  classifying, 93–97
  in cyberspace, 90–93
  nonobscene, 98
  sexually explicit text, 92, 103, 104
  state laws governing, 97–98
Advertisement
  of adult materials, prurient interests
    and, 95–96
  false or deceptive, 84–85
Americans Communicating Electronically
    (ACE), 133–134
America Online, 3, 10
Animated sequences
  child pornography and, 99, 102–103
  description of, 91–92
  file descriptions of, 96
Anonymity
  anonymous Internet file transfer proto-
    col and, 16
  anonymous remailers and, 16
  anonymous servers and, 16

handles and, 14–15
  pseudonyms and, 14–15
  right to associate and, 15
ANSI Bombs, 115
Anti-Semitism, 70–71
Antivirus software industry, 114
Anxiety, from involvement with sexually
    explicit on-line materials, 89
Archie, 7
Archival copies of software, creation of, 62
Association, right of, 15
Attempt of computer crime, 119–120
Attribution right, 52
AUPs (acceptable use policies), 44–45
Authors
  of e-mail, 56–57
  of messages, 57–58
  rights of, 52
  of shareware, 63–64

Bargained-for-exchange, 38–39
BBS. *See* Bulletin board systems (BBS)
Berne Convention, 48
Bill of Rights, 67
B'nai B'rith's Anti-Defamation League, 71
Brandenburg test, 75, 76
Brandenburg v. Ohio, 74, 75
Bulletin board systems (BBS), 3–4, 56
  caller contracts, 44
  downloading of sexually explicit mate-
    rials, 91
  for entertainment, 8
  first software for, 1government investi-
    gations and, 31
  hate speech, 77
  liability for distribution of defamatory
    language, 82

Bulletin board systems *(cont.)*
  number of, 9–10
  Privacy Protection Act and, 87
  public disclosure of private facts, 27
  software exchange and, 7
  software piracy and, 112–113
  software usage in, breach of licensing
    agreement and, 64–65
Business. *See also* Contracts
  cyberspace and, 33–34
  technology and, 33
  transactions in cyberspace, advantages
    of, 41–42

Caller contracts, 44–45
Case citations, 129
CBBS, 10
CCI, 82, 83
CCN/CivicNet (Center for Civic
    Networking), 134
Censorship, 70–71
Center for Civic Networking
    (CCN/CivicNet), 134
CFAA (Computer Fraud and Abuse Act),
    107–109
Chat, 8
  hot, 92–93, 104
  Internet Relay, 8, 78
  live, copyrights and, 61–62
  real-time, 44, 92–93
Chat systems, defamation in, 78
Child pornography, 99, 114
  animated sequences of, 102–103
  digitized images of, 102–103
  federal statute on, 183–185
  First Amendment protection and, 84
  laws governing, 101–102
  possession of, 101
  state statutes, 187–189
  uploading or downloading of, 101
  without children, 99–101
Christensen, Ward, 10
Civil libertarians, 31
Clear and present danger doctrine, 73–76
Clinton administration, 31
Clipper Chip, 31
Collective work copyright, 58
Commercial applications, 9
Commercial on-line services, 2–3
Commercial software copyrights, 63
Common carrier, 83–84

Common law actions, for invasion of pri-
    vacy, 26–28
Communications
  electronic. *See* Electronic communica-
    tions
  indirect, revoking an offer and, 35–36
  stored, access to, 20–22
Communication systems, 31
Community, sense of, 3
Compilations, 50, 58
Complicity of computer crime, 119–120
CompuServe, 3, 10, 44, 58, 71, 82–83
Computer access. *See* Access, computer
Computer crimes. *See also* Cyber-crimes;
    specific crimes
  overzealousness of prosecutors and,
    120–121
  state laws, 201–205
Computer fraud, 118
Computer Fraud and Abuse Act (CFAA),
    72, 107–109, 191–195
Computer Professionals for Social
    Responsibility (CPSR), 134–135
Computer services, theft of, 117–118
Computer trespass. *See* Trespass, computer
Computer underground, 73
Computer viruses, 114–116
Conduct, *vs.* speech, 72–73
Confidential information, protection of,
    28–29
Consent defense, for defamation, 79
Consideration, contracts and, 34, 38–39
Conspiracy, 119–120
Consumer-oriented commercial transac-
    tions, 33–34
Consumer protection laws, 85
Contracts. *See also* Electronic contracts
  consideration and, 38–39
  defined, 34
  elements of, 34
  e-mail ownership and, 57
  issues peculiar to on-line world, 40–44
  law on, 34
  offer and, 34–37
  written requirements for, 39
Cook, Bill, 86
Copying of software, illegal. *See* Software
    piracy
Copyright, 64–65
  author or creator rights and, 52
  creation of, 49–51

in cyberspace, 56–62
derivative work and, 52
digital images and, 60–61
duration, 52
expression and, 49–50
fair use doctrine and, 54–55
formalities and, 50–51
infringement, 53, 61
law, applicability in cyberspace, 47–48
licensing and, 55
live chat and, 61–62
notice requirement, 50–51
orginality and, 50
public domain software and, 64
registration requirement, 51
reproduction of work and, 52
software, 62–64
system development, 48
United States Constitution and, 48
violations, 49, 51
work subject to protection, 51–52
Copyright Act, 48, 60, 61
Counteroffer, 36
CPSR (Computer Professionals for Social
    Responsibility), 134–135
Crackers, 105. See also Hackers
Cracks, 113
Creator rights, 52
Credit card abuse laws, 109–110
Credit cards
    posting numbers of, 73
    transactions, in cyberspace, 45
Criminal liability determination, test for
    sexually explicit materials, 103, 104
Crypto-anarchy, 31
Cryptography, 29, 31. See also Encryption
Cubby, Inc., 82
Cubby v. CompuServe, 82–84
Cyber-crimes. See also specific crimes
    penalties for, 105–106
Cyberspace
    activities in, 5–9
    beginning of, 1
    as business resource, 33
    commercial on-line services and, 2–3
    computer bulletin board systems, 3–4
    computer networks and, 4–5
    credit card transactions in, 45
    differences with noncomputer commu-
        nications, 47
    dimensions, 9–10

future, 10–11
growth of, 10
interaction, mechanics of, 2
private systems, 4
as public forum, 71
Cypherpunks, 31

Damages
    actual, for copyright infringement, 53
    caused by hackers, placing value on,
        121
    punitive, 81
Data
    manipulation, illegal, 117
    tampering, illegal, 117
Databases
    comprehensive, 3
    information ownership, 65
Data highways, 2
Deceptive advertising, First Amendment
    protection and, 84–85
Defamation, First Amendment protection
    and, 78–84
Delphi, 3
Derivative work, copyrights and, 52
DFA, 82
Digital images, copyrights and, 60–61
Digital recordings, copyrights, 65
Digital Telephony, 31
Digitized images
    of adult material, 90–91
    of child pornography, 99, 100, 102–103
    sexually oriented, file descriptions of, 96
Direct communication, revoking an offer
    and, 35
Disclosure, of private communications,
    21–22
Display rights, copyrights and, 52
Distribution
    of shareware, 63–64
    of software, illegal. See Software piracy
Distribution rights, copyrights and, 52
Double jeopardy doctrine, 107
Duplication, instantaneous, 47
Duration, of copyright, 52
Duty to report violations, 119

Echomail, 6
ECPA. See Electronic Communications
    Privacy Act (ECPA)
EDI (electronic data interchange), 34

Editorial discretion, 70

E911 document, 22–23, 110, 121

Educational services, 8–9

EFF (Electronic Frontier Foundation), 77, 131–133

Electronic catalogs, 9

Electronic communications
interception, 17–20
privacy of, EPCA and, 16–25

Electronic Communications Privacy Act (ECPA), 14, 116, 143–175
access provisions, 20–22
interception of electronic communications, 18–20
provisions, 17
Steve Jackson Games v. United States Secret Service and, 22–25
violations, 23

Electronic contracts
acceptance and, 37–38
consideration and, 38–39
defined, 34
issues peculiar to on-line world, 40–44
offer and, 34–37

Electronic data interchange (EDI), 34

Electronic Frontier Foundation (EFF), 77, 131–133

Electronic mail (e-mail), 3, 5–6
acceptance of offer and, 37
copyrights and, 56–57
defamation in, 78
interception of, 24–25
mailbox rule and, 40–41
offers in, 35
sexually explicit materials and, 91

Electronic privacy, 13–14. *See also* Electronic Communications Privacy Act (EPCA)
anonymity and, 14–16
common law actions and, 26–28
cryptography and, 28–31
state laws, 26
U.S. Constitution and, 13–14

Electronic publications libraries, 3

Electronic publishers, 88

Electronic publishing, 7

Electronic shopping, 9

Electronic surveillance, 19

Elite bulletin boards, 73

Elite files, 111

E-mail. *See* Electronic mail (e-mail)

Emergency 911 system, 86

Encoded communication, 28–29. *See also* Encryption

Encryption
constitutionality of, 29
debate over, 28–29
public key, 30–31
routine, for electronic contracts, 42
software, 30–31
widespread usage of, 31

Entertainment, 8

EPCA. *See* Electronic Communications Privacy Act (EPCA)

Export restrictions, on encryption software, 30

Expression, copyrights and, 49–50

Fair use doctrine
copyrights and, 54–55
magazine articles and, 59–60
newspaper articles and, 59–60
statutory concerns, 54

False advertising, First Amendment protection and, 84–85

False light, 27–28

FBI, 31

Federal interest computers, 108

Federal laws
governing adult material, 98
governing child pornography, 101–102

Fees, discussion, in caller contracts, 45

Fidonet, 5, 59
growth of, 11
nodes, 10

Fighting words, 76–77

File transfer protocol (FTP), 4
anonymous, 16

Firm offer, 36

First Amendment, 71, 72
in cyberspace, 67–69
on-line adult materials/activities and, 93
press activity, 8
speech/conduct distinction, 75
violations, 70
zines and, 85–86

Flames, 76–77

Forgery, unauthorized modification of contract and, 41–43

Formalities, in copyright creation, 50–51

Fraud. *See also* Computer Fraud and Abuse Act (CFAA)

computer, 118
Freedom, of press, 85–88
Free-Net, 136–137
FTP (file transfer protocol), 4

Gender hate speech, 77
GEnie, 3, 10
Gibson, William, 1
Gopher, 5, 85–86
Governmental interest, speech posing
    threat to, 75
Government documents, on-line distribu-
    tion services, 60
GURPS Cyberpunk, 23

Hackers, 105, 114
    malicious, 105–106
    Phrack newsletter and, 86
Hacking. *See also* Unauthorized access
    access to and disclosure of stored com-
        munications, 20–22
    trespass and. *See* Trespass, computer
Hacking attempts, 119–120
Handles, 14–15
Harassment, telephone, 179–181
Hash function, 42–43
Hate crimes, 77
High Performance Computing Act, 10–11
Homosexual acts, digitized images of, 91
Hot chat, 92–93, 104
Hustler magazine, 75–76

Indecency, 93
Indirect communication, revoking an
    offer and, 35–36
Information infrastructure, 10
Infringement, on copyright, 53
Injunction, 20
Innocent infringement defense, for copy-
    right violation, 51
Inquiry, about offer, 36
Integrity right, 52
Intellectual property, 47
Intent to access, 108–109
Interception
    defined, 17–18
    of electronic communication, 17–20
    of electronic mail, 24–25
Internet, 4–5, 10
    anonymous file transfer protocol, 16
    file transfer protocol (FTP), 85

growth of, 10
node, 4
Protocol (IP), 10
Internet Relay Chat (IRC), 8, 78
Internet Worm, 108, 115
Interstate transportation, of obscene
    material, 98
Intrusion, wrongful, 28
Invitations for offers, 35
IRC (Internet Relay Chat), 8, 78

Language, defamatory, 78
LAN (local area network), 4
Law review articles, 131
Legal research, 129–131
Legal treatises, 131
Legal value, 38, 39
Legion of Doom (LOD), 22–23
Libel
    defamation and, 78, 79–80
    pecuniary harms from, 79
    vs. false light, 27–28
Library of Congress, 51
Licensing agreements, 58
    breach of, 65
    copyrights and, 55
    for shareware, 64
    for software copyrights, 63
Live chat, copyrights and, 61–62
Local area network (LAN), 4
Logic bombs, 115
Log-in contract, e-mail ownership and, 57

Magazine articles, 59–60
Mailbox rule, 38, 40–41
Manipulation, of computer data, 117
MEDphone, 81–82
Message bases, 6
    copyrights and, 57–59
    sexually explicit text on, 92
Messages
    flames, 76–77
    posting, 58–59
Michelangelo virus scare, 115
Miller test, 99, 101
Miller v. California, 93
Modems, 9
Moderator, 58
Moore, Geoffrey, 70
Morris, Robert T., 108, 115, 116
Multiuser dungeons (MUDs), 8, 73, 78

National Online Media Association
    (NOMA), 135–136
National Public Telecomputing Network
    (NPTN), 136–137
National Science Foundation Internet, 44
National Stolen Property Act, 110–111
National Telecommunications and
    Information Administration (NTIA),
    77
Negligence, 75, 81
Neidorf, Craig, 86
Networks, 4–5
  government investigations and, 31
  growth of, 10
Neuromancer, 1
Newsgroups, 6
  messages, copyrights and, 58–59
  sexually explicit text on, 92
Newspaper articles, 59–60
New York Times v. Sullivan, 80
NEXIS database, 7
Node, 4, 10
NOMA (National Online Media
    Association), 135–136
Noncommercial cyberspace, 33
Notice requirement, for copyrights, 50–51
NPTN (National Public Telecomputing
    Network), 136–137
NTIA (National Telecommunications and
    Information Administration), 77

Obscenity, 114
  community standards definition of,
    94–95
  definition of, 93–94
  First Amendment protection and, 84
  Miller test, 96–97
  possession of obscene materials, 98
  significance of determination, 97
  in telephone calls, 179–181
  transportation of matters for sale or dis-
    tribution, 177
  vs. indecency, 97
Offeree, 35
Offeror, 34–35, 36
Offers
  acceptance of, 37–38
  contracts and, 34–37
  firm, 36
  invitations for, 35
  rejection of, 36

revoking, 35–37, 40
termination of, 36, 37
who may accept, 37–38
Ohio Bell Telephone Company, 28
Omnibus Crime Control and Safe Streets
    Act, 17
On-line chat systems, 61–62
On-line services, 33
  government investigations and, 31
  user bases, 10
Operation Longarm, 102
Operation Sundevil, 120–121
Opinions, defamation and, 79
Optical Character Recognition software, 59
Orginality, copyrights and, 50
Osborn v. Ohio, 102

Paraphrasing, of newspaper or magazine
    article, 59–60
Patently offensive material, 96–97
Paternity right, 52
Penalties
  for cyber-crime, 105–106
  for software piracy, 112
Performance rights, copyrights and, 52
PGP *(Pretty Good Privacy)*, 30–31
Phone systems
  government investigations and, 31
  hacking of, 73
Photographing, wrongful, 28
Phrack newsletter, 86, 121
Phreaking, 73
Playboy magazine, 61
Pornography. *See also* Adult material
  child. *See* Child pornography
  hard-core, 96
Possession
  of child pornography, 101
  of illicit computer information, 118
  of obscene material, 98
Posting of messages, 58–59
PPA (Privacy Protection Act of 1980), 24,
    86–88
President, threats to, 75
Press, freedom of, 85–88
Pretty Good Privacy (PGP), 30–31
Privacy
  of electronic communications, EPCA
    and, 16–25
  invasion of, common law actions for,
    26–28

issues, in caller contracts, 45
rights, from U.S. Constitution, 13
state laws, 26
Privacy Protection Act of 1980 (PPA), 24, 86–88
Private facts, public disclosure of, 26–27
Private systems, 4
Privileges, 79
Prodigy, 3, 10, 70–71, 81–82
Prurient interests, 95–96
Pseudonyms, 14–15
Public concern issues, defamation and, 80–81
Public disclosure of private facts, 26–27
Public distribution, performance or display rights, copyrights and, 52
Public domain, 60, 64
Public figures
defamation suits and, 80
disclosure of facts about, 27
Public forum doctrine, in cyberspace, 71
Public interest groups
national level, 131–137
state level, 137–142
Public key encryption, 30–31
Public messaging systems, 6
Punishment, for access to stored communications, 21
Punitive damages, 81

Racial messages, 77
Radio, regulation, 68
Random monitoring, 18
Real-time chat, 44, 92–93
Recreational activities, 3, 8
Registration fee, 63
Rejection, of offer, 36
Religious messages, 77
Remailers, anonymous, 16
Reproduction of work, copyrights and, 52
Research services, 8–9
Revoking, of offer, 35–37, 40
Right
to associate, 15
to privacy, 13–14
Rights
to free speech, See also Speech, 29, 67
to privacy. See also Privacy
Rumorville USA, 82, 83
Rusty & Edie's BBS, 113

Sadomasochist materials, 91, 95
Searches, unreasonable, protection against, 29
Search warrant, in looking for documents, 87
Secondary publishers, 82–83
Secrecy, breach of, 26–27
Secret Service, violation of ECPA, 22–25
Seizures, unreasonable, protection against, 29
Servers, anonymous, 16
Sex, in cyberspace, 89
Sex-change operation, public disclosure of, 26–27
Sexual exploitation of minors. See Child pornography
Sexually explicit text, 92, 103, 104
Sexually oriented materials. See Adult material; Child pornography
Sexual orientation hate speech, 77
Shareware, copyrights and, 63–64
Sierra Network, 8
Signatures, for contracts, 36, 44
Slander
defamation and, 78, 79–80
vs. false light, 27–28
Software copyrights, 52, 62–64
Software exchange, 7
Software piracy, 111–114
Software Publisher's Association (SPA), 112
Speech
posing a clear and present danger, 73–76
freedom of, 29, 67
hate, 77
posing threat to governmental interest, 75
sysop violation of First Amendment and, 69–71
vs. conduct, 72–73
warranting no First Amendment protection, 73–85
State laws, 129
on adult material, 97–98
on child pornography, 101, 187–189
on computer crime, 116–120, 201–205
on computer trespass or unauthorized access, 116–117
on privacy, 26
State public interest groups, 137–142

Statute of frauds, 39, 43–44
Statutes. *See* State laws
Statutory damages, for copyright
    infringement, 53
Steve Jackson Games v. United States Secret
    Service, 14, 22–25, 87
Stored communications, access, 20–22
Subpoena, in looking for documents, 87
Summarization, of newspaper or maga-
    zine article, 59–60
System operators (sysops), 3, 15, 88
    as custodian of records, 42
    divulging contents of electronic com-
        munication, 18
    engagement in hot chat, 104
    immunity to defamation suits and,
        83–84
    interception of private messages and, 20
    involvement with sexually explicit on-
        line materials and, 89–90
    liability, caller contracts and, 45
    software monitoring, 112–113
    violation of First Amendment and,
        69–71
    wrongful intrusion by, 28

Tampering, with computer data, 117
Telephones
    adult services on, 98
    obscene language usage and, 104
    obscene or harassing calls on, 179–181
    wiretaps, 17, 18
Television, regulation, 68
Telnet program, 4
Termination, of offer, 36, 37
Texas Computer Crime Law, 197–200
Theft, of computer services, 117–118
Thread, message, 6
Tort, 75
Trespass, computer. *See also* Unautho-
    rized access
    laws governing, 106–107, 116–117
    state laws governing, 116–117
Tribe, Laurence, 68
Trojans, 115
Tutors, on-line, 9
27th Amendment, 68

U.C.C. (Uniform Commercial Code), 36
Unauthorized access, 20, 107–108. *See also*
    Trespass, computer

exceptions to prohibitions, 21
intent and, 22
punishment for, 21
state laws governing, 116–117
Underground hacker community, 85
Uniform Commercial Code (U.C.C.), 36
United States Code (U.S.C.), 98, 101, 103,
    129
    Title 18. *See also* Computer Fraud and
        Abuse Act (CFAA)
    Title 18 - section 1465, 177
    Title 18 - section 2252, 183–185
    Title 47 - section 223, 179–181
United States Constitution
    Bill of Rights, 67
    copyrights and, 48
    encryption and, 29
    First Amendment, 29, 67–69, 71
    Fourteenth Amendment and, 69
    Fourth Amendment, 29
    freedom of speech and, 67
    privacy rights, 13
    privacy rights in, 26
    speech protection by, 73
    27th Amendment, 68
United States Copyright Act, 111
United States State Department, 30
United States v. Nolan, 100
U.S.C. *See* United States Code (U.S.C.)
USENET, 31, 59, 73, 77, 85, 91
Usenet newsgroup, 6
User registries, 14

Value of work, in obscenity determina-
    tion, 97
Victim
    of improper disclosure, 22
    of violation of access, 22
Viewers, 90
Viruses, computer, 114–116

WAIS, 5, 86
Warez, 111
Wire Fraud Act, 110
Wiretapping, wrongful, 28
Work-for-hire doctrine, 57
Worm, 108
Written contracts
    requirements for, 39, 43
    unauthorized modification by one
        party, 41–43

Wrongful intrusion, 28
WWIV BBS software, 23
WWIVnet, 10

Zimmerman, Phil, 30
Zines, 7, 85–86